INTERNATIONAL RELATIONS AND POLITICS
Diplomatic History between Two World Wars

Other Books by the Same Author
1. Comparative Politics
2. Contemporary Political Theory
3. The Indian Constitution (A Politico-Legal Study)
4. International Relations and Politics (Theoretical Perspective)
5. Governments and Politics of South Asia (with others)
6. Great Radical Humanist — M.N. Roy
7. Political Thought — Ancient and Medieval
8. Political Thought — Modern and Recent
9. Traditions of Political Thought — Western and Eastern
10. Reflections on Indian Politics
11. Indian Government and Politics
12. Indian Politics
13. Major Modern Political System (U.K., U.S.A., China, Switzerland, Australia, Canada, France, Japan, Germany and Russia)
14. Foundations of Political Science
15. Indian Freedom Movement, Constitution and Administration
16. Principles of Modern Political Science
17. Naxalite Politics in India
18. Voices of Indian Freedom Movement (16 Volumes) (Hindi)
19. Tulnatmak Rajniti
20. Samkaleen Rajnitik Siddhant
21. Adhunik Rajniti Vigyan ke Siddhant
22. Rajniti Vigyan ke Adhar
23. Bharatiya Shasan aur Rajniti
24. Bhartiya Rajniti
25. Bharatiya Samvidhan evam Prashasan
Edited Books
26. Indian Freedom Movement and Thought (1919-1929) *by Dr. Lal Bahadur*
27. Indian Freedom Movement and Thought (1929-1947) *by Dr. R.C. Gupta*
28. Struggle for Pakistan (1906-1947) *by Dr. Lal Bahadur*
29. Introduction to International Relations *by Pierre-Maire Martin*
30. An Introduction to the Methods of Social Sciences *by S.L. Boyle*
31. The History of the Indian National Congress (1885-1947) *by Dr. B. Pattabhi Sitaramayya* (Abridged Version).

INTERNATIONAL RELATIONS AND POLITICS
(Diplomatic History between Two World Wars)

J.C. JOHARI
M.A., LL.B., Ph.D.

STERLING PUBLISHERS PRIVATE LIMITED
A-59, Okhla Industrial Area, Phase-II, New Delhi-110020.
Tel: 26387070, 26386209; Fax: 91-11-26383788
e-mail: mail@sterlingpublishers.com
www.sterlingpublishers.com

International Relations and Politics:
Diplomatic History between the Two World Wars
© 2004, J.C. Johari
ISBN 978 81 207 1560 8
Reprint 2004, 2006, 2012, 2013, 2015

All rights are reserved. No part of this publication may be reproduced, stored in a retrieval system or transmitted, in any form or by any means, mechanical, photocopying, recording or otherwise, without prior written permission of the publisher.

PRINTED IN INDIA

Printed and Published by Sterling Publishers Pvt. Ltd., New Delhi-110020.

Preface to the Second Edition

I am happy to place this work in the hands of the readers in a thoroughly revised and enlarged form. Keeping in view the comments and suggestions of a good number of readers, I have added chapters on Japan, China and the Middle East in this edition. I hope it shall serve well the requirements of the students offering this course at the degree and post-graduate levels as well as of those preparing for some competitive examination.

—J.C. Johari

Preface to the First Edition

Ever since the University of Wales established the Woodrow Wilson Chair in 1919 (that was successfully held by eminent figures like Prof. Alfred Zimmern and his distinguished successors like Prof. C.K. Webster and Prof. E.H. Carr), the study of the subject of international relations and politics has assumed an importance of its own. Other leading centres of Europe and the United States followed the monumental lead of the Wales. More and more researchers and commentators jumped into this field of study that was immensely enriched by the working of the League of Nations. In the course of a few years, abundant literature appeared on the study of the foreign policies of major powers of the world giving an indication of the remarkable development likely to push things towards the taking of such a study to the level of a scientific investigation. The names of G.M. Gathrone-Hardy, P.A. Reynolds, T.E. Evans, L.W. Martin, Quincy Wright, F.P. Walters, F.L. Schuman and H.J. Morgenthau may be specially referred to in this important direction.

A study of the international relations and politics during the inter-War period, however, looks like a study of the diplomatic history of the major European powers. The reason behind it is that Britain, France, Germany and Italy dominated the scene and most of the events of the international sphere took place as a consequence of their initiative. To a considerable extent, the United States remained 'inasmuch as her concern remained confined to consolidating her hold in the Western Hemisphere and in the Far East while keeping herself very much involved in the politics of European powers to the extent it was conducive to the successful persecution of her economic foreign policy. Obviously, during this period 'world' largely meant 'Europe'. As such, a study of international relations and politics remained, by and large, a study of the diplomacy of the major European powers. I have taken note of the plausible opinions of a well-known authority on this subject like Prof. Quincy Wright that the USA, the USSR and other countries of the Middle East, during this period, were generally obliged to accept, or respond, as best as they could, to the initiatives taken by as well as to the conditions resulting from the rivalries of major European powers.

Several important books have appeared on this subject, I have, in my humble way, ventured to tread the path with a view to make the task of my readers easier and more interesting. For this purpose, I have followed my own way of classifying the subject-matter into different chapters and sought to make each almost self-contained. It is on account of this that the readers may complain about the overlapping of some matter at different places. For this, however, I crave their indulgence in view at my consistent effort to make the study of each momentous event of international importance complete as well as comprehensive, as far as possible, at one place. I do not claim any originality in the writing of this textbook, though I ardently hope that this venture will receive appreciation at the hands of those to whom it is addressed and thereby my labours be suitably rewarded. I shall feel thankful to those who will oblige me by conveying their critical observations in the light of which necessary changes or improvements will be made in the next edition of this book.

Saroj Bhawan,
II-A, 112, Nehru Nagar,
Ghaziabad (U.P.)

—**J.C. Johari**

Contents

Preface to the Second Edition   v
Preface to the First Edition   vii

1. First World War   1
   The Pre-War World: Scramble for Empire-Building and Formation of Antagonistic Alliances
   Specific Causes: Prelude to the Great Global Holocaust
   The Prologue: The Balkan Wars and Their Aftermath
   The Course of War: Turning of the Tide after American Participation and Russian Revolution
   Consequences: Emergence of a New State System and Triumph of Internationalism

2. Paris Peace Settlements   33
   Paris Peace Conference: Organisation, Working and Initial Limitations
   Major Peace Settlement: Treaty of Versailles with Germany
   Other Treaties: Peace Settlements with Smaller States in Central Europe and Near East
      Treaty of St. Germaine with Austria
      Treaty of Trianon with Hungary
      Treaty of Neuilly with Bulgaria
      Treaties of Sevres and Lausanne with Turkey
   Peace Settlements and the Question of Minorities
   Critical Appreciation

3. Reparations and Inter-Allied Debts   65
   Reparation: Meaning and Nature of the Problem: Divergent Motives of the Allied Powers
   Fixation of German Liability: War-Guilt Clause and the Reparation Commission
   Determination and Realisation of Reparation: British and French Endeavours of Cross-Roads

The Dawes Plan: Success of Anglo-American Strategy
of 'Business, not Politics'
The Young Plan: Final Settlement of the Reparation
Question
Treag Economic Depression: Hoover's Moratorium as
a Windfall for Germany
Inter-Allied War Debts: A Supplementary Problem to
the Politics of Economic Realism
Critical Appreciation

4. **Phase of Pacification**   97
Draft Treaty of Mutual Assistance: Attempt for General
Guarantee of Security
Geneva Protocol: Addition of Arbitration to the Tenets
of Security and Disarmament
Locarno Agreements: Measures for Substitute Regional
Security
Kellogg-Briand Pact: Illusion of Peace without Security

5. **Phase of Crisis**   118
Rape of Manchuria: Commencement of the Collapse of
Collective Security System
Conquest of Ethiopia: Accomplishment of Italian
Colonial Irredentism
Annexation of Austria: Conclusion of the Prohibited
Anschluss
Dismemberment of Czechoslovakia: Climax of the
Anglo-French Policy of Appeasement
Civil War in Spain: A Trial-Ballon of International
Power Politics
Invasion on Poland: End of Appeasement and Outbreak
of the Second World War

6. **Germany**   156
Germany after the Versailles Treaty: Severe Economic
Crisis and the Policy of Passive Resistance
The Stresemann Era: Revival of Economic Stability and
Rewards of the Policy of Fulfilment
Great Economic Depression and the Rise of Hitler:

Contents

　　　Trend towards Inauguration of the Policy of Blood
　　　　and Iron
　　　The Nazi Political Testament: Role of Ideology in German
　　　　Foreign Policy
　　　Main Propositions of Hitler's Foreign Policy:
　　　　Transformation of the *Mein Kampf's* Words into Deeds
　　　German Diplomacy under Hitler: First Phase of
　　　　Resurgence and Consolidation of Nazism
　　　The Second Phase: Course of Conquest and Annexation
　　　　leading to the Second World War
　　　Berlin-Moscow Non-Aggression Pact: Abandonment
　　　　of the Ideological Basis of Foreign Policy
　　　Concluding Observations

7. **France**　　　　　　　　　　　　　　　　　　　　　　　　191
　　　Search for Security: Keynote of the Real Desire of France
　　　　for Hegemony
　　　Struggle for Productive Guarantees: Pursuance of an
　　　　Obstinate Policy of Coercion
　　　Franco-German Accord: Brilliant Phase of Briand's
　　　　Foreign Policy
　　　Physiology of Paralysis: Inauguration of the Policy of
　　　　Appeasement
　　　The Abyssinian Crisis: Experiment with Appeasement
　　　　of Option
　　　Spanish Civil War: Experiment with Appeasement of
　　　　Principle
　　　Austrian and Czechoslovakian Tragedies: Experiment
　　　　with Appeasement of Compulsion
　　　Germany's Invasion on Poland: Termination of the
　　　　Appeasement Policy
　　　Concluding Observations

8. **Italy**　　　　　　　　　　　　　　　　　　　　　　　　　223
　　　Aftermath of Peace Settlement: Resurgence of Italian
　　　　Irredentism
　　　Rise of Fascism: Role of Ideology in Italian Foreign
　　　　Policy
　　　Mussolini's Dynamic Foreign Policy: Abandonment of
　　　　the Course of Abdication and Retrenchment

Struggle for Treaty Revisionism: Italy's Cautious Policy of Friendship with France and Germany
Conquest of Abyssinia: Last Triumph of Mussolini's Colonial Policy
Rome-Berlin Axix: Mussolini's Drift towards Subservience to Hitler
Conquest of Abyssinia and the Pact of Steel: Italy jumps into the Second World War

9. **Great Britain** 255
Balance of Power: The Most Basic and Most Enduring Principle of British Foreign Policy
Peace Settlement and After: Britain's Search for Peace, Protection and Prosperity
The Chamberlain Era: Policy of the 'Restoration of Europe'
Formula of No Commitments and No Entanglements: Prelude to the Course of Appeasement
Resort to the Course of Retreat and Compromise: Bases and Ramifications of Appeasement Policy
Appeasement in Practice: Britain's Dealings with Japan, Italy and Germany
End of Appeasement Policy: Formation of the 'Peace Front' and Inauguration of the 'Stop Hitler Movement'
Concluding Observations

10. **Soviet Russia** 291
Combination of Ideology and National Interest: Distinctive Characteristics of Soviet Foreign Policy
The Great Revolution and After: Phase of War Communism and Western Military Intervention
New Economic Policy and Defensive Isolationism: Inauguration of the Policy of Peaceful Co-existence
'Socialism in One Country': Stalin's Strategy of Offensive Isolationism
Strategy of United Front: Facing the Grim Challenge of Facism
Resort to Neutrality and Defence: A Complete Revolution in Soviet Diplomacy
Concluding Observations

Contents

11. **United States** — 328
    Broad Aims and Objectives of American Foreign Policy: Predominance of Economic Interest
    Policy towards Latin-America: The Monroe Doctrine and the Movement for Pan-Americanism
    Policy towards the Far East: The Washington Conference on Naval Disarmament and After
    Economic Foreign Policy: Dilemma of Aloofness Versus Commitment
    Policy towards Europe: Adherence to the Course of Splendid Isolationism
    The Course of Appeasement: Triumph of Isolationism over Internationalism
    Critical Observations

12. **Japan** — 366
    World War I and After: On the Path of Glory and Disgruntlement
    Achievements of New Diplomacy: Phase of Democratic Reformism versus Traditional Authoritarianism
    Japan's Monroe Doctrine: Rise of New Japanism in the Warpath
    From Glory to Grave: Militarism on the Path of War
    Concluding Observations

13. **China** — 384
    Feudalism versus Modernism: New Cultural Movement and the Leadership of Sun Yat-sen
    Reactions to Peace Settlement: Emergence of Assertive Nationalism in China
    Partial Success in Diplomacy: Termination of the Soviet Influence
    Manchurian Crisis and After: Formation of the United Front against Japan in a Grim Struggle for Survival
    Concluding Observations

14. **Middle East** — 404
    Turkey: Disintegration of the Ottoman Empire and the Establishment of a Secular Republic
    Egypt: From a British Protectorate to a Sovereign State

Iraq: From a British Mandated Territory to an Independent State
Palestine: Jewish Zionism versus Arab Nationalism
Transjordan: From a British Mandated Territory to an Independent State
Syria: From a French Mandated Territory to an Independent State
Concluding Observations

15. League of Nations 428
Birth of 'A Living Thing': Triumph of Wilsonian Idealism
Structure: Principal and Allied Organs of the League
The Mandate System: Inauguration of the Decolonisation Process under the Auspices of International Organisation
Achievements of the League: Maintenance of International Peace and Cooperation
Failure of the League: Breakdown of the System of Collective Security
Concluding Observations

Appendix A: Covent of the League of Nations   470
Appendix B: Pact of Paris   487
Bibliography   490

Index

LIST OF TABLES AND CHARTS

1. States involved in World War I — 19
2. Wilsonian Idealism — 22-25
3. European State System before and after the War — 30
4. Main Provisions of the Treaty of Versailles — 42-43
5. Losses of Germany — 44
6. Illustration of Keynes regarding Expected Bills — 68
7. Categories of Damages — 70-71
8. Calculations of Keynes — 72
9. Calculation of Keynes about Payments to Allied Powers — 76
10. The Revised Schedule of Payment according to Dawes Plan — 79
11. Calculation of Keynes about Inter-Allied Debts — 89
12. American Loans — 90
13. German Payments — 93
14. Alliances and Pacts (1920-1939) — 154
15. Lenin's Peace Proposals — 299-301
16. Proportionate Naval Strength of Major Powers vide Five-Power Treaty at the Washington Conference — 343
17. American Loans and Interest Thereon — 350
18. American Loans — 351
19. Mandate System — 447
20. Membership of the League of Nations — 464-65

Contemporary international relations are going through a reorganisation in which the old national state and the old state system are being slowly moulded into new political forms. Colonies are gaining independence as empires are breaking up. National states are being merged into great federations. National economies are being completely remoulded. The nation-state is being forced to yield the complete freedom of action which it has long held under the guise of unbridled sovereign power. New forms of political control are evolving. States by voluntary means or under pressure are being gathered into regional groups and in that form promise to be great forces either for peace or for wars of even greater destruction and horror than in the past.

—Thorsten V. Kalijarvi
"The Persistence of Power Politics" in *The Annals*, American Academy of Political Sciences, May, 1948, pp. 10-11.

1

FIRST WORLD WAR

The world as it emerged from the war, though bleeding and exhausted, contained within itself the elements of stability and life. Three emperors and half a dozen kings, the chiefs of the servants of the great military autocracies, had fallen. But constitutionalism, whether in the form of limited monarchy or of a republic, had endured the terrific strain. Kaiserism or military despotism was dead, if Bolshevism or democratic despotism was still alive. Great new principles had been enunciated which implied far-reaching change.

—H.W.V. Temperley[1]

The history of international relations and politics finds its significant start from the First World War that rang out the old epoch and instead rang in the new one. To a chronologist, the nineteenth century ended in December 1899, but to a student of world politics or diplomacy it had its termination in 1914 when the first great war, called World War, entailed the exit of old state system. Instead, a new pattern emerged on the scene after the peace settlements of 1919. A historian may say that even before the first great war, the 'European international system' had worked with several intermittent crises which had provoked jingoistic outbursts in the states concerned, but a critical student of international politics would say that for the most part neither the mass of ordinary people nor even the ruling few were much concerned with, what we now term, 'foreign affairs'. As a matter of fact, the war of 1914-18 "closed the door for ever on that world of automatically functioning international system and general unconcern with politics between nations. Above all, the First World War began the

---

1. See Temperley (ed.): *A History of the Peace Conference of Paris* (London: Oxford University Press, 1920), Vol. 1, p. xxvi.

destruction of the primacy of Europe in international system and its empires overseas which the Second World War completed."²

The Pre-War World: Scramble for Empire-Building and Formation of Antagonistic Alliances

The history of battles is as old as mankind. Whether it is the ancient period finding its termination in the fifth century, or it is the era of the middle ages winding itself up after the fifteenth century followed by the most momentous epoch of the modern age, every phase of people's life has been full of fights, big and small. But the story of the war of 1914-18 has an unprecedented importance in view of the fact that a holocaust of such a massive magnitude occurred for the first time. It "was a total-war in the sense that to ensure victory the belligerents were finally compelled to mobilise totally their resources, their manpower, manufacturing and extractive industries, their farming, shipping transport and communications system."³ Besides, after American President Wilson raised the call of making democracy 'safe' in the world, it assumed a form of its own.⁴ Henceforth, the war looked like a conflict between the principles of liberty and autocracy, between the norms of moral influence and material force, between the ideals of a government by consent and a rule by compulsion.

A study of the First World War, both general and particular, informs us to have a brief look into the conditions of the pre-war times. Broadly speaking, the war was a definite result of three factors—insatiable imperialism, aggressive nationalism, and ebullient militarism—all combined together to have their motivating force in the diplomatic manoeuvres of the great powers of that time. Maintaining 'balance of power' on the continent, France's

---

2. F.S. Northedge and M.J. Grieve: *A Hundred Years of International Relations* (London: Duckworth, 1971), p. 91. Jawaharlal Nehru testified to the same thing in these words: "So with the coming of the war, ended the epoch of the nineteenth century. The majestic and calmly flowing river of western civilisation was suddenly swallowed up in the whirlpool of war. The old world was gone for ever. Something new emerged from that whirlpool more than four years afterwards." *Glimpses of World History* (Bombay: Asia Pub., 1964), p. 641.
3. Northedge and Grieve, op. cit., p. 90.
4. It may be noted here that President Wilson used the term 'democracy' to cover those states, whether monarchic or republican, that had a government by 'consent' as opposed to those under personal or militarist governments. See Temperley, op. cit., p. xxiii, n 1.

claim of embarking on a 'civilising mission' having its essential impact on keeping the menace of German aggression in check, Italy's irredentism manifesting itself in the form of having its own fruits of colonial exploitation in Africa, Germany's stress or *kultur* finding its expression in Kaiser's bombastic utterances of military might, and Japan's ambition to have a free area for colonial exploitation in the Far East all had their cumulative effect on pushing things to the brink of the first global holocaust.

The empire-building activity of Britain informed her statesmen to adhere to the expedient policy of `balance of power' that issued the injunction: 'Thou shalt not grow formidable; thou shalt not resort to war'. Thus, British statesmen strove to maintain a 'just equilibrium' between the nations as could prevent any one of them from being in a position to dominate the rest. "Reduced to practical politics, it involved collective action against such a threat to the security of the community as was involved in the disproportionate strength of a potential aggressor."[5] In order to implement this policy successfully, Britain followed the course of entering into bilateral and multilateral alliances in the face of imperialistic antagonisms.[6] When she failed in having such an alliance with Germany, she had one with Japan in 1902. When she signed the Anglo-Russian Convention in 1907, the 'Triple Entente' or *Entente Cordiale* (involving the membership of Britain, France and Russia) came into being. As we shall see later, German attack on Belgium in August, 1914 was deeply resented by the British government and that forced her to take to the path of war so as to restore the

---

5. G.M. Garthorne-Hardy: *A Short History of International Affairs, 1920-1939* (London: Oxford University Press, 1964), p. 11. The real strength of Britain lay in her navy that ascribed to her the title of the 'mistress of the seas'. It is said that up to 1900, she followed the path of 'splendid isolation'. But the growth of German naval power informed her statesmen to seek an alliance with Germany. For instance, in 1899, Joseph Chamberlain publicly expressed the view that "while we should not remain permanently isolated on the continent of Europe ... the natural alliance is between ourselves and the great German Empire." ibid., p. 12.

6. As W.P. Hall and W.S. Davis observe: "France and the British Empire clashed at many points in Siam, in Egypt, in Oceana, north of Gulf of Guinea, and along the headwaters of Nile. The British Lion and the Russian Bear growled at one another across half a dozen Asiatic frontiers; and the Trans-Caucasian Railway had brought Russian Cossacks within striking distance of the Khyber Pass." *The Course of Europe since Waterloo* (New York: Appleton-Century-Crofts, 1957), p. 493.

balance of power on the continent.

The role of France has its genesis in the conditions arising after the great revolution of 1789. It unleashed the forces of French imperialism. For our purpose what is important is the great humiliation that the French people had suffered in the battle of Waterloo in 1814. After the 'total defeat of Napoleon' and his exile to St. Helena, the statesmen of Britain, Russia, Austria and Prussia held the Vienna Congress in 1815 to divide, what the Secretary of the meet (Gentz) termed, 'the spoils of victory'. But the Vienna settlement could not prove a lasting affair in view of the fact that leading victors had their own axes to grind. Then, France had another humiliating experiment when she lost the provinces of Alsace-Lorraine to Germany in the Franco-Prussian war of 1871. As a result of this, she was deprived of the iron-rich areas that entailed a heavy loss to her industrial power. To take revenge naturally became the determination of the French people. Moreover, when they tried to compensate their loss with colonial adventures in Morocco in 1905, they were once again checked by the power of German imperialists. For this reason, France acted like the most important member of the *Entente Cordiale* formed in 1914 and played the most crucial role in the First World War that entitled Paris to become the venue of peace settlements. However, one should not feel astonished at such an alliance of France with Britain and Russia in view of the fact that the cementing force was the common danger to all from the side of Germany and Austro-Hungarian empire.

The hunger for imperial exploits and traditional rivalry towards France were the two significant factors that determined the role of Germany in this great war. "If England, the fortunate, was not satisfied, the others were even more dissatisfied. And especially Germany, which had joined the great Powers rather late in the day and found all the ripe plums gone."[7] Ever since the unification of the country under Bismarck, Germany emerged as a strong power of the continent. With the capture of Alsace-Lorraine, she had already given a shocking defeat to France. Now a great historian like Trietschke could tell his countrymen that 'the days of England's greatness are over'. Conscious of the eventual confrontation with Britain and France in time to come, the 'iron

---

7. Nehru, op. cit., p. 612.

Chancellor' (Bismarck) played a very important part in the formation of the League of Three Emperors (Germany, Russia and Austria-Hungary) in 1873. But when, five years after, at the Berlin Congress, Austria-Hungary and Russia grappled with each other over the 'Near-Eastern Question', Bismarck threw his lot with the emperor of Austria without caring at all for the resentment of the Russian czar.[8] Not only this, in 1879 he signed a 'dual alliance' with the Austrian Chancellor that obliged Germany to defend Austria against Russia. In 1882 it became the 'Triple Alliance' with the joining of Italy.

And yet Bismarck struggled hard to maintain terms with Russia that culminated in signing the Reinsurance Treaty of 1887. It failed to have a lasting effect, for the Emperor abrogated it after the exit of Bismarck in 1890. The new Emperor followed the course of challenging the power of Britain, France and Russia and instead establishing closer connection with Austria-Hungary, Italy and Turkey. He ridiculed the fact of vast British empire in the face of her small territorial make-up. The Navy Act of 1900 frankly declared: "Germany must have a fleet of such strength that a war against her would involve such risks even for the mightiest naval power, as to jeopardise the supremacy of that power." Moreover, the German government, in this way, could throw a formidable challenge to the British naval power. The British authorities could never forget the fact that Germany had annexed Schleswig-Holstein without their consent and that she had supported Austria-Hungary against Russia in the Balkan wars of 1912-13 like, as the German Emperor said, "a king in the shining armour."[9] Obviously, the British statesmen viewed with disfavour the German tariff system, embryonic German navy, the Teutonic demands for colonies and the commencement of German competition overseas in steel and iron products.[10]

---

8. Vide this agreement, Austria was allowed to 'occupy' and 'administer' the two Balkan principalities of Bosnia and Herzegovina. Thus, the Russian diplomat (Ivan Aksakoff) in an accusing tone cried out: "The Congress is a conspiracy against the Russian people in which the Russian representatives have taken part."
9. See F.L. Schuman: *International Politics* (New York: McGraw Hill, 1941), Ed. III, p. 76.
10. Hall and Davis, op. cit., p. 492. F. Fischer regards the German navy laws of 1898 and 1900 as an inevitable product of German economic expansion and straining after world power." *Germany's Aim in the First World War* (London, 1967), p. 17.

The year 1870 is important in the diplomatic history of Italy. The era of her 'unification' was now replaced by the era of her 'irredentism'. The endeavours of Cavour (a statesman), Garibaldi (a warrior), Mazzini (a poet and prophet of nationalism) and Emmanuel (a tactful ruler) succeeded in bringing about the unification of the country. It, however, led to the movement for 'Unredeemed Italy' that comprised Trieste, Tentino and the eastern coast of the Adriatic sea still under the control of the Austro-Hungarian empire. It became a source of rivalry between Rome and Vienna and yet Bismarck could make Italy a member of the 'Triple Alliance' in 1882. As Italy felt like an unsatiated power in matters of colonial expliots, she looked towards Africa for exporting her population as well as for collecting resources for the purpose of her economic development.

In this direction, Italian statesmen could not make much headway as their ambition was baulked at Tunis in 1881 and then in Abyssinia (now Ethiopia) in 1896, though they could have some satisfaction after capturing the sterile area of Tripoli in 1911. However, the way Italy defected from the 'Triple Alliance' and went over to the side of the Allies in 1915 after making the secret treaty of London (1915) confirmed the old impression of Bismarck: "Insatiable Italy, with furtive glances, roves restlessly hither and thither, instinctively drawn on by the odour of corruption and calamity—always ready to attack anybody from the rear and make off with a bait of plunder. It is outrageous that these Italians, still unsatisfied, should continue to make preparations and to conspire in every direction."[11]

Whereas the 'unification' of Germany and Italy created conditions leading to the first great war, the want of the same in the case of Austro-Hungarian empire could have its own effect in this connection. The Habsburg rulers had a ramshackle empire, big on the map but full of discordant elements. The rising tide of nationalism appeared as a challenge to its polyglot character. The Serbs, the Slavs, the Maghyars, the Croats and the Ruthenians developed aggressive nationalistic aspirations, but the Habsburg rulers failed to satisfy their sentiments. Rather their policy of repression added fuel to fire. The southern part of the empire became affected with the 'pan-Slav movement' led by the people of Serbia. The people of

---

11. See Schuman, op. cit., p. 455.

Serbia had their own grievances towards this empire ever since it had grabbed its provinces of Bosnia and Herzegovina soon after the Berlin Treaty of 1878. Besides, the Russians could not tolerate their loss of concessions in Turkey after signing the Treaty of Stefano in March, 1878.

Thus, the Czar supported the 'bigger Serbia movement' and acted like the 'big brother' of the Slavs. The Russian government also looked in the success of such a movement her eventual gain over the port of Constantinople and the straits of Dardenelles and Bosphorus. As a matter of necessity, Germany supported the Austro-Hungarian empire. She had her own interests in the Near East and, for this purpose, wanted to curb the growing power of Russia that was a great obstacle in the way of launching the most ambitious project in the form of Berlin-Baghdad railway line. For this reason, the Balkan area became the most coveted prize that, in terms of international politics, looked like a 'powder box'. It is here that the two Balkan wars took place that sharpened movement towards the occurrence of the great war; it is here that the most immediate cause of it (in the form of assassination of the heir-apparent to the throne) found its place.[12]

The role of Russia finds its place in what we have seen in the case of other European countries. She was in a very peculiar position because of her own imperialistic designs in the Near East and in the Far East. Keeping in view the menace coming from the side of Germany and Austro-Hungarian empire, Russia joined the Entente Cordiale in 1904 and thereby strengthened the bond of friendship with Britain and France. She adhered to it in spite of the fact that Britain had signed an alliance with Japan in 1902 and then Japan had given her a crushing defeat in 1904. However, the most pressing situation prevailed in the Balkan area where she was face to face with the Austro-Hungarian empire. She supported the Serbians against any possible attack from the side of Vienna. The basic cause of difficulty here was the existence of rival ambitions of Russia and Habsburg empire in the areas that were being released from the Turkish control. Economic as well as nationalistic groups in the Austro-Hungarian empire were committed to a policy of expansion southward through Bosnia and Macedonia to

---

12. W.H. McNeill: *The Contemporary World* (Atlanta: William Morrow and Co., 1967), p. 2.

the Aegian sea. Here it all coincided with the interest of German financiers who had obtained from the Sultan of Turkey the right for a projected railway line across the region of Asia Minor.

All this turned the Balkan area into a theatre of conflict. The Russians could not tolerate any further encroachment of the German or the Austro-Hungarian rulers in the direction of crushing the people of Serbia and Montenegro. Thus, the movements of Germany and Austria-Hungary produced formidable trends. These were viewed with Russia with misgivings, for they threatened her own ambitions in pushing Turkey out of Europe and herself taking over the Balkans whose Slavic peoples she had long hoped to be able to dominate. In this way the "world's trouble spot at this time, however, was in the Balkan peninsula, and this turned out to be the place where World War I was brewed."[13]

Though a non-European power, Japan had her own share in fomenting conditions leading to the outbreak of the first great war. After defeating China in 1894-95 and then Russia in 1904-05, the Japanese successfully crashed the exclusive club of imperialistic nations by annexing Korea in 1910. Having defeated Russia, Japan could secure all privileges of colonial exploitation in Korea (that she had converted into a 'protectorate' in 1905) and her hold over Manchuria also became unassailable. Now she made herself ready to start an aggressive programme of her own in Asia. However, the most noticeable thing about the role of Japan in the first great war is that, in spite of being a victorious power and then gaining some fruits in the peace settlements of Paris, she had to bear the results of an 'unhappy diplomatic denouement' at the Washington peace settlements.[14]

All these factors had their cumulative effect on creating a war psychosis in the early phase of the present century. It is well observed that the twentieth century "opened with thunder and lightning in the air of Europe, and as year succeeded year, the weather grew stormier. Complications and entanglements grew, the life of Europe was tied up more and more in knots—knots which were to be cut ultimately by war. All the Powers expected war to come and prepared for it feverishly, and yet perhaps none of them was keen on it. They all feared it to some extent, for no one

---

13. Norman Hill: *Contemporary World Politics* (New York: Harper and Brothers, 1954), p. 124.
14. C.A. Buss: *The Far East* (New York: Macmillan, 1955), p. 352.

could prophesy with certainty what the result of war would be. And yet fear itself drove them on to war."[15] The system of alliances in the form of Triple Alliance (Germany, Austria-Hungary and Turkey) and *Entente Cordiale* (Britain, France and Russia) signified the clear-cut division of great European powers into two camps capable of picking up the gauntlet at any time and settle the matter by the force of arms. In the initial stages it could be surmised that although the military significance of these two understandings was not clear, it was widely suspected that they might be the framework for military cooperation, should war begin. "Together these alignments meant that a war begun in a small way could easily spread to involve most of Europe and even more remote parts of the world."[16]

Specific Causes : Prelude to the Great Global Holocaust

From the above, it necessarily follows that the eruption of the first great war was conditioned by several factors that had an integrative effect of their own. Insatiable imperialism, aggressive nationalism and ebullient militarism may be pinpointed as the three main factors whose combined effect brought about conditions that terminated the old state system and instead inaugurated a new one under the long desired control of an international organisation. When the present century opened, it appeared that the world "had within and among its nations a multitude of forces and movements crowding for expression. In the field of international relations, it was turning the corner on to a wider street with faster traffic. Little did the nations realise that some among their number, unable to keep up with the pace, would be struck and crushed."[17]

An analysis of the three specific factors may briefly be made in the following manner :

1. *Insatiable Imperialism*

The industrial revolution changed the economic sphere altogether that had its natural impact on the social and political spheres. The old feudal order was replaced by the capitalist order that necessarily led to the system of empire-building. The new entrepreneurs of major European countries like Britain, France, Holland, Portugal,

---

15. Nehru, op. cit., pp. 616-17.
16. Hill, op. cit., p. 125.
17. Ibid., p. 123.

Spain and Germany looked toward the poor and backward parts of the world for the sake of collecting raw materials and converting them into profitable markets. It led to the exploitation of Latin-American, African and Asian countries. The shrewd scholars of the new system justified their advances in the name of 'civilising mission' or 'white man's burden' or 'spreading 'Kultur' and the like and fully thrived on the prevalence of blind superstitions in the subjugated areas. As Hill says : "In those days empire-building was little criticised, most people accepting as a kind of law of nature that the great and powerful nations should govern the weak. Governments were not concerned over any problems that might arise a few decades later within the empires when native peoples would be fired with the desire for self-government."[18]

By its very nature the capitalistic industry was dynamic by virtue of thriving on the development of science.[19] Its distinguishing mark was acquisitiveness; it was always out to acquire and hold more and more and such a hunger could never be satisfied. At first it led to the creation of empires—British, French, German, Spanish, Italian, Portuguese, Dutch, American, Japanese and the like. But when it reached a point of saturation, it naturally led to the condition of scramble for colonial exploitation. Lenin understood this point when he said that 'imperialism is the final stage of capitalism' and, as such, the real cause of the First World War was 'economic'. An ever-growing demand for markets and raw materials made the capitalist Powers race around the world for empire and when there remained nothing more for them in the regions of Africa and Asia, it led to the emergence of national rivalries. "Having covered the world, there was nowhere else to spread, so the imperialistic Powers began glaring at each other and coveting each other's possessions. There were frequent clashes between these great Powers in Asia and Africa and Europe, and angry passions flared up, and war seemed to hang in the balance."[20]

2. Aggressive Nationalism

The French revolution unleashed the force of strong nationalism

---
18. *Ibid.*, p. 121.
19. H.W. Baldwin remarks that the first World War "provided a pre-view of the Pandora's box of evils that the linkage of science with industry was to mean." *World War I: An Outline History* (New York, 1962) p. 159.
20. Nehru, *op. cit.*, p. 612.

that had its definite impact on the fate of other European countries. Such a movement resulted in the 'unification' of Germany and Italy in 1870. The Italians threw off the hold of the Austrians. It turned the Austro-Hungarian empire into a hodgepodge of nationalities—Czechs, Poles, Slovens, Ruthenians, Serbs, Croats, etc. These nationalities developed the sense of nationalism and the people of Serbia resented the annexation of their province of Bosnia with the Austro-Hungarian empire. Herein lies the reason of the assassination of the king and queen of Austria in 1914 at the hands of Gavrilo Princep (a member of the terrorist organisation called 'Black Hand') on June 28, 1914 that lighted the spark and kindled the blaze of the first great war.

Towards the end of the last century and thereafter, the trend of nationalism became irresistibly aggressive. Its spirit turned the heads of statesmen with a feeling of national superiority. The English nationalists prided themselves with being the controllers of the centre of the world; the French claimed themselves to belong to the 'Holy Nation' ; the Germans invoked the teaching of Hegel that the state of Prussia alone had the 'march of God on earth'. The Russians glorified Slavdom as the Germans did for Teutonism. Moreover, while the 'have-nations' (like Britain and France) expressed their ebullience in missionary terms, the 'have-nots' (like Germany and Italy) clamoured for 'irredentism'. In this way, nationalism crossed its liberal framework and rushed towards an aggressive direction. Not only this, in order to justify their aggressive action, great statesmen thoroughly sacrificed the basic norm of enlightened nationalism (having its proper reconciliation with internationalism desiring all national groups to live side by side in freedom and independence) and made it like 'a tool of imperialism and tyranny'.[21]

3. Ebullient Militarism

The trends of insatiable imperialism and aggressive nationalism naturally led to the trend of potentially ebullient militarism. The success of the industrial revolution not only signified invention of

---

21. W. Friedman: *Introduction to World Politics* (London: Macmillan, 1965), p. 31. Sir Winston Churchill says: "National passions, unduly exalted in the decline of religion, burned beneath the surface of nearly every land with fierce, if shrouded, fires. Almost one might think the world wished to suffer. Certainly men were everywhere eager to dare." *The World Crisis, 1911-1914*, p. 188.

new machines for the production of goods, it also found expression in the sphere of armaments. New means of destruction were invented for the sake of capturing the poor and backward parts of the world. Conscription became the order of the day and military aeronautics, submarines, battleships, howitzers, chemicals and germs became powerful instruments of destruction of all that human civilisation and culture stood for. In every major European country defence expenditure increased tremendously. Statistics show that such an increase took place by 335 per cent in Germany, 214 per cent in Russia, 185 per cent in Italy, 180 per cent in England, 155 per cent in Austria-Hungary, and 133 per cent in France during the period of fifty years preceding the First World War. It showed that power "came to be harnessed in the service of diplomacy and war was now looked upon as a mere continuance of policy. Absence of power was looked upon as a failure and a humiliation. Armed conflict was preferred to doubtful negotiation."[22]

The most violent form of potential militarism appeared in Germany where the Prussian landlord and military class was in power. The leaders of this class were aggressive and ruthless and took pride in knowing nothing about humility. Their aggressive pride grew more sharp when they had their supreme leader in their emperor Kaiser Wilhelm II of the house of the Hohenzollern. He "went about proclaiming that Germany was going to be the leader of the world; that she wanted a place in the sun; that her future was on the sea; that it was her mission to spread the *Kultur*, or culture, throughout the world."[23] The writers and intellectuals of other countries also justified the way of war in different terms for the sake of keeping the system of empire-building intact. For instance, John Ruskin, otherwise known as a man of undoubted nobility of the English mind, wrote : " I found, in brief, that all great nations learned their truth of words, and strength of thought, in war, and wasted by peace; taught by war, and deceived by peace; trained by war, and betrayed by peace; in a word, that they were born in war, and expired in peace. "[24] It represented the typical British attitude towards problems of war and peace. Though not so frank and outspoken like the German emperor in respect of making professions

---

22. M.G. Gupta: *International Relations Since 1919*, Part I (Allahabad: Chaitanya, 1969), p. 2.
23. Nehru, op. cit., 613.
24. Ibid., p. 628.

of war, the British statesmen made full preparations and their role in the armed conflict of 1914-18 proved that, as Kamal Ataturk commented, " Britain may lose battles, but never wars."[25]

The causes of the First World War became a favourite subject of study at the hands of scholars after 1919. Thus, Sidney B. Fay enumerated them as militarism, nationalism, economic imperialism and the newspaper press. However, after examining the confidential papers of the belligerent Powers, he concluded that "the greatest single underlying cause of the War was the system of secret alliances which developed after the Franco-Prussian War."[26] Another leading writer on this subject (Quincy Wright) sums up the whole situation in these words : " Writers have declared the cause of the World War I to have been the Russian or the German mobilisation; the Austrian ultimatum; the Serajevo assassination; the aims and ambitions of the Kaiser; Poincare, Izolsky, Berchtold or someone else; the desire of France to recover Alsace-Lorraine or of Austria to dominate the Balkans; the European system of alliances, the activities of the munition-makers, the international bankers of the diplomats, the lack of an adequate political order; armament rivalries; colonial rivalries; commercial policies, the sentiment of nationality; the concept of sovereignty; the struggle of existence; the tendency of nations to expand; the unequal distribution of population, the resources, or of planes of living; the law of diminishing returns; the value of war as an instrument of national solidarity or as an instrument of national policy; ethnocentrism or group egotism; the failure of the human spirit; and many others."[27]

Prof. F. L. Schuman sums up the whole situation in these words: "The great war marked the culmination of the struggle for power in which the coalitions had engaged for the preceding twenty years. For the ambitions of conflicting nationalisms, the strivings of competing imperialisms, the rivalries and tensions between hostile and acquisitive economies, the universal quest of the nation-states for power, profits and prestige came the bloodiest and most catastrophic combat of recorded history, sweeping country after country into its vortex and shattering utterly, per-

---

25. See Warner Moss: "Britain and the Empire" in F.J. Brown, C. Hodges and J.S. Roucek (ed.s): *Contemporary World Politics* (New York: John Wiley, 1939), p. 128.
26. Fay: *The Origins of the World War* (London: Macmillan, 1929), Vol. I, pp. 32-49.
27. Wright: *A Study of War* (Chicago: University of Chicago Press, 1942), Vol. II, pp. 727-28.

haps beyond all hopes of repair, the great world society which Western civilisation had created. The roots of war were deep and ineradicable in the very nature of Western State System itself. The genesis of the conflict of 1919 lay in the irreconciliable aspirations of Teutons and Slavs, Frenchmen and Prussians, Britishers and Germans, struggling for empires, competing for armaments, searching for markets, dreaming of power, security, self-determination, and a brighter place in the sun."[28]

The Prologue: The Balkan Wars and Their Aftermath

The breaking out of the First World War in 1914 finds its genesis in the nerve-racking events that started in the first phase of the present century. As we shall see, all discredit, in this direction, goes to Germany. Ever since her 'unification' under Bismarck, she made remarkable progress as a world power with her enlarged army and navy that naturally became the source of ample anxiety to the British statesman. Enthused with all this, emperor Kaiser Wilhelm II threw his weight about endangering peace of Europe and the neighbouring world with reckless abandon. Thus, the first event took place in the form of Moroccon crisis where German might could give a setback to French power in 1905. However, as a result of some diplomatic efforts, the matter could be referred to an international conference at Algeciras in 1906 where an acceptable compromise could be negotiated. Now the sovereignty of the Sultan was preserved and France was permitted to maintain special rights over the native police force.

Even after this, the Moroccon crisis could not come to an end just on account of the obdurate intentions of the German emperor. The crisis reopened in 1908 when at Casablanca the German consul gave asylum to the deserters from the French Foreign Legion. Once again, resort to diplomacy paid rewards to France vide terms of the treaty of 1909. The third and the last important crisis occurred in 1911 when a German warship landed at Agidir in Morocco with an ostensible purpose to protect German mining property there. Its real purpose was to protect the French occupation of the capital of Morocco (Fez). Once again, the threat of war could be averted by the efforts of the diplomats who worked out an agreement recognising a French protectorate there and ceding to Germany

---
28. Schuman, op. cit., p. 76.

two strips of the French Congo. In short, the three crises of Morocco made it very clear that the German emperor was bent upon showing his fighting power which excelled that of France. It all upset the statesmen of Britain who wanted a successful implementation of their policy of 'balance of power'. Obviously, to the "unprovoked nature and the intensity of the German pressure on France was added confirmation of Britain's own incipient anxieties over Germany."[29]

While the Moroccon crises could be contained by means of successful diplomatic endeavours, the same thing could not happen in the Balkan region. Here German and Austro-Hungarian ambitions coincided that provided ample concern to the Russian government. Taking advantage of the weak position of Turkey, the Austro-Hungarian empire annexed the provinces of Bosnia and Herzegovina in 1908 that were inhabited by the Serbs. Naturally, Serbia resented it. Moreover, it occurred in violation of the Treaty of Berlin of 1878. Apprehending the consequences of such an advance, Russia came to the support of a small state like that of Serbia. At once, Germany declared her support to the emperor of Austria-Hungary. Under these conditions, and also on account of her earlier defeat at the hands of Japan just a few years back Russia however, reluctantly compromised with the situation and dared not support Serbia to the extent of having a full-fledged war with Germany and Austria-Hungary.

A second crisis, though of a smaller proportion, developed in 1911-12 when Italy and Turkey were involved in the tussle over Tripoli. In spite of the support of Germany and Austria-Hungary to Turkey, Italy could weaken the power of the Ottoman emperor and her success in this direction could go to some extent in satisfying her appetite for expansion in the Aegian and in Asia Minor. In 1912 the first Balkan war broke out over the question of Macedonia. It was fought by Turkey on the one hand and Serbia, Montenegro and Greece on the other. It resulted in the defeat of

---

29. D.C. Watt, Frank Spencer and Neville Brown: *A History of the World in the Twentieth Century* (New York: William Morrow & Co., 1968), p. 143. In France, the long-drawn Moroccon crisis deeply affected public opinion. In 1910 Barres was bewailing that the idea of 'revanche' was forgotten or dead. But E. Weber remarks that the events of 1911 persuaded "many of the pacific, the hesitant and the indifferent that the threat to France was real, and that war was only a matter of time." *The Nationalist Revival in France, 1905-1914* (Berkeley, 1959), p. 11.

Turkey so much so that she was virtually pushed out of Europe. Late in the war, the fall of Scutari to the Allies brought about a threat of war by Austria-Hungary, backed by Italy and Germany. Once again, Russia felt enraged and as a consequence of her support to the state of Montenegro culminated in latter's agreeing to withdraw troops from Scutari. Such an action of Russia was certainly conditioned by the sentiments of Pan-Slavism. In this way, the problem was resolved and a war between the Central Powers and Russia was narrowly averted.

But the second Balkan war of 1913 paved the way for the breaking out of the first great war in the following year. It broke out between an alliance of Serbia, Montenegro, Greece, Rumania and Turkey on the one side, and Bulgaria on the other, over the disposition of the territories snatched from Turkey a year before. In this fight over the booty of 1912, other major European powers showed their own diplomatic interests. While Austro-Hungarian empire resented any advantage to Serbia that would amount to her territorial gain, Russia favoured it. The point of difficulty was that the treaty of London (1912) had no provision as to how the spoils of victory were to be dealt with. Italy and Austria-Hungary coveted Albania, but Bulgaria stood firm on her demand for Macedonia. However, the treaty of Bucharest (1913) ended the conflict. Bulgaria left Macedonia; Serbia got nearly 15,000 sq miles of Macedonia, while an area of 18,000 sq miles was given to Greece.

The two Balkan wars intensified the conditions of cleavage between Austria-Hungary (supported by Germany) on the one side and Russia on the other. Now the danger of a general European conflict in a short time to come had become very well apparent. "The war jitters of the nation were intensified when Germany in 1913 increased the size of her protective army. France took up the challenge and lengthened the period of military service from two to three years for her soldiers. Russia and Austria-Hungary too began to strengthen their armed forces. All seemed well aware that a showdown was inevitable."[30] Even the minor countries of the Balkan regions could not remain behind in sharpening the trend of cleavage. "The victorious Serbs and the

---

30. Hill, op, cit., p. 127. The experts viewed the chances of Dual Alliance (France and Russia) "in a great outbreak with great optimism." L. Albertini: *The Origin of the War of 1914* (Translated into English by I.M. Massey), Vol. I (London: Oxford Univ. Press, 1952), p. 373.

Montenegrins thought that they would have to fight Austria-Hungary before they could rest on their laurels. The defeated Bulgers made ovetures for an alliance both with Austria-Hungary and the Turks so as to be revenged on their former allies. The Greeks hovered uncertainly between the Entente and the Austro-German alliance. All of them expected a new war very soon and thought any treaties made in 1913 to be the merest scraps of paper."[31]

The Course of War: Turning of the Tide after American Participation and Russian Revolution

The Balkan crises came to an end with this bold indication that all were ready for a great combat. All major countries of Europe, the Near East and the Far East of that time looked like having lost their balance and filled with blood lust and hatred of the enemy peoples. The occasion came on June 28, 1914 when Archduke Francis Ferdinand, nephew of the Emperor Francis Joseph of Austria-Hungary and heir to the Habsburg throne, with his queen was assassinated while on an official visit to Serajevo—capital city of Bosnia. The ruler of Austria-Hungary placed all blame on the Serbian terrorists and thus handed Serbia an ultimatum with accusations and demands of an exorbitant nature. Naturally, the government of Serbia could not satisfy the terms of the ultimatum as a result of which the Emperor of Austria-Hungary declared war on Serbia on July 28, 1914 against the advice of his Chief of Staff and under German pressure.[32] When Russia resented the action of the Austro-Hungarian empire, Germany invoked the name of the Triple Alliance and, taking advantage of the prevailing situation, declared war on France on August 3, 1914. Same day France declared war on Germany. At first Great Britain hesitated, but when Germany attacked Belgium and thus violated the latter's neutral position, she also joined the war the next day. Thus, in a very short span of time, it became a fight of the unprecedented magnitude in which 26 countries of the world, big as well as small, took part at different stages for their own interests. "The outbreak

---

31. A.J. Grant and H. Temperley: *Europe in the Nineteenth Century* (New York: Longmans, 1952), p. 436.
32. Albertini, op. cit., Vol II, p. 457.

of the war was greeted with wild scenes of popular enthusiasm throughout Europe."[33]

Though a world war, Europe became its principal theatre with Germany playing the role of the villain of peace.[34] She took it as the best opportunity to crush her traditional rival (France). Moreover, owing to the inefficient performance of the Austro-Hungarian empire, Germany alone became the principal figure of the Triple Alliance. As such, France had to play the role of a hero of the Allied powers. The Germans had an occasion to rejoice when, in the beginning, they could have much advances in France, though in the Battle of Marne in early September, 1914 they were pushed back by the French army and thereby Paris could be saved. It came as a source of relief to Britain as well. The Germans had a great occasion to rejoice when in the Battle of Tannenburg, under the command of von Hindenburg, they could defeat Russian forces.

Meanwhile, Russian troops started attacking East Prussia to somehow distract the German attention from the western front. It could satisfy France and Britain who were treating Russia as a 'steam-roller'.[35] But this move could not succeed owing to the corrupt and incompetent staff of the Czar whose results had become obvious in the Battle of Tannenburg. Curiously, while the Russian troops were defeated by the Germans, they could defeat the troops of Austria-Hungary. Among others, while the Turks tried to attack the Suez canal, they were repulsed by the British

---

33. Watt, Spencer and Brown, op. cit., p. 216.
34. Germany moved ahead enthusiastically according to her Schleiffen Plan of campaign. "It contemplated a swift and decisive blow at France, which would release German armies to face Russian invasion from the east. Now all German patriots rallied to the sacred cause of the Fatherland, feeling certain that Germany had been attacked by the scheming enemies and that then only course was to back their way to victory through encircling foes." See Schuman, op. cit., p. 79. When the war was in progress, Schleiffen felt that Germany's power position "was slowly being altered for the worse" and he "would have welcomed an opportunity to stop its decline by a victorious war against France." Holstein "shared Schleiffen's fears for the future and he would also have welcomed a trial by arms." G.A. Craig: *Europe since 1815* (New York, 1966), p. 480.
35. France was bound to give Russia diplomatic support, but she "was in a position to have exercised friendly restraint and proferred counsels of prudence which might have averted the catastrophe. What the French representative at St. Petersburg did was, on the contrary, to fan the flames and thus expose his own country to the most serious risk." Albertini, op. cit., II.p. 457.

States Involved in World War I

States	Dates of Joining the War	Remarks
	(Against Germany)	
1. Russia	August 1, 1914	Separate peace on March 14, 1918
2. France	August 3, 1914	
3. Belgium	August 4, 1914	
4. Great Britain	August 4, 1914	
5. Serbia	August 6, 1914	
6. Montenegro	August 9, 1914	
7. Japan	August 23, 1914	
8. Italy	August 28, 1914	
9. San Marino	May 24, 1915	Against Austria-Hungary
10. Portugal	March 9, 1916	
11. Rumania	August 27, 1916	Separate peace on May 6, 1918
12. Greece	November 28, 1916	
13. United States	April 6, 1917	
14. Panama	April 7, 1917	
15. Cuba	April 7, 1917	
16. Nicaragua	May 7, 1917	
17. Siam	July 22, 1917	
18. Liberia	August 4, 1917	
19. Brazil	October 6, 1917	
20. Guatemala	April 21, 1918	
21. Costa Rica	May 24, 1918	
22. Haiti	July 12, 1918	
23. Honduras	July 19, 1918	
	(With Germany)	
1. Austria-Hungary	August 5, 1914	
2. Turkey	November 5, 1914	
3. Bulgaria	October 14, 1915	

troops. Faced with such a situation, Britain adopted a policy of repression in her 'protectorate' over Egypt and opened fronts of attack on Turkey in Syria, Mesopotamia (now Iraq) and Palestine. Col;. T. E. Lawrence spent a very huge amount of money and thereby fomented a nationalist revolt in Arabia against Turkey. In February 1915, British forces gave a crushing defeat to Turkey by capturing the strait of Dardenelles and the port of Constantinople.

Thereby they could cut off German influence from Western Asia. This success, however, failed from becoming a long-standing affair as the young leader Mustafa Kemal could give a setback to British ambition after a couple of months.

The German colonies in Western and Eastern Africa were also attacked by the Allies and they were cut off from her. In China Germany was deprived of her concessions in Kiachow by the advance action of Japan. The Bulgarians joined Germany a bit late, but they were happy to see that, within a very short time, Serbia could be crushed completely by the Austro-German forces the same thing happened with Rumania when the Austro-German forces occupied her in 1916. Thus within a span of about two years, the Austro-German forces, called Central Powers, came to occupy Poland, Serbia, Rumania, Belgium and a part of France in the northeast region. Now they looked towards the western front where they had to be in the embrace of mortality on account of strong naval power of Britain. At this stage submarine warfare started. Apart from using huge Zeppelin aeroplanes to throw bombs on London, the Germans decided to intensify the use of submarines. Thus, they celebrated a great triumph in May, 1915 when they sank the great English Atlantic liner *Lusitania* that resulted in the massacre of a very large number of English and American people. The submarine warfare brought unexpected gains to Germany, though its incidence provoked the Americans to combat the increasing German menace without any more loss of time. Thus, when in January, 1917 Germany proclaimed that her forces would sink even neutral ships in certain waters, the way for the entry of the United States was opened.[36]

---

36. On January 31, 1917, a German note sent to the United States announced unrestricted submarine warfare. It declared that the attempt of Great Britain "to force Germany into submission by hunger" compelled women and children, the sick and the old, to support grievous privation for the fatherland's sake." To end the 'starvation war', the German government "must abandon the limitations which it has hitherto imposed upon itself in the employment of its weapons at sea." The plea that Germany was justified in counteracting the British blockade by sinking neutral vessels—if they engaged in commerce with Great Britain—was unequivocally rejected by the United States. She at once severed diplomatic relations with Germany and on April 6, 1917 declared war on her. The United States entered the war, because, in the words of President Wilson, "she was made a partner in the sufferings and indignities inflicted by the military masters of Germany", yet her intervention was not intended alone to safeguard American interests. In memorable phrases, President Wilson gave

First World War

The Russian Revolution of November 7, 1917 created a peculiar situation that at first went to the advantage of Germany and then proved her a counter-productive affair. As a result of the victory of the Bolsheviks under Lenin, the role of Russia came to an end (vide treaty of Brest-Litovsk of March 3, 1918) and this was really a factor of help to the Germans in an indirect way. Lenin gave the call of 'Land, Peace, and Bread' and termed the prevailing war as a 'bourgeois affair'. But it had its own disastrous effect on the morale of the German forces. Lenin's statement that the workers must not allow themselves to become the cannon-fodder for the advancement of imperialistic aims of the bourgeois powers changed the minds of the German soldiers, for many regiments had actually fraternised with the Russian army after the revolution. "Germany was war-weary and utterly disheartened, and the seeds from Russia fell on the ground that was prepared to receive them. In this way, the Russian revolution made Germany weak internally."[37]

While the Russian revolution had a negative effect, the change in the American attitude had its positive effect on the course of war.[38] President Wilson took stock of the prevailing crisis that was affecting the American commercial interests to an unprecedented extent. He gave his message to the Congress in which he outlined his historic Fourteen Points and then American involvement became a natural development. It may be said that the changes in the American foreign policy and Russian political system at this stage looked like injecting an ideological element into the First World War. Whereas Lenin declared war as a 'bourgeois combat' and exhorted all workers to dissociate themselves from it, Wilson in his various utterances (as Fourteen Points of January 18, Four Principles of February 11, Four Ends of July 4, and Five Points of September 27 in 1918) "treated democratic self-determination as

---

utterance to the lofty aims which inspired his conception of the war of 1914-18. "The world must be made safe for democracy"; its peace must no longer be endangered by "autocratic governments backed by organised force, which is controlled wholly by their will and not by the will of the people." E. Lipson : *Europe, 1914-1939* (London; Adam and Charles Black, 1957), pp. 300-01.

37. Nehru, op. cit., p. 636.
38. After America jumped into the War and revolution broke out in Russia, "a progressive paralysis gripped the eastern front." Z.A.B. Zeman: *A Diplomatic History of the First World War* (London: Weidenfeld and Nicolson, 1971), p. 207.

WILSONIAN IDEALISM

Fourteen Points of January 8, 1918

1. Open Covenants of peace openly arrived at after which there shall be no private international undertakings of any kind, but diplomacy shall proceed always frankly and in public view.

2. Absolute freedom of navigation upon the seas outside territorial waters, alike in peace and war, except as the seas may be closed in whole or in part by international action for the enforcement in international covenants.

3. The removal, so far as possible, of all economic barriers and the establishment of an equality of trade conditions among all the nations consenting to the peace and associating themselves for its maintenance.

4. Adequate guarantees given and taken that national armaments will be reduced to the lowest point consistent with domestic safety.

5. A free, open-minded and absolutely impartial adjustment of all colonial claims based upon a strict observance of the principle that in determining all such questions of sovereignty the interests of the populations concerned must have equal weight with the equitable claims of the Government whose title is to be determined.

6. The evacuation of all Russian territory, and as such a settlement of all questions affecting Russia as will secure the best and freest cooperation of the other nations of the world in obtaining for her an unhampered and unembarrassed opportunity for the independent determination of her own political development of national policy, and assure her of a sincere welcome into the society of free nations under institutions of her own choosing; and more than welcome, assistance also of every kind that she may need and may herself desire. The treatment accorded to Russia by her sister nations in the months to come will be the acid test of her goodwill, of their comprehension of her needs as distinguished from their own interests, and of their intelligent and unselfish sympathy.

7. Belgium, the whole world will agree, must be evacuated and restored without any attempt to limit the sovereignty which she enjoys in common with all other free nations. No other single act will serve as this will serve to restore confidence among nations in the laws which they have themselves set and determined for the government of their

relations with one another. Without this healing act, the whole structure and validity of International Law is for ever impaired.

8. All French territory should be freed and the invaded portions restored and the wrong done to France by Prussia in 1871 in the name of Alsace-Lorraine which has unsettled the peace of the world for nearly fifty years, should be righted, in order that peace may once more be made secure in the interest of all.

9. A readjustment of the frontiers of Italy should be effected along clearly recognisable lines of nationality.

10. The peoples of Austria-Hungary, whose place among the nations we wish to see safeguarded and assured, should be accorded the freest opportunity of autonomous development.

11. Rumania, Serbia and Montenegro should be evacuated; occupied territories restored; Serbia accorded free access to the sea; and the relations of the several Balkan states to one another determined by friendly counsel along historically established lines of allegiance and nationality, and international guarantees of the political and economic independence and territorial integrity of the several Balkan states should be entered into.

12. The Turkish portions of the present Ottoman empire should be assured a secure sovereignty, but other nationalities which are now under Turkish rule should be assured of an undoubted security of life and an absolutely unmolested opportunity of autonomous development, and the Dardenelles should be permanently opened as a free passage to the ships and commerce of all nations under international guarantees.

13. An independent Polish state should be erected which should include the territories inhabited by indisputably Polish population, which should be assured a free and secure access to the sea, and whose political and economic independence and territorial integrity should be guaranteed by international guarantees.

14. A general association of nations must be formed under specific covenants for the purpose of affording mutual guarantees of political independence and territorial integrity to great and small States alike.

Four Principles of February 11, 1918

1. That each part of the final settlement must be based upon the essential justice of that particular case and upon such adjustments as are most likely to bring a peace that will be permanent.

2. That peoples and provinces are not to be bartered about from sovereignty to sovereignty as if they were mere chattels and pawns in a game, even the great game, now for ever discredited, of the Balance of Power; but that;

3. Every territorial settlement involved in this war must be made in the interest and for the benefit of the population concerned, and not as a part of any mere adjustment or compromise of claims amongst rival States;

4. That all well-defined national aspirations shall be accorded the utmost satisfaction that can be accorded to them without introducing new or perpetuating old elements of discord and antagonism that would be likely in time to break the peace of Europe, and consequently of the world.

The Four Ends of July 4, 1918

1. The destruction of every arbitrary power anywhere that can separately, secretly, and of its single choice disturb the peace of the world; or, if it cannot be presently destroyed, at least its reduction to virtual impotence.

2. The settlement of every question, whether of territory, of sovereignty, of economic arrangement, or of political relationship, upon the basis of free acceptance of that settlement by the people immediately concerned, and not upon the basis of mutual material interest of advantage of any other nation or people which may desire a different settlement for the sake of its now exterior influence or mastery.

3. The consent of all nations to be governed in their conduct toward each other by the same principles of honour and of respect for the common law of civilised society that govern the individual citizens of all modern States in their relations with one another, to the end that all promises and covenants may be sacredly observed, no private plots or conspiracies hatched, no selfish injuries wrought with impunity, and a mutual trust established upon the handsome foundation of mutual respect for right.

4. The establishment of an organisation of peace which shall make it certain that the combined power of the free nations will check every invasion of right and serve to make peace and justice the more secure by affording a definite tribunal of opinion to which all must submit, and by which every international readjustment that cannot be amicably agreed upon by the peoples concerned shall be sanctioned.

The Five Points of September 27, 1918

1. The impartial justice meted out must involve no discrimination between those to whom we wish to be just and those to whom we do not wish to be just. It must be justice that knows no favourites and knows no standards but equal rights of the several peoples concerned.

2. No special or separate interest of any single nation or any group of nations can be made the basis of any part of the settlement which is not consistent with the common interest of all.

3. There can be no league or alliances or special covenants and understandings within the general and common family of the League of Nations.

4. And, more specifically, there can be no special selfish economic combinations within the League and no employment of any form of economic boycott or exclusion, except as the power of economic penalty, by exclusion from the market of the world, may be vested in the League of Nations itself as deans of discipline and control.

5. All international agreements and treaties of every kind must be made known in their entirety to the rest of the world. Special alliances and economic rivalries and hostilities have been the prolific source in the modern world of the plans and passions that produce war. It would be an insincere as well as an insecure peace that did not exclude them in definite and binding terms.

a sacred cause and chose to interpret America's role in the war as that of a crusade: bringing liberty and justice to the war-torn Old World."[39]

American involvement in the War and then Russian revolution had their cumulative effect on turning the tide against Germany. In the later part of 1918, German power looked like rushing towards a disaster in a 'trench warfare.' It is true that when the War broke out, she possessed the most formidable military machine that the world had ever known and that she had the immense advantage of fighting on interior lines. But the vast economic resources commanded by Allied and Associated Powers came to have an upper hand after the Battle of Marne. The German military strength was sapped by the never-ceasing drain on her man-power due to the unparalleled casualties of the war. A despatch from the British commander-in-chief stated: "The rapid collapse of Germany's military powers in the later half of 1918 would not have taken place but for that ceaseless attrition which used up the reserves of the German armies."[40] Her economic strength was sapped by Britain's command of the seas which once again demonstrated in an impressive degree the influence of her naval power. General Ludendorff made the significant admission that if the war "lasted, our defeat seemed inevitable. Economically, we were in a highly unfavourable position for a war of exhaustion."[41]

Under these conditions, the 'key figure of the Central Powers' (Germany) had to surrender on November 11, 1918 and accept the terms of Armistice based on the principles of Wilsonian idealism. Lipson has enumerated these reasons of the defeat of Germany in the great war:[42]

---

39. W.H. McNeill, op. cit., p. 17. The role of Wilson and Lenin in the first World War has been evaluated in different terms. They have been described as the 'two utopians of the early twentieth century'. See A.J.P. Taylor: *From Serajevo to Potsdam* (New York: Harcourt Brace and World, 1965), p. 45. Different from this, A.J. Mayer holds that the First World War was transformed by Wilson and Lenin "from a traditional conflict into a crusade of ideals, thus forming a watershed' from which flow the major opposing currents of twentieth century international politics." *Wilson Versus Lenin: Political Origins of the New Diplomacy* (Cleveland: World Publishing Co., 1964), pp. 368-93.
40. See Lipson, op. cit., p. 306.
41. Ibid.
42. Ibid., p. 307.

First World War

1. The condition of war in the second half of 1918 undermined the spiritual resistance of the German people who could not have endured indefinitely the privations to which they were subjected and it also had repercussions upon those who were fighting at the front.
2. None the less, Germany's capitulation was due to fracture of the military machine under the blows inflicted by the Allied armies, which drove the army chiefs to trade the initiative in demanding peace. The outbreak of popular disturbances in Germany and the overthrow of the civil regime, did not precede, or occasion the military surrender; they followed it when the mortification of defeat was added to the sufferings entailed by semi-starvation.
3. The Russian revolution had its own effect. The German government had encouraged the forces of disruption in Russia in order to relieve the military situation in the eastern theatre, but the momentary relief was duly purchased. The German prisoners of war, released from captivity in Russia and re-enrolled in the fighting forces, produced a decided determination in the army's *morale*. Political ideas recognise no frontier, and the Bolshevik contagion soon spread beyond the borders of the Soviet Union.
4. The intervention of the United States exerted a profound psychological effect on the German people, because it drove home the conviction that they could not hope to win the war.
5. The endurance of the French and the sacrifices of the Russians were vital contributions to the eventual triumph of the Allied cause.

In this way, the first great war came to an end with the most inglorious defeat of Germany and, for that reason, being inherent with a potential menace whose results appeared after about two decades.[43] It all confirmed the observation of Clausewitz: "The

---

43. "The blunders of German diplomacy to this fatal result. The prodigious feats of German armies contributed were in the end unable to rectify diplomatic mistakes and to turn the tide of battle against an anti-German coalition which included all the other great Powers of the world and half of the Minor Powers

stigma of shame incurred by a cowardly submission can never be effaced. The drop of poison which thus enters the blood of a nation will be transmitted to posterity. It will undermine and paralyse the strength of later generation."[44]

Consequences: Emergence of a New State System and Triumph of Internationalism

The termination of the First World War entailed very significant results both for the defeated powers and for the world as a whole. These may be pointed out as under :

1. In terms of power relationships, the chief effect of this world conflict was to upset completely the equilibrium between the pre-war coalitions and to replace it by the imposition upon the continent of Europe the military and diplomatic hegemony of France and her new allies in the east. The post-war alliances among the beneficiaries of the new distribution of power—France, Belgium, Poland and the 'Little Entente' States of Czechoslovakia, Yugoslavia and Rumania—"created a new condition for the preservation of the status quo. Germany disarmed and diminished in size and population was reduced to diplomatic impotence."[45]

2. The old state system was replaced by the new one based largely on the principle of national self-determination as expounded and obdurately stressed by President Wilson. The end of the empires of the Hohenzollerns in Germany, of the Habsburgs in Austria-Hungary, of the Ottomans in Turkey, and of the Czars in Russia entailed the doom of the old monarchical orders and their substitution by the republican system of nation-states. Thus, the new states of Poland, Finland, Yugoslavia and Czechoslovakia came into being, while Austria and Hungary became separate sovereign states in a quite truncated form. A new dimension to the politics of international relations was given by the policy of 'non-isolationism' adopted by the United States. Hence, in the post-war

---

as well. Imperial Germany conquered vaster territories and won a position of military preponderance greater than that enjoyed by the first Napoleon, but in the end this military empire crumbled to pieces even more rapidly and completely than that of Bonaparte." Schuman, op. cit., p. 79.

44. Cited by Hitler in his *Mein Kampf* (Translated from German into English by James Murphy), p. 368.
45. Schuman, op. cit., p. 84.

First World War

world, it seemed that the predominance of Europe and its Concert "were at an end and that the future basis of international government must be world-wide. The system of conference previously employed should continue, but the seats on the board previously monopolised by five or six European Great Powers must now be thrown open to the representatives of some ten times than number of States, small and great, collected from every corner of the earth."[46]

3. The First World War brought untold sufferings to mankind. It stood as the first notorious example of destruction at such a large scale.[47] The German power could hold at bay the greatest coalition of nations the world had ever seen for about four years with no considerable help form their allies. "Russia they had totally defeated; France they had brought to her knees; and the flower of Britain's manhood had fallen as before a scythe in the face of the German army."[48] For about fifty-one months, the whole world lived in a state of acute suspense about the fate of this great holocaust.[49] And ultimately, if the German might came to have an unprecedented humiliation after the involvement of the United States it was just on account of her realisation that if the War "continued, the United States could carry on fighting longer than any other belligerent."[50] If so, Germany deserved a big lesson both for herself and for any other power that might repeat the same disastrous drama in time to come. For this reason, even genuine grievances of Germany

---

46. Gathorne-Hardy, op. cit., pp. 13-14.
47. The total casualties of war have been calculated as under:

Dead Soldiers (known)	10,000,000	Dead Soldiers (presumed)	3,000,000
Dead Civilians	13,000,000	Wounded	20,000,000
Prisoners	3,000,000	War Orphans	9,000,000
War Widows	5,000,000	Refugees	10,000,000

    See Nehru: *Glimpses of World History*, p. 637.
48. See. F.S. Northedge and M.J. Grieve, op. cit., p. 106.
49. For instance, President Wilson's confidential adviser (Col. House) said at one stage: "The saddest feature of the situation is that there is no good outcome to look forward. If the Allies win, it means largely the domination of Russia on the continent of Europe. If Germany wins, it means the unspeakable tyranny of militarism for generations to come." *The Intimate Papers of Colonel House*, Vol. I, p. 285.
50. Northedge and Grieve, op. cit., p. 109.

European State System Before and After the War

Pre-War Phase	Post-War Phase	Independent Statehood (newly created states)
1. Portugal	1. Portugal	1. Austria
2. Spain	2. Spain	2. Hungary
3. Switzerland	3. Great Britain	3. Czechoslovakia
4. Italy*	4. Italy	4. Yugoslavia
5. Austria-Hungary*	5. France*	5. Latvia
6. France*	6. Austria	6. Lithuania
7. G. Britain*	7. Hungary	7. Estonia
8. Serbia	8. Yugoslavia	8. Poland
9. Greece	9. Albania	9. Finland
10. Bulgaria	10. Greece	
11. Rumania	11. Bulgaria	
12. Russia	12. Rumania	
13. Germany*	13. Czechoslovakia	
14. Belgium	14. Belgium	
15. Netherlands	15. Netherlands	
16. Norway	16. Germany	
17. Sweden	17. Poland	
18. Denmark	18. Lithuania	
19. Albania	19. Latvia	
	20. Estonia	
	21. Finland	
	22. Sweden	
	23. Norway	
	24. Denmark	
	25. Russia	
	26. Switzerland	

*Great Powers.

regarding her acute sufferings due to the blockade of all supplies by the Allied Powers in 1917-18 were overshadowed by the magnitude of her great crime. The victorious statesmen of the Allied Powers like Lloyd George of England and Clemenceau of France spoke in sharply vindictive tones at the Paris Peace Conference and they did not bother for these words of protest uttered by the head of the German delegation (Count Brockdorff-Rantzau): "The hundreds and thousands of non-combatants who have perished since November 11 by the reason of the blockade were killed with cold deliberation. Think of that when you speak of guilt and punishment."[51]

4. The first World War enthused a good number of serious statesmen and writers to have a revised look at the subject of war. The use of huge armaments informed them to think about need for putting an effective check on the race for the production of destructive weapons at such a large scale. The use of the propaganda technique and the force of ideological utterances (as made by Wilson and Lenin) enriched the scope of investigation so as to treat them as significant instruments of power politics. Bilateral diplomacy was replaced by its multilateral counterpart; the system of empire-building became a subject of denunciation and the process of decolonisation ushered in having its first manifestation in the Mandate System under the control of the League of Nations. The trial of war criminals added its own contribution to the development of international law. Above all, the war "socialised and democratised foreign policy, as an ideal, if not always as a reality, and as such it was to remain until the present."[52]

5. However, the most important effect of the First World War should be traced in the triumph of internationalism. The new outlook paved the way for the establishment of an international organisation for the purpose of maintaining peace and security in the world. The 'father' of the League of Nations (President Wilson) in his memorable address at the Paris Peace Conference of February 14, 1919 said: "Many terrible things have come out of this war, gentlemen, but some very beautiful things have come out of it. Wrong has been defeated, but the right of the world has been more conscious than it ever was before the majority of right. People that were suspicious of one another can now live as friends and comrades in a single family, and desire to do so. The miasma of distrust, of intrigue is cleared away. Men are looking eye to eye and saying: 'We are brothers and have a common purpose.' We did not

---

51. Carl J. Friedrich: "German Foreign Policy" in Brown, Hodges and Roucek, op. cit., p. 166.
52. Northedge and Grieve, op. cit., p. 94.

realise it before, but now we do realise it, and this is our covenant of friendship'.⁵³

In short, the First World War ended signifying a "revolutionary change that had taken place in the general attitude to it as an institution."⁵⁴ At the same time, it nourished the soldierly spirit inspiring the fire-hot nationalism in the revisionist states from which the Second World War sprang and the dread of the renewed war from which unwillingness on the part of the democracies to resist that nationalism by force also sprang. The victors laid all the blame on Axis Powers, particularly Germany, that reacted to the same in a negative, though mild, tone on account of being in a humiliating position. In the heart of their hearts the vanquished powers waited for the time to take revenge whose disastrous effects appeared some twenty years after.⁵⁵

---

53. Temperley (ed.), op. cit., Vol I, p. 65. L.C.F. Turner is right in holding: "Whatever aims they proclaimed during the conflict, none of the Rulers of Great Powers really knew what they were fighting about in August, 1914." *Origins of the First World War* (London: Edward Arnold, 1970), p. 112.
54. Gathorne-Hardy, op. cit., p. 14
55. Thus, Schuman holds: "Questions of moral responsibility are almost pointless after decades of frenzied debate, for none of the actors willed the war. Each national group of diplomats, imperialists and militarists, simply strove for certain ends which were valued above peace. The ends were those of good patriots everywhere. The striving was not villainy but an act of devotion—blind, stubborn, often muddled and stupid but seldom iniquitous or dishonourable. If the means to the end spelled ruin and death, the guilt of arson and murder fell alike upon all or none." op. cit., p. 76.

2

PARIS PEACE SETTLEMENTS

The European arrangements made at Paris endured rather longer, but, partly through the absence of Russia, they were unstable, and within twenty years had been completely upset, the defeated enemy of 1919 once more dominating the Continent. It may reasonably be held that the failures of 1919 were largely due to the factors beyond the control of any statesman of the time: the immaturity of American policy and the social upheaval in Russia. Yet, had there been a firmer grasp of realities and a more methodical tackling of problems as they arose, more might have been achieved.

—F. S. Marston[1]

The peace settlements made at the Paris Conference of the Allied and Associated Powers and perforce accepted by the vanquished powers of Europe like Germany, Austria, Hungary, Bulgaria and Turkey, in addition to a host of other treaties, big and small, signed by Rumania, Greece and the newly created states of Poland, Yugoslavia and Czechoslovakia, occupy an important place in the long succession of similar occurrences. However, the Paris meet deserves the credit of being the first instance of peace-making on such a large scale. If the combat of 1914-18 gained the title of being the world war, the peace-making after the termination of hostilities, likewise, deserves the credit of being the first instance in the direction of an attempt to bring about an enduring world peace. It is in spite of the fact that the leading statesmen of the victorious powers could not immunise themselves from the shackles of national self-interest and the over all situation that was complicated by the matrix of Wilsonian idealism. Thus, the Paris Peace Conference of 1919 "was dominated by personalities whom the events of the War had made the directing minds of organisations

---

1. F.S. Marston: *The Peace Conference of 1919: Organisation and Procedure* (London: Oxford Univ. Press, 1944), p. 229.

far greater than any that had ever previously existed. They were none of the men who could be fettered by a system; they used and 'scrapped' their materials ruthlessly, and thus continually changed the conference machine to suit the needs of the moments of situation."[2]

Paris Peace Conference: Organisation, Working and Initial Limitations

In a correct sense, a study of the peace-making at Paris should be treated as complementary part of the study of first World War contained in the preceding chapter. What opened at Paris on January 19, 1919 was not something new or spontaneous, it was like a natural development of events having their rise and growth over the last few years. It was a big gathering of 32 countries, big and small, each represented by a very large number of representatives assisted by their staff and press reporters. To make the business possible, more than 50 commissions of various sorts were established and coordination among them was effected by the Council of Ten, also known by the name of the Supreme Council, made up of two representatives each from the United States, Britain, France, Italy and Japan. After some time, it became a Council of Four consisting of one representative each of the US, Britain, France and Italy. When after some time, Italian Prime Minister (Orlando) left Paris in a mood of protest against Wilson's insistence on not taking into recognition any secret treaty made during the times of war, it became a 'group of three'. In this way, the real architects of the peace settlements were President Wilson of the United States, Prime Minister Lloyd George of Britain, and Foreign Secretary Clemenceau of France.

The routine work of the conference was accomplished by a large number of commissions and committees. There were General Commissions to deal with the work relating to the League of Nations as labour, war guilt, reparations, ports, aviation, finance, economics, and treaty drafting; there were Territorial Committees to deal with Polish, Greek, Albanian, Czech, Belgian and Danish affairs; there were ad hoc committees also to deal with the affairs of Baltic region, Alsace-Lorraine, Second Kiel Canal, Luxembourg, Saar, Rhineland, reparations, prisoners of war, Ukraine, financial

---

2. See H.W.V. Temperley (ed.): *A History of the Peace Conference of Paris* (London: Hodder and Stoughton, 1920), Vol I, pp. 236-37.

clauses, Morocco and other overseas territories of the defeated powers. But the Council of Four was the most important of all that controlled Central Drafting Committee, Committees to deal with Enemy Notes and Counter-Proposals, and New States Committees. The Supreme War Council, formed during the times of war, continued to exist so as to exercise control over Council for Supply and Relief, Supreme Economic Council, and Submarine Cabal committee.

For our purpose, not the composition of so many commissions and committees but the working of the conference in the midst of so many limitations and challenging circumstances is important. First, let us have a brief look at the personality of the great leaders who played a decisive role on this occasion. The most important role was played by President Wilson of the United States. His idealism acted like a lengthening chain for the great powers of Europe. "An idealist soaring high in the heavens, with an air of romantic melancholy about him, a brilliant orator, an unskilled statesman from the European standards but unaccustomed to the rough and tumble bargaining with his political equals, having curious capacity to close his eyes to unpleasant facts, Wilson was all the time thinking of something not convincing to the European diplomats. 'His insistence on 'open covenants of peace, openly arrived at' created a problem for the statesmen of Europe, particularly to Orlando, Lloyd George and Clemenceau. Likewise, his advocacy of the principle of national self-determination, as we shall see later, created several thorny problems for the seekers of lasting 'security from German invasion' in time to come. His insistence on not giving Fieume to Italy irked Orlando and his opposition to the proposal of permanent Allied occupation of the Rhineland and Saar basin annoyed Clemenceau. But Wilson could not carry his obduracy to the desired extent in view of several diplomatic limitations. Thus, whenever his idealism "came into sharp conflict with materialism at the conference, in most cases materialism triumphed."[3]

Prime Minister Lloyd George of England deserves the second place of importance in this connection. He was bound by his commitments made to the people of England at the time of elections in 1918 to make Germany pay 'shilling for shilling and ton

---

3. W.C. Langsam: *The World Since 1919* (Delhi: Surjeet Pub., 1981), 8th Ed., p. 8.

for ton' and 'hang the Kaiser'. This 'clever Welsh attorney' was really at a loss to find the most appealing argument to touch the 'vanity weakness or self-interest of his immediate listener.' He could not forget the counsel of Lord Palmerston: "It is the immediately pending future that determines the conduct of governments and not the embalmed past." Thus, he played a role that was justified by some English writers on the plea: "We have moved into a world even more bloody and harsh than that of 1918. Peacemaking will be correspondingly more difficult and the treaties may, perhaps have to be made by quite different methods."[4]

The French delegation headed by Foreign Secretary Clemenceau was described as "uncontrolling and uncontrolled, sleepy and pugnacious; he arose from the long slumbers of sleep only when the interests of France were at stake or when there was an opportunity of strengthening his country at the cost of some smaller power." Nicknamed as 'Tiger' and with a good command over English language, he came to the conference like a disillusioned old man, who seemed to have seen all the evils of life. Until he came to power, he had been known for his violent opposion to censorship and governmental controls. Yet when he became the Premier and Minister of War, he devised an efficient gagging machine of his own. "He probably was the most artful diplomat at the conference. The extent of his realism was indicated by his prudence in paying lip service to Wilson's ideals while pursuing the goal of exalting and securing France as he weakened Germany."[5]

The Italian delegation was led by Prime Minister Orlando who, despite being a learned and eloquent diplomat, lacked command over the English language. His obduracy in giving recognition to secret treaties (particularly the Secret Treaty of London of 1915 whereby Britain had promised Italy major prizes after the termination of war) irritated Wilson to the extent that, feeling incapable of reasoning out the American President, he had to leave Paris for Rome in a 'huff'. Among other delegates, some reference may be made to the Greek delegation headed by Eletherios Venizoles nicknamed as 'the Ulysses of Conference'. Ignace Jan Pederewski headed Polish delegation; Japan was represented by

---

4. C.K. Webster: "Foreword" to Marston, op. cit., p. xi.
5. Langsam, op, cit., p. 5.

Kimmochi Siaonji, Nobuaki and Makino. As a matter of fact, the real architects of peace at Paris were Wilson, George and Clemenceau. The representatives of the defeated powers were not allowed any participation at all; they were brought to the conference hall like captives and made to sign the documents offered to them.

The peace-makers started their task in the midst of several crucial difficulties. In the first places, as already pointed out, it was a problem as to how to reconcile the idealism of Wilson with the materialism of George, Clemenceau, Orlando and others. The war had ended but the challenging question was how to devise a new machinery that could perpetuate peace. Second, the problem of national minorities cropped up as a result of the application of the doctrine of national self-determination. We may say that, in this direction, the authors of the peace settlements could make headway to the possible extent by creating the new states of Poland, Yugoslavia and Czechoslovakia and by allowing the status of independent states to Austria and Hungary after the dismemberment of the Habsburg Empire. It is a different thing that the implementation of the principle of national self-determination was blended with the forces of 'historical claims' and 'economic necessity' ranged within the overall framework of diplomatic bargain. Last, the selection of Paris as the venue of the peace conference in recognition of the great role played by France during the days of war was unfortunate. "Paris was a nightmare and everyone there was morbid. The entire atmosphere was seething with the spirit of discontent, hatred, vengeance, cynicism and spite."[6]

A critical look at the working and achievements of the Paris Peace Conference shows that the great statesmen of the world were really confronted with a large number of cucial issues. "The number of knotty problems facing the conference was legion. The Paris assemblage had to draw up terms to satisfy at least the more important Allies. They had to attempt the feeding of the starving millions in Central and Eastern Europe. There had to be drawn up

---

6. J.M. Keynes: *Essays in Persuasion* (London: Macmillan, 1920), p. 5. President Wilson's Private Secretary (Colonel House) records: "Paris was a bad place for business, where we were hampered by the atmosphere itself; where German guilt was assumed a proved fact; subconsciously the shell shocks of Paris affected the nerves of all the delegates."

a covenant for the League of Nations. And all this had to be done in a Europe which in those dark days immediately following the war, resembled a seething cauldron. Many nations still were involved in combat. The great powers themselves were at odds over policies and viewpoints. In retrospect, it seems miraculous that any treaty was devised in the pandemonium that was Europe in 1919."[7]

It is true that, as we shall see later, the Paris Peace Conference failed in 'making the world safe for democracy' for ever. And yet it did succeed in bringing order out of the prevailing chaos that could have a life of about two decades. Guilt lies on those great powers that played a very decisive role at the time of peace-making and then played an equally criminal role in the devastation of what they had done here. Webster observes well: "Few people had imagined how difficult and complex the process of peace-making was to be. No one had foreseen that the Conference would be the centre of world power while the great figures were present at it, and that a great part of its time and energy would have to be spent on immediate problems rather than on the negotiation of the permanent peace terms. Thus, at the outset, the machinery was strangely amateurish and defective. It was only by desperate hard work and brilliant improvisation that some kind of order was produced out of the chaotic mess of delegates and experts who had to serve and advise their imperious masters, none of whom was anxious to confine himself in the straitjacket of official machinery."[8] In a word, it "was in an atmosphere poisoned by memories of the carnage in the battle fields, of the devastated areas, and of the conference came together in the French capital in 1919 and set their hands to the task of rebuilding the new Europe."[9]

Major Peace Settlement: Treaty of Versailles with Germany
Among all peace treaties signed after the First World War, the Treaty of Versailles occupies an unparalleled importance of its own in the history of international relations and politics. Signed between Principal Allied and Associated Powers (USA, British Empire, France, Italy and Japan) and other Allied and Associated Powers (Belgium, Bolivia, Brazil, China, Cuba, Ecuador, Greece, Guatemala,

---

7. Langsam, op. cit., p. 7.
8. See Marston, op. cit., p. x.
9. E. Lipson: *Europe: 1914-1939* (London: Adam and Charles Black, 1957), p. 308.

Haiti, Hedjaz, Honduras, Liberia, Nicaragua, Panama, Peru, Poland, Portugal, Rumania, the Serb-Croat-Slovene State, Siam, Czechoslovakia and Uruguay) on the one side and Germany on the other on June 28, 1919, it embodied the loud hope that with its coming into force, the 'state of war will terminate'[10]. It appeared as a very comprehensive document running into 440 articles with a score of annexures resulting in the territorial and economic enlargement of other States like those of France, Poland, Belgium, Czechoslovakia, Yugoslavia and Italy at the expense of German empire. The most important provisions of this treaty may be summed up as under.[11]

Territorial Provisions: The German empire was distintegrated in its eastern, western and northern directions. The areas of Alsace and Lorraine (captured by Germany in the Franco-Prussian war of 1871) were returned to France; Morsnet, Eupen and Melmedy were given to Belgium; the rich areas of coal mines in the Saar basin were also given to France with the provision that it would remain under French control for a period of 15 years so as to meet her loss of destruction of mines caused by Germany and then a plebiscite would take place under the supervision of the League of Nations for the final settlement of its political destiny. The city of Danzig was declared 'free' to remain under the sovereignty of the League and in customs union with Poland. Moreover, in order to allow Poland all access to the coastal city of Danzig, a 'corridor' between Pomerania and East Prussia was created that naturally separated the areas of Posen and West Prussia from the rest of the German territory. After a formal plebiscite Lower or Southern Silesia was also given away to Poland. Although Memel was taken away from Germany and placed under the control of Allied Powers, it was grabbed by Lithuania in 1923 and then given away to her by the Allied Powers in 1924.

Germany lost northern Schleswig to Denmark as a result of plebiscite held in two zones. She leased out the ports of Hamburg and Stettin to Czechoslovakia for a term of 99 years. She accepted ban on her union with Austria (Anschluss) and recognised the territorial independence and integrity of the new State of Austria. She also accepted permanent 'demilitarisation of the Rhineland

---

10. Temperley, op. cit., Vol. 3, p. 110.
11. For full text of the Treaty of Versailles see Ibid., pp. 111-336.

and Allied occupation there for a term of 15 years (to be lifted up in three phases after 5,10 and 15 years). Luxembourg ceased to be a neutral state and subsequently she entered into an economic union with Belgium. Besides, she surrendered her special rights and claims in China, Thailand (Siam), Egypt, Morocco and Liberia. Her privileges in Turkey and Bulgaria were forfeited. With the introduction of the Mandate System under the League of Nations, her overseas possessions were taken away and put under the control of other 'advanced' nations subject to the supervision of the League of Nations. Thus, Britain got mandate over German South-West Africa; Britain and France got mandates over Cameroon and Togoland; German pacific islands to the south of the equator were placed under the mandatory control of Australia, while those to the north of the equator went to Japan. Kiachow was also leased out to Japan.

Military Provisions: Equally drastic were other provisions that aimed at crushing the military power of Germany. To limit her military potential, German General Staff was abolished. A ban was imposed on compulsory conscriptions and military training outside the army areas. Manufacture of tanks, armoured cars, military aeroplanes and submarines was prohibited; the strength of the army was reduced to 10,000 soldiers with 4,000 officers. The naval strength of Germany was restricted to 6 battleships of 10,000 tons, 6 light cruisers, 12 destroyers and 12 torpedo boats, and a personnel of 15,000 with 1,500 officers. She was asked to dismantle all fortifications in the islands of Heligoland and Dune. A similar ban was imposed on Baltic and North Sea coasts. The right bank of the Rhine was permanently demilitarised to a depth of 50 kilometres. It was provided that the German government could adopt the method of voluntary enlistment of at least 12 years for the ordinary personnel and 25 years for officers. It was also stipulated that an Allied Control Commission would supervise the execution of the disarmament clauses.

Economic Provisions: No less terrifying were the economic provisons of the treaty that subjected Germany to the payment of heavy fines. Art. 231 of the treaty said: "The Allied and Associated Governments affirm and Germany accepts the responsibility of Germany and her Allies for causing all the loss and damage to which the Allied and Associated Governments and their nationals have been subjected as a consequence of the war imposed upon them by the aggression of Germany and her allies." In Art. 232 it was recognised that the resources of Germany were not adequate to make complete reparation for all such loss and damage done to the civilian population of the Allied and Associated powers and to their property. In addition, Germany would reimburse Belgium with interest at 5 per cent for all the money the latter had borrowed from the Allied governments during the years of war. For this purpose, a reparation commission would be appointed by the Allied Powers to determine the total amount of reparation and to draw up a schedule of payment distributed over 30 years beginning from May 1, 1921. Meanwhile, Germany would pay the equivalent of nearly $ 5,000,000,000 out of which the cost of the army of occupation would be met and the balance applied to the reparation. Since full reparation could not be paid in cash, it was also stipulated that Germany might pay partly in the form of specified commodities.

Moreover, since the resources of Germany were to be devoted directly to the physical restoration of the invaded areas, the Allies were permitted to replace at German expense all merchant-marine ships and fishing boats lost or damaged during the war. It implied that she was made to surrender half of her ships and a quarter of her steam trawlers and fighting boats. The Allied Powers were also allowed to file with Reparation Commission lists showing various articles seized by Germany or destroyed in consequence of military questions as well as lists of building materials that they wished to have manufactured in Germany and delivered to them to permit 'restoration of the invaded areas'. Finally, the Reparation Commission was empowered to recommend action in the case of any German failure to make payment of war penalties. Germany also advanced an assurance that the manufacturers of the Allied Powers would be accorded 'most favoured treatment in her markets'.

Until the reparation question was closed, Germany would supply large quantities of coal to France, Belgium and Italy and build for the Allies a yearly tonnage of 200,000 for 5 years. For 5 years the Allies were also given special concessions in matters of import from and export of goods to Germany. In order to provide some landlocked states (like Switzerland and Czechoslovakia) access to the sea, certain German rivers (like Elbe, Oder, Nieman and Danube) were internationalised and the Rhine was placed

Main Provisions of the Treaty of Versailles

	Territorial	
1.	Germany ceded	Provinces of Alsace and Lorraine to France and control over Saar basin for a period of 15 years as compensation for the destruction of French mines and then a plebiscite was to be held under the League's supervision for the final determination of its political distiny.
2.	" "	Morsnet, Eupen and Melmedy to Belgium.
3.	" "	Posen and West Prussia to Poland, because a 'corridor' between Pomerania and East Prussia was created to give her access to the 'free city of Danzig' placed under the sovereignty of the League and to live in customs union with Poland.
4.	" "	Lower (Southern) Silesia to Poland (after a formal plebiscite).
5.	" "	Memel to the Allied powers that was given away to Lithuania in 1924 as she had already captured it in 1923.
6.	" " Leased out	Hamburg and Stettin ports to Czechoslovakia for a term of 99 years.
7.	" " accepted	ban on *Anschluss*—union between Germany and Austria—and recognised territorial independence and integrity of the new Austrian State.
8.	" "	permanent demilitarisation of the Rhineland and Allied occupation there—of Cologne for 5, of Coblenz for 10, and of Mainz for 15 years.
9.	" " surrendered	special rights and claims in China, Thailand, Egypt, Morocco and Liberia, while her privileges in Turkey and Bulgaria were forfeited.

10. " " overseas possessions for the new Mandate System under the League of Nations. Thus, German South-West Africa went to Britain, Cameroon and Togoland to Britain and France, German Pacific islands south of the equator to Australia and those to the north of the equator to Japan; Kiachow was also leased out to Japan.

Military

1. Ban on conscriptions (voluntary enlistment excluded) and military training outside the army.
2. Prohibition of making tanks, armoured cars, military aeroplanes and submarines.
3. Army reduced to 10,000 soldiers with 4,000 officers.
4. Navy restricted to 6 battleships of 10,000 tons, 6 light cruisers, 12 destroyers and 12 torpedo boats, and a personnel of 15,000 with 1,500 officers.
5. Destruction of fortifications in the islands of Heligoland and Dune and ban on any such activity at the Baltic and North Sea coasts.

under a joint commission. The Kiel Canal was thrown open to the use of all nations. All German properties, whether private or public, in her colonies were confiscated and her pre-war trading concessions available to Egypt, Morocco and China were abolished. Germany was also instructed to return trophies, works of art and flags taken from France in the war of 1871 and compensate the university of Louvain for the destruction of her documents and manuscripts.

Losses of Germany

Population lost to	Total	German-speaking (in thousands)	Other Languages Speaking
1. France	1,874	1,634	240
2. Belgium	60	50	10
3. Denmark	166	40	126
4. Danzig	331	315	16
5. Poland	3,855	1,364	2,491
6. Memel	141	72	41
7. Czechoslovakia	48	7	—
8. Saar Territory	652	652	—
Total	7,127	4,134	2,993

Source: Etienne Mantoux: *The Carthaginian Peace or the Economic Consequences of Mr. Keynes* (New York: Charles Scribner's Sons, 1952), p. 70, n. I.

She was to deliver a very large number of horses, sheep and cattle to Belgium and France and the skull of Sultan M'kwada (that was removed from the protectorate of German East Africa and taken away to Berlin) to England and the original Koran of Caliph Ottoman to the king of Hedjaz.

Legal Provisions: The treaty also contained some clauses relating to war guilt and punishment to the wrong-doers. For this purpose, the German Emperor (Kaiser William II) was arraigned for the supreme war offence against international morality and the sanctity of treaties. Germany also agreed to surrender other persons accused of having committed acts of violation of the laws and customs of war. (The trial of the Emperor could not take place as the government of the Netherlands refused to extradite him. Hindenburg also escaped. Thus, only a few unimportant German officers could be tried and punished by the war tribunals.)

In short, this treaty reduced the European area of Germany by one-eighth and its population by 6,500,000. She was deprived of her major resources at home as well as abroad. Her merchant marine was reduced from more than 5,000,000 tons to fewer than 5,00,000. The navy was virtually wiped out and in respect of military strength it looked like Belgium's counterpart. She heavily suffered in terms of loss of natural and mineral resources like iron, coal, zinc and lead. She was deprived of her overseas possessions that comprised 13,000,000 people and 9,000,000 sq miles of territory. The net result of all was that Germany was crushed and crippled in all respects and by all means. It "so broke down the pre-war industrial complex that for a long time Germany was incapable of producing a healthy economy functioning anywhere near its former level of efficiency. Finally, the defeated nation signed a blank reparation cheque."[12]

Just to maintain some semblance of international courtesy, the draft of the treaty was sent to the members of German delegation who were allowed to offer their 'Observations' on it.[13] It afforded them an opportunity to express their protest in three important directions:[14]

1. The Wilsonian idealism emphasised the principle of national self-determination and Germany accepted it as a basis of surrender. In other words, it constituted the basis of armistice in 1918. And yet it was dishounoured by the victorious powers in view of the fact that predominantly German-inhabited areas like those of Danzig and Memel were taken away from her; the Saar basin was placed under the alien control for 15 years; Rhineland was permanently demilitarised and her union with Austria was forbidden. It was contended that the principle of national self-determination was going to be applied solely to the disadvantage of Germany that must, on the contrary, be equally valid in all states and must be applied specially where a population of German origin desired

---

12. Langsam, op. cit., p. 18.
13. See 'The Observations of the German Delegation on the Draft Treaty of Peace" in *The American Journal of International Law*, Vol. 13 of 1919. For a summary of the same see Lipson: *Europe, 1914-1939*, pp. 311-14.
14. Ibid., pp. 312-14.

adherence to the territory of the German empire.

2. The vexed question of reparation was also touched. It was contended that the obligation of Germany exceeded the scope of initial agreement and if the victorious powers persisted in imposing upon her a debt that robbed her of every possibility of a future, the German people would feel themselves condemned to slavery.

3. The exclusion of Germany from the League of Nations for the 'time being' was also resented. It was, therefore, contended that she be admitted to the international organisation on the 'basis of equality'.

The 'Observations' boldly contended: "This is not the just peace we were promised. It stands in full and irreconcilable conflict with the basis agreed upon for a just and durable peace.... It will be difficult to imagine how harder terms could be imposed upon an imperialistic Germany.... A permanent peace can never be established upon the oppression and enslavement of a great nation. The new peace must be a peace of justice and therefore of voluntary agreement."[15]

The protests of the German delegation were carefully studied by the victorious powers and then a comprehensive 'Reply' was sent rebutting their contentions on the following grounds:[16]

1. If on the territorial settlement the decision in 'certain cases' was against Germany, it was not done with some vindictive motive; it was rather an inevitable result of the fact that an appreciable portion of the territory of the German empire consisted of districts which had in the past been wrongfully appropriated. Every territorial settlement of the peace treaty had been determined upon after a careful and laborious consideration of all religious, racial and lingustic factors in each particular country. The fate of Danzig and Memel, for example, was linked with giving an outlet to the sea to Poland and Lithuania respectively. The forfeiture of overseas German possessions was merited in view of the sufferings of the native population under German colonial administration as well as of necessity for safeguarding against the establishment of bases for military imperialism.

2. Justice demanded that compensation should be made by Germany to all damages sustained by the civilian population of the

---

15. Ibid., pp. 311 and 314.
16. Ibid., pp. 314-17.

Allies. Besides, the defeated country was intact and in no way suffering from the devastation brought upon the land and homes of the Allied people.

3. Germany could not be admitted at once to the membership of the League of Nations, for it was impossible to expect the free nations of the world to sit down immediately in equal association with those by whom they had been so grievously wronged.

On the basis of these counter contentions, the 'Reply' strongly affirmed: "Justice is what the German delegation asks for, and says that Germany had been promised. Justice is what Germany shall have. But it must be justice for all. There must be justice for the dead and wounded, and for those who have been orphaned and bereaved that Europe might be freed from Prussian despotism. There must be justice for the people who now stagger under war debts which exceed thirty thousand million pounds that liberty might be saved. There must be justice for those millions whose homes and land, ships and property German savagery has spoliated and destroyed. That is why, the Allied and Associated Powers have insisted as a cardinal feature of the treaty that Germany must undertake to make reparation to the very utmost of her power; for reparation for wrongs inflicted is of the essence of justice.... It is a peace of right and fulfils the terms agreed upon at the time of armistice."[17]

The lines of rebuttal furnished by the victorious powers can not be appreciated by a detached critic. The Treaty of Versailles was found defective on many counts and, as the later events showed, it was taken as the real cause of pushing conditions towards another global holocaust after twenty years that brought

---

17. Ibid., p. 315. A powerful defence of this stand may be seen in the interpretation of an English writer in these words: "A sedulous propaganda put out by the vanquished Powers, and by the Germany in particular, had led even responsible writers on international affairs constantly to condemn the settlement as a whole, and the Treaty of Versailles in particular as a vindictive and fraudulent departure from the principles on the faith of which Germany had laid down her arms. This legend that the peace was ruined by the substitution of Machiavellian principles of 'Old Diplomacy' for the ideals on which it purported to be based must emphatically be denied. On the contrary, there has surely never been construed a peace of so idealistic a character." G.M. Gathorne-Hardy: *A Short History of International Affairs, 1920-1939* (London: Oxford Univ. Press, 1964), pp. 17-18.

'untold sufferings to the humankind'. Thus it may be criticised on the following grounds:

1. It assumed the form of a 'dictated peace' in view of the fact that the principle of 'reciprocity' was thoroughly dishonoured. The German representatives were not at all taken into consultation. Rather, they were given the draft of the treaty so as to present their 'Observations'. As we have seen, even the notes of protest offered by them were greeted with counter-arguments. Finally, the document was presented to the German leaders who had no other option but to place their signatures on it. Lipson, therefore, comments that it "did not assume the form of a pact freely negotiated between the belligerents; it was an instrument imposed by the conquerors upon a crushed and humiliated foe."[18] An enlightened student of international politics admits that in this case even ordinary courtesies of international intercourses were not observed; the German delegates were treated like captives; they were taken before the peace-makers only two times—once for receiving the draft treaty and then for putting their signatures upon it. For this reason, it "was imposed by the victors on the vanquished, not negotiated by a process of give and take between them. Nearly every treaty which brings a war to an end is, in one sense, a dictated peace, for a defeated Power seldom accepts willingly the consequences of its defeat. But in the Treaty of Versailles the element of dictation was more apparent than in any previous peace treaty of modern times."[19]

2. The principle of national self-determination, as contained in the idealism of President Wilson, was not properly honoured. Rather it was exploited by the victorious powers to crush Germany in every possible way and by all possible means. It attempted to destroy the German reich. Thus, it provided a handle to an aggressive leader like Hitler to raise the call of Pan-Germanism whose effective implementation entailed the destruction of Austria in 1938 and of Czechoslovakia a little after. The ban on

---

18. Lipson, op. cit., p. 311.
19. Carr: *International Relations between the Two World Wars, 1919-39* (London: Macmillan, 1952), p. 4. The Germans could never forget that this treaty was signed by a 'pale and nervous' Foreign Minister Herman Muller. Thus, the German Assembly at Weimar "voted a conditional acceptance, objecting to articles saddling Germany with the guilt of beginning the conflict, demanding the surrender of certain war criminals and accusing her of violating the code of war." Langsam, op. cit., p. 13.

anschluss, for example, was a flagrant violation of the principle of national self-determination. Though Germany accepted the cession of Posen and West Prussia to Poland as these areas had a majority of the Poles, she had every reason to resent the creation of 'Polish corridor' that separated East Prussia from the rest of the country. It showed that the "Polish question was solved in a fashion that left behind a residue of ill-will to trouble Polish-German relations."[20]

3. The terms of the treaty were unduly harsh. Germany was not only politically dismembered to a considerable extent, she was also subjected to excessive burden of reparation. Her great officers were designated as 'war criminals' and plans for their trial were prepared. The total liability of Germany was fixed at a point that was impossible for her to redeem. It was for this reason that the work of calculating her total liability was left for the Reparation Commission that could not function effectively and, as time passed eventually, it had to wind itself up. "The prospects of a crushing reparation amount and of a long military occupation, the forced destruction of the mechanism and equipment of the German national army under the eyes of an Allied Commission and the abolition of conscription were the humiliations difficult to bear."[21]

4. As a matter of fact, the Treaty of Versailles served the purpose of France at the expense of Germany. Besides, other major Allied and Associated Powers (like USA and Britain) did a great wrong by strengthening the argument of Clemenceau to a highly undeserving extent. In doing so, Britain sacrificed its traditional adherence to the principle of 'balance of power,' a mistake for which Lloyd George was condemned by his own people as 'Wilson's puppy dog'. In not much time, British statesmen realised their mistake and reverted to the course of maintaining the 'balance of power' on the continent by giving fresh doses of strength to Germany. A sharp divergence of approach developed and the result was that diplomatic rift between England and France "provided Germany with an escape."[22]

5. Above all, while this treaty punished Germany by all possible means and in every possible way, it could not establish an

---

20. Ibid., p. 11.
21. See F.L. Benns: *European History Since 1870*.
22. Albjerg and Albjerg: *Europe from 1914 to the Present*, pp. 83-84.

effective machinery to preserve its labours. It all depended upon the might of three great Allied Powers (USA, Britain and France) to keep the results of this treaty in existence. However, it could not happen. The burden of responsibility was so great that the USA excluded itself from the League of Nations; Britain reverted to the course of 'balance of power'; France alone remained in the field fighting for maintaining the 'system of security'. The triumph of Bolshevism in Russia and a longing to see its end eventually led to the emergence of the course of 'appeasement' that had its sinister repercussions after 1930. A far-sighted statesman like Gen. Smuts of South Africa could well take it into consideration when he issued a statement soon after placing his signatures on this treaty of peace. He said: "The promise of the new life, the victory of the great human ideals, for which the peoples have shed their blood and their treasure without stint, the fulfilment of their aspirations towards a new international order and a fairer better would, are not written in this Treaty, and will not be written in treaties.... A new heart must be given not only to our enemies but also to us; a contrite spirit for the woes which have overwhelmed the world; a spirit of pity, mercy, and forgiveness for the sins and wrongs which we have suffered."[23]

In short, the Treaty of Versailles caused the deepest humiliation to Germany. It crippled her economically, segregated her politically, humbled her militarily, humiliated her nationally, and exhausted her physically. She stood like a pale person in the comity of nations. An aggressive nationalist like Hitler, for all these reasons, described it as 'an instrument of unlimited blackmail and shameful humiliation'.[24] His 'Political Testament' of 1926 contained in the *Mein Kampf, inter alia*, boldly asserted: "The future goal of our foreign policy ought not to involve an orientation to the East or the West, but it ought to be an Eastern policy which will have in view the acquisition of such territory as is necessary for the German people. To carry out this policy, we need the force which the mortal enemy of our nation (France) now deprives us of by holding us in her grip and pitilessly robbing us of our strength. Therefore, we must stop at no sacrifice in our effort to destroy the French striving towards hegemony over Europe."[25]

23. See Temperley, op. cit., Vol. I, p. 75.
24. Adolf Hitler: *Mein Kampf*, Translated from German into English by James Murphy, (New Delhi: Sagar Publication, n.y.) p. 347.
25. Ibid., p. 367.

Having seen all this, it becomes impossible to feel convinced with the defensive arguments put forth by the great authors of the Treaty of Versailles. For instance, while speaking in the House of Commons on July 3, 1919, British Prime Minister Lloyd George said that it was 'a stern, but a just treaty'. "The terms are in many respects terrible terms to impose upon a country. Terrible were the deeds which it requires. Terrible were the consequences that were inflicted upon the world. Still more terrible would have been the consequences had they succeeded."[26] Likewise, French Prime Minister Clemenceau said these words in the Chamber of Deputies on June 30, 1919: "By France and by our Allies the work of salvation from the danger which placed the word in deadly peril is now accomplished."[27] In the same vein, while appreciating the work of President Wilson, Baker pointed out: "Critics of the Versailles treaty after the event forget that the peace had to be made in an atmosphere still breaking with the fumes of war and still more or less dominated by the military spirit. It could not have been otherwise. For four years the nations had been committed to the use of every agency in building up a war psychology, to giving men the material spirit, instilling hatred as an antidote for fear, driving nations into an artificial unity of purpose by the force of sheer necessity.... Build up such a psychology for four years, inoculate the entire public opinion of the world with it, and then ask for men at Paris—or one man at Paris, to change it all in three months. It was not merely a world peace that had to be made but a world psychology that had to be changed."[28]

---

26. See Temperley, op. cit., p. 84.
27. Ibid., p. 80.
28. Ray Stanard Baker: *Woodrow Wilson and the World Settlement* (London: 1923). We may also refer to the view of T.E. Jessop who says: "Germany was never overrun; only a relatively small and strategically definite part of the country was occupied; apart from the lands restored by the armistice agreement to their inhabitants or historic owners, there were virtually no annexations with the big exception of the colonies (taken on strategic grounds) except to avoid enclaves, no area of anything more than a trifling size with a German majority, except Memel, was placed under non-German rule. The separation of East Prussia from the rest of Germany was, of course, unfortunate but no better alternative presented itself. On the whole, the political settlement was remarkably just to

Other Treaties: Peace Settlements with Smaller States in Central Europe and Near East

Surprisingly, while the First World War had a duration of four years, peace settlements consumed five years beginning with the Treaty of Versailles with Germany in 1919 and ending in the Treaty of Lausanne with Turkey in 1923. The Treaty of Sevres signed in 1920 by the Allied and Associated Powers on the one side and Turkey on the other could not be implemented owing to some revolutionary developments in that country culminating in the overthrow of the Ottoman monarchy and its replacement by a republic under Mustafa Kemal. Thus, it was not until July 1923 that the final treaty of peace was signed with Turkey at Lausanne and with its coming into force on August 6, 1924, peace "was at least formally re-established throughout the world."[29] Though the Treaty of Versailles occupies an importance of its own, other treaties also deserve a brief discussion in this chapter for the reason that all of them may be said to constitute the stock of European peace settlements. More than that, "almost every important political event of an international character in the period between the First and Second World Wars was a direct or indirect product of this settlement."[30] We may, therefore, have a bird's-eye view of them in the following manner:

Treaty of St. Germain with Austria: This treaty "was so completely modelled on the Versailles that whole clauses were taken from the first treaty and reincorporated into the second without changing a word."[31] The reason was that the victors treated Austria as no less guilty than Germany in causing the world war and putting the Allied and Associated Powers to a lot of damage in terms of human lives and material resources. It declared the

---

Europe; to Germany it was not punitive but mild—in startling contrast to the dreadful settlement which her government had planned to impose. It freed oppressed nations, left far more minorities under alien rule than there had been since nation-states came into existence and deprived Germany of the military striking power that had been the chief support of her diplomacy in peace as well as her ruthless weapon in war. It declared the judgement of many nations that Germany was no longer to regard her smaller neighbours as satellites for exploitation." *The Treaty of Versailles: Was it Just?*

29. Gathorne-Hardy, op. cit., p. 122.
30. Carr, op. cit., pp. 3–4
31. Langsam, op. cit., p. 19.

Paris Peace Settlements

dissolution of the Austro-Hungarian empire with its monarchical system. It prohibited the union of Germany and Austria (*Anschluss*) so as to keep Germany in a weak and Czechoslovakia in a safe position. The new state was given the name of "Republic of Austria". The territorial dismemberment of the Habsburg Empire resulted in the cession of South Tyrol up to the Brenner Pass, Trieste, Istria, Trentino and some islands of Dalmatia to Italy. The new state of Czechoslovakia got Bohemia, Moravia, part of lower Austria and nearby all Austrian Silesia. Poland was awarded Austrian Galicia; Rumania got Bukovina; and Yugoslavia received Bosnia, Herzegovina and the Dalmatian coast. Austria surrendered her entire naval force retaining only three boats for police purposes on the Danube; her army was reduced to just 30,000 volunteers. Besides, she gave up all rights and privileges in non-European areas, assented to the proposal of trying her "war criminals" and also yielded to the provision of reparations. However, she was granted access to the Adriatic sea via areas formally included in the erstwhile Austro-Hungarian empire.

It shows that this treaty not only finished the Austro-Hungarian empire under the Habsburg dynasty, it left Austria as a mere shadow of the former image. Hungary became another state, while the Czechs and the Slovaks got their own state with the name of Czechoslovakia. Other parts of the Austro-Hungarian empire were 'looted by Italy, Poland, Yugoslavia and Rumania'. With the collapse of the Habsburg empire in November 1918, this state lived like an isolated and ill-proportioned remnant. Of its 7,000,000 inhabitants more than 2,000,000 were congregated in Vienna, while Bohemia, Moravia and Austrian Silesia were broken away to form the nucleus of the new state of Czechoslovakia. Slovania joined Serbia and Croatia to form the new state of Yugoslavia. Italy had already occupied Trieste and its immediate hinterland. Keeping these facts in view, it may be added that the treaty (signed on September 10, 1919) "did little but register these accomplished facts. Its only two provisions which conspicuously contradicted the principle of national self-determination were the prohibition on union between Austria and Germany, repeated from the Treaty of Versailles, and the cession to Italy of the purely German-speaking

South Tyrol that was designed to give Italy the strategic frontier of the Brenner."[32]

Treaty of Trianon with Hungary: Signed on June 4, 1920, it not only entailed the erection of the dependent state of Hungary out of the old Magyar Kingdom, it also amounted to the cession of its parts to other states of Europe. Thus Rumania received Transylvania; Yugoslavia got Croatia-Slovania; Czechoslovakia received Slovakia, but West Hungary was given to Austria. The Hungarian army was cut to 35,000 men and the navy reduced to a few patrol boats. She was also made liable for the payment of reparation. These provisions reduced Hungary to one-third of her pre-war territory and 40 per cent of her population. Obviously, once again the Treaty of Versailles provided the model inherent with two serious drawbacks. First, it flouted the principle of national self-determination by generating a condition of acute racial disturbances and animosities. Second, in terms of territorial resettlements, it was described as the harshest of all post-war settlements. The new frontiers of Hungary bore witness to a certain eagerness on the part of the treaty-makers to stretch their principles wherever possible to the advantage of the Allied Powers and the detriment of the enemy country.

Treaty of Neuilly with Bulgaria: Though modelled on the Treaty of Versailles, the Treaty of Neuilly signed on November 27, 1919, proved detrimental to the interests of Bulgaria not because of the effects of the First World War as for its own defeat in the second Balkan war of 1913. Though in the first Balkan war of 1912, Bulgaria had combined with Serbia, Greece and Rumania to expel Turkey from the Balkan area and drive her back to about 50 miles from Constantinople, in the second one she was simultaneously attacked by her three former allies and Turkey. The reason of all this was that the victors could not distribute the booty to their satisfaction after the first Balkan war and Bulgaria had to bear its consequences. The Treaty of Neuilly confirmed Bulgarian losses. Thus, Yugoslavia was given four small regions in Western Bulgaria which contained Bulgarian majorities. Greece was awarded Western Thrace and a slight improvement in the Graeco-Bulgarian boundary was made in a way that Bulgaria lost her coast line of the Aegian sea. The strength of the Bulgarian army was fixed at 20,000 men and her

---

32. Carr, op. cit., p. 10.

other armed officials at 13,000; her navy was liquidated though for police and fishery duties she was allowed to retain 4 torpedo and 6 motor boats. She had to accept reparation amounting to 450 million dollars payable in 37 years beginning from 1921. In this way, Bulgaria was made the weakest state of the Balkan area.

Treaties of Sevres and Lausanne with Turkey: Of all the vanquished powers in the First World War, Turkey was described as 'the most thoroughly conquered'. The reason was that not only her provinces but also her capital were under the occupation of the Allied Powers and, more than that, most of her provinces had already been allocated among the Allies by means of secret covenants. Thus, the Treaty of Sevres signed on August 10, 1920, came with its own provisions. The Turkish war was confined to Central Anatolia; Constantinople was returned to Turkey, though the straits were opened and put under international control. Smyrna region was given to Greece. The monarch of Hedjaz was declared independent. Since the Allied Powers had their eyes on the Turkish possessions in the middle east and since Wilsonian idealism had given the commandment of no recognition to secret treaties, the system of 'mandates' under the control of the League of Nations was invented. In this way, Syria was given to France. Palestine and Iraq were placed under British control. Besides, the capitulations and other restrictions on the Turkish sovereignty were restored; Turkey agreed to recognise Armenia as a free state and accord local autonomy to Kurdistan. The army of Turkey was to be reduced to 50,000, the naval fleet was to be disbanded, and aircraft to be surrendered. Though Turkey was charged with war guilt, the reparation clause was not incorporated into the treaty in view of her meagre resources. The Allied Powers were given the right to supervise the budget, financial laws and regulations of Turkey through a financial commission of British, French and Italian representatives. Some important Turkish ports (Constantinople, Smyrna and Alexandria) and river (Maritsa) were placed under international control.

The Treaty of Sevres could not be implemented owing to important political developments in Turkey. The rise of a nationalist leader like Mustafa Kemal turned the tide. He refused to accept the treaty signed by the Sultan under duress and instead led a movement for his abdication. When the Greek forces attacked Turkey and occupied Smyrna, Kemal organised a provisional government. Now he repudiated the terms of the Sevres treaty and demanded the whole of Asia Minor and Thrace. On October 29, 1921, France recognised the new regime and under the Boullin Agreement abandoned her claims in Asia Minor. Then, Italy followed suit. This strengthened the hands of Kemal who defeated Greek troops and recaptured Smyrna on September 9, 1922. A British-Franch-Italian force was still in the occupation of the straits of Dardenelles. Now the Kemalists opened a front in this direction. Since France and Italy as well as British Dominions (except Australia and New Zealand) declined to go on a war against Turkey, the British felt 'isolated' and, for this reason, an armistice was signed on October 11, 1922.

With the abolition of monarchy on November 1, 1922, negotiations restarted between the Allied Powers and Nationalist Turkey at Lausanne. For about ten months negotiations went on in which British, French, Italian, Japanese, Greek, Bulgarian and Yugoslavian representatives and an American observer took part that resulted in the making of 17 agreements out of which the Lausanne treaty, signed on July 24, 1923, deserves some importance. Now the Turkish sovereignty over Anatolia was recognised and the proposals of according independence for the Kurds and the Armenians came to an end. Smyrna, Constantinople and Thrace were restored to Turkey. But nothing was done to upset the mandate system already established under the control of the League of Nations. The Mosul question was shelved, but the northern frontier of Syria (as drawn under the Boullin Agreement) was confirmed. Suprisingly, no control or restriction was placed on the military forces, or naval strength, or finances of Turkey. The non-Muslim communities lost their privileges and immunities that had been granted to them under the rule of the Ottoman kings.

Among all peace treaties signed after the First World War, the Treaty of Lausanne alone has the credit of remaining in force for more than 15 years. It was treated as valid by both the sides and whenever the need to make any alteration in it arose (as in 1936), it could be done by means of voluntary agreement. The reason behind it was that it had taken place in a quite changed atmosphere. The Treaty of Sevres was a product of the same vicious atmosphere in which other treaties were signed. But time had changed in 1922-1923. Moreover, political developments in Turkey culminating in the emergence of a republican system under Kemal at the expense of the Ottoman rule had their own impact which the Allied Powers could not ignore. The negotiations took place at Lausanne (in Switzerland that was a neutral place) and not in any territory of the Allied Powers. The secularisation of Turkey was appreciated by all great Allied Powers like Britain and France. Since the new Turkish state explicitly renounced all claims to territories containing Arab majorities, the conclusion of peace obviously presented no insuperable difficulty. Moreover, the treaty had no irritating provisions like those relating to reparation, war guilt, war criminals, disarmament, etc. All things considered, this treaty alone inaugurated a more lasting settlement than any other that followed the war.[33] It "was not imposed but negotiated and in that fact lay hopeful prospects for its permanence."[34]

Peace Settlements and the Question of Minorities

Thus, the Allied and Associated powers managed to play their game through the conclusion of peace treaties with Germany and other vanquished powers. However, the question of minorities remained. As a result of the redrawing of the political map of Europe, some nationalities became insecure. Its reason lay in the application of the principle of national self-determination. In order to safeguard their interests, the Allied Powers thought in some other directions. For this purpose, the peace-makers at Paris appointed a New States Committee that steered a course which would, on the one hand, avoid giving so much autonomy to minorities as to constitute them 'States within States' and, on the other hand, "providing so little protection for them that their position might become precarious." Success in this direction was achieved when a broad pattern of minority rights and safeguards was prepared and on that basis appropriate provisions were included in the peace treaties with Austria, Hungary, Bulgaria and Turkey. In order to make a concrete advance in this important direction, the Allied Powers signed minority treaties with Czechoslovakia and Yugoslavia on September 10, 1919, with Rumania on December 9, 1919, and with Greece and Armenia on August 10, 1920. Then, the Baltic States and Albania also entered into such agreements with the League of Nations.

---

33. Temperley, op. cit., Vol. 6, p. 15.
34. Gathorne-Hardy, op. cit., p. 122.

In order to secure for the members of the 'minorities' (like the Jews in Poland, Lithuania and Greece, the Muslims in Albania, Greece and Yugoslavia and non-Muslims in Iraq) legal equality with the majority nationals and to avoid discrimination, the Treaties recognised:[35]

1. Full and complete protection of life and liberty irrespective of birth, nationality, language, race or religion;
2. Equality before law and enjoyment of the same civil and political rights without distinction as to race, language or religion;
3. No interference with the enjoyment of civil or political rights such as admission to public employments, functions and honours, or the exercise of professions and industries because of difference of religion, creed or confession; and
4. Free exercise, whether public or private, of any creed, religion or belief, whose practices are not inconsistent with public morality.

Moreover, the Treaties generally separated the recognised special interests of the minorities into following categories:[36]
1. Use of their language in private relations;
2. Use of their own language before the courts;
3. Adequate facilities for primary education in their own language wherever there was a considerable proportion of the minority groups;
4. Establishment of religious and welfare institutions, schools and other educational facilities under their own control and with their own language; and
5. The right to an equitable proportion of State and communal expenditures for educational, religious and welfare purposes.

In this way, "judging the aims of the system of international legal protection for minorities on the basis of the texts and the authentic declarations of its founders, the conclusion seems clear: "The humanitarian and democratic legal consciousness could not reconcile itself to an order which deprived men of their rights because they differed from the majority in race, language or religion. An international public law guarantee for minorities was indispensable to the international and internal peace of Europe

---

35. J. Robinson, N. Robinson, O. Karbach and M. Vichnaik: *Were the Minorities Treaties a Failure ?* New York, Institute of Jewish Affairs, 1943, p. 37.
36. Ibid., p. 38.

Paris Peace Settlements

after the First World War, both for the sake of the minorities with whom they had to live within common frontiers. Such a guarantee served the interests of Europe and the whole world in which these states of many races, faiths and languages formed an internal part."[37]

Critical Appreciation

A study of peace settlements made at Paris after the termination of the First World War, as discussed in the preceeding sections, leaves certain strong impressions on our minds in regard to their validity and reasonableness on the one hand and their excessively harsh and unjust character on the other. While the defenders would say that the victors had to satisfy the strong opinions of their countrymen and also give a lesson to the war-hungry nations of the world so as to realise the idea of unleashing 'a war to end all wars', the critics would say that the victors established the first great instance of a 'dictated peace' that was sure to have its sinister repercussions in time to come.

The main argument of the victors was that "no better results could reasonably have been anticipated by the vanquished powers."[38] However, such a defensive argument cannot be accepted as thoroughly plausible. Prof. Langsam raises the following points of criticism:[39]

1. It probably was unwise to enunciate broad principles that would not be carried out in practice; thus, in the matter of self-determination of peoples, since the victorious powers were willing to grant much rights in only limited fashion, their earlier promises incited minorities to thoughts of revenge against those responsible for the unfulfilled pledges.

2. The victors should not have made promises, such as that to disarm, which they could not really expect to keep.

3. The economic clauses of the settlement, bearing little relation to economic facts, brought on situations, such as prolonged depression in British ship building, because the prolonged depression in British appropriated most of the German merchants fleet as reparation and thus for a long time needed no new ships.

---

37. *Ibid.*, p. 26.
38. Gathorne-Hardy, op. cit., p. 20.
39. Langsam, op. cit., pp. 21-22.

4. It soon became apparent that Western 'democracy' could not arbitrarily be imposed upon people who had few democratic traditions in Germany where it was difficult to convert an autocratic monarchy into a smoothly functioning republic simply because the Allies wished it so.

5. The peace settlements left both Germany and Russia as large, revengeful and potentially powerful nations surrounded by a cordon of small and weak states; the 'balkanisation of Central Europe' made it relatively easy later for Nazi Germany and the Soviet Union to absorb some of their smaller neighbours.

6. The history of events of peace of Paris made it clear that victorious powers needed later to cooperate in upholding whatever peace settlements they had agreed upon at the peace conference itself. The validity of this point soon became apparent as Britain and France began to follow divergent paths. The British wanted to see Germany recover for purposes of trade, whereas the French were anxious to keep Germany weak. And so after 1920 a succession of German treaty modifications was winked at by one or another of the Allies, as each sought to serve its own purposes.

As a matter of fact, the peace settlements made at Paris could not establish grounds for an enduring peace. Its reason was that self-interests of the victorious powers were given an artificial reconciliation with Wilsonian idealism. Following important points, therefore, engage our attention now:

1. With the entry of the United States the situation underwent a change in the course of war. It strengthened the position of the Allied Powers to an unforeseeable extent. It had its natural effect on the course of peace parleys. President Wilson assumed the capacity of a super-prophet with a set of 14 commandments whose number exceeded those once given by Moses. The problem of reconciling these idealistic norms of Wilson with the respective claims of the victors arose and a solution could be discovered in doing the needful as much as possible keeping in view the exigencies of the prevailing situation. Thus, it may be claimed that, broadly considered, the treaties, in fact, "were permeated by Wilsonian principles, and further, it is not in any departures from those principles that grave and lasting dangers to international understanding were to be found. Indeed, it may well be argued that the seeds of future discord lay precisely in those decisions which most faithfully implemented the 'Fourteen Points', and their asso-

ciated 'particulars', 'principles' and ends'."[40] "Understanding the implications of this situation, distinguished commentators pointed out that "political speeches necessarily possess a vagueness and generalised aspect which suit them for diplomatic interpretation."[41]

2. As a corollary to the above point, it may be added that the peace-makers at Paris could not sacrifice their national self-interest at the time of drafting treaties. It is for this reason that the principle of national self-determination was honoured in some and dishonoured in some other cases. For instance, while Poland got the Polish-majority areas of Posen and West Prussia, the creation of a 'corridor' and conversation of German-population area of Danzig into a 'free city' were quite unjustified. Likewise, the formation of the new states of Austria and Czechoslovakia could be justified in the name of this principle, but a ban on the *Anschluss* and cession of Sudetenland (German-majority areas) to Czechoslovakia was by no stretch of imagination convincing. As a matter of fact, it was all done according to the secret decisions of the victors taken during the times of war. The dissolution of the Austro-Hungarian empire was a *fait accompli* before the victors had met at Paris. It must also be acknowledged that by the beginning of 1917, the liberation of the Italians, as also of the Slavs, Rumanes, and Czechoslovaks from foreign domination was a declared part of the Allied war policy. The Allied Powers did not hide this fact in their 'Reply' sent to President Wilson dated January 10, 1917.[42] The British Prime Minister Lloyd George testified to this fact that a leading consideration of the four peace-makers (USA, Britain, France and Italy) at Paris in 1919 was "to free from the clutches of

---

40. Gathorne-Hardy, op. cit., p. 20. A vehement critic of the peace settlements and the role of President Wilson therein, Lord J.M. Keynes, says that he (Wilson) "had no plan, no scheme, no constructive ideas whatever for clothing with the flesh of life the commandments which he had thundered from the White House. He could have preached a sermon on any of them or have addressed a stately prayer to the Almighty for their fulfilment; but he could not frame their concrete application to the actual state of Europe." *Economic Consequences of Peace* (London: Macmillan, 1920), p. 43.
41. Temperley, op. cit., Vol. 6, p. 540.
42. See Temperley, op cit., Vol. I, p. 428.

the successor States, which they had created, territory to which they were not entitled."⁴³

3. To carry the same point further, it may be said that France and Britain played the game of their having an axe to grind in favourable weather at the time of peace-making. Both had their own diplomatic designs and both pulled things in a direction that served their purpose. Tied to the apron strings of idealism and also on account of not being a very good student of European geography and ethnography, Wilson failed in resisting British and French leaders to the desired extent.⁴⁴ The Italians remained unsatiated as Orlando could not become an effective match to Lloyd George and Clemenceau and Wilson refused to take into recognition any secret treaty made during the time of war. Thus, France exploited the doctrine of Wilson as "a useful pretext for dismembering her enemies; to her and to England, it also appeared in the light of a price to be paid, with due caution and reservations, for the advantage attained by fostering disaffection among the suppressed minorities of Central Powers, but the pledges given under this head ranked no higher than those comprised in the secret treaties, in the promises to the Arabs, or the Zionist declaration by which it was sought to win the sympathy and support of Jewish population. All these promises must be kept, and so far as possible—which was more difficult—reconciled; but no illusion was entertained as at the efficacy of self-determination as an instrument of peace. Left to themselves, the European Allies have been trusted to push the doctrine no further than was reasonable."⁴⁵

4. It may be conceded that the Allied Powers established a good precedent by a giving a 'dictated peace' in the form of a lesson

---

43. David Lloyd George: *The Truth About Peace Treaties*, Vol. I, (London, 1938), p. 91.
44. Wilson's ignorance of European geography and ethnography is corroborated with the facts that he thought Prague (capital of Czechoslovakia) to be in Poland and Southern Tyrolese as Italians. "It is, indeed, one of the major tragedies of Versailles that Wilson's personality was so ill-equipped for the role of a prophet." (Kenneth Ingram) While speaking in the House of Commons, Lloyd George referred to Gen. Kolchak as Gen. Kharkhov (the capital city of the republic of Ukraine of the then Soviet Russia). Jawaharlal Nehru says: "The ignorance of elementary geography, however, did not prevent these statesmen from cutting up Europe into bits and making a new map of it." *Glimpses of World History* (London: Lindsay Drummond, 1949), p. 655.
45. Gathorne-Hardy, op. cit., pp. 22-23.

for the war-mongering nations of the world. But, as already pointed out, this course was taken to the most unfair extreme so far as the case of a defeated power like Germany was concerned. The Treaty of Versailles "humbled Germany to the dust and imposed upon her terms so severe as to render her impotent in European international politics for many years."[46] The authors of this treaty were quite aware of the fact that their action would entail its heavy consequences in time to come. For instance, Lloyd George, taking note of the creation of 'Polish corridor', prophesied that 'next war will begin in Danzig'.[47]

5. However, the most solid contribution of the Paris peace settlements should be seen in adopting the Covenant of the League of Nations. It set up the first international organisation and thereby realised the dream of great thinkers of the past like Dante, Grotius, Rousseau, Kant, Bentham and Green. Though the US Senate did not ratify Wilson's commitment to the Versailles Treaty and thereby America did not join the first international organisation, President Wilson got the distinction of being its 'Father'. Immortal is the exhortation of Wilson that he offered in his speech at Paris on February 14, 1919: "A living thing is born and we must see to it what colthes we may put on it. It is not a vehicle of power, but a vehicle in which power may be varied at the discretion of those who exercise it, and in accordance with the changing circumstances of time. And yet while it is elastic, while it is general in its terms, it is definite in the one thing that we called·upon to make definite. It is a definite guarantee of peace. It is a definite guarantee by world against aggression. It is a definite guarantee against the things which have just come near bringing the whole structure of civilisation to ruin."[48]

In short, the peace settlements made at Paris could not do what an idealist would desire to appreciate. Undeniable is the fact that the peace-makers were diplomats and they well knew the doctrine of Clausewitz that war meant continuance of diplomacy and diplomacy meant continuance of war. Thus, they could not free themselves from the shackles of professional diplomacy. In

---

46. F.L. Schuman: *International Poltics* (New York: McGraw Hill, 1941), III Ed., p. 83.
47. See F.S. Northedge and M.J. Grieve: *Hundred Years of International Relations* (London: Duckworth, 1971), p. 104.
48. Temperley, op cit., Vol. 3, p. 63.

spite of this, they could not satisfy the raging public opinion of their respective countries. We may take note of the fact that Wilson was 'bamboozled' in the Senate; Clemenceau was pilloried by the Chamber of Deputies for permitting 'autocratic Wilson' to bully their leader into the surrender of French rights; Orlando was denounced by the people of Italy for showing 'servility'; and Lloyd George was nicknamed as 'Wilson's puppy dog'.

In short, the great Allied Powers failed to do much of lasting significance. Italy emerged like an unsatiated nation with its claim for 'irredintism'; the new regime in Russia under Lenin dubbed it all as a 'bourgeois peace'; Stanley Baldwin later made a trenchant comment that the Allied Powers at Paris were "made up of hard—faced men who looked as if they had done well out of the war."[49] The labours made at Paris led to the emergence of conditions of their own unsettlement. The events of the fourth decade of the present century demonstrated that the crusade for having a war to end all wars was an exercise in futility. "As finally drafted and later applied, the Peace of Paris was neither severe enough to hold down the Germans for ever, nor generous enough to help the vanquished to adjust to the new situation. Consequently, the world eventually was reduced to crying in the manner of Jermiah, 'Peace, peace, when there is no peace'."[50]

---

49. See Northedge and Grieve, op. cit., p. 96.
50. Langsam, op. cit., p. 22. Philip Snowden, who later became Viscount Snowden and a British Cabinet Minister, commented that the Treaty of Versailles "should satisfy brigands, imperialists and militarists. It is the death-blow to the hope of those who expected the end of the war to bring peace. It is not a peace treaty, but a declaration of another war. It is a betrayal of democracy and of the fallen in the war. The Treaty exposes the true aim of the Allies." On the basis of this frank affirmation, Jawaharlal Nehru holds: "Indeed, the Allies, in their hatred and pride and greed, over-reached themselves. They began to repent in after years when the consequences of their own folly threatened to overwhelm them. But it was too late then." *Glimpses of World History*, p. 684.

3

REPARATIONS AND INTER-ALLIED DEBTS

> *There are few episodes in history which posterity will have less reason to condone, —a war ostensibly waged in defence of the sanctity of international engagements ending in a definite breach of one of the most sacred possible of such engagements on the part of the victorious champions of those ideals.*
>
> —Lord J. M. Keynes[1]

A brief survey of the First World War followed by a detailed study of the peace settlements made at Paris, as discussed in the preceding two chapters, deserves its supplementation with an elaborate examination of the problem of reparations and inter-Allied debts in view of the fact that, to a considerable extent, their account looks like a puzzling admixture of the politics and economics in the postwar international relations. The 'war guilt' clause on which the entire edifice of the reparations was based became one of the most effective instruments that eventually brought Hitler to power in Germany and that transformed the 'period of pacification' into the 'period of crisis' culminating in the outbreak of another great war in 1939. The problem of reparation and its solution, as we shall see, became a potential source of friction between the Allied Powers themselves and, for that reason, it contributed its own part to the creation of destabilising conditions in Europe having their definite repercussions in other parts of the world. For this reason, a study of this ticklish problem, as contained in this chapter, will look like "a detailed account of the harassing epistolary tournament that

---

1. Keynes: *The Economic Consequences of Peace* (London: Macmillan, 1920) p. 145.

followed between the imploring Reparation Commission and the dodging German government."²

Reparation: Meaning and Nature of the Problem: Divergent Motives of the Allied Powers

The word 'reparation' implies punitive damages or war fines and their payment in cash or kind or both. In a literal sense, it suggests "compensation either in money or in materials, commodities, capital equipment, merchant vessels, and the like payable by a defeated nation as war indemnity for direct damages and for loss from war expenditures, occupation costs, etc., sustained as a result of aggression by the defeated nation."³ it is, therefore, obvious that the question of reparation is integrally connected with the politics of greed and revenge. The *Oxford English Dictionary* describes 'revenge' as an act of doing harm to another in return for wrong or injury inflicted and satisfaction obtained in the repayment of injuries. Keeping this bold fact in view, a vehement critic of the reparation provisions like Keynes commented that "revenge and greed were at the bottom of Peace Settlement."⁴

However, the victorious powers try to give a justification to their vindictive act in a way that the issue of reparation is cleverly blended with the canons of international law and natural justice. Thus, the Australian Prime Minister (Hughes) said: "This principle of justice on which the right of reparation is founded is that when a wrong has been done and suffered, the wrong-doer should, to the full extent of his capacity, right the wrong. It is based on the idea of justice, not of revenge, on the idea that in so far as possible, the burden of the wrong done shall fall on the wrong-doer, not on the innocent victim. This principle is universally recognised in every system of jurisprudence."⁵ Likewise, a memorandum presented by the British delegation at the Paris Peace Conference in February 1919 said: "Reparation is not a technical word... it is the making good of the losses which an injured party has sustained by wrongful act and their natural consquences, so as to replace him in as

---

2. E. Mantoux: *The Carthaginian Peace or the Economic Consequences of Mr. Keynes* (New York: Charles Scribner's Sons, 1952), p. 139.
3. *Webster's New English Dictionary*, p. 2111.
4. See Mantoux, op. cit., p. 96.
5. See P.M. Burnett: *Reparations at the Paris Peace Conference: From the Standpoint of American Delegation* (New York: Octagon Books Inc.,1965). Vol. I., p. 353.

good a position as that which he occupies before the wrong was done. It is effectuated by material means and affords full compensation for the real effect of the wrong."[6]

However, the notable point that engages our attention at this stage is not that the victors (Allied Powers) and the vanquished (Germany) studied the problem of reparation from fundamentally different aspects; it is that the factor of 'national interest' dominated and that brought about divergence in the stand of the leading Allies like Britain, France and the United States. Let us, first of all, take the case of France. It is a fact that the "primary object of the Treaty of Versailles was to secure France against further German aggression." (Wheeler Bonnet) But in terms of reparation, it meant imposition of huge indemnities—so huge that Germany might not be able to pay and France might be able to harass and dominate her. Thus, through reparation France intended to continue the war on Germany even after the conclusion of armistice. In terms of reparation, it "was thought that realisation of huge sums, on the one hand, will keep down Germany and, on the other, will continue to be a source of security to France."[7]

The British statesmen also favoured imposition of huge reparation on Germany, but they were not prepared to crush her power totally as it would lead to disturbing the balance of power. The total suppression of Germany would entail an excessive increase in the power of France that would become another source of danger to the peace system of Europe. For this reason, they also took into consideration the fact of German capacity to make payment of reparation. Prime Minister Lloyd George explained it as an admission of financial liability for the cost of war and, at the same time, recognised the inability of Germany to meet this total liability. Thus, the British stand on the question of reparation actually limited it to a certain category—' all damage done to the civilian population of the Allied and Associated Powers and to their property.' The items involved in this category amounted to (i) damage for injury to civilians and acts contrary to international law, and (ii) damage to property, with the exception of naval and military works and material as a direct consequence of utilities,

---

6. Ibid., Vol. II, p. 298.
7. M.G. Gupta: *International Relations since 1919*, 'Part I (Allahabad: Chaitanya, 1969) III ed., pp. 45-46.

Illustration of Keynes Regarding Expected Bills

British, French and Belgian Claims
1. Damage to civilian life and property by the acts of enemy Government including damage by air, raids, naval bombardments, submarine warfare and mines, and
2. Compensation for improper treatment of interned civilians.

French and Belgian claims
In addition to these two points, French and Belgian claims were based on the following points as well:
1. Damage done to the property and persons of civilians in the war area, and by aerial warfare behind the enemy lines,
2. Compensation for loot of food, raw materials, live stock, machinery, household effects, timber and the like by the enemy government or their nationals in territory occupied by them,
3. Repayment of fines and requisitions levied by the enemy government or their officers or French municipalities or nationals,
4. Compensation to French nationals deported or compelled to do forced labour, and
5. Expenses of the Relief Commission in producing necessary food and clothing to maintain the civilian French population in the enemy-occupied districts.

Source: Mantoux, op. cit., pp 117-18.

---

and (iii) separation and similar allowances granted during the war to families of mobilised men, and pensions to be paid for death or injury to combatants.[8]

The stand of the United States was different. Caught by the force of idealism on the one hand and confronted with the greater force of political expediency on the other, President Wilson looked at the problem of reparation in a way different from that of other major Allied powers. While speaking in the Congress on February 11, 1918, he had spoken of 'no contributions' and 'no punitive damages'. But in the face of resentment shown to such idealism by

---

8. See Mantoux, op. cit., p. 95.

Reparations and Inter-Allied Debts

Hughes of Australia and Lord Sumner of England at the Paris Peace Conference, he sent a cable stating: "We should dissent and dissent publicly, if necessary, not on the ground that it is clearly inconsistent with what we deliberately led the enemy to expect and cannot now honorably alter simply because we have the power."[9]

It shows that while the three leading Allied Powers had divergent stands on the question of reparation, they all were in agreement on this point that Germany should be severely dealt with and that this was in consonance with the principles of international law and natural justice. However, in this direction, France could have an upper hand on account of the fact that other minor members of the Allied and Associated powers like Belgium and Italy also strengthened her stand. The hands of the British Prime Minister were tied by the weight of public opinion formulated and expressed at the time of 'Khaki elections' of 1918 in which he had promised to make Germany pay 'pound for pound and shilling for shilling.' So was the case with Prime Minister Clemenceau of France. As a matter of fact, the position of George and Clemenceau "was not an easy one, caught as they were between the inflexibility of the President (of America) and the wrath of their respective parliaments, who would very likely hurl them from power if it would not be shown that the maximum had been demanded and obtained. It was, in the last resort, a problem of world opinion."[10]

With the assistance of Lord Summer of England and on the basis of the amplification of the French paper, the Secretariat of the Paris Peace Conference first debated these two categories of damages:[11]

---

9. Ibid., p. 100. At this stage, we may also refer to a Note of March, 1918 addressed by President Wilson to the German government in which he said: "In their present enforced withdrawals from Flanders and France, the German armies are pursuing a course of wanton destruction which has always been regarded as a direct violation of the rules and practices of civilised warfare. Cities and villages, if not destroyed, are being stripped, not only of all they contain, but of their very inhabitants." Ibid., pp. 96-97.
10. Ibid.
11. Burnett, op. cit., p. 38.

Private Damage	Public Damage
(Categories mentioned by the Majority)	
Immovable (buildings, land, mines railways, power lines, etc. and Allied property sequested or liquidated by the enemy)	Private damage 'suffered by the State in its non-military property and in its own resources.
Movables (furnitures, raw materials, machinery, livestock and agricultural implements, ships, documents, etc., and property sequestered or disposed of by the enemy)	State allowances to refugees.
Miscellaneous interests 'in every theatre of operations' (share and securities, forced labour, unenforceable claims, expenses of private relief, disclosure of trade secrets, deprivation of the rights to work, loss of normal profits)	State redemption of depreciated enemy currency.
Exactions of a Financial Character (taxes, fines, levies, etc. and issue or depreciation of monetary instrument)	Military pensions and separation allowance and other war costs.
Damage to Persons (pensions and damages to civilians injured, maltreated etc.)	
Categories not mentioned by the majority	
Miscellaneous interests' outside of every theatre of operations much like above but special Italian demand for increase in prices, freight rate etc.	General damages to the productivity of the nation.
Damage to Persons (damages to persons injured but	Greek demand for claims against Turkey and Bulgaria antedating 1914.

Reparations and Inter-Allied Debts 71

employed against the interests of their country, and damages to persons injured in the war factories)   French demand for the indemnity of 1871.

Speaking generally, the majority categories were accepted for the Final Report of March 31, 1919, although many of the items were amended or clarified. Also speaking generally, the 'non-majority categories were rejected' with the exception of damages to persons.[12]

Fixation of German Liability: War Guilt Clause and the Reparation Commission

The fixation of the total liability of Germany became a problem from the very beginning on account of astronomical claims made by the Allied powers, particularly France. Obviously, any amount thus fixed was sure to be beyond the capacity of Germany to pay. The German delegation on the Conditions of Peace in its note dated May 29, 1919, had made it plain that their country "is ready to make the payments incumbent upon her according to the peace programme agreed upon, up to the maximum sum of 100 billion gold marks of which 20 billion gold marks in annual sums are without interest." But this was not at all acceptable to the victors. Thus, they met at San Remo in April 1920 and then discussed the same matter at Spa in July some three months after. This was the first occasion when the German Chancellor and Foreign Minister were given treatment of equality, though their arguments were not accepted. The importance of the Spa conference is that now the Allied powers, in pursuance of Art. 237 of the Treaty of Versailles, agreed upon this ratio for the distribution of reparation receipts: British Empire 22 per cent, France 52 per cent, Italy 10 per cent; Japan 0.75 per cent, Belgium 8 per cent, Portugal 0.75 per cent; and 6.5 per cent was reserved for Greece, Rumania, Serb-Croat-Slovene State as well as for other powers entitled to reparation which were not signatories to that agreement.

---

12. Ibid.

Calculation of Keynes
(Regarding annual payments to be made by Germany resulting from the provisions of Treaty of Versailles)

Duration	$ Millions	Gold marks (Milliards)
1. 1921-1925: milliards of bonds at 2½ per cent interest	75	1,500
2. After 1925: 40 milliards of bonds at 5 per cent interest	1,803	600
3. After the Commission is satisfied that 40 milliards more bonds can be issued	280	5,600
4. Annual interest charge on total disability of $ 800 millions	430	8,600
5. On the assumption that until 1936 payments cannot exceed 150 millions annually, annual interest after 1936	650	13,000
6. On the assumption, annuity with binding fund amortised over 30 years after 1936	780	15,600
7. On the assumption which no one supports and even the most optimistic fear to be unplausible that Germany can pay the full charge of interst	480	9,600

Source: Mantoux, op. cit; p. 107.

Though the ratio could be determined, the total liability of Germany remained to be ascertained. For this purpose, a conference of the representatives of Britain, France, Italy, Belgium and Japan took place at Paris in January, 1921, that called for 42 instead of 30 annual payments beginning at 2 billion gold marks and rising to 6 billion gold marks per year from May 1, 1932 to May 1, 1963. For this purpose, continued occupation of the German territory as an interim sanction was also contemplated by the Allied Powers. Since this was not acceptable to Germany, they had their meeting at London in the first week of March, 1921 and continued their deliberation until it was dealt with by the Reparation Commission after two months. As a pre-emptory measure, French, Belgian and British troops occupied the three towns of Germany (Duisburg, Ruhrott and Dusseldorf on the right bank of Rhine) and tariffs were levied on imports from Germany.

At this stage, the 'war guilt clause' of the Treaty of Versailles engages our attention. Art. 231 said: "The Allied and Associated Governments affirm and Germany accepts the responsibility of Germany and her allies for causing all the loss and damage to which the Allied and Associated Governments and their nationals have been subjected to as a consequence of the war imposed upon them by aggression of Germany and her allies." Then, in Art. 232 it was recognised that the resources of Germany were not adequate to make complete reparation for all such loss and damage and Germany was required only to make compensation for all damage done to the civilian population of the Allied and Associated Powers and to their property. In addition, Germany was to reimburse Belgium with interest at 5 per cent for all the money the latter had borrowed from the Allied Governments during the war years.

Under the terms of this part of the Treaty, a Reparation Commission was to be appointed by the Allied Powers to determine the total amount of reparation and to draw up a schedule of payments distributed over 30 years beginning from May 1, 1921. Meanwhile, Germany was to pay the equivalent of nearly $5,000,000,000. Out of this advance sum, the cost of the army of occupation was to be met, and the balance applied to reparation. Since full reparation could not be paid in cash, it was stipulated that Germany might pay in pay part in the form of specified commodities. The right of the Allies was recognised to replace at German expense all merchant marine ships and fishing boats lost or damaged during the war. Therefore, Germany was made to surrender one-half of her ships and one-fourth of her steam trawlers and fishing boats. The economic resources of Germany were to be devoted directly to the physical restoration of the invaded areas. As a result, the Allies were permitted to file with this commission lists showing various articles seized by Germany or destroyed in consequences of military operation, as well as lists of building materials that the Allies wished to have produced and manufactured in Germany and delivered to them to permit restoration of the invaded areas. Germany also agreed to make large annual coal deliveries for 10 years to France, Italy and Luxembourg.[13]

Apart from its incorporation into the text of the Versailles Treaty, the implementation of the 'war guilt clause' was no less a tangled problem. For this purpose, a Reparation Commission was set up whose important functions included:[14]

1. to determine the precise figure of the claim against the enemy Powers by an examination in detail of the claims of such of the Allies and this task was to be completed by May 1,1921;

2. to draw up a schedule of payments for the discharge of the whole sum with interest within 30 years and from time to time, revise the schedule within the limits of possibility, considering the resources and capacity of Germany;

3. to demand the surrender of any piece of German property wherever situated with a view to securing the payment of $5,000,000,000 by May, 1921;

4. to decide which of the rights and interests of the German nationals in public utility undertaking operate in Russia, China, Turkey, Austria, Hungary and Bulgaria, or in any territory formerly belonging to Germany or her allies were to be appropriated and transferred to the Commission itself and then to assess the value of the interests so transferred and divide the spoils;

5. to determine how much of the resources thus stripped from Germany must be returned to her to keep enough life in her economic organisation so as to enable her to continue payment of reparation;

6. to assess the value without appeal or arbitration of the property and rights ceded under the Armistice and under the Treaty, rolling stock, mercantile marine rivercraft, cattle, Saar mines, property in ceded territory for which credit was to be given and so forth;

7. to determine the amounts and values of the contributions which Germany was to make in kind every year;

---

13. W.C. Langsam, *The World since 1919* (Delhi, Surjeet Publications, 1981), pp. 17-18.
14. Keynes, op. cit., pp. 211-14.

8. to provide for the restoration by Germany of property that could be identified;
9. to receive, administer and distribute all receipts from Germany in cash or kind and to issue market German bonds of indebtedness;
10. to assign the share of the pre-war public debt to be taken over by the ceded areas of Schleswig, Poland, Danzig and upper Silesia and distribute the public debt of the late Austro-Hungarian empire among its constituent parts;
11. to liquidate the Austro-Hungarian Bank and supervise the withdrawal and replacement of the currency system of the late Austro-Hungarian empire; and
12. to report, if in their judgement, whether Germany was falling short in fulfilment of her obligations and to advise methods of coercion.

In this way, the entire burden of the determination of the amount of reparation and the work of its realisation lay on the Reparation Commission in which France, as we shall see, could have an edge over other members.

Determination and Realisation of Reparations: British and French Endeavours at Cross-Roads

The issue of reparations should be studied not as an economic but as a political problem in which, as we have already hinted, British and French statesmen had their divergent motives. It is because of this that the peace-makers at Paris could not fix Germany's total liability. A roundabout estimate was made whereby Germany was to pay by May 1, 1921 a sum of 20 million gold marks ($ 1 million) before the total amount was to be determined by the Reparation Commission. Political consideration became so powerful at this time that "the safest course for the politicians was, therefore, to mention no figure at all."[15] Not only was the vexed question left to the Reparation Commission, "herefrom the great deal of complications of the Reparation Chapter essentially spring."[16]

On May 5, 1921, the Reparation Commission could fix the total liability of Germany at 132 billion gold marks. By all means, it was too excessive and a strong critic of all these developments

---
15. Ibid., p. 159.
16. Ibid.

like Lord J. M. Keynes had already hinted:[17]
1. That the claims against Germany which the allies were contemplating were impossible for payment;
2. That the economic solidarity of Europe was so close that the attempt to enforce these claims might have ruined everyone;
3. That the money cost of the damage done by the enemy in France and Belgium had been exaggerated;
4. That the inclusion of pensions and allowances in our claims was a breach of faith;[18] and
5. That our legitimate claim against Germany was within her capacity to pay.[19]

But the warnings of the great English economist went in vain. Though Germany could make the payment of first instalment of 150 million gold marks in 1921, she was caught in a great economic crisis just after that. The value of the German currency began to fall steadily and the German budget witnessed a net deficit of 96 billion paper marks. Finding that she would not be able to pay the next instalment under these conditions, the Reparation Commission on March 21, 1922 limited Germany's payment for this year to 720 million gold marks in cash as against 2 billion gold marks called for by Art. 4 of the Schedule of Payments and credited against this amount of 281,948,920'49 gold marks that had already been paid in kind.

---

17. See Mantoux, *op. cit.*, p. 94.
18. The cost of 'pensions and separation allowances' was added to the bill at the insistence of Gen. Smuts of South Africa. It was much criticised in the name of 'arbitrary incidence of the criterion adopted'. G.M. Gathorne-Hardy: *A Short History of International Affairs* (London: Oxford Univ. Press, 1950), IV ed., p. 38.
19. One may not agree with this contention of Keynes. The Foreign Minister of France (Klotz) had estimated the total liability of Germany at $75,000,000,000. Of course, it was too much, but the total liability of Germany as fixed by the Reparation Commission was no less excessive. According to the calculation of Keynes, the Allied Powers were entitled to these payments:

Receipts			Pensions and allowances only	
1. Belgium	$	2,500,00,000	1. Br. Empire	$ 7,000,000,000
2. France	$	4,00,00,000	2. France	$ 12,000,000,000
3. G. Britain	$	2,850,000,000	3. Italy	$ 2,500,000,000
4. Others	$	1,250,000,000	4. Others	$ 4,500,000,000
Total		$ 10,600,000,000	Total	$ 25,000,000,000

See Keynes, *op. cit.*, pp. 134 and 160.

Henceforth, British and French differences came on the surface. While British leaders looked at the helpless condition of Germany in the light of their economic interests as well as in the context of their traditional policy of maintaining the balance of power on the continent, their French and Belgian counterparts adopted the strategy of exploiting a favourable opportunity to weaken Germany as much as possible. The obstinate Poincare of France described German helplessness as deliberate that afforded the Allied powers an occasion to occupy some important German areas as a matter of sanction or coercion for the payment of scheduled reparation. It is, therefore, well observed: "The ink was scarcely dry upon the preposterous settlement when the solidarity of the Allies began to disappear. The warnings of Keynes had exerted a distinct influence upon many Englishmen in public life among whom there was a growing feeling that the financial terms imposed upon Germany were so impossible of fulfilment that they would retard recovery until they were modified.... For them the war was over and, being primarily concerned with the world economic outlook, they knew from their long experience with international economic affairs that the scars of the War would never be healed until Germany was restored to a state of economic health."[20]

France adhered to the policy of force and in its hot pursuance she was backed by Italy and Belgium. Thus, the British representative saw his defeat in the meeting of the Reparation Commission. By 3 votes to 1, Germany was held guilty of non-payment of annuity by her deliberate action. Consequently, on January 10, 1923, the French and Belgian troops made their entry into the industrially rich areas of Ruhr. The German government reacted to this sanction by a policy of passive resistance. Though naturally popular throughout the Reich, it could not delay the financial collapse, then imminent. It crippled German economic position to any imaginable extent. "By June an English traveller could get 500,000 marks for a pound and as the wild orgy of inflation continued, the mark sank until by the middle of August, the exchange rate stood at the fantastic figure of twenty million marks to the pound."[21]

---

20. Sharp and Kirk: *Contemporary International Politics* (New York: Farrar and Rinehart, 1944), p. 331.
21. *Ibid.*, p. 332.

The Dawes Plan : Success of Anglo-American Strategy of 'Business, not Politics'

The question of reparation was like a nightmare for Germany as the matter of 'security' was for France. The blunder of France and Belgium in occupying the area of Ruhr proved like a blessing in disguise for Germany. It afforded a powerful opportunity for the businessmen of England and America to support the case of the restoration of German economy. The American Secretary of State (C. E. Hughes) on December 29, 1922, put an idea before the American Historical Association that a commission of financial and economic experts must be set up to look into the capacity of Germany to clear the burden of reparation. The most important part of his talk was that even some distinguished Americans could be associated with such a committee. It well coincided with the interests of the English and American statesmen who wanted to give a turn to the politics of reparation in their favour at that time. Thus, the Reparation Commission adopted a resolution seeking to establish a committee to consider the resources and capacity of Germany to pay. The committee (with its chairman Charles G. Dawes of the United States and having representatives of Britain, France, Belgium and Italy) was commissioned with the task of recommending the means of balancing the budget and measures to stabilise German currency.

The Dawes Committee met at Paris from January 14 to April, 19, 1924. It submitted its recommendations as under:

1. It recommended the creation of a new currency Reichmark to be controlled by a Bank of Issue independent of the German Government. This Reichbank was to be controlled by a committee of an equal number of Germans and foreigners and was to have a capital of 400,000,000 gold marks and a 50 years monopoly to issue paper money.

2. With the increased stability of her currency, Germany was to pay annually a sum of $ 50,000,000 for 5 years, and afterwards this was to be raised to a maximum of $125,000,000 a year, the standard annual payment varying with the prosperity of Germany.

3. Lest the exchange should have collapsed in the event of the transfer of difficulties, it was recommended that payments were to be made in German currency and that the operation of transfer rest with the creditors.

4. With a view to provide security for payment, it recommended that payment could be made from railway bonds, transport taxes, industrial debentures, and proceeds of revenue of alcohol, tobacco, beer and sugar.

5. A Foreign Agent-General for Reparations Payment was to be appointed to be in-charge of the whole scheme.

6. Germany was to receive a foreign loan of $ 40,000,000 so that she could have a currency reserve and be able to pay the first instalment of reparation.

7. Ruhr was to be speedily evacuated in order to restore Germany's economic sovereignty and permit the new plan to operate without delay.

The Revised Schedule of Payment according to Dawes Plan
(in millions of Gold Mark)

	Resources	Years				
		I	II	III	IV	V
1.	Railways	200	595	550	660	660
2.	Reparation Loss	800				
3.	Transport Tax		250	290	290	290
4.	Industries		125	250	300	300
5.	Sale of Preference Shares of the Railway Company		250			
6.	Ordinary Budget Allocations			110	500	1250
7.	Supplementary Budget Contributions			300		

Then followed the London Conference of July 16, 1924, where the Dawes Plan was signed by the Prime Ministers of England (Ramsay MacDonald) and France (M. Herriot) and Foreign Minister Gustav Stresemann of Germany. After two weeks, it was agreed that future defaults could be declared by a unanimous vote of the Reparation Commission. The German Reichstag passed a law to implement the recommendations of the Dawes Plan. Thus, on October 30, 1924, the Dawes Plan came into operation. Thereupon, the proposed loan by the United States was successfully floated. In January 1925, the Allied Finance Ministers' Conference quickly settled the issue of apportionment of the reparation payments. Then on July 31, 1925, the French and Belgian troops vacated the area of Ruhr.

The Dawes Plan inaugurated a new era in the history of reparation that had subjected Germany to an unduly severe burden. The committeemen who started their work with a slogan 'business, not politics', "approached their tasks as businessmen anxious to obtain effective results."[22] The Plan was widely appreciated for these reasons:

1. It distinguished the issue of reparation from the arena of political controversy and treated it liked an ordinary commercial debt. For this purpose, it extricated the whole problem from the hands of the unsatisfactory Reparation Commission and assured that it would be handled by an 'Agent' who would be an American citizen and, as such, who would be able to deal with this issue from a non-political and impartial standpoint.

2. It separated the question of payment of reparation from the question of transfer and left the latter for the creditors to deal with. In this way, it gave to the creditors the security of certain specified revenues like those of railways, industries, transport tax etc. Thus, the vagueness of the term 'Germany's resources' was done away with.

3. It limited its demands to sums that Germany could pay in favourable conditions. The annuities were to begin at a low figure till the standard annuity of 25,000 million gold marks was reached in the fifth year.

4. It provided against the use of military sanctions except in the event of flagrant German default and even that by concerted agreement of all the Allied powers. For this it was required that the Reparation Commission would take a decision with a unanimous vote and that too with the participation of the American delegate.

5. It resulted in a general economic recovery for confidence in the German economy having been restored, Anglo-American capital started flowing into Germany and other Central European countries.

---

22. Langsam, op. cit., p. 35.

But the Dawes plan was not free from certain shortcomings that may be pinpointed as under:

1. Though it provided for annual payments, it certainly failed to prescribe their duration or to make any pronouncement on total indebtedness of Germany. No French government at this stage would have dared to confess that it had formally abandoned any part of the full reparation claim of $ 6,600,000,000. "Germany was still, therefore, in the hopeless position that any increase in her financial well-being would entail an increased obligation, and she was deprived of any incentive to accumulate savings, which would merely pass into the Allied exchequers."[23]

2. The success of the Dawes Plan compelled Germany to depend upon massive borrowings from the American creditors. Thus, the way was opened for the influx of American capital into Germany that certainly created a wave of prosperity in the country. At the same time, it pushed Germany under the control of American economic imperialism. "Few people had the insight to realise that Germany was paying her debts out of American money, and that her solvency depended on the continued popularity of German loans in Wall Street."[24]

3. The Dawes Plan left Germany in a condition like that of a bucket being filled and emptied simultaneously, the filling by receipt of loans from the English and American, mainly the latter, creditors and emptying by making payments to the Allied. Statistics reveal that during the period of 1924-1928 Germany paid 10.3 million reichmarks in reparation and borrowed 18.2 million reichamarks by foreign, largely American, loans. Thus, Hitler

---

23. Carr, op. cit., p. 84.
24. Ibid., p. 85. Norman Angell says that the principal injuries that the Dawes Plan inflicted upon the Germans "have been psychological rather than economic. They arise from the natural general humiliation as being submitted to any system however friendly in its execution, of protracted supervision and control of foreigners." Actually, German payments had been made possible, at least in part, by the accumulation of exchange derived from foreign speculations in the mark. This was endorsed by the McKenna Report keeping which in view, J.M. Keynes observed: "For five years, Germany's victors have squeezed the lemon with both hands, have heard the 'pips squeak' and felt their own hands ache, have seen a trickle flowing into the bowl,—only to discover in the end that every drop has come, not from the lemon, but from the hands themselves. What Germany has appeared to pay in Reparations is nearly equal to what the foreign world has subscribed in return for worthless mark." Cited in Sharp and Kirk, op. cit., p. 334.

could resent: "Bismarck's Reich never had to shoulder such heavy and entirely unproductive obligations as those to which Germany was subjected under the Dawes Plan."[25]

A critical evaluation of the Dawes Plan, for these reasons, smacks of its qualified success. It marked that the businessmen of America and England were interested more in effectuating recovery of Germany than in patronising the claim of France for keeping her 'prostrate enemy' in an extremely weak position. It also suggested that the 'policy of force' as pursued by Poincare of France had been overshadowed by the 'policy of co-operation' now adopted by Stresemann of Germany. "Agreement was now general that Germany must be restored to economic health as a condition necessarily precedent both to the payment of reparation and at the general recovery of Europe."[26] As the later developments demonstrated, competent observers "began to talk as if the last chapter in the dismal record of the War had actually been written."[27]

The Young Plan: Final Settlement of the Reparation Question
We have already pointed out that the Dawes plan came as a stop-gap arrangement. It was taken for granted by all concerned parties that it was a provisional arrangement that would be replaced by some other arrangement in time to come. Its authors had described it as 'a settlement extending in its application for a sufficient time to restore confidence' and 'framed to facilitate a final comprehensive agreement as to all the problems of reparation and connected questions as soon as circumstances make this possible.' The Agent-General for Reparation Payments (Parker Gilbert) in his report of December 10, 1927, pointed out that the reparation problem would not be solved finally unless 'Germany has been given a definite task to perform on her own irresponsibility, without foreign supervision and without transfer protection.' Afterwards in his another report dated June 7, 1928, he stated that the Dawes Plan "has marked a turning point in the reconstruction of Europe in general and of Germany in particular and that steps should be taken as soon as circumstances made it possible by a mutual agreement among

---

25. Hitler: *Mein Kampf*, p. 314.
26. Sharp and Kirk, op. cit., p. 335.
27. Ibid.,

the creditor powers to a final determination of Germany's reparation liabilities and other connected questions.'[28]

It is true that the Dawes Plan contributed to the economic recovery of Germany, but the problem of the evacuation of the Rhineland remained like a festering wound at this stage. During the session of the League Assembly of 1926, Germany not only witnessed her admission to the world body, her delegate (Stresemann) had an occasion to confer with his French counterpart (Briand) in the village of Thoiry near Geneva in Switzerland where a *communique* was issued to the effect that the two ministers had disclosed all matters of common interest to the two countries. The significant part of the *communique* was that they 'had brought their point of view into agreement in regard to the general solution' and that they were referring it to their respective governments for approval. Though the nature of this provisional agreement was not officially disclosed, it was understood that Stresemann "begged for the immediate evacuation of the Rhineland and the return of the Saar to Germany offering in return concessions in the form of reparation payments, and that Briand was personally disposed to close with this offer."[29]

It well synchronised with what the British statesmen were contemplating at this stage. During the Assembly session of 1928 the delegates of Germany and principal reparation powers (Britain, France, Italy, Belgium and Japan) came to an agreement that negotiations should be opened for the early evacuation of the Rhineland and that a committee of financial experts should be appointed 'to prepare a complete and definite settlement of the reparation problem.' As a result of this, a committee of financial experts consisting of two representatives each of Britain, France, Italy, Japan and the United States came into being. Its chairman was

---

28. On this point, Gathorne-Hardy well observes: "One of these connected questions was, of course, the occupation of the Rhineland, to the termination of which Herr Stresemann's policy of the fulfilment' was mainly directed: so long as it continued, the resumption of cordial relations between Germany and her former opponents was evidently impeded, and, as time went on, the German people evinced increasing impatience at the postponement of this reward of good behaviour. The unexpected case with which the conditions of the Dawes Plan seemed to have been carried out produced, moreover, a widespread impression that the time was now ripe for a final settlement." op cit., p. 263.
29. Carr, op. cit., p. 124.

Owen Young (an American). It deliberated for about four months and on June 7, 1929, it submitted its report. Along with certain revisions made at the Lausanne Conference, it made these important recommendations:[30]

1. Germany was to pay 37 annual instalments of $100,000,000 (as against $125,000,000 under the Dawes Plan) followed by 22 annual small payments that might cover the War debt payments of Allied powers to the United States. The 37 annual instalments were to be derived from the German railways, while the 22 instalments from the Reich budget. Now the total German liability amounted to about $5,750,000,000.

2. The total payment was divided into 'postponable' and 'nonpostponable' parts. Roughly, 2/3 of an instalment was postponable for two years whenever, in the opinion of a Special Advisory Committee, Germany's exchange and economic life might be seriously endangered.

3. The operation of the Plan was no longer to be in the hands of the Reparation Commission. Now a new body (Bank of International Settlements) was provided to act as a trustee for the creditors. It was to collect the annuities, serve as a link between national central banks, and to furnish international commerce and finance with important facilities hitherto lacking and thus to contribute to the stability and the growth of international finance and trade. It was to be administered by a board of directors representing all creditor powers and Germany.

4. The payments to be made by Germany in kind were reduced to 10 annual instalments of gradually decreasing amount.

5. A new 'sanction clause' was included in it so as to ensure the resumption of the 'full liberty' of act on the part of any creditor power if the Permanent Court of International Justice should declare Germany in a state of voluntary default.

6. The responsibility for transferring the sums paid was no longer to rest on the creditors but on the German government.

7. Rhineland was to be evacuated by June 30, 1930, and the cost of occupation after September 1, 1929 was to be borne by the countries concerned (France and Belgium).

---

30. See G.V. Haberler: *The Theory of International Trade* (London: William Hodge and Co., 1933), p. 107.

8. The Belgian claim to cover the loss of the depreciated German marks left in the country after the war was left to be settled by separate and direct negotiations.

9. It made a complete departure from the ratio fixed at the Spa conference obviously to the detriment of Britain. Now 5/6 of the postponable annuities were allotted to France and Britain's share was reduced from 22 to 19 per cent.

10. In a concurrent memorandum signed by all the members of the Committee (excluding the United States) it was provided that the payment of the reparation amount and the inter-allied debts were inter-connected matters.

Now arose the problem of the ratification of the Plan by respective governments. For this purpose, the Hague Conference took place in August, 1929. It broke down because the British delegate (Philip Snowden) fought against the revision of British share from 22 to 19 per cent. Then, another Hague conference took place in January, 1930. (It was here that the 'sanctions clause' mentioned above was inserted at the insistence of France.) Now the agreement took place as a result of which the Bank of International Settlement was opened at Basle and the plan came into force on May 9, 1930.

Viewed from a critical angle, it may be added now that, like the Dawes plan, the Young plan made 'another shot in the arm of Germany's economy'.[31] It was fairly well received, but the presumed continuation of annual payments till 1988 was strongly resented by a good number of German nationalists. "It appeared to involve an unjust transfer of the idea of 'war guilt' and the Versailles restrictions to generations yet unborn."[32] But other nations "were relieved, believing that a complete and final settlement had at least been reached."[33] What, however, entailed the doom of the Young Plan was the emergence of an astounding economic depression in 1930 that forced the American President (Hoover) to declare one year's moratorium to which we refer now.

---

31. Norman Hill: *Contemporary World Politics* (New York: Harper and Brothers, 1954), p. 133.
32. Langsam, *p. cit.*, p. 36.
33. Ibid.

Great Economic Depression: Hoover's Moratorium as a Windfall for Germany

An astounding development in the recent economic history of Europe was the great 'economic blizzard' that began in the autumn of 1929 and lasted till 1933. It was by all means a long-range effect of the First World War. As a matter of fact, the war had left behind it an economic legacy that imposed a heavy mortgage upon the resources of all the belligerents. Heavy industries (such as coal mining, engineering and ship building) were inflated to meet the insatiable demands of the war and upon the cession of these demands there arose the acute problem of the 'distressed areas. In addition, the lavish expenditure of the people and their governments, the emotional reaction unsettling the mind of the post-war generation, fluctuating currencies causing bank balances to melt away swiftly, high rate of taxation discouraging savings, fast changes in the sphere of international trade capable of suddenly sweeping away the accumulated profits of industry, and the orgy of public speculation of the stock exchange markets were the phenomena that "combined to produce a psychological situation in the twenties in which wasteful extravagance was rampant."[34]

The great economic depression brought about an unexpected slump in the sphere of production. It had its effects on the political conditions also. Not only did Britain abandon the gold standard and a very large number of states followed her, it forced several governments to renounce the path of classical liberalism too. As Lipson says: "It induced the United States, where the dying system of *laissez faire* had found its last asylum, to throw her cherished economic enterprise to an unwanted degree of official direction. It induced the Allied Powers to renounce their claims upon Germany for reparation. It induced the German people to substitute an authoritarian government for the political regime established by the Weimar constitution. And, finally, it gave an immense impetus to the movement for economic self-sufficiency."[35]

Under these conditions, President Hoover of the United States on June 20, 1931 gave a statement in which he said: "The American Government proposes the postponement, during one year, of all payments on inter-governmental debts, reparations and

---

34. E. Lipson: *Europe, 1914-1939* (London: Adam and Charles Clark, 1957), p. 473.
35. Ibid., p. 472.

relief debts, both principal and interest —of course, not including obigations of Governments held by private parties. Subject to confirmation by the Congress, the American Government will postpone all payments upon the debts of foreign Governments to the American Government payable, through the fiscal year beginning July next, conditional on a like postponement for one year and of all payments of inter-governmental debts owing the important creditor powers."

It is obvious that "at this juncture, President Hoover came forward as the *dues ex machina* with his proposal"[36] that certainly went to the chagrin of France. Germany could treat it as a grace from the blue, for it provided her with a powerful and legitimate alibi. She frankly regretted her inability to make any payment any more according to the terms of the Young Plan. Thus, the governments of Germany, France, Belgium, Britain, Italy and Japan decided to hold a conference at Lausanne on February 13, 1932 with a view "to agree to a lasting settlement of a questions raised in the report of the Basle experts on the measures necessary to solve the other difficulties which are responsible for, and may prolong present world crises."

The Lausanne Conference opened on June 16, 1932. After three weeks of deliberations, an agreement was signed on July 9, 1932, by the delegates of Britain, France, Italy, Japan, Belgium, Austria, Canada, Greece, India, New Zealand, Poland, Portugal, Rumania, Czechoslovakia, South Africa, and Yugoslavia. It was designed to put an end to the vexed problem of reparation and instead instruct the government of Germany to pay a sum of three milliard Reichmarks gold into a general fund for the reconstruction of Europe. In order to meet this obligation, the Government of Germany was to deliver to the Bank for International Settlements 5 per cent redeemable bonds of that amount. Obviously, as Bennes says, this agreement "constituted one more recession in the series of ever diminishing demands upon Germany for reparation. An Allied demand in 1921 that Germany assume an obligation to pay $ 56,500,000,000 was followed in the same year by the Reparation Commission's decision that the total figure should be $33 billion. This stood legally as Germany's obligations until the Young Plan

---

36. Gathorne-Hardy, op. cit., p. 270.

reduced it to an amount which was equivalent to a cash payment of approximately $ 9 billions. Two years later, came the Hoover Moratorium and then in July, 1932, the Lausanne Agreement which drastically revised Germany's obligations to a total cash of only $ 750 million with the possibility that even this amount might never be paid."

The situation changed fundamentally when Hitler assumed power in 1933. Even the drastically reduced amount of $ 714,000,000 at the Lausanne Conference, what to say of the figure fixed under the Young Plan, became a nullity. The whole issue of reparation "was consigned to the limbo of the forgotten past. Throughout the whole history of German reparation issue, two problems were present:
 i   the indifference of the German government, and
 ii the practical impossibility of converting funds that might be raised through taxation by the German Government towards its account into the currencies of the creditor nations. Only by an enormous export trade could Germany as a debtor pay off her creditors, and those creditors did not favour giving her the trade opportunities she would require in order to accumulate the export balance necessary for payments."[37]

Inter-Allied War Debts: A Supplementary Problem to the Politics of Economic Realism

Closely connected with the problem of reparation was that of inter-allied war debts. It showed that the financial aftermath of the war was far from liquidated."[38] Prior to the entry of the United States in the First World War, Britain and France had advanced loans to their allies. But eighteen days after the US joined the war the Congress authorised the lending of $ 3 billion to the Allies at the interest of 5 per cent per annum. These loans continued even after the end of the war. The approximate position of the inter-allied debts at the end of the war was that the US had lent a sum of $ 2,325,000,000 to her European partners: Britain had lent a sum of $ 2,183,000,000, while France had advanced a sum of about $ 100,000,000. According to the calculations of Keynes, the position was as follows:[39]

---
37. Hill, op. cit., p. 454.
38. Sharp and Kick, op. cit., p. 135.
39. Keynes, op. cit., p. 271.

Inter-Allied Loans

(in million dollars)

Loans to	By US	By UK	By France	Total
1. Britain	4,210	—	—	4,210
2. France	2,750	2,540	—	5,200
3. Italy	1,625	2,335	175	4,135
4. Russia	190	2,840	800	3,830
5. Belgium	400	490	450	1,340
6. Serbia and Yugoslavia	100	100	100	300
7. Other Allies	175	395	250	820
Total	9,450	8,700	1,775	19,925

Naturally, the payment of inter-allied war debts became intertwined with that of the issue of reparation at the time of Paris Peace Conference. The lesser allies came forward with a demand for the cancellation of all these debts. The burden of their argument was that while they took loans for the prosecution of war, they had also paid with their flesh and blood. Among the major allies, France demanded the same with this contention that the question of reparation should not be involved with the issue of payment of inter-allied debts. Britain, being in a position of creditor as well as debtor with balance on the credit side, desired the same with this insistence that 'enormous non-commercial debts were a millstone round the neck of the world in its attempt to recover from the destruction and calamities of war.'

It placed the American financiers in a complex situation. They had their own argument that why they should pay for the cost of a war started and conducted by the 'quarrelsome Europeans'. Moreover, when the European victors were bent upon squeezing Germany, why in return they should not pay their debts to the American creditors. To their success, the Paris Peace Conference could do nothing about the cancellation of debts. Despite the fact that the Senate rejected the Treaty of Versailles, the interest of the American financiers continued in the payment of loans. The American policy was contained in this expression of President Coolidge: 'They hired the money, didn't they?'

Amercian Loans (in dollars)
(as on November 15, 1922)

Borrowing Countries	Principal	Interest	Total
1. Armenia	11,959,917'49	1,677,256'88	13,637,174'37
2. Austria	24,055,708'92	2,886,685'08	26,942,394'00
3. Belgium	377,123,745'94	60,073,383'65	4,37,197,129'59
4. Cuba	7,740,500'00	—	7,740,500'00
5. Czechoslovakia	91,887,668'65	14,404,536'67	106,292,205'32
6. Estonia	13,999,145'60	2,089,625'66	16,088,771'26
7. Finland	8,281,926'17	1,012,436'10	9,294,362'27
8. France	3,340,746,215'16	503,836,035'61	3,844,132,250'77
9. Great Britain	4,135,818,358'44	611,044,201'85	4,746,862,560'29
10. Greece	15,000,000'00	750,000'00	15,750,000'00
11. Hungary	1,685,835'61	202,300'28	1,888,135'89
12. Italy	1,648,034,050'90	284,681,434'61	1,932,715,485'51
13. Latvia	5,132,287'14	643,576'87	5,775,864'01
14. Liberia	26,000'02	3,518'85	29,518'85
15. Lithuania	4,981,628'03	747,244'20	5,728,872'23
16. Nicaragua	170,585'35	—	170,585'35
17. Poland	135,662,867'80	17,618,809'01	153,281,676'81
18. Rumania	36,128,494'94	5,864,104'34	41,992,599'28
19. Russia	192,601,927'37	39,712,670'78	232,313,968'15
20. Serbia	51,104,5959'58	7,994,087'92	59,089,683'50
Total	10,102,140,829'09	1,554,791,908'36	11,656,932,737'45

Source: Sharp and Kirk,. op. cit., p. 329.

It was also argued by the American statesmen that a considerable amount of loans taken by the European countries was utilised for non-war purposes like food and rehabilitation. In pursuance of this policy, therefore, the Congress set up on February 9, 1922, the World War Foreign Debt Commission to collect all loans by 1947 with at least 4½ per cent interest. Thereafter, an agreement was made between the US and Britain stipulating that from 1923 to 1932 the latter would pay to the former a sum of $33,000,000 a year and then from 1933 to 1948 a sum of $38,000,000 a year. On April 29, 1926 a funding agreement between France and the US was also made under which the former was to pay to the latter her debts for 62 years. Similar agreements were made between Britain and other European allies in 1926 and 1927.

Though the issue of inter-Allied war debts could not be bracketed with that of the reparations at the time of Paris Peace Conference, the problem continued to subsist simultaneously. The European allies now invoked the plea that they would not be able to make payment of their debts to the United States until they received their share from the payment of German reparation. Even the British leaders took this argument though in a wider perspective. For instance, the Balfour Note of August 1, 1922 said that the sum Britain would require from her debtors would depend solely upon the amount that she would have to pay to the US and that she would be prepared to forsake her claims in this regard as well as in regard to the payment of reparation along with the payment of her own money from the allies if such renunciation formed part of a general plan by which the highly ticklish problem of war debts and reparation could be dealt with as a whole and taken to the point of a final settlement. In other words, it signifies that in the British point of view, the problem of the payment of American loans could not be separated from the payment of reparation and other loans given by the major allies to their lesser partners.

That the two problems could not be treated independently became obvious when the German government could not make the payment of her second instalment in 1922 and thereafter French and Belgian troops occupied Ruhr that was evacuated afterwards with the intervention of the British and American statesmen. The Dawes Plan failed to solve the tangled issue, but it was wisely dealt with by the Young Committee. The Allied delegates in the Young Committee asserted that being the creditors of Germany, they were desirous of using their receipts from that 'government' to pay for their own indebtedness. Thus, the Young Committee adopted the memorandum of the Experts at the Hague (that did not form part of the Young Plan) in which the payment of inter-Allied war debts was bracketed with the settlement of reparation on a permanent basis. This important document "was based on the principle that all the net liabilities of the Allies between 1931 and 1988, as provided in the funding agreement, should be covered by German reparations."[40]

It is on account of such integration of the two gigantic issues that Hoover moratorium not only effected suspension of the

---
40. Haberler, op. cit., p. 113.

payment of reparation by Germany, it also effected payment of all debts given by the creditors to the debtors during the period of great economic depression. The American government renewed its demand for the payment of debts on June 30, 1932, when the moratorium duration came to an end. They did not appreciate the argument of British and French leaders that the Lausanne Agreement (that practically cancelled all German liabilities) covered their debts also. They frankly said that the Lausanne Agreement was concerned with the European countries and it was not made on the basis of any commitment or undertaking from Washington. While welcoming the Agreement as 'a great step forward in the stabilisation of the economic situation in Europe', the State Department on July 9, 1932, declared that on the question of the war debts there was no change in the policy of the American government.

The American obduracy could not succeed even in the short run. With great uneasiness, the British government paid her instalment of debt to the United States in 1932 in gold, while other debtors, including France, just made 'token' payments. The World Economic Conference of 1933 could not afford success to the American leaders in view of the fact that on this occasion nothing beyond making some references to war debts could be done. In April, 1934 the Johnson Act came into being that closed the security markets to any foreign government that 'defaulted' in payment of American debts. Even this threatening measure failed. With the emergence of Hitler in Germany, the scene changed. The Lausanne Agreement remained unratified in the absence of a war debt settlement and also in view of the fact that by this time all debtors states, except Finland, had defaulted.

The result was that the Young Plan virtually remained in force, though in a truncated form, and even that was thrown to the winds when Hitler adopted the course of repudiation of all what was given in the Treaty of Versailles. The immediate effect of all this was that even the amount of $150,000,000, as stipulated in the Lausanne Agreement, remained unpaid. In a very short time to come, it became clear to all that the issues of war debts and reparations came to an end in the midst of defaults, recriminations and bitterness leaving behind "a sad story of complicated idiocy in the making of which much toil and virtue was consumed". (Churchill) It also demonstrated that the two tangled issues in-

Reparations and Inter-Allied Debts

volved the use of American money to a very large extent by which the Allies had fought and defeated Germany, then realised reparation and then they made payments to their arch-creditor. Thus, in 1926 Keynes commented: "Reparations and inter-Allied debts are being mainly settled on paper, not in goods. The United States lends money to Germany, Germany transfers its equivalent to the Allies, the Allies pay it back to the United States government. Nothing real passes—no one is a penny the worse."[41]

Critical Appreciation

If reparation means a levy imposed upon a defeated nation to compensate the victor in some measure in cash or kind or both for the costs of war, two significant questions arise at this stage. The first is as to how much or what amount did Germany pay in all? The answer is that though she could not pay the full amount, she did pay a considerable part of the reparation as is evident from the following breakdown:[42]

Payments	Reparation Commission	German Government (in million marks)
From Nov. 11, 1918 to Aug. 31, 1921	9,637.8	42,059.00
Under Dawes Plan	7,553.2	4,993.0
Under Young Plan	778.9	14,608.0
Total	20,769.9	67,763.00

But the second question is related to the ethics of the whole problem. Whether it was all just or not still remains a matter of debate. The Allied Powers held their action of fixing total liability of Germany for reparation in accordance with the principles of international law and natural justice. It is said: "Considered from an academic standpoint, there can hardly be a doubt as to the well-established right of a victor to recover, if he can, and in the absence of agreement to the contrary, the whole costs of a war from his defeated antagonist. This right is completely independent of any

---

41. See Mantoux, op. cit., p. 148.
42. Ibid., p. 152.

question as to the moral or legal responsibility of either party for the hostilities; the question of war-guilt is, therefore, wholly irrelevant."[43]

There may be some element of justification in this argument, but the fact stands out that the story of reparation is ridden with these important points of criticism:

1. A dispassionate study of the whole story of peace settlements with the supplementary study of the issues of reparation and war debts leaves this strong impression that it was done with a determination of taking 'revenge'.[44] The victors sought to settle their scores in their own ways so far as the politics as the art of compromise could make it all possible. We may endorse the observation of J. F. Dulles: "The unity of the Allied and Associated Powers with respect to Conditions of Peace had been so different to achieve, and was of so fragile a nature that it was feared, it could not withstand the shock of reviewing the reporting part of the Treaty. Thus what was originally conceived of as a basis of discussion became without discussion the Treaty terms."[45] Again: "So intent were the American, British and French delegates upon finding words that would compromise their own differences. So swayed were they by emotion against Germany, that the permanent effect upon Germany was not adequately perceived or considered....

---

43. Gathorne-Hardy, op. cit., p. 37.
44. While rebutting this charge, a powerful advocate of the reparation provisions like Mantoux observes: "In November, 1918, means of revenge were in the hands of the Allies; and their motives for revenge were not lacking in their hearts. For four years, their countries had been invaded, their fields and cities plundered, their houses destroyed; and they knew that at the back of these disasters there lay something far deeper than the inevitable consequences of the act of war; the systematic destruction of the French and Belgian industries could not be attributed solely to military motives; and whence the German armies retreated in 1917 and in 1918, these acts increased in wild porportions, the more so all hopes of a military victory were gone." op. cit., p. 96. On the basis of this strong affirmation, this writer adds that the charge of a critic like Keynes is irrelevant. He says: "There is not one single clause in the Treaty of Versailles that can be considered as an act of revenge." Ibid., p. 97. An American historian like Prof. R.C. Binkley advanced the argument that Art. 231 of the Treaty "was not properly interpretable as a war guilt clause." Refer to his paper "The Guilt Clause in the Versailles Treaty" in *Current History*, Vol. XXX, New York, 1929, pp. 294-300.
45. See John Foster Dulles: "Introduction" in Burnett, op. cit., Vol. I, p. ix.

Reparations and Inter-Allied Debts 95

In their own minds, they were merely finding a formula for solving different opinions as to Germany's theoretical liability for reparation."[46]

2. Obviously, the amount of injustice perpetrated by the victors in the name of reparation forced the people of Germany to yearn more intensely to retrieve their lost prestige and vindicate themselves before the world. They strongly believed that a lot of injustice had been meted out to them; that "the legend of German war guilt was a hypocritical formula invented by the democracies to excuse Allied extortions and conquests. In dark hours even peaceful Germans doubted if they would ever receive fair treatment unless they rearmed and damned the Treaty."[47] Even an English commentator like Carr holds: "The vast and undefined reparation debt not only made it impossible for Germany to put her financial house in order, but paralyzed her will to make any serious effort to do so; for the sounder her finances, the more she would be able to pay."[48]

3. The question of peace settlements at Paris and then the issue of reparation entailed brisk involvement of the United States in the politics of international relations, hitherto a concern of major European powers. Though the Senate rejected the Treaty of Versailles, the involvement of the American statesmen could not be lessened. The American financiers did their best in keeping the issue of their loans to several European countries aloof from the vexed question of reparation, it could not happen. By 1926 the issue of reparation was entangled with the issue of war debts so much so that the dictate of Hoover affected not only the fate of reparation but also the American debts. The rise of Hitler meant the end of reparation, and that automatically entailed the end of the concurrent issue of war debts.

It well confirmed the impression of Clemenceau that 'America emerged from the war with one great illusion, America, and one great disillusion, Europe.'[49] In short, an account of reparation and allied with that an account of inter-Allied war debts, constitutes a

---

46. Ibid., p. xii.
47. Geoffery Bruun: *The World in the Twentieth Century* (Boston: D.C. Heath & Co., 1957), p. 411.
48. E.H. Carr: *International Relations between the Two World Wars, 1919-1939* (London: Macmillan, 1952), p. 58.
49. See Sharp and Kirk, op. cit., p. 336.

very complicated record of the excessive burden cast by the Allied Powers on Germany that could be shaken off by a strong man like Hitler and that entailed heavy consequences due to the intermixing of politics with economics. After 1930 a new trend developed that was known by the name of 'economic nationalism'. Germany under Hitler followed the policy of 'autarchy'. Through strict economic controls of many sorts, she succeeded in linking the States of Central and Eastern Europe to the Nazi system and in orienting the economies of other States to serve her needs for war purposes. The Nazis relied heavily on a barter system by which they sought to compensate for their lack of foreign exchange and to secure the materials needed for building up their war machine by the export of non-essentials. Naturally, it "disturbed relations between Germany and other nations, but it did serve the political ends of the Nazi state."[50]

---

50. N.D. Palmer and H.C. Perkins: *International Relations: World Community in Transition* (Calcutta: Scientific Book Agency, 1957), p. 577.

4

PHASE OF PACIFICATION

The struggle from 1914 to 1918 had, at its close, become in the minds of most people in great Britain 'a war to end war'; unless this aim had been realised, the effort had been wholly fruitless. What was confidently expected or at least not openly questioned, was the inauguration of a new era, in which nations and races, under governments of their own choosing, would, unselfishly and automatically cooperate in the suppression of the first signs of an appeal to force.

—G.M. Gathorne-Hardy[1]

Peace settlements at Paris culminating in the establishment of the League of Nations could not bear the expected dividends in the time to come widely hailed as the new era of peace. "Left by America as a 'foundling' on the door step of the European Allies, a seriously crippled League began its life."[2] The British statesmen made it very clear that they were not prepared to shoulder the gigantic responsibility of maintaining the system of collective security single-handed. When the first Assembly of the League met at Geneva in 1920, the Canadian delegate proposed the elimination of Art. 10 (relating to the preservation of territorial integrity) and further developed his point of view in 1922 by adding that 'no member shall be under the obligation to engage in any act of war without the consent of its parliament or other representative body.' The second Assembly of 1921 adopted a series of 19 resolutions bearing upon the system of collective security under the League the effect of which was generally to weaken the force of Art. 16.

---

1. Gathorne-Hardy: *A Short History of International Affairs, 1920-1939* (London: Oxford Univ. Press 1964) pp. 60-61.
2. Sharp and Kirk: *Contemporary International Politics* (New York: Farrar and Rinehart, 1944), p. 535.

Naturally it irked France who interpreted it as if the confidence reposed in the collective security system of the League of Nations was being rapidly undermined. In this situation Britain, France and other powers, major as well as minor, looked for certain other arrangements that would strengthen the provisions of the Covenant, or fill up the gaps therein so as to stabilise the foundations of peace.

Draft Treaty of Mutual Assistance: Attempt for General Guarantee of Security

The system of collective security embodied in the Covenant of the League of Nations received an initial setback not only for the reason of American 'foundling' but also in the face of shifting attitude of the then major powers of the world. The reluctance of the British statesmen to shoulder the great responsibility alone and in response to that the attitude of other dominions like those of Canada and Australia coupled with the rise of 'fascism' in Italy caused a basic change in the prevailing situation.[3] These developments which "seemed to threaten a relapse to the pre-war system, brought into rather unexpected alliance the French with their insistence on guaranteed security and the more zealous champions of the League as the last bulwark of civilisation."[4]

And yet some efforts in the direction of plugging the gaps in the Covenant so as to maintain the system of collective security, preferably in alliance with the system of treaties and pacts, persisted. The first Assembly set up a Temporary Mixed Commission with the task of preparing a plan for the execution of the disarmament obligations contained in Art. 8 of the Covenant. In 1922 Lord Robert

---

3. Soon after its establishment, the League became a centre of intra-alignments. Between the 'peace' and 'security' groups, various League members took fluctuating intermediate positions. Following the advent of 'fascism', Italy moved gradually from the *status quo* to the revisionist camp which after the admission of Germany in 1926, became articulate. For many years the Japanese government co-operated loyally with efforts to strengthen the security system—until having fallen under the domination of the military party at home, it decided to defy the League over Manchuria. For the most part, the South American nations displayed an indifferent attitude towards the central issues of League policy, their chief interest being to 'lobby' for the election of as many of their number as possible to the Council, the Court, and various League committees. Ibid., p. 542, n 18.
4. Gathorne-Hardy, op. cit., p. 67.

Phase of Pacification

Cecil of Britain submitted these important propositions to this Commission.[5]
1. That reduction of armaments, to be successful, must be general.
2. That such reduction depended upon satisfactory guarantees of security.
3. That these guarantees should be general.
4. That the provisions of such guarantees should be conditional on an undertaking to reduce armaments.

The proposals of Cecil along with those of Col. Requin of France were taken for discussion at the session of the League Assembly and then from the coordination of the two texts was produced the Draft Treaty of Mutual Assistance. Its main features were:

1. It imposed upon Council of the League of Nations the task of indicating what military or financial assistance should be furnished to the victim of aggression, but with the definite proviso that such miltary assistance should be confined to the states situated on the same continent as the aggressor state. It branded 'war of aggression' an international crime and made automatic the obligation of the signatory powers to go to the aid of any state which, having reduced its armaments, should find itself a victim of aggression. In other words, it provided that if the Council believed that there was a reasonable ground for thinking that a menace of aggression had arisen, it could apply economic sanctions against the aggressor state. In such a situation, it could call upon any of the contracting parties, whose military assistance was required, to assist, determine the forces which each state furnishing assistance should place at its disposal, prescribe measures for the communication and transport connected with such operations, prepare a plan for financial cooperation so as to provide funds for the states attacked and appoint the higher command and also define its objects and duties.

2. It made more precise the method of determining the 'aggressor'. The League Council could fix neutral zones which the parties were forbidden to cross and, if it ever happened, the case of the aggressor could be easily located. Further, the Council could propose an armistice and invite the disputants to put their claims

---
5. Ibid.

before the League or the Permanent Court of International Justice, as the case might be, and refusal to accept this invitation would provide additional evidence for determining an 'aggressor'.

3. At the insistent request of France it was inserted that, with the approval of the Council, the states were to be permitted to conclude mutual assistance agreements of a regional character.

4. It also provided that the aggressor would bear the entire cost of operations undertaken by the powers to prevent aggression and would pay reparations for damages caused by an act of aggression.

5. It was proposed that the signatories would cooperate in the general disarmament scheme that the League Council might propose and mutual assistance would be given only to the parties which had reduced their arms.

The Draft Treaty of Mutual Assistance "designed to strengthen Covenant and, at the same time, to meet American objections, lay in the nature of these defence measures."[6] Though it contained somewhat vague provisions for future disarmament, it certainly had "extremely precise guarantees for present security."[7] But it went into the pages of history like a rejected or futile exercise. In the autumn of 1923, the Labour Government of England under Ramsay MacDonald rejected it on the ground that "the apportionment of liability on continental lines cut fatally across the structure of the British Commonwealth with its worldwide responsibilities. Some parts of the Empire might be at war, while others remained at peace (a situation regarded at that time as intolerable), or Great Britain and her Dominions would be subjected to a wholly disproportionate share of the burden of resisting aggression in all parts of the world."[8]

Other sates of the world, including the United States and Soviet Russia, had their own reasons for rejecting it. It was widely asserted that the proposed Treaty had too much emphasis on 'sanctions' and too little on the pacific settlement of international disputes. Most of the big powers having their place in the League of Nations did not appreciate the amount of load put on the executive functions of the Council of the League in the form of

---

6. Sharp and Kirk, op. cit., p. 543.
7. E.H. Carr: *International Relations between the Two World Wars* (London: Macmillan, 1952), p. 89.
8. See Gathorne-Hardy, op. cit., p. 68.

defining an aggressor in precise terms and then proposing effective action against it. Keeping it in view, a group of American intellectuals led by Prof. James T. Shotwell pointed out with force that what had been to many governments the real stumbling block in the Draft Treaty of Mutual Assistance was the provision which left to the Council the duty of deciding, with full and unlimited discretion, which party to any given war had been guilty of aggreession."[9]

Geneva Protocol: Addition of Arbitration to the Tenets of Security and Disarmament

Generally, serious labours do not go in vain. The rejection of the Draft Treaty of Mutual Assistance hit at the inherent weaknesses of the existing machinery for the prevention of war. Focus was thrown on certain gaps in the system of collective security enshrined in the Covenant of the League of Nations. "If the Draft Treaty had to be sacrificed, it was felt that some acceptable alternative method of establishing the security at which it aimed must rise from its ashes. The method chosen was a return to the Covenant, and an endeavour to improve the machinery of the League as an instrument to preserve peace and deter aggression. It was sought to achieve this result in two ways — by supplying a satisfactory test of aggression, and by closing the 'gap in the Covenant' which still left war legitimate in the event of a failure of the machinery for settlement laid down in Art. 15. The key to both difficulties was sought in compulsory arbitration.[10] The utility of this expedient as a test of aggression was emphasised by the British Prime Minister (Ramsay MacDonald) in his opening speech at the fifth Assembly of the League in September 1924 when he said: "The one method by which we can secure, the one method by which we can approximate to an accurate attribution of responsibility for aggression is arbitration."[11]

In addition to this, some other constructive developments in the international sphere also took place. Reference may be made to the meeting of the Reparations Conference in London, adoption of the Dawes Plan, and evacuation of the Ruhr. Now international situation had eased to a considerable extent. The way for closer

---

9. See P.J. Noel-Baker: *The Geneva Protocol* (London, 1925), p. 18.
10. Gathorne-Hardy, op. cit., p. 69.
11. Ibid.

Anglo-French collaboration was paved. Thus, taking inspiration from the suggestion of his British counterpart about the principle of 'compulsory arbitration', the Premier of France (M. Herriot) adopted on October 2, 1924, a new plan based on the famous trilogy of arbitration, disarmament and security. The two statesmen had well in their mind the schemes of Dr. Benes (Foreign Minister of Czechoslovakia) and M. Politis (a Greek scholar of International Law and delegate of Greece at the General Assembly) regarding effective steps for the maintenance of collective security system. But the novelty of MacDonald-Herriot collaboration was further emphasis on the principle of compulsory arbitration to avert the situation of war, though one may point out that they had certainly picked up a thread from the proposals of the group of Shotwell.

As a result of this, the Geneva Protocol for the Pacific Settlement of International Disputes came into being with these important features:[12]

1. Compulsory arbitration was to be the only legal means of settling international disputes. If a nation refused to accept the procedure of pacific settlement or to accept a decision of a recognised third party, including the Council of the League of Nations, or violated provisional measures laid down by the Council, it would be deemed an aggressor. In the event of a difference of opinion, the Council could require an armistice of belligerents by a two-thirds majority vote and the party, which rejected the armistice or violated it, was to be regarded as an aggressor.

2. The Council could try to persuade the parties themselves to submit the issue of arbitration or judicial settlement, or failing that, as a last resort, it must refer the matter to a committee of arbitrators of its own choosing whose decision would be binding upon the disputant parties.

3. After the Council had designated an aggressor, it could also invite the signatory states to apply immediate economic and military sanctions. But whereas the Draft Treaty had provided that the Council should have a voice in directing these measures, the Protocol provided that each signatory power should remain in control of its own forces.

---

12. For full text of the Geneva Protocol see Fredrick W. Hartmann (ed.); *Basic Documents in International Relations* (New York: McGraw Hill, 1951), pp. 98-109.

4. It required every signatory state to accept 'compulsory jurisdiction' of the Permanent Court of International Justice over all disputes covered by the 'optional clause' of the Court's Statute. The decision of the Court would be binding and any violation thereof would be punishable as an act of aggression.

5. Disputes about matters of 'domestic jurisdiction', though excluded by the Covenant from a formal judgment of the Council under Art. 15, should be submitted to the procedure of conciliation under Art. 11, and that no power should be judged as an aggressor in such a dispute if it had brought the matter before the League under that Article.

6. In order to keep the balance between security and disarmament, it proposed that the Disarmament Conference should meet on June 15, 1925 for the reduction of armaments. The Protocol was to come into effect after the conclusion of a disarmament convention.

It was signed by Albania, Brazil, Bulgaria, Chile, Estonia, France, Greece, Latvia, Poland, Portugal, Yugoslavia and Czechoslovakia and subsequently by seven other states.

The merit of the Geneva Protocol should be seen in the fact that it "stigmatised aggressive war as an international crime. To prevent such conflicts, it stipulated that the nations adhering to its terms must agree to a variety of commitments aimed especially at defining the aggressor and thus reducing the likelihood of war."[13] Carr says: "The principal novelty of the Protocol was its attempt to improve on the Convent and to provide additional security through compulsory resort to arbitration. The Covenant left the door open for war, and not only in cases when the subject of the dispute was ruled to be a matter within the domestic jurisdiction of one of the parties. The Protocol sought to close these two gaps."[14]

In spite of the fact that the Geneva Protocol represented the most important attempt to strengthen the League of Nations, it had the same fate what we have seen in the case of the Draft Treaty of Mutual Assistance. Britain and other Dominions did not appreciate the provision of compulsory arbitration in the repugnance of which economic and military sanctions could be imposed at the behest of the Council of the League of Nations. Canada, Australia

---

13. W.C. Langsam: *The World Since 1919* (Delhi: Surjeet Pub., 1981), p. 42.
14. Carr, *op. cit.*, p. 90.

and New Zealand followed the reaction of the United States in resenting the control of the League or some other international body of conciliation or arbitration or the World Court over a matter falling within their domestic jurisdiction. The new Conservative Government of England having its Foreign Secretary in Austen Chamberlain looked at with great concern the contents of the Zinoviev letter wherein the President of the Third International in his secret note dated September 15, 1924, had directed to the Central Committee of the British Communist Party to stir up the working class against the government so as to pressurise it to ratify the Anglo-Soviet treaty.

The charge of rejecting the Geneva Protocol lay mainly on Great Britain for two reasons. "First, there were objections from the overseas Dominions, partly because of the fear that their domestic policies relative to Oriental immigration might be brought within the purview of the League, and partly because they preferred not to become involved any further in a system of collective sanctions, through their Imperial connection with Great Britain which might entangle them in European political quarrels. Basically, this reluctance was but a continued manifestation of the 'isolationist' position of Canada, in particular, because of its proximity to the United States, and maintained ever since the First League Assembly. In the second place, public opinion in Britain itself soon began to express the fear that, with the United States out of the League, the British navy might find itself in collision with America in case the League undertook to blockade a continental aggressor. Under the circumstances, the British hesitated to accept international commitments which might leave them, so to speak, 'holding the bag'. Nor were they enamoured of the proposal to extend the technique of arbitration to what were essentially political controversies."[15]

Britain got the bad name for administering a death-blow to the Geneva Protocol in not much time, though other leading states of the world did not remain behind in doing the same. National interest dominated the thinking of leading statesmen of the world and they saw with certain lurking apprehensions the serious attempts done to plug the loopholes of the Covenant. Speaking in ideal terms is one thing, doing in actual terms is quite different. Thus, the powers that pretended to remove the inherent

---

15. Sharp and Kirk, op. cit., p. 547.

shortcomings of the Covenant showed that they were really interested in maintaining the *status quo*. For this reason, the Geneva Protocol that "represented the most important attempt made to strengthen the League of Nations... failed of adoption completely because of the unwillingness of all the League members to see the gaps in the Covenant closed and a system of automatic sanctions introduced."[16]

Locarno Agreements: Substitute Measures for Regional Security
The rejection of the Geneva Protocol once again indicated that the labours had gone waste. But as the maxim goes that sincere labour never goes in vain, we may say that the Locarno Agreements of 1925 registered the fulfilment of what had been contemplated and done in the preceding two or three years. Credit for this goes to the trio of the Foreign Ministers of Britain (Austen Chamberlain), France (Briand) and Germany (Gustav Stresemann). By his stroke of statesmanship at Locarno, Chamberlain could remove the stigma of Britain's giving death-blow to the Geneva Protocol.[17] Likewise, the new Foreign Minister of France showed a changed attitude towards Germany.[18] Then, the new Foreign Minister of Germany succeeded in terminating the policy of 'passive resistance' and in stead launching a new policy of 'fulfilment'.

The agreements signed at Locarno in 1925 were a product of certain circumstances. By committing a mistake in occupying the areas of Ruhr, then facing the onslaughts of 'passive resistance' and, finally, vacating it, France had learnt a lesson. After signing the Treaty of Rappallo in 1920 Germany had been able to improve

---

16. Hartmann, op. cit., pp. 98-99.
17. Sir Alfred Zimmern fairly concluded that a more statesman-like course on the part of Britain would have been "not to repeat gesture of objection, thus for the second time throwing the work of a whole Assembly of some fifty delegations on the scrap heap, but to draw up a reasoned series of objections, accompanied by corresponding amendments. Had this been done, the real underlying differences between the British and the Continental view of the League would have been thrashed out in a favourable atmosphere, rather than as an embittering by-product of a Disarmament Conference." *The League of Nations, 1918-1935* (New York: Macmillan, 1939), p. 357.
18. Briand said: "The Treaty of Versailles will always be a source of irritation. It was the fruit of war, of victory. It can be called, and is called, a treaty imposed by force, under duress, that the defeated party is morally justified in repudiating when it can do so."

her relations with Soviet Russia. It came as a factor of apprehension for the British and French statesman alike who studied herein some long-range dangers to their economic gains. Besides, it was also feared by the British and French statesmen that the growing relationship between the two non-League members might create some complications for the international organisaion. It created an atmosphere for the benefit of Germany in particular. Thus, in October, 1925, the statesmen of seven states (Britain, France, Germany, Italy, Belgium, Poland and Czechoslovakia) assembled in the city of Locarno in Switzerland. They discussed several agreements that were signed two months after.

The Locarno agreements may be grouped into three parts in which the first one titled Treaty of Mutual Guarantee (also known by the name of the Rhineland Pact) has its outstanding importance.[19] These may be enumerated as under:[20]

1. *Treaty of Mutual Guarantee*
As said above, it was the most important of all treaties signed by Great Britain, France Italy, Germany and Belgium. It provided:
i) The signatories collectively and severally guaranteed the maintenance of the territorial *status quo* resulting from the frontiers between Germany and France and the inviolability of the said frontiers as fixed by the Treaty of Versailles.
ii) Germany and Belgium and Germany and France mutually undertook that they would in no case attack or invade each other or resort to war against each other. However, this stipulation was not to apply in the case of the exercise of the right of legitimate defence action or an action as a result of a decision of the Assembly or Council of the League of Nations.
iii) Germany and Belgium and Germany and France undertook to settle by peaceful means questions of every kind that might arise between them and that might not be possible to settle by normal methods of diplomacy. Any question with regard to which the parties were in conflict as to their respective rights was to be submitted to judicial decision and the parties under

---

19. Sharp and Kirk described it as 'the capstone of whole structure." op, cit., p. 550. Norman Hill calls it 'the heart of this system of peace." *Contemporary World Politics* (New York: Harper and Brothers, 1954), p. 135.
20. For full text of the Locarno Pacts, see Hartmann, op. cit., pp. 110-14.

Phase of Pacification

took to comply with that decision. All other questions were to be submitted to a Conciliation Commission. If the proposals of the Commission were not accepted by the two parties, the question was to be brought before the Council of the League of Nations for disposal.

iv) In the event of a flagrant violation of this Agreement or of the Treaty of Versailles, the signatories undertook to come immediately to the help of the party against whom such a violation of breach had been directed. As soon as the said Power had been able to satisfy itself that by reason either of crossing the frontier or of the outbreak of the hostilities or of the assembly of the armed forces in the demilitarised zone immediate action was necessary, the League Council was to issue its findings and the signatories undertook to act in accordance with the recommendations of the Council provided these were concurred in by all members other than the representatives of the parties which had encouraged any hostilities.

v) Where one of the powers refused to submit a dispute to peaceful settlement or to comply with arbitral or judicial decision, the other party must bring the matter before the League Council and it was the duty of the Council to propose what steps were to be taken. And it was the duty of the signatories to comply with those proposals.

vi) Its provisions did not effect the rights and obligations of the signatories under the Treaty of Versailles or other agreements like one signed at London on August 30, 1924.

vii) Though designed to ensure the maintenance of peace and being in conformity with the Covenant of the League, this Treaty was not to be interpreted as restricting the duty of the League to take whatever action might be deemed wise and effectual to safeguard the peace of the world.

viii) It was a to remain in force until the Council, acting on the request of one or other of the signatories, notified to other parties three months in advance and that it was to terminate on the expiry of a period of one year from such decision.

ix) It was not to impose any obligation upon any of the British Dominions or upon India, unless the government of such Dominion or India signified its acceptance thereto.

In short, this treaty provided that Germany, Belgium and France would regard their existing frontiers and the demilitarised zone of the Rhineland as inviolable and they would, in no case, attack or resort to war against each other. They would resort to pacific settlement of international disputes on the lines suggested in the Geneva Protocol. These obligations were placed under the supervision of Britain and Italy. Any complaint regarding the breach of this treaty was to be made to the Council of the League and in case the Council confirmed it, the guarantors were bound to rush immediately to the help of the aggressor. Moreover, they were required to obey the decision of the Council. The standard of the Geneva Protocol was adopted for the location of an 'aggressor' in that a state that refused to submit to arbitration or to carry out the arbitral award was to be declared an 'aggressor'. In this way, this treaty sought to supplement the provisions of the Covenant guaranteeing the territorial integrity and security of every member of the League of Nations by pledging automatic sanctions against any designed aggressor. For this reason, it has been pointed out: "In essence, the Locarno agreements may be described not inaccurately as an attempt to apply the principles of the Geneva protocol to a restricted area —the borderland separating Germany from France and Belgium."[21]

2. *Arbitration Treaties between Germany and Poland and between Germany and Czechoslovakia*
Germany signed artitration treaties with Poland and Czechoslovakia. By these agreements, the signatories agreed to refer their international disputes, with a view to their amicable settlement, to a Permanent Conciliation Commission to be constituted in accordance with the provisions of these treaties. In case the dispute could not be settled, the parties were to refer the matter either to an arbitral tribunal or to the Permanent Court of International Justice. However, this provision was not to apply to disputes arising out of the events 'prior to the present conventions and belonging to the past' and, for this reason, was not binding in the case of problems that arise out of the peace settlement.

3. *Treaties of France with Poland and Czechoslovakia*
Finally, France signed separate treaties with the states of Poland and Czechoslovakia in which it was provided that in the event of

---

21. Sharp and Kirk, op. cit., p. 549.

an attack on any one of them, the other signatories would come to the aid of the 'aggressed' in the event such a failure was accompanied by an unprovoked recourse to arms.

It is, therefore, obvious that for the first time in the post-War period France could achieve remarkable success in her search for security and, more important than that, Germany could have the honour of standing on a pedestal of equality with other European powers. It paved the way for her entry into the League of Nations in the following year. France was satisfied to a great extent because the Western frontiers of Germany, as determined under the Treaty of Versailles, were guaranteed. Briand expressed his ideas in these words: "Peace for Germany and for France that means that we have done with the long series of terrible and sanguinary conflicts which has stained the pages of history.... True, differences between us still exist, but henceforth, it will be for the judge to declare the law.... Away with rifles, machine guns, cannon. Clear the way for conciliation, arbitration, peace."[22]

The English press and commentators loudly appreciated the achievements at Locarno. When the discussions were taking a successful turn, the leading English daily commented that the "worst of the long travail is over at last ... the light of a new dawn is at last breaking upon the world."[23] Later, a well-known commentator observed: "The immediate effect on international relations in Europe was undoubtedly most favourable. The sense of improved security which the British guarantee implanted in the minds of Germans and Frenchmen had an importance far outweighing that of the question whether, on occasion arising, it would prove for Great Britain to fulfil her obligations. A democracy can hardly resort to war without the support of national opinion, and, what is comparatively easy to enlist this on the side of a known ally, the existence of two alternative allies or opponents complicates the situation. During the crisis preceding an outbreak of war, sympathy may very well have rallied to the side which eventually proves to be the aggressor; a sudden *volte-face* is then difficult. It is more probable that in such a case public opinion would be hopelessly divided on the merits. So long, however, as British intervention was feared by the potential aggressors of both sides, it seemed

---
22. Ibid., p. 551.
23. *The Times* (London), October, 17, 1925.

unlikely that the reality of the pact would be put to test. To scare the war-maker from his purpose is a more useful task than to arrest or defeat him when his offence has been committed. At the time of its adoption, at any rate, the Locarno Pact was a most effective and formidable-looking scarecrow which went far to justify the opinion of its creator, Mr. Austen Chamberlain, that its erection marked 'the real dividing line between the years of war and years of peace."[24]

The real significance of the making of these agreements lay in the fact that, for some time, leading statesmen of the world invoked the 'Locarno Spirit'. It signified that the agreements made at Locarno "represented the greatest diplomatic achievement of the peace years 1918-1939."[25] And yet it must not be lost sight of that the Locarno agreements had some shortcomings. For instance, they settled the point of Germany's western frontiers and thereby satisfied France and Belgium; they did not provide the same about her Eastern frontiers. It paved the way for the eventual dismemberment of Austria and Czechoslovakia at the hands of Hitler some ten years after. Thus, the leaders of Poland and Czechoslovakia had evey reason to feel dissatisfied with the magnificent achievements of Locarno. They had no other expedient course than to have some treaties of mutual assistance with France and Germany and this they did in the situation of a Hobson's choice.

Above all, it all went to the positive advantage of a weak Germany that could elevate her position in the comity of nations. When Hitler assumed power and started acting in flagrant violation of the Locarno Agreements, the Pact of Paris and the Covenant of the League of Nations, it became clear that the peace established by such diplomatic efforts was as brittle as a looking glass. It is thus critically remarked: "The Locarno achievements were widely hailed as precursors of a new era in world history. But neither the pacts nor the spirit of Locarno were actual guarantees of peace.... The spirit of friendliness, moreover, was only sporadically evident in international affairs after 1925."[26] Likewise, Carr says: "In the

---

24. Gathorne-Hardy, op. cit., p. 76. David Thompson lauds it as the 'Locarno Honeymoon' for five years, 1924-29. *Europe since Napoleon* (Middlesex: Penguin Books, 1978), Ch. 25.
25. E. Lipson: *Europe, 1914-1939* (London: Adam and Charles Black, 1957), p. 381.
26. Langsam, op. cit., p. 238.

Phase of Pacification

long run, the Locarno Treaty was destructive both of the Versailles Treaty and of the Covenant."[27]

Viewed in a long-range perspective, it may be argued that the Locarno agreements could not make a really durable success in the direction of outlawry of war. The signatory powers pledged to resort to the use of pacific means of international disputes, but they reserved the right to go to war in the events of legitimate self-defence action, flagrant breach of demilitarised zone agreement, and in pursuance of League action against a state charged with aggression. We may, however, add at this stage that this achievement was made just two years after, to which we shall refer now.

Kellogg-Briand Pact: Illusion of Peace without Security

Also known by the name of the Pact of Paris for the outlawry of war, this agreement of universal security should be lauded as the acme of idealistic diplomacy pursued by the great pacificator of France (Foreign Minister Briand) and having its synchronisation with the movement for the same purpose going on in the United States. During the session of the General Assembly of the League of Nations at Geneva in 1927, the Polish delegation had proposed a solemn declaration that "all wars of aggression are, and shall always be, prohibited." The great event of 1928 has, however, nothing to do with it in spite of the fact that the proposal of the Polish delegation was accepted with a unanimous vote. All credit for this goes to the powerful American legal and political opinion on this subject that found its timely coincidence with the diplomacy of Briand.[28] It, however, goes to the credit of the American Secre-

---

27. Carr, op. cit., p. 97.
28. At this time, a popular movement to 'outlaw war' had been making steady headway in the United States. The names of Prof. James T. Shotwell, Senator Borah and S.O. Levinson (a lawyer of Chicago) were associated with it. Though they had opposed the Covenant of the League of Nations a couple of years ago, now they had come to emphasise that war was something 'more than a crime'. It was rather a sin ! When the draft of the Geneva Protocol for the pacific settlement of international disputes was under consideration, a group of leading American figures like Shotwell, David Hunter Miller and General Bliss (who had attended the Paris Peace Conference of 1919 under the leadership of President Wilson) had formulated a plan for the outlawry of war or any sort of aggressive activity based upon the same general idea but with this significant addition that if a state "was adjudged an aggressor, its commerical, trade, financial and property interests... shall cease to be entitled... to any privileges,

tary of State (Kellogg) that instead of keeping the great ideal confined to the two countries (USA and France), he thought it expedient as well as worthwhile to circulate it so as to have its universal acceptability. It boldly demonstrates the fact that "the range of Briand's peace horizon was not limited to Europe."[29]

As a result of the success achieved by the 'fathers' of this solemn move, the Pact was signed by 15 states of the world at Paris on August 27, 1928.[30] The preamble said:[31]

"Deeply sensible of their solemn duty to promote the welfare of the mankind;

"Persuaded that the time has come when a frank renunciation of war as an instrument of national policy should be made to the end that the peaceful and friendly relations now existing between their people may be perpetuated;

"Convinced that all changes in their relations with one another should be sought only by pacific means and be the result of a peaceful and orderly process, and that any signatory power which shall hereafter seek to promote its national interests by resort to war should be denied the benefits furnished by this Treaty;

"Hopeful, that encouraged by their example, all the other nations of the world will join in this humane endeavour and by adhering to the present Treaty as soon as it comes into force bring their peoples within the scope of its beneficent provisions, thus uniting the civilised nations of the world into a common renunciation of war as an instrument of their national policy;

"Have decided to conclude a Treaty...."

---

protection, rights or immunities accorded by either international law, national law or treaty." From this, it may be gathered that the purpose of such a proposal "was to find a formula which might bring the United States into a limited but official relationship with the Geneva system. Even though American opinion might not be prepared to accept rigid sanction's obligations, it was felt that on the question of banning war, the United States might be persuaded to commit itself to a position even more unqualified than that taken by the League members under the Covenant." Sharp and Kirk, op. cit., p. 556.

29. Ibid., p. 555.
30. The signatories to this Pact were: USA, France, Germany, Belgium, Great Britain, Ireland and the British Dominions, India, Italy, Japan, Poland and Czechoslovakia. By 1933 it was ratified by 55 States of the world.
31. For full text of the Pact of Paris see Hartmann, op. cit., pp. 115-17.

The Treaty, in short, aimed at declaring renunciation of war as an instrument of national policy and instead seeking pacific settlement of international disputes. By it the High Contracting Parties made two important commitments to

1. "Solemnly declare in the names of their respective peoples that they condemn recourse to war for the solution of international controversies, and renounce it as an instrument of national policy in their relations with one another;

2. Agree that the settlement or solution of all disputes or conflicts of whatever nature or of whatever origin they may be, which may arise among them, shall never be sought except by pacific means."

The Pact of Paris came as an outstanding indication of the changed international atmosphere. It was heralded as a declaration of revolutionary significance in view of the fact that it was the first time in the history of world politics that such a solemn move was undertaken by all the then great powers to which a very large number of other states subscribed after a couple of years. It looked as if the idealism of Wilson had found its resuscitation through the efforts of Kellogg and Briand. "An upsurge of mass idealism had forced the governments to affix their seals to a sweeping pledge of good behaviour which, if it had been suggested fifteen years earlier, would have provided only cynical and raucous laughter from every foreign office. But now the peoples of the world might take hope: peace had at last universally been proclaimed. For on the face of it, this Pact contained no reservations. Nor could the states subscribing to the agreement renounce it individually at will. There was no provision, as in the Covenant, for withdrawal after notice."[32]

But, in not much time, the inherent weaknesses of this pact became evident. Norman Bentwich called it an 'international kiss purely Platonic promising nothing for the future'. Others denounced it as 'a tiger without a teeth', 'a high sounding nothing' and 'an instrument of international confusion'. It was said to have three serious weaknesses:

1. Though it condemned war and exhorted the states of the world to 'renounce war as an instrument of national policy', it did not precisely define the term 'war' and, for that reason, it failed to

---

32. Sharp and Kirk, *op. cit.*, pp. 557-558.

distinguish between an aggressive move and a defensive action. It left a convenient handle in the hands of the powerful states of the world to justify their stand in the name of honouring the terms of this treaty and, at the same time, justifying their action of 'war' in the name of self-defence. Committed to the observance of the Monroe Doctrine, the American statesmen like Senator Borah minced no words in making it above board that even at the risk of a war they would not tolerate any foreign interference in the region of the New World. Likewise, Japanese Foreign Minister declared in 1929 that Manchuria and Mongolia "are, of course, within the sphere where our right of self-defence can be exercised." The British Foreign Secretary (Austen Chamberlain) had already made it clear on May 19, 1928, that there are "certain regions of the world the welfare and integrity of which constitute a special and vital interest for our peace and security." Though one of the principal architects of the Pact, Kellogg himself said that every nation alone "is competent to decide whether circumstances require recourse to war in self-defence." These reservations came on the surface after a couple of years when Japan attacked Manchuria and thereby paved the way for other aggressors like Italy and Germany. Sharp and Kirk, therefore, point out: "There was no test, judicial or otherwise, by which aggression in its various forms, short of declared war, might be identified. The diplomatic correspondence that preceded the signing of the Pact clearly indicated that wars of self-defence would still be permissible and that each party would be judge of what constituted self-defence."[33]

2. While the Pact boldly desired resort to the pacific settlement of disputes, it certainly failed to elaborate what was meant by it in practical terms. Nor, for that matter, "did the signatory states accept any *positive* obligation to settle their controversies by pacific means. They agreed merely to seek a peaceful settlement which was a negative and less iron-clad way of restricting national

---

33. Ibid., p. 558. E.M. Borchard put the situation in these words: "Considering these reservations, it would be difficult to conceive of any wars that nations have fought within the past century or are likely to fight in the future that can not be accomodated under these exceptions. Far from constituting an outlawry of war, they constitute the most solemn sanction of specific wars that have ever been given to the world." *Twentieth Century Europe*. Likewise, Norman Hill comments that "the significant fact is that the Pact has not made the war impossible." Op. cit., p. 588.

behaviour."[34] It overlooked the fact that as long as force is the only mechanism for assuring international changes, then a purported renunciation of force or an optimistic resort to the pacific settlement of disputes are all like wishful thinking. In the period following the Second World War, the American Secretary of State (John Foster Dulles) said that, far from being sacred, such a pledge would be iniquitous even if it were practicable, and thus to put shackles on the dynamic peoples and condemn them for ever to acceptance of conditions that might become intolerable and by all means warrant use of force for the settlement of international disputes. With the force of this argument he concluded that a treaty like the Paris Pact would seek to realise "a desirable result without taking any of the steps essential to achieve it."[35]

3. But the most serious defect of the Pact was that while it contained very high and noble commitments, it provided no effective machinery for their protection and realisation. All depended upon the clean conscience of the then super-powers of the world. Moreover, since the United States was not a member of the League of Nations and USSR (at that time not a big power at all) joined it in 1933, one could not go beyond hoping that Britain and France would act as the custodians of international peace in case any major power broke the solemn commitment of this Pact. "So far as the Pact itself was concerned, no arrangements for joint consultation by the signatory states, in case the threat of war, were provided for. The riddle of security remained unsolved."[36] A critic, for this reason, observed that one of the chief effects of this Pact "was the appearance of the so-called undeclared war."[37]

These points of attack, however, lose much of their weight when we study the effects of the Paris Pact on the international politics in the years to come. Despite the weaknesses that this treaty had, the fact remains that for a time it "gave a pronounced impetus to the campaign to expound and strengthen the world's peace structure. At the least, the Pact was a magnificent gesture toward a new ethical evaluation of war; at the most, it might have supplied

---

34. Sharp and Kirk, *op. cit.*, p. 558.
35. See Palmer and Perkins: *International Relations* (Calcutta: Scientific Book Agency, 1957), p. 227.
36. Sharp and Kirk, *op. cit.*, p. 558.
37. W.C. Langsam, *op. cit.*, p. 45.

the key to effective American (and Soviet) cooperation with the League system."[38] In order to substantiate this view, Sharp and Kirk furnish the following evidence:[39]

1. It had its constructive effect on the working of the League of Nations. At Geneva, where preparatory work for the Disarmament Conference was in progress, the Ninth Assembly (1928) adopted a General Act for the Pacific Settlement of International Disputes which was definitely designed to implement this Pact. In three separate chapters, this Act provided (i) for a procedure of conciliation for all disputes, (ii) for a procedure of judicial settlement or arbitration for disputes of a legal nature, and (iii) for the application of the principle of arbitration to disputes for which the machinery of the Permanent Court was not appropriate.

2. The League now took steps to encourage development in this direction by drafting model treaties based upon the Locarno precedent that two or more states might follow. By the beginning of 1930, some 130 new bilateral conciliation and arbitration conventions were registered with the Secretariat at Geneva. By and large, these treaties were so construed as to cover all cases not settled by direct diplomacy except for domestic questions, disputes involving prior facts and definitely specified subject matter such as territorial status or third party interests. Its positive result can be seen in the expansion of the compulsory jurisdiction of the World Court. By the early 1930s, 40 states were bound by the 'optional clause.'

3. It was also contemplated to revise the Covenant of the League of Nations in a way so that it could become in tune with the spirit of the Pact of Paris. For this purpose, the British delegation in 1929 submitted to the League Assembly a number of proposals which could not be accepted. Undeclared by such discouragement, the British government proposed that the sanctions of Art. 16 should be broadened to include all wars—a change which, if adopted, would have obliged the League to punish any and all violators of the Paris Pact, at least among its own members. Even this move remained unsuccessful, for by this time great powers like the United States were more concerned with the solution to the problem of great economic depression.

---

38. Sharp and Kirk, op. cit., pp. 558-59.
39. Ibid., pp. 559.-61.

Phase of Pacification

Keeping such evidence in view, Carr has observed: "Impertect, though it was, the Pact of Paris was a considerable landmark. It was the first political agreement in history of almost universal scope."[40] So oberves another English commentator: "As a gesture indicative of a new ethical attitude to war, the Pact of Paris was undeniably impressive. It was particularly important in that it created a basis upon which the great nations outside the League, the United States and Russia, could take a direct interest in the collective organisation of peace.... It served at the moment as a magnificent advertisement of the pacific disposition of the world, and might have been thought to constitute a great step forward on the road to international security."[41]

Now the 'period of pacification', as termed by Carr, came to an end. After 1930 the state of international relations rapidly deteriorated. Gradually the influence of the League waned not as much due to the path of aggression adopted by the 'fascist' powers like those of Japan, Italy and Germany as owing to the policy of 'appeasement' pursued by the statesmen of London, Paris and Washington. The trio of Briand, Stresemann and Austen Chamberlain also went out of existence. Thus the 'period of crisis', another term coined by Carr, followed. It witnessed rapid occurrence of events that pushed things to the situation of another global holocaust in 1939. Now new men and new methods "came upon the scene. The League suffered a series of reverses which culminated eventually in its complete eclipse. The reign of international law was brought to an abrupt close. The prevailing fashion of the unilateral repudiation of treaties rode roughshod over the sanctity of covenanted agreements. From a dream of universal peace men suddenly awoke to the crude realities of naked aggression. Almost overnight the political landscape of Europe was transformed and the stage was set for a fresh chapter in history—the retreat from Versailles."[42]

---

40. Carr, op. cit., p. 119.
41. Gathorne-Hardy, op. cit., pp. 183-84.
42. Lipson, op. cit., pp. 31-32.

5

PHASE OF CRISIS

For 'war' consists not in battle only, or the act of fighting; but in a tract of time wherein the will to contend by battle is sufficiently known.... For, as the nature of foul weather lies not in a shower or two of rain, but in an inclination thereto of many days together, so the nature of war consists not in actual fighting, but in the known disposition thereto all the time there is no assurance to the contrary.

—Thomas Hobbes[1]

The phase of consolidation of peace or the 'period of pacification', as termed by E.H Carr, came to an end in 1930 and then started the new phase of crisis or of 'collapse of peace' as termed by G.M. Gathorne-Hardy. Henceforth, the trend of 'return to power politics' witnessed its irresistible growth. The coming events in the form of great economic crisis followed by failure of the efforts for disarmament, Japan's rape of Manchuria in the Far East, Italy's aggression over Ethiopia in Africa, and Germany's conquest of Austria coupled with the dismemberment at her hands of the State of Czechoslovakia, the murder of democracy in Spain as a result of the successful revolt of Gen. Franco with the ostensible support of Mussolini and Hitler and, finally, Germany's unprovoked invasion on Poland were the great events demonstrating in bold terms that the peace settlements made after the First World War and the mechanism which they devised for the elimination of war 'lay in irretrievable ruin'.[2] To the astonishment of all serious observers, British Prime Minister Ramsay MacDonald's optimistic note that the risk of war was 'practically nil' in 1930 was contradicted by the fact that the shadows of another holocaust had started

---

1. Hobbes: *Leviathan*, Chapter 13.
2. Gathorne-Hardy: *A Short History of International Affairs, 1919-1939* (London: Oxford Univ. Press, 1950), IV Ed., p. 257.

darkening the globe. The imminence of another grim fight now became a staple subject of conversation. Gathorne-Hardy hints at three important developments in this regard. "The first world began to be traced in 1929, with the financial crash in the United States; the second in September 1931, with the failure to curb Japanese aggression in Manchuria; and the last in January 1933, with the accession of Adolph Hitler to the Chancellorship of the German Reich."[3]

Rape of Manchuria: Commencement of the Collapse of Collective Security System

The first important episode that led to the inauguration of a series of aggressions and thereby disintegration of the League of Nations was the Manchurian crisis of 1931-32. The upper hand of the military leaders in the State structure of Japan brought about a fundamental change in the course of her diplomacy. It is rightly said that while the civilian leaders desired to achieve the goal of making Japan great by following the policy of cooperation with the West, the militarists pinned their faith in the course of armed conquest. They well knew that the public opinion of their country had been rendered desperate by the economic depression and also grown furious by the recurrence of Chinese boycotts and that they needed some space in a neighbouring area to export their population that had crossed the point of 70 million by that time. The natural and mineral resources of Manchuria were also a source of great attraction for the Japanese leaders. Though Japan had signed the Nine-Power Treaty at Washington in 1922, her leaders could never be oblivious to the fact that, in strategic terms, the control of Manchuria would afford them a peculiarly favourable base for the offensive and defensive operations against any powerful country like China or Russia.

Then, there was the railway politics. The Chinese leaders desired to run their own railways so as to compete with the South Manchurian Railway (SMR) that was an establishment of the Japanese. For this reason, they opposed the Japanese project of installing a railway line from Tunhua to Kwainei that would link Central Manchuria with the North Korean border and its ports. In view of all these considerations, Manchuria became the next affair

---

3. Ibid., pp. 259 and 261.

for Japan after her successful adventure in Korea. "The existing economic privileges there of Great Britain and the United States aroused her indignation and envy. Increasing Russian penetration aroused her fear. Growing Chinese nationalism and imminent consolidation and industrialisation of China prompted urgent action. Chinese weakness offered the opportunity. Economic need and imperialist aspirations provided the incentive and the excuse. Cooperation with the great powers had so far done little for her. Japan determined to take her fate in her own hands."[4]

The Mukden episode provided the coveted opportunity for the ambitious Japanese leaders to realise their projected aim of raping Manchuria. After defeating Russia in 1905, Japan signed the Treaty of Portsmouth whereby she acquired the right to maintain some 15,000 troops in Manchuria for the safety and protection of the SMR. Already provoked by the murder of Captain Nakamura,[5] the Japanese troops went into action after alleging that in the night of 18-19 September, 1931 a detachment of the Chinese soldiers had attempted to blow up the main railway line. Naturally, a major fight ensued in which about 10,000 soldiers were disarmed and within a few days all towns within a radius of 200 miles north of Mukden were occupied by the Japanese troops. The Chinese provincial government was driven out of Mukden and thereafter it maintained a shadowy existence at Chinchow. The Japanese forces also moved southward in the areas outside the railway zone. Aerial bombardment resulted in the fall of Chinchow on 28 December and on January 4, 1932, the Japanese reached Shanhaikwan on the Great Wall that signified completion of the Manchurian conquest. In this way, to the great surprise of all major powers of that time, the Japanese plan of campaign "had been carried through without regard to the embarrassments of the Council of the League of Nations, which had been in almost continuous session during this time."[6]

4. C.D.M. Ketelbey: *A History of Modern Times*, p. 533.
5. Nakamura was a Japanese military officer on a mission in Manchuria. On June 27, 1931 he was killed by some Chinese soldiers in the north-western part of Manchuria. The military leaders of Japan described it as 'a wilful insult to the Japanese army' and demanded its explanation from the Chinese government.
6. E.H. Carr: *International Relations between the Two World Wars, 1919-1939*, (London: Macmillan, 1950), p. 163.

Phase of Crisis

Faced with this terrible situation the Chinese government lost no time in appealing its case to the Council of the League of Nations under Art. 11 of the Covenant. As pointed out above, already in session, the League Council managed to secure a prompt assurance from the Japanese delegate that his country "had no territorial designs on Manchuria and that she would withdraw her troops within the South Manchurian Railway Zone subject to the sole condition that the safety of the lives and property of Japanese nationals was assured."[7] Thus, by proceeding in a cautious manner, the Council hoped to bring about an immediate cessation of hostilities before going into the substance of the dispute itself. These were the tactics that had worked with signal success in the Graeco-Bulgarian affair of 1925. Facing for the first time (since Corfu) the duty of imposing "restraint upon a great power in a truculent mood', the Council hesitated even to discuss the possibility of sanctions, at any rate for the time being."[8]

However, to some satisfaction of China, the Council could go to the extent of passing a resolution on Sept. 30, 1931. It asked Japan to withdraw her troops immediately and restore normal relations Surprisingly, the delegates of Japan supported the decision of the Council just to strengthen his plea that, as bound by the terms of the Nine-Power Treaty of 1922 as well as by the Pact of Paris of 1928, the act of the Japanese government was not one of aggression but a piece of 'police action' necessary to protect the Japanese lives and property from Chinese bandits. Thereafter, the Council appointed a commission of the Five Great Powers (Britain, France, USA, Germany and Italy) under the chairmanship of Lord Lytton "to investigate on the spot any circumstance which affecting international relations threaten to disturb peace between China and Japan."

The Report of the Lytton Commission frankly affirmed that the attack of Japan on the barracks of Mukden was entirely unprovoked and came as a 'complete surprise'. For this reason, the military operations of the Japanese troops could not be regarded as 'measures of legitimate self-defence.' It admitted that Japan had certain grievances against China like disorder in Manchuria, boy-

---

7. M.O. Hudson: *The Verdict of the League* (Boston: World Peace Foundation, 1933), p. 22.
8. Sharp and Kirk: *Contemporary International Politics* (New York: Farrar and Rinehart, Inc., 1944), p. 576.

cott of Japanese goods by the Chinese, spread of communism, etc. Therefore, a restoration of the *status quo ante* would be no solution, even if this were possible. A satisfactory settlement must be compatible with the interests of both parties, together with those of the Soviet Union. At the same time, it must conform to the principles of the Covenant, the Paris Pact, and the Nine-Power Treaty. With these objects in view, the Commission in very concrete terms recommended:[9]

1. That new treaties between China and Japan should restate their respective rights, interests and responsibilities in Manchuria;
2. That the government of Manchuria should be modified so as to allow as large measure of autonomy as possible, and that to aid in this task a number of foreign advisers should be attached to the autonomous regime, one of whom, in particular, should have control over a constabulary for the preservation of civil disorder, and another of whom should supervise finance;
3. That Japan and China should conclude a new treaty regulating their commercial relations, and
4. That following the 'demilitarisation' of Manchuria, the two countries should pledge themselves, by a treaty of non-aggression, not to encroach upon another's territory, and should settle all future controversies by resort to conciliation and arbitration.

In conclusion, the Report declared that "the final requisite for a satisfactory solution is temporary international cooperation in the internal construction of China, as suggested by late Dr. Sun Yat-sen."

The irony of the international situation at this stage should be traced in the fact that while the Lytton Commission was doing its job, the Japanese users were going ahead with their project. The reason was that no other great power (like Britain and France) was prepared to take a bold stand against the Caesars of Tokyo. Inquires in the Whitehall led British Foreign Secretary Sir John Simon to declare that "under no circumstances will the Government authorise this country to be a party to the conflict."[10] President Hoover of the United States refused "to go along... on any sanction, either economic or military, for these are the roads to war."[11] The

---

9. Ibid., pp. 579-80.
10. C.A. Beard: *American Foreign Policy in the Making* (New Haven: Yale Univ. Press, 1946), p. 133.

Phase of Crisis

Secretary of State, Henry L. Stimson, could only formulate a declaration that the United States would not recognise any situation or treaty, or agreement, entered into by... Governments in violation of those treaties which affected the rights of America in China.'[12] Now came the Stimsonian doctrine of 'no-recognition' implying that the US would not recognise any situation, treaty, or agreement which would be brought about by means contrary to the Covenant of the League of Nations and the Pact of Paris.[13]

The Stimsonian doctrine could not go beyond offering a mild moral condonation of Japanese action. In reply to what Stimson said, the rulers of Japan contended that the Chinese inhabitants of Manchuria were 'not destitute of the power of self-determination' implying that the real answer of Japan to the prevailing dilemma lay in the total independence of the Manchurians. Thus, in flagrant disregard to the resolutions of the League, Japanese forces went on marching so much so that by the end of the year (1932) the whole region of Manchuria was occupied and a new state was established there with the name of 'Manchukuo' under the presidentship of Pu Yi—the last survivor of Manchu dynasty—as a model of Japanese puppet state. In this way, in September 1932, shortly before the Report of the Lytton Commission was made public, Japan, "affronted the League by recognising the State of Monchukuo. The motive presumably was to confront the League with a *fait accompli*, and the procedure called forth a sharp rebuke from the President of the Council, who happened to be the Irish (Eamon de Valera). Recognition was accorded through a Japanese-Manchukuo proto-

---

11. Ibid., p. 156.
12. C. Yanaga: *Japan since Perry* (New York: McGraw Hill, 1949), p. 559.
13. It may be pointed out here that though not a member of the League of Nations, an invitation was sent to the United States. Thus, an American (Prentiss Gilbert) participated officially in the meeting of the Council. However, he was instructed by his Government to take part in the discussions relative to the Pact of Paris, otherwise he was to sit like an 'observer'. The participation of the United States led to enormous enthusiasm. "Optimism whispered that the League, if it had lost Japan, had won America. But events soon showed that optimism was premature. The American government was so frightened of anti-League opinion in the United States to permit its delegate to play any active part; and when the Council resumed its meetings in the following month, American cooperation was once more confined to private and unofficial conversations with individual members of the Council." Carr, op. cit., pp. 165-66.

col, wherein the former Chinese domain, in return for an endorsement of its 'independent' status, promised Japan a long series of favours, including the right to station troops at any desired point in Manchukuo."[14]

From the standpoint of the League, the final stage of the Manchurian drama commenced in September 1932, with the consideration of the Lytton Report that was heralded as one of the most statesman-like international documents under the obtaining conditions. But by that time, it "was too late for the sensible suggestions of the Lytton Commission to have any chance of acceptance by the military clique in power at Tokyo. The die had been cast and no face-saving formula satisfactory to the Oriental mind could be found—despite patient efforts of the League Council and the Assembly Committee of Nineteen.[15] Throughout the autumn of 1932 Geneva nourished the illusion that Japan might still be induced to negotiate with China in accordance with the Lytton Commission's suggestion; but to no avail. All hope of bringing the controversy to a peaceful conclusion was dashed to pieces when Japan, early in January, 1933, launched an attack upon Shanhaikwan, gateway to Great Wall of China, and then proceeded to occupy the Province of Jehol and annex it to Manchukuo. Came May and the invading forces were threatening Peiping."[16]

The rape of Manchuria, it may be easily seen, had very serious results. Its virtual effect was like serving notice on the world that Japan would not accept any solution of the Manchurian question which involved even a partial acceptance of the *status quo ante*.[17] It, in very clear terms, established that the League "had failed and the collective security system received a tremendous shock from which it never fully recovered. Equally by refusing to put teeth into the Paris Pact, the United States and Great Britain had failed to secure its observance and to protect the territorial integrity of

---

14. W.C. Langsam: *The World since 1919* (Delhi: Surjeet Pub., 1981), p. 269.
15. After adopting the Lytton Report, the League Assembly appointed a committee "to follow the situation ... and to aid the members of the League in concerting their action and their attitude among themselves and with the non-member states."
16. Sharp and Kirk, op. cit., p. 580.
17. H.M. Vinacke: *A History of the Far East in Modern Times* (London: George Allen and Unwin, 1964), p. 514.

China as required by the Nine-Power Treaty."[18] Likewise, says Carr: "The Japanese conquest of Manchuria was one of the most important historical landmarks since the First World War. In the Pacific, it denoted the resumption of the struggle for power which had been suspended by the Washington Conference. In the world at large, it heralded a 'return to power politics', which had been in abeyance, at any rate in this naked form, since the end of the war. For the first time since the peace settlement, war had been waged, (though under the guise of police operations) on an extensive scale, and a vast territory had been annexed (though under the guise of an independent state) by the conqueror. For the League of Nations, whose Covenant had been flouted, the consequences were incalculable. It was difficult to resist the conclusion that members of the League (and in particular the Great Powers on whom the main burden of upholding the Covenant must necessarily fall) were not prepared to resist an act of aggression committed by a powerful and well-armed state."[19]

Conquest of Ethiopia: Accomplishment of Italian Colonial Irredentism

The second important event leading to the collapse of peace in the fourth decade of the present century finds place in repudiation of peace settlements at the hands of the Fascist ruler of Italy. It synchronised with the similar repudiation of peace settlements at the hands of the Caesar of Germany (Hitler) and, for this reason, it is pointed out that the events of 1935-36 culminated in the realisation of a great plan conceived by Mussolini some three years back. Italy's plan to settle scores with Abyssinia (Ethiopia) "was taken with an eye on the development of the German situation: assuming—which turned out to be correct—that France and Britain would not nip the German danger in the bud, the three years would provide a period of uncertainty and confusion which could be exploited with safety and skill: it might not be prudent, on the other hand, to allow so much time to pass that Italy might find herself embroiled in a colonial adventure when it would be desirable to be free to move on the European scene."[20]

---

18. Sharp and Kirk, op. cit., p. 581.
19. Carr, op. cit., pp. 171-72.
20. Rene Albrecht-Carrie: *Italy from Napoleon to Mussolini* (New York: Columbia Univ. Press, 1950), p. 244.

Italy's choice of Abyssinia was dictated by several considerations. This country was rich in raw materials and mineral wealth that was not fully exploited by that time. She could also find in this country a place for the export of her growing population. Then, it was the only independent country in Africa where she could make an experiment with her colonial irredentism. Ever since the treaty of Ucciali of 1889 the Italian rulers had been regarding Ethiopia as their 'protectorate' in spite of the fact that their claim was challenged by Menelik in 1893 and that she had seen her most inglorious defeat at the hands of the Abyssinians at Adowa in 1896. However, the most covenient factor was that this country was sandwitched between two Italian colonies of Eritrea and Somaliland. Finally, as a highly unsatiated power since the making of the peace settlements, Italy strongly desired some colonial achievement for the sake of her psychological satisfaction. For this reason, it "should be borne in mind that the chief Italian interest in Ethiopia has been not so much economic as spiritual, the saving of face."[21]

The Walwal incident of December 5, 1934, provided a pretext for Mussolini to embark on his ambition of destroying the independence of Ethiopia. On this date a minor clash occurred between Ethiopian troops and a detachment of the Italian forces near the village of Walwal in Somaliland. In the skirmishes a few Italian solders engaged in the work of marking out boundary lines were killed. Soon the Italian government showed its intentions. Mussolini demanded an apology as well as substantial indemnity from Abyssinia. Faced with this situation, the government of Ethiopia appealed to the League of Nations and requested that the matter should be placed on the agenda of the Council under Art. 11 of the Covenant. But the League Council adjourned the matter in January, 1935, when the Italian delegate deprecated discussion of the Walwal incident on the ground that it did not affect the peaceful relations between two countries and that his government might be willing to settle the matter by peaceful means under the Treaty of 1928.[22]

---

21. H.R. Spencer: "Expanding Italy" in F.J. Brown, C. Hodges and J.S. Roucek (ed.s): *Contemporary World Politics: An Introduction to the Problem of International Relations* (New York: John Wiley & Sons, 1939), p. 195.
22. Apart from being a party to the Pact of Paris of 1928, Italy was also a party to the Treaty of 1906 signed with Britain and France whereby she with others had

But insincere were the professions of Italy at this time. In Walwal Mussolini saw his Mukden. It is evident from the fact that, for the next three months, the Italian government deliberately delayed the appointment of arbitrators. Moreover, large reinforcements of men and material from Italy to her African colonies surrounding Ethiopia showed that serious military operations were imminent. In the meantime, Mussolini also repudiated any idea of submitting the matter to arbitration as it would constitute 'a humiliating admission of equality with Ethiopia which is intolerable and unthinkable.' Under these conditions the statesmen of Britain and Italy, who were very keen to maintain relations with Mussolini, offered the course of a non-League settlement on the basis of 1928 treaty. Reluctantly, Mussolini agreed to this course. Thus, a commission was set up. As feared beforehand, the Italian government did not give full cooperation to the Walwal Arbitration Commission. Surprisingly, on 3 September, 1935 the Walwal Arbitration Commission submitted its report exonerating both parties from responsibility.

The report of the Walwal Commission coupled with the ostensibly appeasing role of Britain and France came as a great booster for the colonial ambitions of Mussolini. Knowing it well that the Italian troops were engaged in more and more serious concentration in the colonies of Eritrea and Somaliland, British and French statesmen did not study the issue of Abyssinian crisis at the Stressa meet of April, 1935. At the most, they made a roundabout reference to the prevailing crisis and resolved that 'any unilateral repudiation of treaties which may endanger the peace of Europe' would be opposed by them. Such a silence of the major power in the face of an undisguised Italian preparations of war "was interpreted by Mussolini to mean that Great Britain, like France, was content to regard his African venture with a benevolent, or at

---

declared 'to maintain the integrity of Abyssinia'. In 1928 Italy concluded a treaty with Abyssinia in which the two parties promised each other 'constant peace and perpetual friendship' and at the same time mutual undertaking to submit all disputes to 'a procedure of conciliation and arbitration'. In the same year Italy had signed the Kellogg-Briand Pact for the renunciation of war as an instrument of national policy. Above all, Italy had been one of the principal supporters of the admission of Abyssinia to the membership of the League of Nations in 1923. See Carr., op. cit., pp. 222-23.

least an indifferent eye."²³

Instead of catching the bull by the horns, the statesmen of London and Paris adhered to the course of appeasing the Caesar of Rome. In June 1935 Anthony Eden visited Rome and made a proposal that Great Britain should cede to Abyssinia the port of Zeila in British Somaliland, while in exchange Abyssinia should cede her southern province of Ogaden to Italy. But this proposal could not be accepted by Mussolini who took it as a very meagre concession for Italy and a substantial gain for Abyssinia. After being successful in such a mediatory effort, the representatives of Britain, France and Italy had a meeting at Paris in August, 1935 in accordance with the terms of the Treaty of 1906. Here another proposal was mooted that Abyssinia should be requested to apply to the League 'for collaboration in promoting the economic development and administrative reorganisation of the country', and that in according such collaboration, the League should take 'particular account of the special interests of Italy'. Even this proposal had the same fate.²⁴

Curiously, instead of honouring the pledges made by her in the past, just one day after the submission of the Walwal Arbitration Report, Italy on September 4, 1935 presented to the League Council a general memorandum of its claims against Ethiopia. It unabashedly asserted that Ethiopia was such an uncivilised and backward state that it had lost every right to invoke the protection of the Covenant against other League members and in return any civilised state was under no obligation to observe the provisions of the Covenant in dealing with such a 'barbarous' state. On this plea, the Italian delegate walked out of the Council when the Ethiopian delegate submitted his counter-claim and requested the Council to invoke Art. 15 of the Covenant so as to prevent an impending war. At this stage, the Council appointed a Committee of Five to examine the problem and seek a pacific settlement of the matter. However, a satisfying instance was a statement of 'unexpected firmness' made by British Foreign Secretary (Sir Samuel Hoare) in the Assembly of the League that was not liked by his French counterpart who was not at all prepared to alienate Italy for the

---
23. Ibid., p. 224.
24. Ibid., p. 225.

Phase of Crisis

sake of a 'barbarous' African country.[25]
The tone of Hoare's statement was not liked by Mussolini as well. Sensing that some sort of sanctions may be imposed against Italy, he warned that such a step taken by the League would be met with force. Paying no heed to the efforts of the Committee of Five regarding introduction of reforms in Ethiopia (like suppression of slavery and control of traffic in arms) under the supervision of foreign 'observers', he inaugurated the long-anticipated invasion of Ethiopia. Under these conditions the action of the Council became unavoidable. On the report of its Committee, the Council on October 7 branded Italy as an 'aggressor' and took a decision for the imposition of 'sanctions' against a great power. This action was approved by 51 out of 58 states in the Assembly of the League. Proposals for economic sanctions elaborated at once by a Committe were put into operation with remarkable speed. These sanctions included arms embargo, refusal to grant any financial assistance to Italy, prohibition on all imports from Italy, and a prohibition on the export of certain commodities to Italy.[26] It was, indeed, a great event. "On November 18th, 1935, for the first time in the history of the League, sanctions—though only of an economic character, and these far from complete—came into operation."[27]

Mere taking of such an important decision was not enough. What was needed more than this was a sincere determination to put it into practice. The appeasers of London and Paris were not interested in going to that extent. In spite of the fact that British and French Foreign Ministers (Hoare and Laval respectively) had said before the Committee of Coordination (that had been set up by the League Assembly to enforce its decision of sanctions) that further efforts would be made by their governments to settle Italo-Ethiopian dispute in a peaceful manner, they met at Paris and chalked out a

---

25. Hoare said: "In conformity with its precise and explicit obligations, the League stands, and my country stands with it, for the collective maintenance of the Covenant in its entirety, and particularly for steady and collective resistance to all acts of unprovoked aggression. The attitude of British nation in the last few weeks has demonstrated the fact that this is no variable and unreliable sentiment, but a principle of international conduct to which they and their government hold with firm, enduring and universal persistence." Sharp and Kirk, op. cit., p. 620.
26. Sharp and Kirk, op. cit., p. 622.
27. Carr, op. cit., p. 226.

plan for its presentation to the belligerents. Herein it was proposed to cede Italy more territory than what had actually been invaded by her by that time, while Ethiopia was to be placated by a corridor to the sea through British Somaliland. It came to be known as the notorious Hoare-Laval Plan. The disclosure of this scheme in the month of December, 1935 caused a storm of indignation on the ground that the plan "had been designed to help Italy to extract herself with credit from a hazardous position; and it was felt to be no part of the duty of Great Britain, as a member of the League, to help an aggressor reap the fruits of his aggression."[28]

It certainly boosted the morale of the Fascist aggressor yet more. He could draw from it the big inference that neither Britain nor France could stand against his plan of advancing in Ethiopia in spite of the fact that he had committed an act of aggression for which economic sanctions were imposed by a decision of the Council of the League of Nations and that his other inhuman actions (like slaughter of Abyssinian tribesmen by means of poison gas) had created a storm of resentment all over the world. No tangible change could occur even after the resignation of Hoare and his succession by a Conservative like Anthony Eden, widely known for his vigorous advocacy of the League system. The Italian forces went on moving more rapidly after March, 1936. Internal order broke down and the Emperor (Haile Selassie) had to escape from Addis Ababa on May 1, 1936. On May 9, the King of Italy was proclaimed Emperor and the whole country was officially annexed to Italy.

The story of the conquest of Ethiopia by Italy, therefore, made it very clear that the statesmen of London and Paris bent their knees before the insolent might of the Fascist Caesar. They deliberately overlooked the fact that, from beginning to end, the bad faith of Italy remained manifest for all sensible leaders to take notice of it. "From the Italian point of view, Abyssinia made things more difficult by consistently playing the part of Aesop's lamb—this was, indeed, her best and only hope—forcing ever more clearly her antagonist to assume the role of the wolf. The results were the same as in the fable."[29] Such a policy of appeasement was bound to result in the destruction of the League. After the birth of the Italian empire

---

28. Ibid., p. 227.
29. Rene Albrecht-Carrie, op. cit., p. 245.

was announced to the world with suitable and self-conscious fanfare, the League feeling defeated in the half-hearted attempt at coercion could do little else than acknowledge the fact. Surprisingly, in July 1936 the League retraced; it recommended the dropping of sanctions as its members gradually came to accept the Italian title based on the right of conquest. In this way, the Abyssinian conquest "may be said to have marked the real death of the League."[30]

Viewed in a different perspective, it may be pointed out that the politics of major powers at this stage was much influenced by the interest of the big business community that, as Laski had said, viewed Fascism as the last remedy to save the system of capitalism. The American financiers vigorously asserted that the Neutrality Resolution passed by the Congress in 1935 did not authorise the President to embargo petroleum, iron and steel in their trade with Italy. Thus, they made enormous profits by export of such things to Italy. Likewise, British and French businessmen thought it expedient to support the Fascists of Germany and Italy with a long-range view of using them against the demon of Communism. Noticeably, the French statesmen had another game in supporting Mussolini against Hitler so as to keep their system of security intact. "Laval and his successors blessed Italian designs against the ancient empire of Haile Selassie in the hope of securing continued Italian support against the Reich—at the cost of destroying the League of Nations as an agency of collective security."[31]

Annexation of Austria: Conclusion of the Prohibited 'Anschluss'
After Japan and Italy, we turn to Germany under Hitler who made his first experiment with the fate of Austria. We have seen in Chapter 2 that the Treaty of St. Germain had prohibited the 'Anschluss' (Germany's Union with Austria). However, as Hitler was determined to pursue his policy of *Drang Nach Osten* (move towards the east) with as much force as possible and as he was conscious of the fact that the rulers of Britain and France were sticking to the policy of appeasement, he took to the course of the repudiation of peace settlements. Any student of his spiritual

---

30. Ibid., p. 248.
31. F.L. Schuman: *International Politics* (New York: McGraw Hill, 1941), III Ed., p. 540.

biography (*Mein kampf*) could now safely take it for granted that the Caesar of Germany would claim to incorporate into the German Reich all scattered German minorities living beyond her present borders and treat Eastern Europe as a suitable field for German colonisation.

However, the rashness with which Hitler acted in completing the 'Anschluss' proved a blunder. The success of the Nazis in Germany in 1933 became a source of great inspiration and enthusiasm for the Nazis of Austria. Ever since the making of the Treaty of St. Germain a good number of people of Austria were in favour of the union of their country with Germany and they had, in very clear terms, criticised the ban on the 'Anschluss' in the name of Wilson's principle of national self-determination. But the way Hitler started his autocratic rule in Germany created his critics in Austria. The Social Democrats, the Catholics, the Jews and others of a liberal disposition did not appreciate the brutal and ruthless efficiency of the new regime in Germany. Thus, with a mind to put a heavy hand on the menacing activities of the Nazis in Austria, Chancellor Dollfuss suspended the constitution and relied largely on the support of a private military organisation—Heimwehr.

Faced with this challenging situation the German government frankly entered into the field. German aeroplanes started dropping leaflets on the Austrian territory in favour of the Nazi propaganda. Money and arms were also sent to the Austrian Nazis and a prohibitive visa fee was imposed on intending German visitors to Austria. The Radio Munich took active part in instigating the Nazis of Austria for a *coup* against the established order. It all forced the Government of Dollfuss to suppress the activities of the Nazis by force. In retaliation the Nazis of Austria became more active. With the help of the German government, they created a *coup* on July 25, 1934, in which Chancellor Dollfuss was assassinated. But the *coup* failed as the governments of Italy, Britain and France came to the rescue of the new government under Chancellor Schuschnigg. It is, for this reason, pointed out: "Notwithstanding the resistance of the Heimwehr and of certain sections of the population, Austria might soon have yielded to German pressure but for the intervention of great powers."[32]

---

32. Carr, op. cit., p. 205.

Phase of Crisis

Thus, the first experiment of Hitler failed. Rather his "decision to make Austria the first object of his foreign policy proved in many respects unfortunate."[33] Italy's immediate help to the government of Austria turned the tables against Germany. The reason behind it was that Italy had taken the territory of South Tyrol under the peace settlement that was a largely German-inhabited area and, more than that, she did not like to see her frontiers close to those of Germany at the Brenner Pass. "As for Italy the fly in the ointment was Austria. Mussolini could not tolerate at the Brenner Pass a Germany of 75 million people pushing southward towards Bolzano and Trieste."[34] Moreover, as Britain and France were tied to Italy with the bonds of their political interest and, more particularly, they were not prepared to alienate Italy at this stage the Three-Power declaration came on 27 September, 1934. It was publicly stated: "After having proceeded to a fresh examination of Austrian situation, the representatives of France, the United Kingdom and Italy have agreed in the name of their Governments to recognise that the declaration of February 17, 1934, regarding the necessity of maintaining the independence and integrity of Austria in accordance with the Treaties in force, retains its full effect, and will continue to inspire their common policies."[35]

In particular, Mussolini took a very serious view of the cold-blooded end of Dollfuss. On October 6, 1934, he gave a statement: "We have defended and will defend the independence of the Austrian Republic, an independence which has been consecrated by the blood of a Chancellor, who may have been small in stature but whose spirit and soul were great. Those who assert that Italy has any aggressive aims, or that she wishes to establish some kind of Protectorate over the Republic are either ignorant of the facts or are consciously lying."[36] In this way, Hitler committed a blunder by antagonising a Fascist power with whom Britain and France had already established strong diplomatic links. More than this, he alienated the natural sympathy and support of a large number of Austrians to whom Nazi techniques and doctrines "were so unpalatable that any governmental policy other than that of strict

---

33. Ibid., p. 204.
34. Schuman, op. cit., p. 563.
35. See A.B. Keith (ed.): *Speeches and Documents on International Affairs, 1918-1937* (London: Oxford University Press, 1938), Vol. II, p. 8.
36. Ibid., pp. 8-9.

independence would have torn the country asunder and in all probability plunged it into fratricidal strife."[37]

Now Hitler realised his diplomatic error and took to the course of winning time for repeating his step in a successful way so as to implement his *Drang Nach Osten* policy. He tried to improve the relations of Germany with Austria and, for this purpose, had very cordial meetings with Schuschnigg. In a speech on May 21, 1935, he specifically declared that Germay "neither intends nor wishes to interfere in the internal affairs of Austria, to annex Austria, or to conclude an Anschluss." Then, in the document of Rome-Berlin Axis of July 11, 1936, he recognised 'full sovereignty of the Austrian Federal State.' It also bound Berlin not to support the Nazis of Austria. Herr Schuschnigg "took this bait and hailed the agreement as a diplomatic victory which provided a foundation stone for the future peaceful cooperation of the two states declaring jubilantly that the problem of Austrian independence has been eliminated."[38]

A dramatic turn in this situation took place in the following year when Italy had her full sway over Ethiopia. Germany recognised this conquest and, in return, got a promise of economic concessions from Italy. Now the great hurdle was removed; rather two great Fascists had come closer. "Italy agreed with the Reich that any Locarno must be limited to Western Europe; that Art. 16 should be removed from the Covenant, and that the two Fascist Powers must cooperate against Bolshevism."[39]

In this favourable opportunity Hitler re-enacted the drama of completing the 'Anschluss'. On February, 12, 1938 he invited Schuschnigg to meet him at his personal residence at Berchtesgaden. There under the threat of making an invasion without any loss of time, he forced the Austrian Chancellor to grant amnesty and full freedom of action to the Austrian Nazis and to enlarge his cabinet so as to have some Nazi ministers. It led to the induction of Seyss-Inquart as the Minister of Interior (along with two more Nazi leaders) and making of an important announcement by the Vienna government on March 9, 1938, that a plebiscite would be held in the country on the question of the 'Anschluss'. Events moved very fast. Just two days after the official annoucement, Seyss-Inquart pre-

---

37. Sharp and Kirk, op. cit., p. 650.
38. Ibid., p. 651.

sented an ultimatum to the Chancellor asking him to postpone the plebiscite and quit, otherwise German troops already in motion would cross into the country. Schuschnigg obliged by resigning and then Seyss-Inquart became the new Chancellor who not only cancelled the plebiscite but invited Hitler to come to Vienna and restore order in the country.[40]

Of course, the time chosen by Hitler for the second *coup* was quite propitious from an international point of view. In Britain as well as in France, the leaders were scrupulously sticking to the course of appeasement, while the latter, in addition to this, was in the throes of a cabinet crisis. Jubilant over her victory of Ethiopia, Italy had been tied to Germany by the bond of the new Axis. Hitler had his way through without any hurdle. So he announced the holding of the plebiscite on the question of Austria's union with Germany simultaneously with the election for the first Reichstag of Great Germany. However, before the plebiscite was held, two laws legalised the 'reunion' of Austria with the Reich and introduced the Four-Year Plan into the new province. Moreover, anti-semitic decrees were quickly put into force in Austria that entailed the tale of a horrible cruelty. On April 10, 1938, the so-called plebiscite was held in which more than 99 per cent of votes were said to have been cast in the affirmative. In this way, about 7,000,000 more German-speaking people were added to the population of the German state.

The annexation of Austria demonstrated that, from this time on, Germany became a force of undeniably great importance in all the affairs of south-eastern Europe. It is, indeed, an irony of the situation that the statesmen of Britain and France did not pay heed to the last pathetic expressions of Chancellor Schuschnigg.[41] Tied

---

39. Schuman, op. cit., p. 564.
40. W.L. Shirer noted in his diary dated 11-12 March, 1938 at 4 a.m.: "The worst has happened. Schuschnigg is out. The Nazis are in. The Reichwehr is invading Austria. Hitler has broken a dozen solemn promises, pledges, treaties. And Austria is finished." *Berlin Diary* (1934-41) (London: Hamish Hamilton, 1941), p. 82.
41. After laying down his office, Schuschnigg said these words in his farewell speech: "The German government today handed to the President an ultimatum ordering him to nominate as Chancellor a person designated by the German Government, and to appoint members of an Austrian Government on orders of the German Government, otherwise German troops would invade Austria. I declare before the world that the news launched in Germany concerning disorders by workers, the shedding of streams of blood and the creation of a

firmly to the course of appeasement, sir Austen Chamberlain (Prime Minister of Britain) did nothing to materialise his own warning that the "independence of Austria is a key position. If Austria perishes, Czechoslovakia becomes indefensible. Then, the whole of the balkans will be submitted to a gigantic new influence."[42] Hitler's wrong of 1934 was righted in 1938 and the way for the dismemberment of Czechoslovakia was opened. "By the annexation of Austria the programme of *Mein Kampf* was brought considerably nearer realisation through the acquisition of important strategic and economic advantages. Direct contact was established with Italy, Hungary and Yugoslavia. A wedge was driven deeply into the heart of the Little Entente, and the Bohemian and Moravian districts of Czechoslovakia were enclosed as between the jaws of a pair of pincers."[43]

Dismemberment of Czechoslovakia: Climax of the Anglo-French Policy of Appeasement

The annexation of Austria with the Third Reich "at once reacted upon the position of Czechoslovakia, for the ease with which the German *Fuhrer* had fulfilled the first of his aspirations served but to whet his ambitions."[44] Hitler could never be oblivious to the farsightedness of Bismarck's judgment that "who holds Bohemia is the master of Europe" as well as to the fact that Wilsonian principle of national self-determination had its most deplorable contradiction in the formation of the state of Czechoslovakia.[45] Besides, some favourable factors were also there to enthuse Hitler to go ahead with the policy of *Drang Nach Osten*. By his fortification of the

---

situation beyond the Austrian Government's control, are lies from A to Z. The President has asked me to tell the people of Austria that he has yielded only to force." See E. Lipson: *Europe, 1914-1939* (London: Adam and Charles Black, 1957), p. 405.
42. Cited in D. Reed, *Disgrace Abounding* (London: Cape, 1939), p. 146.
43. Gathorne-Hardy, op. cit., p. 456.
44. Lipson, op. cit., p. 405.
45. Gathorne-Hardy says that the state of Czechoslovakia "produced in miniature the racial jigsaw of the pre-war Austro-Hungarian empire." According to the census figures of 1930 it had a population of 7,447,000 Czechs; 3,231,6000 Germans; 2,309,000 Slovaks; 691,900 Magyars; 549,000 Ruthenians and 81,700 Poles. Thus, it afforded the case of a badly blended population of different stocks. "If we dissect the tadpole from which the state assumed on the map, the head, corresponding to Bohemia and Moravia, was a Czech brain with a German rash on its face and skin, and a virulent but isolated patch in the back

Rhineland, he had made it almost impossible for France to come to the rescue of the ally (Czechoslovakia) and the 'barrier policy' of Poland and Rumania stood in the way of any assistance to this state from the side of the Soviet Union. Czechoslovakia was surrounded by indifferent and unfriendly neighbours on all sides except on the tiny side of Rumania. The League had already exposed its hollowness in the cases of Manchurian and Abyssinian crises. Above all, the existence of a militant German minority in the state of Czechoslovakia with a strong base in the Sudetenland could be used as a convenient tool for an imperialistic adventure. All these factors played their part in placing Czechoslovakia in a grim queue after the tragedy of Austria. Now she "was a tempting field for another sudden *fait accompli*."[46]

In the matter of Czechoslovakia Hitler adopted the same course that had paid him rewards in the case of Austrian conquest. Here he found his reliable tool in Konard Henlein—leader of the Sudeten German party. Funds were supplied and guidance given to him from Berlin. It strengthened his hands so much so that he issued an appeal for all Sudeten Germans to join his party. After some time, he succeeded in forcing the Sudeten Germans to quit the cabinet and take an active part in creating problems for the government of Prague. Mob violence and clashes between Germans and non-Germans living in Czechoslovakia became the order of the day. The German press and other propaganda machinery exploited the situation by publicising 'horrible tale of atrocities' on the innocent Germans of Czechoslovakia.

On March 28, 1938, Henlein visited Berlin and had a meeting with Hitler and his Foreign Minister Ribbentrop. He then publicly declared: "We must always demand so much that we can never be satisfied." On April 23 in a speech at Carlsbad, he presented a 'Charter of 8 Demands' as a minimum to the government of Prague. Among these were full autonomy for the Sudeten German

---

of the neck, to the south of Silesia. The body was Slovak, with a Polish infection of the spine and a belly full of indigestible Magyars. The slender tail was Ruthenian. To Germany, the position of Bohemia and Moravia, the parts of the country in which she was interested, was not that of a Czech majority and a German minority, but of a small Czech island in a intense Teutonic ocean. After the Anschluss with Austria, that island was almost surrounded by the rising tide of Nazidom." Gathorne-Hardy, op. cit., pp. 463-64.

46. Ibid., p. 466.

areas with complete liberty to profess German nationality and German political philosophy, and complete revision of Czech foreign policy with special reference to her alliance with the Soviet Union. During the course of his oration, he openly affirmed that all this was inspired by the ideas and principles of the National Socialism of Hitler. The main objective of the Carlsbad address was "to rally the Sudeten Germans to keep the Czech Government in play and bamboozle public opinion abroad."[47]

Henceforth, Hitler remained in search of some pretext to interfere in the affairs of Czechoslovakia. An occasion came on 20-21 May, 1938, on the eve of municipal elections when two Sudeten Germans were shot dead while attempting to pass a frontier post without halting in response to a challenge. However, the German government could not exploit this chance on account of some firmness shown by the British and French Prime Ministers in expressing their sympathy with the state of Czechoslovakia. In this way, a most serious chance of crisis could be very narrowly averted. And yet the German motives could not remain concealed. Hitler's Propaganda Minister (Goebbels) said on June 21, 1938: "We will not look on much longer while 3,500,000 Germans are maltreated. We saw in Austria that one race cannot be separated into two countries, and we shall soon see it somewhere else."[48]

Though a matter of minor significance, the German government magnified the question of the Sudeten Germans to such an extent just for certain reasons subserving its imperialistic designs.[49] With a view to satisfy the agitating Sudeten Germans, the Government of President Benes and Prime Minister Hodza prepared a 'Nationalities Statute' specifying legitimate grievances of a minority and trying to redress them within the framework of territorial security and national independence. The Nazi-inspired leaders of the Sudeten German Party scoffed at it and instead they retaliated with a memorandum of 14 Points.

Now the British government tried to bridge the gap between the offer of the Czech government and the demands of the Sudeten

---

47. Allan Bullock: *Hitler: A Story in Tyranny* (New York: Harper, 1935), p. 406.
48. Cited in Gathorne-Hardy, op. cit., pp. 468-69.
49. Sir Alfred Zimmern frankly noted: "So far as the larger issues are concerned, the grievances of the German minority in the Historic Provinces are simply a pretext. If they did not exist, they would have needed to be created or invented." *International Affairs*, London, July 1938, p. 467.

Phase of Crisis

Germans by deputing Lord Runciman to act as a mediator. However, behind this diplomatic move the appeasement policy of London remained at work. It is event from the fact that Runciman offered a plan to the Prague government in which almost all demands of the Sudeten Germans were met. Willy-nilly, the government of Czechoslovakia accepted the Runciman Plan, but Henlein rejected it on the plea of being unsatisfactory. Then he took the course of visiting Berlin to derive further strength for the sake of worsening prevailing situation that alone could satisfy his German boss. It was, therefore, aptly commented that the "real purpose of the mission was to prepare the Czechs for an ultimate sacrifice rather than to find a satisfactory compromise."[50]

The crisis went on developing. In a much anticipated speech to the Nuremberg Party Congress on 12 September, 1938, Hitler officially promised all help to the Sudeten Germans saying that "if these tortured creatures cannot obtain rights and assistance by themselves, they can obtain both from us... The Germans in Czechoslovakia are neither defenseless.... nor forsaken."[51] It encouraged the Sudeten Germans to any imaginable extent. The result was that they intensified their struggle and the government had to declare martial law in all the affected areas so as to prevent skirmishes between a militant minority of the Germans and the rest of the population. Henlein secretly moved to Berlin and therefrom made a major announcement that the Czechs and the Sudetens could not live together any more and that the latter, under these conditions, demanded their amalgamation with the Reich. The government of Prague "replied by declaring Henlein a traitor and dissolving the Sudeten German party. Germany responded by moving more troops to the frontier. The crisis had reached such an intensity that it was difficult to see how any party could retreat from its advanced position without an impossible sacrifice of prestige."[52]

Caught up in such a war of nerves and at the same time desiring to prevent the outbreak of another war, British Prime Minister Chamberlain flew to Germany and had a meeting with Hitler at Berchtesgaden on September 15, 1938. On this occasion

---

50. H.F. Armstrong: *When There is no Peace* ? (New York, 1939), p. 30.
51. *The New York Times*, September 13, 1938.
52. Sharp and Kirk, op. cit., p. 659.

Hitler made it quite clear that there was nothing that anybody could do to prevent German invasion on Czechoslovakia unless the right of self-determination was granted to the three million Sudeten Germans. Chamberlain returned to England and there he conferred with French Prime Minister (Daladier) and his Foreign Minister (Bonnet). There it was decided to move a proposal that all districts containing more than 50 per cent of the German inhabitants should be directly transferred to Germany without any plebiscite. The French public described it all as a matter of 'shameful necessity'. The government of Czechoslovakia showed its willingness to accept the proposal as a Hobson's choice when British and French statesmen coerced it to accept on the assurance that they would come to its rescue in the event of any German invasion.

Feeling encouraged at this fake success, Chamberlain visited Berlin on 22 September. But in his meeting with Hitler at Godesberg, he had to face another shock when, instead of appreciating the gift of Anglo-French appeasers, the Fuhrer came forward with a set of some more demands like:[53]

1. Withdrawal of all Czech forces, including police and customs officials, from area defined in an attached map and roughly corresponding to the whole area to be ceded, and the cession of this area to Germany on 1 October;
2. The territory to be handed over in its existing state, with all fortifications and commercial installations, railway rolling-stock, etc., and without the removal of foodstuffs, cattle or raw material;
3. The discharge of all Sudeten Germans serving in the Czechoslovak military or police forces and of all German political prisoners; and
4. Final delimitation to be decided by a plebiscite under the control of an international commission and settled by a German-Czech or an international commission.

It led to the rejection of all demands by the Prague government and with that of the breakdown of the Godesberg conference that left Chamberlain reproaching the Fuhrer in quite bitter terms.

Now came the occasion when appeasement policy witnessed its climax. President Roosevelt of the United States made a proposal

---

53. See Gathorne-Hardy, op. cit., pp. 472-73.

of 'peace by conference' to settle the growing controversy. Repudiating his previous endeavors, Chamberlain said it publicly: "We cannot in all circumstances undertake to involve the whole of British Empire in a War simply for the sake of Czechoslovakia." He conveyed his proposal of holding an international conference for stilling the raging controversy to Mussolini who transmitted it to Hitler. Thus, the historic Munich Meet took place in which the statesmen of Britain, France, Italy and Germany took part and on September 20, 1938 signed a pact that was remarked as "one of the most remarkable documents of our times."[54] The main features of the Munich Pact were as follows:[55]

1. The evacuation of the Sudeten German territory would begin on 1 October and be completed within 10 days without any existing installations having been destroyed.
2. The conditions of evacuation would be specified by a commission consisting of the German, Italian, French, British and Czech representatives.
3. The occupation by stages of the predominantly German territory by the German troops would begin on 1 October and be completed within 10 days and the Five Power Commission would determine the territories in which a plebiscite would be held, but till then these territories would be held by an international commission.
4. From the date of this agreement till next six months there would be a right of option into and out of the transferred territories.
5. Within 4 weeks of this agreement the government of Prague would release from its police and military force any Sudeten German who desired to quit and all Sudeten Germans in preventive detention would also be freed.

In the Annexure appended to this historic document, the statesmen of Britain and France assured their help to Czechoslovakia for the maintenance of her new boundaries.

The pact of Munich caused the tragedy of Czechoslovakia. To the astonishment of all peace-lovers of the world, great wrong was done by the appeasers of London and Paris. Surprisingly, while the

---

54. F.W. Hartmann: *Basic Documents in International Relations* (New York: McGraw Hill, 1951), p. 123.
55. Ibid., pp. 124-26.

fate of this small state was decided, her representative was not invited to participate in the Munich conference. More surprisingly, France agreed to the partition of Czechoslovakia in spite of the fact that she was bound by the terms of a defensive alliance with the Little Entente powers. No necessity was felt for the participation of the USSR. Thus, the Soviets "felt that they had been given ample grounds for distrusting the motives of the Western powers. They construed the agreement as an attempt to turn German aggression towards the East. With this the seeds were sown for the mutual distrust whose harvest was reaped with the signing of the Nazi-Soviet Non-Aggression Pact."[56]

At Munich the odious task of communicating the terms of the pact was left to the Prime Ministers of Britain and France. Thus, the two Prime Ministers conveyed to the Government of Prague what Hitler so impatiently waited for. Not only this, they exercised pressure on President Benes who, like a broken-hearted man, accepted the Anglo-French ultimatum. Giving vent to his agonised feelings he simply reacted to it as something without precedent in history and his minister (Hugo Vavrecka) uttered these pathetic words: "Nothing else remained, because we are alone. It is a case without parallel.... We shall not blame those who left us in the lurch, but history will pronounce a judgement about these days."[57]

In pursuance of the terms of the Munich Plan, the German armies moved into the Sudetenland on October 1, 1938. Two days later, Hitler visited Eger—the unofficial capital of Sudetenland and then he threw all other conditions of the Munich Pact to the wind. The promised plebiscite was never held in the frontier areas and the international guarantee of the new frontiers never materialised. The new boundary lines, when finally drawn, followed strategic,

---

56. Ibid., p. 124. The Munich Pact was widely denounced. Schuman says: "The Peace of Munich was the greatest triumph to date of Hitler's strategy of terror. It was the culmination of appeasement and the warrant of death for the Western Powers... The Munichmen of Paris and London comforted themselves with the hefty thought that the Third Reich would now strike towards Kiev and the Black Sea and clash with Moscow. In this assumption, which was the whole meaning of Munich, they were completely and tragically mistaken." op. cit., pp. 571-72.
57. See Schuman, op. cit., p. 569. W.L. Shirer in his diary dated 30 September, 1938 noted: "Hitler gets everything he wanted except that he has to wait a few days longer to all of it. His waiting 10 days has saved the peace of Europe—a curious commentary on this sick, decadent continent." *Berlin Diary*, p. 120.

Phase of Crisis

much more than ethnographic, lines leaving 250 thousand Czechs in the land ceded to Germany. Czechoslovakia lost her system of fortifications that greatly impressed the German generals when they visited them together with 11,000 sq miles of territory under their sway. Other neighbouring states also took advantage of the tragic situation. Poland demanded and then got an area of Teschen covering 499 sq miles with a population of 240,000 Poles. Through Italo-German arbitration Hungary had her claim adjusted and got an approximately 4,800 sq miles of territory inhabited by the Magyars. In this way, Czechoslovakia suffered heavy territorial losses as a result of the non-fulfilment of pledges advanced by the British and French statesmen at the Munich meet.[58]

Even after seizing the Sudetenland, Hitler did not stop. The Nazis encouraged the two eastern provinces of Slovakia and Ruthenia to declare their independence. For this sake, Hitler accorded a grand reception to Bela Tuka (the leader of the National Party of Czechoslovakia) on February 12, 1939, and assured him of his full support for staging a revolt. Under these conditions, President Hacha (who had succeeded Benes after his resignation following acceptance of the Munich Pact) dismissed the Ruthenian minister and sacked the provincial government of Slovakia for its separatist intrigues. It afforded another opportunity for Hitler. Now he invited the deposed Premier of Slovakia (Tiso) and another Slovak leader (Durcansky) on 13-14 March and incited them to rise in revolt against the government of Prague. Soon Hacha and his Foreign Minister (Chavalkovsky) visited Berlin to sort out matters with Hitler. Hitler accorded all honour to the heads of the Prague government and then his ministers Ribbentrop and Goering put before Hacha a document containing some new demands of the Fuhrer that were to be accepted by him in order to avoid the invasion of German troops. Hacha fainted and he had to be brought back to senses with the help of an injection. Then he put his signatures that enthused Hitler to dance with joy on the 'greatest day' of his life.[59]

Consequently, the German troops moved into the provinces of Bohemia and Moravia. On the evening of March 15, 1939, Hitler reached Prague and declared German Protectorate over these two

---

58. See Bullock, op. cit., p. 445.
59. Ibid.

provinces that had now become 'part of the German *Lebensraum* for a thousand years'. Slovakia was also taken under German protection; at the same time, Hungary was permitted to occupy and annex the Carpatho-Ukraine tip. In explanation of this step, Hitler said that the republic of Czechoslovakia had not succeeded "in the sensible organisation of the common life of national groups, which were arbitrarily united within its borders, it had proved its inability to live and actually fell to pieces.... Germany already has proven its 1,000-year old historical part that, by reason of its size and the characteristics of the German nation, it alone is predestined to solve these problems."[60] In short, the inevitable conclusion of the Munich Pact manifested itself in the disappearance of the republic of Czechoslovakia from the political map of Europe and the notorious agreement, being another resounding victory for the Nazi techniques, "constituted an armistice rather than a final settlement."[61]

Civil War in Spain: A Trial Balloon of International Power Politics

Spain is said to have played an inconsiderable role in international affairs. But the civil war conditions here (1936-39) provided an occasion for the Fascist powers of Germany and Italy to cash capital out of the domestic politics of this country. At the same time, the appeasers of London, Paris and Washington added fuel to fire by taking to the course of 'non-intervention' that was appeasement in a different guise. Once again, the USSR alone remained in the field to champion the cause of the aggrieved party. The result was that the conditions of internal struggle in Spain between the right and the left afforded one more chance to the statesmen of England, France and the United States to strengthen the hands of the Fascist powers in the long-range hope that one day their combined strength would play a a decisive part in the destruction of the communist system of Soviet Russia. Naturally, the civil war of this country procreated conditions for the positive and negative role of other major powers of the world. In this way, it should be described as the first phase of the Second World War that broke out in 1939. "In theory, a civil struggle, the Spanish war rapidly assumed the

---
60. *The New York Times*, March 17, 1939.
61. Sharp and Kirk, op. cit., p. 662.

Phase of Crisis

appearance of an international conflict which, though disguised, was nonetheless painfully real."[62]

Infamous for being destitute of democratic traditions,[63] Parliamentary system established in Spain after the First World War broke down in 1923 when Capt. Primo de Rivera staged a military coup and established his military rule that survived till 1930. Still different elements like the Socialists, the Republicans, the separatists of the Province of Catalonia, the landowners, the church leaders, the moderate Republicans, the Fascists, etc., were at loggerheads. As a matter of fact, it was a struggle between the rightist and the leftist forces. On November 12, 1933, elections were held in which the leftists (mostly Republicans) were defeated and the rightists (landowners, church leaders, moderate Republicans and the Fascists) formed a coalition government under the leadership of Senor Lerroux. But when they started undoing what the Socialists had done in the last three years, the Socialists offered resistance. They openly incited the people of Asturias to revolt. Though their revolt was suppressed, the province of Catalonia declared its independence. Under these conditions President Lerroux dissolved the Parliament and held its new elections in 1936. Now the leftists (socialists, communists and anarchists) came to power and a new government under the leadership of Senor Azana was formed. Naturally, the rightists rose in revolt. Taking advantage of this situation, Gen. Franco on July 17, 1936 raised the banner of revolt in Morocco against the Madrid Government. On 20 November, 1937, the capital was moved from Valencia to Barcelona, but on January 26, 1939 even Barcelona fell to the rebels. In April 1939, civil war came to an end when the entire country passed under the control of Gen. Franco.

What did immediately provoke Gen. Franco to revolt? The answer is that the government of the leftists proved its incompe-

---

62. Ibid., p. 633.
63. While taking stock of the political history of this country, it was well observed: "In 1874 it was a military *pronunciamiento* which brought about the restoration of the Bourbons. It was the same device which inaugurated the dictatorship of General Primo de Rivera, in 1923, which lasted till 1930. General Franco's *coup*, in July 1936, was intended as a further use of the same time-honoured expedient which is almost entitled to be regarded, in Spain, as a recognised instrument for the achievement of constitutional changes." Gathorne-Hardy, op. cit., p. 431.

tence by not being able to maintain law and order in the country. In not much time 251 churches were burnt, 324 newspaper offices and political clubs were attacked of which 79 were completely damaged, 339 persons were murdered and 1,287 wounded. Robbery became rife and not less than 331 strikes occurred. But the most heinous event was the assassination of Senor Calvo Sotelo (the most prominent figure of the rightist forces) on July 13, 1936. It may also be admitted that the government of the leftists not only failed in maintaining conditions of law and order, it took positive interest in the suppression of the rightist forces. On both sides, the really powerful elements "sought to use the difficulties in which the republic found itself in 1936 as an opportunity to overthrow liberal inculcations and to capture the Spanish State."[64]

However, what made this event a matter of international significance was the role played directly or indirectly by the great powers of the world. The Fascist ruler of Italy saw herein another grand occasion to have foothold in western Mediterranean waters so as to offer a potential challenge to the British power in time to come. But one point that motivated the powers of Italy and Germany was the victory of their creed. Fascism first triumphed in Italy under Mussolini, then it surfaced itself in Germany under Hitler; now it was going to have the same fate in Spain under Franco. Both Mussolini and Hitler studied it as a favourable development to be made use of eventually against the power of the USSR. Moreover, since it was studied by other major powers (like Britain, France and the United States) in the same manner, it got its strength from their policy of appeasement. "In 1936 Italy and Germany treated the Spanish Civil War, on somewhat unconvincing grounds, as a struggle between Communism and Fascism, and thought it appropriate that they should support the insurgents."[65]

The dictators of Rome and Berlin did not conceal their role in this civil struggle. It demonstrated that the fight at once assumed the form of an Axis invasion of Spain. In June, Italian and German fighters returned to their homelands and enjoyed triumphal receptions in Rome and Berlin. Ciano and Goering revealed that Axis soldiers, sometimes disguised as 'tourists', had gone to Spain at the outset of the rebellion and had been prepared for action long in

---

64. *The Round Table*, London, June, 1938, p. 443.
65. Carr, op. cit., p. 260.

advance. "The courageous struggle of the Spanish people to defend their liberties in the face of the united opposition of the Vatican, the Caesars of the Axis, and the appeasers and isolationists of Paris, London and Washington were foredoomed to failure. No government, save only that of the USSR, would give or even sell them arms to resist the enemies."[66]

It may also be found that the great appeasers certainly sought to help Gen. Franco in an indirect way by sticking to the course of 'no-intervention'. In agreement with Chamberlain, Premier Blum of France proposed an international agreement to ban all shipments of arms and war materials to both groups of the contestants. An International Non-Intervention Committee came into being that had its first meeting in London on September 9, 1936. The government of Spain did not like this stand of Britain and France and instead sought to take the matter to the League of Nations. Surprisingly, the Spanish delegate was dissuaded from making specific accusation against Italy and Germany. Then, on December 12, 1936, the League Council sidestepped the dangerous issue by resolving that "every state is under an obligation to refrain from intervention in the internal affairs of another state." Even the Non-Intervention Committee became ineffective when Italy and Germany recognised the regime of Gen. Franco in November 1936, and after a couple of months stopped playing to the tune of English and French plans of setting up a naval patrol for a system of frontier supervision.[67]

British interest collided with that of Italy at this juncture. While Mussolini was rendering full support to Gen. Franco, the British statesmen were afraid of the growing power of Italy so as to become a menace to her hold in the Mediterranean region. For this sake, Chamberlain was keen to have Italy in the Non-Intervention Committee and also play her positive role for the localisation of the conflict. He could succeed in concluding a 'gentleman's agreement' with Mussolini on January 2, 1937 whereby both

---

66. Schuman, op. cit., p. 543.
67. It is rightly said: "An effort was made to include Germany, Italy and the Soviet Union in a non-intervention agreement, but, after long negotiations and violent recriminations, non-intervention remained a dead letter except for France and Great Britain." See Graham H. Stuart: "The Struggle of France for Hegemony and Security" in Brown, Hodges and Roucek (eds..): *Contemporary World Politics*, p. 162.

governments agreed that "freedom of entry into, exit from, and transit through, the Mediterranean is a vital interest both to the different parts of the British Empire and Italy and that these interests are in no way inconsistent with each other." It failed to prove a successful step. Ships after ships were being torpedoed and sunk without warning, particularly by the submarine attack of the Italian naval power. Obviously, such a campaign "was another move in the half-veiled policy of pinpricking the British and French, until they would be willing to make substantial concessions in order to stop these annoying tactics."[68]

Sporadic events of attack by Italian and Spanish submarines continued. On June 19, 1937, the German government complained about an attack on its cruiser (Leipzig) by Spanish submarines that was denied by Britain and France. Taking advantages of the opportunity, Germany and Italy withdrew from the patrol and Portugal withdrew facility for the observation of her frontier. Then, on 10 July, supervision of Pyrenean frontier was suspended by France. It is obvious that "the measures of control so far taken to ensure non-intervention were materially interfered with."[69] Thus, the British delegate on the Non-Intervention Committee put forward a note of compromise on 14 July, stating:[70]

1. The naval patrol should be withdrawn and observers established in Spanish ports, while the supervision of land frontiers should be resumed.
2. A commission should be constituted to superintend the withdrawal of foreign nationals from the forces of both sides.
3. After substantial progress with the withdrawals had been reported, both sides should be recognised as belligerents, and granted, the rights accorded to that status by international law.

Since the French government agreed with the British emphasis on necessity of a retaliatory action to deal with the nuisance of sporadic submarine warfare, they jointly convened a conference at Nyon in Switzerland to consider measures for the abatement of the menace. In September 1937, Nyon Agreement was signed by 9 states. It authorised an Anglo-French naval patrol to attack and

---

68. Sharp and Kirk, *op. cit.*, p. 637.
69. Gathorne-Hardy, *op. cit.*, p. 440.
70. Ibid.

destroy any submarine surface vessel, or aircraft which had illegally attacked a non-Spanish merchant vessel. Consequently, sporadic attacks by submarines ceased to a considerable extent.

Nothing substantial could be achieved, however, by the British and French leaders in stopping secret assistance being given to Gen. Franco by Mussolini and Hitler. The course of blackmail continued and the Italian government began the official distribution of medals to the families of soldiers who had lost their lives in the Spanish war. The Duce had given his mind to the liberal democracies of England, France and the United States, first by paying a state visit to Berlin in September (1937) in the course of which he proclaimed the solidarity of the two Fascist powers, and later by adhering to the Anti-Comintern Pact already signed by Germany and Japan. But the most astounding act of Mussolini was to withdraw Italy's membership of the League of Nations in December 1937, that made him free from any liability to honour the decision of the Non-Intervention Committee. According to an official admission of Rome, more than 40,000 Italian troops were in Spain in October 1937. Franco's victory with such a massive help from a Fascist power became a foregone conclusion. For all these reasons, in 1939, the civil war in Spain or the 'little world war' ended in 'a victory of the Axis'.[71]

Invasion on Poland: End of Appeasement and Outbreak of the Second World War
The dismemberment of Czechoslovakia did not, and could not, imply an end to the imperialistic designs of Hitler. Poland could not remain unaffected by such developments in view of the fact that she had taken her own share out of German losses when the Treaty of Versailles was dictated. Germany under Hitler could never resign herself to the loss of the Corridor that had separated East Prussia from the rest of the country and the additional loss to Poland of the valuable mining areas of Upper Silesia. Then, there was the perennial question of the city of Danzig that had been made free and put under the charge of a High Commissioner appointed by the League of Nations. The location of this city at the mouth of River Vistula made it of paramount significance to Poland and the

---
71. Langsam, op. cit., p. 121.

Polish Corridor. All this arrangement had left both Germany and Poland in a state of distress after the conclusion of peace settlements. "Germany continued to look upon the whole Corridor and especially Danzig, as an irredentist area, while Poland, dissatisfied with the inadequacy of her controls over Danzig, finally determined to break the resistance of the Danzigers by constructing a new seaport, Gdynia, a few miles away, which was to take as much of the seaport traffic as possible."[72]

The fate of Czechoslovakia had made two things very clear which the anti-Fascist heroes failed to take note of deliberately. First, the dynamics of Nazism lay in its inability to stop anywhere. Second, Poland should have taken it for granted that the next step of the firm follower of the *Drang Nach Osten* policy would be to deal with her in not much time. Unfortunately, the statesmen of London and Paris overlooked this fact deliberately as their eyes were set on inciting the great Fascist powers to move ahead so as to fight ultimately with the demon of communism. The leaders of Poland could, however, take a lead in the matter and requisition the support of Britain and France even before an attack on their own country had taken place. That is, their determined opposition to the destruction of the neighbouring states of Austria and Czechoslovakia could have succeeded in putting the sworn enemy at a distance. Taking note of this fact, Amery had said in 1938 that "the mere threat of Polish intervention would have made it impossible for Hitler to attack Czechoslovakia.... To grab the Teschen coalfield... the Poles let the keystone be pulled out of the Arch of Versailles structure and signed their own death warrant."[73]

Adhering to the strategy that ultimately succeeded in the annexation of Austria and then in the destruction of Czechoslovakia, Hitler provoked the Germans of Poland to rise in revolt against the Polish government. Thus came into being a Nazi party there. In not much time it controlled all key elective posts and gained a majority in the Senate. And yet with a view to cheat the Polish government, he signed a 10-year pact of amity and non-aggression on January 26, 1934 and reiterated in 1938 that this agreement would bring lasting pacification. But in March 1939, he presented to the Warsaw government a set of demands like immediate return of Danzig city

---

72. Sharp and Kirk, op. cit., p. 668.
73. L.S. Amery: *My Political Life*, Vol. III, p. 294.

Phase of Crisis 151

to Germany and a passage from the existing Polish territory including a railway and road across the Corridor that would join Germany with East Prussia. In return, Germany would recognise all existing economic rights of Poland in Danzig, give Poland a free port in Danzig, recognise the new political frontiers between Germany and Poland, and conclude a 25-year non-aggression pact with Poland. It clearly demonstrated that now Poland, too, "must be made to come to Canossa and do her penance."[74]

These designs of Hitler were resisted by the leaders of the major democratic countries. For instance, President Roosevelt of the United States conveyed a message to Mussolini and Hitler requesting not to make use of armed forces for a war-like purpose for at least 10 years and, if they followed it, America would render her full cooperation in a subsequent world conference to reduce the burden of armaments and increase the flow of international trade by lowering artificial barriers. But more meaningful was the stand of British Prime Minister (Chamberlain) who on August 22, 1939, warned Hitler against launching an aggression on Poland. For this purpose, he instructed his ambassador in Berlin (Sir Neville Henderson) to seek a personal meeting with Hitler in this regard. But Hitler minced no words in scoffing at the stand of the British Prime Minister.

Since the USSR had opposed German advances in Austria and Czechoslovakia, her support for the Polish government looked like a certainty under these conditions. But it all changed suddenly when Ribbentrop signed at Moscow on August 23, 1939, a treaty of non-aggression between Germany and the Soviet Union. By such an act Germany could throw a bombshell into the Allied camp. All hopes of Britain and France to count on the Russian cooperation in the event of Germany's attack on Poland were shattered. "The jubilation in Berlin was equalled only by the gloom in Paris and London. If Germany now chose to fight it out, she would face no enemy save Poland in the East, thus avoiding the one thing which Nazi strategists had dreaded: a powerful enemy on two fronts at the same time. Britain and France made haste to reiterate their intention to support Poland despite this new development, but it was generally recognised that the situation had taken a serious turn for the worse. Allied chagrin was not lessened

---
74. Sharp and Kirk, op. cit., p. 679.

by the realisation that in all probability Germany and the Soviet Union had been negotiating secretly while Molotov had been pretending to negotiate with the Allies. Duplicity could have gone no further."[75] First to isolate Poland and then to devour her independence was the immediate objective of German diplomacy at this stage. By making a pact of non-aggression with the USSR, Hitler could avoid the possibility of any Russian help to Poland. Then he made an effort to conciliate with Britain by offering that after the Polish question was solved, Germany would guarantee the existence of the British Empire and that she would render all help to Britain wherever necessary. It could not work. Then, Hitler publicised his view of settling the question with Poland if her top spokesman visited Berlin and had a direct talk with him on this count. In return the Polish government desired to have the matter talked over by her ambassador posted at Berlin. Hitler declined and made it clear that very soon his troops would invade Poland. Now the British envoy (Henderson) expressed his desire to convey the German proposal to Poland if it was given to him in writing. Hitler declined on the plea that it was too late. Similarly, when the Polish Minister (Beck) rushed to Berlin in the evening of August 30, 1939, to have direct negotiation with Hitler, he declined to meet him. Bent upon settling every controversy by the use of force, Hitler mobilised his troops on September 1. Invasion on Poland began. Now Britain abandoned the course of appeasement. Chamberlain sent a note of warning to Hitler to suspend military operations against Poland and when he declined to honour it, Britain jumped into the war two days after. The Second World War started and the prophecy of H.G. Wells (given in 1933 in his *The Shape of Things of Come*) proved true that the next world war would begin over the Polish Corridor.

Hitler's unprovoked aggression on Poland should be regarded as the last heinous act in the series of aggressions—first committed by Japan in Manchuria, then by Italy in Abyssinia, and then by Germany in Austria and Czechoslovakia coupled with her as well as her ally's (Italy's) hand in the Spanish civil war. It ultimately entailed the end of twenty years' armistice. After an interval of twenty years, we saw another global combat as 'the

---

75. Ibid., p. 673. For a detailed study of this subject see R.L. Buell: *Poland, Key to Europe*.

Phase of Crisis

greatest unresolved riddle in politics'.[76] The system of alliances and pacts devised by the Allied and Axis Powers to prevent the recurrence of the tragedy of 1914-18 but more particularly to perpetuate their own interests proved a failure. The appeasement policy designed to have the destruction of communism ultimately at the hands of Fascist powers recoiled. Britain and France had to join hands with the USSR in a determined bid to checkmate the dictators of Tokyo, Rome and Berlin. Moreover, the advancement of Japanese troops in the Far East forced the United States to strengthen the position of the Allies. The net result of all this was that the Fascist powers, after having some imperialistic gains in the period of pacification, had to face their Waterloo one day. In a word, the collapse of the mechanism of peace and return to the course of power politics culminating in the occurrence of another great war confirmed the impression of Fosdick: "It is doubtless safe to say that half the tragedies in the long story of the human race have been due to the inability of men to find any method except organised slaughter as a means of solving their rivalries and antagonism."[77]

Prof. Roth sums up the whole story in these words: "The major developments of the inter war period beginning with Versailles were at the very least, war-related if not war-dominated: the post-war economic difficulties, the disillusionment, the rise of Communism and Fascism, the Crash of 1929 and Great Depression, the Manchurian war, the totalitarianism of the thirties, the destruction of the Versailles system, the outbreak of war in 1939 and in broad outline, even the Second World War. All were heart of the same development, all had their roots in the First World War. But the persistence of the war long after the official cease-fire only points to its inconclusive character. The war had failed to make a clean sweep—that is why, contemporaries so little understood its consequences. The war had resulted in a blurring of distinctions which in an earlier framework had been reasonably clear-cut. Warfare and diplomacy, war and peace, military and civilian, international and domestic, political and economic nationalism and socialism. Few could see or even wanted to see clearly. The

---

76. E.M. Earle: "The Influence of Air Power on History" in *The Yale Review*, Vol. XXXV, Summer, 1946, p. 592.
77. Raymond Fosdick: "We Need New Words and New Faiths" in *New York Times*, Magazine, December 19, 1948.

Alliances and Pacts (1920-39)

Powers	Nature	Years	Countries	
France	Alliances and pacts	1920	Belgium	
		1921	Poland	1922
		1924	Czechoslovakia	Little
		1926	Rumania	Entente
		1927	Yugoslavia	(1920-21)
		1932,1935	USSR	
		1935	Italy	
Soviet Union	Non-aggression and neutrality pacts	1925,1935	Turkey	
		1926	Germany	
		1926	Afghanistan	
		1926	Louisiana	
		1927	Iran	
		1931	Finland	
		1931	Estonia	
	″		Poland	
		1932,1935	France	
		1933	Latvia	
	″		Czechoslovakia	
	″		Yugoslavia	
	″		Rumania	
	″		Italy	
Italy	Neutrality and friendship pacts	1924	Czechoslovakia	
		1924,1929	Yugoslavia	
		1926	Rumania	
	″		Spain	
		1926,1927	Albania	
		1927	Hungary	
		1928,1930, 1933	Turkey	
		1930	Austria	
		1933	USSR	
		1935	France	
		1937	Germany and Japan (Axis)	
Poland	Alliances and pacts	1921	France	
	″		Rumania	
		1922	Little Entente	
		1931,1934	USSR	
		1934	Germany	
Balkans	Pacts	1934	Greece	
	″		Rumania	
	″		Turkey	
	″		Yugoslavia	

Phase of Crisis

inter-war era, consequently, was one of monumental blunders and within each nation and within the international community generally. In effect, what the Second War did was to sweep away much of the unfinished business of the First thereby clarifying its meaning."[78]

---

78. Jack J. Roth: 'Conclusion' in his *World War I: A Turning Point in Modern History* (New York: Alfred A. Knopf, 1967), p. 132.

6

GERMANY

One must have the simple mind of a child to believe that the revision of the Versailles Treaty can be obtained by indirect means and by beseeching the clemency of the victors; without taking into account the fact that for this we should need somebody who had the character of a Talleyrand among us... The sword is the only means whereby a nation can thrust that clutch from its throat. Only when national sentiment is organised and concentrated into an effective force, can it defy the international menace which tends towards an enslavement of the nations. But this road is and will always be marked with bloodshed.

—Adolf Hitler[1]

What we have seen in the preceding two chapters on the phases of 'pacification' and 'crisis' constitutes a rich context in which a study of the foreign policies of major countries of the world can be made. The cases of major countries like Britain, France, Germany, Italy, Soviet Russia, United States, China and Japan immediately engage our attention at this stage. However, it is Germany that deserves its treatment in the first place in view of the fact that the conditions of the inter-war period (1919-39) were basically governed by the fall and rise of this country.[2] The peace settlements made at Paris

---

1. Hitler: *Mein Kampf*, Translated from German into English and annotated by James Murphy, (New Delhi: Sagar Publication; n.y.), p. 358.
2. F.H. Simonds and B. Emeny hold the view that Germany deserves to be studied 'first in a survey of the Great Powers of Europe'. *The Great Powers in World Politics* (New York: American Book Co., 1939), p. 191. In support of such a contention, they cite Richard von Kuhlmann who observed: "Germany's central position in the heart of Europe is chiefly responsible for the disastrous reverses which have been so frequent in history. They have baulked her progress at every step, nipped every growing bud, doomed every hopeful development to a tragic ending. No one recognised this more clearly than did Bismarck himself." Ibid., p. 192, n 2.

Germany

happily designated as 'a war to end all wars' procreated conditions that entailed another great war after an interlude of twenty years. However, as the Treaty of Versailles was the *magnum opus* of the peace-makers assembled at Paris, and as this important instrument of peace was related to the case of Germany, it was taken by the aggrieved party as "a millstone round the neck of the Weimar republic."[3] Germany that was sought to be crushed by this Treaty could arise from the ashes to undo all that was done at Paris. In other words, the developments of European politics after 1930 demonstrated the bold fact that the peace-makers had created a 'peaceless Europe.'[4]

Germany after the Versailles Treaty: Severe Economic Crisis and Policy of Passive Resistance

German foreign policy during the inter-war period runs between the two poles of the acceptance of the notorious peace settlement embodied in the Treaty of Versailles at the pleadings of a weak Chancellor like Bauer to its frank repudiation alongwith a powerful retaliation at the hands of a strong Chancellor like Hitler. A study of the matter contained in the preceding chapters makes it above-board that Germany came out of the First World War like a pale person just out of the game. Economically crippled, politically segregated, militarily humbled, and potential resources exhausted, she fit herself like an outcaste, a moral leper among the nations of the world. (Lipson) President Friedrich Ebert and his Chancellors like Bauer and Cuno behaved like a prisoner of the circumstances in trying to discover a way out of the impasse created by the unwisdom of the rulers serving the Hohenzollern dynasty, who plunged the country into the First World War, followed by a still greater act of unwisdom committed by the statesmen of the Allied and Associated Powers in dictating a peace settlement that ulti-

---

3. Gerhard Schultz: *Revolution and Peace Treaties, 1917-20*, Translated from German into English by Marian Jackson (London: Methuen, 1972), p. 224. He elsewhere says: "The peace-makers failed to establish a permanent order. Their work continued the political transformation of the world begun with the war; but they did not find the lasting state of calm for which humanity longed after experimenting to the full horrors of war and after making such terrible sacrifices. The great movements of the age did not come to a stop." Ibid., p. 222.

4. Ibid., p. 224.

mately became the cause of its own unsettlement with far-reaching results.

The German people could never be oblivious to the fact that at the Paris Peace Conference their delegates were denied any semblance of proper treatment the like of which was accorded to France at the Congress of Vienna about 100 years back. To their eternal regret and national humiliation, they were brought to the Conference room like criminals and then sentenced without ever having been permitted the ordinary justice of their say in the court.[5] They had every reason to take it for granted that while professing the idealism of a new world, the Allies had reverted to the Roman example to make another Punic Peace. The Reparation Clauses of the Treaty condemned the Germans to the condition of a tribute-paying nation. The provisions which imposed perpetual disarmament reduced them to the circumstances of a defenceless people. The territorial decisions definitely shattered their unity. Revsion became henceforth the fixed, enduring, immutable purpose of the nation and policy of the successive governments".[6]

The end of the First World War brought about important political changes in Germany. With the abdication of the monarch (Kaiser Wilhelm II) the rule of Hohenzollern dynasty came to an end. Germany became a Republic and a new constitution drawn up by a Constituent Assembly at Weimar came into force on August 11, 1919. In the meantime, the first problem before the new government of President Ebert was the ratification of the Versailles Treaty. Since Chancellor Scheidemann disagreed with the majority view of accepting the terms of the dictated peace, he resigned. He was succeeded by Bauer. Then, the work of accepting the treaty was accomplished on June 23, 1919, under the shadow of the threats issued by the victorious powers. Herein lay the source of the most important factor of German foreign policy—fight for its revision. Taking this fact in view, it was rightly pointed out: "German foreign policy since World War I has revolved around one central goal : to redress the balance of power in Europe as established by the Treaty of Versailles. In this urge towards

---

5. See Victor Schiff: *The Germans at Versailles* (London: Williams and Norgate, 1930).
6. F.H. Simonds and B. Emeny, op. cit., p. 228.

throwing off the fetters of a treaty believed to be iniquitous and imposed by force, German action in the international sphere bears a certain resemblance to French policies after 1871."[7]

The opening phase of German foreign policy (1920-23) is marked by the prevalence of a great economic crisis which put her in a state of heavy inflation. It was an immediate result of huge budget deficits caused by the payment of first instalment of reparation. The situation reached a point of crisis when she could not pay the second instalment of reparation in 1922. The argument of the French and Belgian representatives that it was an act of deliberate and voluntary default of Germany prevailed. Consequently, the Reparation Commission took the decision of holding Germany guilty on January 9, 1923, that entitled France and Belgium to advance their troops into the area of Ruhr. Soon the German government adopted the policy of 'passive resistance'. The people of the coal-rich area were forbidden to cooperate in any way with the invaders; and all voluntary reparation payments and deliveries were stopped. The French "replied with a counter-boycott, drawing a line between occupied and unoccupied German territory across which nothing was allowed to pass. Recalcitrant officials and industrialists in the occupied area were expelled or imprisoned; and an organisation was set up to extract reparation from the output of the Ruhr industries."[8]

The act of Ruhr occupation proved a blessing in disguse to Germany. Still adhering to the policy of maintaining the balance of power, Britain felt forced to come to the rescue of Germany on the plea that unless her economic condition was improved, she would never be in a position to pay reparation. It well coincided with the American point of view. But at the national level, the people resented the weak stand of Chancellor Cuno in dealing with the governments of France and Belgium. Thus, he resigned. Stresemann became the Chancellor of Germany on August 12, 1923, and gave a new direction to the foreign policy of his country by adhering to the course of 'fulfilment' and 'reconciliation'. In not much time, it became clear to all that the rash step of the Ruhr

---

7. Friedrich: "German Foreign Policy" in Brown, Hodges and Roucek (eds.): *Contemporary World Politics: An Introduction to the Study of International Relations* (New York: John Wiley & Sons, 1939), p. 165.
8. E.H. Carr: *International Relations between the Two World Wars, 1919-1939*, (London: Macmillan, 1950), pp. 56-57.

occupation proved a disaster to France and Belgium in view of the fact that the forces of occupation "resorted to reprisals, arrests, courts-martial and other repressive measures; but coal could not be mined with bayonets, and occupation was fruitless. The German government was, however, reduced to bankruptcy, and in August of 1923 Chancellor Stresemann abandoned passive resistance and surrendered."[9]

The Stresemann Era: Revival of Economic Stability and Rewards of the Policy of Fulfilment

"The Ruhr occupation, which completed Germany's ruin, was however a turning point in the post-war history of Europe."[10] The formation of the Stresemann government signified introduction of a new element in the foreign policy of Germany. It was the policy of national reconstruction through international cooperation. Instead of merely crying for the defence of the downtrodden, or sticking to the distractive course of passive resistance, or repeatedly yielding to external pressures, Stresemann and his associates regarded international cooperation as a positive method and goal though well tied to the task of national reconstruction. On one occasion the new Chancellor said: "International cooperation for national reconstruction.... If you try to find a general formula for German foreign policy, you must discover it in the international agreements in which we are and must be involved....The task before us is to devote all our strength to the maintenance of peace in Europe.... The road ahead of us is clear; we must strengthen our own national life by the advancement of peaceful understanding."[11]

Stresemann assumed office at a time when French leaders had grown impatient of Anglo-American check on their desire to keep Germany in a state of complete suppression. Disgusted with the non-cooperative attitude of Britain and the United States in regard to complete suppression of Germany, France (with the cooperation of Belgium) had won her point in the Reparation Commission and occupied the Ruhr. But when this move proved

---

9. F.L. Schuman: *International Politics* (New York: McGraw Hill, 1941), III Ed., p. 556.
10. Carr, op. cit., p. 59.
11. See Friedrich, op. cit., p. 171.

Germany

counter-productive, the leaders of France took to the course of Rhineland occupation. They instigated a 'separatist movement' in the Rhineland. Its purpose was to instigate the local people to rise in revolt against the government of Berlin and declare their independence so as to come under French patronage one day. Such a movement was brewing in the Rhineland with the cooperation of some traitors since 1920. But in the autumn of 1923 events took an ugly turn. In the Palatinate (which formed part of Bavaria and not of Prussia) the local French representative of the Rhineland High Commission recognised the separatists as an independent government. They expelled all German officials and in January 1924 the Rhineland High Commission by a majority vote (with the cooperation of the Belgian delegate) officially recognised the 'autonomous government' of the Palatinate. It was strongly disapproved by the British government. Thereupon, under British pressure, the government of France had to convey orders to its representative in the Rhineland to abandon all support for the 'separatists'. "The result was shattering. The whole movement collapsed in a few hours. There were riots in the principal towns of the Palatinate; and a score of more of the separatists were lynched by the population before the troops could intervene. After February 1924, no more was heard of the separatist movement in the Rhineland."[12]

The British opposition first to the occupation of the Ruhr by France and then at her hands to the intensification of separatist movement in the Rhineland came to the unexpected advantage of Germany at this stage. The British government played a very important role in the adoption of the Dawes Plan on September 1, 1924, that put Germany back on the road to economic recovery. Shortly thereafter, Britain and France advanced loans to Germany whose tangible results appeared some five years after when it could be found that Germany, instead of remaining a debtor, had become a creditor nation. However, more important was the event of British cooperation that appeared in the role of Lord D'Abernon—a far-sighted English diplomat posted as English ambassador at Berlin at that time. He had very close and cordial meeting with Stresemann and, for this reason, the German Chancellor made a move for the guarantee of existing boundaries between Germany, Belgium and France combined with treaties of

---

12. Carr, op. cit., p. 52.

friendship and cooperation with Britain and Italy. It paved the way for the conclusion of Locarno Agreements of 1925.[13]

The Locarno Agreements have an importance of their own at this stage. For the first time, German delegate (Stresemann) was treated at par with his British and French counterparts (Chamberlain and Briand respectively). Now Germany pledged herself to accept permanently her Western frontiers with France and Belgium as laid down in the Treaty of Versailles that amounted to her abandonment of the claim upon Alsace-Lorraine. She also bound herself to maintain the Rhineland as a demilitarised zone. Both Germany and France agreed that neither would resort to war against the other; and each had the right to invoke the military aid of the remaining parties to the treaty in the event of unprovoked aggression. Now the pacification of Europe "seemed on the point of complete attainment when the Treaty of Locarno gave to France the security which was the goal of her policy, and to Germany the status which admitted her into the comity of nations."[14]

Its best upshot was the admission of Germany to the League of Nations in 1926 in an atmosphere of great enthusiasm. Stresemann

---

13. On this point, G.M. Gathorne-Hardy makes a fine observation: He says: "The favourable atmosphere created by the London Conference and the adoption of the Dawes Plan inaugurated an era of the improved understanding not only between Allies and Germany, but between Great Britain and France. The subordinate question of apportionment of the reparation payments was quickly and happily settled during a conference of Allied Finance Ministers which took place in January 1925.... The 'Locarno Spirit' which did much in the ensuing years to encourage a more hopeful sense of security, was thus a logical outcome of the Dawes settlement, and, since the appeal to American cooperation of which this was the culmination was occasioned by the catastrophic experiences of the Ruhr occupation and it was this sharp lesson which brought the protagonists nearer together, it appeared, for the moment at any rate, that good had been born out of evil." *A Short History of International Affairs, 1920-1939* (London: Oxford Univ. Press, 1950), IV Ed., p. 59.

14. E. Lipson: *Europe: 1914-1939* (London: Charles Adam and Clark, 1957), VII Ed., p. 82. As Louis L. Snyder says: "For the first time since the close of the World War I, the statesmen of Europe seem to have caught a fleeting vision of a peaceful continent. Locarno with its skilfully managed attempt to abolish the psychology of Versailles made a tremendous impression." Thus, he cites Stresemann who jubilantly affirmed: "We are citizens each of his own country... but we are also citizens of Europe and are joined together by a great conception of civilisation. We have the right to speak of a European idea. Hatred and illwill were to be replaced by mutual understanding and peace." *Documents of German History*, p. 398.

took this occasion to declare: "The cooperation of the peoples in the League of Nations must and will lead to just solutions for the moral questions which arise in the conscience of the people. The most durable foundation of peace is a policy inspired by mutual understanding and mutual respect between nation and nation."[15] Those who witnessed this historic occasion were well impressed with the obvious sincerity of the three architects of Locarno (Chamberlain, Briand and Stresemann). It certainly brought the League to the peak of its strength. Each Assembly and Council meeting now served to bring the foreign ministers of four major European powers together regularly for face-to-face discussion of Europe's problems. In spite of marked differences in temperament and background, Briand, the nimble-minded Breton, and Stresemann, the hard-headed German, developed a confidence in each other that enabled them to speak frankly and honestly about the issues still dividing their two nations—reparations, disarmament, the return of the Saar, and the evacuation of the Rhineland."[16]

Apart from making the first impressive debut in the Assembly in September, 1926, Stresemann had a close meeting with Briand at Thoiry—a place near Geneva—where the two could take several important decisions on matters of pressing concern to their countries. Although the contents of the Thoiry Meeting remained undivulged, it could be guessed that Stresemann begged for the immediate evacuation of the Rhineland and the return of the Saar territory to Germany, offering in return concessions in the form of regular reparation payments. But the more impressive feature of the Thoiry Meet was that Briand was personally disposed to close the chapter of Franco-German ill-will. It is true that though neither of the two statesmen could induce his government to accept such an arrangement at that time, "Franco-German good feeling continued without abatement. In January 1927, France consented to the withdrawal of the Inter-Allied Military Commission from Germany."[17]

As a genuine lover of international peace, Stresemann also looked towards the Soviet Union. He extended *de jure* recognition to the USSR. With a view to make a further advance on the Treaty

---

15. Ibid., p. 405.
16. W.R. Sharp and G. Kirk: *Contemporary International Politics* (New York: Farrar and Rinehart, Inc., 1944), p. 553.
17. Ibid., p. 554.

of Rapallo (signed by German Foreign Minister Walter Ratheneau on April 16, 1922, with the Soviet Union whereby both had renounced their war claims and pre-war debts and established normal diplomatic relations), he signed a treaty of friendship with Russia on April 24,1926 that was further strengthened by the Treaty of Conciliation signed on January 24, 1929. The desire of Stresemann to make friendship with the USSR, however, stood as a source of irritation to the statesmen of London and France. Besides, when it was given that Germany would be offered a seat in the League Council, it was feared by her that she might sometimes be called upon not only to allow League troops to cross her territory for action against the Soviets but even to contribute to such an action herself. Impressed with the anti-Soviet complexion of the Baldwin-Chamberlain cabinet, Moscow also had misgivings about the 'seemingly western orientation' of German policy which, it was feared, might result in Soviet isolation from Europe. "After protracted *pourparlers* between the various chancellories, Germany agreed to accept interpretation of her obligations under Art. 16 of the Covenant in the sense that she would be bound to join in collective League action only in so far as her 'disarmed' condition and geographical position allowed."[18]

It is now clear that by this time the initiatives of Stresemann could achieve certain diplomatic gains which, though less tangible, were nevertheless very real. Germany, instead of remaining like a passive object of international diplomacy, had re-entered the family of nations. She had become a full-fledged member of the League Assembly and given a semi-permanent seat in the Council with this understanding that she would be given a 'permanent' seat in a very short time to come. The pace of improvement continued. At the League Assembly of 1928, Germany and her creditors agreed that a committee of financial experts should be appointed to work out 'a complete and definite settlement of the reparation problem'. If this were realised, France declared that she would be willing to effect the Rhineland evacuation without delay. The successful consequence of all this was the Young Plan that provided a final settlement of the question of reparations.

In August 1928, Germany along with other nations of the world signed the Kellogg-Briand Pact that stood for the renuncia-

---

18. Ibid., p. 549.

tion of war as an instrument of national policy. Then, at the Hague Conference of August 1929, Stresemann persuaded his French counterpart to lift military occupation from the Rhineland. His pleadings proved successful. Thus, the last important achievement of the Stresemannian diplomacy was the evacuation of the Rhineland in 1930—five years earlier than the completion of the terms as laid down in the Treaty of Versailles. It all enables us to endorse that the evacuation of the Rhineland and the final settlement of the reparation question, that was destined to be so soon undone, were the two great and successful consequences of the diplomacy pursued by Stresemann and, as such, "the last important events of the period of pacification".[19]

Great Economic Depression and the Rise of Hitler : Trend Towards Inauguration of the Policy of Blood and Iron

The Stresemann era came to an end on October 13, 1929, when the architect of the policy of national reconstruction and reconciliation through international cooperation passed away. He was succeeded by Muller who resigned on March 19, 1930, and thus cleared the way for Dr. Heinrich Bruning who gave a new direction to German foreign policy that had its confluence with the line of Hitler. Inspired by the nineteenth century ideal of Greater Germany, he looked towards what was explicitly prohibited by the peace settlements. For instance, he desired Germany's union with Austria, her resort to the path of armament, and termination of the payment of reparation instalments. Not only this, with a view to materialise his designs, he assumed extra-constitutional powers. As we shall see, it all paved the way for the emergence of a strong man like Hitler that effected the end of the Weimar Republic and instead inauguration of the system of totalitarianism of the right.

Distinctly in violation of the terms of the Treaty of St. Germain, Bruning looked upon Austria as a bridge into the Balkans. For this purpose, he sponsored the proposal for a customs union with Austria that was published in Vienna on March 21, 1931.[20] It was vehemently opposed by Britain, Italy, France and Czechoslovakia. The British government brought the issue before the League of Nations and the latter at the proposal of France referred the

---
19. Carr, op. cit., p. 129.
20. See A.B. Keith (ed.): *Speeches and Documents on International Affairs, 1918-1937*, (London: Oxford Univ. Press, 1938), Vol. I, pp. 212-16.

matter to the Permanent Court of International Justice for having its advisory opinion. By a narrow margin of 8 to 7 votes, the Court ruled against the proposal of customs union. As a result, Dr. Curtius, the last representative of the line of Stresemann resigned in disgrace and his portfolio of Foreign Affairs was taken over by Chancellor Bruning. Its immediate effect was that the Nazis "redoubled their propaganda against the Versailles Treaty."[21]

Another bold step taken by Bruning was to resort to secret rearmament of Germany. In clear violation of the Military Decree of March 18, 1921, passed in pursuance of the implementation of the Treaty of Versailles, Bruning's Minister for the Reichwehr (General von Schleicher) started equipping the army with new weapons and providing them with the means of anti-tank defence.[22] In September 1931, large-scale manoeuvre took place in the city of Frankfurt and on July 26, 1932, Schleicher announced the details of his military re-organisation plan designed to convert the 100,000 troops into a modern army. Thus when the World Disarmament Conference opened in Geneva on February 2, 1932, Bruning frankly advanced the proposal that all weapons prohibited to Germany by the Treaty of Versailles be regarded as aggressive and they be internationally abolished. In any event, he insisted, Germany "was entitled to and would demand 'equality of status' in whatever convention might be negotiated."[23]

But the great worldwide economic depression came to Bruning as the most handy factor. In repudiation of several provisions of the Weimar Constitution he assumed semi-dictatorial powers in the name of dealing with the problems of a severe economic crisis. Now he found a natural alibi for the non-payment of reparation under the obtaining conditions. To his great satisfaction the creditor powers took such a decision at the Lausanne Conference of June 1932, when they cut down Germany's obligations to a total cash of only $750 million. Even this amount was not paid. In spite of this,

---

21. Carr, op. cit., p. 139. It may be added at this stage that France became critical of such a proposal in spite of the fact that it had been mooted by Briand in the recent past. The reason was that such a manoeuvre "was viewed as an attempt not only to sabotage the Briand project but also to achieve the Anschluss by an indirect route." Sharp and Kirk, op. cit., p. 566.
22. By this decree, conscription was abolished; the strength of the army was reduced to 100,000 volunteers with 4,000 officers; and the naval strength was limited to 15,000 men with 1,500 officers.
23. Sharp and Kirk, op. cit., p. 596.

the deteriorating economic condition of the country had its direct impact upon the political conditions. Most of the people were looking forward to a leader who could restore the conditions of political and economic stability in the country. Highlighting the prevailing condition, it was well commented: "The middle class had been turned into a proletariat and the working masses had fallen to the rank of a disqualified 'fourth estate'. Disillusioned and rebellious youth ran to either Communism or Nazism seeking refuge either in a Totalitarian State of German inspiration or in that which the Russian Revolution had conjured up."[24]

The short period of Bruning's Chancellorship not only marked a change in the course of German foreign policy, it laid the foundations on which Hitler could build his edifice as designed in his *Mein Kampf* a couple of years back. The labours of the Weimar constitution-makers came to an end when Hitler was appointed as Chancellor in 1932 after the forced exit of Schleicher by President Hindenburg. The Nazi party swept the polls of March 1933 and then Hitler became the Chancellor again with the so-called massive mandate of the people, though it was all manipulated after the suppression of all dissident forces in the time preceding the election on the charge of setting fire to the Reichstag.[25] More astounding was the day when after the death of Hindenburg, on August 2, 1934, Hitler assumed the office of the President as well. "The supreme and final authority in all matters was Hitler himself, later to be known officially as *Der Fuhrer* (an appellation he had assumed some years before the Nazis gained control of the government). This principle of leadership (*Fuhrerprinzipo*) was calculated to emphasise the unity of purpose of the whole nation."[26]

Thus came to an end the Weimar Republic and with it a foreign policy of national reconciliation and reconstruction in keeping forcibly with the dictates of peace settlements devised at Paris. Instead, a new era started that undid what was done so far.

---

24. Edmond Vermeil: *Germany in the Twentieth Century* (New York: Harper, 1956), p. 52.
25. In December 1933 a young Netherlander (Marinus von der Lubbe) was arrested on the charge of setting fire to the Reichstag. He was found guilty and executed in January 1934. Lubbe had set the fire in the hope that it would trigger an uprising against the Nazis, but it went to their advantage. See Fritz Tobias: *The Reichstag Fire* (New York: G.P. Putnam's Sons, 1964).
26. W.C. Langsam: *The World since 1919* (Delhi: Surjeet Pub., 1981), p. 143.

Once again it became evident that the world politics would revolve around the Third Reich. It is well observed: "In summary, Republican Germany's foreign policy encountered a succession of defeats at the hands of France and attained none of its major objectives. The circumstances helped to discredit Germany. The psychic insecurities bred of national defeat and impotence were aggravated by social insecurities engendered by currency inflation and general impoverishment ..... When the great depression descended upon the Reich, it created potentially revolutionary conditions once more....The Nazi Messiah appealed to the masses by combining the vocabulary of socialism with the language of impassioned chauvinism and racial hatred."[27]

The Nazi Political Testament : Role of Ideology in German Foreign Policy
The growth of the National Socialist (Nazi) Party dates from 1919 when Hitler joined the German Workers' Union founded by Drexler a year before. Some of the important items of the 25-Point Programme of this party announced in 1920 were:
1. We demand the union of all Germans to form a Great Germany on the basis of the right of self-determination enjoyed by nations.
2. We also demand equality of rights for the German people in their dealings with other nations, and abolition of the peace treaties of Versailles and of St. Germain.
3. Land and territories (colonies) should be acquired for the nourishment of our people and for settling our excess population.
4. None but members of the nation may be citizens of the state; none but other than those of German blood, whatever their creed, may be members of the nation. No Jew, therefore, may be a member of the nation.
5. Anyone who is not a citizen of the state may live in Germany only as a guest.
6. The right of voting on the leadership and legislation is to be enjoyed by the state alone.
7. Foreign nationals (non-citizens) must be excluded from the Reich.

---
27. Schuman, op. cit., pp. 557-58.

8. All non-German immigration must be prevented.
9. The activities of the individual may not clash with the interests of the whole, but must proceed within the frame of the community and before the general good.
10. In view of the enormous sacrifices of life and property demanded of a nation by every war, personal enrichment due to a war must be regarded as a crime against the nation.[28]

Soon after joining this organisation, Hitler laid stress on the unleashing of a New Order by invoking National Socialism capable of preparing for war-like revenge. In 1920, the organisation became National Socialist German Workers' Union. It adopted a 3-Point Programme of foreign policy—union of all people of the German race by the right of self-determination in one Great Germany, cancellation of the Treaties of Versailles and St. Germain, and acquisition of more territory for the settlement of surplus German population. Apart from giving such an ambitious programme to the organisation, Hitler also made efforts for the materialisation of his plans. In August 1921, he organised Assault Groups that rendered to the organisation the character of a para-military body. In September 1923, the German Fighting Front was created to avenge the defeat of Hitler in the unsuccessful coup of May 1923 and his consequent detention in the Fortress of Landsberg. Here he wrote the first part of his *Mein Kampf* that was supplemented with the second part after his release in 1926.

That Germany would follow a policy of blood and iron under Hitler could be easily understood if one had a chance to go through his 'Political Testament of the German Nation' as contained in the Second Part of his *Mein Kampf*. It embodied these rules which would, as the author confidently affirmed, always be valid for its conduct towards the outside world:[29]
1. "Never permit the Continental Powers to arise in Europe. Should any attempt be made to organise a second military Power on the German frontier by the creation of a State which may be a Military Power, with the prospect of an aggression against Germany in view, such an event confers on Germany not only the right but the duty to prevent by every means, including military means, the creation of such a State and to

---

28. See Louis L. Snyder: *Documents of German History* (Brunswick, New Jersey: Rutgers University Press, 1958), pp. 393-94.
29. Hitler, op. cit., pp. 366-67.

crush it if created. See to it that the strength of our nation does not rest on colonial foundations but on those of our own native territory in Europe. Never consider the Reich secure unless, for centuries to come, it is in a position to give every descendent of our race a piece of ground and soil that he can call his own. Never forget that the most sacred of all rights in this world is man's right to the earth which he wishes to cultivate for himself and that the holiest of all sacrifices is that of the blood poured out of it.

2. "In speaking of the German alliance problem, England and Italy are the only two countries with which it would be worthwhile for us to strive to form a close alliance. But the military consequences of forming this alliance would be the direct opposite of the consequences of an alliance with Russia. Most important of all is the fact that a *rapprochement* with England and Italy would in no way involve a danger of war. The only Power that could oppose such an arrangement would be France; and France would not be in a position to make war.

3. "But the alliance should allow Germany the possibility of making those preparations in all tranquillity which, within the framework of such a coalition, might in one way or another be requisite in view of a regulation of accounts with France. For the full significance of such an alliance lies in the fact that on its conclusion Germany would no longer be subject to the threat of a sudden invasion. The coalition against her would disappear automatically : that is to say, the Entente which brought such disaster to us. Thus, France, the mortal enemy of our people, would be isolated. And even though at first this success would have only moral effect, it would be sufficient to give Germany such liberty of action as we can not now imagine. For the new Anglo-German-Italian alliance would hold the political initiative and no longer France.

4. "A further success would be that at one stroke Germany would be delivered from her unfavourable strategical situation. On the one side, her flank would be strongly protected; and, on the other, the assurance of being able to improve her foodstuffs and raw materials would be a beneficial result of this new alignment of States.

5. "But almost of greater importance would be the fact that this new League would include States that possess technical quali-

ties which mutually supplement each other. For the first time, Germany would have allies who would not be as vampires on her economic body but would contribute their part to complement our technical equipment.
6. "And we must not forget a final fact: namely, that in this case we should not have allies resembling Turkey and Russia today. The greatest World Power on this earth and a young national State would supply for other elements for a struggle in Europe than the putrescent carcasses of the State with which Germany was allied in the last war.
7. "The future goal of our foreign policy ought not to involve an orientation to the East or the West, but it ought to be an Eastern policy which will have in view the acquisition of such territory as is necessary for our German people. To carry out this policy we need that force which the mortal enemy of our nation, France, now deprives us by holding us in her grip and pitilessly robbing us of our strength. Therefore, we must stop at no sacrifice in our effort to destroy the French striving towards hegemony over Europe. As our natural ally today, we have every Power on the Continent that feels France's lust for hegemony in Europe unbearable. No attempt to approach those powers ought to appear too difficult for us, and no sacrifice should be considered too heavy, if the final outcome would be to make it possible for us to overthrow our bitterest enemy. The minor wounds will be cured by the beneficent influence of time once the ground wounds have been cauterised and closed.
8. "We must oppose that current of public opinion which will be driven mad by Jewish cunning in exploiting our German thoughtlessness. The waves of this public opinion often rage and roar against us; but the man who swims with the current attracts less attention than he who buffets it. Today we are but a rock in the river.

"Therefore, it is necessary that in the eyes of the rest of the world our movement should be recognised as representing a definite and determined political programme."

The 'Political Testament' had a chance to be put to implementation after Hitler came to power the reasons for which may be given as under:

1. The rise of Nazism is gererally traced to the severity of the terms imposed upon Germany by the peace settlements of Paris. It is held that the degrading conditions of the peace settlements destroyed the self-esteem of the German people. "They had drained the cup of national humiliation to its dregs, and their feelings grew embittered towards their victorious adversaries. In their despondency, they blindly followed the leader who raised the banner of revolt and flung defiance in the face of their unconscionable taskmasters."[30]
2. More important than this was the fear of the rise and growth of communism in Germany. In the elections to the Reichstag the strength of the Communists increased from 77 in 1930 to 89 in 1932 and then to 100 in the new elections of the same year. Big businessmen supplied funds to the Nazis to beat the growing power of the Communists and others belonging to the extreme left. Even after the seizure of power in 1932, the Nazis "continued to exploit the prevailing dread of Communism and pose as a bulwark against a world revolution."[31]
3. The economic conditions of Germany played their own part in this regard. Nazis exploited with marked success the diverse elements of unrest which were seething in the cauldron of disaffection. They worked upon the anti-capitalist feelings of the lower middle class, composed of peasants and small tradesmen, to whom they made lavish promises. They drew to their side the victims of inflated currency whose incomes had been wiped out by the depreciation of the Mark. Above all, they enlisted in their cause the battalions of unemployed youth. The great 'economic blizzard' "shook the pillars of the unstable regime in Germany and brought them crashing to the ground. The old political parties were forced to give way before the onslaught of the young and confident upstart which

---

30. Lipson, op. cit., p. 388. This writer is not in favour of attaching prime importance to the factor of peace settlements in the rise of Nazism in Germany in the light of certain facts like emergence of her status after the Locarno agreements of 1925 culminating in her membership of the League of Nations in 1926, evacuation of the Rhineland in 1930, end of the payment of reparation in 1932, even her equality with other Powers in respect of armament etc. These facts lay down that the Versailles Treaty was the 'subsidiary cause' of the success of the Nazis. Ibid.
31. Ibid., p. 389.

Germany

claimed to have a panacea for every economic malady."[32]

4. Reference should also be made to the resurgence of militant German nationalism aiming at anti-Semitism and Pan-Germanism. They looked for a strong man who could restore the international status of their country after taking revenge from her sworn enemies like France. Since Hitler had already given his political testament, he became people's favourite choice. They loudly admired the aphorism of their leader: "To forge a mighty sword is the task of the internal political leadership of a people; to protect the forging and to seek allies in arms is the task of a foreign policy."[33]

Keeping all these factors in view, Langsam says: "The war and the peace settlement left Germany crashed, spiritually and materially. The Germans could not easily forget the humiliation of the defeat and the 'dictate' of Versailles. The continuing hostile attitude of France, the quarrels over the Ruhr, the Rhineland occupation, the Saar and reparation, the wrangling over disarmament—all these fed the anger of many Germans. In such circumstances, the republic's policy of reconciliation and its fulfilment, and its apparent inability to assert itself more strongly in international affairs rankled in the hearts of many, especially the younger and veterans and the youth that believed itself deprived of a glamorous and secure future by the 'treachery' and 'cowardice of seemingly complacent republican politicians. During a temporary economic revival from 1924 to 1929, these factors remained somewhat in the background. But they continued to exist, and it required only few years of hard times and increasing unemployment to bring them out in full force. Many of the Germans, too were weary of the manner in which the democratic parliamentary system functioned. Those Germans who could remember the days when order and discipline prevailed in the Reichstag, and many of those who had merely heard or read about such days, were impatient with the bickering and quarrelling that characterised the republican lower house. Increasingly, many Germans became convinced of the need for a 'strong man' to restore German prosperity and prestige."[34]

---

32. Ibid., p. 391.
33. See Schuman, op. cit., pp. 560-61.
34. Langsam, op. cit., p. 142.

Main Propositions of Hitler's Foreign Policy: Transformation of Mein Kampf's Words into Deeds

If the keynote of German foreign policy in the period of 1920-32 was how to throw off the burden of unjust reparation by pursuing the policy of national reconstruction and reconciliation, in the period of 1933-39 it became how to re-establish a Great Germany by sticking to the policy of blood and iron. The apparent difference between the two phases may be highlighted in other words by pointing out that while in the first phase of the Weimar Republic the German statesmen cautiously pursued the policy of national resurgence with the cooperation of friendly states like Britain and the United States, in the phase of the Third Reich they took to the course of a tooth for a tooth and an eye for an eye with certain deep motives like revision of the peace settlements not only for the sake of getting back what had already been lost but, more than that, for the sake of satisfying an aggressive nationalism, that stood for the restoration of the German Empire. Now it shall be worthwhile to have a study of the main propositions of German foreign policy as outlined in the *Mein Kampf* put to implementation after the assumption of power by Hitler. These are:

1. Pan-Germanism

The central theme of this proposition was the establishment of great state including all people of the superior German race. The movement of *Pax Teutonica* meant the creation of a Great German State with a powerful government organised according to the provisions of a new constitution and based on the political beliefs and values of the German nation. Called by the name of the 'German Reich', it signified the formation of a Great German nation-state. It automatically implied that territorial areas belonging to other states but inhabited by the majority of the German people belonging to the Aryan race should form part of the German Reich. Taking inspiration from the Wilsonian principle of national self-determination, it insisted that the German people living in other countries like Austria and Czechoslovakia be permitted to decide their political destiny by means of a plebiscite. In short, it demanded the union of all people of the Nordic race by the right of self-determination in one Great Germany.[35]

---

35. Gathorne-Hardy, op. cit., p. 362. On this point, Sir Eyre Crowe says: "The vague and undefined schemes of Teutonic expansion are but the expressions of the

2. Treaty Revisionism

Allied with what we said above was the point of treaty revisionism. The peace settlements made at Paris had destroyed the great German empire ruled by the Hohenzollern dynasty. Several areas of Germany were given to other states of Europe, while her extra-colonial possessions were placed under the charge of the League of Nations. Hitler demanded that all this should be revised. On March 1, 1937, Nazi Foreign Minister (Ribbentrop) declared at a Leipzig fair: "Germany claims in the world, even the smallest, has this right. She, therefore, repudiates all arguments which deny this right to her .... The question of raw materials, i.e., the necessity for Germany to possess territories where she can develop sources of raw materials by means of her own German currency and from which she can buy raw materials for the supply of the German industries and pay for them in her own currency of which we have not a sufficient quantity .... Quite apart from the fact that every colony in itself must in case of war be considered lost for Germany, the recently signed naval agreement between Germany and Great Britain is certainly the best and most practical proof against such contentions."[36]

3. Move Towards the East

To establish a grand reich of the German people and also to seek a restoration of the lost German territories made it essential for Hitler to lay down the policy of *Drang Nach Osten*. Austria, Czechoslovakia and Poland fell prey to the advancing German troops on account of their being in the east. Moreover, since the Soviet Union was the last state in the east and as she had a

---

deeply rooted feeling that Germany has by the strength and purity of her national purpose, the fervour of patriotism... the successful pursuit of every branch of public and scientific activity and the elevated character of her philosophy, art, and ethics, established for herself and the right to assert the primacy of German national ideals. And as it is an axiom of her political faith that right, in order that it may prevail, must be backed by force the transition is easy to the belief that the 'good German sword' which plays so large a part in patriotic speech, is there to solve any difficulties that may be in the way of establishing the reign of those ideals in a Germanised world" See G.P. Gooch and H. Temperley (ed.): *British Documents on the Origin of the War* (London: H.M.S.O., 1926-1938), Vol. III, p: 397.

36. Cited in Simonds and Emeny, op. cit., p. 214, n 1.

Communist order, Hitler's last ambition was to deal with the 'enemy of liberalism'. It is here that the roots of the policy of appeasement followed by Britain, France and the United States lay embedded.[37]

4. France as Germany's Mortal Foe

Hitler's proposition of 'move towards the east should, however, be studied in the light of his equally forceful assertion that France was the deadliest enemy of Germany. Since France lay in the West, one could take it for granted that by following the policy of 'move towards the east' Hitler would not attack any country like Britain, Belgium and France, since they existed in the west. In a public speech on January 30, 1937, he said: "As to France, Germany has repeatedly and solemnly declared—and I desire to reiterate here—that between Germany and France there are no humanly conceivable points of dispute and there can be none. The German government has assured also Belgium and Holland that it is prepared to recognise and guarantee the inviolability of their territories."[38] The coming events showed that it was all an exercise in deceit. After 1937 the method of Germany "followed the historic precedent set by Bismarck in settling accounts with one adversary after another, while in the meantime she carefully declaimed all

---

37. Many of the ideas expounded in the *Mein Kampf* conflicted with each other when their realisation was attempted. S.H. Roberts, a skilful commentator of the Nazi foreign poicy, depicted it as 'torn between three alternatives—the opportunist, the Eastern, and the Western'. In the post-1933 period, while Hitler's 'eastern' conception frankly emphasised expansion, the 'western' conception apparently desired collaboration. However, it was all like a makeshift arrangement. There could be no sense in believing that Hitler would stick to the course of collaboration with France in a sincere way for the reason that he had specifically written in the *Mein Kampf*: "French nation, which is slowly dying out, not so much through depopulation as through the progressive disappearance of the best element of the race, can continue to play an important role in the world only if Germany be destroyed. French policy may make a thousand detours on the march towards its fixed goal but the destruction of Germany is the end which it always has in view as the fulfilment of the most profound yearning and ultimate intentions of the French. Now it is a mistake to believe that if the will on one side should remain only *passive* and intent on its own self-preservation it can hold out permanently against another will which is not less forceful but is active." op. cit. Ch. XV.
38. Cited in Simonds and Emeny, op. cit., p. 221.

Germany

aggressive intentions in other quarters.[39]

5. Anti-Communism

Since Hitler justified the case of totalitarianism of the right, he had no reservations in being the sworn enemy of Communism at home and abroad. Shortly after coming to power, he suppressed all opposition elements, including the Communists, and manifested the anti-Russian stance of his foreign policy. The anti-Bolshevism of Hitler synchronised with his anti-Semitism. He considered Russia, once a great state built by the people of the Nordic race fallen under the rule of the Jews. Thus, he put : "In delivering Russia over to Bolshevism, Fate robbed the Russian people of that intellectual class which had once created the Russian state and were the guarantee of its existence. For the Russian state was not organised by the constructive political talent of the Slav element in Russia, but was much more a marvellous exemplification of the capacity for State-building possessed by the Germanic element in a race of inferior worth.... And the end of the Jewish domination in Russia will also be the end of Russia as a State. We are chosen by Destiny to be the witnesses of a catastrophe which will afford the strongest condemnation of the nationalist theory of race."[40]

6. Anti-Internationalism

Last, Hitler preferred the course of making Germany a big power in the world by taking to the path of armed struggle in flagrant violation of all rules of international law and morality. Thus, he remilitarised the Rhineland and denounced the League of Nations as a 'dreamy discovery' of the Allied powers. The re-occupation of the Rhineland was described by Ribbentrop not as a preparation

---

39. Lipson, op. cit., p. 402.
40. Hitler, op. cit., pp. 360-61. While hitting at the ideas and successes of the Communists, Hitler recorded: "Today Germany is the next battlefield for Russian Bolshevism. All the force of a fresh missionary idea is needed to raise up our nation once more, to rescue it from the coils of the international serpent and stop the process of corruption which is taking place in the internal constitution of our blood, so that the forces of our nation, once liberated, be employed to preserve our nationality and prevent the repetition of the recent catastrophe from taking place even in the most distant future. If this be the goal we set to ourselves it would be folly to ally ourselves with a country whose master is the mortal enemy of our future." Ibid., pp. 364-65.

for another attack on France rather as the German bolting of the back door so as to insure eventual freedom of action on the eastern front. After remilitarising the Rhineland, Hitler proudly declared on September 9, 1936: "Our greatest achievement is that we have broken the last shackles of Versailles and re-established our supremacy in the Rhineland." In his great work, Hitler had already recorded: "Thus the German nation could assure its own future only by being a World Power. Germany is not at all a World Power today. Even though our present military weaknesses could be overcome, we still would have no claim to be called a World Power. At an epoch in which the World is being gradually portioned out among states many of whom almost embrace whole continents, one cannot speak of a World Power in the case of a State whose political motherland is confined to territorial area of barely five hundred thousand square kilometres."[41]

The *Mein Kampf* had shown Hitler's mind in 1926. But the way Hitler dissolved the Reichstag and contested re-election in 1933 after liquidating all opposition elements, that caused the quasi-withdrawal of some other moderate elements, were the bold events signifying that "mysterious warnings were soon current of some remarkable occurrence in the days immediately preceding this event."[42] By sticking to the course of appeasement, the lovers of liberalism sitting in London, Paris and Washington failed to grasp 'a golden opportunity never to be repeated.'[43] Things went on moving so much so that Hitler's deputy (Herr Hess) said on June 19, 1938: "It had not been possible under the old democratic system to rearm secretly in defiance of the Treaty of Versailles, because pacifists.... were always ready to reveal these designs to the world."[44]

German Diplomacy under Hitler: First Phase of Resurgence and Consolidation of Nazism

Generally, it is said that German diplomacy underwent a basic

---

41. Ibid., p. 354.
42. See J.W. Wheeler-Bennett: "The New Regime in Germany" in *International Affairs*, London, 1933, p. 315.
43. Gathorne-Hardy, op. cit., p. 365.
44. Ibid.

change after the termination of the Weimar Republic in view of the explanation that Hitler abandoned the course of national reconciliation and reconstruction through international cooperation and instead took to the way of 'blood and iron' so as to restore the grandeur of the German Reich. Such a view is not correct, however, if we take into consideration the fact that ever since the imposition of a dictated peace, the people of Germany on account of suffering from persecution complex wanted to repudiate all what was done at Paris. It is a different matter that while Stresemann struggled and succeeded in resurging the status of his country by following a policy of conciliation and compromise, Hitler could do the same by adhering firmly to the policy of blood and iron. A sort of continuity may, therefore, be discovered in the diplomacy of Germany in the period following the First World War. This fact is corroborated with this plausible interpretation that "to understand the national policy of a great power, it is necessary to see into the soul of its people. Deep in the German soul has been the corroding sense of wrongs remediable only by the force of German arms and constituting in themselves the enduring evidence of the relentless purpose of the victors of the Versailles."[45]

However, a study of the German diplomacy under Hitler may be put into two phases. While the first phase of 1933-36 displays his endeavour for consolidating his position by resorting to the strategy of pacts and alliances, the second phase of 1937-1939 shows his open attempt for implementing the principles of Pan-Germanism, anti-Semitism, anti-Communism, anti-internationalism and the like as so boldly outlined in his *Mein Kampf*. The main events of this period may be enumerated as under:

1. When British Prime Minister (Ramsay MacDonald) and his Foreign Secretary (Sir John Simon) visited Rome in March, 1933

---

45. Simonds and Emeny, op. cit., p. 231. So says Schuman: "The Third Reich pursued the same general diplomatic objectives as the Weimar Republic but utilised in place of conciliation and compromise the methods of treaty-breaking threats and defiance. But to these old objectives were added new ones far more alarming to Germany's neighbours. Mystical racial Pan-Germanism contemplated the ultimate liberation of all Germans abroad and the nation with the Reich of Austria, German Switzerland, the Sudeten Deutsch of Czechoslovakia, the Germans of Danzig, the Corridor, the Baltic States, and other irredentist areas. Beyond these lived other 'Nordics' who ought also willy-nilly, to join the Reich—the Flemings, the Dutch, the Scandinavians." op. cit., p. 560.

and had a meeting with Mussolini, a proposal was mooted for concluding a pact of understanding and cooperation. Now the Duce presented a draft seeking revision of the peace treaties, Germany's right to disarm in the event of failure of the disarmament conference, and co-ordination of the policy of the signatory powers (Britain, France, Italy and Germany) in all extra-European ques- tions. In opposition to this, the French draft desired cooperation of all states within the framework of the League of Nations and joint consideration for dealing with the problem of armament in case the disarmament conference broke down. Hitler rejected these terms, but he gave his consent on the pleadings of Mussolini. As a result, the representatives of Britain, France, Italy and Germany met at Rome and signed a pact on July 15, 1933 (called Four-Power Pact) wherein they expressed their faith in the Covenant of the League, the provisions of the Locarno Treaty and the Pact of Paris, and cooperation to each other in dealing with the problems of peace and disarmament.

2. But the insincerity of such a move was clear for all when Hitler, in the midst of the professions of peace and further pleas for equality of the German nation, proclaimed the withdrawal of Germany from the League of Nations and International Labour Organisation on October 14, 1933. In this way, he could absolve his country from all international obligations. On May 11, 1934, President Hindenburg said: "In their foreign politics the German people have to travel the road to cavalry. A frightful Treaty has weighed heavily upon us and has threatened, in its ever-increasing consequences, to bring our nation to a point of collapse. For a long time, the world around us has failed to understand that Germany must live, not only for her own sake, but also as the standard bearer of western civilisation, for the sake of Europe."[46]

3. The same day Hitler declared withdrawal of his country from the World Disarmament Conference in session at Geneva. Later, on March 10, 1935, the world was told that German Air Force was in existence. A few days after, promulgation of the Law for the Reconstruction of the National Defence Forces was announced and military conscription was introduced. Then, in the month of October, the German General Staff with General Ludwig Beck as Chief was re-established. In pursuance of the same policy, he

---

46. See Snyder, op. cit., p. 422.

Germany

announced the abrogation of the Locarno agreements and remilitarisation of the Rhineland. On August 24, 1936, German military service was extended from one year to two years.

4. On January 26, 1934, Germany signed a 10-year non-aggression pact with Poland. Ever since the conclusion of the Locarno pacts (whereby Germany had recognised her western frontiers touching France and Belgium), Poland had become critical of the French diplomacy in view of the fact that the question relating to the eastern frontiers of Germany was ignored. Moreover, after the conclusion of the Four-Power Pact in 1933, Poland had become more concerned with the problem of her safety from the side of any German attack. For this purpose, Poland accepted the course offered by Germany.

5. According to the peace settlement, Saar with a German population of nearly three-quarters of a million was put under a League of Nations Commission for 15 years after which the people of this area were to decide their political destiny through a referendum. In early January 1935, the plebiscite took place under the control of the Plebiscite Commission. As a result of this, Saar was merged with Germany on March 1, 1935.

6. When Hitler's rash move in seeking annexation of Austria with Germany proved abortive owing to strong opposition of Mussolini, he changed the course of his diplomacy. On July 16, 1936, Germany entered into an accord with Austria recognising her independence and reopening of German trade and travel with Vienna.

7. Now Italy and Germany came closer as the latter had supported the action of the former in the Abyssinian war. On October 25, 1936, Germany and Italy signed an agreement providing for collaboration of the two states in all matters affecting their 'parallel' interests, economic co-operation in the Danubian region, and defence of the European civilisation against Communism. For this sake they rendered support to the revolt of General Franco in Spain.

8. With a resolve to fight Communism, Germany made another pact with Japan on November 25, 1936 whereby the two parties agreed to inform each other about the activities of the Comintern and to consult each other in matters concerning fight against this menace before taking any important and effective step.

A study of all these developments shows that German diplomacy during the last three years had become highly dynamic. The achievement of the Weimar Republic, which in the view of the Nazis was a symbol of defeat in war and of humiliation in peace had been overthrown as the French for the same reason had dismissed the Bourbons fifteen years after Waterloo".[47] The League of Nations which she joined in 1926 became "like a Trojan horse of Allied diplomatic strategy and when Hitler assumed power, his delegate came to Geneva with a mind to move the League in the direction of treaty revisionism so as to test its sincerity as a measure of its idealistic nature. But when to them the right of self-defence was denied, the German people followed Hitler out of the League, disillusioned and disgusted."[48]

The Second Phase: Course of Conquest and Annexation Leading to the Second World War

As already pointed out, the second phase of Hitler's diplomacy (1937-1939) looks like a culmination of what he could do over the last three years. The pace of the policy of blood and iron became more rapid and now the Fuhrer did not hesitate in revealing the real meaning of his *Mein Kampf*. First Austria, then Czechoslovakia and, finally, Poland became the victims of Nazi aggression. Ultimately, the statesmen of Britain and France had to give up the counter-productive strategy of appeasement and, surprisingly, while being the enemies of Communism, they had to join hands with the Soviet Union. The net result was the second World War in which Germany witnessed her doom. If so, let us enumerate major events in the following manner:

1. Hitler made a rash move to destroy the independence of Austria in 1934 but retraced his step in 1936 and even signed an accord with this small state to recognise her territorial sovereignty and integrity. But he could never lose sight of the fact that the keys to Vienna were the keys to the gateway of the Near East. Thus, for releasing such a grandiose conception, Germany's union with Austria ('Anschluss') was the essential step. What he could not achieve in the first move, he did it in the second one. Austria became a part of the German Reich in 1938.

---

47. Simonds and Emeny, op. cit., p. 227.
48. Ibid., p. 229.

2. Then came the chance of Czechoslovakia. Bismarck had once said that the possessor of Bohemia held the two keys to Germany. But as a result of the peace settlements, the 'two keys' were placed in the hands of a newly created state of Czechoslovakia and that promptly aligned herself with France, the mortal foe of Germany. "From the Bohemia plateau Czech armies, borrowing the passes which had been famous in the wars of Fredrick the Great, could arrive in the Silesian plain and joining hands with the Poles above or below Breslau, open for them a safe passage of the order and a clear road to Berlin. In the same way, moving West along the valley of the Main, they could join hands with the French at Frankfurt, opening for them the passage of the Rhine and isolating South Germany from the North. Finally, Czech troops descending the Elbe could reach the Leipzig and Dresden which are unfortified, and beyond them penetrate to the very heart of Germany following the roads employed by Tilly and Wallenstein in Thirty Years War. Berlin had thus become a frontier town and an equally vulnerable target for Polish and Czech aircraft, which could easily be reinforced by French."[49] If so, Hitler could not resist himself from destroying the independence of Czechoslovakia after the annexation of Austria in 1938. At the Munich meet he got a big share of the Sudetenland and the rump was devoured in a couple of months.

3. Since the Spanish uprising afforded a timely opportunity for the Fascist powers to intervene and strengthen the hands of their ally for the cause of an eventual struggle with the Communism of Russia, Hitler joined hands with Mussolini. The result was that the duly elected government of Spain was subverted by the rule of a military junta under Franco with the support of Germany and Italy. It attracted Hitler for one more reason. He now could have a strong friend on the other side of France already declared by him as the 'mortal enemy' of his country.

4. Last came the chance of Poland. The Nazi leader could not stop after the destruction of Czechoslovakia. Without caring for the threats and warning issued by the statesmen of Britain and France, he moved ahead to play with the independence of a small country. Invasion on Poland illustrated that the 10-year non-aggression treaty signed in 1934 was not done with a sincere intent.

---

49. Ibid., p. 203.

"The truce with Poland was a truce of necessity and not of reconciliation."[50]

It could all happen on account of the fact that by the end of 1938 Germany's power had enhanced to such an extent that, as compared to the power of other major nations of the world, it looked like a race between a lame man and an athlete. By all means, it now looked like promising to develop into a catastrophe. The moving step could not be checked by any force, whether internal or external, and a sensible student of international politics could register his impression in 1939 in these words: "The German people will have to pay for the sins of their 'leader'. Unhappily, this time they will not be able to excuse themselves by saying that the leader was not of their own choice.... The role of the man of violence is an unlovely one at best; it is foolish when the resources are so limited that the bullying and braggadocio turns into empty bluff or into calamitous defeat. Anyone considering the present German policy cannot help weeping at the way in which the future of Germany, Europe and the world is being recklessly jeopardised by incompetence, thirst for glory, and an indisciplined disregard of all the vital facts."[51]

Berlin-Moscow Non-Aggression Pact : Abandonment of the Ideological Basis of Foreign Policy

By this time, it had become quit clear that Germany's hunger for irredentism was not limited to the realisation of the oft-repeated goal of pan-Germanism. Instead it covered everything in the name of acquiring living space (*Lebensraum*) for her people. That is, it was another instrument of German imperialism. The destruction of Czechoslovakia in 1938 "had given a moral shock to the world not only because it had proved the falsity of assurances that the Sudetenland was the last demand in Europe, but because it gave lie also to the claim of the Fuhrer that his object was simply the recovery of German populations for the Reich. If in October 1938 three million Sudeten Germans were freed, in March 1939, eight million Czechs paid the price in enslavement. Here indeed was naked aggression, deprived of any disguise.... For the doctrine of 'self-determination' for the Germans outside the Reich was substi-

---

50. Ibid., p. 221.
51. Friedrich, op. cit., pp.185-86.

Germany

tuted the insistence on *Lebensraum* for the Reich itself—a claim for national self-fulfilment for which the plea on behalf of the German minorities served only as a cloak."[52]

Now Poland was to be conquered. But as British and French Premiers had shown their full preparedness to come to her rescue, it was required that she be isolated at least from the side of the Soviet Union. In this situation Stalin could also foresee some gains in the Baltic. Negotiations between Ribbentrop and Molotov proved eminently successful when the Berlin-Moscow Treaty of Non-Aggression was signed on August 23, 1939. Its terms were:[53]

1. The contracting parties obligated themselves to refrain from every act of force, every aggressive action and every attack against one another, including any single action taken in conjunction with other powers;
2. In case one of them should become the object of warlike acts by a third power, the other would in no way support the third party.
3. The two parties in future would remain in consultation constantly with one another in order to inform each other regarding questions of common interest.
4. Neither of the parties would associate itself with any other grouping of powers that, directly or indirectly, was aimed at the other party.
5. In the event of any conflict between the two parties on any question, they would adjust such a difference exclusively by friendly exchange of opinions or, if necessary, by an arbitration commission.
6. This treaty would remain in force for a period of ten years that, if neither of the parties announced its abrogation within one year of the expiration of this period, it would continue in force automatically for another period of five years.

The Nazi-Soviet non-aggression treaty came as a major 'bombshell', as commented by Chamberlain, into the Allied camp. Britain and France were seriously taken aback. Their efforts for having an alliance with the USSR as a measure to deal with the Nazi menace stood suddenly defeated at this juncture. With a single

---

52. A.J. Grant and H. Temperley: *Europe in the Nineteenth and Twentieth Centuries, 1789-1950* (London: Longmans, 1964), VI Ed., p. 35.
53. For text of the treaty see Sharp and Kirk, op. cit., p. 806.

stroke, Germany "had destroyed all this effort by an agreement which made it certain that the Soviet Union would not join in any anti-Nazi coalition."[54]

By all means, the conclusion of such a pact demonstrated a great diplomatic success for Hitler. Now he realised that a two-front war against Poland and Russia in the east with England and France in the west involved great strategic risks that he preferred to avoid. His calculation was that if Russia could be kept out of the conflict at least for some time, Poland would remain isolated and thus be crushed in a short time after which German forces would run Westward and then either conquer France or conclude peace with the Western powers. Consequently Hitler decided a *rapprochement* with Stalin. The latter also "perceived the advantages of the situation: it offered him easy territorial aggrandisements in the Baltic and at least a temporary breathing spell in the face of growing Nazi menace."[55]

Despite this all, Hitler failed in cashing capital out of this diplomatic victory on account of his bad motives. The pact signified abandonment of all ideological pretensions on both sides. But it was not to last for a considerable duration. The treaty completed the transformation, and gave a new shock to Europe. For both countries it meant renunciation of the ideological basis of foreign policy, for which few people outside the circles of high politics were prepared. As recently as May (1939), common ideologies "had vied with solidarity of interests as the foundation of the Italo-German alliance, and how could the new treaty be reconciled with the hatred of communism and of Russia which underlay the Anti-Comintern pact ? To the western democracies, at least, the logic of the situation was that German policy would henceforth be one purely of aggression."[56]

For such reasons, it was well remarked : "The cynical Nazi-Soviet Pact not only removed Hitler's last hesitation about attacking Poland but had other far-reaching repercussions. It was obviously a temporary arrangement, for it contravened Hitler's long-planned eastward expansion by allowing Russia to move west-

---

54. Ibid., p. 673.
55. John E. Rodes: *A Short History* (New York: Holt, Rinehart and Winston, 1964), p. 367.
56. Grant and Temperley, op. cit., p. 533.

Germany

ward. For a short while, by giving it access to Russian food and raw materials, particularly petroleum, it freed Germany from the fear of total war time blockade. But these transitory advantages could not conceal the fact that Hitler had violated the spirit and letter of the anti-communist ideology. Expediency had reached its high point. Rosenberg, the party philosopher, feared the consequences of Hitler's actions."[57] In his diary, two days after the signing of the Pact, he wrote : "I have the feeling that the Moscow pact will someday backfire National Socialism."[58]

The truth became clear just after a week when Germany put these proposals to Poland:
1. Danzig should return as a Free State into the framework of the German Reich.
2. Germany should receive a route through the corridor and a railway line at her own disposal having the same extra-territorial status for Germany as the corridor itself has for Poland.

In return Hitler said that Germany was prepared to
1. recognise all Polish rights in Danzig,
2. ensure for Poland a free harbour in Danzig of any size as disired and to which she (Poland) would have completely free access,
3. Thereupon to accept the frontiers between Germany and Poland to regard them as final,
4. Conclude a 25-year non-aggression pact with Poland, and
5. Safeguard the independence of Czechoslovakia jointly with Poland and Hungary, which meant in practice the renunciation of any unilateral German hegemony in this territory.

The Polish government rejected these proposals and showed its preparedness to negotiate concerning the question of a substitute for the League Commissioner, and consider facilities for thorough traffic across the corridor.[59]

---

57. J.E. Rodes, op. cit., p. 367.
58. Ibid.
59. See *Official German Documents relating to the World War* (New York; Oxford University Press, 1923), Volumes I and II and *Preliminary History of the Armistice*, Official Documents published by the German National Chancellory by order of the Ministry of State (New York: Oxford University Press, 1924, both works translated into English under the auspices of the Carnegie Endowment for International Peace Division of International Law).

Hitler's invasion on Poland confirmed the aphorism of Tacitus that 'hitherto no one, who has acquired power criminally, has used if for good ends.' The darkest chapter of German history became an epilogue to the story of the Second World War. It came to an end after revealing that the method of Hitler's strategy was first to create disorder and use terror, if necessary, in order to produce counter-terror and then to intervene allegedly with the aim of preventing civil war and chaos and of helping one's friends.[60]

Concluding Observations

A study of German foreign policy and diplomacy during the interwar period, particularly after the rise of Hitler in 1933, leaves these important impressions:

1. The foreign policy of Germany looks like a diplomatic record ranging from the forced acceptance of and compliance with the Treaty of Versailles by the rulers of the Weimar Republic to its frank denunciation and repudiation at the hands of the Nazi Fuhrer. All norms of international decency were thrown to the winds when the peace was dictated at Versailles in 1919. It was, indeed, a deplorable act on the part of the victors that they did not even allow the German Foreign Minister (Count Ratinjo) to say a few words on this occasion who, in stead, had to issue this statement in writing: "We are fully aware of the hatred which we have to face here and we have also heard passionate demands that the victorious nations will realise all the indemnities from us, who are defeated, and severely punish as criminals. It has been demanded from us to confess that we alone bear the responsibility for the war, but any such confession on my part would be a falsehood."[61] The zeal of victory made the victors blind to the long-range consequences of their actions, for they had comforted themselves with this emphatic assertion that Germany "was never given the assurance that the peace would be based on the Fourteen Points of Wilson."[62]

2. It is obvious that such a dictated peace was bound to be overthrown in due course when the people would discover a man

---

60. See Golo Mann: *The History of Germany since 1789* (London: Chatto and Windus, 1968), p. 454.
61. See Lord Ridel: *Intimate Diary of the Peace Conference and After*, p, 73.
62. D.C. Somervell: *Between Two Wars*, p. 70.

Germany

of iron and steel like Hitler. Though he professed to move in the east for the sake of satisfying his imperial hunger, he could never give up his design of destroying France so as to avenge the losses of 1919. The drive towards the east was just a ruse to mislead the west. Although German strategists "preferred a new Schleiffen Plan to crush France through Holland and Bulgaria, Hitler's professed objective was to keep peace in the west, while he moved forward in the east... With France checkmated and British neutrality assured, the *Drang Nach Osten* could be carried forward, until the Western powers should be outmanoeuvred, and made ripe for conquest."[63]

3. The policy of drive towards the east constituted the backbone of the policy of appeasement so obdurately pursued by Britain and France interested in seeing the destruction of Russian Communism. Had the statesmen of these major democracies, including the United States, under-stood the follies of such a policy, they could have easily checked the growing power of Hitler in time and thereby avert the great disaster that occurred in the form of the Second World War. The success of Hitler also suggested the bankruptcy of British and French diplomacy. "Step by step, the two democracies had retreated: when Hitler defied them by declaring conscription in 1935, when he occupied the Rhineland in 1936, when he demanded and got the Sudetenland, they had sat by weeks when he occupied the rest of Czechoslovakia in March 1939. With the Soviet Union on their side, they still might have dissuaded the German dictator from launching war or, if they failed, have fairly quickly defeated him in an armed conflict."[64]

In a word, the guiding principle of Hitler's foreign policy was 'divide and conquer'. An alliance with any country, whether France or the USSR, would serve the same purpose as her destruction.[65] Strategy informed him to win confidence of any country first and destroy her afterwards. Repudiation of all unjust treaties lost its justification in the end. Until the tragedy of Czechoslovakia, it could be admitted that Nazism was and could be a menace to world peace, for it was the child of opposition to the defeat of 1918 and

---

63. Schuman, op. cit., p. 562.
64. W.L. Shirer: *The Rise and Fall of the Third Retich: A History of Nazi Germany* (London: Sacker and Warburg, 1960), p. 543.
65. Robert Dell: *Germany Unmasked* (London: Martin Hopkins. 1934), p. 121.

the humiliation of the Treaty of Versailles "grasping at the stab-in-the-back theory to explain why the unbeatable Germany had not been victorious."66 But later events revealed the insatiable imperial hunger of the Fuhrer. "At first glance, the earlier policies of the Nazi regime give the appearance of being merely rectifications of what the Treaty of Versailles had done to the Germans and the Austrians. But closer study reveals that Hitler had never meant to leave it all that."67

---

66. Ralph Flonley: *Modern German History* (London: J.M. Dent & Sons, 1968), p. 380.
67. Peter H. Merkl: *German Foreign Policies: East and West: On the Threshold of a Neo-European Era* (Santa Barbara, California: American Bibliographical Centre, 1974), pp. 74-75. Also see Gerhard L. Weinberg: *The Foreign Policy of Hitler's Germany* (Chicago: University of Chicago Press, 1970), Ch. 2.

7

FRANCE

France must be preserved intact in order to remain France.... It was this observation for security that dictated French policy at the Paris Peace Conference. Clemenceau was not merely a vindictive old man imposing impossibly harsh terms upon a vanquished foe, he was also a realistic leader of France who had seen his country's territory ravaged twice in his life time and who intended to prevent a repetition if it were in his power.

—Graham H. Stuart[1]

In a work on international relations and politics during the inter-war period, a study of the foreign policy and diplomacy of France deserves a place after that of Germany. The reason behind it is that the rise of one remained dependent upon the fall of the other. That is, the low position of Germany remained a condition-precedent for the ascendancy of France. Moreover, as a victor power in the First World War, France had achieved much in political and economic terms for the suppression of her neighbour that was to be consolidated and preserved. In this way, any possibility of the resurgence of Germany stood as a nightmare for France. 'Security' became the watchword of French foreign policy. It is, therefore, rightly observed: "The most important and persistent single factor in European affairs in the years following 1919 was the French demand for security. Since 1870—and still more since 1914—France had been morbidly conscious of her weakness in face of Germany. She had turned the tables on the victor of 1871. What could be

---

1. Stuart: "The Struggle of France for Hegemony and Security' in Brown, Hodges and Roucek (ed.s): *Contemporary World Politics: An Introduction to the Study of International Relations* (New York: John Wiley & Sons, 1939), p. 146.

contrived to prevent Germany one day turning the tables on the victor of 1918?"[2]

Search for Security : Keynote of the Real Desire of France for Hegemony

As given in the preceding chapters and also hinted above, it may be asserted in the beginning of our study of French foreign policy that, to a very large part, it "was inspired by the desire to escape from the nightmare of another German invasion on the soil of France. It was as a measure promoting security from this that French statesmen had originally clamoured and schemed for a natural defensive frontier on the Rhine: the alliances of France with eastern European countries were similarly assumed in the interests of French security from German aggression, and French interest in the League of Nations was equally concentrated on its potentialities as a further reinforcement against the same danger."[3] Obviously, the demand for French security implied keeping Germany in a position of weakness so as to avoid every possible danger of invasion from the side of an eastern neighbour. In this way, security of the country became another term for the real desire of hegemony over the continent. "The attainment of security, i.e., the maintenance of hegemony over the Continent required that Germany be kept weak and that France be kept strong."[4]

Viewed in another perspective, it appears that the problem of security having its obverse side in the real desire for hegemony found its natural solution in the maintenance of the *status quo*. Let there be no revision of the peace settlements of 1919 that had crushed Germany to an extent so that she could never recover. French yearning for peace, for this reason, was informed not by any principle of internationalism as with the satisfaction of her own appetite now curiously synchronised with the condition of a happy international order. Prof. F.L. Schuman is, therefore, justified in holding: "Security became at once the guiding slogan of the Quai d' Orsay. Security meant assurance against invasion from the east.

---

2. E.H. Carr: *International Relations between the Two World Wars, 1919-1939* (London: Macmillan, 1952), pp. 25-26.
3. Gathorne-Hardy: *A Short History of International Affairs, 1920-1939* (London: Oxford Univ. Press, 1964), IV Ed. p. 423.
4. Schuman: *International Politics* (New York: McGraw Hill, 1948), IV Ed., p. 737.

Assurance against invasion was not to be had, in the opinion of the most patriotic Frenchmen, unless the prospective invader were kept in a position of political inferiority and military helplessness."[5] Again, "Security demanded peace. Peace demanded the *status quo* in its broad essentials. Preservation of the status quo demanded the maintenance of French hegemony; and, paradoxically, France was prepared to fight to maintain peace, i.e., French ascendancy, rather than yield the fruits of victory."[6]

Aware of this fact, the French statesmen demanded at the Paris Peace Conference several important arrangements like permanent demilitarisation of the Rhineland, fixation of the western frontier of Germany at river Rhine with its bridges under the control of French administration, and, above all, creation of a new state virtually under French protection covering 10,000 sq miles of territory between the Rhine in the east and the Netherlands, Belgium and France in the west. But Wilsonian idealism coupled with Georgian realism stood in the way. Both Wilson and George came forward with the argument that the materialisation of the French demand would involve separation of more than five million German people from their homeland and, as such, it would amount to the violation of the principle of national self-determination. And yet French demands could be satisfied to some extent. The Treaty of Versailles provided for permanent demilitarisation of the Rhineland and its placement under the charge of a Commission for 15 years—northern sector for 5 years, central sector for 10 years, and southern sector for 15 years.[7]

---

5. Ibid., pp. 736-37.
6. Ibid. p. 739.
7. The French desire for 'physical guarantees' meant the possession in perpetuity of the Rhineland and its bridges across which any invader from the east might pass. A French memorandum presented at the Paris Peace Conference in February 1919 said: "The danger comes from the possession by Germany of the left bank and the Rhine bridge.... The safety of the Western and Overseas Democracies makes it imperative, in present circumstances, for them to guard the bridges of the Rhine." See Carr, op. cit., p. 26. At the same time, Marshal Foch made this prophetic statement: "If we do not hold the Rhine permanently, there is no neutralisation, no disarmament, no written clause of any nature, which can prevent Germany from breaking out across it and gaining the upper hand. No aid could arrive in time from England or America to save France from complete defeat." Cited in W.L. Shirer: *The Collapse of the Third Republic*, p. 127.

Though the Treaty of Versailles could not satisfy French appetite for security to her desired extent, British and American statesmen adopted another way for this sake. After the conclusion of the Versailles Treaty, Britain signed a treaty with France on June 28, 1919, in which she agreed to come immediately to the latter's assistance in the event of any unprovoked aggression against her from the side of Germany.[8] At the same time, the United States signed a treaty with France stipulating that the former would be bound to come immediately to the latter's assistance in the event of any unprovoked attack on her from the side of Germany.[9]

But the failure of the United States to ratify the peace settlement made at Paris "rendered both the British and the American undertaking void. France felt herself cheated. She had abandoned her claim on the strength of a promise which was not honoured; and this grievance was an underlying factor through the subsequent discussions between France and Great Britain on the question of security. Having thus compelled to abandon her hope of a 'physical guarantee', France worked feverishly during the next four years to find compensation for her natural inferiority to Germany, and to allay her fear of German vengeance. She followed two separate and parallel methods: a system of treaty guarantees, and a system of alliances."[10]

At this moment French desire for security witnessed its coincidence with the universal quest for the same. The provisions of 'collective security', as enshrined in the Covenant of the League, provided some satisfaction to France. For instance, Art. 10 of the Covenant said: "The Members of the League undertake to respect and preserve as against external aggression the territorial integrity and existing political independence of all Members of the League. In case of any such aggression or in case of any threat or danger of such aggression the Council shall advise upon the means by which this obligation shall be fulfilled." To give effect to such a momentous provision, Articles 16 and 17 provided for sanctions or penalties against any state that resorted to war in disregard of its obligations.

---

8. For text of the treaty see H.W.V. Temperley (ed.): *A History of the Peace Conference of Europe* (London: Oxford University Press, 1920), Vol. 1, pp. 337-38.
9. Ibid., pp. 339-40.
10. Carr, op. cit., p. 27.

As per the decision of the Council, the members of the League were bound to break off economic and financial relations with an aggressor.

France took all these arrangements as inadequate. Her proposal to create an international army, that alone could make the decision of sanctions effective against an aggressor state, had been emphatically negatived by Britain and the United States. More shocking event was the withdrawal of the American commitment that cast serious doubts on the efficiency, or even possibility, of a financial or economic blockade. Even this small measure of confidence in the machinery of the League received a serious jolt when the first international organisation started its work. In the first session of Assembly in 1920 the provisions of collective security became the subject of heated discussion. The Canadian delegate insisted on the abrogation of Art. 10 of the Covenant, while the Scandinavian delegate desired to provide exceptions to the automatic application of sanctions under Articles 16 and 17. Since, after the defection of the United States, the whole burden of maintaining the system of collective security fell on the British shoulders, her delegate offered a new interpretation of Art. 16 of the Covenant. At the second session of the Assembly in 1921, he put a resolution stipulating:

1. Each member would be free to decide for itself whether or not an actual breach of the Covenant had occurred in a given situation, and was only then under an obligation to apply sanctions.
2. If the Council took a decision that there was a breach, and conveyed its opinion to members, that opinion would not be binding. Each government would decide for itself that which form of sanctions—diplomatic, economic or military—should take place and that such sanctions would have a gradual application.
3. Resort to war would not automatically create a state of war with all members of the League.
4. A complete breach of diplomatic relations need not occur immediately but in stead the heads of missions might be recalled while consular relations be maintained.

To the great disappointment of France, this resolution was adopted by the Assembly on October 24, 1921.[11]

These developments could convince France with the fact that a practical use of the provisions of collective security would lag considerably behind the strict letter and spirit of the Covenant. That is, the "machinery of Geneva was evidently not likely to set in motion that prompt military action which alone could save France from invasion."[12] Thus, recourse to the system of making military alliances became a matter of greater importance. Such an alliance was made with Belgium on September 7, 1920, and with Poland on February 19, 1921.[13] (An alliance was made with Little Entente Countries—Czechoslovakia, Rumania and Yugoslavia—on November 11,1927.) Such a move was in keeping with the traditions of this country as well as with the dictates of national interest at this juncture. As Carr observes: "A policy of military alliances was more congenial to French temperament and French tradition than the more abstract security of guarantees against aggression.... It was this policy by which she now sought to encircle Germany.... Out of this material France built up, in the three years after the war, an effective and closely knit system of alliances."[14]

Struggle for Productive Guarantees : Pursuance of an Obstinate Policy of Coercion

Apart from demanding 'physical' guarantees directly aimed at the maximum possible suppression of Germany, France also insisted on certain 'productive' guarantees amounting to an indirect struggle for the same purpose. Mere guarantees of mutual assistance by a major power, like Britain or the United States were of a negative

---

11. Technically, such a resolution had to be passed unanimously, but for being opposed by Persia (Iran), it was not passed. But it is certain that all other Powers approved it. See A.J. Grant and H. Temperley: *Europe in the Nineteenth and Twentieth Centuries, 1789-1950* (London: Longmans, 1964), VI ed., p. 506 n. 1. Then, in 1923 a resolution was moved declaring that the decision of what measures were necessary to carry out the obligations of Art. 10 must rest with the constitutional authorities of each member of the League. The effect of this resolution was to leave the whole matter of military assistance to the discretion of individual governments. It could not be passed.
12. Carr, op. cit., p. 29.
13. See A.B. Keith (ed.): *Speech and Documents on International Affairs, 1918-1937* (London: Oxford Univ. Press, 1938), Vol. I, p. 67.
14. Carr, op. cit., p. 30.

character. Instead a guarantee of a positive or constructive character was needed. It found its manifestation in the form of France's struggle for imposing heavy reparation on Germany. Here we may refer to Point 5 of the Protocol supplement to Treaty of Versailles signed on June 28, 1919, which said: "From the signatures of the Treaty and within the ensuing four months Germany will be entitled to submit for examination by the Allied and Associated Powers documents and proposals in order to expedite the work connected with reparation, and thus to shorten the investigation and to accelerate the decision."[15]

Henceforth, it became one of the most important items of French diplomacy to beat Germany with the stick of reparations. French statesmen like Clemenceau and Poincare sought to honour the public opinion of their country by forcing Germany to pay, what the English people said, 'shilling for shilling and pound for pound.' We have already seen in Chapter 3 that France did her best to maximise the burden of reparations on Germany. The Foreign Minister of France (Klotz) fought against the British and American assessment and, though he could not win the point to his satisfaction, he certainly succeeded in imposing heavy war fines on Germany. His calculations could not be accepted on account of being too heavy and at the Paris Conference he was critically nicknamed as 'the only Jew who could not count.'

However, the representative of France could have a better position in the Reparation Commission in view of the fact that United States now became lukewarm and the Italian and Belgian delegates came to the side of their French counterpart. Thus, the British delegate remained alone. But such a favourable position of France enthused her to take the rash step of making the Reparation Commission take a wrong decision when Germany could not pay the second instalment in 1922. By holding Germany guilty of withholding payment of the second instalment of reparation by her deliberate action, France and Belgium manufactured an alibi for the occupation of the Ruhr that had to be vacated in a short course of time on account of British and American pressure. The British government frankly disapproved of such a drastic measure on the plea that it would cripple Germany to a point that payment of any more instalment of reparation would become impossible. Thus, it

---

15. Temperley, op. cit., pp. 345-46.

branded such an action as 'fault of the unrealistic, vindictive, selfish French.'[16]

Another grave mistake of France at this time was instigation of a separatist movement in the Rhineland. To make the situation more fraught with disaster for Germany and therefore more appalling in its prospect, the French carried on an intensive propaganda for the separation of the Rhineland from the German republic and the establishment of an independent state with the name of Rhenania. "Money was poured out to bribe agitators to carry on this work, and some of the most insidious elements of the German population became active in the pay of the invader. At the same time, a vigorous movement was being carried on in Bulgaria for the secession of that country and the establishment of the independent Catholic monarchy there, under vassalage to France, as Napoleon had done when he made Maximilian the first king of Bavaria in 1805."[17]

Both the rash steps of France had counter-productive effects. The humiliation of these two adventures drove home this fact to the statesmen of France that while a weak Germany could pay no more reparations, British and American leaders stood in their way whenever they demanded full execution of the economic and financial clauses of the Treaty of Versailles. More impelling was the consideration that a strong Germany could threaten French security. An obstinate leader like Poincare worked on this assumption that while the reparation problem was a concern of the Reparation Commission in which Britain and the United States had their participation and who would obstruct measures going to make Germany thoroughly impotent, some corresponding measures could be devised to make France powerful. Thus, new fortifications were erected along the eastern frontier and the French army, though reduced in numbers, was maintained at what was believed to be the highest possible level of technical efficiency. The French government "steadfastly refused to reduce its armaments further, except in return for an international police force or some alternative arrangement which would afford an equal degree of security."[18]

---

16. D.W. Brogan: *The French Nation: From Napoleon to Petain, 1814-1940* (London: Hamish Hamilton, 1960), p. 259.
17. James Murphy's 'Introduction' to his English translation of Hitler's *Mein Kampf* (New Delhi: Sagar Publication n.y.), p. 9.
18. Schuman, op. cit., p. 737.

France

In brief, during the period of 1918-24, France failed to make major diplomatic achievements owing to her adherence to a policy of maximum possible 'coercion of Germany'. Her obstinate leaders like Poincare and Herriot demanded too much that their English and American counterparts were not prepared to concede. It is for this reason that the Geneva Protocol (banning all recourse to an aggressive action and emphasising pacific settlement of international disputes by means of arbitration) appreciated by France became a dead affair in the face of opposition of Britain and other Dominions. It demonstrated that another attempt to straighten the security system failed and, once again, in the French reckoning, Great Britain became the villain of peace. It gravely shocked the Herriot Government that had signified its willingness to accept the new security plan taking into its consideration that the whole orientation of the Geneva Protocol "was towards a system which would guarantee the territorial *status quo* in Europe. This was still the primary concern of France and her Allies."[19]

Franco-German Accord : Brilliant Phase of Briand's Foreign Policy

A new international situation developed in 1925. By this time most of the problems involved in the peace treaties either appeared to have been liquidated or in a fair way to become so and the leading statesmen of world "were free to direct more undistracted attention to the constructive word of the new regime in laying the foundations for a durable tranquillity."[20] It had its definite manifestation in France when in April 1925, Aristide Briand assumed the charge of Foreign Ministry. He had seriously noted that with the rejection of the Geneva Protocol the security of his country through international cooperation was jeopardised, if not destroyed. But the Locarno meet reversed the trend of setback. By signing the Rhineland Pact with Germany, France could secure her frontiers on the eastern side and make the latter resolve for a peaceful settlement of international disputes by means of arbitration.

The Locarno pacts should be taken as a remarkable achievement of French diplomacy in the period following the First World War. The credit for this goes to the new Foreign Minister

---

19. Sharp and Kirk: *Contemporary International Politics* (New York: Farrar & Rinehart Inc., 1944), p. 546.
20. Gathorne-Hardy, op. cit., p. 60.

(Briand) who could establish an excellent rapport with his foreign counterparts like Austen Chamberlain of England and Gustav Stresemann of Germany. Now Germany frankly accepted her western frontiers touching France and Belgium as determined under the Treaty of Versailles and that naturally implied her abandonment of any claim over Alsace-Lorraine. She also surrendered her wish for the fortification of the Rhineland. Now the jubilant French Foreign Minister could describe the Locarno Agreements as 'fragments from the broken mirror which was the 1924 Geneva Protocol.' By all means, it was "the first real guarantee of security which France could accept implicitly."[21]

A milestone in the way of Franco-German *rapprochement* was established in 1925. It led to another great event of the following year when Germany became the member of the League of Nations with a semi-permanent seat for her in the Council. Welcoming Stresemann at Geneva in September 1926, Briand commented that the spirit of Locarno was undoubtedly a sentient reality and a permanent milestone in this series is the Pact of Paris of 1928. In collaboration with his American counterpart (Kellogg), Briand could drag a very large number of states in the direction of renouncing war as an instrument of national policy. It was no less an astounding development that the United States, that had taken an isolationist stand by rejecting the Treaty of Versailles, had now joined hands with all peace-loving nations of the world. As Stuart comments: "Nevertheless, France had finally drawn the United States from its shell of isolation and, in so doing, had obtained world-wide denunciation of aggressive warfare."[22]

Encouraged with the conclusion of the Pact of Paris, Briand offered a grand plan of Pan-European Union. He desired to have a League of European States within the League of Nations more or less on the lines suggested by the leaders of the Pan-European Movement drawing inspiration from the idealism of Count Coudenhove-Kalergi with their headquarters at Vienna. When Briand attended the session of the League Assembly at Geneva in September, 1929 he circulated his proposal among the delegates for their reactions. Then, he prepared a Memorandum of 'regional entente within the terms of Art. 21 of the Covenant' and invited

---

21. Stuart, op. cit., p. 152.
22. Ibid., p. 153.

comments of 27 other European states who were members of the League of Nations. It received different reactions ranging from full approval by states as Poland, Belgium, Yugoslavia, Czechoslovakia and Rumania to its qualified appreciation by Germany, Italy, Hungary, Bulgaria, Britain and Ireland. When the Briand project came up for discussion at the Assembly session in 1930, France held that political security and economic cooperation were indispensable if other problems, including those of treaty revision and disarmament, were to be dealt with in a spirit of European solidarity.

In spite of the fact that his proposal was not favoured by a good number of major states, Briand could succeed in convincing his fellow counterparts with the idea that there should be set up within the framework of the League of Nations a supplementary machinery for the furtherance of intra-European collaboration that should range over a broad front covering matters as rationalisation of production, freeing of trade, communications and transit, finance, labour regulation, public health measure, intellectual activity, inter-parliamentary relations, and public administration. It emphasised that all states would possess equal voting power. There would be a European committee composed of a certain number of members of the European Conference. In short, the Briand plan "appears to have contemplated a loose association or entente of European states operating in and around the worldwide Geneva system."[23]

Impressed, though half-heartedly, with the Briand Plan, the Assembly set up a Commission of Inquiry for European Union under his chairmanship to study the implications of the scheme in conjunction with the League Secretariat. Unfortunately, nothing could materialise in this regard. International situation changed so rapidly that the Briand Plan had to see its doom. Owing to the death of Stresemann in Germany and the fall of Chamberlain in England, Briand remained as the last 'great European pacificator'. His own resignation in the autumn of 1931 sealed the fate of such a grand project. Thus, the era of Briand came to an end having its last noble manifestation in the evacuation of the Rhineland in 1930 that had marked a great achievement of German diplomacy at the hands of Stresemann.

---

23. Sharp and Kirk, op. cit., p. 564.

At this stage, it shall be worthwhile to make a reference to the efforts of the new Foreign Minister (Barthou) for effectuating, what was described as the 'Eastern Locarno Agreement'. In the early summer of 1934 he paid a series of visits to Warsaw, Bucharest, Prague and Belgrade and discussed the prospects of an Eastern Pact of Mutual Guarantee on the lines of the Locarno Agreements of 1925. The parties proposed to such a pact were the USSR, Poland, Baltic States, Czechoslovakia and Germany. Herein it was specifically provided that the USSR be admitted to the League of Nations. In this direction, Barthou had drawn inspiration from a recent treaty signed at Athens by the representatives of Greece, Yugoslavia, Rumania and Turkey under which they had agreed mutually to guarantee their Balkan frontiers, to consult together on measures affecting their common interests, not to embark on any political action towards a non-signatory Balkan country without previous discussion and not to assume political obligations towards such countries without their general consent.

The French project won the appreciation of Italy and Britain, but both declined to shoulder the great responsibility that might fall on them. Besides, it was opposed by Poland on the plea that it would add to her obligations without materially adding to her security and that it might open passages for either Russia or Germany across her territory. More formidable was the opposition of Germany. Hitler did not appreciate the inclusion of the USSR in such a pact. Stalin also opposed it both on account of being caught up in a number of domestic problems and in its broad range covering a Fascist country like Germany. Thus, the scheme of the French Foreign Minister for the defensive encirclement of Germany patently based on the assumption of strict mutuality could not be realised. The proposed partners took different stands that could not be reconciled. The move failed, for the proposed pact could be "compared to one between a wolf, some sheep, and a buffalo; the reluctance of the first to join might no doubt be explained by the fact that he could hardly derive any positive advantage from it, but, assuming that his carnivorous nature was unreformed, he would also clearly prefer bilateral pact, which would depend merely on his own good faith, and would isolate one victim from another in the event of his deciding to break his promise."[24]

---

24. Gathorne-Hardy, op. cit., p. 372.

France

Till now the foreign policy of France may be said to have succeeded on two counts. First, she could strengthen her position with the network of alliances. The French statesmen were justified in turning for support to those nations whose future existence depended either upon an impotent Germany or upon an unified action for defence against an aggressive country once more restored to influence and power. The success of France, in this direction, gave the Germans ample cause for concern who had not forgotten the fact that their Bismarck's fear was coalitions and Kaiser's nightmare was the encirclement of their country. The French policy of making bilateral alliances with potential enemies of Germany "not only gave her hegemony in Europe but also, at the same time, provided a *cordon sanitaire* which guaranteed her security by the maintenance of the political *status quo*."[25]

Second, while France carried out her policy of alliances with other European states so as to encircle Germany, she did not overlook additional safeguards of international organisation and cooperation. In spite of the fact that she had little faith in the League of Nations as an absolute protection for her territorial integrity, she willy-nilly appreciated its possibilities as a valuable reinforcement. As a permanent member of the Council, with a large number of her nationals working in the Secretariat as well as with the support of a good number of states, she was in a position to dictate her policy in the international organisation. As a matter of fact, French authority "became so pronounced that Great Britain almost broke with her on several occasions, and neutral opinion could appreciate the accusation of the vanquished powers that, in practice, the League of Nations was a league of victors."[26]

Physiology of Paralysis : Inauguration of the Policy of Appeasement
The disastrous phase of French foreign policy begins after 1930. The great economic depression wiped out reparations. It amounted to the end of even truncated payments from Germany that could have added to the economic strength of France. Political developments at home in the form of cabinet crises added to the weakening of her political power. These had their natural development on the

---
25. Stuart, op. cit., p. 150.
26. Ibid.

gradual disintegration of her security. Above all, after the advent of Hitler as the Chancellor of the Third Reich in 1933 with a programme of his own, boldly declared in the *Mein Kampf* a couple of years ago, the French leaders could foresee a complete debacle of their political hegemony unless drastic counter measures were taken by them. In the international sphere, the power of the League was seriously weakened by the resignation of Japan and the prospective withdrawal of Germany. Under these conditions, a new and disastrous epoch was inaugurated in French diplomacy that has been described as the 'physiology of paralysis' by Schuman. He says : "As German truculence increased and German military power grew, French willingness to resort to force to maintain the *status quo* diminished. French opinion was so firmly attached to peace that it would no longer approve recourse to preventive violence to meet the menace of the new militarism now dominant in the Reich.... The great issue before the Republic was no longer that of keeping a weak Germany in subjection but that of preserving the remnants of security and checkmating a strong, rearmed and defiant Reich."[27]

Political developments at home played their own part in weakening the position of France at this stage. The murder of her Foreign Minister Barthou and of King Alexander of Yugoslavia on October 9, 1934, at Marseilles by a Croatian terrorist, amounted to the loss of an able and competent Foreign Minister as well as of a reliable friend in the Balkan area. Barthou's successor (Laval) proved a misfit, while the successor of Alexander (Peter II) was just a boy-king having no strong position in the Balkan region. The death of Philippe Berthelot (who had served as the Secretary-General of the Quai d'Orsay for a very long time) on November 22, 1934, removed another able diplomat from the scene. Inspired by the wave of Fascism of Italy, a section of the politicians staged riots in the country on February 6, 1934,, that awakened the socialist and communist forces to face the challenge of right reaction. The liberals and the radical socialists also became anti-Fascists. Thus, a 'popular front' having a distinctly anti-Fascist orientation came into being. It swept the polls of April-May, 1936, as a result of which a socialist like Leon Blum became the Prime Minister with Pierre

---

27. Schuman, op. cit., p. 739.

Laval as his Foreign Minister. It appeared that "French democracy was apparently saved. French security was apparently secured."[28] The Blum government certainly failed in taking a bold action to face the challenge posed by Fascism at home and abroad. A treaty of friendship had already been signed with the USSR in May, 1935 and the new government looked towards Poland for the same purpose. In August 1936, General Gamelin, Chief of the French General Staff, visited Warsaw. In return, in the following month General Edward Rydz-Smugly (who had succeeded Marshal Pilsudski on May 12, 1935) visited Paris. The fear of Nazi militarism brought France and Poland closer. So deep was the impact of Hitler's *demarche* at this stage that the treaty of friendship signed with the Soviet Union in May 1935 could be ratified by the new government after about a year in the face of its opposition by the rightist elements. Moreover, as French statesmen were still determined to keep the bond of friendship with Italy and as the Fascist leader had frankly expressed his anti-Communist orientations, Laval sought to conciliate the Italian dictator on the assumption that these powers (like Poland and USSR) "could be counted upon for support against Berlin."[29]

Pursuance of a weak policy in the face of a challenge posed by Hitler became obvious when the government of Sarraut did not resent Hitler's military action in the Rhineland. It limited itself to protests in accordance with the example set a year before when the Paris government had acquiesced in Hitler's repudiation of the military clauses of the Treaty of Versailles. The Blum cabinet continued the same policy hoping fondly that French inaction in the Rhineland would avoid deterioration of her relations with Italy. It was by all means a betrayal by its own illusions inherent with long-range effects. Remilitarisation of the Rhineland took place in clear violation of the Versailles Treaty and the Locarno Pact—the latter accepted voluntarily by the government of Berlin. Hitler just played a trick, perhaps the biggest gamble of his career. "The officers in the operation, it is now known, carried sealed orders to withdraw at once if they met with French resistance. But none came, because the government of Sarraut was weak and tottering to its fall, and because it delayed while it consulted Britain

---

28. Ibid., p. 740.
29. Ibid.

and lodged protests with the League of Nations. There is little doubt that vigorous military reprisals taken by a strong French government would at the moment, have checked Hitler for a time and maybe for ever."[30]

One striking feature of French foreign policy at this juncture may be traced in the determination of her statesmen to remain tied to the movements of English government that had already taken to the course of appeasement for more or less similar reasons. Sarraut, Blum and Daladier overlooked several points when their British counterparts (Baldwin and Chamberlain) refused to accept any commitment in Central or Eastern Europe in which France had an unshakable stake. An obsession to maintain friendship with Italy under a Fascist government and with Britain committed to a liberal-democratic system forced a statesman of France like Laval to follow the course of appeasement, no matter it proved disastrous in a couple of years. "In order to placate Downing Street and 'preserve peace', he acquiesced in German rearmament and supported Britain in imposing sanctions on Italy. In order to placate Rome and 'preserve peace', he acquiesced in Italian designs on Ethiopia and undermined the League system of collective security. In the execution of this devious course, Paris fell between two stools. Rome and London were both alienated. Berlin was strengthened, and French power and prestige was diminished."[31]

A peculiar development at this stage took place that found its manifestation in integration of the policy of appeasement with the protection of the 'class interest'. That is, instead of studying each issue on its own merit and giving utmost importance to the consideration of 'national interest', the men in power showed their concern with the protection of their class interest. It became quite vivid in 1936 when civil war broke out in Spain. In deference to the Tory Britain and the pro-Franco parties of the right in his own country, Blum favoured the course of 'non-intervention'. Thus, instead of saving the duly elected government of Madrid, Blum indirectly strengthened the hands of Gen. Franco. When the critics of the non-intervention course insisted that France should give help to the legitimate government of Spain, Blum remained imperturbable and maintained his policy of forbidding all arms

---

30. David Thompson: *Europe since Napoleon* (London: Penguin Books, 1978), p. 734.
31. Schuman, op. cit., p. 740.

shipment to the government of Madrid. Naturally, the policy of appeasement became the policy of extreme right that frankly defended the wrong action of a Fascist leader like Franco. The rightists fondly hoped that Franco in alliance with Mussolini would be able to destroy the demon of Bolshevism one day. The influence of Fascism deepened in France. Secret Committees of Revolutionary Action called by the name of 'Cagoulards' Hooded Men') involving leaders like Laval and Petain came into existence with the aim of setting up a Fascist Directory with the help of secret arms and money supplied by Rome. Once again, French statesmen committed a blunder by supporting a dictatorship against a democracy and thereby creating another enemy of liberalism on the western side of their country. As Schuman says: "The ensuing collaboration with the Axis in conquering Spain drove more nails into the coffin of France's eastern alliances and left *la grande nation* discredited and weakened."[32]

The Abyssinian Crisis : Experiment with Appeasement of Option

Though Italy was a victor power like France in the post-war period and she belonged to the class of the Allied and Associated Powers, an undercurrent of differences was also discernible there for the reason that while France adhered to the course of maintaining the *status quo* following the peace settlements of 1919, Italy remained interested in effecting the revision. Thus, as a revisionist power, Italy's eventual leanings towards another revisionist power like Germany could never be nipped in the bud. Moreover, the sources of Franco-Italian rivalry in the Balkan region, in the Danubian basin, in the western Mediterranean zone and, above all, in North Africa could never be lost sight of. However, the most impelling

---

32. Ibid., pp. 742-43.
33. On this point, Gathorne-Hardy observes: "The creation of the Fascist dictatorship inevitably tended to throw Italy and France into opposing camps. France was a prototype of democratic government, loyal to the principles of her great revolution; Italy was now the exponent of a new despotism, the anti-thesis of popular government, a possible source of infection to democracies, whose ideals she repudiated with scorn. The ground of friction was intensified by the fact that a large proportion of the anti-Fascist refugees had sought asylum in France which thereby became a base of propaganda hostile to the Italian government, and even for plots and attempts against the life of the Duce." op. cit., p. 161.

factor was the rise of Fascism in Italy in 1922.[33] And yet Franco-Italian relations could not reach the verge of disintegration on account of the fact that France scrupulously sought to keep Italy in good humour as a reliable ally to be made use of against Hitler in any time to come.

To maintain friendship with Italy was like an obsession for France. It can be evident from the fact that, while breathing hard under the phobia of Nazi aggression, France became a party to the Four-Power Pact of July 1933, whereby she (along with Britain, Italy and Germany) undertook to carry out between themselves an effective policy of cooperation in order to ensure the maintenance of peace in the spirit of the Pact of Paris.[34] Surprising here is not the fact that Hitler accepted this pact, it is that France became a party to it at the proposal of Mussolini seconded by MacDonald. It shows that France was so keen to ditto the line of England and Italy that she failed to foresee the consequence of such an action, particularly in view of Hitler's being a party to a pact of this nature. It could be seen without any difficulty that such an action of France was founded upon fear rather than hope, for by signing the Four-Power Pact she alienated Poland and the Little Entente without any corresponding advantage to herself. "It never had a chance of success, and its failure pushed Italy close towards Germany and the revisionist camp."[35]

Viewed in this perspective, we may study the policy of appeasement as pursued by France at the time of the crisis in Abyssinia. When the matter was taken up by the League of Nations, it became a ticklish affair for Britain and France. The Conservative statesmen of Britain preferred the survival of a Fascist system in Italy lest it should be overthrown after some debacle in Africa and thereby pave the way for the emergence of a regime of the 'left'. Faced with this reality, Britain could not go beyond accepting limited economic sanctions against Italy. The apparently bold stand taken by Sir Samuel Hoare in the Assembly of the League was diluted when he had some secret negotiation with Laval of France in preparing a notorious plan to appease the dictator of Italy. This plan showed Anglo-French willingness to

---

34. See Rene Albrecht-Carrie: *Italy from Napoleon to Mussolini* (New York: Columbia University Press, 1950), p. 202.
35. Stuart, op. cit., p. 158.

give approximately two-thirds of Ethiopia to Italy at a time when she had been designated as an aggressor by the League; when she was being subjected to economic sanctions; and when the slaughter of the native tribesmen by means of poison gas had horrified world opinion.[36]

If Anglo-French collaboration at this stage be examined in a critical manner, a line of difference may be drawn in that while the former (which had been less hostile to Germany and even made a naval treaty with her in June, 1935)[37] now set the pace for imposing economic sanctions against Italy, the latter had been more insistent on pressing for resistance to Germany and was anxious to placate Italy so as to rob Hitler of an ally. It is true that both adhered to the course of appeasement so as to satisfy the imperial hunger of the Italian dictator, but neither of them could think in terms of saving the League of Nations from such a fatal challenge. The process of the dilution of sanctions remained at work despite the exit of Hoare and succession by Eden. In the first instance sanctions were imposed, in the second one they were made 'limited', and in the last one they were abandoned curiously by the League Council in July 1936. In this way, the whole idea of sanctions "was discredited by their partial application and their failure to save Abyssinia".[38]

The role of France in the Abyssinian crisis smacks of her adherence to a policy of appeasement of choice. It was the first important occasion when her statesmen could have stuck to the right side of the problem. Instead of assisting the Duce in an indirect manner, they could have come to the rescue of Haile

---

36. Sharp and Kirk, op. cit., p. 623.
37. The naval pact was signed in London on June 18, 1935, without the British government's having the courtesy to consult either France or Italy, or later to inform them of the secret agreement which stipulated that the Germans could build in certain categories more powerful warships than any of the three Western nations then possessed. The French "regarded this as a treachery which it was. They saw it as a further appeasement of Hitler, whose appetite grew on concessions and they resented the British agreeing, for what they thought a private gain, to scrap further the Peace Treaty and thus add to the growing overall military power of Nazi Germany." Shirer, op. cit., p. 230.
38. Thompson, op. cit., pp. 733-34. Subsequently on June 25, 1939 Laval gave a statement that economic sanctions "were imposed, because we did not want to break with Britain and the League of Nations, and they were implemented in moderation, because we did not want to annoy Italy". S.P. Varma: "Between Two World Wars—1920-1939" in C.D. Hazen: *Modern Europe upto 1945* (New Delhi: S. Chand & Co., 1971), p. 669.

Selassie and thereby demonstrated the proof of their being the defenders of the peace of the world. Even after the publicity of the notorious plan (that led to the exit of Hoare in England), Laval remained in office. It could convince Mussolini with the fact that in no case France would stand in his way of imperial aggrandisement. He took it all as Laval untruthfully asserting that 'nothing in the Rome Agreement tampers with the sovereignty, independence and territorial integrity of Ethiopia', and in repudiating the charge that he had given *carte blanche* in advance to Italian aggression. In the light of all this, the Duce appeared to have concluded rightly that if French interests "were no bar to his plans, Ethiopian interests were not a matter in which France would be greatly concerned."[39]

Spanish Civil War : Experiment with Appeasement of Principle

The role of French diplomacy in the Abyssinian crisis set the pace. It found its repetition in the civil struggle of Spain. The result was that now it became a matter of principle for her to align her fate with another Fascist power. The advancement of the troops under Gen. Franco so as to destroy the constitutionally established government of Madrid in the hands of the 'Left' placed British and French statesmen in a state of dilemma whose solution was discovered by them in sticking cautiously to a middle course. The Tory Prime Minister of England (Baldwin) did not face any division in his cabinet on this issue. But different was the case with Blum of France. Heading a 'popular front' consisting of the rightist as well as leftist elements, it became very difficult for him to take the whole cabinet with him. The 'Right' had already shown its highly critical attitude towards Franco-Soviet alliance of 1935 and it had also displayed its sympathetic inclinations for the liquidation of a 'Left ' government in Spain. On the other hand, the 'Left' was in favour of giving all help to the legitimate government of Madrid so as to frustrate the design of a military leader. "Consequently, Premier Blum resisted quite keenly, that if he made any attempt to come openly to the aid of the embattled Spanish liberals, France would

---

39. Gathorne-Hardy, op. cit., p. 394. Laval had been pungently described by Lord Vansittart, who had first-rare opportunity of studying him at close quarters, as—in the category of 'rotters'—'one of the few in whom the microscope has revealed nothing but more teeming decomposition.' *Lessons of My Life* (London: Hutchinson, 1943), p. 45.

be split asunder politically and the entire social programme of the Popular Front would be wrecked irretrievably."⁴⁰

The way out was discovered by Blum. It was the course of 'non-intervention in a local conflict that was going to be an international civil conflict of the first magnitude. The British government readily responded to an appeal issued by Blum on August 1 for the 'rapid adoption and immediate observance of an agreed arrangement for non-intervention in Spain.' After preliminary soundings, the French cabinet proposed an international agreement to ban all shipment of arms and war material to both groups of contestants. To give effect to such a decision, a Non-Intervention Committee was set up at London with 27 states that in its first meeting held on September 9, 1936, registered the decision of embargo measures.

The strategy of non-intervention in the affairs of Spain put her legitimate government in a very helpless situation. It then took the matter to the League of Nations where British and French representatives sought to discourage their Spanish counterpart in their own ways. At Geneva the Spanish delegate was dissuaded from making specific accusations against Italy and Germany for the reason that while France wanted to shield the guilt of Mussolini, Britain desired the same for that of Hitler. In such a situation he could not do anything more than arranging the conduct of the two dictators in thinly veiled terms. The government of Spain promptly published a 'White Book' containing documents in support of its stand that was supplied to the members of the League at Geneva. But so strong was the position of France and Britain in the League Council that it, in its meeting of December 12, 1936, sabotaged the explosive issue by resolving that 'every state is under an obligation to refrain from intervening in the internal affairs of another state.' In other

---

40. Sharp and Kirk, op. cit., p. 634. On September 6, 1936, Blum ssaid: "There is not a single piece of circumstantial evidence to show that the (non-intervention) agreement has been violated.... Do you think my heart is not torn when I think what is happening down there in Spain ?... Undoubtedly, the legal government that has arisen from the expression of universal suffrage, the Government of the Spanish Republic would assure us complete security on our Pyrenees frontier, while it is impossible to foresee the ambitions of the Rebel generals. On the one hand, safety; on the other, danger.... But should we undertake a competition of armaments on Spanish soil ? If certain powers furnish arms and planes to the Rebels, should France furnish them to the Popular Front?... No." See Schuman, op. cit., p. 742.

words, the Council sidestepped the 'dangerous issue' by 'praising the policy of non-intervention.'[41]

The course of non-intervention proved gainful to Gen. Franco who, with the help of Hitler and Mussolini, went ahead confidently in the face of appeasement shown by Britain and France. An effort was made to include Germany, Italy and the USSR in a non-intervention agreement, but after long negotiations and violent recriminations, non-intervention "remained a dead letter except for France and Great Britain."[42] Franco's grand success revealed that the aggressive nationalistic dictatorships of Germany and Italy would and could ally together in order to defeat democratic governments and that they might in the face of democratic weakness and disarray succeeded in their purposes.... The success of their concerted action in Spain sealed the alliance of Fascism which was to operate in 1940 when Italy attacked a reeling France."[43]

The role of French government in the Spanish civil war clarified it beyond any doubt that in the steadily deteriorating international situation, it, beset as it was by internal difficulties, "made it the first axiom of its foreign policy not to become separated from Britain. This was sound calculation, save that, by failing to stress that France was as important to Britain as Britain was to France, it tended to surrender to an unnecessary degree the guidance of French policy into British hands."[44] After taking note

---

41. Sharp and Kirk, *op. cit.*, p. 635. "We may take note of the fact that at this stage the spirit of Art. 11 of the Covenant was not honoured which declared it 'to be the friendly right of each member of the League to bring to the attention of the Assembly or of the Council any circumstance whatever affecting international relations which threatens to disturb international peace or the good understanding between nations upon which peace depends. 'Hence, the embarrassment of he League was reflected in the vote of the Council taken in May 1938, on the resolution of Spain that League members should consider ending the lgal monstrosity of the formula of non-intervention which the open intervention of Germany and Italy rendered a mockery'. It was rejected by 4 to 2 votes with 9 abstentions. It seemed as if the Spanish Foreign Minister (Senor Alvarez del Vayo) was justified in his declaration before the League Assembly on September 19, 1938, that there had grown up at Geneva 'a strange theory according to which the best method of serving the League was to remove from its purview all questions relating to peace, and the application of the Covenant.' See Grant and Temperley, op. cit., p. 513.
42. Stuart, op. cit., p. 162.
43. Thompson, op. cit., p. 178.
44. Albrecht-Carrie, op. cit., pp. 253-54.

of the fact that while to the 'leftists' the triumph of Fascism in a neighbouring country was obvious and terrible and to the 'rightist' danger from a Communist Spain was immediate and terrifying, Blum discovered the solution to such a dilemma in staying close to Britain stuck to the path of non-intervention. Moreover, France supported the resolution of the Nyon Conference of September 1937 for a 'piracy patrol system' that solved the problem of the safety of British commercial vessels.

Obviously, the guilt of defending an aggression at the expense of an aggressed lay with both Britain and France. Being the major powers of the world at that time, they, even after being well aware of the fact that the situation in Spain was a creation of the intervention of Fascist Powers of Italy and Germany, failed to formulate a policy which they were expected to put into effect.[45] In fine, the impact of the Spanish civil war, the enormous frustration it brought to French policy abroad, the dismay it caused at home, the feeling of moral guilt on the 'Left' that France had let down the democracy across the Pyrenees and helped Fascism to triumph in still another Western country to the detriment of France's position in Europe "broke Blum's heart and the heart of the *Front Populaire*, hastening its end and leaving the Republic more divided and poisoned by hatred than it had been. The unity and the impetus of the Popular Front was shattered. To the traditional division between Right and Left were added divisions within political parties and among Catholics and intellectuals. And in the paroxysm of ideological passion everyone lost sight of the national interest of France."[46]

Austrian and Czechoslovakian Tragedies : Experiment with Appeasement of Compulsion

The policy of appeasement in dealing with the movement of Germany under Hitler after 1936 became a matter of compulsion for France. The situation took a turn after Mussolini's victory in Ethiopia with the result that in the face of Italy's support to Hitler in establishing the *Anschluss* confronted France with an optionless situation. So strong was the obsession of France for maintaining friendship with Italy that she played a two-pronged role in the

---

45. Grant and Temperley, op. cit., p. 513.
46. W.L. Shirer, op. cit., p. 285.

Austrian crisis. While in the first phase of 1933-34, she opposed Hitler's move in the name of being violative of the Treaty of St. Germain and got success on account of Mussolini's firm opposition to the Fuhrer's move, in the second phase of 1938 she studied the annexation of Austria with the Reich like a select and horrified spectator, for Mussolini had now changed his stand in favour of his German counterpart.

We have already noted the fact that Mussolini did not appreciate Hitler's action in Austria in 1933 in view of keeping the danger of German menace away from the frontiers of Italy. France fully supported Mussolini in this direction as Germany became a common enemy. When Hitler made his first move towards Austria the government of France not only protested against it, rather it lodged an appeal with the Secretary-General of the League of Nations. An emergent meeting of the League Council was summoned. But before it Italy, Britain and France had a meeting at Stressa on April 11, 1935, to demonstrate a common front against Hitler. Now France with two other allies invoked the peace settlements of 1919 and Locarno agreements of 1925 to denounce the Nazi action and "recognised that the necessity of maintaining the independence and integrity of Austria would continue to inspire their common policy." It had its definite effect on the proceedings of the League Council when on 17 April it resolved that Germany "has failed in the obligation which lies upon all the members of the international community to respect the undertaking which they have contracted." The significance of the resolution is that France along with other members of her bloc gave a hint that "verbal reproof might be supplemented by positive action, if any further action of the kind condemned were to take place."[47]

Hitler had to retrace in his first rash action. But credit for this should not be attributed to French diplomacy that had now made itself like a handmaid to the dictates of Italy. It may be said at this stage that it was Mussolini's bold action that could place an effective check on the ambition of Hitler. But when tables were turned after Duce's triumph in Abyssinia with Hitler's full-throated appreciation of the same, France could do nothing for defending the independence of Austria. On March 13, 1938, Hitler's troops moved into Austria, but Blum did nothing after informing his

---

47. Gathorne-Hardy, op. cit., p. 398.

ministry the same day. He resigned on April 8 and then his successor (Daladier) proved a still more unfortunate choice. "The culmination of Anglo-French impotence seemed to have been reached on March 13, 1938, when Chancellor Hitler marched his Nazi troops into Austria and consummated the *Anschluss*, while neither democracy dared more than protest verbally."[48]

However, the tragedy of Czechoslovakia effected at the Munich meet furnished the climax of the policy of appeasement. It is true that after the tragedy of Austria, France had taken a very serious view of the real designs of Hitler, but as she was firmly tied to the apron-strings of Britain, she remained helpless altogether. The course of appeasement became a matter of Hobson's choice for her. For instance, in their talks in London on April 28-29, 1938, Prime Minister Daladier and his Foreign Minister (Bonnet) emphasised that Hitler's real design was not to gain concessions for the Sudeten Germans but "to use their grievances as a pretext to destroy Czechoslovakia and eventually to secure a domination of the Continent in comparison with which the ambitions of Napoleon were feeble."[49] Daladier said : "Today it is the turn of Czechoslovakia. Tomorrow it will be the turn of Poland and Romania. When Germany has obtained the oil and wheat, she will turn on the West. Certainly we must multiply our efforts to avoid war. But that will not be obtained unless Great Britain and France stick together, intervening in Prague for new concessions but declaring at the same time that they will safeguard the independence of Czechoslovakia. If, of the contrary, the Western powers capitulated again they will only precipitate the war, they wish to avoid."[50]

Instead of getting the sense, the British statesmen remained stuck to their policy of appeasing the dictator of Germany who would eventually collide with the power of Bolshevism without moving his face to the West. Rebutting the argument of Daladier, Lord Halifax sent a message stipulating these important corrections for France:[51]

1. It is of utmost importance that French government should not be under an illusion as to the attitude of His Majesty's Govern-

---

48. Stuart, op. cit., p. 163.
49. Shirer, op. cit., p. 320.
50. Ibid., pp. 320-21.
51. Ibid., pp. 325-26.

ment...... in the event of failure to bring about peaceful settlement of the Czechoslovakian question.
2. His Majesty's Government have given the most serious warnings to Berlin. But it might be highly dangerous if the French government were to read more into these warnings than is justified by their terms.
3. His Majesty's Government would, of course, always honour their pledge to come to the assistance of France if she were the victim of unprovoked aggression by Germany.
4. If, however, the French government were to assume that His Majesty's Government would at once take joint military action with them to preserve Czechoslovakia against German aggression, it is only fair to warn them that our statements do not warrant any such assumption.
5. In view of His Majesty's Government the military situation is such that France and England, even with assistance, as might be expected from Russia, would not be in a position to prevent Germany over-running Czechoslovakia. The only result would be a European war, the outcome of which, so far as can be seen,.. would be at least doubtful.
6. His Majesty's Government fully realise the nature and extent of the French obligations, but they feel that in the present highly critical situation the French government should take full account of the preceding considerations.

In the face of British stubbornness, a weak partner like France thoroughly yielded. At Munich Daladier supplied the knife with which Chamberlain butchered the lamb of Czechoslovakia. A big chunk of this small state was ceded to the Nazi aggressor along with certain guarantees made by the great appeasers to protect the revised frontiers keeping which in view the government of Prague was commanded to accept the ill-fated Munich injunction. While communicating the decision of the Munich meet, the French Prime Minister sent this note to Prague : "France in agreement with England has set forth the only procedure which it judges in the actual circumstances can prevent the Germans from marching into Czechoslovakia. In rejecting the Franco-British proposal the Czech government assumes the responsibility for Germany resorting to force. It thus ruptures the Franco-British solidarity which has just been established and by doing so it removes any practical effectiveness of assistance from France.... Czechoslovakia thus assumes the risk which we believe to have been removed. She must herself understand the conclusions which France has the right to draw if the Czechoslovak government does not accept immediately the Franco-British proposal."[52] Indisputable is the fact that Munich represented climax of the folly of appeasement policy. Bonnett publicly pledged support to Prague but "privately worked for an *entente* with Hitler at Prague's expense."[53] Daladier and Bonnett "were destined to bring France and the Republic to distruction. Munich was the symbol of their folly. They made the Quai d'Orsay completely subservient to Chamberlain's designs."[54] Now the diplomacy of the Western Powers "lost all prestige in the East; the Munich decision had been reached without Russian agreement, and because of this mistake Russia was irretrievably alienated. France had bled white between 1914 and 1918 and feeling her military and economic exhaustion still remained blind to the imminence of the danger and folly of such compromises."[55]

Germany's Invasion on Poland : Termination of the Appeasement Policy

Curiously, Daladier defended his action at Munich as a successful endeavour to save the country from Bolshevism. The anti-Communist posture of French policy remained at the base so much so that now France was more interested in establishing friendship with Germany than having a genuine alliance with the USSR. Such a posture had virtually made her statesmen blind who, instead of getting meaning of the *Mein Kampf*, "moved after Munich to surrender the Continent to Hitler's fancied *Drang nach Osten*."[56] On December 6, 1938, Bonnett signed with German Foreign Minister (Ribbentrop) a declaration of pacific and good neighbourly relations. In justification of such a stand, he endorsed: "It is the struggle against Bolshevism which is essentially at the basis of the common German and Italian political conception, and without saying so

---

52. Ibid., p. 348. See V.M. Dean: "Diplomatic Background of Munich Accord" in *Foreign Policy Reports*, Part 24, No. 20, December 15, 1938.
53. Schuman, op. cit., p. 743.
54. Ibid.
55. Andre Maurois: *A History of France*, Translated from French into English by Henry L. Binsse (London: Jonathan Cape, 1956), p. 489.
56. Schuman, op. cit., p. 744.

without saying so formally, Ribbentrop perhaps wished to give us to understand that there is no other objective to be attributed to it."[57]

But the eyes of the appeasers of France and England opened when Hitler yielded Carpatha-Ukraine to Hungary on March 16, 1939, immediately after the seizure of Prague. It now became certain that the Nazi forces would move towards Poland in the east or towards France in the west to translate the words of the *Mein Kampf* into deeds. In such a desperate situation France looked towards Poland and the members of the Little Entente for restoring the system of alliances. For France the result of this hasty action was securing reaffirmation of alliance with Poland, support of Britain in guaranteeing Rumania and Greece, and conclusion on June 23, 1939, of an alliance with Turkey paid for by the cession of Hatay to her. A rightist leader like Flandin warned that Hitler's aim towards Danzig was merely an exercise of the revision of the Peace Treaty. Now French policy vacillated between sticking to the fallacious path of appeasement and abandoning it after grasping the reality of the situation. When Germany mobilised her troops into Poland on September 1, 1939, Bonnett sought to make an effort for satisfying the imperial hunger of Hitler by arranging another Munich on the Polish question. Paying deference to the dictates of Mussolini, he accepted the Italian proposal for peace through a conference with German troops remaining where they were on the Polish soil. So firm was the move of Bonnett that he declined to join his English counterpart (Halifax) in issuing a common warning to Hitler. Instead of apprecating and endorsing the counsel of Halifax that there could be no conference with Hitler without withdrawal of German aggression from Poland and evacuation of Nazi troops therefrom, he insisted upon a separate course of action. However, Daladier vacillated and yet, in a state of fix, he told the Parliament on 2 September that France would not abandon her ally (Britain). Bonnett reluctantly accepted it.

At this stage, the policy of appeasement saw its end. Bonnett conveyed an important instruction to French emissary (Coulondre) to bring it to the notice of the German government that in case Nazi troops did not stop, French government "would be compelled to fulfil as from today September 3 at 5 p.m. the engagements France

---

57. Ibid.

France

dishonoured by Ribbentrop in a quite contemptuous way. In stead came the German ultimatum that if France attacked the Reich, this would be on her part an act of aggression. Thus, on September 3, 1939, at 5 p.m. France entered into war against Germany. The appeasement policy having its climax at Munich came to an end illustrating grand failure of the course adopted by Chamberlain and Daladier and instead proving the accuracy of Churchill's judgement given after the declaration of Munich, that "France and Britain had to choose between war and dishonour. They chose dishonour. They will have war."[58]

Concluding Observations

The following important impressions may be gathered after making a detailed study of the French foreign policy and diplomacy during the inter-war period:

1. A struggle for self-preservation remained the sheet-anchor of French foreign policy. Even after emerging as a victor in the First World War, France looked like a prostrate, exhausted and internally disrupted country. The menace of German resurgence loomed large on her horizon. So poignant was its impact that it "hypnotised French policy-makers" and their "search for security exhibited an almost hysterical nervousness and a sort of pathological obsession".[59] For this reason, this 'country's idol in 1918' (Clemenceau) strained every nerve to materialise that the "years of French supremacy were also the years of Germany's deepest humiliation."[60] When the Peace Conference opened on January 18, 1919, in the gilded hall of the Quai d'Orsay in Paris, President Poincare in his high-pitched nasal voice and in his usually chilly manner said: "Justice is not inert.... When it has been violated, it demands first of all restitutions and reparations for peoples and individuals who have been despoiled and maltreated. In formulating this legitimate claim it shows neither hate nor an instinctive and thoughtless desire for reprisals. It pursues a durable object: to render to each his due and to discourage the renewal of the crime any impunity."[61]

---

58. Ibid.
59. M.G. Gupta: *International Relations since 1919* (Allahabad: Chaitanya, 1969) III Ed., p. 257.
60. Carr, op. cit., p. 44.

his due and to discourage the renewal of the crime any impunity."[61]

2. Despite being a victor power, France emerged from the Peace Conference like an unsatiated hero. Several provisions of the Paris peace settlement left her in a disgruntled condition. For instance, the Rhineland could not be separated from Germany so as to be converted into a separate state and the arrangement of its placement under an international Commission was made only for 15 years, in three instalments of 5 years each. The coal-rich area of Saar was not permanently ceded to her and instead placed under the control of the League whose political destiny was to be decided by means of a plebiscite after 15 years. As we have seen, it also went to Germany in 1935. Though Britain and the United States had made guarantees of mutual assistance at the time of signing the peace treaties, these remained unfulfilled in the event of American defection and British reluctance to shoulder such a heavy responsibility. The changed attitude of Britain weakened the effectiveness of the system of collective security as enshrined in the Covenant and it made the attitude of France towards the League of Nations quite sceptical.[62]

3. Britain's adherence to the policy of 'balance of power' created a source of ample irritation to the statesmen of France. After the conclusion of the peace settlements, British statesmen tried to put more weight on the side of Germany so as to weaken relatively the position of France. Whenever France made an effort

---

61. Cited in Shirer, op. cit., p. 126. French policy-makers started with a programme of restitution, reparation and guarantee. "Restitution implied the recovery of the provinces of Alsace-Lorraine. Reparation meant that Germany should contribute to the reconstruction of the devastated areas. Guarantee implied that Germany should fulfil its obligations and that the Allies must establish some material and diplomatic guarantees for French security." Gupta, op. cit., p. 257.

62. It is true that France shared the guilt with Britain in pursuing the destructive policy of appeasement, but the evaluation of Shirer is quite plausible. Says he: "But whatever the shortcomings of a friend and ally, and in the case of Great Britain they were calamitous, a nation in the end must shoulder responsibility for its own failure. Because of its hesitations and devious policies of Laval, the French government had lost all; Italy as an ally against Germany, the military backing of Russia, Great Britain as a close partner, the League of Nations as a potential force in halting aggression. These grievous consequences opened the eyes of Hitler to his opponents and strengthened his determination to seize them." Shirer, op. cit., p. 230.

to strengthen the system of security to her desired extent, British opposition stood in the way. Thus, Prime Minister Herriot's scheme to put teeth into the system of collective security in the name of the Geneva Protocol of 1925 went in vain. However, a change occurred in 1925 when Briand became the Foreign Minister of France. As a man of compromise and insight, a great imperturbable artist of diplomacy and the rostrum, he could make manysuccessful efforts for the re-establishment of peace. The Locarno Agreements of 1925 and the Pact of Paris of 1928 deserve special mention here.

4. A great change in the foreign policy of France occurred after the exit of Briand. In the face of several grim challenges, his successors had to take to the ill-fated path of appeasement. Now France saw an increase in the number of her enemies and decline in the strength of her friends. The growing force of the rightist elements in the country also forced the government to have softer relations with totalitarianism of the right represented by Mussolini of Italy and Franco of Spain. So deep was their aversion towards Communism that toward the end of 1938 Bonnett preferred a pact of friendship with Ribbentrop in stead of joining hands with the USSR to beat the challenge of Nazi aggression. Ultimately, the policy of appeasement entailed its destructive effect. France had to declare war on Germany after wrongly dealing with the crises of Abyssinia, Austria, Spain and Czechoslovakia. As Prof. Gupta says: "When Daladier put his signatures on the Munich Pact on 30 September, 1938, by one stroke of pen he killed the whole framework of French security by alienating the Soviet Union and by making German invasion of Poland a certainty. When Bonnett signed with Ribbentrop the Franco-German declaration of friendship on 6 December, 1938, he accepted a cheque from Germany on a bank that never existed. France lost both Italy and the Soviet Union. In 1939, Germany and the Soviet Union invaded the French ally, Poland; in 1940, Germany and Italy had a joint feast of France."[63]

5. Above all, a determination to have security and avoid the risk of another war coupled with seeing the defeat of Communism haunted the minds of the foreign policy-makers of France from

---

63. Gupta, op. cit., pp. 263-64.

Clemenceau to Daladier. A thread of continuity may, for this reason, be discovered in The French foreign policy during the inter-war period. As Langsam says: "In international affairs, the attitudes of all post-war ministries in France were determined by a desire to make the Republic secure against foreign aggression. French foreign policy, therefore, was an integrated foreign policy designed to maintain the *status quo* internationally, preserve the Versailles Treaty, and develop a favourable climate of world opinion for the French case as it developed in diplomatic confrontations. In carrying out this policy, some French leaders were unyielding, others were conciliatory. Nevertheless, since the same end always was kept in the view, there was a marked degree of unity in the French foreign policy."[64]

In retrospect, France could never fully recover from the pangs of a defeat turned into that of a victory in 1918. The struggle was so fierce that it sapped her resources and energy. In the post-war period, she realised that she would be unable to find security by herself. Hence, she fought for the system of guarantees and alliances. But the statesmen committed a wrong by alienating the Soviet Union just for the sake of being a Communist power and instead leaning towards the totalitarian powers of the right whose hunger for territorial aggrandisements was above board. When these aggressors started on their mission, the statesmen of France sacrificed security to peace. "Her failure to act when German troops moved into the Rhineland in 1936 may be regarded as a turning point, and the capitulation at Munich two years later exposed her physical and psychological weakness and unpreparedness; weak and distracted France entered the Second World War, and the mood of appeasement created the atmosphere for the collaborationism of Vichy regime. For five bitter years, while the fate of free world hung in the balance, France in effect was blotted out as an independent state."[65]

---

64. W.C. Langsam: *The World since 1919* (Delhi: Surjeet Publications, 1981), VIII ed., p. 74.
65. N.D. Palmer and H.C. Perkins: *International Politics: World Community in Transition* (Calcutta: Scientific Book Agency, 1965), p. 751.

8

ITALY

The fundamental orientations of our foreign policy are as follows: the Peace Treaties, good or bad as they may be, when once they have been signed and ratified, are to be executed. A State which respects itself can have no other doctrine. But treaties are not eternal and not irreparable. They are chapters in, not epilogue to, history. To execute them means to test them. It is in the course of execution that their absurdity becomes manifest that may contribute a new fact which opens up the possibility of a further examination of the respective positions.

—Benito Mussolini[1]

A detailed discussion of the foreign policy and diplomacy of Italy in a study of international relations and politics during the interwar period deserves a place of its own after that of Germany and France. The reason behind it is that after of peace settlements of 1919 while Germany became the arch-revisionist country and France behaved like a great anti-revisionist power, Italy stood between the two poles. At first a partner of the Central bloc (Germany, Turkey and Austro-Hungarian Empire) in World War I and then a defector to join the side of the Allies (Britain, France and Russia) on the basis of a secret treaty signed in 1915, Italy emerged as a victorious power in 1918 without having the capability to share the spoils of war so as to satisfy her territorial claims to the aspired extent. Woodrow Wilson and Lloyd George stood in the way with the result that the Italian claims could be satisfied to

---

1. Mussolini's speech in the Italian Parliament on November 16, 1922, cited in Rene Albrecht-Carrie: *Italy from Napoleon to Mussolini* (New York: Columbia University Press, 1950), p. 187.

a limited extent. As later developments revealed, the total effect of the peace settlements "was to leave her dissatisfied, disappointed, and considerably wounded in her self-esteem. The result was to place her in a special intermediate position between the revisionist and anti-revisionist Powers."[2]

Aftermath of Paris Peace Settlement : Resurgence of Italian Irredentism

As already hinted, Italy faced an unexpected opposition to her territorial claims at the Paris Peace Conference. The opening item of Wilson's 14-Points derecognised consideration of any secret agreement arrived at during the period of war.[3] Moreover, as a staunch exponent of the principle of national self-determination, Wilson informed the Italian Prime Minister (Orlando) that he did not feel free to differentiate the application of his doctrine from one case to another. He made it very clear that constancy demanded application of the same principle to all treaties signed with Germany, or with Austria, or with Turkey and the like.[4] Such a stand created an unforeseen problem for Italy; it did the same for Britain and France in view of the fact that they felt morally bound to

---

2. Gathorne-Hardy: *A Short History of International Affairs, 1920-1939* (London: Oxford Univ. Press, 1950), IV ed., p. 159.
3. Under the Secret Treaty of London (signed on April 26, 1915) Italy's possessions in Africa were only slightly increased; but she made extensive acquisitions in Europe—the Trentino and the rest of South Tyrol as far as Brenner Pass, Trieste, Gorizia, Istria, Northern Dalmatia (except Fieume), the Adriatic Islands, etc. Art. 8 of the Treaty provided that the temporarily occupied Dodecanese Islands should pass under full Italian sovereignty. Art. 9 said: "Generally speaking, France, Great Britain and Russia recognise that Italy is interested in maintenance of the balance of power in the Mediterranean and that, in the event of the total or partial partition of Turkey in Asia, she ought to obtain a just share of the Mediterranean region adjacent to the province of Adalia.... The zone which shall eventually be allotted to Italy shall be delimited, at the proper time, due account being taken of the existing interests of France and Great Britain." Then, Art. 13 said: "In the event of France and Great Britain increasing their colonial territories in Africa at the expense of Germany, these two Powers agree in principle that Italy may claim some equitable compensation, particularly as regards the settlement in her favour of the question relative to the frontier of the Italian colonies of Eritrea, Somaliland and Libya and the neighbouring colonies belonging to France and Great Britain". See Rene Albrecht-Carrie, op. cit.; p. 228.
4. H.W.V. Temperley (ed.): *History of the Peace Conference* (London: Oxford University Press, 1920), Vol. 5, p. 397.

honour what was given in the secret Treaty of London. They worked hard for an acceptable compromise but, at the same time, regarded themselves as bound by the Treaty of London in the event of a voluntary agreement not being arrived at.'[5]

It is for this reason that, for some time, British and French representatives had an argument with the American President. It showed that relations at the Paris Conference "were, however, difficult and strained, and at one time resulted in the temporary withdrawal of the Italian delegation."[6] The consistency of President Wilson had its way to a very large extent. Italy could gain Tyrol, Trieste, part of the Dalmatian coast and certain islands of the Aegean and Adriatic seas. She could not get Fieume, nor any mandate over former German colonies in Africa. It is, therefore, obvious that while being one of the five principal Allied and Associated powers, who dictated the terms of peace in 1919, 'Italy's appetites, like those of Japan, were whetted, not satisfied, by the results of the War; and throughout the subsequent period she must be ranked, like Japan and like the ex-enemy countries, among the discounters, among the discontented and 'troublesome' states."[7]

The rejection of the Italian claims to such an unexpected extent enthused a poet and an aviator like D'Annunzio to lead an unofficial army to capture Fieume with the tacit connivance of the Italian government in September 1919. It, however, proved a short-lived affair. As David Thomson describes: "The dashing romanticism of the escapade—D'Annunzio garbed his men in cloaks, crested them with eagle's feathers, armed them with daggers, and flew them to Fieume in aeroplanes—stirred memories of the hectic days of Garibaldi and the *Risorgimento*. The Italian government of Gioletti had the unhappy and unpopular task of driving him out on Christmas Eve, after three months of wild heroics and of restoring Fieume to the inter-Allied authorities, who later made it a 'free city'."[8]

5. Ibid., p. 426.
6. Gathorne-Hardy, op. cit., p. 160.
7. E.H. Carr: *International Relations between the Two World Wars, 1919-1939* (London: Macmillan, 1952), p. 66.
8. Thomson: *Europe since Napoleon* (London: Penguin Books, 1978), p. 594. Fieume was partitioned between Italy and Yugoslavia in 1924. Muriel Grindrod observes: "The episode of Fieume, unimportant and indeed well-high comic opera in itself, nevertheless had its place in contributing to the climate of the

As Italian discontent became a disturbing factor in the international affairs in the period following the peace settlements of 1919, some explanation may be given of its causes:

1. Thanks to the efforts and sacrifices of great figures like Cavour (the statesman), Garibaldi (the warrior) and Mazzini (the poet and prophet of nationalism) that Italy became a strong nation-state in the later part of the nineteenth century. "Her dead bones were conjured back to life and became a living body. In the middle third of the nineteenth century Mazzini preached the word, Garibaldi wielded the sharp sword, and Cavour contrived the diplomatic and political process of redemption. The vigorous impulse having been given by Piedmont, *Italia irredenta* was redeemed bit by bit in successive stages (1859, 1866, 1870, 1919) until substantial completions had been achieved so far as the peninsula and continent and island were concerned. There remain as still unredeemed fragments only in Corsica, Nice and Savoa in French hands, the British islands stronghold of Malta and Dalmatia, where the traces of Venice's ancient empire have been almost completely submerged under the rising Jugoslav tide."[9]

2. As already said, partiotic Italians resented the non-fulfilment of the terms of the secret Treaty of London at the Paris Peace Conference. The principle of national self-determination as so strongly defended by Wilson denied the whole of Tyrol to Italy as it had a majority of the German population, while Trieste with its hinterland and the Dalmatian coast was inhabited mainly by the Slavs. To some extent Italian claims were accommodated here, but the case of Albania became a source of irritation. By the Treaty of London it was stipulated that Italy should receive the port of Valona and be charged with the conduct of Albania's foreign relations. Though Albania had become an independent state in 1913, she had fallen in a state of chaos during World War I and come

---

immediate post-war years in Italy.... In the drabness of the war and the dsillusionment of the peace each daring action stood out as a splash of colour, firing the imagination of the generation of youths who, growing up just too late to take part in the war, shared their elders' disappointment at its outcome and sought an outlet for their pent-up energy." *Italy* (New York: Fredrick A. Praeger, 1968), p. 67.

9. Henry R. Spencer: "Expanding Italy" in Brown, Hodges and Roucek (eds.): *Contemporary World Politics: Introduction to the Problem of International Relations* (New York: John Wiley and Sons, 1939) p. 187.

Italy

under Italian occupation. In 1920 Italian troops were withdrawn and Albania was made a member of the League of Nations. But now Italy demanded her 'special status' in Albanian affairs. The matter could be settled to the satisfaction of Italy when the Italo-British Ambassadors' Conference took place in London in November 1921, and then it was resolved that the task of maintaining the independence of Albania be entrusted to Italy in a moment of crisis as per the direction of the League Council.[10]

3. Another factor that contributed to Italy's discontentment was related to her colonial hunger in Africa. It was given to understand that after the conclusion of war, she would receive 'equitable compensation' when Britain and France would distribute the booty of German possessions in Africa. That is, she desired a favourable adjustment of the frontiers between her existing colonies in Africa vis-a-vis those of France and Britain. Nothing could be achieved by her at the Paris Peace Conference in this regard. Naturally, Italo-British relations became strained and it was not until 1924 that London obliged Rome by ceding a small strip of the territory of Jubaland to Italian Somaliland out of her colony of Kenya. But France could not do even that much. A mere frontier rectification in North Africa made by her failed to satisfy Italy's extensive claims with the result that Italian grievance "continued until 1935 to inject a further element of poison into Franco-Italian relations."[11]

In short, Italy emerged from the Paris Conference like a highly unsatiated victor. It put her in a strange position of being a defender as well as a critic of the peace settlement. It had its definite impact on the foreign policy-makers of Rome and in not much time it was instrumental in the rise of Fascism. Prof. F.L. Schuman well observes: "At the Peace Conference Italy found her claim thwarted by Wilsonian idealism, by Serbian aspirations in the Adriatic, by the French and British reluctance to permit Italy to dominate the Mediterranean.... All Italian patriots felt that Italy had won the war

---

10. Carr makes an interesting observation in this regard. "In form this resolution had no immediate application, whatever. It was, indeed, something of an absurdity, since the only power likely to threaten Albania's independence was Italy herself. But Italy interpreted it as a recognition of her right to intervene in Albanian affairs to the exclusion of any other Power; and this claim was a source of constant irritation and apprehension in Yugoslavia". op. cit., p. 70.
11. Ibid.

but had lost the peace. Italy, despite her gains, emerged from the Conference an unsatiated state."[12]

Rise of Fascism : Role of Ideology in Italian Foreign Policy
Italian foreign policy underwent a fundamental change after the emergence of Mussolini in October 1922. The Fascists had given a programme of their own in the Proclamation issued on August 28, 1919, in which it was boldly specified: "Italian Fascism in its new national life wants to continue to realise the value of the great soul fused and tempered in the great cement of war; it also was to keep united—in the form of an anti-party or super-party—those Italians of all persuasions and of all the productive classes in order to sustain them in the new inevitable battles which must be fought to complete and realise the value of the great revolutionary war. The *Fasci di combattimento* want that the sum of sacrifices accomplished may give to Italians in international life that place which victory has assigned to them."[13]

The Fasists could not make their mark through parliamentary procedure. They suffered heavy defeat in the elections of 1921. But the conditions of the country deteriorated to such an extent that induction of the great Black Shirt Leader (Mussolini) as the Prime Minister after demonstrating his strength in the Great March of October 28, 1922, became a certainty. Premier Facta resigned and the King invited Mussolini to form government. Now came into being the first instance when a highly ambitious leader assumed the office of the working head of the Italian state. His passion was 'quest for power'. As he said: "I am possessed by this mania. It inflames, gnaws and consumes me like a physical malady. I want to make a mark on history like a lion with his claws."[14]

Three important factors may be enumerated to show their role in the sudden rise of Fascism under Mussolini:

1. Italy emerged from the First World War as a victor with highly deteriorated political and economic condition at home and national humiliation abroad. An Italian historian of distinction (G. Salvemini) described the picture of his nation slipping into anarchy

---
12. Schuman: *International Politics* (New York: McGraw Hill, 1948), IV Ed., p. 651.
13. Cited in Albrecht-Carrie, op. cit., p. 156.
14. See Schuman, op. cit., p. 652.

Italy

as 'legendary' at this time. The country badly suffered from 'post-war neurasthenia' inasmuch as there "were disturbances, strikes, riots—but there never occurred a breakdown in the economic machinery of the country."[15] Under these conditions the people needed a strong government that could give a better administration to the country. Mussolini thus filled the bill. It is rightly pointed out:"The situation in 1920 was in the highest degree painful for Italy in both the material and spiritual senses. Almost destitute of coal and iron she had acquired no new industrial resources at the peace. And the results of Versailles were in fact distinctly humiliating to her, and had aroused the nations to fury. During the actual negotiations they overthrew Orlando and Sonnino and substituted Nitti and Tittoni for them. But they were simply politicians of the old type and what Italy needed was something really new, leaders possessed of dash, of boldness and of decision."[16]

2. There was the 'population problem' with its pressure standing like a justification for territorial expansion. During the period of four years preceding the First World War (1910-1914), it was given that 3,500,000 Italians migrated to foreign countries and in the post-war period more than 10,000,000 Italians were reported to be living abroad. In the face of such a danger, American government made a law to control the immigration of foreign nationals. Emigration was no solution. Mussolini took it in a different way. He looked into the fact of population explosion as a powerful instrument for the building of a great empire. It was appreciated by the countrymen. The huge manpower would supersede the excellence of French imperialism and establish the new Roman Empire. A Fascist paper dated 27 December, 1925 said: "A block of 80,000,000 Romans from the Atlantica to the Mediterranean under the mighty fist of Mussolini would solve the hard and obscure problem of Europe. In a year France would be France again, a worry collaborator for the eternal restoration of the glory that was Rome. And if the French people is irremediably destined to disappear despite our efforts to give it new blood, it will have the joy of fainting in the immortal arms which fondled it when

---

15. Lipson: *Europe, 1914-1939* (London: Adam and Charles Black, 1957), VII ed., p. 415.
16. A.J. Grant and H. Temperley: *Europe in the Nineteenth and Twentieth Centuries* (London: Longmans, 1964), VI ed., p. 484.

young—not destroyed by barbarians but absorbed in the immortal breast of Rome."[17]

3. But the most impelling factor was national humiliation received at the Paris Peace Conference. The patriotic people resented the attitude of Wilson, George and Clemenceau in showing a casual regard to the claims of Orlando. They took strong exception to the fact that the Italian delegation had to withdraw from peace parleys in a mood of frustration and, in spite of that, the attitude of the United States, Great Britain and France remained unchanged. More than this, the weak government of Gioletti surrendered what was seized by the zealous patriods under D'Annunzio in Fieume. Though the government yielded to the Anglo-French pressure in leaving Fieume, it became clear that after "this fantastic mutineering adventure in Fieume had upset the nation's mental balance, *Sacro Egoismo* (Holy Egoism) was developed with emotional inflation beyond all rational consideration of due limits. 'Italy will carry on by herself' came to have a new meaning...."[18]

All these factors had their cumulative effect on the emergence of Mussolini after a successful Grand March to Rome.... In not much time the 'Father of Fascism' revealed his inclinations to the world. A strong government committed to the cause of establishing a great Roman empire by means of arms became the sheet-anchor of Italian foreign policy. For instance, on August 24, 1932, he said: "The Fascist State is a will to power and empire. The Roman tradition is the idea of force. In the Fascist doctrine, the imperial idea is not only territorial, military and mercantile expression, but also one of spiritual and moral expansion. For Fascism, the tendency to the imperial idea means expansion of the nation and is a manifestation of vitality."[19]

---

17. See Sharp and Kirk: *Contemporary International Politics* (New York: Farrar and Rinehart Inc. 1944), p. 136. In 1927 while inaugurating the new policy, Mussolini declared that "to count for something in the world, Italy must have a population of at least sixty million when she reaches the threshold of the second half of this century.... It is a fact that the fate of nations is bound up with the demographic power.... Let us be frank with ourselves: What are forty million Italians compared with the forty million of France and the ninety million of her colonies, or with the forty six million of England and the 450 million inhabitants of her colonial possessions ?" See D.V. Glass: *The Struggle for Population* (London, 1936), p. 34.
18. Spencer, op. cit., p. 188.
19. Cited in Schuman, op. cit., p. 649.

With this view, Mussolini vehemently hit at the role of Britain and France played at the Paris Conference. He denounced the League of Nations and frankly reiterated his claim for colonial expansion in Africa. As he said: "We won the war and then our poltron statesmen at Paris lost us the peace; they even helped build the League as an insurance institution for guaranteeing Britain's and France's illegal gotten imperialist gains; we had been promised respectable shares of the loot, instead we were thrown mere inconsiderable scraps of desert in Jubaland and Sahara."[20] In order to realise the goals of a foreign policy of this type, he laid emphasis on two important counts—a huge population and recourse to the path of war. In his address to the Parliament on May 26, 1927, he desired to retain the sons of Italy, for she "must appear on the threshold of the second half of the century with a population of not less than 60,000,000 inhabitants. If we fall off.... we cannot make an Empire."[21] Prof. Schuman puts the same thing in these words: "Empire-building involves war. War requires manpower. Manpower requires not emigration or birth control, but a population which will grow to the bursting point. More colonies must be acquired at all costs. Italian power must be extended over the Mediterranean. Only in this way can Italy attain that 'place in the sun' to which she has long aspired."[22]

Thus, Mussolini frankly repudiated the norms of internationalism. With him as a new imperator and conqueror, Italy should be made strong, powerful, respected and a new empire won with all other interests to be subordinated to the supreme end of the power of the Fatherland. As he boldly declared: "Fascism sees in the imperialistic spirit—i.e., the tendency of nations to expand —a manifestation of their vitality. In the opposite tendency, which would limit their interests to the home country, it sees a symptom of decadence. Peoples who rise or re-arise are imperialistic; renunciation is characteristic of dying peoples. The Fascist doctrine is that best suited to the tendencies and feelings of a people which, like the Italian, after lying low during centuries of foreign servitude, is now reasserting itself in the world."[23]

---

20. See Spencer, op. cit., p. 189.
21. Schuman, op. cit., p. 653.
22. Ibid., pp. 653-54.
23. Mussolini: *Fascism, Doctrine and Institutions* (Rome, 1935), pp. 30-31.

Mussolini's 'Dynamic' Foreign Policy: Abandonment of the Course of Abdication and Retrenchment

"What else may be thought of Fascism, its inner qualities and nature, there can be no doubt about its dynamic character."[24] Europe as well as the League of Nations had a taste of Mussolini's quality in not much time. By the Treaty of Lausanne (1923) Italy obtained legal recognition of her possession of the Dodecanese island which she had ceded to Greece three years back. But what immediately delighted the people of Italy was Mussolini's action in the Corfu case. An international commission was demarcating the boundary line between Greece and Albania in August 1923. Some Greek bandits fired shots that took the life of Italian representative on the commission (Gen.Tellini) with three of his assistants. Soon Italy bombarded the island of Corfu and demanded an unqualified apology from Greece along with the payment of a huge amount of indemnity. The Ambassadors' Conference, that took place at Paris shortly thereafter, endorsed Italy's stand.

In such a situation Greece appealed to the League of Nations, but Mussolini refused to accept its jurisdiction in the matter. Private negotiations then started. It was decided that Greece deposit a sum of 50,000,000 lire with the Permanent Court of International Justice at the Hague pending an award by the Court on the validity of the Italian claim. Again he rejected this move. The Ambassadors' Conference went on exercising its pressure on Greece with the result that she was forced to pay the huge amount of indemnity direct to Italy. Such a triumphant success in such a minor matter enhanced Mussolini's image among his people who were anxious to see their country under a strong leader, but it definitely smacked of the weakness of the League of Nations. "The moral of these proceedings appeared to be that the Allied Governments were not prepared, through the League of Nations or otherwise, to take action against one of their members in defence of a small Power."[25]

---

24. Albrecht-Carrie, op. cit., p. 187.
25. Carr, op. cit., p. 72. As a matter of fact, Mussolini's real aim was to win the appreciation of his people and discredit the League of Nations in the eyes of the people of the world. Thus, he said in the Senate: "In my opinion, the Corfu episode is of the greatest importance in the history of Italy, because it has put the problem of the League of Nations before the public opinion of Italy in a way which no number of books could have done. Italians have never been very

The aggressive course of Italy's foreign policy continued. On January 27, 1924, the Treaty of Rome was signed whereby the Free State of Fieume was divided between Italy and Yugoslavia in a way that the former secured Fieume proper, while the neighbouring towns of Porto Baros went to the latter. It was said to have solved the problem of Fieume—'an original apple of discord'. Now Mussolini seemed bent on a thorough-going liquidation of his quarrel with a neighbouring country like Yugoslavia without taking to the path of abdication and retrenchment as followed by his predecessors. The annexation of an important part of Fieume with Italy was followed by the conclusion of a five-year pact of friendship and collaboration with Yugoslavia and the following year (1925) witnessed the drawing up of so-called Nettuno Convention designed to implement this collaboration in the domains of economic and cultural relations.[26] In 1924, Mussolini astonished Europe by formally recognising the new Soviet regime and concluding a commercial treaty with it. "It was an unexpected reversal of policy, but a good commercial move, opening the straits and the Black Sea to Italian shipping and industrial products."[27]

It may be pointed out at this stage that while taking such steps, Mussolini kept in his mind the strong position of France that might be a source of obstruction to his long-range designs. Resurgence of Germany was, therefore, to be a matter of delight for the Italian dictator. With this view Italy took part in the deliberations at Locarno in October, 1925. She signed the Rhineland pact and thereby pledged to come to the help of either France or Germany in the event of an unprovoked attack on them. Italy also signed a

---

much interested in the League of Nations: they believed that it was a lifeless academic organisation of no importance.... In the point of fact the League is an Anglo-French duet; each of these powers has its satellites and its clients, and Italy's position, so far, has been one of absolute inferiority. The problem may be stated in these terms: should Italy leave the League of Nations?" See Albrecht-Carrie, op. cit., p. 208.

26. It may be given here that by the Rapallo Treaty of November 1920, Italy and Yugoslavia composed their differences. Italy gained the line of Julian Alps, including Monte Nevoso, Istria with Pola, Trieste, and Julian Venetia. Fieume was declared an independent state. But by the agreement of 1924 Italy acquired the enclave of Zara on the Dalmatian coast.
27. H. Herder and D.P. Waley (eds.): *A Short History of Italy* (Cambridge: Oxford University Press, 1963), p. 216.

commercial treaty with Germany that opened a large market for Italian goods on the continent. At the same time, with a view to implement his *'drang nach osten policy'*, he kept his eyes fixed at the position of Albania. In November 1926 Italy signed the Treaty of Tirana by which Albania became virtually an Italian dependency.

The Franco-Yugoslavian Treaty was signed at Paris in November 1927, and within two weeks a treaty of defensive alliance between Italy and Albania was concluded. Now Mussolini created a situation that annoyed France, Yugoslavia and Greece as well as other members of the Little Entente like Czechoslovakia and Romania. Against the prospective enemy in the Adriatic (Yugoslavia), Italy "was obliged to proceed cautiously, for Yugoslavia was the ally of France and a member of the Little Entente. Fascist Italy was long obliged to modify Theodore Roosevelt's advice to 'speak softly and carry a big stick' by speaking loudly and recognising that the Italian big stick was ineffective against the bigger stick of French hegemony over the Continent."[28]

The French system of alliances aimed at the defensive encirclement of Germany witnessed its natural clash with the Italian foreign policy at this stage. The reason behind it was that Mussolini did not appreciate growing French strength through the instrumentality of military alliances. Moreover, he well took into his account the fact that there was no place for Italy in the French system of alliances. The undue rise of French supremacy would upset the balance of power in the Continent. For this sake, Germany's power should be restored upto a point. What irked him most was the fact that in the destruction of the power balance in Europe, Italian policy "had been robbed of its most effective lever. France, indeed, would have welcomed Italian adherence, but neither would nor could pay the price of it; nor is there reason to believe that, whatever the price and had the price been paid, this adherence would have been either lasting or dependable for the simple reason that national interest would always make Italy sympathetic to any possibility of re-establishing the balance."[29]

A way out to this dilemma was discovered in looking towards the anti-revisionist powers or those countries that had

---

28. Schuman, op. cit., p. 654.
29. Albrecht-Carrie, op. cit., p. 198.

Italy

suffered at the hands of the Allies in the name of 'peace settlement'. Mussolini moved cautiously after realising that it would be imprudent to espouse too soon and too vigorously the German cause. There were smaller countries also like Hungary, Austria and Bulgaria towards whom Italy could turn her sympathetic attention. Since Hungary was the biggest sufferer after Germany in the peace settlements of 1919, Mussolini gave first-rate importance to friendship with her. Thus, a pact of friendship between Italy and Hungary was signed in early 1927. In 1928, Italy signed the Kellogg-Briand Pact for the renunciation of war as an instrument of national policy, though taking it as 'a tiger without teeth'. In 1928, Mossolini signed a treaty of peace with Turkey and another similar treaty with Abyssinia that was to last for 20 years. At the Naval Conference of 1930, he appreciated disarmament and declared that Italy preferred to reduce her armament to any level provided the rest of the world did the same.

This softly aggressive course of Italian foreign policy continued till 1930. In 1931 Mussolini frankly came forward with the call of treaty revision and along with that denunciation of the League of Nations that stood as a custodian for the protection of the peace settlements. Now he thundered: "Revision of the peace treaties is not a predominantly Italian interest; it is a European interest, a world interest. This possibility of revision ceases to be something absurd and unrealisable from the moment when it is envisaged in the very Covenant of the League of Nations. The sole absurdity lies in the pretense that the treaties are immovable."[30]

Struggle for Treaty Revisionism : Italy's Cautious Policy of Friendship with France and Germany

A new change occurred in the foreign policy of Italy after the rise of Nazism in Germany under Hitler. While Mussolini appreciated the Nazi movement for being a potential source of challenge to the hold of the anti-revisionist powers like Britain and France, he also studied therein some danger to the position of his own country. An implementation of Hitler's plan of Germany's union with Austria would bring the frontiers of Germany close to those of Italy at the Brenner Pass and then create a problem for her South Tyrol that had

---

30. Ibid., p. 200.
31. Gathorne-Hardy, op. cit., p. 366.

a majority of the German people and had been given to her in 1919 in violation of the principle of national self-determination. The common danger of Nazi Germany brought Italy and France close to each other. At the same time, Mussolini could not lose sight of the fact that the maintenance of peace in Europe depended on the revision of Peace Treaties in a way satisfactory to his claims. It is obvious that now Italy's advocacy of revision "was genuinely founded on a desire for peace—peace especially between France and Germany, a contest between whom would raise awkward problems of alliance. With this motive the scope of the contemplated revision was narrowed; as involving an immediate risk of war, neither the grievance of Hungary, Austria nor Bulgaria were really vital."[31]

The new dimension of Italian foreign policy in 1933 were, therefore, to restore Germany as rapidly as possible to a position of equality with other great Powers as well as to weaken France and her satellites like Poland and Little Entente countries (Czechoslovakia, Rumania and Yugoslavia) and in the midst of both promote a revision of peace settlements so as to redeem the plan of *Italia irredenta*. These designs were very cleverly incorporated by Mussolini in the form of a pact desired to be accepted by all the four great powers of that time—Great Britain, France, Italy and Germany. Mussolini offered the idea to British Prime Minister (Ramsay MacDonald) who discussed it with his French counterpart (Herriot). Though Hitler showed some serious reservations in the beginning, but at the pleadings of Mussolini he also gave in. Thus, on July 15, 1933, the Four-Power Pact was signed which had these important provisions:[32]

1. "The Four Western Powers (France, Germany, Great Britain and Italy) undertake to carry out between them an effective policy of cooperation, in order to ensure the maintenance of peace in the spirit of Kellogg Pact and of the 'no resort to force pact', and undertake to follow such course of action as to induce, if necessary, third parties, as far as Europe is concerned, to adopt the same policy of peace."

2. "The Four Powers confirm the principle of the revision of treaties, in accordance with the clauses of the Covenant of the

---

32. Albrecht-Carrie, op. cit., pp. 202-03.

League of Nations, in cases in which there is a possibility that they will lead to conflict among the states. They declare at the same time that the principle of revision can not be applied except within the framework of the League and in a priority of mutual understanding and solidarity of reciprocal interests."

3. "France, Great Britain and Italy declare that, should the Disarmament Conference lead only to partial results, the parity of rights recognised to Germany ought to have an effective import, and Germany pledges herself to realise such parity of rights in a gradual manner, as the result of successive accords to be taken between the Four Powers, in the normal diplomatic way. The Four Powers pledge themselves to reach similar accords as regards 'parity' for Austria, Hungary and Bulgaria."

4. "In all questions, political and non-political, European and extra-European, and also as regards the colonial sector, the Four Powers pledge themselves to adopt, within the measure of the possible, a common line of conduct."

Examined critically, the language of the pact was full of diplomatic mischiefs played by Italy. For instance, despite the diplomatic verbiage and the homage paid to the League, it was "tantamount to a destruction of the foundations of that institution, for it aimed at bringing into existence a four-power directorate of Europe. Such a concept was not novel: Matternich's Quadruple Alliance, Tsar Alexander's Holy Alliance, and the Concert of Europe itself were, in one form or another, expression of the same idea."[33] But it had certain tricks for the benefit of Italy. The terms of the pact were such that they drew a wedge in Franco-Polish relations and had a very adverse effect on the sympathy of the Little Entente powers towards France. In a way, Germany and Italy drew closer. The effort, however, proved a failure when France and Germany declined to ratify it. The whole affair ended after showing that Mussolini, eager to assert Italy's new position as a front-rank world power—and perhaps eager to avoid being pushed out of the limelight by his new fellow-dictator—had made the first move.

Conquest of Abyssinia : Last Triumph of Mussolini's Colonial Policy

The period of 1930-36 covered the "halcyon years of

---
33. Ibid., p. 203.

Fascism."[34] The worldwide economic crisis of 1930-31 and the breakdown of the World Economic Conference of 1932 provided a timely opportunity for the Duce to embark of the path of 'autarchy'. The Disarmament Conference had the same fate. Mussolini frankly declined to take to the path of disarmament unless it was accepted faithfully by other major European powers. Now he could declare his colonial ambitions in bold terms. On one occasion in 1932 he said: "...we shall march with sure and Roman step towards infallible goals. No force can stop us, because we do not represent just a party or a doctrine or a mere programme; we represent much more than that. We bear in our hearts the dream that stirs also within our souls; we want to forge the great, proud, majestic Italy of our dreams, of our poets, our worries, and our martyrs. Sometimes, I see this Italy in its unique, divine geographical expression. I see it constellated with its marvellous towns, I see it surrounded by its fourfold sea, I see it populated by an ever more numerous people hard-working and vigorous, seeking its paths for expansion in the world. Salute this Italy, this divine land of ours protected by God...."[35]

Thus, in violation of previous international commitments, Mussolini looked towards Abyssinia.[36] As a shrewd statesman, he could calculate that Britain and France, for the reason of being a victim of Naziphobia, would not stand in his way.[37] The invasion was launched in October 1935. Hitler's occupation and militarisation of the Rhineland became an important development now that contributed yet more to effect Ethiopia's desertion by London and Paris and by their joint efforts under the auspices of the League of Nations. The great appeasers acted completely in the hope of

---

34. Mauriel Grindrod: *Italy* (New York: Fredrick A. Praeger, 1968), p. 79.
35. Ibid., p. 80, n 1.
36. For instance, by an accord of December 13, 1906, Britain, France and Italy had agreed to maintain the *status quo* and to make every effort to preserve the integrity of Ethiopia. An Anglo-Egyptian agreement of July 20, 1934, extended the frontiers of Libya at Egypt's expense. By the Laval-Mussolini accord of January 7, 1935, 44,500 sq. miles of the Tibesti desert were ceded to Libya and strip of French Somaliland was added to Eritrea all in fulfilment of the Treaty of London of 1915. "Laval and his successors blessed Italian designs against the ancient Empire of Haile Selassie in the hope of securing continued Italian support against the Reich—at the cost of destroying the League of Nations as an agency of collective security." Schuman, op. cit., p. 654.

bringing the Italian dictator back into the Stresa Front of April 1935. Surprisingly, British and French statesmen, instead of codemning the move of Mussolini or understanding his real motives, adhered to the path of appeasement so much so that even the decision of economic sanctions taken by the League remained ineffective. In a mood of sheer enthusiasm, he rejected the Hoare-Laval plan whereby Italy was offered a very large part of Abyssiania along with some portion of the adjacent British colony in Africa.[38]

In flagrant violation of the norms of international law and the half-hearted reaction of the League of Nations, Italian forces moved on. By July 1936, Abyssinia was made a part of the Italian empire. At this stage, Mussolini in a thundering voice said: "I announce to the Italian people and to the world that the war is finished... that peace re-established... Abyssinia is Italian—Italian in fact, because occupied by our victorious armies, Italian of right, because with the sword, it is civilisation which triumphs over barbarism.... At the rally of October 2, I solemnly promised that I would do anything possible in order to prevent an African conflict from developing into a European war. I have maintained the pledge.... But .... we are ready to defend our brilliant victory with the same intrepid and inexorable decision with which we have guided it."[39]

---

37. Gen. de Bono of Italy has put on record that Mussolini had been preparing to invade Abyssinia since 1932, though the invasion "was subsequently sold to the world as an answer to the unprovoked aggression by the Abyssinians in 1934." Denis Mack Smith: *Italy: A Modern History* (Ann Arbor: University of Michigan Press, 1959), p. 448.

38. The Hoare-Laval proposal bearing the deceptive title of the 'exchange of territories' was that Italy should be granted most of the Tigre district in the north and most of the Ogaden district in the south. Selassie would, however, be allowed to keep in the holy city of Axum in the Tigre district. In return Abyssinia would be compensated by a strip running down to the sea. According to Eden's plan of six months before, this strip was to be at British expense and run to Zeilah; according to the new plan, it was to be at Italian expense and run to Assab, to the north of French Somaliland. The whole of rest of Southern Abyssinia, while still remaining under Selassie's sovereignty, was to be constituted into a 'zone of economic expansion and settlement resolved to Italy.' Christopher Hollis says that the plan "was not as wicked as outcry made it out to be, but it was a great deal sillier." *Italy in Africa* (London: Hamish Hamilton, 1941), pp. 222-23.

39. Ibid., p. 231.

Four days after, he said: "Italy has her empire at last, a fascist empire, because it bears the indestructible tokens of the will and of the power of the Roman victors, because this is the goal towards which during fourteen years were spurred on the exuberant and disciplined energies of the young and dashing generations of Italy—an empire of peace, because Italy desires peace, for herself and for all men, and she decides upon war only when it is forced upon her by imperious, irrepressible necessities of life—an empire of civilisation and of humanity for all the populations of Abyssinia. That is in the tradition of Rome who after victory associates the people with her own destiny. Here is the law, O Italians, which closes one period of our history and opens up another as a vast pass opens on all the possibilities of the future. The territories and the peoples that belonged to the empire of Abyssinia are placed under the full and entire sovereignty of the Kingdom of Italy. The title of Emperor has been assumed for himself and his successors by the King of Italy."[40]

Mussolini's conquest of Abyssinia had some very important effects. In the first place, such a successful aggression "placed her in a far stronger international position than she had hitherto enjoyed. Having effectively played off Berlin against Paris and London, Mussolini could retain a foot in both camps and bargain with each for concessions under the threat of joining the other."[41] Second, it sharpened the trend of Italy's hatred towards Britain in view of the fact that it was Sir Anthony Eden's emphatic assertions in the League Assembly that Italy's antipathy towards the English became marked as 'a residue of Mussolini's influence.'[42] Third, the success of the course of aggression made the League of Nations a major victim. The international organisation received another serious jolt after the Manchurian crisis of 1931. Last, it added to the colonial ambitions of Italy yet more. On November 30, 1938, the Italian deputies made 'loud outcries of Tunisia, Nice, Savoy, Corsica, Djibouti.'[43]

---

40. Ibid., pp. 231-232.
41. Schuman, op. cit., p. 655.
42. See Norman Kogan: *The Politics of Italian Policy* (New York: Fedrick A. Praeger, 1963), p. 23.
43. Schuman, op. cit., p. 658.

Italy

Rome-Berlin Axis : Mussolini's Drift Towards Subservience to Hitler

The distinctly rightist character of Italian Fascism under Mussolini became manifest after the successful aggression of Ethiopia. Now the Duce jubilantly reiterated his intention of expanding the empire and, at the same time, finishing Communism in the world. On August 30, 1936, he declared: "We can mobilise 8,000,000 men.... We reject the absurdity of eternal peace, which is foreign to our creed and to our temperament. We must be strong. We must be always stronger. We must be so strong that we can face any eventualities and look directly in the eye whatever may befall." And then on November 1, 1936, at Milan he said: "Collective security never existed, does not exist and will never exist.... The League of Nations can perish.... Today we raise the banner of anti-Bolshevism...."[44]

The frankly anti-Bolshevik affirmation of Mussolini brought him very close to his German counterpart. On November 25, 1936, Italian and German Foreign Ministers (Vicomate Kintomo Mushakoji and Joachim von Ribbentrop respectively) signed the Anti-Comintern Pact "declaring the purpose of the Communist International, called Comintern, is to destroy and subdue the existing States by all available means, and assured that the interference of the Communist International in the internal affairs of nations threatens not only their domestic tranquillity and social welfare but threatens world peace in general, and thus have agreed to co-operate against the communist activity of destruction in the following manner:
1. To share information concerning the activities of Third International, to consult in regard to necessary defence measures and to execute the same in full cooperation with each other; and
2. To invite the Third Powers, whose domestic tranquillity is threatened by the activity of the Communist International, to take defensive measures in the spirit of understanding or to participate in the agreement."

It was to remain in force for a term of five years within which the two parties with mutual consent were to decide in regard to the

---
44. Ibid., p. 656.

form of their continued cooperation.⁴⁵

Thus, came into being Rome-Berlin Axis or a union of the two dictatorial powers both committed to the revision of the peace settlement and the destruction of Communism. For the latter aim, they could well thrive on the Anglo-French policy of appeasement. The word 'axis' "came as the first clear indication of a new orientation of the two powers—Germany and Italy."⁴⁶ But, as later events showed, this union meant subservience of Mussolini's moves to those of Hitler. It is rightly commented: "Italy's foreign policy was now definitely drawn into the orbit of Nazism. The formation of the Axis in 1936 thus entangled the policy of Mussolini with that of Hitler. This new political term meant that round the directing policy of either Rome or Berlin, the States of Central and Eastern Europe should rotate, while retaining their own governments, composed of men sympathetic to the Axis policy, their political and economic life was to be controlled and directed from the Centre round which they revolved."⁴⁷

As a matter of fact, the Rome-Berlin axis of 1936 "was born partly of Mussolini's long-standing illusion that the growth of German power could be made to save Italy's interests and partly his taste for an ideological foreign policy."⁴⁸ But, as events proved in a short time to come, it proved a wrong step on the side of Italy. It can be said in extenuation that at the time of signing the axis, Mussolini "could hardly have foreseen the rash and impetuous action of Hitler in 1939 that later involved Italy in a ruinous war."⁴⁹

---

45. For text of treaty see Sharp and Kirk, op. cit., Appendix IV, pp. 804-05.
46. H. Hearder and D.P. Waley (eds.): *A Short History of Italy*, p. 224.
47. Ibid., pp. 224-25. The term 'axis' was a peculiar euphemism at this stage. Keeping its impact in view, it was remarked that it "is a strange new phrase, unfamiliar in international relations. An axis is not an instrument, nor is it a human relation. It is a line between two points, a line about which something is in revolution. An axis is not an alliance, it is not even an *entente*. Yet in this case there may be something of cooperation and sympathy." Stuart, op. cit., p. 197. For this reason, it was commented that the "aim of the two Centres (Germany and Italy) did not coincide. Rome wanted Austrian independence and the revision of the boundaries of Hungary and Bulgaria while Berlin meant to have ultimate dominance everywhere including Rome." See Hearder and Waley, op. cit., p. 225.
48. Alan Cassels: *Mussolini's Early Diplomacy* (Princeton, New Jersey: Princeton University Press, 1970), p. 395.
49. Luigi Villari: *Italian Foreign Policy under Mussolini* (New York: The Devin-Adair Co., 1956), p. 162.

In clear disregard to all that he had said about Hitler in the recent past, he virtually reduced himself to a dummy of his German counterpart and that made Italy like a satellite of Germany from 1936 till the close of the Second World War. Thanks to the personal fascination which he (Hitler) henceforth inspired in the Duce, Fascism in Italy "lost its character and became poor, half-hearted, imitation of German National Socialism."[50]

It is well evident from the following instances of great international significance:

1. *Annexation of Austria with the Reich*

We have already seen in Chapter 5 that Mussolini, who had opposed Hitler's rash step towards destruction of Austrian independence in 1934, changed his stand after his conquest of Abyssinia. The reason was that he willy-nilly wanted to reciprocate Hitler's sympathy for Nazi imperial aggrandisements in Central Europe. Though Italy was a party to the decision of Stresa Conference of 1935 where she with France and Britain had pledged to preserve Austrian independence, Mussolini ignored all this during the course of his meeting with Hitler in Germany towards the end of September, 1937. The result was vociferous proclamation of the Rome-Berlin axis, as a political combination of high importance

---

50. Elizabeth Wiskemann: *Fascism in Italy* (London: Macmillan, 1969), p. 70. Compare it all with what Mussolini had said on earlier occasions. For instance, in 1933, he said: "The Germans should allow themselves to be guided by me if they wish to avoid unpardonable blunders. In politics it is undeniable that I am more intelligible than Hitler." See Christopher Hibbert: *Benito Mussolini: A Biography* (London: Longmans, 1962), p. 66. The biographer of the Duce says that he despised Hitler as a horrible sexually degenerate creature, a dangerous fool, leader of a barbarous and savage system capable only of slaughter, plunder and blackmail. While hitting hard at Hitler's purge of June 1934, he reacted. "I should be pleased. I suppose, that Hitler has carried out a revolution on our lives, but they are Germans, so they will end by ruining our idea. They are still the barbarians of Tactius and the Reformation is in eternal conflict with Rome." Ibid., p. 72. But it all changed after he had personal contact with Hitler. Thus, it is said by his biographer: "Not only Mussolini's policies but even his character seemed to have been effected by his association with Hitler, by his unwilling but growing dependence upon him, his reluctant admiration, his patent jealousy. Whereas in the past he had been willing to listen to advice and even occasionally to criticism, now he attacked with an alarming venom those who presumed to advise him or to question his political sense." Ibid., pp. 101-02.

and value.⁵¹ It afforded a grand opportunity for Hitler to win over Mussolini to his side with the force of his usual adroitness. It made the latter accept the action of the former in accomplishing the Anshchluss in March, 1938.⁵²

2. *Anti-Semitism*

Another important direction in which Mussolini dittoed the line of Hitler in clear disregard to what he had said a little earlier was his resort to the path of anti-Semitism. In 1932 he despised Hitler's professions of anti-Semitism as 'arrant nonsense, stupid, and idiotic'. In September 1934, in a speech at Bari, he said: "Thirty centuries of history enable us to look with majestic pity at certain doctrines taught on the other side of the Alps by the descendants of people who were wholly illiterate in the days when Rome boasted a Caesar, a Virgil, and an Augustus."⁵³ But in the summer of 1938 he followed Hitler in vigorously launching an anti-Semitic campaign after knowing it well that his country had a population of about 70,000 Jews and that his countrymen would never appre-

---

51. See E. Wiskemann: *The Rome-Berlin Axis* (London: Oxford University Press, 1949).
52. Grant and Temperley, op. cit., p. 515. About the real reactions of Mussolini on this point, it is well remarked. "In Italy the *coup* had caused much popular and official indignation. Hitler made an effort to smooth over this situation by reminding Italy of his support during the sanctions period and by immediate promises to respect scrupulously the new Italo-German frontier. Ostensibly at least these assurances were accepted by Italy, but the Duce countered by concluding a new agreement with Great Britain and he let it be known that he was far from pleased by this action of his axis partner. He may never have trusted Hitler before, but it seems obvious that his distrust was greatly intensified by this enhancement of German strength in the region which Italy had hoped to keep as her own private reserve." op. cit., pp. 653-54.
53. Christopher Hibbert, op. cit., p. 76. In 1932 Mussolini told Ludwig in an interview thus: "Of course, there are no pure races left; not even the Jews have kept their blood unmingled. Successful crossings have often promoted the energy and beauty of a nation. Race ! It is a feeling, not a reality; ninety-five per cent at least is a feeling. Nothing will ever make me believe that biologically pure races can be shown to exist today. Amusingly enough, not one of those, who have proclaimed the 'nobility' of the Teutonic race was himself a Teuton. Gobineau was a Frenchman; Houston Chamberlain, an Englishman; Woffman, a Jew; Lapouge another Frenchman. Chamberlain actually declared that Rome was the capital of chaos. No such doctrine will ever find wide acceptance here.... National pride has no need of the delirium of race." See Emil Ludwig: *Talks with Mussolini* (London: George Allen and Unwin, 1932), Translated from Roman into English by Eden and Cedar Paul, pp. 73-74.

Italy

ciate such a barbarous move. A group of some University professors published a report, apparently phrased largely by Mussolini, that outlined the scientific basis for an Aryan racial policy. It contained 10 propositions that became the platform for an Italian anti-Semitic campaign. New decrees followed in rapid succession barring Jews from the schools and institutions of the Italians—pure Aryans. Mussolini dispensed with the services of a good number of high officials who were Jews. Even marriages between the Romans and the Jews were forbidden. Thus, Mussolini "officially brought Italy into ideological harmony with Nazi Germany."[54]

3. *Destruction of Czechoslovakia*
When Hitler made another experiment of his policy of 'drive towards the east' and made Czechoslovakia the next target of his attack, Britain and France adhered to the course of winning peace at any price. Taking note of the fact that the prospects of a European war over Czechoslovakia were extremely distasteful, Mussolini entered the scene. Prompted by appeals from London and Washington, he managed to persuade Hitler to hold up military action for some time and sort out the matter with him in conference with Chamberlain and Daladier at Munich. The conference itself "was destined to be anti-climatic, for it was understood that by consenting to confer on the question, Hitler had decided to accept a compromise rather than to force his own solution by resort to arms."[55] If examined from a critical standpoint, it appears that the Munich settlement of 1939 "was in effect the application of the policy advocated in Mussolini's Four-Power Pact of 1933; it was, indeed, the application of this policy with a vengeance. The Little Entente members had shown a sound instinct in raising the loudest outcry against Mussolini's proposals in 1933; Munich was the confirmation of their worst premonitions, preserving the peace among the great powers through the device of agreement among them at the expense of a small nation."[56]

---

54. W.C. Langsam: *The World since 1919* (Delhi: Surjeet Publications, 1981), p. 96.
55. Sharp and Kirk, op. cit., p. 661.
56. Albrecht-Carrie, op. cit., p. 262.

4. Spanish Civil War

The civil war in Spain afforded another timely opportunity for the dictators of Germany and Italy to strengthen their hands with a view to create a powerful anti-Communist front in Europe. Mussolini gave all support to Gen. Franco. When a resolution passed by the Assembly of the League of Nations declared that there were veritable foreign army corps on the Spanish soil, it was guessed that there were about 100,000 Italian troops operating in Spain, while Rome acknowledged 40,000 only. Whatever the strength of the Italian troops, it was sure that Mussolini was more interested in saving his face first and then having a friend to combat communism. So strong was his determination to support Gen. Franco in league with Hitler that he went to the length of playing a game without any prospects of immediate gain to his people. Italian involvement in the civil war of Spain, therefore, went straight to the pleasure of Hitler. Certainly Italy could cash no tangible advantage after having a hold in the Mediterranean. It is critically pointed out: "In return for all the money and effort expended on intervention in Spain, Mussolini received nothing for his pains. When the Italians suffered a minor defeat on the Guadalajara, the foreign press began to suspect that fascism was more bark than bite, and this irritated him exclusively, because not being taken seriously was his greatest fear, as it was also the greatest danger to his government. He, therefore, soon made Roatta's expeditionary force less 'voluntary' and replaced the black-shirted militiamen with more regular soldiers. Seventy thousand Italians were engaged in Spain during 1937, and the initial promise of arms had led by degrees to an inextricable involvement. While victory would bring little reward, defeat would mean a loss of face which he dared not contemplate. Here was a political mistake which was as elementary as it was now irreparable."[57] It had its definite repercussions. When the Spanish trouble came up, it was Spain rather than the distant memories of Abyssinia which was responsible for the complications of Italy's international relations."[58]

---

57. Denis Mack Smith, op. cit., p. 457.
58. Christopher Hollis, op. cit., p. 238.

Keeping all these important facts in view, a critic says that "from 1936 until the end, nothing can be discerned that deserves the name of Italian foreign policy, nothing but a surrender to pressure from Hitler with no regard for Italy's interest or capacity."[59]

Conquest of Albania and Pact of Steel: Italy Jumps into the Second World War

Henceforth, Italy behaved like a satellite of Germany. When Hitler seized from Lithuania the port of Memel given to her in the peace settlement of 1919, Mussolini certainly anxious to claim some compensatory glory when his partner was gaining so much, invaded Albania on April 7, 1939. The Italian troops drove King Zog and Queen Geraldine out of their backward Balkan kingdom and King Victor Emmanuel of Italy assumed the Albanian crown. This action amounted to the violation of several agreements, ranging from the Treaty of Tirana of 1927 (which had made a defensive alliance between the two countries) to the recent British-Italian 'gentlemen's agreement' about the Mediterrranean. Once again, British and French governments gave a show of their adherence to the course of appeasement. Although this action was a flagrant violation of the Ciano-Perth accord, they took no counter-action beyond extending guarantees to Greece and Rumania and concluding an alliance with Turkey about a week after. However, the most deplorable fact was that Mussolini devoured an orphan state placed under the vassalage of his own country. The invasion on Albania on Good Friday "bore the perfect hallmark of Fascist Machiavellianism and carelessness."[60]

But the last and the most important event of Italo-German collaboration, that signified unscrupulous subservience of the former to the latter, is the Military Pact of May 22, 1939, signed by the German and Italian Foreign Ministers (Ribbentrop and Ciano respectively). Known by the name of the 'Pact of Steel', it came as a bold mark of Nazi-Fascist collaboration in a way that the "futility of Fascist diplomacy was completed by rushing into these obligations as drafted by the Germans with no written safeguards as to

---

59. Elizabeth Wiskemann, op. cit., p. 65.
60. Denis Mack Smith, *op. cit.*, p. 465.

the delay for which the Italians had asked."⁶¹ As coming events soon revealed, in point of fact by this treaty Mussolini "gave him (Hitler) *carte blanche* to attack Poland and to plunge into the second world war."⁶²

By this treaty Germany and Italy considered that the moment had come to bear testimony by a solemn act to close relationship of friendship and community of interests existing between them and now that a secure bridge towards mutual aid and support had been constructed by the common frontier fixed for all time between Germany and Italy. They declared anew their faith in the policy, the foundations and aims of which had already at an earlier date been agreed upon and which had proven successful as well for the advancement of the interests of both and for securing the peace of Europe. Firmly bound to each other through the inner relationship of their philosophies of life and the comprehensive solidarity of their interests, the German and Italian peoples were determined in the future also to stand side by side with united strength to secure their space for living and for the maintenance of peace. Proceeding along this path pointed out to them by history, both desired in the midst of a world of unrest and distintegration to serve the task of rendering safe the foundations of European culture.

The treaty had some important provisions whereby Germany and Italy resolved to:

1. Remain in constant contact with each other in order to arrive at an understanding on all matters touching their common interests or the general European situation,
2. Immediately enter upon consultations concerning the measures to be taken for safeguarding these interests if their common interests be endangered by international events of any sort whatsoever, and to give the threatened party full political and diplomatic support in order to remove a threat if the security or other essential interests of the other party be threatened from outside,
3. Immediately rally to the side of the partner as ally and support him with all military resources on land, sea and air, if contrary to their wishes and hopes it should happen that either of them

---

61. Elizabeth Wiskemann, op. cit., p. 75.
62. Wiskemann: *Rome-Berlin Axis*, p. 181.

be involved in military entanglements with some other Power or Powers,

4. Further deepen their cooperation in the realm of the military and war economy in order in any given case to make sure that the duties of an ally undertaken in accordance with above articles would be carried out speedily; to constantly arrive at understandings concerning other measures necessary for the practical execution of the provisions of this treaty in a similar manner; to form standing Commissions for the purposes indicated above under the jurisdiction of their Foreign Ministers; and

5. Conclude an armistice or peace only in full agreement with each other in the event of war conducted jointly.

The document ended with the note that the two parties were conscious of the importance which attached to their common relations to Powers with whom they were on terms of friendship and that they were determined in the future too to keep up these relationships and jointly give them a reform consonant with the mutual interests that bound them initially for a period of 10 years.[63]

Matters started deteriorating fast after the signing of this military pact. The notes of President Roosevelt, scoffed at as 'Messiah-like messages' conveyed to Hitler and Mussolini to refrain from attacking their neighbours, went in vain. Likewise, the mission of his envoy (Sumner Welles) to see if there was anything that Mussolini could be persuaded to do to bring Britain and France to terms with Germany proved an exercise in futility. When Hitler attacked Poland on September 1, 1939, and when Britain and France renounced their policy of appeasement, the Second World War started. Soon the Italian government announced that it would take no initiative whatever toward military operations, for the Fascist formula was 'no-belligerency' which "meant in practice all aid to Germany short of war and blackmail against the Allies."[64]

Now Mussolini depended upon the calculation of safety. "To attack while the Allies could still counter-attack would be too late. To attack after the Reich had got complete victory would be too late. To attack after the Allies had been decisively defeated, but

---

63. For full text of the treaty see Schuman, op. cit., pp. 665-66.
64. Ibid., p. 667.

before they had capitulated, would be to attack at the right moment."[65] Since Italy did not go to war simultaneously with that of German action, Britain, France and the United States made serious efforts to bribe or cajole Mussolini into continued neutrality. But all such efforts went in vain.[66] On June 10, 1940, Mussolini informed a cheering crowd in the Piazzade Venezia that Italy had declared war on Britain and France. In a thundering voice he said: "The hour destined by fate is sounding for us. The hour of irrevocable decision has come.... We went to break the territorial and military chains that confine us in our sea.... It is a conflict between two ages, two ideas.... Now the die is cast and our will has burned our ships behind us.... We will conquer in order, finally, to give a new world of peace with justice to Italy, to Europe, and to the universe."[67]

Though belatedly, Italy's plunge into the Second World War was by all means governed by the will of one man—Mussolini. He preferred to materialise his ambition by honouring his commitment to his German partner more than for paying proper heed to the counsels of his most vocal lieutenants like Count Ciano (Minister for Foreign Affairs), Count Grandi (Minister for Justice and former Italian ambassador to England) and Giueseppe Bottai (Minister for Education) who had made no secret of their dislike for German alliance and of the disastrous policy of linking Italy's fate with

---

65. Ibid.
66. On May 16, 1940, Prime Minister Churchill sent a secret message of goodwill coupled with a plea and a warning saying: "Whatever may happen on the Continent, England will go on to the end, even quite alone as we have done before; and I believe, with some assurance, that we shall be aided in increasing measure by the United States and, indeed, by all the Americans. I beg you to believe that it is in no spirit of weakness or of fear that I make this solemn appeal which will remain on the record.... Hearken to it. I beseech you in all honour and respect, before the dread signal is given." Through his ambassador (William Phillis) President Roosevelt offered to Mussolini his good offices to adjust Anglo-Italian differences. Said he: "I propose that if Italy would refrain from entering the war, I would be willing to ask assurances decision so reached that Italy's voice in any future peace conference would have the same authority as if Italy had actually taken part in the war as a belligerent." Ibid., pp. 667-68.
67. Ibid., p. 668. Hearder and Waley rightly comment: "At last as the German armies approached Paris, an attack on the disorganised French forces seemed to assure a splendid Italian victory and taking courage in both hands Mussolini declared war on 10 June." *A Short History of Italy*, p. 230.

Germany's in a war of which the outcome, whatever it might be, could only bring with it a weakening of Italy's position.[68] As a matter of fact, at this stage, Mussolini integrated his irresistible ambition with the bond of the pact of steel that obliged to fight the Italians alongside Germany if war broke out and Hitler thus had in his possession an unconditional warrant which he could present at any time."[69]

Concluding Observations
A detailed study of the Italian foreign policy and diplomacy under the Fascist rule of Mussolini during the inter-war period, as contained in the preceding sections, leaves these important impressions:

1. The tradition of Italian policy was opportunist and its direction remained constantly changing and unpredictable. Since her strength was unequal to that of Germany, France and Great Britain—the principal opponents to her expansionist dreams on the continent, or around the Mediterranean—her statesmen knew that their ambitions could be fulfilled only during the periods of confusion when the relationship of these powers were conflicting and their attention distracted from the Italian purposes.[70] It is for this reason that the case of Italy was dubbed as 'the misery of the impotent' by Schuman.[71] In order to substantiate his view, this writer banks on the critical observation of Chancellor Otto von Bismarck of Germany who once said: "Insatiable Italy, with furtive glances, roves restlessly hither and thither, instinctively drawn on by the odour of corruption and calamity—always ready to attack anybody from the rear and make off with a bit of plunder. It is outrageous that these Italians, still unsatisfied, should continue to make preparations and to conspire in every direction."[72]

2. It shows that the statesmen of Italy gave a proof of their 'jackal' mentality in dealing with the countries of the world.

---

68. Muriel Grindrod: *The New Italy: Transition from War to Peace* (London: Royal Institute of International Affairs, 1947), p. 4. Also see *The Ciano Diaries* (New York: Doubleday, 1946).
69. Denis Mack Smith, op. cit., p. 469.
70. Simonds and Emeny: *The Great Powers in World Politics* (New York: American Book Co., 1939), p. 295.
71. Schuman, op. cit., pp. 649-78.
72. Ibid., p. 649.

Mussolini bombarded Corfu in 1923 and secured huge indemnities from a small state like Greece; then in 1936 he raped a backward state of Africa like Abyssinia and established Roman empire there; then, in 1939, he annexed the orphan state of Albania that was already under the vassalage of his country. When the Second World War broke out, he preferred the course of apparent neutrality to hoodwink the statesmen of London, Paris and Washington. But, after some time, when Germany made some successful advances, Italy also joined the war. "As the tempo of Germany's war accelerated with Hitler's lightning series of invasions into Western Europe, Mussolini began to fear that Italy would be left behind altogether; the war, he believed, might soon be over and he must act quickly if Italy were to qualify for any of the spoils—he had his eye on Nice, Corsica and Tunis. He, therefore, declared war on Britain and France on 10 June, 1940."[73]

3. In spite of the fact that Fascism was a movement of the right, the element of opportunism could not be discarded by Mussolini. He played fast and loose with his anti-Bolshevik orientations. The Fascist foreign policy typically cut itself from tradition and veered unstably from ideological arguments to momentary whims and intuitive fancies. But all this was compounded with a modicum of shrewd realism and a real virtuosity in propaganda and showmanship. Though he had come to power on the pretext of opposing Bolshevism, he was realistic enough to be almost the first to recognise the revolutionary government in Russia. He said: "Both we and the Russians are opposed to liberals, democrats, and parliaments." Not until Russia joined the League and seemed to abandon revisionism, did Mussolini turn to prefer German help. "Evidently, the central core of Fascism was not anti-Bolshevism. (Mussolini was himself more like a Bolshevik than were most Italian socialists.) But rather the deliberate intention to blow sky-high the peace of Europe: anti-Bolshevism had just been a pretext for tricking the ingenuous at home and abroad into becoming his accomplices."[74]

4. Personal egoism as well as political opportunism played their decisive part in the formulation of Italian foreign policy under

---

73. Muriel Grindrod: *Italy*, p. 83.
74. Denis Mack Smith, op. cit., p. 447.

the Duce. His feelings towards the dictator of Germany and his official ideology were a mixture of envy, fear, dislike and admiration. Thus, while he rabidly denounced Hitler's anti-Semitism in 1932-34, he did the same four years after. Likewise, while he desired the Germans to follow his path, he virtually made Italy a satellite of Germany after his successful colonial experiment in Africa. In spite of the fact that he had formed an axis with Hitler in November, 1936 and had concluded the Pact of Steel in May, 1939, he did not resent the action of Hitler in signing a non-aggression treaty with Russia in August, 1939 and, more than that, of keeping him uninformed of such an important development in advance. He treated Italy's membership of the League of Nations as a matter of form, he never made any constructive contribution to its spirit. Particularly after 1936, the tragedy of Italy was "the working out of these misconceptions to their bitter end. Mussolini shared both the illusion and the subsequent disillusion though few, if any, people had been better placed than her for knowing the real truth. Flattery went into his head."[75]

5. Above all, Mussolini lost the sense of proportion so much so that after his triumph in the Abyssianian war, he preferred to lose much than gain anything in return for war-like sacrifices. For instance, Italian losses "had been heavier in Spain than in the Ethiopian campaign. No territories had been won. Fascist Spain was dominated more by Germany than by Italy."[76] Unnecessarily, he took to the inhuman way of suppressing the Jews in 1938 and in the following year he made a direct assault on France by declaring that his aim was to free the Italians from the last servitude—their attitude towards Paris. He told Ciano that he wanted to make the Italians nastier, more Prussian, hard, implacable, hateful, in other words, 'masters'.[77] Throughout the period of his stay in power, he lived in a world of miscalculations and confusion that eventually brought about undoings in his foreign policy. It is, therefore, commented: "From the very beginning he was dangerously muddled between, on one hand thinking that he could convince foreign admirers that Italy was a safe and stabilising force in Europe and, on the other, hand, incessantly proclaiming that the

75. *Ibid.*, p. 452.
76. Schuman, *op. cit.*, p. 665.
77. Wiskmemann: *Fascism in Italy*, p. 72.

settlement of 1919 must be smashed in order to allow further Italian expansion."[78]

In short, Mussolini "showed a lamentably small sense of the high European loyalty of which he sometimes made profession and of that sense of destiny of imperial Rome, which alone gave justification to his philosophy. He would have done well to have read a little more Dante and a little less Machiavelli."[79]

78. Denis Mack Smith, op. cit., p. 446.
79. Christopher Hollis, op. cit., p. 234.

9

GREAT BRITAIN

Observe that the policy of England takes no account of which nations it is that seeks the overlordship of Europe. The question is not whether it is Spain, or the French Monarchy, or the French Empire or the German Empire, or the Hitler regime. It has nothing to do with rulers or nations; it is concerned solely with whoever is the strongest or the potentially dominating tyrant. Therefore, we should not be afraid of being accused of being pro-French or anti-German. If the circumstances were reversed, we could equally be pro-German and anti-French. It is a law of public policy which we are following, and not a mere expedient dictated by accidental circumstance, or likes and dislikes or any other sentiment.

—Sir Winston Churchill[1]

In spite of the fact that passing references have been made to the foreign policy and diplomacy of Great Britain in the preceding chapters, it shall be in the natural fitness of things to present its detailed account so as to highlight the role of British statesmen in the politics of Europe as well as of the whole world during the inter-war period. The striking point, in this direction, is that while the English leaders could faithfully adhere to the 'wonderful unconscious tradition' of their foreign policy contained in the celebrated principle of the 'balance of power' during the phase of pacification (1920-1930), they steadily shifted to the notorious course of appeasement during the phase of crisis (1931-1939). The obdurate course of purchasing 'peace at any price' ultimately led to a ruinous war. It forced Prime Minister Neville Chamberlain to say these words in the House of Commons on September 3, 1939:

---

1. Statement of Churchill at the Conservative Members Committee on Foreign Affairs in March, 1936 contained in his *The Second World War: The Gathering Storm* (Boston: Houghton Mifflin Co., 1948), Vo. I, pp. 207-8.

"This is a sad day for all of us, and to none is it sadder than to me. Everything that I have worked for, everything that I have hoped for, everything that I have believed in during my public life, has crashed into ruins."[2]

Balance of Power: The Most Basic and Most Enduring Principle of British Foreign Policy

The central aim of British foreign policy from the time of the Tudor monarchs had been to prevent the domination of Europe by a single power. Britain opposed the strongest, most aggressive, most dominating power on the Continent of Europe and particularly prevented the Low Countries from falling into the hands of any such power. For this sake, she had taken to the most difficult course. "Faced by Philip II of Spain against Louis XIV under William III and Marlborough, against Napoleon, against William II of Germany, it would have been easy and must have been very tempting to join with the stronger and share the fruits of his conquest. However, we always took the harder course, joined with the less strong Powers, made a combination among them, and thus defeated and frustrated the Continental military tyrant, whoever he was, whatever nation he led. Thus, we preserved the liberties of Europe, protected the growth of its vivacious and varied society, and emerged after four terrible struggles with an ever-growing fame and widening Empire and with the Low Countries softly protected in their independence. Here is the wonderful unconscious tradition of British foreign policy."[3]

Simply stated, it implies that Britain "has viewed with ever-watchful suspicion any state which threatened to upset the balance of power; at crucial moments she has intervened on the continent with all her might—against France under Louis XIV and under Napoleon, and against Germany under William II and under Adolf Hitler."[4] So firm has been the adherence to this course that British statesmen have followed the counsel of Lord Palmerston in keeping their national interest above consideration of permanent friendship or enmity with any country of the world. It is evident from the fact

---

2. Cited in F.L. Schuman: *International Politics* (New York: McGraw Hill, 1948), IV Ed., p. 847.
3. Churchill, op. cit., pp. 207-8.
4. N.D. Palmer and H.C. Perkins: *International Relations: The World Community in Transition* (Calcutta: Scientific Book Agency, 1965), p. 733.

that for centuries Britain and France "had been the best of enemies, but under the altered conditions of the nineteenth century they began a cautious friendship and collaboration in many ways; and in the twentieth century the blood of Englishmen and of the Frenchmen has flowed in a common cause of many battlefields. During this period Germany and not France threatened to upset the balance in Europe."[5]

This 'guiding principle of historic British foreign policy' has its classic representation in the Memorandum of Sir Eyre Crow that *inter alia* said: "The first interest of all countries is the preservation of national independence.... History shows that the danger threatening the independence of this or that nation has generally risen, at least in part, out of the momentary predominance of a neighbouring State, at once militarily powerful, economically efficient, and ambitious to extend its frontier or, spread its influence, the danger being directly proportionate to the degree of its power and efficiency, and to the spontaneity or 'inevitableness' of its ambitions. The only check of the abuse of political predominance derived from such a position has always consisted in the opposition of any equally formidable rival, or of a combination of several countries forming leagues of defence. The equilibrium established of such a grouping of forces is technically known as the balance of power, and it had become almost a historical truism to identify England's secular policy with the maintenance of this balance by throwing her weight now in this scale and now in that, but ever on the side opposed to the political dictatorship of the strongest single State or group at a given time."[6]

The observance of such a guiding principle in the sphere of international politics had ascribed to British foreign policy the character of 'splendid isolationism'. It signified a sort of 'no-alignment' or independence of action so that British "would be free to commit her power as her interest dictated."[7] At the same time, it placed her in the most enviable position of being the 'balancer'.

---

5. Ibid.
6. Memorandum on the Present State of British Relations with France and Germany dated January 1, 1907 in G.P. Gooch and H. Temperley (eds.): *British Documents on the Origin of the War, 1898-1914* (London: H.M.S.O. 1928), Vol. III, p. 403.
7. C.P. Schleiher: *International Relations* (New Delhi: Prentice-Hall of India, 1963), p. 363.

"To hold the balance, a state must be flexible and relatively powerful. Flexibility is necessary, because it must always be ready to throw its weight to the lighter side. It must be strong in order to tip the balance."[8] A cautious pursuance of such a policy placed Britain in the position of acting as the holder of the balance in Europe rather than as an active participant in European power politics. "This was wholly in keeping with her long-standing dualism of approach to continental affairs—that is, her concern in the affairs of Europe and at the same time her desire to remain aloof from them."[9]

It is for this reason that British statesmen took different stands at different times that could be identified with different alternatives like placing more weight into the side of the scale that was sinking, or preventing a state from adding more weight to its side of the scale so as to effectuate the maxim that 'none shall grow formidable', or that 'none shall resort to war'. Sometimes, it assumed the form of a collective security mechanism so that the challenge of the predominant power could be met effectively. That is, it "involved collective action against such a threat to the security of the community as was involved in the disproportionate strength of a potential aggressor."[10] It also founded itself upon an involuntary acceptance of a given distribution of power as in the peace settlements of 1919 whereby a nation or a group of nations had been obliged to acquiesce after having a defeat in the war.[11] In certain situations, it signified commitment to the measures of peace and security (like those devised at Locarno in 1925 or at Paris in 1928) and rendering support to the machinery of the League of Nations. Thus, after the peace ballot of 1935, Prime Minister Stanley Baldwin declared: "The League of Nations remains the sheet-anchor of British policy."[12]

Unfortunately, British statesmen completely forgot the lessons of the past in the late thirties of the present century and brought upon their people so painful an aftermath of folly. The lone

---

8. Ibid.
9. Palmer and Perkins, op. cit., p. 733.
10. G.M. Gathorne-Hardy: *A Short History of International Affairs, 1920-1939* (London: Oxford University Press, 1950), IV. Ed., p. 11.
11. Norman Hill: *Contemporary World Politics* (New York: Harper and Brothers, 1954), p. 261.
12. Schuman, op. cit., p. 839.

voice of a great leader like Churchill went unheeded. As we shall see, English government under Stanley Baldwin and Neville Chamberlain, in particular, sacrificed the policy of balance of power at the altar of appeasement. It did not denounce acts of aggression when Japan raped Manchuria, Italy annexed Abyssinia, Germany conquered Austria and Czechoslovakia and a military junta seized power in Spain with the ostensible support of Mussolini and Hitler. Ultimately, the will of Churchil had its way. As Prime Minister he said in the House of Commons on May 13, 1940: "I have nothing to offer but blood, tears, toil and sweat.... Our policy? It is to wage war by land, sea, and air. War with all our might and with all the strength God has given us, and to wage war against a monstrous tyranny never surpassed in the dark and lamentable catalogue of human crime.... Our aim? It is victory,.. for without victory there is no survival."[13]

Peace Settlement and After: Britain's Search for Peace, Protection and Prosperity

Britain emerged from the Paris Peace Conference as a satiated as well as an unsatiated power in her own ways. As a victor power, her statesmen could achieve much that had been pledged by Lloyd George in the 'khaki elections' of 1918. Though Kaiser William II (the monarch of Germany) could not be tried and hanged as demanded by the English public opinion, it was a no less happy development that he left the country with the result that Germany became a republic. Moreover, German strength could be crushed to a great extent so much so that she could not be in a position to upset the balance of power on the Continent. But what placed her in the position of an unsatiated power was the reaction of France. Clemenceau's pleadings could not be set aside to the last extent as a result of which France could get much more than appreciated by Britain. The suppression of Germany placed France in a position that she could upset the balance of power on the Continent. To the critics it appeared that Britain "was a victor in name only, for she was economically crippled and her allies took the principal spoils. To France went the hegemony of the Continent. To the dominions went the principal but not very valuable German colonies. To the

---

13. Ibid., pp. 848-49.

unscathed Americans and Japanese went the preponderance of naval power and the markets of the East."¹⁴

Search for peace, protection and prosperity became the goal of British foreign policy within the overall framework of the system of balance of power. After the conclusion of war, British statesmen turned towards what was for them the greatest possible gain of victory—an enduring peace that was a condition precedent to the enjoyment of political security and economic prosperity. An atmosphere of peace alone was conducive to the prospects of trade and commerce. "Peace had long been the supreme objective of British Continental policy. Of the things which in the main dictate national policies, security and prosperity, only the first was for the British Empire a European problem of primary importance; and both security and prosperity, in their European phase, turned upon peace. Since the real affair of the British was imperial, the trade was the life-blood of Empire; peace in Europe, as elsewhere, was essential to British prosperity."¹⁵

Pursuance of the policy of balance of power under these conditions, therefore, required that Germany should be crushed through the mechanism of peace settlement to a point that she could not be a source of menace to the peace of Europe. But it should not be done to a point that France were a beneficiary at British expense and thereby pose a formidable challenge to the position of Britain. Thus, at the close of the First World War, the paramount consideration of Lloyd George and Balfour "was to see

---

14. Warner Moss: "Britain and the Empire" in Brown, Hodges and Roucek (eds.): *Contemporary World Politics: Introduction to the Problem of International Relations* (New York: John Wiley and Sons, 1939), p. 137. "British politicians, Conservative and Labour alike, considered that France, Britain's hereditary enemy, was the most likely trouble-maker in Europe because of her innate fear of Germany. It was Germany, not France, whom they came to think of as having been hardly done by at the Peace Conference. They suspected France's East European Allies either as French client States or as incorrigible meddlers in great power affairs which they did not understand. Even before the Treaty was signed, they entertained an unabashed sympathy for Germany's territorial losses to Poland through the peace settlement. This fact is indispensable to an understanding of British attitudes towards German revisionism in Eastern Europe in the 1930s." See F.S. Northedge and M.J. Grieve: *A Hundred Years of International Relations* (London: Duckworth, 1971), p. 104.
15. Simonds and Emeny: *The Great Powers in World Politics* (New York: American Book Co. 1939), p. 262.

Great Britain

to it that Germany's power to renew the challenge of 1914 was abolished; next, Germany had to be made to pay for her war; but, finally, extreme care had also to be taken to curb the ambitions of France. To that end, the balance of power was to be restored on the Continent, as it had been re-established after the Napoleonic downfall.... The business of the British statesmanship was to see that parity existed not only among the Great Powers individually but also between any two coalitions into which these powers might be divided, in order that the danger of any pursuit of hegemony by an individual state should be abolished."[16]

With such considerations set on his mind, Lloyd George stood as a formidable barrier in the way of Clemenceau. Support of Wilson and repeated invocation of his principle of national self-determination strengthened the hands of the English Prime Minister. For these reasons, France's appetite for security could not be satisfied to the desired extent. For instance, the Rhineland could not be converted into a separate and sovereign state, nor could it be placed under permanent demilitarisation. The interim arrangements of having it under an international commission for 15 years to be abolished in a phased manner (in three instalments of five years each) was a poor consolation for France. Likewise, in the face of British opposition, Germany could not be subjected to heavy reparations to the extent Klotz (French Finance Minister) had calculated. At the instance of Lloyd George, the tangled problem of total German liability could be left to be settled by the Reparation Commission. The reason behind it all was that Lloyd George "was interested not merely in saving Germany territorially but also in insuring her economic recovery. It was to British interest, to European advantage, to world profit, that the Great German people should be brought back into normal economic and financial life and international trade as soon as completely as possible. It was, moreover, the single prescription for peace, because only a properous Germany could be a contented nation."[17]

And yet friendship with a country like France was deemed to be in the British national interest. Keeping this important consideration in view, Lloyd George signed a treaty of guarantee of security (after signing the Treaty of Versailles) whereby Britain

---

16. Ibid., p. 269.
17. Ibid., p. 272.

pledged to come to the assistance of France in the event of any unprovoked aggression from the side of Germany. It, however, proved abortive when the United States Senate rejected the Treaty of Versailles and along with that a similar commitment of America to France became infructuous. Under these conditions, Britain declined to shoulder alone the great responsibility of providing security to France against any possible German attack. However, in the face of repeated French insistence for some additional guarantee of assistance against a possible German aggression, the British government at length plucked up courage in January 1922, to offer France a guarantee on approximately the same terms as those of the abortive treaty of 1919. It could not satisfy the obstinate French Prime Minister (Poincare) who, as a believer in the policy of all or nothing, "demanded that the guarantee should be supplemented by a military convention defining the precise nature of the assistance to be rendered by the British army, and declared that failing this, a mere guarantee treaty was worthless to France. The British government was not prepared to commit itself so far. "It had discharged its debt of honour; and it now abandoned for some time to come the apparently hopeless task of satisfying the French appetite for security."[18]

It was, therefore, natural for Britain to oppose the contentions of France in the deliberations of the Reparation Commission. When in 1922 the French delegate could have his point in the meeting of the Commission with the support of his Belgian counterpart (that the non-payment of the second instalment of reparation by Germany was a proof of deliberate wrong on her part), the British delegate felt alone as the American representative was not there to come to his rescue. As a result of this, French and Belgian troops occupied the Ruhr. The British government denounced this action on the plea that it would further cripple the economic position of Germany and thereby render her incapable of making any payment of reparation afterwards. The French statesmen came to realise the mistake of their hasty action after a year and then Ruhr had to be evacuated. By such an action Britain won the appreciation of Germany. Moreover, the role that Britain played in the formulation

---

18. E.H. Carr: *International Relations between the Two World Wars, 1919-1939* (London: Macmillan, 1952), pp. 29-30.

of the Dawes Plan had its more impressive impact upon the government of Berlin.[19]

It is, therefore, clear that during the first four years of the postwar period Anglo-French relations remained strained. The obvious reason was that the French leaders adhered to the course of obduracy; they "completely refused to make any concession to their former allies. Affirming that they knew the Germans better than did any other nation and that they found them thoroughly untrustworthy, they felt unable to attempt conciliation."[20] However, as Britain was the greatest power on the continent, French leaders could not take matters to a point of total rupture of relations with her."Relations with Britain became one of their major proccupations. But even then she (Britain) had to cope not merely with resistance in minor matters, but with a complete lack of agreement on what was for France the crux of the whole matter, namely, the necessity of enforcing the treaties upon Germany and of supplementing the guarantees of security through which they contained."[21]

The Chamberlain Era : Policy of the Restoration of Europe

Since Britain emerged from the war "nevertheless wounded and weakened from its most perilous ordeal of a thousand years,"[22] her foreign policy-makers endeavoured to "heal the wounds of war, to establish better relations all round."[23] Prime Minister Bonar Law looked at the American defection with great anxiety and he sent Stanley Baldwin to Washington D.C., to negotiate a settlement of the British war debts, incurred very largely on account of other nations. In February 1924, the Labour government under Prime Minister Ramsay MacDonald surprised his critics by according *de jure* recognition to the Communist regime of Russia. Just three months after, he convened a conference in London having as its object the conclusion of treaties for settlement of outstanding loan

---

19. See Reginald Mackenna: *Reparations and International Debt*, International Goodwill Communique, No. 131, December, 1923, p. 571.
20. I.C. Hannah: *British Foreign Policy* (London: Nicholas and Watson Ltd., 1938), p. 199.
21. Arnold Wolfers: *Britain and France between Two World Wars: Conflicting Strategies of Peace since Versailles* (New York: Harcourt Brace & Co., 1940), p. 17.
22. Schuman, op. cit., p. 833.
23. Hannah, op. cit., p. 197.

granted by the British Government.[24] However, progress in the direction of improving relations with Russia received a severe setback after a short while with the disclosure of the notorious 'Zinoviev Letter' in October 1924 wherein, as alleged, the President of the Comintern (Zinoviev) had advised the British workers to stage an armed insurrection in their country after the pattern of Lenin.

The induction of the Conservative Government in 1925 under Stanley Baldwin had, therefore, its own effect on the progress of British relations with other European countries. The fate of the Geneva Protocol (that had sought to fill up certain gaps in the Covenant by banning all recourse to an aggressive war, by laying down a formula for the detection of an aggressor, and by reiterating pacific settlement of international disputes by men of judicial adjudication or compulsory arbitration) was sealed when the Tory government sought to decline the heavy responsibility that might befall on her under the auspices of the League. By doing so it also sought to placate the claim of the Dominions.[25] The new Foreign Secretary (Austen Chamberlain) formally announced in the Council

---

24. It may be pointed out here that as early as May 1920, a Russian trade delegation under M. Krassin had visited England. Though his mission bore some fruit in the shape of the Anglo-Russian Trade Agreement of March 1921, this did not effect any substantial improvement, since it was unaccompanied by *de jure* recognition, and made no provision for the re-establishment of that credit which the Russians had forfeited by the confiscation of foreign property and the repudiation of external debts. The British government at this time was fully alive to the necessity of promoting the resumption of international trade, and it was due to the action of Mr. Lloyd George at the Cannes Conference of January 1922, that Russia was enabled to attend the general Conference which succeeded it in Genoa in April of the same year. See Gathorne-Hardy, op. cit., pp. 102-3.

25. One important feature of British foreign policy that should be taken note of at this stage is that London could not thoroughly ignore the wishes of the governments of the British Dominions. "Of equal significance also is the political influence exerted by the Dominions upon British policy. While the prestige of Great Britain in European Councils is immeasurably enhanced when backed by the United Commonwealth, yet insistence by the Dominions that the mother country assume no new responsibilities on the Continent enormously accentuates British desire for permanent peace; for it is by no means beyond the limit of possibility that if events like those of 1914 should again expose the British Empire to the hazards of a European war, refusal of the Dominions to repeat the services and sacrifices of the World War might lead to parting of the ties that bind them to Great Britain. Canada's failure to offer its

of the League of Nations that Britain had decided not to accept it.[26]

However, the new Foreign Secretary earned a name by sticking to the constructive course of reconstruction of Europe and strengthening the League of Nations without deviating from the basic policy of maintaining the balance of power.[27] His most outstanding achievement found place in the conclusion of Locarno agreements in the autumn of 1925. By the Rhineland Treaty, Germany's western frontiers (as revised under the Treaty of Versailles) were permanently recognised and Britain stood as one of the important sureties to see that the momentous agreement would not be dishonoured by the unilateral action of Germany. Thus, by all means, it "was the most serious commitment undertaken by Britain since the war, and it is significant that it led to a very great improvement in the international situation. Britain had at last found the means of reconciling the necessity for cooperation with her dislike of formal military commitments and it may well be that British policy in the future will revert to this Locarno system of limited guarantees, which incidentally, won the strong approval of Viscount Grey. It is now generally recognised that by undertaking these obligations to France and Germany, Britain was not intervening unnecessarily in Continental affairs; she was playing her part in the protection of that peace of Western Europe which,

---

full support to the mother country in the dispute with Italy over Ethiopia emphasised this possibility." Simonds and Emeny, op. cit., p. 266. These writers refer to the statement of the Canadian Prime Minister (Mackenzie King) who on assuming his office on November 2, 1935 said: "The Canadian government desires to make it clear that it does not recognise any commiment binding Canada to adopt military sanctions (against Italy), and that no such commitment could be made without the prior approval of the Canadian Parliament," Ibid., n. 2.

26. For instance, an official Memorandum criticising the Geneva Protocol said: "The fresh emphasis laid upon sanctions, the new occasions discovered from their employment, the elaboration of military procedure, insensibly suggest that the vital business of the League is not so much to promote friendly cooperation and reasoned harmony in the management of international affairs as to preserve peace by organising war and (it may be) war on the largest scale." See Maurice Bruce: *British Foreign Policy: Isolation or Intervention ?* (London: Thomas Nelson and Sons, 1938) p. 132.

27. For instance, on 24 March, 1925, Austen Chamberlain said in the House of Commons: "All our greatest wars have been fought to prevent one great military power dominating Europe, and at the same time dominating the coasts of the channels and the parts of the Low Countries." Simonds and Emeny, op. cit., p. 259 n3.

as our survey of previous centuries has shown, is no less a vital interest to Britain than it is to France."²⁸

What really motivated the British government at this stage? Two reasons may be advanced. First, the realisation that the insular position of Britain could no longer serve as a bulwark against continental attack by sea or air was to have a profound influence upon future British strategy. Taking it in his view, Chamberlain said: "The development of aeronautics has further impaired our insular security and has given fresh force to the secular principle of British policy that the independence of the two countries is a British interest, that their frontiers are in fact our frontiers, their independence is the condition of our independence, their safety inseparable from our own.... Here, at any rate, we find a permanent basis of British policy, recognised and reaffirmed by the guarantee we have given in the Treaty of Locarno to the frontiers of Germany and her neighbours on the west."²⁹

Second, the Tory government was deeply interested in improving the position of Germany so as to improve British commercial prospects. Thus, in the name of yearning for universal peace Chamberlain could bring Germany back to the comity of nations and that paved the way for her entry into the League of Nations in the following year. It was just to put a mask on his real motives that the British Foreign Secretary made a solemn invocation to the cause of world peace when he said in the House of Commons on November 18, 1925: "I believe that a great work of peace has been done. I believe it, above all, because of the spirit in which it has been engineered. It could not have been done unless all the governments and, I will add, all the nations had felt the need to start a new and better chapter of international relations, but it could not have been done unless this country was prepared to take her sphere in

---

28. Maurice Bruce, op. cit., p. 143. It may be noted here that the Locarno Treaty signed in 1925 and brought into force in 1926 specifically excepted the self-governing Dominions and India from the obligations undertaken in these instruments by Great Britain on behalf of the British Empire, "unless and until any of these specified communities in the Empire voluntarily adhered, by their own act, to the instrument in question. See A.J. Toynbee: *The Conduct of British Empire Foreign Relations since the Peace Settlement* (London: Oxford University Press, 1928), p. 3.
29. See Simonds and Emeny, op. cit., p. 261. n 2.

guaranteeing the settlement so to come."[30]

The Locarno agreements certainly came as 'the high watermark of European restoration'.[31] But they revealed one more important thing. So far it was taken that as the British people were insular, they saw Europe only as far as their own immediate security was involved and, for this reason, their concern did not cross the Rhine. But now Chamberlain widened this perspective. He also took into his consideration the case of Germany's eastern frontiers. It is true that he supported the case of Germany to the extent that she got a seat in the League of Nations. But when the issue of filling up the seat of a permanent member in the Council (given to the United States but lying vacant owing to American abrogation of the Treaty of Versailles) came up, he supported the case of Poland. Owing to this Germany could have a newly manufactured status of a semi-permanent member of the Council in the first instance that was upgraded to full status in 1926. In 1928 Britain signed the Pact of Paris aimed at the renunciation of war as an instrument of national policy.

A critical study of the British foreign policy up to this stage suggests that nothing in the post-war history "can be more interesting or more illuminating than the Anglo-French battle of policy, fought over the prostrate body of Germany, and its ultimate results; for in this conflict, triangular at least in its implications, there is presented an accurate picture of post-war Europe."[32] At Locarno "the wounds of the war were healed, at least in part. Unfortunately for Britain, the Dominions could do no more than congratulate; they refused to be parties to the treaty."[33] Hence, it was too rash an observation to offer that under the Foreign Secretaryship of Austen Chamberlain, there "has been no British policy at all. Britain has not yet been able to decide exactly what her role is to be in the changed conditions of the post-War world."[34]

Formula of No Commitments and No Entanglements: Prelude to the Course of Appeasement

Even after signing the Kellogg-Briand pact aiming at the renuncia-

---

30. Sir Austen Chamberlain: *Peace in Our Time* (London: Philip Allan & Co., 1928), p. 102.
31. Churchill: *The Second World War*, Vol. 1, p. 27.
32. Simonds and Emeny, op. cit., p. 282.
33. Hannah, op. cit., p. 201.
34. Maurice Bruce, op. cit., p. 147.

tion of war as an instrument of national policy, the keynote of British foreign policy remained almost the same. A slight change occurred with the installation of Labour Government in 1929, because Prime Minister MacDonald once again preferred the course of improving relations with Soviet Russia and sticking to the formula of 'no commitments and no entanglements' that went definitely to the detriment of France. The Labour Government took the view that "the true role of Great Britain was not to play the part of a 'shining second' to France, but that of an impartial arbiter between France and Germany. In a word, British Labour demanded that Great Britain should henceforth occupy the centre of the 'teeter' and not always sit heavily on the French end."[35]

When the great economic depression gripped the countries of the world, including the United States, Britain supported the stand of President Hoover of the United States as a result of which his 'moratorium' came into effect in 1930. Much against the wishes of France, Germany could get some reprieve in the payment of further instalments of reparations as held under the Young Plan of 1929. The Manchurian crisis of 1931 afforded a test case. Britain did not appreciate the course of shouldering all responsibility alone contained in the Covenant of the League of Nations. The problem of enforcing actions against an aggressor like Japan "presented such difficulties that the reluctance of the Great Powers to resort to such length became increasingly apparent, and the Japanese were encouraged accordingly. Of the three powers principally interested in the Pacific, neither Russia nor the United States were members of the League, and it appeared that the brunt of any naval operations required would fall exclusively upon Great Britain."[36]

Similarly, on the issue of disarmament, Britain incurred the displeasure of France by affirming the idea of comparable reduction of armaments of all nations and along with that application of this principle to the case of Germany. In a statement given in the House of Commons on July 29, 1934, Baldwin reiterated: "Because of our commitments under the Covenant of the League and the Locarno Treaty, the many symptoms of unrest in Europe and elsewhere and the failure of other governments to follow our example by comparable reductions, we have for some time felt that

---

35. Simonds and Emeny, op. cit., p. 277.
36. Gathorne-Hardy, op. cit., p. 319.

the time has come when the possibility of keeping our armaments at the present level must be reconsidered in the absence of comparable reduction by other powers."[37] While referring to the case of Germany, L.S. Amery, former Colonial Minister, said: "The first condition of European peace today is the frank acknowledgement that Germany's armaments are now her own affair and nobody esle's."[38]

Such a soft view towards German rearmament found its culmination in the Anglo-German naval treaty effected by exchange of notes on June 18, 1935. It provided that the total German naval tonnage would never exceed 35 per cent of that of the British Commonwealth. This percentage was also accepted 'in principle' as applying to the various categories of vessels individually, with the exception of submarines. The German submarine tonnage could equal 45 per cent of that of the British. But in the event of a situation which in their opinion made it necessary, the German government could increase this tonnage to equal that of the British Commonwealth. It was natural that to the French this bilateral treaty "seemed both a stupid and a perfidious betrayal of the 'Stresa Front' in the face of a common enemy. Once more, the British had allowed Germany to drive a wedge between the two powers that, indeed, could ensure the peace and stability of Europe. But the British at this time had no intention of undertaking the involved and onerous duties of policing the Continent in the interest of the *status quo*."[39]

So far as the attitude of British government towards the League of Nations is concerned, we find that right from the time of its inception, its statesmen preferred to avoid every occasion of shouldering the great responsibility alone embodied in the doctrine of collective security.[40] It is for this reason that all serious

---

37. *The New York Times*, July 20, 1934.
38. *The Forward Review* (1935), p. 71. As early as on July 24, 1924, Viscount Grey said in the House of Lords that "you cannot make control of a great nation's armaments permanent in that way, and sooner or later, unless there be some reduction of armaments in other countries, you will find it impossible to prevent Germany from beginning again to increase her armaments." See Arnold Wolfers, op. cit., p. 41.
39. Simonds and Emeny, op. cit., p. 281,
40. A critic of this subject like Prof. H. Kantorowicz in his book *The Spirit of British Policy* made a comment in 1929: "It was touching to see the fervour with which

efforts of France went in vain. However, as France sought to strengthen the League as much as possible and for that reason her statesmen played a leading role, the first international organisation was looked at by the British as an institution meant mainly for the benefit of France. Among the British people the League steadily lost its popular favour in confidence inasmuch as it came increasingly to be identified as an instrument of French diplomacy rather than as a mechanism of international accommodation and collaboration.

Thus, half-hearted remained the role of the British delegates in the League of Nations until the Abyssinian crisis exploded in 1935 that threatened British interests in Africa and in the Mediterranean. Now the British statesmen strongly espoused the principle of collective security.[41] Anthony Eden (Minister for the League Affairs) denounced the action of Italy and vigorously pleaded for the imposition of economic, political and military sanctions against the aggressor. It was quite surprising to see that while Britain had not espoused the same point when Japan had raped Manchuria, she did in so clear-cut terms now for no other reason than to fight for the sake of her own interests. But this time, it was, however, the French "who held out a policy of conciliation rather than coercion, for their interests were only remotely affected."[42]

The Abyssinian crisis created a peculiar situation. The friction arising out of the disagreement between Britain and France on the role of the League in implementing the measures of 'collective security' against an aggressor was removed by the adoption of

---

these (English) people believed in the ideals of the League of Nations, and to witness their total ignorance of the fact that England stands alone within a Europe that is supposed to benefit by this faith." Cited in Bruce, op. cit., p. 136.

41. It shall be worthwhile to say at this stage that such a change in the British foreign policy towards the League was a result of the changed public opinion. In 1934-35, the British League of Nations Union, under Lord Robert Cecil, conducted a National Peace Ballot in which no less than 11,500,000 votes were cast, giving an overwhelming majority for support of the League and disarmament and a heavy majority was in favour of military and economic sanctions against aggressors. Accepting this result as an accurate index of the national public opinion, Baldwin declared: "The League of Nations will remain as before the keystone of British policy.... We shall continue to do all in our power to uphold the Covenant.... There will be no wavering." See Schuman, op.cit., p. 839.

42. Simonds and Emeny, op. cit., p. 286.

common policy towards Italy. It was reflected first in the gradual abandonment of 'sanctions' and then in the conclusion of Anglo-Italian and Franco-Italian Agreements of 1938. The resort to appeasement stood as a bond between Britain and France that had its manifestation in the form of the notorious Hoare-Laval Plan of 1936. Avoidance of war at any cost resulted in pursuance of the course of appeasement and, during the period of next three years, it appeared to all that the European policies of Britain and France "were again almost identical. They aimed at postponing war at the cost of a series of concessions to Axis countries."[43]

A critical study of the British foreign policy up to this period, therefore, shows that Anglo-French standpoints could not have a harmonious reconciliation on account of divergent national interests. "Britain never showed her willingness to share the Continental commitments of France. The idea of a Europe dominated by an alliance under French leadership and directed explicitly against Germany seemed completely out of harmony with the tradition of British policy. This difference was revealed in many ways but especially in the different attitudes adopted respectively by Britain and France towards the League of Nations. Up to 1938 the British view of the League emphasised its potentialities as an instrument of conciliation rather than its function as an organisation for the forcible maintenance of law. Its task was conceived to be the defence of an existing order against law-breakers. Thus, repeated French proposals designed to give the League the backing of effective military force excited strong suspicion in this country and invited the criticism that France wished to use the League exclusively as an instrument of French policy."[44]

Resort to the Course of Retreat and Compromise : Bases and Ramifications of Appeasement Policy

The host of uneasy, fleeting and contradictory affirmations entertained and professed by the policy-makers of London and Paris in the 1930s, particularly after 1934, give a reflection of their serious embarrassment on various counts ranging from abhorrence of war to the destruction of Communist and Fascist powers. Different

---

43. *France and Britain*, A Report by Chatham House Study Group (London: Royal Institute of International Affairs, 1945), p. 22.
44. Ibid., p. 20.

ramifications of such a policy like those of serious yearning for world peace, reassertion of national self-respect and exasperation with any one trying to probe the mass of emotional pretence and questionable reasoning were the offshoots of the same policy of retreat and compromise. These basic points determined British foreign policy not only towards friends (like France, the United States and the Dominions of the British Commonwealth of Nations) but also towards the foes having a dictatorial system whether of the left (like the USSR) or of the right (like Japan, Italy and Germany).

Let us now examine the bases or determining factors and ramifications of the policy of appeasement. These were:

1. *Internal Weakness*

In fact, the gradual erosion of the genuine norms of the policy of balance of power and rather their supplementation with the counter-productive consequences of appeasement was a definite offshoot of the conditions after the First World War. Britain emerged from the war like a victor with a shattered economy. Her rulers knew it well that they did not have the same resources that had placed their country in the position of a super-power for the last few hundred years. This realisation informed them to follow the lead of the United States. But after the rejection of the Treaty of Versailles by America, British statesmen trembled at the thought of shouldering any major responsibility alone either for the security of France or for the maintenance of the system of collective security under the auspices of the League of Nations. Some of the Dominions also adopted a discouraging attitude. Restoration of economic and military strength remained the standing consideration. It required ample time. It is for this reason that Britain sought to improve her commercial relations by supporting the resurgence of the Germany much against the wishes of France. The Labour leaders went to the length of improving economic relations with Soviet Russia much against the wishes of their Tory counterparts. Appreciable progress could be achieved in this direction, but deficiency in the sphere of military strength continued. Prime Ministers like Baldwin and Chamberlain well took into their account this fact and, just to put a mask on it, they clamoured for world peace until they had to accept the course of war as a matter of Hobson's choice. It is, therefore, aptly commented: "The policy

Great Britain

of appeasement, while it was partly based on a sincere belief that a permanent basis could be built upon peace, was also formulated on the realisation that Britain's defence programme due to its tradition in getting started, would not come to harvest until 1939. Munich was to be the price she had to pay for this year of grace."[45]

2. Fear of Communism

The success of Bolshevism in Russia in 1917 created a great menace for the capitalist class. The activities of the Comintern were looked at with great apprehension. It is for this reason that the Labour Government had to go after the disclosure of the Zinoviev letter in November 1925. The Tory leaders desired the end of the Communist system. When they took note of the fact that Fascism could serve this purpose, they supported the dictators of Japan, Italy and Germany. If world revolutionary communism was the gravest of menaces to the British ruling classes and to the integrity of the Empire and if the Fascist Triplice (Japan, Italy and Germany) promised to hold the menace in check, Britain could well afford to boycott the USSR and lend comfort to Hitler, Hirohito and Mussolini.[46] One may ask that Fascism could also become a danger to the British power. But its explanation is that it was a lesser evil. "If the Triplice should attack and conquer the Soviet Union, it might, to be sure, become a danger to the Empire. But this danger was envisaged as negligible by comparison with the danger to the Empire of any extension of Communism beyond the Soviet frontiers or any major enhancement of the power of the Soviet State, hence, the wisdom of appeasement."[47]

---

45. J.F. Kennedy: *Why England Slept?* (London: Sidgwick and Jackson, 1940), p. 148.
46. See Viscount D'Abernon: *The Diary of an Ambassador: Versailles to Rapallo, 1920-22* (New York: Doubleday, 1929), pp. 21-22. The bourgeois class appreciated rise of Fascism as an antidote to the spectre of Communism. G.L. Mosse makes an apt observation: "Fascism shared throughout Europe and its various forms shared common elements deriving from a commonly felt need to transcend a banal bourgeois world." *The Crises of German Ideology: Intellectual Origins of the Third Reich* (Universal Library, Grosset and Dunlop), p.312.
47. Schuman, op. cit., p. 836. The typical Tory point of view can be seen in the affirmation of the Marquess of Londonderry, Lady Desborough and G.W. Price: "Our Foreign Office appears to condone the associations with Communism and Bolshevism through our affiliation with France, while paying but little regard to robust attitude of Germany, Italy and Japan which wholeheartedly condemn Communism and Bolshevism. Bolshevism is a world-wide

3. Liquidation of Fascism

A study of the above factor should be made with this important consideration in mind that while Britain desired destruction of the Communism of Russia with the force of Fascism, she also desired liquidation of Fascism inasmuch as it was the enemy of democracy and constitutionalism. Let the two fight and destroy themselves so that liberalism is preserved, was the basic consideration of British statesmen. They worked on this presumption that ultimately the Fascists of Japan, Italy and Germany and lately of Spain would destroy themselves in a bid to remove Communism from the world. Thus, Schuman is justified in holding: "This policy which was clearly suicidal in its consequences and apparently mad or muddled in its motivation, was not primarily a product of popular isolationism or pacifism, although these sentiments won public support for a programme which otherwise might have been repudiated. The Tory line had a logic of its own in *Realpolitik*, albeit one seldom acknowledged. That logic presupposed that the great protagonists of the future would be Japan and the USSR in Asia and the Reich and the USSR in Europe. If these powers were likely to checkmate one another and ultimately engage in a death grapple, Britain could well afford to stand aloof and to protect itself from involvement by pressing France to abandon the Allies which stood in the way of the German 'Drive to the East".[48]

4. Anglo-French Differences

The fact of differences between the views of English and French statesmen had its own impact on resort to the course of appeasement. We have already seen that while France desired to crush Germany to the last possible extent, Britain wanted to weaken Germany up to a point only. That is, while France was interested in total suppression of Germany that would be a source of her security for ever, Britain apprehended that the materialisation of the French plan would be a source of upsetting the balance of power. "A weak Germany would be an open invitation to commu-

---

doctrine which aims at the internal disruption of all modern systems of government with the ultimate object or what is termed World Revolution. That Germany, Italy and Japan condemn Bolshevism is an attitude of mind which is not properly appreciated in this country... The anti-Communist platform was (and still is) invaluable." *Ourselves and Germany* (1938), p. 129.

48. Schuman, op. cit., p. 836.

nist expansion; a reasonably strong Germany would strike an all-round balance of power in Europe by working as a bulwark against Russia and by counteracting the hegemony of France."[49] Curiously, the undercurrent of differences continued even after the establishment of Anglo-French reconciliation in the period following the Italo-Abyssinian war. A shrewd leader like Hitler could grasp the reality of the situation. In a bid to cash capital out of it, he took matters to a point that Britain and France had to give up the course of appeasement and eventually take up arms against their pampered child, surprisingly with the collaboration of the Communist Russia. It is, therefore, convincingly remarked: "From 1919 to 1933 the French policies largely prevailed and this brought Hitler to power, from 1933 to 1939 the British policies dominated and this brought the world to a war. Just as Hitler paralysed all possible opposition by seizing upon the Western fear of communism, similarly he made full capital out of the Anglo-French differences. Just as Germany's object was to isolate the Soviet Union by gaining Anglo-French goodwill, similarly it was her object to isolate France by gaining Britain's goodwill."[50]

5. *War Phobia*

Above all, there was the fear of war that haunted the minds of British and French statesmen. Purchasing of peace at any price became their motto. So unshakeable was the obsession of Neville Chamberlain for the avoidance of war that he was called 'a go-getter for peace'. It afforded him a pretext for justifying his action at the Munich meet that came as the climax of the policy of retreat and compromise and ascribed to him the title of being the 'king of appeasement'. In justification of it, in the House of Commons on November 11, 1938, he said: "I feel all the more convinced of the soundness of this policy, because I believe that the influence which this country can exert for peace is more powerful than that of any other that I can think of."[51] In January 1939, he reiterated: "War today is so terrible in its effects on those who take part in it, no

---

49. M.G. Gupta: *International Relations since 1919* (Allahabad: Chaitanya Publishing House, 1969), III Ed., p. 245.
50. Ibid., p. 246.
51. Neville Chamberlain: *In Search of Peace* (New York: G.P. Putnam's Sons, 1939), p. 232.

matter what the ultimate outcome may be; it brings so much loss and suffering even to the bystanders that it ought never to be allowed to begin unless every practicable and honourable step has been taken to prevent it. This has been the view of the Government from the beginning and the Munich Agreement, though it is the most important illustration of its practical working was only an incident in a consistent unwavering policy of peace."[52]

It may, however, be emphasised by way of drawing an inference from what we have said above that British statesmen took conflicting stands in different situations for the sake of maintaining the balance of power or bringing about a situation conducive to the protection and promotion of the political and economic interests of their country. It is a different matter that they miserably failed in establishing a proper and workable reconciliation between divergent stands that ultimately revealed shocking failure of the basic touchstone of their foreign policy. Matters reached such a point after 1938 that every attempt to avoid a war led to its advent without fail. A critic like Norman Angell noted his impression in these words: "Peace will not come by sporadic, partial, piecemeal refusals to fight about anything at all; by refusing to be moved by any measures or any horror. Nor will it come by arousing in panic without knowing to what end. It will come when men are clearer to what Right is, and decide that their force shall be the instrument of naught else but that purpose. There is no refuge but in the maintenance of that purpose. To surrender it, to bargain it away for a momentary immunity from the violence of those who would destroy it, is, in the end, to destroy ourselves."[53]

Appeasement in Practice: Britain's Dealing with Japan, Italy and Germany

The policy of appeasement, as resorted to by the Tory statesmen of Britain, showed that its justification was sought in different directions ranging from those of sympathy and despondency to those of observance of the principle of equality of all nations in matters of rearmament and an honest invocation of the principle of national self-determination. It shall, therefore, be worthwhile to make a

---

52. Ibid., p. 251.
53. Angell: *Peace with the Dictators?* (London: Hamish Hamilton, 1938), p. 328.

brief study of Britain's dealings with the totalitarian systems of Japan, Italy and Germany. In this direction, a critical student of British foreign policy may come across a very large number of self-contradictory situations that smack of utter hollowness of the British Foreign Office and leave an impression that, during the phase of crucification of peace, British government had mortgaged itself to the dictate of the great dictators, particularly the Fuhrer of Germany.[54]

Britain and Japan
Since the story of appeasement policy is integrally connected with the aggressive conduct of the Axis powers, let us first of all refer to the case of Japan. The ruling British class fondly remained under the impression that the collapse of the power of 'the land of rising sun' would open the way for Russian hegemony over China, Inner Mongolia and Manchuria. For the sake of the protection of British commercial interests a strong Japan could neutralise the force of growing nationalism in China that was working against foreign dominance. In addition to this all, it was also taken into consideration by the British statesmen that a war against Japan would entail very heavy burden on their exchequer. For these reasons, "the task of checking by force a Great Power like Japan at the other side of the world was an experiment and a risk that Britain would very properly have hesitated to undertake, even if she had been at the

---

54. Two outstanding instances may be referred to at this stage. First, despite his knowledge of the fact that Hitler's Foreign Minister (Ribbentrop) appointed on February 4, 1938, had anti-British convictions, on February 20, 1938, Chamberlain sacrificed his Foreign Secretary (Eden) who was widely known for his anti-Fascist orientations. Second, when on January 13, 1938, President Roosevelt of the United States made a proposal of calling a conference of neutral nations to prepare a set of principles that should govern international relations (ostensibly an attempt for the creation of a force to fight for the maintenance of collective security system with American cooperation), Chamberlain could not foresee the long-range implications of the move. He declined the historic offer. It went to the definite gain of the dictators of Italy and Germany. On this point Churchill makes a comment: "That Mr. Chamberlain with his limited outlook and inexperience of the European sense, should have possessed the self-sufficiency to waive away the proffered hand stretched out across the Atlantic leaves one, even at this date, breathless with amazement." *The Second World War*, Vol. I, p. 199.

height of her military and economic security."[55]

For such reasons, Japan's action of conquering Manchuria went unchecked by a great protector of the collective security system like Britain in spite of the fact that the Lytton Committee (appointed by the League to investigate the matter) had frankly declared Japan as an aggressor and subsequently the League Assembly without dissent indicted Japan of aggression as defined in the Covenant of the League and the Nine-Power Treaty signed at Washington in 1922. Eventually the British government recognised the act of Japanese aggression when a mission of the Federation of British Industries, and an official mission under the leadership of Sir Fredrick Lieth-Ross was sent to Tokyo to conciliate the dictators of the Far East. The British press lauded the action of Japan.[56] The business circles thankfully appreciated the role of the British delegate (Sir John Simon) in the League Assembly whose 'wise and moderate' affirmations ruled out the possibility of putting an embargo on shipment of arms to Japan inasmuch as it would mean ominous interference with British industry.

The Japanese rulers grasped the weakness of the British foreign policy-makers and they tried to exploit it in their own ways. Thus, Japan flouted British desire with impunity and her invasion of China went on along with humiliation and losses being heaped on the British subjects and traders in the Far East. Even when the Japanese in August 1937, inflicted physical injuries on the person of the British ambassador (Sir Hugh Montgomery Knatchbull-Hughesson), the British government did not resent. The invasion of the Yangtse valley "extinguished British trade hegemony dating back for seventy years. Following the Munich surrender, Japan's army overran the Canton Delta, sealing it from Hong Kong, and her navy seized the Spratly islands off French Indo-China. Gross

---

55. Maurice Bruce, op. cit. A little after L.S. Amery (who had the privilege of being the Colonial Minister) recorded his impression thus: "It would be no concern of ours... to prevent Japanese expansion in Eastern Siberia." *The Forward Review* (1935), p. 288.
56. For instance, it was commented that "Japan, broadly speaking, is the only element making for order and good government in the Far East."*Morning Post*, January 30, 1932. Another paper remarked that Japan's presence in Manchuria "has been a benefit to the world." *Daily Mail*, November 5, 1931. After a short while, it admired that Japan "is rendering good service to the civilisation by restoring law and order in Manchuria." Ibid., December 10, 1932.

insults were inflicted upon the Europeans by Japanese occupation forces in Tientsin, Amoy, and Shanghai and HBM ambassador's official motor car was machine-gunned near Nanking."[57]

It well indicates that, despite the abrogation of the Anglo-Japanese treaty of 1902 in 1921, Britain thought it expedient to keep Japan in good humour against the growing menace of Russian Communism and Chinese nationalism. The adherence to the course of appeasement forced the British statesmen to acquiesce in the Japanese declaration of 1934, warning all European powers to keep their 'hands off' from China. Rather like a coward and dishonest gambler, Britain preferred to enact the drama of the conference at Brussels in November 1937, where it was decided to goad the USSR to combat the Japanese aggression in China. But the Russian dictator caught the point and he declined to pick up the chestnuts out of fire for the appeasers of London and the aggressors of Tokyo. "In short, working on the false assumption that Japan would act as Britain's watchdog in the Far East and would amicably settle the division of China with them, the National Government of Britain openly backed up Japan "as the champion against the Soviet Union and even against the United States."[58]

Britain and Italy
British appeasement policy towards Italy failed to have a consistent character in view of the fact that in dealing with the dictator of Rome, London sometimes showed an attitude of retreat and compromise and at other times made some imbecile efforts to condemn and check the tide of Fascist aggression. Ever since the advent of Fascism in Italy in 1922, British feelings towards the new system were of a mixed character. While the business circles appreciated the emergence of a dictatorial system as a bulwark against the growth of leftism in the country and also as a powerful counter-force to the menace of Communism abroad, they also disdained the existence of a system inimical to the principles of democracy and constitutionalism. And yet the two never came to a loggerhead. While Italy after the peace conference of 1919 demanded rewards in accordance with the terms of the Secret

---

57. Alfred Crofts and Percy Buchanan: *A History of the Far East* (Bombay: Allied Pub,, 1958), pp. 393-94.
58. M.G. Gupta, op. cit., p. 249.

Treaty of London of 1915, Britain preferred to honour the moral commitment whenever so possible. Above all, the imperialistic tone of the foreign policy stood as a cementing factor that found its clear manifestation in 1935 when Mussolini made his experiment in Ethiopia. "Italian foreign policy regarding Britain had until 1935 one continuing principle: vulnerability of the peninsula as regards the great sea power compelled deference. In other words, an isolationist Britain, postponing to the distant future any realisation of the League ideal, shares imperialism with Fascist Italy, makes no trouble for her and finds one in her."[59]

Waiting impatiently to realise the plan of Italian irredentism since his coming into power in 1922 and feeling much encouraged with the British attitude of appeasement first towards Japan during the Manchurian crisis in 1931-32 and then towards Hitler's remilitarisation of the Rhineland in 1935, Mussolini now turned "to twist the tail of the British Lion."[60] He studied with ample apprehension the role of Britain in using the machinery of the League against his colonial advancement in Africa. The reason was that such an act of Italian aggression was inherent with dangers to British position in the Mediterranean, in North Africa and in the Middle East. Thus, the British delegate (Sir Anthony Eden) denounced the action of Italy in harsh terms and managed to influence the League Council with the decision of imposing 'sanctions' against the aggressor state. One may say that such an action amounted to the abandonment of the course of appeasement. But later developments spoke otherwise. Since France revealed her reluctance to implement the decision of sanctions against Italy, Britain preferred to renounce it and take to a different path. The decision of sanctions against an aggressor remained unhonoured. On January 2, 1937, Britain signed a 'gentlemen's agreement' with Italy whereby both agreed that "freedom of entry into, exit from, and transit through, the Mediterranean is a vital interest both to the different parts of the British Empire and to Italy, and that these interests are in no way inconsistent with each other." By this agreement, both disclaimed "any desire to modify, or so far as they

---

59. Henry R. Spencer: "Expanding Italy" in Brown, Hodges and Roucek (ed.s), op. cit., pp. 196-97.
60. Walter R. Sharp and Grayson Kirk: *Contemporary International Politics* (New York: Farrar and Rinehart, Inc., 1944), p. 636.

are concerned, to see modified the *status quo* as regards national sovereignty of territories in the Mediterranean area."[61]

Actually, this smoothly worded document did not in any way affect the character of the Anglo-Italian relations. The Duce was fully aware of the fact that the declaration did not in any way enhance the Italian position, rather it "merely confirmed the *status quo*. Indeed, its ambiguity of phraseology was such that each signatory could regard the agreement as a triumph."[62] Naturally, it forced the Duce to discover some way out so as to gain something at the cost of British appeasement. However, he was forced to stop and strengthen Italian relations with Britain after Hitler annexed Austria in March 1938 with the Reich. It strengthened the position of Germany to a greater extent. In a bid to counteract it, Italy signed a new agreement with Britain on April 16, 1938, that went beyond the vague terms of the gentlemen's agreement of a year before.

According to the terms of the new agreement, the signatories agreed to exchange information about their respective troop movements in North African territories, to refrain from air or naval base construction in the Eastern half of the Mediterranean without notifying it to each other, to respect the sovereignty of and to refrain from seeking any favoured position in Saudi Arabia, and to ban propaganda injurious to each other. Great Britain was assured that Italy would not impede the use of Lake Tsana's water so as to interfere with Sudanese irrigation and both parties agreed to respect the International Convention of 1888 guaranteeing that the Suez Canal would be kept open both in peace and in war. In accompanying letters, Great Britain insisted that the agreement could not enter into force until the final and satisfactory settlement of the Spanish question was found, and in order to encourage Italy to comply with this demand, Chamberlain agreed to take steps at Geneva to clear the way for general recognition of the Ethiopian conquest. In turn, an Italian letter gave assurances of respect for Spanish independence and a categorical promise to withdraw all troops and material at the end of the war.[63]

However, British appeasement policy towards Italy assumed a genuine character after she, in collaboration with Germany,

---

61. Ibid.
62. Ibid.
63. Ibid., p. 641.

played a decisive role in the Spanish civil war on behalf of the military junta under Gen. Franco. Instead of coming to the rescue of the legitimate government of Madrid and denouncing the role of Franco and his great supporters like Hitler and Mussolini, Chamberlain adopted the course of 'no-intervention' in the domestic affairs of Spain. Obviously, it was another guise of appeasement, for the role of the non-intervention committee formed in London under the chairmanship of Lord Plymouth indirectly strengthened the hands of Fascist powers. It became clear for all to see that the appeasers were blinded by the 'delirium tremens of Bolshevism gnawing its way into their bank cellars'. Surprisingly, Chamberlain took no pains to discourage the rise of Fascism in Spain in spite of the fact that he confessed in a letter written to the Dutchess of Atholl that "a considerable number of regular Italian troops have been in Spain since the early days of the war."[64]

Britain and Germany
British appeasement policy towards Germany was informed by same important considerations now marked with two alibis—finding fault with the peace settlement of 1919 and invocation of the principle of national self-determination. After the emergence of Hitler's despotism in 1934 and his declaration of adopting the policy of 'drive to the east', British leaders and press took to the course of appeasement for reasons already given in the preceding section of our study. However, with a view to offer a plausible justification of their notorious policy, they found alibi in the great injustice done to Germany at the time of making treaties of peace[65] and, at the same time, insincerely honouring the prin-

---

64. *The Times* (London), April 29, 1937. Prof. Schuman makes an observation: "In Rome as in Berlin, it was obvious to the tyrant in power that his ambitions could be furthered by converting Spain into a fascist ally or a vassal. To threaten Gibraltar from Algeceras and Ceuta, to menace French communications from the Beleric Islands, to control the coasts of Spain would enable the Axis to levy further blackmail against France and Britain and perhaps automatically to destroy them... Mussolini and Hitler assumed correctly that most men of Property and Piety in France, Britain and America would be deceived by this slogan and would, therefore, acquiesce or even cooperate in the destruction of the Spanish Republic." op. cit., III Ed., p. 542.
65. For instance, in 1935 the official standpoint was that it "must be recognised that whatever the justice of national aspirations, the peace settlement at the end of the world war produced monstrosities in central Europe... If central Europe is

ciple of national self-determination. Along with this, the traditional reasons of avoiding war and purchasing peace at any cost remained at work. In this direction, we may refer to the crises of Austria and Czechoslovakia.

When Hitler made first attempt to destroy the independence of Austria in 1934, Britain's purpose of checking the Nazi menace was served by the action of Italy. Mussolini's formidable opposition to the design of Hitler (as the annexation of Austria would bring German frontiers close to those of Italy and then create a problem for the German majority area of South Tyrol) forced the Fuhrer to retrace. But when Mussolini adopted an attitude of acquiescence after his victory in Ethiopia and his desire to reciprocate for the sympathy of Hitler in his African adventure, consummation of the Anschluss became a certainty. A clear indication was given to Germany that Britain would not resist expansion of the Reich to the east when Sir Anthony Eden gave a public statement on November 20, 1936: "These British arms will never be used in a war of aggression.... They may, and, if the occasion arose, they would be used in our defence and in the defence of the territories of the British Commonwealth of Nations. They may, and, if the occasion arose, they would be used in the defence of France and Belgium against unprovoked aggression in accordance with our existing treaty obligations. In addition, our armaments may be used in bringing help to a victim of an aggression in any case where, in our judgement, it would be proper under the provisions of the Covenant to do so. I use the word 'may' deliberately, since in such

---

viewed in this light, the only possible policy was that of appeasement leading to a reorganisation satisfactory to Germany." Warner Moss, op. cit., p. 143. The leading English daily commented: "It is regrettable that no allowance should have been made by a body like the League Council for the special circumstances in which Germany incurred her obligations. It would have enhanced the reputation of the League for impartiality, if one voice at least had been raised to recall the manner in which this particular treaty (of Versailles) had been imposed. Germany signed it literally at the point of bayonet. Hitlerism is largely a revolt against Versailles, and until this fundamental truth is taken fully into account there will be no real peace in Europe. For the present, no doubt, the peace must be kept by a close combination of the powers which, satisfied by the war, have no temptation to break it. But it will be a mere uneasy truce until their main purpose can be changed from the negative policy of organising security against war into the positive policy of negotiating an agreed peace." *The Times* (London), April 17, 1935.

an instance there is no automatic obligation to take military action."[66] On March 3, 1937, Lord Halifax asserted in the House of Lords: "... we are unable to define beforehand what might be our attitude to hypothetical complication in Central or Eastern Europe."[67]

Thus, the British government indirectly regretted its inability to keep the Treaty of St. Germain intact. When Henderson had a meeting with Hitler on March 3, 1938, he discussed several important issues like disarmament, question of Anschluss, and Germany's demand for colonies, but he did not like to discourage the ambitions of the Fuhrer by asserting the stand of his government. When the poor and helpless Chancellor of Austria (Schuschnigg) appealed to Chamberlain, the latter promptly replied that the British government "could not take any responsibility of advising the former to take any course of action which might expose his country to the dangers against which His Majesty's Government are unable to guarantee protection." It shows that the Austrian crisis found the British government "stranded between the abandoned policy of collective security and an unachieved settlement with Italy. All Chamberlain could do was to make a show of various indignation and to submit to an insolent rejoinder that this was an internal affair of the German people, and no concern of his."[68]

The Austrian independence was destroyed in March, 1938. Soon it was to be followed by the tragedy of Czechoslovakia that signified the denouement of the policy of appeasement. Here British statesmen invoked the principle of national self-determination for the Sudeten Germans and fondly hoped that after the annexation of the Sudetenland with the Reich, the danger of war would be averted. Implicit herein was the plea of not involving in a war of no concern to Britain. Thus, Chamberlain said on September 27, 1938, that it "was horrible, fantastic, incredible that we should be digging trenches and filling gas masks because of a quarrel in a far away country among people of whom we know nothing. I was taken completely by surprise (by Hitler's demand for immediate military occupation). I must say that I find that

---

66. Schuman, op. cit., p. 841.
67. Ibid.
68. L.S. Amery: *My Political Life*, Vol. III. Also see G.F. Elliott: "The Military Conquerors of Munich" in *Foreign Policy Reports*, Part 24, No. 20, December 15, 1938.

attitude unreasonable.... But if we have to fight, it must be on larger issues than that.... But if I were convinced that any nation had made up its mind to dominate the world by fear of its force, I should feel that it must be resisted."[69]

The Munich Pact came as the most deplorable instance of Chamberlain's notorious policy of appeasement. After signing the Munich pact, he proposed a three-term document as a model of Anglo-German declaration. It stipulated:

1. "We are agreed in recognising that the question of Anglo-German relations is of the first importance for the two countries and for Europe;
2. "We regard the Agreement signed last night and the Anglo-German Naval Convention as symbolic of the desire of our two peoples never to go to war with one another again; and
3. "We are resolved that the method of consultation shall be the method adopted to deal with any other questions that may concern our two countries, and we are determined to continue our efforts to remove possible sources of differences and thus to contribute to assure the peace of Europe."[70]

It went unhonoured by Hitler. However, as we have already seen in the preceding chapters, Chamberlain and his collaborator of France (Daladier) partitioned Czechoslovakia in a way that the German majority area of Sudetenland was given away to Germany. More unfortunate is the fact that neither Britain nor France came to the rescue of Prague to materialise their assurances when Hitler devoured the rump Czechoslovakia after a couple of weeks.

End of Appeasement Policy: Formation of the 'Peace Front' and Inauguration of the 'Stop Hitler Movement'

The role of Chamberlain and his collaborator(Daladier) at the Munich meet displayed the height of the policy of surrender to the claims of the Nazi gangsters. The dictators of Germany and Italy with the help of Britain and France could impose their will. Not only this, after the making of the pact, they could force Chamber-

---

69. Schuman, op. cit., p. 842. The leading daily opined that self-determination for the Sudetens "would afford a welcome example of peaceful change... It would be a drastic remedy for the present unrest but something drastic may be needed." *The Times* (London), June 6, 1938.
70. R.W. Seton-Watson: *From Munich to Danzig* (London: Methuen & Co., 1939), III Ed., p. 106.

lain and his craven ally (Daladier) to do the more sinful job of follow-up action. The two Prime Ministers then conveyed an ultimatum to the government of Prague to honour the terms within 10 days, or face the consequences themselves. The helpless victim had to yield. It well demonstrated the fact that if ever there "was a settlement to which the title of 'Dictat'—that method against which the Germans protested so vigorously at Versailles and after—could be applied, it was the triple and progressive surrender of Berchtesgaden, Godesberg and Munich. Mr. Chamberlain, however, continued to maintain that this was 'peace by agreement'—if this was so, then words lose meaning."[71]

At last came the day when Chamberlain had to realise the folly of his course of appeasement. After annexing the Sudetenland with the Reich, Hitler devoured the independence of the rump Czechoslovakia. Now it became clear to the 'king of appeasement' that Germany's demands were unsatiable. On March 31, 1939, he said in the House of Commons: "In order to make perfectly clear the position of H. M. 's Government.... I have now to inform the House that... in the event of any action which clearly threatened Polish independence and which the Polish government accordingly considered it vital to resist with the national forces, H.M.'s Government would feel themselves bound at once to lend the Polish government all support in their power."[72]

Henceforth, British government made it clear that German attack on Poland would not be tolerated. With a view to check further Nazi action, similar assurances were given to Greece and Rumania. Thus Britain sought to establish a 'peace front' with the cooperation of anti-Nazi forces. To give vent to such a changed policy, Chamberlain said in the House of Commons on 3 April, 1939: "Therefore, we welcome the cooperation of any country,

---

71. Seton-Watson, op. cit., p. 105. A caricature in the *News Chronicle* of March 14 1938 hit off the situation well. It represented Germany in the likeness of a wolf's head, with the upper or Silesian jaw closing over the western end of Czechoslovakia from one side, while the Austrian or lower jaw encircled it from the other. 'The Jaws of the German wolf are closing in' ran the sentence below, and six months later the jaws did actually close and separated the Sudetens from Czechoslovakia." See A.J. Grant and H. Temperley: *Europe in the Nineteenth and Twenieth Centuries* (London: Longmans, 1964), VI Ed. p. 516.
72. Cited in Simonds and Emeny, op. cit., p. 724, n 1.

whatever may be its internal system of government, not in aggression but in resistance to aggression."[73] However, behind such a categorical affirmation lay reservations towards honouring the cooperation of Soviet Russia. The 'usual mixture of concession and hesitation, of endeavour and reluctance', as remarked by L.B. Namier, continued with the result that in the changed course of commitments and involvements, Britain ignored the hand of friendship extended to it by the Soviet Union. Thus, by the middle of 1939, the fact "remained, however, that no adequate counterpoise to German power in the east of the Continent had been established and these guarantees, which were in the first instance unilateral and could not become effectively reciprocal were an argument for rather than against securing an alliance with Russia."[74]

In the summer of 1939, Chamberlain looked like groping in the world of confusion so far as requisitioning Russian cooperation for the 'stop Hitler movement' was concerned. In a statement in the House of Commons on 29 June Lord Halifax made it above board: "We have assumed obligations and are preparing to assume more, with full understanding of their causes and with full understanding of their consequences. We know that if the security and independence of their countries are to disappear, our own security and our own independence will be gravely threatened. We know that if international law and order is to be preserved, we must be prepared to fight in its defence."[75] At the same time, an attitude of misgivings towards the USSR continued. As a result of this, Hitler could give a shock to the world by entering into a non-aggression pact with the USSR on 24 August. In this way, even after discarding the foolish and self-delusive course of appeasement, the British government endeavoured to cash more capital out of her commitments to Poland, Greece, Rumania and other Baltic States rather than accepting the offer of Soviet friendship.[76]

---

73. Neville Chamberlain, op. cit., p. 287.
74. *France and Britain*, A Report by Chatham House Study Group, p. 23.
75. H.H.F. Craster: *Speeches on Foreign Policy by Viscount Halifax* (London: Oxford University Press, 1940), p. 287.
76. It was really unfortunate on the part of Chamberlain that instead of understanding the seriousness of the situation and complexity of the Russian offer, he took it in a different way. He deputed a junior official of the Foreign Office

As a matter of fact, a disillusioned Prime Minister of Britain now endeavoured to "rebuild a coalition against the Reich upon the ruins of appeasement."[77] With an obsession to make correction of his serious mistakes, he observed with some anxiety the Japanese occupation of the Hainan and the Spratly Islands. On April 13, following the Italian annexation of Albania, he told the House of Commons that he was 'disappointed' and declared that the H.M.'s Government was prepared to lend Greece and Rumania all support in its power 'in the event of any action being taken which clearly threatens the independence of either, and which the Greek or Rumanian Government respectively consider it vital to resist with their national forces.'[78] In his Albert Hall Address on 12 May, 1939, he forcefully reiterated that 'no more deadly mistakes would be made.'[79] The truth of such reiterations became evident when Britain opposed Germany's attack on Poland on September 1, 1939, and soon after declared war on Germany.[80] In fine, the conflict

---

(Strang) to conduct negotiations with Stalin on such an important matter in June, 1939. A grand opportunity was, therefore, lost. A critic of this policy like Namier observes: "It had been a mistake on the part of the British Government, so quick, unstinting, and easy about terms when handing out guarantees to second and third-rate powers, to have treated Soviet Russia like a suppliant, and to have started off with suggestions which were both ludicrous and humiliating: it was a further mistake to have gone on haggling about every concession, which rendered it ungracious and unconvincing; it was a third mistake to have sent a junior official to negotiate with Russia and later on, servicemen of less standing than him were sent, for instance, to Poland or Turkey. Behind it all was a deep, inseparable aversion to Bolshevist Russia such as was not shown in dealings with Hitler or Mussolini; and whether it was justified or not, it certainly was not conducive to success in very difficult negotiations." *Diplomatic Prelude, 1938-1939*, pp. 187-88.

77. Schuman, op. cit., p. 844.
78. Ibid. When Chamberlain failed in honouring the assurance of protection given to the rump republic of Czechoslovakia after the secession of the Sudetenland, and when Hitler occupied the rest of the country, he realised that the invocation of the principle of national self-determination to appease the Nazi dictator was a blunder. Thus, when on 16 March 1939, Hitler gave Carpatho-Ukraine to Hungary, the next day Chamberlain questioned: "Is this the last attack upon a small State, or is it to be followed by others ? Is this, in fact, a step in the direction of an effort to dominate the world by force ? ... I am sure that they will require grave and serous consideration." Ibid., pp. 843-44.
79. Simonds and Emeny, op. cit., p. 726.
80. See G.J. Hains and R.J.S. Hoffman: *Origin and Background of Second World War*.

which Hitler "had willed and which he hoped to localise had now become a European war."[81]

Concluding Observations

A detailed account of British foreign policy and diplomacy, as contained in the preceding sections, leaves these important impressions:

1. British statesmen adhered to the pursuance of the policy of balance of power which unfortunately took a wrong turn after 1930. Thus, while they achieved success in putting a check on the growing power of France by giving doses of strength to the weak power of Germany, they certainly failed in putting a check on the imperialistic ambitions of their pampered child after it developed into a man. The traditional norms of their foreign policy were sacrificed at the altar of sheer expediency. Conflicting threads were sought to be interwoven just for the sake of appeasing the aggressors with a view to have their eventual confrontation with the demon of Communism and that might lead to the destruction to both. Misgivings towards the motives of the USSR continued so much so that her offer of friendship was not happily reciprocated in June 1939. It afforded a good chance for Hitler to neutralise the power of Russia in his search for capturing Poland. It also illustrated the bold fact that "only sheer infatuation with appeasement at almost any price can explain the cold-shouldering of Russian offers of help when things were already on the eve of war, even if that help had amounted to no more than sending aeroplanes to help the Czechs and holding back the Poles."[82]

2. As the Tory statesmen remained in power for most of the time during the inter-war period, protection and promotion of British commercial interests haunted their mind. They deliberately surrendered political dominance in exchange for the trade dominance of the world, but with the distinct provision that no other nation could be allowed to exercise such a political dominance to Britain's disadvantage. It is for this reason that Britain opposed France in the meetings of the Reparation Commission and then her

---

81. Ralph Flonely: *Modern German History* (London: J.M. Dent & Sons, 1968), IV Ed., p. 387.
82. Amery, op. cit.

occupation of the Ruhr. Britain's role in the formulation of the Dawes Plan of 1924 and of the Young Plan of 1929 was informed by similar objectives. Finally, Britain's role behind the declaration of the Hoover Moratorium and the closing of the chapter of reparations at the Lausanne Conference of 1932 were governed by the consideration of helping Germany in a way that the commercial interests of the Englishmen could be safeguarded. It had its own manifestation in the Far East where, instead of checking the growth of Japanese imperialism, British statesmen adopted the policy of appeasement as a safety-valve to check the pace of Russian Communism and Chinese nationalism for the sake of British iconomic onterests.[83]

3. After the defection of the United States, Britain did not appreciate the proposal of implementing the provisions of collective security single-handed. She preferred to declare support for the League of Nations as the corner-stone of her foreign policy. But it was all in theory. In practice, British statesmen sought to use the first international organisation in their own national interest. Whenever the crucial occasion arose, they tried to invoke and interpret the provisions of the Covenant in a way that their own imperial interests were served. Thus, Geneva Protocol was dishonoured. The clause of sanctions was not invoked when Japan raped Manchuria. Moreover, while a decision of applying 'sanctions' against Italy was taken in 1935, nothing could be done in practice to show that Britain was not interested in protecting the machinery of collective security under the auspices of the League. According to official standpoint, the strength of the League was that it sought "to import new and much needed element of idealism into international affairs," but its main weakness was that it attempted "to freeze into immutability the present distribution of the earth, in many ways singularly unsatisfactory."[84]

4. After 1930, British foreign policy may be criticised for being a storehouse of blunders. By appeasing Japan's aggression in Manchuria, British statesmen annoyed Russia as well as China; by applying sanctions against Italy and then not implementing them in a sincere manner, they pushed Mussolini into the lap of Hitler; by not opposing the accomplishment of the Anschluss, they

---

83. Warner Moss, op. cit., pp. 129-30.

emboldened Hitler to move ahead with the policy of destroying the independence of Austria; by taking to the course of non-intervention, they cleared the way of Gen. Franco to seize power in Spain with the open support of Mussolini and Hitler and thereby strengthening the Fascist bloc; above all, by making the peace of Munich, they gave a proof of their impotence to challenge at all the formidable menace of Fascism. The inherent weaknesses of the policy of appeasement became vivid after irreparable loss had been done to the cause of international peace and security. "The tragedy of this policy, however, was with every concession allowed to the Axis powers Britain allowed the destruction of that balance of power which she was traditionally wedded to uphold and without which she could not retain that diplomatic initiative which was the basis of her world supremacy. The truth is that any policy of appeasement, to be successful, presupposes a sound balance of power without which appeasement degenerates into servility."[85]

Hence, we can not agree with the observation of a protagonist of British foreign policy that it "is mysterious—beyond the comprehension of Continentals. The Geneva documents on the origin of the World War reveal that Germany utterly failed to understand British policy. Throughout the world Britain's reputation is as bad as that of a Pope in the Belfast.... It cannot be denied that Britain appears on the European stage as a much bullied old woman bewildered by the taunts of upstarts."[86]

---

84. Hannah, op. cit., pp. 187-88.
85. M.G. Gupta, op. cit., p 245. In justification of the policy of appeasement a great American politician like J.F. Kennedy says: "I believe Chamberlain was sincere in thinking that a general step had been taken towards healing one of Europe's fever sores. I believe that English public opinion was not sufficiently aroused to back him in a war. Most people in England felt it's not worth a war to prevent the Sudeten Germans from going back to Germany. They failed at that time to see the large issue involving the domination of Europe, but though all these factors played a part in the settlement at Munich... I feel that Munich was inevitable on the grounds of lack of armaments alone... Taking all these factors into consideration the Munich Pact appears in a different light from that of a doddering old man being completely taken in. It shows that appeasement did have some realism; it was the inevitable result of conditions that permitted no other decision." *Why England Slept ?*, pp. 149-54.
86. Moss, op. cit., p. 128.

10

SOVIET RUSSIA

Since October Revolution we have been 'defencists'; we have won the right to defend the fatherland. We are not defending secret treaties; we tore them up and exposed them to the entire world; we are not defending our great Power status—nothing remains of Russia but great. Russia--our national interest--since for us the interests of world socialism rank higher than national interests; we are defending the socialist fatherland....

—V.I. Lenin[1]

While making a study of the foreign policy of Soviet Russia after the successful October Revolution of 1917 under the leadership of Lenin we find ourselves in a different world. It is said that national interest is the basis of the foreign policy of a country. But in the case of Soviet Russia we could see a peculiar blending of the ideology of Marxism-Leninism with the vague term of 'national interest' so much so that one was sought to be forcibly harmonised with the other. All existing states of the world not subscribing to the 'Soviet' model were discredited as 'bourgeois' destined to disappear in course of time. As such the question of a 'socialist' state having permanent relations with the 'bourgeois' states of the world did not arise. At the same time, the 'socialist' state was committed to contribute its part to the realisation of the goal of international socialism. The socialist revolution of a country became a part of the ultimate international socialist order. It is because of this that a fundamental change was said to have occurred in the sphere of

---

1. Lenin's speech at the Central Executive Committee of the Communist party of Russia on May 14, 1918, contained in Jane Degras (ed.): *Soviet Documents on Foreign policy, 1917-24* (London: Oxford University Press, 1951), Vol. I, p. 78.

foreign policy after the successful socialist revolution in Russia in 1917.[2]

Combination of Ideology and National Interest: Distinctive Characteristics of Soviet Foreign Policy

To say that Russian foreign policy under the great Marxist leaders like Lenin and his successors was like the continuation of the old Czarist policy is altogether absurd even if we stick to the fact of its expansionist or imperialist character. The reason behind it is that the new Soviet leaders not only repudiated the line of their predecessors, they sought to give a basically new shape to the foreign policy of their country by reconciling the premises of Marxism with the national interest of the 'fatherland of socialism'. Naturally, the canons of expediency and opportunism had their way into the formulation of this new policy. As a shrewd interpreter of Marx as well as a competent strategist, Lenin in the name of implementing the principles of scientific socialism made several important modifications in the school of Marx and Engels so much so that the new ideology became known by the name of Marxism-Leninism. It had its ramifications in national as well as international spheres. In justification of this, Stalin once forcefully asserted: "Marxism as a science cannot stand still, it develops and improves.... Marxism does not recognise invariable conclusions and formulae obligatory for all epochs and periods."[3]

If so, certain distinctive characteristics of the Soviet foreign policy may easily be earmarked as under:

1. The foreign policy of a country is formulated according to the interest of the ruling class that is euphemistically described as 'national interest'. We have already seen in the preceding chapter that the nature of the British foreign policy changed with the shift

---

2. "For the first time in the history of mankind there appeared an entirely new foreign policy which began to serve not the exploiters, but workers, the working class which came to power and represents the interests of the whole working people. This could not fail to change, as it did, the nature of foreign policy, its aims and tasks, the source of its strength and the influence, and its methods." *Soviet Foreign Policy, 1917-1945* (contributed by I.N. Zemskov. I.F. Ivashin, V.L. Israelyan, M.S. Kapitsa, I.K. Koblyakov, I.I. Mints, V.I. Popov and A.A. Roschin) (Moscow: Progress Publishers, 1980), Vol. I, p. 9.
3. Stalin: *Concerning Marxism in Linguistics* (London: Soviet News, November, 1950), pp. 39-40.

in the nature of the class rule. It had its special manifestation in the attitude of the British government towards the Soviet Union. While the Labour Government accorded *de jure* recognition to Soviet Russia in 1924, the Conservative Government severed relations with her in 1925; similarly, what was done by MacDonald in 1929 was reversed by Baldwin after 1930. Since the working class got power for the first time in Russia in 1917, a fundamental change in the foreign policy of the country was bound to occur. In a technical sense, the foreign policy of a country like Russia came to be determined in the final analysis by its social and economic system. Thus, Lenin said: "The economic interests and the economic position of the classes which rule our state lie at the root of both our home and foreign policy."[4]

2. Since socialism is the anti-thesis of capitalism, the purpose of the foreign policy-makers became denunciation of the bourgeois system and assertion of its replacement by the socialist model of their own. It is for this reason that the new Russian statesmen exposed and condemned the moves of imperialist powers and instead championed the cause of world peace and fraternity of the international working class. Diplomacy, for this reason, became the extension of class struggle in the international sphere. Lenin pointed out that "only a thorough and consistent break with the capitalists in both home and foreign policy can save our revolution and our country, which is gripped in the iron vice of imperialism."[5] It was this kind of break that was made by the Great October Socialist Revolution as a result of which "the international policy of the working class became a state policy for the first time in history."[6]

3. Since workers know no fatherland and workers of the world have to unite for bareaking the chains of slavery existing all over the world, it became the mission of the foreign policy-makers to denounce the network of imperialism and support struggles for national liberation. It also became essential for them to make efforts for the successful 'export of revolution'. For this purpose, Lenin formed the Third Communist International (Comintern) in 1919.

---

4. Lenin: *Collected Works* (Moscow: Progress Publishers, 1965), Vol. 27, p. 365.
5. Ibid., Vol. 25, p. 363.
6. S.P. Sanakoyev and N.I. Kapchenko: *Socialism: Foreign Policy in Theory and Practice* (Moscow: Progress Publishers, 1976), p. 26.

Its statute said that it "has for its purpose the struggle by all available means, including armed force. For the overthrow of the international bourgeoisie and the creation of an international Soviet republic as a transitional stage to the complete abolition of the state."[7] Then, a manifesto issued by its Second Congress of 1920 added that "the international proletariat will not lay down its sword until Soviet Russia has become a link in the federation of the Soviet republics of the world."[8]

However, the most perplexing feature of the Russian foreign policy finds place in a dexterous combination of the high principles of Marxism with the tactical norms of flexibility as sanctioned by the strategy of Leninism. Expose secret diplomacy of the 'bourgeois' states and, at the same time, follow it for its own purpose became the most perplexing feature of Soviet diplomacy. The preaching of the doctrine of peaceful co-existence, and, at the same time, working for the subversion of other political systems had their simultaneous flow. It was on account of this that Russian relations with major 'bourgeois' countries of the world like Britain, France and Germany witnessed rise and fall at successive stages during the inter-war period.

Reference should be made to the role of Comintern at this stage. Its programme boldly included: "In view of the fact that the USSR is the only fatherland of the international proletariat, the principal bulwark of its achievements and the most important factor for its international **emancipation** that international proletariat must on its own part facilitate the work of socialist construction in the USSR and defend her against the attacks of the capitalist powers by all means in its power."[9] Shortly after its creation, it could be ascertained that it had at its disposal a number of information bureaus, special missions and other agencies as operational bases. Besides, the official diplomatic offices, the trade missions in particular were first and foremost used as espionage and agitation centres. More astounding is the fact that protests regarding the propaganda and other activities of the agents of the

---

7. See K.M.T. Florinsky: "Soviet Foreign Policy" in R.A. Goldwin, Gerals Stourzh and Marvin Zetterbaum (eds.): *Readings in Russian Foreign Policy* (New York: Oxford University Press, 1959), p. 189.
8. Ibid.

Comintern were usually countered by Moscow with the observation that the Soviet government was not responsible for the activities of its organs.[10] Repudiating all this, a critic asserts: "The official policy of the Soviet Government has always been to deny any connection between itself and the Third International. The undeniable fact is that the Russian Communist Party controls the Soviet government and completely dominates the Third International. It is, therefore, not surprising to find a fairly close correlation between their policies."[11]

The Great Revolution and After: Phase of War Communism and Western Military Intervention

Certainly, a new epoch opened in the history of Russian foreign policy after the establishment of the new regime in November, 1917.[12] The liquidation of the old order marked the occurrence of the "most revolutionary and far-reaching social upheaval of modern times, demolishing utterly the existing economic and social fabric of Russia and shaking all of Western society to its foundations."[13] With their slogan of 'All Power to the Soviets' and 'Peace, Land and Bread', as coined by Lenin, the Bolsheviks secured ascendancy in the Soviets and organised the new proletarian revolution. On November 7, the provisional government of Kerensky was overthrown by the workers of Petrograd and the Second All-Russian Congress of Soviets approved the creation of a Council of People's Commissars of which Lenin became the President. The next day he proclaimed the 'Decree of Peace' saying: "The Government considers it greatest crime against humanity to continue this war for the sake of dividing among the people of

---

9. Max Beloff: *The Foreign Policy of Soviet Russia, 1929-1941* (London: Oxford University Press, 1947), p. 10.
10. George von Rauch: *A History of Soviet Russia*, Translated into English by Peter and Annettee Jacobson (London: Pall Mall Press, 1967), p. 200.
11. Florinsky, op. cit., p. 189.
12. We may not fully agree with the observation of an American critic of the Russian foreign policy like I.J. Lederer who says that there "has been a tendency by some to think of 1917 as a rigid dividing line in modern Russian history. This view in recent years has been modified with regard to intellectual and social history." *Russian Foreign Policy* (New Haven: Yale University Press, 1962).
13. F.L. Schuman: *International Politics* (New York: Mc Graw Hill, 1948), IV Ed., p. 866.

wealthy nations the weaker nationalities which they have conquered, and the Government solemnly declares its determination to sign immediately terms of peace which will put an end to this war on the conditions, here stated, which are equally just for all nationalities without exception."[14]

In this way, immediately after being in power, Lenin declared firm adherence of his government to the path of peace. The new regime at once opened peace negotiations with the Central Powers (Germany, Austro-Hungarian Empire, Bulgaria and Turkey). When the Allied Powers (Britain, France and the United States) refused to participate, the Russian government published all secret treaties in order to expose their imperialistic war aims. An armistice was concluded on the eastern front in the month of December 1917. For this sake, Russia signed the most humiliating treaty of Brest-Litovsk on March 3, 1918, whereby she on the one part and Central Powers on the other declared termination of the state of war between them and henceforth resolved to live in peace and friendship with one another.[15] Just two days after, Germany imposed on Russia the Treaty of Buftea and Rumania did the same on 7 May by the Treaty of Bucharest. Now Germany got the fertile lands of Ukraine, access to oil wells of Azerbaijan and Rumania, and the way was opened for the intensification of anti-British activities in Iran, Afghanistan and India.

Naturally, the foreign policy of the new republic led to immediate friction with the 'bourgeois' governments like Britain, France and the United States. While the Bolsheviks "regarded their revolution as but a step towards world revolution of the international proletariat leading to the universal overthrow of capitalism, nationalism and imperialism", the bourgeois governments "re-

---

14. See Degras, op. cit., p. 2. Meticulous adherence to the path of peace continued. Thus, in an interview, Leon Trotsky (Lenin's War Minister) affirmed on January 2, 1918: "Our task is clear: we shall continue negotiations on the basis of the principles proclaimed by the the Russian revolution. We shall do all we can to bring the results of these negotiations to the notice of the popular masses of all European countries, despite the truly humiliating censorships which the European governments have imposed on our military and diplomatic communications. We do not doubt that the negotiations themselves will make us stronger, and the imperialist governments of all countries weaker." Ibid., p. 28.
15. How humiliating were the terms of this treaty is evident from the fact that hereby Russia ceded to Germany Russian Poland, Lithuania, Courland, Livo-

garded the communists as dangerous fanatics, whose subversive assault on the existing order must be met by ruthless suppression at the hands of the 'sane' elements in Russia, i.e. the expropriated classes, aided by the outside world."[16] The command of the allied armies drew up plans for armed intervention in Russia. One such plan dated 12 November 1918, read in part: "It is essential to destroy Bolshevism.... It is also important to obtain a good guarantee for Russia's debts to the Entente." On 15 February 1919, Britain's War Minister (Winston Churchill) proposed the setting up of a special body (called the Allied Council of Russian Affairs) that would direct the struggle of the international counter-revolution to overthrow Soviet power in Russia.[17] This Council was to consider the practical possibilities of joint military action against Soviet Russia in which alongside the Entente countries and the Russian white guards the troops of the bourgeois states bordering on Russia would also take part.[18]

Such a sinister proposal of Churchill was supported by the Commander of the Allied troops (Marshal Foch) who outlined a scheme for a vast attack on Soviet Russia by the people of Finland, Estonia, Latvia, Lithuania and others lying in the fringe of Russia (like Poles, Czechs and White Russians) all under Allied direction. At a meeting of the Allied Supreme War Council, Foch announced: "These young troops in themselves not well organised... would, if placed under a unique command, yield a total force sufficient to subdue the Bolshevik forces and to occupy their territory. If this were done, 1919 would see the end of Bolshevism."[19] Thus, occurred the blockade and intervention of the Western powers. It certainly put the new regime in a very difficult situation. Taking note of it, Lenin said: "We have never been in such a dangerous situation as

---

nia, Estonia and the islands of the Moon Sound, while the areas of Kars, Aradhan and Baturm were ceded to Turkey. Russia also recognised the independence of Finland, Ukraine and Georgia and also agreed to pay reparations to the tune of 120,000,000 marks to Germany. Thus, Russia lost 34% of her population, 32% of her agricultural land, 85% of her beet sugar, 54% of her industrial undertakings, and 89% of her coal mines. For text of the treaty see Degras, op. cit., pp. 50-55.

16. Schuman, op. cit., p. 867.
17. Churchill: *The World Crisis: The Aftermath* (London, 1929), Vol. I, pp. 173-74.
18. See David Lloyd George: *The Truth about the Peace Treaties* (London, 1939), Vol. I, p, 370.

Proposals for Peace Submitted by Lenin to the Paris Peace Conference on 12 March, 1919

1. All existing *de facto* Governments which have been set up on the territory of the former Russian Empire and Finland to remain in full control of the territories which they occupy at the moment when the armistice became effective, except in so far as the Conference may agree upon the transfer of territories until the peoples inhabiting the territories controlled by these *de facto* Governments shall themselves determine to change their governments. The Russian Soviet Government, the other Soviet Governments, and all other Governments, which have been set up in the territory of the former Russian Empire, the Allied and Associated Governments, and the other Governments which are operating against the Soviet Governments, including Finland, Poland, Galicia, Rumania, Armenia, Azerbaijan, and Afghanistan, to agree not to attempt, to upset by force the existing *de facto Governments* which have been set up on the territory of the former Russian Empire and other Governments signatory to this agreement.

   The Allied and Associated Governments undertake to see to it that the *de facto* Governments of Germany do not attempt to upset by force the *de facto* Governments of Russia. The *de facto* Governments which have been set up on the territory of the former Russian Empire to undertake not to attempt to upset by force the existing *de facto* Governments of Germany.

2. The economic blockade to be raised and trade relations between Soviet Russia and Allied and Associated countries to be re-established under conditions which will ensure that supplies for the Allied and Associated countries are made available on equal terms to all classes of the Russian people.

3. The Soviet Governments of Russia to have the right of unhindered transit on all railways and the use of all ports which belonged to the former Russian Empire and to Finland and are necessary for the embarkation and transportation of passengers and goods between their territories and the seas.

4. The citizens of the Soviet Republics of Russia to have the right of free entry into the Allied and Associated countries as well as into all countries which have been formed on the territory of former Russian Empire and Finland; also the right of sojourn and circulation and full security, provided they do not interfere in the domestic politics of these countries.

It is considered essential by the Soviet Governments that the Allied and Associated Governments shall see to it that Poland and all neutral countries extend the same right as the Allied and Associated countries.

Nationals of the Allied and Associated countries and of the other countries above-named to have the right of free entry into the Soviet Republics of Russia also the right of sojourn and of circulation and full security, provided they do not interfere in the domestic politics of the Soviet Republics.

The Allied and Associated Governments and other Governments which have been set up on the territory of the former Russian Empire and Finland to have the right to send official representatives enjoying full liberty and immunity into the various Russian Soviet Republics. The Soviet Governments of Russia to have the right to send official representatives enjoying full liberty and immunity into all Allied and Associated countries which have been formed on the territory of former Russian Empire and Finland.

5. The Soviet Governments, the other Governments which have been set up on the territory of former Russian Empire and Finland, to give general amnesty to all political opponents, offenders, and to their own nationals who have been or may be prosecuted for giving help to Soviet Russia. All Russians who have fought in or otherwise aided the armies opposed to the Soviet Governments, and those opposed to the Soviet Governments which have been set up on the territory of the former Russian Empire and Finland, to be included in this amnesty.

All prisoners of war of non-Russian powers detained in Russia, likewise all nationals of those powers now in Russia to be given full facilities for repatriation. The Russian prisoners of war in whatever foreign country they may be; likewise, all Russian soldiers and officers abroad and those serving in all foreign armies to be given full protection for repatriation.

6. Immediately after the signing of this agreement all troops of the Allied and Associated Governments and other non-Russian governments to be withdrawn from Russia and military assistance to cease to be given to anti-Soviet Governments which have been set up on the territory of the former Russian Empire.

The Soviet Government and the anti-Soviet Governments which have been set up on the territory of the former Russian Empire and Finland to begin to reduce their armies simultaneously, and at the same rate, to a peace footing immediately after the signing of the agreement. The conference to determine the most effective and just method of inspecting and controlling this simultaneous de-mobilisation and also the withdrawal of the troops and the cessation of military assistance to the anti-Soviet Governments.

7. The Allied and Associated Governments taking cognisance of the statement of the Soviet Government of Russia, in its note of 4 February, in regard to foreign debts propose an integral part of this agreement that the Soviet Government and other Governments which have been set up on the territory of the former Russian Empire and Finland shall recognise their responsibility to the financial obligations of the former Russian Empire, to foreign States parties to this agreement and to the nationals of such states. Detailed arrangements for the payments of these debts to be agreed upon at the conference, regard being had to the present financial position of Russia. The Russian gold seized by the Czecho-Slovaks in Kazan or taken from Germany by the Allies to be regarded as partial payment of the portion of the debt from the Soviet Republics of Russia.

The Soviet Government of Russia undertakes to accept the foregoing proposals, provided it is made not later than April, 1919.

The Soviet Governments is extremely desirous of receiving semi-official guarantees from the American and British Governments that they will do all that lies in their power to get France to observe the conditions of armistice.

we are now. The imperialists were busy among themselves, but now one group has been wiped out by the Anglo-French-American group, which considers its main task to be the extermination of world Bolshevism and the strangulation of its main centre, the Russian Republic."[20]

But the Allied plan of totally destroying the communist regime of Russia could not succeed to the desired extent. An attack from all sides by 14 bourgeois states in the form of 'blockade' and 'intervention' continued for about three years. The reason was that great leaders of the Allied bloc had their own differences in this regard. For instance, British Prime Minister Lloyd George said that the 'mere idea of crushing Bolshevism by a military force is pure madness.' Prime Minister Clemenceau of France suggested the idea of 'cordon sanitaire'.[21] The result was that after an interlude of about three years the blockade and military intervention of Russia in which Kolchak, Yudenich and Denikin played a very important role failed to achieve the desired purpose. The bourgeois governments of the Baltic states did not like to fight for long against Soviet Russia; "they waited, temporised, sent delegation, formed commissions, sat in conference, and did so until Yudenich, Kolchak and Denikin had been crushed and the Entente defeated in the second campaign too."[22]

Diplomatic hostility of the Allied powers towards the Communist regime had its own effect on not extending it an official invitation to take part in the Paris Peace Conference. None of them wanted Russian participation. Clemenceau cautioned that "Bolsheviks would convert France and England to Bolshevism." Lloyd George simply desired to summon the Russians to Paris 'somewhat in a way that the Russian Empire summoned chiefs of

---

19. *Papers Relating to the Foreign Relations of the United States: The Paris Peace Conference, 1919* (Washington, 1943), Vol. IV, p. 122.
20. Lenin, op. cit., Vol. 28, pp. 160-61.
21. Louis Fischer makes it clear that, for practical purposes, the British "had not accepted the French *cordon sanitaire* idea. This, indeed, became the policy of the entire western world: help the Russian border states and help the Russian whites fight their battles without foreign troops." *The Soviets in World Affairs: A History of Relations between the Soviet Union and the Rest of the World* (London: Jonathan Cape, 1930), Vol. I, p. 187.
22. Lenin, op. cit., Vol. 30, pp. 388-89.

outlying tributary states to render an account of their actions."[23] Wilson prepared a secret plan that was approved by the Council of Ten, i.e., by all the Allied and Associated Powers wherein it was suggested to divide up Russia among the Russian white guards and the bourgeois nationalists of other nations of the former Russian Empire. More shocking than this was the fact that the Allied Powers sent an invitation to the 'Whiteguard governments' that were involved in the game of destroying the Communist regime of Lenin by the techniques of armed blockade and military intervention.

In such a situation, Lenin's Minister for Foreign Affairs (Chicerin) brought this matter to the notice of President Wilson not so much with the aim of getting representation in the Peace Conference as for driving home the fact that "the absence of an answer on our part should not be misinterpreted."[24] It was done to defeat the propaganda going on in some Allied countries that the Bolsheviks had declined to take part in the work of peace settlement. However, finding no reply to such a request, he addressed another note to the heads of the governments of Britain, France, United States, Italy and Japan on 4 February 1919. It had the same fate. The net result of all this was that Wilson deputed his envoy (Bullitt) to have some preliminary clarifications from Lenin. Parleys continued for some time. It was through Bullitt that Lenin could submit his proposals for peace to the Paris Peace Conference on 12 March, 1919. It all went in vain despite the affirmation of Bullitt: "No real peace can be established in Europe or the world, until peace is made with the revolution. This proposal of the Soviet Government presents an opportunity to make peace with the revolution on a just and reasonable basis—perhaps a unique opportunity."[25]

For the survival of the Communist regime in the midst of such difficult and humiliating situations, Lenin made three important steps. First, he adhered to the path of seeking peace at any price. Thus, Russia concluded humiliating treaties with the Central Powers during the days of First World War. After that she made

---

23. See Ray Stanard Baker: *Woodrow Wilson and World Settlement* (London, 1923), Vol. I, p. 166.
24. *Soviet Foreign Policy Documents* (Moscow, 1958) Vol. II, p. 52.
25. *The Bullitt Mission to Russia*, p. 54. Despite the fact that no official invitation was sent to the new regime of Russia to represent itself at the Paris Peace Confer-

similar proposals to the Baltic states of Estonia, Latvia, Lithuania and Finland so as to weaken their determination to fall into the trap of the Allied powers. In order to allay their fears Lenin also reiterated the principle of self-determination for all nations and nationalities of the world.[26] Second, he went ahead with the policy of thorough collectivisation of national economy what he termed 'war communism' that was interpreted as his counterpart to Walter Rathenau's 'war socialism' in Germany before 1919.[27] Above all, he set up the Third Communist International in March, 1919 with its centre at Moscow as a federation of revolutionary Communist parties throughout the world. Its chief aim was to serve as the general staff of the 'world revolution' that "would attack from the rear the bourgeois governments seeking to strangle the Russian proletarian dictatorship."[28]

New Economic Policy and 'Defensive Isolationism': Inauguration of the Policy of Peaceful Co-Existence

The First World War ended in 1918 but the Russian civil war came to a close in 1920 with the defeat of bourgeois intervention and counter-revolution. It marked the termination of a crucial period in the history of Soviet Russia. The bourgeois states of the world ultimately realised that Soviet Russia could stand up for itself and be reckoned with. It also signified the beginning of a new and peaceful period—a period of economic rehabilitation and the

---

ence, it is a fact that its existence had its own effect on the minds of the peacemakers. As Wilson himself revealed on one occasion: "The effect of the Russian problem on the Paris (Peace) Conference was profound; Paris cannot be understood without Moscow. Without ever being repesented at Paris at all, the Bolsheviks and Bolshevism were powerful elements at every turn. Russia played a more vital part at Paris than Persia." See Baker, op. cit., Vol. II, p. 64.

26. Lenin had carefully taken note of the fact that while carrying on political and economic blockade of the Soviet state, the Allied powers had actively drawn up plans for a concentric attack on Soviet Russia: Kolchak from the east, Denikin from the south, the troops of the interventionists and General Miller from the north, and Yudenich, the White Poles and the Baltic bourgeois nationalists from the west. Besides, the *de facto* rrecognition, which followed soon afterwards, of Kolchak's 'government' by the USA, Britain, France and Italy provided further confirmation of the fact that they were counting on armed struggle against Soviet Russia. *Soviet Foreign Policy, 1917-1945*, pp. 110-12.
27. David Thomson: *Europe since Napoleon* (London: Penguin Books, 1978), p. 584.
28. Schuman, op. cit., p. 868.

creation of technical and economic prerequisites for the building of socialism in Soviet Russia. Under these conditions in March 1921, Lenin astonished the world by introducing his New Economic Policy (NEP) that allowed revival of the capitalist system in agriculture and industry at a limited scale in the national and signified commitment of the state to the policy of peaceful coexistence in the international spheres. In short, the new line of Lenin desired all peace-loving states of the world to live in friendship and cooperation without undermining other's social, economic and political systems.

It had its special impact in the economic field. When Lenin desired international economic cooperation, it came to have its natural reconciliation with the interest of other states of the world. The statesmen of Britain, Germany, France and Italy well took note of this new development and they sought to make a bold experiment in establishing economic relations with a socialist state. The British statesmen took the lead in this direction. Already taking note of the new development in Russia, Prime Minister Lloyd George and his great colleagues like Churchill (War. Secretary) and Lord Curzon (Foreign Secretary) hounoured the proposal of R. Horne (President of the Board of Trade) that "the only way we shall fight Bolshevism is by trade." A little after, Lloyd George rebutted the argument of his critics by asserting: "I have heard predictions about the fall of the Soviet government for the last two years. Denikin, Yudenich, Wrangel, all have collapsed, but I can not see any immediate prospect of the collapse of the Soviet Government."[29]

As a matter of fact, now economics dominated politics. The British bourgeois statesmen thought it expedient to make capital out of restoring economic relations with the communist state of Russia. Thus, the Anglo-Russian trade agreement of March 1921, came into being. It amounted to according *de facto* recognition to the new republic of Russia by the greatest capitalist country of Europe. It facilitated the development of Russian foreign trade and British industry found new markets in a socialist country. In appreciation of it, Lenin said: "The important thing for us is to force windows one after another. The agreement with Britain was that of a Socialist Republic with a bourgeois state.... The consequences

---

29. *Soviet Foreign Policy*, p. 129.

have shown that thanks to this agreement we have forced open a window of sorts."³⁰

The policy of making peace and restoring economic relations with other states of the world subscribing to any social, economic and political system now moved with great success. In March 1921 Russia signed the Treaty of Riga with Poland and (another with Ukraine) whereby she ceded Ukrainian and Byelorussian territories to Poland so as to offset the danger of further blockade or attack on her territory from that side. In April 1922 an important international conference, second only in size to Versailles Peace Conference itself, met at Genoa in Italy to form a European 'consortium', or a kind of Economic League of Nations, which would undertake the restoration of Europe with Russian collaboration. It afforded the first occasion for the Russian Foreign Minister (Chicerin) to be face to face with his European counterparts. When they demanded payment of Russia's debts and compensations to expropriated investors as the price of recognition, their bill of $ 13,000,000,000 was met by a Soviet counter-claim of $ 60,000,000,000 for damage done by the Allied and Associated Powers during the period of armed blockade and military intervention. "Neither side would yield and no general agreement was possible."³¹

However, the Genoa meet proved successful in another way to the statesmen of Russia and Germany. Chicerin and Rathenau secretly moved to Rapallo on 16 April, 1921, and there signed a treaty—a consortium of their own. By this agreement all claims and counter-claims were cancelled and mutually advantageous economic relations restored. The real significance of this treaty lay in the fact that Russo-German *rapprochement* took place that stood as 'a source of fear to France.'³² It is well observed: "The terms of the treaty were unimportant. But its signature was a significant event. It secured for the Soviet Union its official recognition by a Great Power; and it was the first overt attempt by Germany to break the ring which the Versailles Powers had drawn round her. The

---

30. Lenin, op. cit., Vol. 42, p. 289, Already on February 21, 1920, Lenin had affirmed: "I know of no reason why a Socialist commonwealth like ours cannot do business indefinitely with capitalistic countries. We do not mind taking their capitalistic locomotives and farming machinery, so why should they mind taking our Socialistic wheat, flax and platinum." Ibid., p. 177.
31. Schuman, op. cit., p. 869.
32. Louis L. Snyder (ed.): *Documents on German History* (Brunswick, New Jersey: Rutgers University Press, 1958), p. 402.

indignation with which this treaty was greeted by the Allied Powers was understandable. But it was the direct consequence of their own policy of treating Germany and the Soviet Union as inferior countries. The two outcastes naturally joined hands; and the Rapallo Treaty established friendly relations between them for more than ten years."[33]

The fact of Russo-German collaboration through this treaty of friendship informed British leaders to understand the reality of the situation and cash advantage out of it.[34] Thus, the British government accorded *de jure* recognition to the Communist state of Russia on 2 February, 1924. It forced a good number of other bourgeois states to follow suit.[35] The Soviet leaders appreciated the action of Labour Prime Minister MacDonald and, at the same time, described it as a matter of necessity for the British government in the light of growing labour movement in their country coupled with the protection and promotion of their economic interests.[36] That is, the act of according *de jure* recognition had a two-sided effect. If Britain recognised Russia in legal terms, it was also recognised by Russia in the same way. Thus, Chicerin expressed his reaction: "They need *de jure* recognition as much as we do ... simply because they know

---

33. Carr: *International Relations between the Two World Wars* (London: Macmillan, 1952), p. 75.
34. Strongly opposing the policy of armed blockade and military intervention of Russia by the Allied Powers and, at the same time, defending the course of rendering help to Germany to restore her economic position as the condition precedent for the impovement of British commercial relation, one of the best representatives of the British bourgeois class noted: "Let us then in our Russian policy not only applaud and imitate the policy of non-intervention which the Government of Germany has announced, but, desisting from a blockade which is injurious to our own permanent interests, as well as illegal, let us encourage and assist Germany to take up again her place in Europe as a creator and organiser of wealth for her Eastern and Southern neighbours." Lord J.M. Keynes: *The Economic Consequences of Peace* (London: Macmillan, 1920), p. 294.
35. The USSR was recongised by Italy on 8 February, by Norway on 13 February, by Austria on 25 February, by Greece on 8 March, by Sweden on 15 March, and by Denmark on 18 June in 1924.
36. For instance, on 29 January 1924, there was a certain impatience among the working class over delay in the expected recognition of the Soviet government. London workers sent a deputation to the government demanding immediate recognition of the USSR. In its issue of January 1924, the Labour monthy paper pointed out that 'recognition was extended, but only under pressure from the masses.' *Soviet Foreign Policy*, p. 192.

and they feel that Britain itself needs our market. needs our raw materials."[37]

However, it should be borne in mind that behind the facade of pursuing the policy of peaceful co-existence the strategy of gradually and secretly infiltrating socialism in the bourgeois states continued unabated. The method of Bolshevism "was that of the Boig in *Peer Gynt*, to win without fighting; it was for this reason that the Soviet Government had been prepared to offer to Poland, in the summer of 1920, far better territorial terms than the Allies at the time were contemplating. By thus conciliating rationalistic aspirations they hoped to rally to their cause the workers of Poland, and thus to bring another country within their political orbit and it may well be that their object would have been achieved but for unexpected success of the Polish army."[38]

In this respect the French occupation of the Ruhr in January 1923, presented an excellent opportunity for the leaders of the Comintern to steer the agitation of the working masses into proper channels. At their secret instance, on March 25, a district party congress was convened in Essen to chalk out a programme for the seizure of local power by the communists. A workers' republic in the Rhineland and in the Ruhr was to be the base for which a Red Army was to advance on Central Germany and seize power in Berlin.[39] Leo Schlageter organised acts of sabotage in the Ruhr area. He was arrested and tried by a French court martial and then shot on 26 May. Then, the great Bolshevik expert on Germany (Karl Radek) honoured his memory as 'a brave soldier in a counter-revolution.'[40]

The Communists organised military formations and called upon factory workers and farm labourers to go on a strike. In the

---

37. Ibid., p. 190.
38. G.M. Gathorne-Hardy: *A Short History of International Affairs, 1920-1939* (London: Oxford University Press, 1950), IV Ed., pp. 103-04.
39. Ruth Fischer: *Stalin and German Communism: A Study in the Origins of the State Party* (Combridge, Mass., 1948), p. 329.
40. The Comintern dispatched Karl Radek to Germany to maintain contact with the German Communist Party. There "seems a strong probability that a serious revolution would, in fact, have broken out in the course of 1923 had not the Russian emissary, who regarded such an outbreak as premature, exerted his influence to restrain the movement." Gathorne-Hardy, op. cit., 107-08.

year 1923 alone more than 1 million dollars were smuggled into Germany. Definite dates had been set for the outbreak of a communist uprising in Germany. The details of the plan were arranged during a special session of the Executive Committee of the Communist International which Zinoviev had convoked in Moscow at the end of September. On October 10, the communists, as planned, formed a government in Saxony; four days later, President Ebert ordered the occupation of Saxony and Thuringia by German troops. A handful of extremists arose on 22 October in Hamburg. Led by E. Thaelmann, the Communists attacked the police precinct states.[41]

The implementation of the policy of secret infiltration and of communism into the bourgeois states so as to subvert their socio-economic systems was looked at with great apprehension by the statesmen of Britain. Zinoviev (the President of the Comintern) "was quite undeterred in his task of permeating the world with Communist principles and propaganda, by any consideration of its reactions upon Russian prosperity."[42] While he frankly appreciated the role of Labour Prime Minister (MacDonald) as 'of great assistance to me and the Government,' he "yet valued it as an organism in whose constitutions the red bacillus of Communism might hopefully be injected."[43] On one occasion in July 1924, he said at the congress of the Cominern: "A Labour Government is the most alluring and popular formula for listing the masses in favour of dictatorship of the proletariat.... The worker, peasant, railwayman will first do their revolutionary 'bit', and only afterwards realise that this actually is the dictatorship of the proletariat."[44] It was on account of this that Anglo-Soviet relations witnessed a severe setback with the exposure of notorious 'Zinoviev Letter' in October 1924, that was described by Chicerin on 19 October as "gross

---

41. George von Rauch, op. cit., pp. 192-95. On 30 September, 1923 Trotsky plainly uttered: "We do not hide our sympathies for the German working class in its heroic struggle for its liberation.... We are entirely on the side of the victims of rapacious and bloody French imperialism. We are with the German working class with all our soul in its struggle against foreign and domestic exploitation. But, at the same time, we are entirely for peace." Cited in Louis Fischer, op. cit., Vol. I, pp. 456-57.
42. Gathorne-Hardy, op. cit., p. 105.
43. Ibid.
44. Ibid.

forgery and an audacious attempt to prevent the development of friendly relations between the two countries."[45]

'Socialism in One Country': Stalin's Strategy of Offensive Isolationism

An important shift in the Russian diplomacy appeared after the passing away of Lenin in January 1924. "To the rank and file of the Communists, his tomb in Moscow became a shrine; to the party leaders, his passing signalised a struggle for control."[46] A war of succession ensued. While Joseph Stalin led one camp, the other was led by Leon Trotsky. "The rival leaders, both of whom professed to be loyal Leninists, expressed anti-thetical views on several major points. Stalin believed capitalism to be so firmly entrenched in the West that any effort to bring about its immediate overthrow would be futile. He preferred to concentrate on 'socialism in one country' rather than upon uncertain attempts to dislodge capitalism from the West. Trotsky, on the contrary, was intolerant of any let up in the world revolutionary movement."[47] In this war of succession, ultimately the Stalin line emerged triumphant. "The growing weight attached to the defensive aspects of Soviet foreign policy was reinforced by the final acceptance into the canons of social orthodoxy of the hotly disputed doctrine of socialism in one country."[48]

Soviet regime became more ruthless under the hold of Stalin. With the inauguration of the First Five Year Plan in 1927, the degree

---

45. Degras, op. cit., p. 472. On 10 October, 1924, the British Foreign Office came into possession of a document allegedly representing a letter from Zinoviev to the British Communist Party. In it the Party was ordered to go beyond ordinary agitation and to form special cells in the British army as well as in armament factories and munition supply depots. It said: "In the event of an imminent War, one can with the help of the latter and in co-operation with the transport workers, paralyse all war preparations of the bourgeoisie, thus transorming the imperialist war right from the start into a class war." Finally, steps were to be taken to train millitary specialists of the British Red Army. Ruth, op. cit., p. 561. It may, however be added here that the authenticity of the Zinoviev letter could not be proved. An investigation commission set up by the Labour Party arrived at this conclusion. However, the mischievous element of the Soviet foreign policy could not be ignored that they were interested in supporting MacDonald 'as the rope supports the hanged.' George von Rauch, op cit., p. 200.
46. W.C. Langsam: *The World Since 1919* (Delhi: Surjeet Publications, 1981), p. 203.
47. Ibid., p. 204.
48. Max Beloff, op. cit., pp. 3-4.

Soviet Russia

of liberalisation introduced in the NEP was abolished. A very heavy hand was put on all dissident and deviationist elements. Now the Russian leaders took to the course of openly condemning the diplomacy of bourgeois states and their role in maintaining peace through the League of Nations. While attacking the League of Nations on November 23, 1925, Litvinov said in a press interview that it "is a cover for the preparation of military action for the further suppression of small and weak nationalities. To a considerable degree, it is only a diplomatic house, where the strong powers arrange their business and conduct their mutual accounts behind the back at the expense of the small and weak nations. The USSR, as a state of working masses, cannot take responsibility for the League of Nations, which sanctifies the enslavement and exploitation of foreign nations. Inspired solely by the desire to avoid any complications which might break the general peace and, in particular the progress of its great work by the internal construction, and pursuing its policy of non-intervention in the internal affairs of other nations, the USSR does not feel the slightest desire to enter an organisation in which it would have to play the part either of hammer or of anvil."[49]

Likewise, efforts made by the statesmen of Britain and France for the maintenance of peace were looked upon with great apprehension by the Russian foreign policy-makers. For instance, when the Locarno agreements were made in October 1925, its news in the Kremlin at first caused ample alarm. Speaking at the XIV Party Congress in December 1925, Stalin commented that it "was pregnant with a new war in Europe, that it was nothing but a continuation of the Versailles."[50] The fact that while western frontiers of Germany (revised under the Treaty of Versailles) touching France and Belgium were recognised permanently and Britain gave the guarantee for their protection, her eastern frontiers touching Poland, Czechoslovakia, Austria and other Baltic states were left untouched. It revealed that the great bourgeois powers were interested in nothing more than their own defence against a possible German attack in time to come. Thus, Soviet leaders could understand the long-range motives of the statesmen of Paris and

---

49. See Degras, op. cit., Vol. II (1925-32), p. 65.
50. V.P. Potemkin: *History of Diplomacy* (Moscow, 1947), Vol. III, pp. 329 ff.

London. At the same time, they noted the fact that Locarno agreements "limited the sphere of activity of Soviet foreign diplomacy. It left Russia an approach only to Turkey, Lithuania and in part to France. By narrowing the possibilities in the West, it put a premium on Bolshevik efforts in Asia."[51]

The Soviet reaction to the Kellogg-Briand pact of August 1928 must be studied against this background. Stalin and other Russian leaders took strong exception to the fact that the negotiations that culminated in the conclusion of a pact for the renunciation of war as an instrument of national policy had no representation of the USSR. It made it above board that the main idea behind the conclusion of such a momentous moral declaration was to isolate the Soviet Union or to make a covert attempt for its encirclement. Thus, the Commissar for Foreign Affairs (Chicerin) commented: "The omission of the Soviet Government from those taking part in the negotiations brings us in the first place to the thought that the real aims of the initiators of the pact obviously included and include the desire to make it a means of isolating the USSR and of fighting against it. The negotiations for the conclusion of the pact are clearly a constituent part of the policy of encircling the USSR which is at the present moment at the centre of the international affairs."[52] Since the lead in this regard was taken by the French Foreign Minister (Briand) and since Russian relations with this country had not improved, Stalin critically reacted: "The most striking representative of the bourgeois movement towards intervention against the Soviet Union is the bourgeois France of today, the fatherland of Pan-Europe, the cradle of the Kellogg Pact, the most aggressive and militaristic country among all aggressive and militaristic countries of the world."[53]

While one could disagree to some extent with the points raised by the Russian leaders in regard to the usefulness of the Pact

---

51. Louis Fischer, op. cit., Vol. II, p. 612. The Locarno Agreements were hailed by the peace-makers of London as 'the dividing line between the years of war and the years of peace.' But Gen. Smuts of South Africa dubbed them as 'a new Holy Alliance between the spectres of Empire.' An ex-Premier of Italy (Nitti) warned that the question of the pact of guarantee "is one of the worst instances of mistaken effort, and may develop into a very dangerous one." Ibid., p. 611.
52. Degras, op. cit., Vol. II, p. 322.
53. See Max Beloff, op. cit., p. 43.
54. Degras, op. cit., Vol. II, p. 324.

of Paris, this much of their attack was justified that a mere declaration for the abandonment of war as an instrument of national policy was inadequate in the absence of a commitment to disarmament. Thus, Chicerin reacted: 'Our Government notes that the Pact already inadequate, is rendered still less valuable by the reservations made by France and England, and the right granted to all signatories to interpret the pact in the spirit of their own national or imperialist policy. In particular, our Government would emphasise that the Kellogg Pact is made less valuable in the first place by the circumstances that it is not accompanied by undertaking in regard to disarmament."[54] And yet the USSR signed the Pact on 6 September, 1928. It gave the Soviet Government "a new possibility of forwarding its security policy, and began a new era of activity in Soviet diplomacy."[55] As subsequent developments showed, after the signing of this Pact, Soviet diplomacy "was once more able to resume its plan for a treaty system in Eastern Europe.[56]

However, the most important achievement of Russian diplomacy during the later part of the 'period of pacification' (1925-30) was a steady improvement in her relations with Germany. Reference should now be made to the Neutrality Agreement signed by the two powers on April 24, 1926. Its preamble said that the two Governments "animated by the desire to do all they can to contribute to the maintenance of general peace and convinced that the interests of the peoples of two countries demand conscientious and constant collaboration have come to an agreement to confirm the friendly relations existing between them." Its main provisions were:[57]

1. "The Treaty of Rapallo remains the basis of relations between Germany and the USSR. They remain in friendly contact in order to settle amicably all questions of a political and economic nature concerning their two countries.
2. If one of the contracting parties, despite its peaceful attitude, should be attacked by a third power or by several third powers, the other contracting parties shall observe neutrality during the period of the conflict.

---

55. Max Beloff, op. cit., p. 9.
56. George von Rauch, op. cit., p. 207.
57. L.L. Snyder, op. cit., p. 403.

3. If in the event of a conflict of the nature foreshadowed in above article, occurring at a time when either of the two contracting parties is not involved in an armed conflict, a coalition should be formed by third parties with a view to imposing economic and financial boycott of one of the two contracting parties, the other contracting party will not participate in such a coalition."

With the conclusion of this treaty, the entire Western world was taken aback. But the German Foreign Minister (Stresemann) jubilantly said: "This Treaty has nothing sensational in it. An age-old friendship unites our two countries."[58]

The conclusion of this treaty should be attributed to the successful diplomacy of the Foreign Ministers of Germany and Russia who ardently desired to improve the position of their countries in the comity of nations in the midst of prevailing conditions of Anglo-French hegemony. Both parties sought to make capital out of it in their own ways. While Germany cautioned the major capitalist powers (like Britain, France and the United States) to come to her help so as to save her from falling into the trap of a Communist State,[59] the Soviet Union managed to establish its foothold in the Central Europe whose results appeared some three years after.[60] The East Pact, also known by the name of the 'Litvinov Protocol,' was signed on 9 February 1929 by Poland, USSR, Rumania, Estonia and Latvia. (Subsequently it was accepted by Turkey, Lithuania and Persia.) It certainly came as a significant success for Soviet foreign policy. "It was mainly due to Litvinov's astute tactics of a negotiator. For the first time since the revolution, the

---

58. *Gustav Stresemann: His Diaries, Letters and Papers,* edited and translated from German into English by Eric Sutton (London, 1937), pp. 379-80.
59. Stresemann was widely regarded as a German statesman who was also a good European, as the architect of the 'spirit of Locarno' and as the prophet of a new, peaceful Germany. The posthumous publication of his *Memoirs,* however, revealed that he was a master of power politics whose main object "was to bring about the restoration of Germany to the status of a major power and who knew how to use the weapon of fear of the Soviet Union to bring the Western allies to terms." See Snyder, op. cit., p. 404.
60. Even after signing the Neutrality Treaty with Germany, the USSR remained somewhat doubtful of the 'spirit of Locarno.' The news of Germany's entry into the League of Nations in September, 1926 was received with equanimity. It was only later that Germany's efforts to maintain the middle ground between West and East were depicted as a deceitful game in which Germany used its relations

nations of Eastern and Central European intermediate zone had joined a treaty system which, although originally conceived in the West, was put into effect and signed in Moscow. Soon the fear would arise that this system would also find its pivot in Moscow."[61]

Anglo-Soviet relations during this period witnessed a curious rise and fall. The act of according *de jure* recognition to the Soviet State in 1924 by the Labour Government received a severe setback after the exposure of the 'Zinoviev Letter.' The Conservative leaders could thrive on the exploitation of, what Lord Curzon said, MacDonald's 'biggest mistake in the world'. The attitude of other great Tory leaders remained quite critical in this regard. However, as *de jure* recognition had been given, there was no sense in retracing a diplomatic step in this important direction. Thus, Baldwin and Asquith defended it in the House of Commons and Lord Grey did the same in the House of Lords. Since 1921 the two countries were represented by the *charge d'affaires*, but after the conferment of *de jure* recognition, their status was raised to that of ambassadors. Christian Rakovsky was appointed as the first Russian ambassador to Great Britain.

Yet the diehard British conservative elements reiterated the plea of not going beyond maintaining economic relations with the Soviet State. King George V ignored the representation of a regime, that had killed his cousin Czar Nicholas II, at a social function. In 1927 a Tory Secretary of State for India (Lord Birkenhead) described Bolshevism as 'a serious and strange epidemic'. The police made a raid at the London office of a British-Soviet concern 'Arcos' that yielded substantial material showing it as a regular centre of Bolshevik espionage and subversive propaganda in England. It led to the breakdown of diplomatic relations, but the deteriorating condition could improve a little after the installation of another Labour Government under MacDonald in 1929. It demonstrated that "the policy of Great Britain in regard to the Soviet Union unfortunately became a shuttlecock of party politics."[62]

As a matter of fact, the relations of the USSR with the 'bourgeois' states of the world improved after the triumph of

---

with the Soviet Union as a bargaining object in its dealings with Western powers." See George von Rauch, op. cit., p. 197.
61. Ibid., p. 208.
62. Carr, op. cit., p. 75.

Stalin's edict of 'socialism in one country'. The expulsion of the arch-protagonist of the world-revolution (Trotsky) and Zinoviev in 1927 came as a concrete proof of the eventual victory of the Stalin line. It also illustrated that "the hopes of world-revolution, while not formally abandoned, would not in future be allowed to interfere with the establishment of normal relations between Soviet government and capitalist States. The Soviet Union had thus at length accepted the fundamental basis of international relations, and its full return to the international community of states was only a matter of time."[63] The acceptance of the Pact of Paris of 1928 corroborated the same trend. It now appeared that the "seal to Stalin's policy of co-operation with the democratic capitalist powers of Europe against the Fascist opponents of communism was set."[64]

Strategy of 'United Front': Facing the Grim Challenge of Fascism
After 1930 the Soviet statesmen in their usual fashion insisted on adhering to the line of international peace.[65] However, two momentous developments occurred that brought about a change in the nature of Russian diplomacy. The first was the great economic depression that hit the United States badly and forced the American administration to come to economic terms with the Soviet Union. President Hoover preferred to abandon the traditional line of Coolidge and Harding.[66] Now it became apparent to him that it was extremely difficult to exclude permanently so tremendous an economic area as the Soviet Union from world trade without exposing the capitalist economic system itself to certain unwarranted hardships. Thus, in the early thirties a resumption of normal trade relations and the diplomatic recognition of the Soviet Union "was increasingly demanded in the United States."[67]

---

63. Ibid., pp. 77-78.
64. F.H. Simonds and B. Emeny: *The Great Powers in World Politics* (New York: American Book Company, 1939), p. 337.
65. For instance, Karl Radek endorsed: "The object of the Soviet Government is to save the soil of the first proletarian state from the criminal folly of a new war. To this end the Soviet Union has struggled with the greatest determination and consistency for sixteen years. The defence of peace and the neutrality to the Soviet Union against all attempts to drag it into the whirlwind of a world war is the central problem of Soviet foreign policy." Refer to his paper "The Bases of Soviet Foreign Policy" in *Foreign Affairs* (Moscow), January, 1934, p. 206.

Soviet Russia

The second event was the rise of Fascism in Germany under Hitler. Already in his *Mein Kampf* he had boldly declared his programme of effacing Bolshevism from the world. The suppression of the Communist party in Germany in 1933 had come as a concrete proof of the ultimate mission of the great Nazi leader. Naturally, the peace problem of the USSR was fundamentally altered. Instead of hating or condemning the bourgeois systems of the world, it was needed that the USSR adhere to the strategy of a 'united front' to face the challenge of Fascism. "To prevent assault from Berlin, Moscow must arm in the teeth and find allies. To prevent destruction of the Communist movement throughout the world, Moscow must co-operate with socialists and liberals against Fascism. The Narkomindel (Foreign Minister's Office) and the Comintern faced the new task realistically. The result "was a revolution in Soviet diplomacy and a reorientation of international Communism."[68]

Under these conditions the bourgeois states, feeling afraid of a possible German attack, came closer to the USSR. The Franco-Soviet Non-Aggression Pact of 29 November 1932, was supplemented with a commercial treaty of 11 January 1934. Similar non-aggression pacts were signed by the Soviet Union with Poland and other Baltic states. Closer relations were cultivated with Britain and Turkey as well. The Litvinov mission proved eminently successful in getting recognition of the USSR by the USA in 1933 as a result of which the Soviet Union got a seat in the League of Nations in 1934. Now the USSR, more than any other nation, strove "to uphold and apply the principle of collective security."[69] It was officially given: "The Soviet government is entering into the League of Nations in order to support those Powers which will struggle for the preservation and consolidation of peace."[70]

---

66. In a message to the American Congress on December 6, 1923, the President made it clear that his government did not propose "to enter into relations with another regime which refuses to recognise the sanctity of international obligations." *Soviet-American Relations, 1919-1933*, p. 58.
67. George von Rauch, op. cit., p. 332 n 1.
68. Schuman, op. cit., p. 873.
69. W.P. Coates and Zelda Coates: *World Affairs and the USSR* (London: Lawrence and Wishart Ltd, 1939), p. 32.
70. *Izvestia* (Moscow), September 20, 1934.

However, the great bourgeois powers of Britain, France and the United States in the heart of their hearts desired liquidation of communism at the cruel hands of Fascism. For this sake, they desisted from giving their sincere cooperation to the strategy of 'United Front' so assiduously pursued by the Soviet Union. They condemned the ruthless policy of Stalin in crushing dissidents like Radek, Sokolnikov, Yagoda, Kharakhan, Bukharin, Rykov, Krestinsky, Piatakov, Serebriakov, Tukhachevsky, Rakovsky, etc. The Fascist leaders could well understand the real motives of the great 'appeasers' of London, Paris and Washington and they strove to exploit the opportunity for their imperialistic aggrandisements. Thus came into being an axis of the Caesars of Rome, Berlin and Tokyo in 1936 that revealed to the Soviet leaders what the enemies of Communism had really desired. As time passed, Britain, France and the United States "took their own threats less seriously, and the Kremlin became less concerned with them. Fascist mouthings of 'anti-Bolshevism' were intended for ears in London, Paris and Washington where they were taken quite seriously—to the ruin of Western Powers. Under these conditions, Soviet hopes of a 'United Front' with the West against the Triplice, and Communist hopes of a 'United Front' with socialists and liberals against Fascism, were alike doomed to frustration."[71]

The story of 'betrayal' shown by the bourgeois states to the USSR during this phase of crisis may be corroborated with a passing reference to four important events:

1. *Rape of Manchuria*

When Japan raped Manchuria in 1931 and the great Powers of London and France desisted from invoking the provisions of collective security in the deliberations of the League of Nations in spite of the fact that the Lytton Commission had declared Japan guilty of the act of aggression, the USSR thought it expedient to denounce the action of Japanese imperialism in very cautious terms and, at the same time, try to gain some time for preparing herself for any future contingency. For this purpose, she desired to abide strictly and consistently by its policy of peace and strict non-interference into the internal affairs of other states with the hope

---

71. Schuman, op. cit., p. 876.

that the Japanese government would also seek "to preserve the existing relations between the two countries and would ensure that none of its actions or orders violated the interests of the USSR."[72] It went unhonoured by the Caesars of Tokyo. Then, the Soviet leaders expressed their full sympathy with the Chinese people who had taken a stand against Japanese aggression for the independence of their country. Fraternal relations based on the principles of proletarian internationalism developed between the USSR and the Provisional Central Workers' and Peasants' government set up in the liberated areas of China. The USSR gave all assistance to the Communist Party of China and the armed forces led by it. The public demand and the fear of further Japanese aggression in China compelled the Nanking government to restore relations with the USSR. It helped to strengthen ties between the two countries and provided the Chinese people with certain political support in their struggle against the Japanese aggressors.[73]

2. Conquest of Ethiopia

The aggression of Italy over Ethiopia in 1935 provided another occasion for the Soviet leaders to denounce the dangerous trend of imperialistic aggradisements. Once again, when the Caesars of Rome went ahead with their plan of subjugating a weak and undeveloped state of Africa, the appeasers of London and France deliberately failed in checking this aggression in spite of the fact that Litvinov now fought for honouring the provisions of collective security in the deliberations of the League of Nations. The lukewarm attitude of Britain after the decision of the League Council to impose 'sanctions' against Italy warned the Soviet leaders to move ahead in this matter very cautiously. Now the only way out for the Russian diplomats was to show more concern to their national interest than to fight blindly for saving the real objective of the League of Nations. It is aptly remarked: "Once inside the

---

72. *Izvestia* (Moscow) November 21, 1931.
73. M.S. Kapitsa: *Soviet-Chinese Relations* (Moscow, 1958), p. 255. The evidence furnished by the Japanese criminals at the time of Tokyo Trial (1946-48) revealed that in 1931 Manchuria was regarded by the Japanese military leaders as a base in case of war with the Soviet Union. It all stemmed from Japan's ultimate strategic aim of war against the USSR. *Pravda* (Moscow), November 13, 1948.

League, the Soviet Union acted as a loyal and even enthusiastic member, but it was obviously no more willing than any other power to risk vital national interests for the sake of demonstrating its devotion to League principles. Thus, in the matter of sanctions against Italy, it was prepared to go at least as far as any other power, but not to bear more than its fair share of the burden. On the other hand, it refused to help create a dangerous precedent by recognising the conquest of Abyssinia."[74]

3. Spanish Civil War

When Gen. Franco staged a revolt in Spain in 1936 so as to destroy the legitimate government of the leftists, the Soviet government condemned the action of another dictator who was moving ahead with full support of Mussolini and Hitler. Likewise, when Britain and France adopted the strategy of 'non-intervention' in the civil war of Spain, the Soviet Union denounced it as a camouflaged attempt to help the Fascist forces. Thus, the Soviet statesmen preferred the course of supplying arms to the legitimate government of Madrid so that the revolt of a military junta may be checked effectively. The embarrassment of the League was reflected in the vote of the Council in May 1938, on the Spanish Government's resolution that members of this international organisation should consider 'ending the legal monstrosity of the formula of non-intervention', which the open intervention of Germany and Italy rendered a mockery. The resolution was rejected. The Spanish republican government continued the struggle until March, 1939, but the amount of assistance which Germany and Italy were openly giving to the nationalist side made the victory of Gen. Franco a foregone conclusion. The civil war in Spain ended on 30 March and on 20 April, 1939, the non-intervention committee with its office at London was formally dissolved.[75] It all showed that "the courageous struggle of the Spanish people to defend their liberties in the face of the united opposition of the Vatican, the Caesars of the Axis,

---

74. Max Beloff, op. cit., p. 137. In his speech in the League Council, the Russian delegate (Manuilsky) said on 14 September 1935 that "only the USSR would lose if it applied sanctions against Italy with other powers abstaining." Ibid., n 2.
75. See A.J. Grant and H. Temperley: *Europe in the Nineteenth and Twentieth Centuries* (London: Longmans, 1964), VI Ed., p. 513.

and the appeasers and isolationists of Paris, London and Washington was foredoomed to failure. No government, save only that of the USSR, would give or even sell them arms to resist their enemies."[76]

4. Destruction of Austria and Czechoslovakia

The Soviet government was well aware of the grave danger to peace in Europe presented by Germany's seizure of Austria in March 1938. Reacting sharply to this tragic incident, Russian Foreign Minister commented: "This time the violation has been committed in the centre of Europe, thus creating an indisputable danger not only for the 11 countries which at present have common borders with the aggressor but also for all the states of Europe, and not only of Europe."[77] Hitler's move towards the east was seen with particular concern. While Japanese aggression on Manchuria and Italian conquest of Abyssiania took place in a distant land, Hitler's invasion created a more serious problem for the Soviet leaders in view of the factor of vicinity. After Austria came Czechoslovakia. Thus, to check the menace of Nazi aggression Stalin advanced the proposal of immediately holding an international conference of all major powers including the United States. But no progress could be made in this regard as the great appeasers were interested in their own diplomatic game. Its climax reached in the Munich Pact whereby the helpless state of Czechoslovakia was butchered with the open blessings of London and Paris. The Soviet leaders sought to avoid another chance of inviting war for the sake of obliging Prague with the bond of their treaty of friendship. To them the Munich Agreement of September 30, 1938, was like a blackout defeat and a timeshed between two epochs in their foreign policy. The statesmen of four Western Powers (Britain, France, Germany and Italy) not only "blueballed Russia from the club; they dynamited the Soviet diplomatic defences to the West. Such a Homeric repudiation of a friendly great power invoked equally Homeric retaliation."[78]

76. Schuman, op. cit., p. 661. Also see Charles A. Thompson: "Spanish Civil War" in *Foreign Policy Reports*, Part II, No. 21.
77. *Soviet Foreign Policy*, p. 328.
78. Bruce Hopper: "Potentials of Soviet Foreign Policy" in Brown, Hodges and Roucek (eds.): *Contemporary World Politics: An Introduction to the Study of International Relations* (New York: John Wiley & Sons, 1939), p. 204.

It is, therefore, clear beyond any iota of suspicion that all sincere efforts of the Soviet Union to check the menace of Fascist aggressions first in the Far East, then in Africa and finally in Europe had their doom for the sole reason of the policy of appeasement adopted by the 'bourgeois' states of Britain, France and the United States. It is beautifully summed up by Prof. F.L. Schuman in these words: "When the USSR sought to use the League to save Ethiopia from Mussolini, London and Paris preferred to save Mussolini at the cost of destroying Ethiopia and the League. When the USSR sought to save the Spanish republic by observing the 'non-intervention' agreement only in the measure to which it was observed in Rome and Berlin, the Western appeasers preferred to cooperate with the Axis in destroying the Republican regime. The Spanish People's Front died. The French People's Front followed it to the grave. After Anschluss, Litvinov proposed a conference to consider ways and means of halting Hitler. Downing Street and Quai d'Orsay refused. When Litvinov proposed joint defence of Czechoslovakia in 1938, Chamberlain and Halifax, with the support of Daladier and Bonnet, preferred to abandon Prague. Immediately after the fall of Prague, Litvinov proposed a conference to consider joint action to halt aggression, London and Paris refused."[79]

Resort to Neutrality and Defence: A Complete Revolution in Soviet Diplomacy

As a matter of fact, the Munich Pact fully and finally disillusioned the Soviet leaders with the real designs of the great 'bourgeois' powers. Hitler thoroughly exploited the opportunity to thrive at the cost of Western appeasement and then make Poland the next target of his policy of 'drive to the east'. Stalin willy-nilly thought in terms of befriending the great Nazi leader so as to gain some time for the preparation of the eventual fight with the sworn enemy of Bolshevism. Thus, he made a vehement attack on the diplomacy of the Western powers. On March 10, 1939, he spoke at length at the Eighteenth Congress of the Communist Party of the Soviet Union thus: "The majority of the non-aggressive countries, particularly England and France, have rejected the policy of collective resistance to the aggressors, and have taken up a position of non-intervention,

---

79. Schuman, op. cit., pp. 876-77.

a position of neutrality.... The policy of non-intervention reveals an eagerness, a desire, not to hinder the aggressors in their nefarious work; not to hinder Japan, say, from embroiling herself in a war with China, or, better still, with the Soviet Union.... Take Germany, for instance. They let her have Austria, despite the undertaking to defend her independence; they let her have the Sudeten region; they abandoned Czechoslovakia to her fate, thereby violating all their obligations; and then they began to lie vociferously in the press about the weakness of the 'Russian army', 'the demoralisation of the Russian Air Force', and 'riots' in the Soviet Union, egging the Germans on to march farther east, promising them easy pickings and prompting them: 'Just start war on the Bolsheviks, and everything will be all right.'"[80]

With this affrmation, Stalin declared the following main aims of the Soviet foreign policy:[81]

1. "We stand for peace and the straightening of business relation with all countries. That is our position; and we shall adhere to this position as long as these countries maintain like relations with the Soviet Union, and as long as they make no attempt to trespass on the interests of our country.

2. "We stand for peaceful, close and friendly relations with all the neighbouring countries which have common frontiers with the USSR. That is our position as long as these countries maintain like relations with the Soviet Union, and as long as they make no attempt to trespass, directly or indirectly, on the integrity and inviolability of the frontiers of the Soviet State.

3. "We stand for the support of nations which are the victims of aggression and dare fighting for the independence of their country.

4. "We are not afraid of the threats of aggressors, and are ready to deal two blows for every blow delivered by instigators of war who attempt to violate the Soviet borders."

Now Moscow demanded a binding alliance against Berlin which London and Paris refused to conclude; in return they showed their eagerness to have some flexible formula that would leave them option to come to the help of the USSR in the event of

---

80. Ibid., p. 877.
81. Ibid., p. 878.

the Nazi attack to an extent they deemed proper. Besides, they demanded frank and firm commitment from the Soviet Union to come to the help of Poland and Rumania in the event of any attack on them by the Nazi troops.

Unfortunately, the British and French statesmen still cultivated a deep distrust in the bona fides of the Soviet leaders. They could not draw any implication when Litvinov (an advocate of collective security in cooperation with Britain and France) resigned and Molotov (a champion of nationalistic Soviet policy) became the new Foreign Commissar. Circumstances led to the conclusion of the Nazi-Soviet Non-Aggression Pact of 23 August, 1939, whereby the two parties obligated themselves to refrain from every act of force, every aggressive action, or every attack against one another, including any single action or that action taken in conjunction with other powers. It confirmed the general impression that by this time the military conversations between the Western democracies and the Soviet Union had virtually come to a standstill and for this intransigence of the Poles was largely to blame.[82] The astonishing feature of this development was that Stalin took this step in the face of two evils—open declarations of Hitler and concealed motives of his appeasers. He naturally chose the first after taking it as a lesser evil and knowing fully that Hitler would not keep his words. "Despite such warm exchanges between those who until recently had been such mortal enemies, Stalin appears to have had mental reservations about the Nazis keeping the pact."[83]

Certainly, the Nazi-Soviet pact came as "a diplomatic bombshell. The burying of Nazi-Communist hatchet was a bitter, though hardly unexpected, blow for Britain and France. It made war inevitable, as Hitler now saw no obstacle in the way of his attack on Poland. The feverish diplomacy which was pursued to the end could not deflect the course of events."[84] On 1 September, Hitler attacked Poland and just two days after Britain and then France declared war on Germany. Now the Soviet Union adopted the course of 'neutrality' and 'defence' with a firm determination to

---

82. W.L. Shirer: *The Rise and Fall of the Third Reich: A History of Nazi Germany* (London: Secker and Warburg, 1960), p. 533.
83. Ibid., p. 540.
84. Ralph Flonley: *Modern German History* (London: J.M. Dent & Sons, 1968), IV Ed., p. 387.

sell neutrality to Hitler at a price which would greatly strengthen the defences of the USSR against the Reich. The first step was to seize the former Russian territories of Poland and to reach new agreements with Berlin on the division of the carcass of the victim of the blitzkrieg. On 17 September, Moscow declared that the Polish state had virtually ceased to exist and that the 'Red Army' must undertake the protection of its abandoned 'Blood Brothers', the Ukrainians and Byelorussians.[85]

In this way, the Soviet leaders could ultimately have the tables turned on the appeasers of London and Paris. Those who endeavoured to push Germany to the point of a war against the USSR had to declare a war on her, while the fatherland of socialism had to take to the path of neutrality and defence in the autumn of 1939. Chamberlain's policy of fostering a German-Soviet war with the Western powers neutral in it was a failure, ending in Soviet neutrality in a war in which Britain was soon without allies against the most formidable foe of all time. Stalin's policy of self-protection against the Tory-Nazi threat was a success inasmuch as it led to an Anglo-German war in which the USSR was neutral.[86]

Concluding Observations

Following important impressions may be gathered from what we have critically discussed in the preceding sections:

1. Since a new type of political system emerged in Russia in 1917, a new development naturally took place in the sphere of foreign policy. The Bolshevik regime adopted a new approach to the politics of relations among states. In a way, it extended the doctrine of class struggle from the domestic to the international setting. It interpreted the politics of the world in terms of imperialism as the 'final stage of capitalism' and took upon itself the onus of internationalising the victory of socialism. Russia became the 'fatherland of socialism' and her statesmen endeavoured for the successful export of revolution. For this purpose, they set up the Comintern. They tried to improve relations with all states of the world and, at the same time, sought to infiltrate Bolshevism

---

85. Schuman, op. cit., p. 880.
86. F.L. Schuman: *Soviet Politics: At Home and Abroad* (London: Robert Hale Ltd., 1948), p. 379.

secretly. For this reason, Russian diplomacy assumed a dualistic character. The Russian leaders justified their action in their own way that amounted to the refutation of the charge of working for secret infiltration of Bolshevism in other countries of the world and affirmation of the argument that their foreign policy "combines class and universal human principles, which explains its profound and powerful impact on international relations."[87]

2. The foreign policy and diplomacy of the Soviet Union ever sought to establish a workable bond between the ideological premises of Marxism and the workable strategies of Leninism. That is, they scrupulously adhered to the course of reconciling the official ideology with the national interest of the fatherland of socialism. It is for this reason that, despite preaching the policy of peaceful co-existence, the Soviet leaders did not desist from openly denoucing the capitalist systems and desiring their eventual substitution with the system of scientific socialism. At the base of their affirmations, lay the edict of Lenin prononuced in March 1919: "We live not only in a state but in a system of states, and the existence of the Soviet Republic side with the imperialist states for a prolonged period of time is unthinkable. In the meantime, a series of frightful collisions will occur."[88]

3. There occur numerous ups and downs in politics, whether national or international. The foreign policy of a country, in order to make it a success, must be formulated and reformulated in the light of the exigencies of the situation. The Russian statesmen gave a proof of their realisation as well as of capability in this important direction. Soon after coming into power Lenin issued the decree of peace and signed the Treaty of Brest-Litovsk at the expense of national honour. In 1921, he decreed the New Economic Policy that

---

87. O. Byekov, V. Razmerov and D. Tomashevsky: *The Priorities of Soviet Foreign Policy Today*, English translation by Stainslav Ponomarenko (Moscow: Progress Publishers, 1981), p. 11.
88. See Geoffery Stern: "The Foreign Policy of the Soviet Union" in F.S. Northedge (ed.): *The Foreign Policies of the Powers* (London: Faber and Faber, 1968), p. 77. At the Seventh Communist Party Congress of March 1918, Bukharin said that there "could be no peaceful cohabitation between the Soviet Republic and international capital and the war against international capitals is the one and only one possible and necessary prospect for the future." Trotsky said that "deals with the imperialists are inadmissible for the revolutionary class." *The Priorities of Soviet Foreign Policy Today*, p. 9.

violated some of the essential tenets of his earlier affirmations. The Russian delegate in the deliberations of the League of Nations pleaded for attaching sancitity to the provisions of the Covenant. He rabidly denounced the aggressive actions of Japan and Italy. But the Russian delegate never agreed to defend the international organisation at the cost of his national interest. Though Stalin denounced Hitler in quite umistakable terms, he had the non-aggression pact with Germany in 1939 just for strategic reasons. Thus occurred the paradox of 1938: "The Soviet Russia that was excluded from the Paris Peace Settlement, that established the new territorial set up, became the one forthright defender of that settlement."[89]

Undeniably, the Anglo-French appeasers miserably failed in grasping the reality of the situation. They should have understood the real motives of the dictators of Italy, Germany and Japan and thus came closer to the USSR so as to checkmate the ambitions of the real enemies of peace. Faced with a danger on both sides, the Soviet leaders did well by making a non-aggression pact with Hitler. It at least temporarily relieved the USSR of the danger of war on two fronts and gave time to strengthen her defence. The Soviet Union agreed to this treaty after it had finally become apparent that Britain and France were unwilling to cooperate with her in resisting the Nazi aggression. The subsequent developments yielded dividends. In the later part of 1939 the Soviet Union certainly succeeded in avoiding the trap "into which the Munich policymakers had hoped to lure it, and skilfully used the contradictions in the imperialist camp to preserve and strengthen its defence capacity."[90]

---

89. Bruce Hopper, op. cit., p. 211.
90. *Soviet Foreign Policy*, p. 379. The Central Committee of the CPSU (B) and the Soviet Government "based themselves on the fact that the pact did not guarantee the USSR against the threat of Nazi aggression, but did give them the opportunity of gaining time to strengthen our defences and prevented the creation of united anti-Soviet front." G.L. Zukhov: *Reminiscences and Reflections* (Moscow, 1974). Vol. II. p, 253. In conversation with the French ambassador in Moscow (Naggier), Molotov stated that a non-aggression pact with Germany "was not inconsistent with a neutral defensive alliance between Great Britain, France and the Soviet Union." *Foreign Relations of the United States: Diplomatic Papers of 1939* (Washington), pp. 313-14.

11

UNITED STATES

Every nation has its pet illusions. The Germans have the illusion of self-pity; the French have the illusion of being universally loved by all civilised people; the English have the illusion of being always morally right and, in the long run, always victorious. The Americans have the illusion of being invincible, right or wrong; of being disinterested spectators of a world on which they descend like the god in a Greek tragedy to unite the knot the Europeans or Asiatics have tied in their malignant fashion.

—D. W. Brogan[1]

A study of international relations during the period of two world wars is, by and large, regarded as an account of the politics of major European countries in which involvement of the United States is said to have just been incidental in view of the 'isolationist' character of her foreign policy. Such a generalised statement is, however, faulty in many respects. As a matter of fact, the role of the US in European affairs remained overshadowed by her wholehearted involvement, first in the Latin-American, and then in the Far Eastern affairs for the most important reason of her obsession to protect and promote her economic interests. It could well continue until her entanglement in the First World War. A great, rather a fundamental, change occurred after 1917 when, as we shall see in this chapter, this 'highest, best, richest, most productive, most powerful, most gigantic, stupendous, titanic and super-colossus country beyond all questions,'[2] "was pushed or dragged into extensive interventions, by diplomacy and by arms, in Europe,

---

1. See his 'Introduction' to Walter Lippmann: *U.S. Foreign Policy* (London: Hamish Hamilton, 1943), p. x.
2. F.L. Schuman: *International Politics* (New York: McGraw Hill, 1948), IV Ed., p. 766.

Africa and Asia, and compelled, willy-nilly, by considerations of security, prosperity and self-interest and by the sheer fact of its own overwhelming power, to assume a role of world leadership."³

Broad Aims and Objectives of American Foreign Policy : Predominance of Economic Interest

Foreign policy, like domestic policy, is a mirror of various competing national purposes and pressures conditioned by the fixed facts of geography and the fluid facts of economic interests and power relationships in an unstable state system. Moreover, as national interest is the base of the foreign policy of a country, so the determining factor is national character. The American people are neither thrifty like the Scots, or quick-tempered like the Italians, emotional like the Latin-Americans, or conservative like the English, or radical like the French, nor aggressive like the Germans and like. But they have an essential feature of their own culture. It is 'individualism' that informs them to place individual interest over social interest. Materialism governs the mode of their life. As such, success is measured in terms of material gains that a man makes for himself. Self-interest is the basis of American way of thinking, though it is covered with the tapestry of moral values for the sake of giving a logical justification to the brazenly materialistic pursuits of the people. Its glorious instance can be found in America's involvement in the First World War in the name of 'making democracy safe in the world'.⁴

Protection and promotion of the economic interests of the people, therefore, constitutes the foundations of American foreign policy. It is, however, a different matter that leading American writers and commentators try to put the same in a well-classified manner in which factors of ethical and humanitarian considerations come to have a superficial place of their own. For instance, a leading diplomatic historian enumerates the fundamentals of American foreign policy right from the inauguration of the American Republic in 1789 to the commencement of the Second World War as follows:⁵

---

3. Ibid., p. 768.
4. See Stephen V. Monsma: *American Politics: A Systems Approach* (New York: Holt, Rinehart and Winston, 1969), pp. 36-42.
5. Samuel Flagg Bemis: *John Quincy Adams and the Foundations of American Foreign Policy* (New York: Alfred A. Knopf, 1949), pp. 567-70.

1. Sovereign independence to preserve the rights of the English freemen;
2. Freedom of the sea;
3. Freedom of commerce and navigation;
4. Abstention from the ordinary upsets and ordinary combinations and collisions of European politics;
5. Principle of non-transfer of territories;
6. Continental expansion;
7. Self-determination of peoples;
8. No further European colonisation in the New World;
9. Non-intervention;
10. Right of expatriation and nationalisation and the wrong of impressment;
11. Suppression of the African slave trade;
12. Pan-Americanism;
13. International arbitration; and
14. Anti-imperialism.

In other words, from the days when the American leaders were fighting for making their independence secure to those of the second World War, the broad objectives of American foreign policy may be thus enumerated in a different way:[6]

1. To secure independence with satisfactory boundaries that would contribute to the national security;
2. To extend those boundaries in the interest of security, navigation and commerce, space for a growing population, and the spread of democracy;
3. To promote and protect the rights and interests of American citizens in commerce with, and investments in, foreign lands; to safeguard trade on the high seas in peace and in war; and, as a special application of this aim in the nineteenth century, to open the Far East to American trade and American influence;
4. To preserve neutrality and peace, to keep out of the wars of Europe (and Asia) as long as non-participation is compatible with preservation of American security and vital interests, and to devise means for the peaceful settlement of international controversies;

---

6. J.W. Pratt: *A History of United States Foreign Policy* (Englewood Cliffs, New Jersey: Prentice-Hall, 1965), II Ed., p. 3.

5. To prevent the powers of Europe from further colonising in the Western hemisphere and from interfering in the affairs of the United States and of the Americans in general; and
6. To do good with a humanitarian desire in the world, to spread democracy, to put an end to the slave trade, to halt the massacres or persecutions of racial and religious minorities, to raise standards of living in backward countries, etc.

However, behind the facade of all these broad aims and objectives of the American foreign policy, a critical student of this subject may discern the predominant position of the economic factor. As we shall see, the so-called 'isolationism' towards the politics of Europe, the struggle for the cause of Pan-Americanism, and the forced entanglement of the United States in the affairs of the Far East were mainly motivated by a persistent struggle for promoting the economic interest of the ruling class. In a statement given on 3 December, 1912, President Taft frankly confessed: "The diplomacy of the present administration has sought to respond to modern ideas of commercial intercourse. This policy has been characterised as substituting dollars for bullets. It is one that appeals alike to idealistic humanitarian sentiments, to the dictates of sound policy and strategy, and to legitimate commercial aims."[7]

One may ask about the reason behind this. The answer is that the people of the United States are the descendants of those Europeans who came to this country and then exploited it just for the sake of earning economic gains. It is an historical fact that most of the settlers and immigrants came to the New World to find out a better material existence. The society they created emphasised economics. Thus, John Jay "viewed political conflict in economic terms and regarded political power as a means for securing economic privilege."[8] A great leader like James Madison believed that "in the absence of armed forces, power went with property."[9] The revolt of the Americans against the English rule was made with an economic slogan: 'No taxation without representation'. Thereafter for a century, the people of the United States "had a

---

7. See Thomas A. Bailey: *A Diplomatic History of the American People* (New York: Appleton-Century-Crofts, 1955), Ed. V, p. 577.
8. H.B. Parkes: *The American Experience*, p. 106.
9. C.A. Beard: *The Economic Basis of Politics*, p. 33.

unique opportunity of exploiting an empty continent of almost infinite resources. Labour and luck led to wealth. Wealth could and generally did lead to political power. Political power unscrupulously exerted brought more wealth. Small wonder that the number of American economaniacs multiplied, that professors looking rather upon the experience of their nation than upon that of mankind came to consider politics as the handmaid of economics."[10]

Policy towards Latin America : The Monroe Doctrine and the Movement for Pan-Americanism

If the endeavour for economic and financial expansion behind the facade of political aloofness remained the basic touchstone of American foreign policy from the inauguration of the Republic to the occurrence of the Second World War, it had its best manifestation in the Latin-American region. The principle of 'Ameri-ca for the Americans' implied gradual control of the United States over the weak and small states of the Caribbean region and of South America so much so that their independence was curtailed to a considerable extent by the clutches of 'dollar imperialists'. On the plea of inoculating the 'American way of life' against European Fascism, the American administration adopted the policy of declaring 'Hands off' for some powers of Europe like France, Spain, Austria and Prussia. Certainly, this policy saved the Latin-American countries from the interference of the European governments; at the same time, it placed them under the suzerainty of 'the holder of the big stick.' The charge of American imperialism in the name of propagating and implementing the call of 'Pan-Americanism' could not be diluted until Frankin D. Roosevelt formulated his 'Good Neighbour Policy' in 1933. Now the resentment of the Latin-American states against the Colossus of the North "was mitigated by the new orientation at Washington."[11]

It had its first bold manifestation in the address of President Monroe on December 2, 1823, when he said : "The occasion has been judged proper for asserting, as a principle in which the rights and interests of the United States are involved, that the American

---

10. E.A. Mowrer: *The Nightmare of American Foreign Policy* (London: Victor Gollancz, 1949), p. 39.
11. Schuman, op. cit., p. 777.

continents, by the free, and independent condition which they have assumed and maintain, are henceforth not to be considered as subjects for future colonisation by any European powers.... We owe it, therefore, to candour and to the amicable relations existing between the United States and those powers to declare that we should consider any attempt on their part to extend their system to any portion of this hemisphere as dangerous to our peace and safety. With the existing colonies or dependencies of any European power we have not interfered and shall not interfere. But with the Governments who have declared their independence and maintained it, and whose independence we have, on great consideration and on just principles, acknowledged, we could not view any interposition for the purpose of oppressing them, or controlling in any other manner their destiny, by any European power in any other light than as the manifestation of an unfriendly disposition toward the United States."[12]

The declaration of Monroe, called the Monroe Doctrine, had a two-sided effect. It was a warning of the US to some of the European powers to keep their hands off from the countries of the Western hemisphere; at the same time, it was a pledge of the US for the neighbours to come to their rescue in the event of any attack on them by the powers of Europe particularly France, Prussia, Spain and Austria. Curiously, it was not directed against Great Britain for the reason that behind this historic declaration the support of the English government had its secret role. However, the imperialistic undertones of the Monroe Doctrine became vivid in not much time. A number of new territories were annexed to the American

---

12. L.L. Leonard: *Elements of American Foreign Policy* (New York: McGraw Hill, 1953), pp. 225-26. A great critic of the American foreign policy observes: "This new and different and momentous chapter of our history begins in 1823. In that year the United States assumed an obligation outside of its continental limits. President Monroe extended the protection of the United States to the whole of Western hemisphere, and declared that at the risk of war, the United States would thereafter resist the creation of new European empires in this hemisphere." This momentous action was taken after the President had consulted Madison and Jefferson who were assured by the British Foreign Secretary that British navy would support the United States. It reveals that the "Founding Fathers understood the realities of foreign policy too well to make commitment without having first made certain they had the means to support them." Lippmann, op. cit., p. 11.

federation as Texas in 1845. When it was resented by Mexico, battle ensued as a result of which the US occupied New Mexico and upper California under the treaty of 1848.

This trend not only continued in time to come, rather it had a more sinister development in the form of a 'corollary' invented by President Theodore Roosevelt on December 6, 1904. This time, in order to put Britain and Germany at bay, the President in his annual message said: "Any country whose people conduct themselves well count upon our friendship. If a nation shows that it knows how to act with reasonable efficiency and decency in social and political matters, if it keeps order and pays its obligations, it need fear no interference from the United States. Chronic wrongdoing, or an impotence which results in a general loosening of the ties of civilised society, in America, as elsewhere, the adherence of the United States to the Monroe Doctrine may force the United States, however reluctantly, in flagrant cases of such wrong-doing or importance to the exercise of an international police power."[13] This revised interpretation of the Monroe Doctrine signified that while its author had denied the right of interference in the affairs of the Latin-American countries to some European powers, the author of its 'corollary' frankly reserved it to the United States. By all means, the principle of defence became the instrument of offence. Now the United States "assumed the right to intervene in the domestic affairs of the Latin-American countries and adjust their political disorders and economic distress in order to prevent European interference."[14]

Henceforth, the movement of American imperialism had a faster pace. Panama became a 'protectorate' of the US in 1904 and then came the chance of Dominican Republic, Nicaragua and Haiti. It boldly manifested that now "Uncle Sam assumed the role of the international policeman kindly to the law-abiding, but apt to lay a stern hand upon little nations that fell into disorder or defaulted on their obligations, since disorder or default, if allowed to continue, might invite intervention from outside the hemisphere."[15] A little change for the better, however, occurred during the days of President Wilson when he declared that the United States would

---

13. See Pratt, op. cit., pp. 228-29.
14. J.H. Landman and H. Wender: *World Since 1914* (New York, 1958), p. 305.
15. Pratt, op. cit., p. 252.

welcome the establishment of democratic regimes alone in the Latin-American countries. With optimism he remarked to a British visitor that he would 'frown upon revolutions in the neighbouring republics' and 'teach the South American Republics to elect good men.'"[16] Such remarks foreshadowed a new turn in the American interventionist policy in which the promotion of democracy would take its place as an objective beside the preservation of the Monroe Doctrine and the protection of the economic and strategic interests of the United States."[17]

The new line of Wilson paid its dividends during the days of the First World War.[18] New treaties were signed with the republics of Nicaragua, Haiti, Costa Rica, Honduras and Dominican Republic for conserving peace and solidarity among themselves as well as for important purposes like free trade, disarmament, elaborate educational programmes, labour legislation, social welfare, transportation and reciprocal rights of citizenship. President Coolidge took some steps to discard the Roosevelt 'corollary' and dispel the ghost of 'Yankeephobia'. In 1927 an Inter-American Commission of Jurists adopted a resolution to the effect that no State 'can interfere in the internal affairs of another.' At the Sixth International Conference of American States held at Havana in 1928, former Secretary of State (Hughes) made it clear that the intervention of the United States in the affairs of any neighbouring state was only for the purpose of ensuring stability as a means of securing independence. After signing the Pact of Paris, the new Secretary of State (Kellogg) reiterated what his predecessor had said.

A Memorandum on the Monroe Doctrine (prepared by the Under-Secretary of State J.R. Clark) published in 1930 outrightly affirmed: "The Monroe Doctrine states a case of United States v. Europe, not of United States v. Latin-America. Such arrangements as the United States has made, for example with Cuba, Santo

---

16. Ibid.
17. Ibid.
18. It is evident from the fact that out of 21 Latin-American states none declared war against the United States. Brazil, Cuba, Costa Rica, Guatemala, Haiti, Honduras, Nicaragua and Panama declared war against the Central Powers; Peru, Bolivia, Uruguay, Ecuador and Dominican Republic cut off diplomatic relations with the enemies of the United States; Argentina, Chile, Colombia, Mexico, El Salvador, Venezuela and Paraguay remained neutral.

Domingo, Haiti, and Nicaragua, are not within the Doctrine as it was announced by Monroe."[19]

The real meaning of the Clark Memorandum should, however, be understood in the light of the fact that while it expressed no intention on the part of the United States to intervene in the affairs of the neighbouring countries, it certainly implied that it could be done so as to protect the economic interests of the American ruling class. President Hoover simply asserted that it could be done without resorting to the means of force. However, a softer dimension to such a policy was given for the first time by President Roosevelt who, in his inaugural address of 4 March, 1933, said: "In the field of world policy I would dedicate this Nation to the policy of the Good Neighbour—the neighbour who resolutely respects himself and, because he does so, respects the rights of others."[20] More significant was his affirmation at the Woodrow Wilson Foundation dinner on December 28, 1933 that "the definite policy of the United States from now on is one opposed to armed intervention."[21]

The Seventh Pan-American Conference held at Montevideo in 1933 marked the success of this line now forcefully advanced by new Secretary of State (Cordell Hull). Now a Convention on the Rights and Duties of States was signed whose Art. 8 said: "No state has the right to interfere in the internal or external affairs of another state." The new line yielded some results. The protectorate of the United States over Haiti was withdrawn as a result of which American marines left this country. In 1934, Cuba became free from the burden of the Platt Amendment of 1901 whereby the US could intervene in the domestic affairs of this country. In 1936, the US signed a treaty with Panama whereby it relinquished her right to interfere in the domestic affairs of Panama. On September 4, 1940, a treaty was signed between the US and the Dominican Republic whereby the former relinquished right to name the general receiver of customs and, in return, the latter guaranteed services on its bonds by a lien on its general revenues. Only in Nicaragua did an American Collector-General of customs continue to administer the customs and services on the national debt.

---

19. Pratt, op cit., p. 369.
20. Ibid., pp. 370-71.
21. Ibid., p. 371.

Reference should be made at this stage to the Buenos Aires Conference for the Maintenance of Peace held in 1936 where a convention was signed pledging consultation among all the American nations in the event of their peace or security, should it be threatened from any internal or external source. This agreement is important, for it "intended to remove any stigma of inferiority that might be fit by the South American countries in relation to the United States."[22] However, most important of all is the Lima Conference of 1938 held under the shadow of an imminent world war. By this time, the deterioration of international morality in Europe and the Far East imparted an additional point to a vigorous proclamation of inter-American solidarity. In the face of menace to the peace of the world created by the aggressive moves of the Fascists of Japan, Italy and Germany, it was realised that mere talks of co-operation among the American nations was not enough. Now it "was also believed essential to agree upon concerted action against any and all subversive activities intended to undermine the domestic institutions of the Western Hemispere."[23]

Thus came into existence the historic Lima Declaration highlighting these points of resolution:[24]

1. "The intervention of any State in the internal or external affairs of any other State is inadmissible.
2. All differences of an international character should be settled by peaceful means.
3. The use of force as an instrument of national or international policy is proscribed.
4. Relations between States should be governed by the precepts of international law.
5. Respect for and the faithful observance of treaties constitutes the indispensable rule of the development of peaceful relations between States, and treaties can only be revised by agreement of the contracting parties.
6. Peaceful collaboration between representatives of various States and the development of intellectual interchange among their peoples is conducive to an understanding by each of the

---

22. W.R. Sharp and Grayson Kirk: *Contemporary International Politics* (New York: Farrar and Rinehart, 1944), p. 689.
23. Ibid.
24. Ibid., p. 817 (Appendix VIII).

problems of the other as well as of problems common to all, and makes more readily possible the peaceful adjustment of international controversies.
7. Economic reconstruction contributes to national and international well-being, as well as to peace among nations.
8. International cooperation is a necessary condition to the maintenance of the aforementioned principles."

In this way, the Lima Declaration "at once affirms the spiritual solidarity of the American republics in the face of the Fascist challenge and pledges their determination to protect the solidarity not only against armed attack, but against subversive propaganda and other types of indirect interference as well."[25]

Despite this all, the domineering role of the United States in the Pan-American Union continued. The policy of the United States overshadowed the policy of the Latin-American republics. When the Second World War started in September 1939, shortly thereafter Ninth Inter-American Conference took place. Now the American representative insisted that the 21 American republics could not permit their security, their nationals, or their legitimate commercial rights and interests to be jeopardised by belligerent activities in close proximity to the shores of the New World. A 'neutrality zone' was set up including all of South America, south of Canada and extending out to sea 300 to 1,000 miles. On the initiative of the United States, the Foreign Ministers of the countries of the Pan-American Union met again at Havana in Cuba from 21 to 30 July, 1940. This Tenth Conference of the Inter-American Union approved a Convention and a supplementary act 'continentalising' the Monroe Doctrine and declaring that when islands or regions in the Americas now under the possession of non-American nations "are in the danger of becoming the subject of barter of territory or change of sovereignty, the American nations may set up a regime of provisional administration pending eventual independence, or restitution to their previous status whichever of these alternatives shall appear the more practicable and just."[26]

Indisputable is the fact that the policy of President Roosevelt proved eminently successful and even his most severe critics

---

25. Ibid., p. 689.
26. Schuman, op. cit., p. 779.

"credit him with a magnificent achievement in Latin-America."[27] The Monroe Doctrine laid the foundation for permanent hemispheric cooperation. Theodore Roosevelt set down the right of intervention by the US in any other American republic to defend life and property and prevent 'chronic war-doing'. Successive Presidents right up to Hoover followed this 'corollary'. But in a series of Pan-American conferences, Franklin Roosevelt reversed the traditional line who made it above board in January, 1934 to his neighbours that 'we seek with them future avoidance of territorial expansion and of interference by one nation in the internal expansion and of interference by one nation in the internal affairs of another'. After two years, he reiterated: "This policy of the Good Neighbour among the Americas is no longer a hope—no longer an objective remaining to be accomplished—it is a fact, active, present, pertinent, and effective." The Declaration of Lima of 1938 "transformed the one-sided Monroe Doctrine into a Pan-American policy. The new policy worked so well that in the Word War II all but one of the American republics (Agrentina) stood together for the defeat of the aggressors."[28]

Policy towards the Far East : The Washington Conference on Naval Disarmament and After

No less active was the involvement of the United States in matters relating to the Far East. Here American interests were seriously threatened by the growing power of Japan. Though the United States and Japan had fought on the same side in the first World War, the partnership became one of discord between them after the conclusion of Paris peace settlement. By the Treaty of Versailles Japan acquired from Germany the leased territory of Kiachow in the Shantung province of China in protest against which China refused to place signatures on the treaty. In addition to this, Japan also got mandate over Germany's former island possessions in the Pacific, like Guam and Yap. After the eclipse of Russia, Japan had

---

27. Mowrer, op. cit., p. 74.
28. Ibid., p. 75. In his Pan-American Day address on 14 April 1939, Roosevelt said: "The past generation in Pan-American matters was concerned with constructing the principles and the mechanisms through which this hemisphere would work together. But the next generation will be concerned with the methods by which the new world can live together with the old." See Commager (ed.): *Documents on American History*, p. 595.

become the only great power on the borders of China and after simultaneous destruction of the Russian and German navies, she had been left not only the greatest naval power in the Far East, but the third naval power in the world. Thus, Japan's threat to China and her bid for naval supremacy in the Pacific were highly disquieting to the American interests."[29] Under these conditions, in the Far East, the United States "could not afford to preserve the same attitude of serene detachment."[30]

The immediate source of friction with Japan was her occupation of Eastern Siberia and northern Sakhalin. Secretary of State Hughes opposed Japanese expansion at the expense of Russia and China. He warned that the US would not recognise any claim or title arising out of the present occupation nor acquiesce in any action that might impair existing treaty rights or the political or territorial integrity of Russia.[31] Moreover, despite the promises of the Lansing-Ishii Agreement,[32] the menace of Japanese domination still hung over China as a whole. The fifth group of the '21 Demands' had been shelved for the time being but not renounced. Besides, the Japanese promise to observe the 'open door principle' in her sphere of interest had been found not wholly dependable.[33]

---

29. In his address to the Senate on 22 January 1917, President. Wilson said: "It is a problem closely connected with the limitation of naval armaments and the cooperation of the navies of the world in keeping the seas at once free and safe. And the question of limiting naval armaments opens the wider and perhaps more difficult question of limitation of armies and of all programmes of military preparation." See Commager, op. cit., p. 307.
30. E.H. Carr: *International Relations between the Two World Wars* (London; Macmillan, 1952), p. 19.
31. See M.J. Pusey: *Charles Evan Hughes* (New York: Macmillan, 1951), Vol. II, Chapter 43.
32. By an exchange of notes on 2 November, 1917 the Japanese Foreign Minister (Ishii) and his American counterpart (Lansing) declared continued adherence of their governments to the policy of respecting the independence and territorial integrity of China and the preservation there of the 'open door' for trade, commerce and industry.
33. On January 18, 1915 Japan served on China a document embodying fantastic demands as there would be three centres (Manchuria, Shantung and Fukein) from which Japanese influence would be exercised. The nothern sphere of Japan was to be extended by including Inner Mongolia. From the Shantung sphere of influence could be made to radiate to the interior by means of railway extensions to Honan and Shansi. Similarly, from the Fukein sphere, railway concessions would carry Japanese influence into the provinces of Kiangsi, Hupe and Kwangtung. Most important of all was Group V that included

In 1919 the United States moved the major part of the battle fleet to the Pacific and announced that it would remain there. In retaliation Japan adopted a programme calling for a fighting fleet of eight battleships and eight battle cruisers with annual replacement of one ship of each type. Thus, there developed a naval rivalry that "involved not only the United States and Japan but Great Britain also, for Great Britain would not willingly surrender her traditional mastery of the sea, and this mastery was threatened by the naval programme of the United States."[34]

The prevailing state of affairs became a source of anxiety for the United States as well as Great Britain.[35] The American government, that under President Theodore Roosevelt had looked upon Japan as the defender of the faith against Russia and upon the Anglo-Japanese agreement as a beneficent instrument to preserve the peace in Eastern Asia, became engaged in the thankless task of attempting to restrain Japan. America's opposition to her efforts to consolidate her position in Manchuria embittered Japan against the United States, and the failure of the policy of the United States enhanced its distrust of Japan. This estrangement was further emphasised by the immigration controversies.[36] Under these

---

demands like employment of effective Japanese advisers in political, military and finacial affairs of China, the joint Chinese-Japanese organisation of the police forces in important places, purchase by China from Japan of a fixed amount of munitions of war, and effective control of Japan over the armament and military organisation of China. See H.M. Vinacke: *A History of the Far East in Modern Times* (London: George Allen and Unwin, 1964), pp. 367-68.

34. Pratt, op. cit., p. 323.
35. How to keep Japan as well as the US in the bond of friendship was a great problem for the English statesmen. Lloyd George had yielded to the wishes of the American leaders to renounce the alliance of Britain with Japan. But he and other British statesmen remained concerned with the idea of devising a suitable alternative arrangement. It was also, taken into recognition that such a substitute could be found, if at all, only through an understanding with the US in regard to the Far East and the Pacific. Pratt, op. cit., p. 323.
36. Vinacke, op. cit., p. 414. The Japanese had begun to come to the US in large numbers only after 1900, when there were upwards of 2,000 in the country. By 1910 their number had increased to slightly over 72,000, and by 1920 to more than 110,000. In proportion to the total population this was certainly not a threatening flux. But the concentration of the Japanese settlers in California and in other Pacific Coast States led to an exaggeration of the danger, an apprehension which was enhanced, because the Japanese had settled on the land. Ibid., pp. 360-61.

conditions the Congress adopted the resolution of Senator Borah calling upon the President to invite Great Britain and Japan to a conference to sort out defferences on this subject. In accordance with this, President Harding announced that some powers were being invited to a conference on the Far East and naval armaments to meet in Washington on November 11, 1920.[37]

The deliberations at Washington culminated in the conclusion of three important treaties:

1. *The Four-Power Treaty*

It was concluded between US, France, Japan and the British Empire. By it the signatories agreed to respect each other's rights in relation to their insular possessions in the Pacific and to consult together in the event of any controversy between them regarding these rights, or any threat to them through the aggressive action of any other power. Signed on December 13, 1921, it was to remain in effect for 10 years and thereafter until one of the parties should terminate it by giving a year's notice in advance. "The importance of this treaty is twofold. It drew the United States for the first time (since their rejection of the Covenant of the League) into a limited system of consultation with other Great Powers on matters of common concern and it provided a decent pretext for bringing to an end the now superfluous Anglo-Japanese alliance, which had become highly unpopular in the United States, in the Dominion, and among a large section of public opinion in Great Britain."[38] It was a definite result of the successful diplomacy of the Secretary of State (Hughes) who could secure British and French endorsement to Japan's promise of respecting the sovereignty of the United States over the Philippines."[39]

2. *The Five-Power Treaty*

Signed on February 6, 1922, by the US, Great Britain, Japan, France and Italy, it provided for naval parity between British Empire and

---

37. Invitations were sent to Great Britain and the British Empire (Canada, Australia, New Zealand, South Africa and India), France, Italy, Japan, China, Portugal and the Netherlands and to Belgium at her own request. That is, invitations were sent to all states having stake in the Far Eastern interests.
38. Carr, op. cit., p. 20.
39. Pratt, op, cit., p. 328. For text of the treaty see Commager, *op. cit.*, pp. 363-64.

the United States and the fixing of the strength of Japan in capital ships to 60 per cent of the American and British figures. The French and Italian quotas were fixed at 35 per cent as is evident from the following breakdown:

Countries	Number of Capital Ships	Tonnage
United States	15 (18)	525,000 (525,850)
Great Britain	15 (20)	525,000 (558,950)
Japan	9 (10)	315,500 (301,320)
France	5 (10)	175,000 (201,170)
Italy	5 (10)	175,000 (182,800)

N.B. Figures given in the brackets indicate immediate strength after scrapping and before replacement.

As for the maintenance of status quo in fortifications, Japan agreed to exempt the Hawaiian islands, which she had at first included, and also Singapore, Australia and New Zealand. Japan herself would agree not to fortify the Kuriles, the Bonins, the Ryukyus, Formosa or the Pescadores. This treaty was to remain in force till December 31, 1936, and thereafter subject to two years' notice of termination by any of the signatories. The significance of this treaty is that while there "were professional outcries against her 'inferior allotment', Japan was generously treated. She was obliged to scrap only half as many vessels as was the United States; and to increase her security, Britain and the United States agreed to add no new naval bases west of Hawaii to their installations at Manila and Singapore. To limit their striking range, battleships could not exceed thirty-five thousand tons in size, nor cruisers, ten thousand tons."[40]

3. The Nine-Power Treaty

It was signed on February 6, 1922, by all the nine participants. The signatories (except China) agreed to respect the sovereignty, independence and territorial integrity of China and to allow China the

---

40. Alfred Crofts and Percy Buchanan: *A History of the Far East* (Bombay: Allied Publications, 1958), p. 343.

fullest opportunity to develop and maintain for herself an effective and stable government. They also agreed to use their influence for establishing and maintaining the 'open door' for industry and commerce throughout China. In addition to this, they agreed not to do anything or support their subjects or citizens in doing anything that would infringe the principles here stated, or that would tend to create spheres of influence or exclusive opportunities in any part of China. On her part, China agreed not to discriminate in any way between nationals of different countries. The real significance of this treaty should be traced in the fact that while the US could have the acceptance of 'open door policy' by other concerned powers of the world, in particular China gained a lot. She "came from the conference not only without any new administrative or other limitations upon its autonomous powers, but with the formal and unqualified assurance that the Powers would not take any advantage of existing conditions to impose any new restraints upon her freedom of action."[41]

In addition to these three important treaties, the Washington Conference also made some other contributions to the settlement of Far Eastern and Pacific problems. A treaty between China and Japan was signed on 4 February, 1922, that provided for the restoration of Chinese sovereignty over Shantung, withdrawal of Japanese troops, and the purchase by China from Japan of principal railroad in the province. A treaty signed between the US and Japan on 11 February, 1922, assured the former of free access to the island of Yap for purposes connected with cable and radio communications, and rights of residence and property holding for American citizens. Japan also signed a document whereby she pledged to return Kiachow to China that had been ceded to her by Germany under the Treaty of Versailles.

The work of the Washington Conference was hailed as a monumental contribution to international understanding and human progress. The Far Eastern and Pacific matters could be sorted out with the agreement of all concerned powers. However, the conference results were inadequate in some other respects also.

---

41. W.W. Willoughby: *China at the Conference: A Report (1922)*, pp. 338-39.
42. A critic like T.A. Bailey holds: "Yet the Washington Conference interfered with the effort of the League of Nations at Geneva to achieve genuine arms reduction. The Washington Conference also befogged disarmament by strengthening the assumption that armaments are the basic cause of the

For instance, in not much time Japanese ambition resorted and took to the course of repudiating the settlements. Later developments showed that Japan merely agreed to postpone and not to renounce her imperialistic ambitions in the Far East. It was also commented that the Conference could not make a permanent solution to the problem of disarmament.[42] While it put a check on big instruments of warfare like battleships, it did not bother for the use of minor instruments like cruisers, destroyers and submarines that were no less harmful for the cause of international peace. Above all, the Conference could not establish an effective machinery for the implementation of its decisions.[43] The fundamental question whether the dominant influence in the Far East was to be Anglo-Saxon or Japanese remained undecided. However, "thanks to the Washington conference that it remained in abeyance for ten years."[44]

American relations with Japan improved after the conclusion of the Washington Conference. The Americans generously contributed to relief of the victims of the destructive Japanese earthquake of September 1, 1923. But the Johnson Act of the following year gave a setback to progress in this regard in view of the fact that it put a severe restriction on the immigration of the foreign nationals that affected the Japanese in particular.[45] However, owing to the

---

international distrust. A current belief was that big warships bring big wars; small warships, small wars; no warships, no wars. But armaments are not ordinarily so much a disease as a symptom of a disease, and no regulation of the size, shape and number of thermometers is likely to reduce fever or cure the disease. The 'ever-logical' French were right when they insisted that security would have to precede disarmament. And in the end French insecurity proved to be so much a problem as a world problem." *A Diplomatic History of the American People* (New York: Aplleton-Century-Crofts, 1958), pp. 647-48.

43. Critical evaluations of the Washington treaties range from a deprecatory characterisation as a "face-saving retreat of the United States from active diplomacy in the Far East," (S.F. Bemis, op. cit., p. 696) to its enthusiastic praise as the "apotheosis of the traditional Far Eastern policy of the United States." A.W. Griswold: *The Far Eastern Policy of the United States* (New York: Harcourt Brace and World, 1938), p. 331.

44. Carr, op. cit., p. 22.

45. To the Japanese it was clearly against the Gentlemen's Agreement of 1907. The Immigration Act of 1924 allowed after 1 July, 1927, a maximum annual immigration of 15,000 (exclusive of immigrants from Western hemisphere countries and certain other non-quota immigrants) and assigned to each European nationality a fraction of the 15,000 equal to the percentage of persons derived from that nationality in the total population of the US in 1920. If Japan had been placed on this basis, her quota would not have exceeded 185 in a year. Pratt, op. cit., p. 346.

conciliatory attitude of the Foreign Minister, Baron K. Shidehara, the situation was not allowed to drift to an unpalatable extent. In spite of the pressure of the military generals, the government of Japan signed the London Naval Treaty of 1930 by which it continued to maintain naval limits inferior to those of Great Britain and the United Sates.[46] The murder of the Prime Minister (Hamaguchi) in November, 1930 and the exit of Foreign Minister Shidehara, however, entailed the upper hand of the military as a result of which Japanese government took to the path of aggression in violation of the Washington treaties, the Pact of Paris, and the Covenant of the League of Nations.

Thus, the Manchurian crisis of 1931 strained the American relations with Japan. Secretary of State Hughes 'pulled his punches' and with the agreement of President Hoover preferred the course of 'non-recognition' of a state that would come into existence as a result of such aggression. It was like a moral sanction against the action of Japan in Manchuria. Though not a member of the League of Nations, the US had its representative in the Lytton Commission (R. McCoy) that held Japan guilty of aggression in Manchuria. Now if Stimson "was unable to deflect Japan from her course, he did have the satisfaction of seeing his doctrine officially adopted by the League of Nations."[47] Since Japan spurned all conciliatory efforts of the League, the new Secretary of State (Cordell Hull) under President Roosevelt insisted that the US had a "definite interest.... in maintaining the independence of China and in preventing Japan from gaining overlordship of the entire Far East."[48] Moreover, as the United States had by now taken to the course of 'appeasement', Hull made every effort to avoid the prospect of an open war with Japan so as to offset application of the 'Japanese Monroe Doctrine'.[49]

---

46. See Griswold, op. cit., pp. 378-79.
47. Pratt, op. cit., p. 352.
48. Cordell Hull: *The Memoirs* (London: Hodder and Stoughton, 1948), Vol. I, p. 270.
49. For instance, when the League of Nation took up the issue of Manchuria, President Hoover expressed his reaction in these words: "This is primarily a controversy between China and Japan. The United States has never set out to preserve peace among other nations by force and so far as this part is concerned, we shall confine ourselves to friendly counsel.... These acts do not imperil the freedom of the American people, the economic or the moral feature of our people I do not propose ever to sacrifice American life for anything short of

Heceforth, the record of the American foreign policy towards the Far East looks like a tragic account of follies and failures. While brazenly violating territorial and administrative integrity of China, Japan started encouraging disregard for the 'open door principle' by the puppet state of Manchukuo in 1934. Hull simply protested to Tokyo over discriminations against American trade in that area. When in December 1934, Japan served notice that she would not renew the naval limitation treaties of Washington and London when they expired on December 31, 1936, it brought the United States to the 'Oriental crossroads of decision'. Now the US was faced with two options. First, she should withdraw gradually with dignity from the Far East acquiescing in the closing of the 'open door', the nullification of treaty rights, the appropriation by Japan of additional portions of China and other territory and in effect turning over the entire Pacific Ocean west of Hawaii. The other was to continue to insist on the maintenance of law, on legitimate American rights and interests in the Far East, and on observance of the treaties and declarations that guaranteed an independent China and pledged equality to all nations, non-intervention, non-aggression, and peaceful settlement of disputes in the Orient.

The American government was thus confronted with two options. While the first option could win the support of many who wanted to avoid the course of war and stick to the way of continuing trade in the Far East, the latter signified a firm, though not an aggressive, policy toward Japan. Of course, it meant military preparedness, close contact and parallel action with other powers interested in the Orient, particularly Great Britain, and friendship and cooperation with China. The President and his Secretary of State chose the second course that on account of being enforced with the determination to 'keep peace at any price' proved a disaster. "Thus, rightly or wrongly, the United States chose the course that was to lead, seven years later, to Pearl Harbour, and

---

As the League of Nations has already taken up the subject, we should co-operate with them in every field of negotiation or conciliation. But that is the limit. We will not go along on war or any of the sanctions, either economic or military, for those are the roads to war." See Charles A. Beard: *American Foreign Policy in the Making (1932): A Study in Responsibilities* (New Haven: Yale University Press, 1946), p. 136.

eventually to the destruction of Japan's empire and her military and naval power."⁵⁰

Economic Foreign Policy : Dilemma of Aloofness Versus Commitment

A study of the American foreign policy towards Europe during the inter-war period presents a strange dilemma of aloofness versus commitment. It is on account of the fact that while the 'isolationists', rather the 'insulationists', did not permit the Administration to involve itself into the contentions of European powers, they strove hard for forcing it to fight for the protection and promotion of their economic interests. That is, the US adopted a peculiar economic policy so as to reap benefits from trade with the European countries while maintaining an attitude of political aloofness so far as the contentious matters of European politics were concerned. So intense was the burden of this standpoint that the US indirectly helped Germany after witnessing her ruthless suppression at the Paris Peace Conference under the Treaty of Versailles. More than that, the Roosevelt administration took to the course of improving commercial relations with the USSR that had so far been an untouchable ever since the establishment of the communist regime in 1917.

The motivating force behind this was the issue of inter-allied War debts and reparations.⁵¹ During the First World War, the US had lent huge sums to the European countries and their realisation was one of the great problems.⁵² Moreover, "a consequence of the First World War, whose significance was little realised, was the sudden trasformation of the United States from a debtor to a creditor nation."⁵³ Without counting interest, the United States government at the close of the war was a creditor of its war time associates to the extent of $ 10,350,000,000. Most important of all was the fact that although the war impoverished Europe, it "brought

---

50. Pratt. op. cit., p. 355.
51. See B.H. Williams: *The Economic Foreign Policy of the United States* (New York: McGraw Hill, 1929), p. 17.
52. Pratt, op. cit., p. 334.
53. Ibid. As a matter of fact, the protagonists of the 'new economics' "regarded International relationships as an incident to primary interests, the distinctive completeness of the national state." See C.A. Beard: *The Idea of National Interest*, Ch. XI.

sudden wealth to the United States and thereby created a large fund of surplus capital ready to seek investment abroad."[54]

However, the first baffling question was the stand of the major allied powers that the US had no moral right to claim recovery of her loans from them in view of the fact that while she had paid with money, they had paid with the blood of their people in the war. For some time, it appeared that if the United States adhered to her stand, it might create ill-will with other Allied Powers. But Wilson and his advisers rebuffed all such contentions at the Paris Peace Conference. Instead, the Administration insisted that any proposal of the cancellation of loans was unacceptable, for the United States had gained no territory or other advantages from the war, like other Allied Powers and, for this reason, the American tax-payer "would not willingly shoulder the burden of paying off the Allied indebtedness."[55]

President Harding had the same stand. His argument was that the total or partial cancellation of the war debts was not possible, for the Allied governments had 'hired the money'. The Congress made a law on February 9, 1922, whereby the World War Foreign Debt Commission was created with the Secretary of Treasury as its chairman. The Act authorised him to negotiate settlement with the debtor nations of Europe. It was made clear that no portion of the debts could be cancelled, the interest rate not to be less than 4 per cent, nor the date of maturity later than 1947. Despite this, the Commission failed to make the desired progress for the obvious reason that the debtor nations adopted a non-cooperative attitude. They took plea that unless they recovered reparations from Germany, they would not be in a position to pay further to the United States. Naturally, it forced the American Administration to help Germany for the sake of recovering her own debts through the allied powers. It is for this reason that

---

54. H.G. Moulton and Pasvolsky: *War Debts and War Prosperity* (Washington: Brookings Institution, 1931), pp. 52-70.
55. This category included (i) loans to governments for balancing of budgets as a result of insufficient taxation, (ii) loans for military purposes, (iii) loans for assistance to monopolies where their conduct was such as to maintain prices against the American consumer, (iv) loans to governments not recognised by the US, and (v) loans to governments or citizens in countries who have failed to maintain their obligations to the US. Herbert Feis: *The Diplomacy of the Dollar: First Era, 1919-1932* (Baltimore: The John Hopkins Press, 1950), pp. 18-19.

America played a very important part in the formulation and implementation of the Dawes Plan of 1924 and then the Young Plan of 1929.

While the Debt Commission was engaged in its uphill task, the Administration adopted the strategy of encouraging foreign investments unless they were of an 'objectionable' nature.[56] This category also covered the peculiar cases of the Soviet Union, as it was an 'unrecognised' state, and of France as she was a defaulter. But the steadily deteriorating economic condition of the world could not be arrested by the American subsidies. President Hoover had to declare one year's moratorium in 1931 so as to deal with the conditions of Great Depression. Despite this all, after the Lausanne Conference of 1932, the whole chapter of reparations and inter-allied war debts had to be closed. Thus, the US had to bear the consequences of huge cancellation of her debts as is evident from the following breakdown:[57]

Countries	Principal Amount (in dollars)	Rate of interest	Percentage of Cancellation
1. Austria	24,614,885	—	70.5
2. Belgium	417,780,000	1.8	53.5
3. Czechoslovakia	115,000,000	3.3	25.7
4. Estonia	13,830,000	3.3	19.5
5. Finland	9,000,000	3.3	19.3
6. France	4,025,000,000	1.6	52.8
7. Great Britain	46,000,000,000	3.3	19.7
8. Greece	32,467,000	0.3	67.3
9. Hungary	2,939,000	3.3	19.6
10. Italy	2,042,000,000	0.4	75.4
11. Latvia	5,77,000	3.3	19.3
12. Lithuania	6,030,000	3.3	20.1
13. Poland	178,560,000	3.3	19.5
14. Rumania	44,590,000	3.3	25.1
15. Yugoslavia	62,850,000	1.0	69.7
Total	11,579,435,885		

---

56. Pratt, op. cit., p. 336.
57. Ibid., p. 337.

American Loans

(in dollars)

Countries	Date of Agreement	Funded Principal	Interest (to be received)	Total	Interest* (per cent)
1. Bulgaria	August 18, 1925	417,780,000.00	310,050,500.00	727,830,500.00	1.8
2. Czechoslovakia	October 13, 1925	115,000,000.00	197,811,433.88**	312,811,433.88	3.3
3. Estonia	October 28, 1925	13,830,000.00	19,501,140.00	33,331,140.00	3.3
4. Finland	May 1, 1923	9,000,000.00	12,695,055.00	21,695,055.00	3.3
5. France	April 29, 1926	4,025,000,000.00	2,822,674,104.00	6,847,674,104.17	1.6
6. G. Britain	June 6, 1923	4,600,000,000.00	6,505,965,000.00	11,105,965,000.00	3.3
7. Hungary	April 25, 1924	1,939,000.00	2,754,240.00	4,693,240.00	3.3
8. Italy	November 14, 1925	2,042,000,000.00	365,677,500.00	2,407,677,500.00	0.4
9. Latvia	September 24, 1925	5,775,000.00	8,183,635.00	13,958,635.00	3.3
10. Lithuania	September 22, 1924	6,030,000.00	8,501,940.00	14,531,940.00	3.3
11. Poland	November 11, 1924	178,560,000.00	257,127,550.00	435,687,550.00	3.3
12. Romania	December 4, 1925	44,590,000.00	77,916,260.00**	122,506,260.05	3.3
13. Yugoslavia	May 3, 1926	62,850,000.00	32,327,635.00	95,177,635.00	1.0
	Total	522,354,000.00	10,621,185,993.10	22,143,539,993.10	

* Average interest rate approximate over the whole period of payments.
** Includes deferred payments to be funded into principal.
Source: Latene and Wainhouse: *A History of American Foreign Policy,* p. 792.

In short, the economic foreign policy of the United States relating to the recovery of her war loans proved a failure. "No one foresaw apparently that Uncle Sam himself would supply a large share of the funds which would be used by Germany to pay reparations and then by the recipients of reparations to pay war debts to the United States."[58]

Policy towards Europe : Adherence to the Course of Splendid and Selective Isolationism

It is said that ever since the times of George Washington 'isolationism', proudly called by some as 'splendid isolationism', had been the most outstanding feature of the American foreign policy in so far as her attitude towards the European powers was concerned. The first President of the United States in his farewell address said: "Nothing is more essential than that permanent, inveterate antipathies against particular nations and passionate attachments for others should be excluded, and that in place of them just and amicable feeling should be cultivated. The nation which indulges towards another an habitual hatred or an habitual fondness is in some degree a slave."[59] It was reiterated by President Jefferson in his inaugural address. Since then it became the basic touchstone of the American foreign policy with particular reference to her relations with the European powers. The main reason behind this was that the American statesmen were really concerned with the protection and promotion of their economic interests and for this, while keeping themselves away from European contentions, they could well bank upon "twisting the tail of British lion."[60] "They could defend American interests abroad in negative terms of neutrality and abstention from power politics and positive terms of promoting commerce by championing neutral trading rights,

---

58. Ibid.
59. See T.A. Bailey, op. cit., p. 81. The philosopher of the American Revolution, Thomas Paine, in his tremendously effective work *Common Sense* (1776) said: "Any submission to, or dependence on, Great Britain tends directly to involve this Continent in European wars and quarrels, and sets us at variance with nations who would otherwise seek our friendship, and against whom we have neither anger nor complaint. As Europe is our market for trade, we ought to form no partial connection with any part of it. It is the true interest of America to steer clear of European contentions." Ibid., p. 4.
60. Schuman, op. cit., p. 770.

freedom of the seas, most favoured nation treatment, and the Open Door in the Orient."[61]

For this reason, the United States observed neutrality when the First World War broke out in 1914, but she plunged into it in 1917 when her economic interests were threatened. President Wilson declared his Fourteen Points on the basis of which Germany surrendered unconditionally in 1918 and then America took an active part in the Paris Peace Conference. But soon after that, the 'isolationists' had their day when the 'evil men of the Senate' rejected the Treaty of Versailles and along with that the Covenant of the League of Nations. Naturally, it gave a rude shock to the 'internationalists' who labelled it as an act of great 'betrayal'.[62] It signified that the American policy of isolationism implied "rejection of the membership of the League of Nations, non-entanglement in the political controversies of Europe and Asia, non-intervention in the wars of those Continents, neutrality, peace and defence of the United States through measures appropriate to those purposes, and the pursuance of a foreign policy friendly to all nations disposed to reciprocate. An isolationist may favour the promotion of goodwill and peace among nations by any and all measures compatible with non-entanglement in any association of nations empowered to designate 'aggressors' and bring engines of sanction and coercion into action against them."[63]

As a matter of fact, the course of 'isolationism' did not amount to the way of complete aloofness from European politics;

---

61. Ibid.
62. Thomas A. Bailey made a scathing attack on such a heinous action of the Senate. He described it as a 'betrayal' on 14 counts: of the League of Nations, of the Treaty of Versailles, of the Allies, of France, of Germany, of liberal opinion in the world over, of American boys who died and yet unborn, of the masses everywhere, of our humanitarian, missionary and educational interests of American merchants, manufacturers, bankers and investors, of America's responsibility to assume that world leadership which had been thrust upon, of nations plighted word and of good faith in international dealings, of our clear moral obligations to finish the job, and of the American people. *Woodrow Wilson and the Great Betrayal* (New York: Macmillan, 1945). Prof. C.A. Beard takes a different view when he defines betrayal as an act "to give up to a place in the power of an enemy a person or thing by treachery or disloyalty. Betrayal is a treacherous surrender to a foe, a violation of a trust or confidence, an abandonment of something committed to one's charge. A betrayal is commonly regarded as a human and moral act of lowest and vilest kind." op. cit., p. 7.
63. Ibid., p. 17 n 2.

it simply suggested non-involvement in conflict among European powers while as much engagement as possible with them for the protection and promotion of their economic interests. That is, soon after the war, the American people "forgot their noble professions and resolutions, let their war idealism 'slump', grew weary of hearing about the woes of the world, turned selfishly to their own affairs, and sank into the mire of isolationism."[64] Thus, even after rejecting the Treaty of Versailles in 1920, the United States signed a treaty of peace with Germany on August 25, 1921, that reserved to the American nationals all rights, privileges, immunities, reparations or advances together with a right to seek their enforcement.[65]

The policy of continued economic involvement behind the facade of political isolationism continued. The American statesmen minced no words in making it above board that if the League powers ever committed themselves to the economic boycott of an aggressor, they would face the alternative of seeing the same dishonoured by American ships and goods or provoking sharp controversies with Washington by challenging the rights of the Americans to trade with any other power of the world even if a lawbreaker. When the Secretary of State (Hughes) discussed this issue with the British ambassador (Sir Esme Howard) in 1925, having in view the provisions of the Covenant of the League of Nations, the abortive Geneva Protocol and the successful treaties of Locarno, he made it clear that there "was one thing he believed could be depended upon and that was that his government from its very beginning had been insistent upon the rights of neutrals and would continue to maintain them. The Secretary did not believe that any Administration, short of a treaty, concluded and ratified, could commit the country against assertion of its neutral rights in case there should be occasion to demand their recognition."[66]

However, as conditions of peace are required for the promotion of commercial relations, the US government remained serious about making efforts for the same cause. In 1927 it sought to promote further naval disarmament in the abortive Coolidge Conference at Geneva. But more important than this was the

---

64. Ibid. p. 17.
65. H. Commager (ed.): *Documents on American History* (New York: Appleton-Century-Crofts, 1949), V. Ed., pp. 352-53.
66. See Schuman, op. cit., p. 773.

United States

support of the Secretary of State (Kellogg) for the proposal of his French counterpart (Briand) as a result of which the Pact of Paris for the renunciation of war as an instrument of national policy came into being in 1928. It was widely appreciated by the American people, though some hard-headed cynics registered their reservations. "Some insisted that the treaty was a dangerous step towards membership in the League. Others noted that the pact permitted defensive war; and whoever heard of the nation that did not fight defensively? Others sneered that the treaty had no teeth, except the feeble pressure of world opinion; it was just a 'New Year's resolution' or 'a letter to Santa Claus'.... The Kellogg-Briand pact proved to be a monument to illusion. It was not only delusive but dangerous, for it further lulled the public already prepared to lag behind in the naval race into a false sense of security. Instead of outlawing wars, the treaty merely outlawed declarations of wars."[67]

Nevertheless, the signing of the Paris Pact indicated that the US "began to return to the policy which had led to America's most active foreign development and leadership in the Hague Peace Conference."[68] The line of Hoover and Stimson received a break when Roosevelt assumed the office of the President. His first startling act was negotiations with Russian Foreign Commissar (Litvinov) that led to the recognition of the Soviet State in 1933. William C. Bullitt became the first American ambassador to Moscow. A joint Congressional resolution dated 19 June 1934 authorised, the President to accept the membership of the International Labour Organisation, provided no obligations were assumed under the Covenant of the League of Nations. When the President took note of the fact that in Europe things started deteriorating as a result of the aggressive actions of Italy and Germany, he issued increasingly urgent warnings to his people that 'neutrality' "was not enough, but he never felt—without doubt correctly—that he could afford to move too far ahead of public opinion, for he was actually aware of the disaster which had overtaken Wilson and his policies had lost touch with the people."[69]

Early in October 1937, Roosevelt took a stand showing that the US had departed from its policy of impartiality to join with the

---

67. Bailey: *A Diplomatic History of the American State*, p. 650.
68. Arthur Sweetser: *American Year-Book* (1928), p. 71.
69. H.C. Allen: *A Concise History of the USA* (London: Ernest Benn, 1964), p. 249.

League of Nations in labelling Japan as a treaty-violator. It was really a startling event when, on 5 October in a speech at Chicago, he deplored the fact that "the epidemic of world lawlessness is spreading" and suggested a 'quarantine' for those nations infected with it. Although he did not name any nation, he was clearly alluding to Japan.[70] What he meant by 'quarantine', he did not spell out, but there is good evidence that he had in mind complete severance of relations with a nation adjudged to be an aggressor.[71]

Certainly, the 'quarantine speech' fell upon the American people like a bolt from the blue. The 'internationalists' greeted it with rejoicing as a conclusive evidence of the fact that the President had at last spurned the principle of the non-entanglement and non-intervention in the political and military operations of the European and Asiatic powers and thereby had aligned himself on the side of full cooperation with 'peace-loving nations' in designating and taking collective action against the aggressors—Germany, Italy and Japan. With this interpretation of the speech, the 'isolationists' also agreed, but they criticised the President in blunt language. They accused him of having violated the pledges he had repeatedly made to the people and charged him with "setting out on the road to war".[72]

However, the isolationists once again had their way. Most of the Americans adhered to the course of non-involvement in other people's quarrels by 'running away', by 'minding their own business' and, if need be, 'by abandoning business which might drag them into war'. In the full blast of isolationism, its protagonists adhered to the contents of the Neutrality Acts with the result the quarantine address of the President "backfired and slowed down the realities."[73] And yet the isolationists had to take into account that the complexities, confusions, and frustrations en-

---

70. Pratt, op. cit., p. 382.
71. W.L. Langer and S.E. Gleason: *The Challenge to Isolation, 1937-40* (New York: Harper and Row, 1952), p. 19.
72. Beard, op. cit., p. 187.
73. Allen, op. cit., p. 249. A great critic of the course of US 'isolationism', like Prof. F.L. Schuman in *Nation* (12 February, 1936) described neutrality legislation as a "one part lunacy, one part stupidity, and one part criminal ignorance of diplomatic and economic realities." See Beard: *American Foreign Policies in the Making*, p. 19.

countered in the course of this effort revealed the impossibility of achieving isolation in a world in which American trade and investments were scattered over the five continents of the Seven Seas."[74]

Course of Appeasement: Triumph of Isolationism over Internationalism

The isolationists strongly emphasised the course of neutrality after the Manchurian crisis that implied complete impartiality between belligerents without any distinction between the aggressors and the victims of aggression. It took a shape of its own in the Neutrality Act of 31 August 1935, formulated hastily in the face of what looked like an impending war in Africa and Europe. This important legislation resolved that upon the outbreak or during the progress of war between or among two or more foreign States, the President "shall proclaim such fact, and it shall thereafter be unlawful to export arms, ammunitions, or implements of war from any place in the United States or possessions of the United States to any part of such belligerent states, or to any neutral port for trans-shipment to, or for the use of a belligerent." The President could, from time to time, by proclamation extend such embargo to other States as and when they were involved in such war. The violators were to be punished by forfeiture of property as well as imprisonment. It established a National Munitions Control Board (consisting of the Secretaries of State, Treasury, War and Navy) with which all importers of arms, their manufacturers and exporters were obliged to register their names, goods and places of business.

In this important direction, the aims of the Congress dominated by the isolationists differed from that of the President (Roosevelt) and his Secretary of State (Hull) who desired a legislation flexible enough to empower the Administration to forbid the exportation of arms and ammunitions to an aggressive government while permitting their sale to the victim of an aggression. It was not acceptable to Congress in whose view such an action would have meant taking sides in a conflict and possible involvement in a war. It is for this reason that President Roosevelt prohibited the exportation of arms and ammunitions or implements of war to either party involved in the Italo-Ethiopian war in

---

74. Schuman, op. cit., p. 782.

1935-36. But Italy needed no arms. She wanted oil and since it was not classified as a prohibited item under the Neutrality Act, the President had no authority to forbid its export. At the most what he could do was to place a 'moral embargo' on oil and other commodities appealing to the exporters of his country to hold their shipment to Italy to normal pre-war levels.[75]

The implementation of the economic sanctions against Italy in a half-hearted manner by the statesmen of London and Paris coupled with the scope of the Neutrality Act of 1935 (that did not cover export of essential items like oil, coal, iron and steel) went certainly to the advantage of the Italian dictator in his aggression over a poor and backward country of Africa. By all means, the American attitude swelled the course of appeasement adopted so frankly by Britain and France. More than that, the new Neutrality Act of 1936 embodied a new feature that was hardly encouraging to those who might consider using stronger sanctions against the autocratic power of Rome. Apart from saying what had already been given in the first neutrality legislation, it further laid down that no loan was to be given to a belligerent state by any American person or firm. It exempted from the ban on ammunitions, loans and the like an American republic engaged in war with a non-American state, provided the American republic was not co-operating with a non-American state or states in such a war.

The second neutrality legislation strengthened the hands of Gen. Franco who was fighting a 'civil war' in Spain. Here the American government had a pretext to distinguish between a war and a civil war. The President in his usual manner desired that the exporters of his country would refrain from shipping war material to either side in the civil war. Since his appeal of laying a moral embargo had no effect, he appealed to the Congress to make a legal provision in this regard. Accordingly, on 6 January, 1937, the Congress passed a resolution (that became third Neutrality Act) whereby it prohibited the export of any arms, ammunition or implements of war to either of the opposing parties in Spain. It put the loyalists or the legitimate rulers of Spain in a position of disadvantage, for they were deprived of the help from a big power like the United States, whereas Gen. Franco was receiving all

---

75. See Hull: *Memoirs*, Vol. I, Chapter 31.

United States

assistance from the dictators of Italy and Germany. It, therefore, "appears certain that American policy, like British and French non-intervention policy, played into the hands of Hitler and Mussolini enabling them to assist in establishing a friendly Fascist government in Spain. There is, on the other hand, a strong probability that a Loyalist victory would have meant eventually a Spain under Communist domination."[76]

The foreign policy of America towards Spain at this time looked like a grave act of self-contradiction. Everyone could see that after Ethiopia another legally established and duly recognised government was equated with a powerful aggressor. "A friendly government wedded to democracy and fighting to uphold it, not including a single communist face to face with a fascist rebellion, instigated and actively assisted by Hitler and Mussolini, was yet denied the benefit of obtaining the necessary supplies to defend itself. In this case, the American appeasement can be explained in terms of the Spanish Government's supposed sympathies and affiliations with Communism, the sympathy of a large number of American Catholics for Gen. Franco, Roosevelt's unwillingness to alienate the Catholic votes for Democratic candidates in the Congressional elections of 1938, the American desire to prevent the enlargement of the Spanish Civil war into a general European conflict, and the suspicion of the Soviet Union which was helping the Loyalists."[77] Roosevelt's Under-Secretary of State (Sumner Welles) points out that the American Administration "committed no more cardinal error than the policy adopted during the civil war in Spain."[78]

The hands of the President remained tied by the terms of the neutrality legislation. Curiously, the third Neutrality Act of 1937 not only retained what was given in the first two of the preceding two years, it embodied a temporary cash and carry provisions (to

---

76. Ibid., Vol. II, Chapter 34. Hull holds that the Congress recognised that the American aid to the Spanish government might lead to a spread of war and that our peace and security required our keeping aloof from the struggle." Ibid., p. 491. Schuman rightly points out: "The destruction of Spanish democracy was a direct consequence of 'non-intervention' by the European democracies and of a specious 'neutrality' on the part of the United States." op. cit., p. 787.
77. M.G. Gupta: *International Relations Since 1919* (Allahabad: Chaitanya, 1969), III Ed, p. 271.
78. Sumner Welles: *The Time for Decision* (New York: Harper & Row, 1944), pp. 60-61.

expire in May 1939) that empowered the President, as per his discretion, to prohibit the export to a belligerent country of commodities not included in the lists of arms, ammunitions and implements of war in any American vessel until ownership had been transferred to the foreign purchaser. The obvious intent was to prevent 'incidents' that might arise from the destruction of American property by one of the belligerents. In this way, the United States "was now fortified, or so it seemed, against being drawn into any 'foreign war' through such violations of 'freedom of the seas' as had involved it in 1812 and 1917."[79]

Now the most compelling reason that engaged the attention of the American foreign policy-makers was to eliminate the danger of a world war. Thus, Roosevelt in a letter dated 26 September, 1938, made an appeal to Hitler: "Whatever may be the differences in the controversies at issue and however difficult of pacific settlement they may be, I am persuaded there is no problem so difficult that it cannot be justly solved by the resort to reason rather than by resort to force."[80] Two days after, in a similar appeal to the King of Italy, he said: "The question for the world today is not the question of errors of judgement or of injustices committed in the part. It is the question of the fate of the world today and tomorrow. The world asks of us who at this moment are heads of nations, the supreme capacity to achieve the destinies of nations without forcing upon them as a price the mutilation and death of the millions of citizens."[81]

These strong appeals failed to have any effect. The Nazi engine of violence went on crushing the independence of the people of Austria and Czechoslovakia with the blessings of London and Paris. Thus, Roosevelt tried again to have an effect of his appeal on the minds of the dictators of Berlin and Rome. In a letter to Hitler dated 14 April 1939, he said: "We recognise complex world problems which affect all humanity, but we know that study and discussion of them must be held in an atmosphere of peace. Such an atmosphere of peace cannot exist if negotiations are overshad-

---

79. Pratt, op. cit., 365.
80. Robert Birely (ed.): *Speeches and Documents on American History* (London: Oxford University Press, 1951), IV, p. 264.
81. Ibid., p. 265.

owed by the threat of force or by the fear of war."[82] Then, on 24 August, 1939, he wrote to the King of Italy pleading: "The governments of Italy and the United States can today advance those ideals of Christianity which of late seem to have been obscured. The unheard voices of countless millions of human beings ask that they shall not be vainly sacrificed again."[83]

Such appeals went in vain for the obvious reason that they were made by a head of the state that had taken to the path of neutrality and non-intervention. When the Second World War broke out on September 1, 1939, and Britain and France declared war on Germany just two days after, Roosevelt declared that "this nation will remain a neutral nation."[84] As could be guessed in advance, it was certain that the United States would have to repeat what was done by her in 1917. And it happened. As the course of appeasement forced Britain and France to pay its price, so the US could not remain unaffected by it. Ultimately, America had to jump into the second global holocaust. It illustrated the fact that "no one knew better than F.D. Roosevelt in 1940 that passive defence of the US or of the Western hemisphere would become a strategic impossibility, mathematically certain to insure defeat, the moment Britain surrendered."[85] The impression that the Administration could, however, give was that "from 1933 to 1939 the US Government followed the policy of attempting to improve international relations and thus prevent the collapse of world peace. President Roosevelt and Secretary Hull were avowed internationalists."[86]

Concluding Observations

A critical study of the American foreign policy and diplomacy during the inter-war period, as contained in the preceding sections, leaves these strong impressions:

1. It is said that from the early days of the Republic, the US adhered to the course of 'isolationism'. It was certainly a misleading statement. It simply signified political aloofness behind the facade of which the US statesmen tried to protect and promote the

---

82. H.S. Commager, op, cit., p. 597.
83. Ibid., pp. 597-98.
84. *Ribbentrop Memoirs*, p. 105.
85. Schuman: *Night over Europe* (New York: Alfred A. Knopf, 1941), p. 553.
86. Walter Johnson: *The Battle against Isolation*, p. 10.

economic interests of their people. At the most, it may be found applicable to America's non-entanglement into the contentious affairs of European politics. As a matter of fact, at no time during the inter-war period had the US remained cut off from the crosscurrents of diplomacy, alliances and wars in other parts of the world. During this period, the signs pointed to a weakening of the hold of the isolation. For instance, the covening of the Washington Conference in 1921-22, the conclusion of a peace treaty with Germany in 1921, the signing of the Kellogg-Briand Pact in 1928, the formulation and implementation of the Dawes Plan in 1924 and the Young Plan in 1929, the declaration of Moratorium for one year in 1931 and the restoration of diplomatic relations with Soviet Russia in 1933 are the leading instances of the same. The 'quarantine address' of President Roosevelt of 1937 could not become the policy of the nation both on account of its vague implications and the hold of the isolationists on the Congress that led to the enactment of neutrality legislation in 1935, 1936 and 1937. But the way the President stressed it and subsequently made fervent appeal to the heads of German and Italian states did mark the waning of the sign of isolation.[87]

2. While the appellation of 'isolationism' could be applied to the American policy towards Europe to some concocted extent, it could not at all be said about American policy towards the Latin-American region. Behind the dexterous plea of saving the weak states of the Western hemisphere from the colonial exploitation of the European powers (like France, Spain, Austria and Russia), the statesmen of the United States sought to perpetuate their exclusive hold over them. For this, the US was deprecated as 'Colossus of the North' or the follower of a 'big stick policy.' In the name of Pan-

---

87. L.L. Leonard: *Elements of American Foreign Policy* (New York: McGraw Hill, 1953), p. 221. As R.C. Snyder and E.S. Furniss, Jr. observe: "The US rejected the League of Nations and the Versailles Treaty of which it was a part. Instead, the American government separately concluded peace with the Central Powers in July and August 1921. In so doing the US entered upon the twenty, year interwar period of what has erroneously been described as a 'state of isolation'. This term does justice neither to the situation as it existed in fact nor to the ideas and attitudes of those Americans who repudiated Wilsonian idealism". *American Foreign Policy* (New York: Rinehart & Co., 1954), p. 33. In form it remained 'nonentanglement', but in fact, it was veering, by the logic of events, towards a cautious form of international co-operation." Latane and Wainhouse, op. cit., p. 794.

Americanism, the US not only managed to keep the hands of some European powers off from the Western hemisphere, it could also manage to establish her suzerainty over the weak states like those of Cuba, Mexico, Nicaragua and Haiti. This line can be traced consistently right from the frank affirmations of Monroe and elder Roosevelt to those of Wilson and younger Roosevelt. It is, therefore, aptly observed: "The term isolation could never be applied to the inter-war policies of the United States towards Latin-American countries. The economic power of the United States placed the American government and certain private businesses in the position of virtual arbiters of the destinies of small and weak states in the Central American and Caribbean areas. The United States continued its policy of intervention which had placed it in the control of the Dominican Republic, Haiti and Nicaragua."[88]

3. Likewise, American foreign policy towards the Far East was dominated by the consideration of imperialistic interests. It was for this reason that the Washington Conference was convened to put a check on the growing power of Japan. Similarly, it was for the sake of protecting the economic interests of the people that the Administration adopted the Stimson doctrine in 1931. A critic could take note of the fact that Stimson, though well advertised as an advocate of international peace, was, in fact, an imperialist of The odore Roosevelt-Lodge-Mahan-Beveridge school. He advocated strong policy in the Far East and was vehemently hostile to the independence of the Philippines."[89] In the name of having an 'open door' in China , the Americans sought to have another version of their Monroe Doctrine in retaliation to the expansionist policies of Japan. But the weak and meek attitude of the United States in regard to maintaining the territorial integrity and independence of China went to strengthen the case of Japan's ambitions yet more. That is, an attitude of appeasement towards the aggressive behavior of Japan proved counter-productive to the interests of the United States. Thus, it is critically pointed out: "The Hoover-Stimson non-recognition doctrine had no deterrent effect on Japan. It had antagonised the Japanese government and people without achieving its purpose. The generalisation seems sound that to

---

88. Ibid., p. 37.
89. Beard, op. cit., p. 113.

oppose international aggression with weapons that are irritating but ineffectual is worse than not to oppose it at all."[90]

4. The notorious course of appeasement adopted by the United States in dealing with the aggressors of Japan, Italy and Germany made it clear that she, like Britain and France, had "become a victim of impotence."[91] Japan's seizure of Manchuria had proved that the collective opinion of mankind was no deterrent to the aggressor. Then the Italian conquest of Ethiopia, the successful intervention of Germany and Italy in Spain, the rearmament of Germany, the recuperation of the Rhineland, the anti-Comintern Pact which, in fact, allied Germany with Japan, and the invasion of China in 1937, these events made it unmistakably clear that Germany, Italy and Japan were on the march and that they would dominate the world if they were not successfully resisted. "The surrender of the Rhineland in 1936 and that of Austria and Czechoslovakia in 1938 were then strategic preliminaries to the neutralisation of Russia and the conquest of Poland in 1939. What was surrendered by our allies in the name of peace became the strategic foundation upon which Hitler prosecuted his war."[92]

5. The foreign policy of the United States remained tied to the economic interests of the people. Economic motives determined all other objectives of the foreign policy-makers from Wilson to Roosevelt. Negotiations were conducted, treaties were concluded, and wars had been fought not for the sake of giving effect to great moral considerations but to break down commercial barriers, to protect traders and their ships in peace and in war, and eventually to safeguard American investments in foreign lands. Instead of making and realising political and ideological commitments, the statesmen of the United States "turned to outworn theories and tried to build the security of the United States upon the cardboard

---

90. See R.E. Osgood: *Ideas and Self-Interest in America's Foreign Relations* (Chicago: University of Chicago Press. 1953), p. 356.
91. As L.T. Mowrer and H.H. Cummings observe: "Actually, neither the Kellogg Pact, nor the Stimson doctrine, nor the Neutrality Acts either deterred aggressors or prevented war. Many students believed that they did just the opposite. By giving the aggressors the impression that the United States would not intervene in any conflict short of direct attack no matter what happened, these attempts to maintain peace may have helped bring on the very conflict which they planned to prevent." *The US and World Relations* (New York: Harper & Bros., 1952), p. 345.
92. Lippmann, op. cit., p. 34.

foundations of physical distance and disarmament, accompanied by moral exhortation and plaintive appeals to world public opinion. Yet, while eschewing any real responsibility for the world, the Americans indulged in an orgy of financial and economic expansion, saddling the country with overseas physical investments they were unable and unwilling to defend."[93]

Keeping all these points in view, a great critic on this subject says that it "is hard to avoid the conclusion that from 1920 to 1937, almost every major American diplomatic decision or undertaking was either abortive, futile, or dead wrong."[94] The world's most powerful nation "conducted its foreign relations in the manner of a nervous woman compelled to pass through a dark corridor infested with man-eating mice."[95] Curiously, the misleading nature of isolationism was lauded as 'splendid' by the supporters of the traditional course and President Harding went to the extent of calling it 'triumphant nationalism.' One historian has indicated that "no less than in Cleveland's day Americans in the twenties insisted on the unique mission of the United States, the need to maintain independence of action and avoid permanent alliances...."[96] But this neo-isolationist position, this return to the pattern of foreign relations that had been interrupted briefly by America's European adventure of 1917-18 "was not to endure. The new technology, the new politics, and the new social currents at work in the world created powerful forces that drew the United States inexorably back into the arena of world power."[97]

---

93. Mowrer, op. cit., pp. 52-53.
94. Ibid., p. 52.
95. F.H. Simonds: *Can America Stay at Home?* (London: Harper & Brothers, 1932), p. 136.
96. T.N. Bonner: *Our Recent Past* (Englewood Cliffs, New Jersey: Prentice-Hall, 1963), p. 248.
97. W.C. Langsam: *The World Since 1919* (Delhi: Surjeet Pub., 1981), p. 309.

12

JAPAN

The position of Japan in the Far East could be compared to that of Germany and Italy in Europe. Her native resources were insufficient to maintain a rapidly growing population. She felt that she was treated as an upstart, and that the other Great Powers jealously resisted the fulfilment of her aspirations.

—E. H. Carr[1]

Japan, a small archipelago country of the Far East, also nicknamed as the Hermit Kingdom, became a modern state as a definite result of the trend of modernisation unleashed by the entry of an American naval commander (Commodore Matthew Parry) with his ship into Yedo Bay in 1853. Her doors were opened to the ambitious adventurers of the West. Apprehensive of the growing influence of Russia over China threatening her imperial interests in the Far East, Britain sought friendship with Japan as a result of which an alliance was concluded on 30 January, 1902, whereby the signatories affirmed the principle of 'open door' implying reciprocal help in the event of an attack on either by some power. The real importance of this Anglo-Japanese alliance was stated in Clause I which recognised 'special interests' of Japan politically as well as commercially and industrially in Korea.[2] The alliance made Japan so strong that she could defeat Russia in the battle of 1904-1905. As Schuman says: "Victory in the Russo-Japanese war enabled Japan to achieve the status of the Great Power without qualification and to prepare the way for a further extension of her empire. The Anglo-Japanese Alliance was renewed in 1905, and by agreements

---

1. Carr: *International Relations between the Two World Wars (1919-1939)*, (London; Macmillan, 1952), p. 153.
2. See S.F. Bemis: *A Diplomatic History of the United States* (New York, 1950), p. 490.

Russia in 1907 Japan became practically a fourth member of the Triple Entente. Japan achieved a free hand in Korea and South Manchuria; and if an occasion presented itself in war between Germany and the Entente, she could displace Germany in Shantung as she had already displaced Russia farther north."[3]

World War I and After: On the Path of Glory and Disgruntlement
During the Great War Japanese rulers had held the view that military preparations of Germany at Kiachow were a menace to the peace of the region and so they resolved to seize German possessions in the Far East. When Britain and Germany were involved in the war, Japan exploited the coveted opportunity to destroy German influence from eastern Asia and thereby improve her own position in the Far East. In not much time Japan could succeed in seizing Kiachow, occupying railway line from Tsingtao to Tsinan, and taking over German islands north of the equator as the Marianas, the Carolines, and the Marshalls. Thus, emboldened, a Japanese minister posted at Peking (Hioki) presented to the President of China (Yuan Shih-kai) a set of 21-Demands on 18 January, 1915 which aimed at ensuring Japan's colonial position in China.[4] The terms were so fomidable that, if accepted, would have converted China into a vassal of Japan. China immediately sought American support. But the US in a roundabout manner declined to take into view the terms of an earlier alliance of Japan with Britain. A little after, the Japanese Foreign Minister (Ishii) visited the US and signed an agreement on 2 November, 1917, with his American counterpart (Lansing) whereby the US recognised that the territorial propinquity created special reactions between the two coun-

---

3. F.L. Schuman: *International Politics: The Destiny of the Western State System* (New York : McGraw Hill, 1948), IV ed., p. 612.
4. The demands were in five groups. The first group was related to Shantung, the second one covered Manhuria and Eastern Inner Mongolia, the third one to certain coal and iron concessions, the fourth one to non-alienation of territory, gulfs, harbours and coasts, and the fifth one demanded the appointment of Japanese advisers, purchase of munitions, privilege of religious propaganda, police control and an economic preference amounting in Fukien to practical dominance. In fact, all these demands were designed to close China to Europe and to keep it reserved for Japan. As Langsam says: "These demands were calculated to make China a Japanese protectorate." *The World since 1919*, p. 260.

tries and "Japan had special interests in China particularly in the parts to which her possessions are contiguous." It implied that the US recognised Japan's imperial claims upon the Shantung province of China. Surprisingly it saw its endorsement in the Treaty of Versailles signed in 1919.

Japan emerged as a victor after the First World War on account of being on the side of the Allied Powers. But the Paris Peace settlement left her in a state of shock and frustration. Major powers like USA, Britain and France did not appreciate what the Japanese leaders had now desired and the concession of the Shantung province was nothing more than a sop for them. As Buss says : "They encountered determined hostility from Chinese, who were in no mood to surrender Shantung to the Japanese. They were not able to obtain a clear-cut international recognition of the principle of racial equality to which they were dedicated. They were not able to get outright title to the German possessions north of the equator in spite of war-time agreements. Mandates, subject to supervision by the League of Nations, seemed poor substitutes for colonies which Japan had expected to receive and to develop strictly for its own benefit. The Japanese signed the Covenant of the League of Nations, but they were not too happy about commitments, to respect and preserve against external aggression the independence and integrity of Member-States, including China. They disliked the obligation to settle dispute by arbitration, conciliation or adjudication before resort to war.... Japan was equally frustrated in its venture into Siberia. It had not been able to gain a military or diplomatic victory over the Russians and it had stirred up suspicion in the minds of its allies because of the blatant exposure of its expansionist ambitions on the Asian mainland."[5]

Since the United States had played a very important part in formulating the terms of the Paris peace settlement which had left Japan in a disgruntled state, her anxiety to put effective checks on the colonial ambitions of Japan inspired her to settle such a score at the Washington Conference of 1922.[6] The treaties signed on this occasion could well serve the purpose of the United States, but to Japan they were like an addition of insult to injury. As Schuman says : "These developments constituted a postponement, not a

---

5. C.A. Buss: *The Far East* (New York, 1955), p. 351.
6. See Chapter 11.

renunciation, of the efforts to enhance Japanese power on the Asiatic mainland. Japan, like all other Great Powers in the Western state system, sought to extend its domination over as wide an area as possible. Japan's threat of action in Eastern Asia was remote from the centres of power of other great states. Japan—westernised and militarised—found the huge disintegrating bulk of the Celestial Empire an easy prey. She was able to dominate the western Pacific with the naval power and to dominate the Asiatic mainland with her army. The specific objectives of her quest reflected the interests of her ruling classes—the new bourgeoisie, the old nobility, and the military naval and diplomatic bureaucracy."[7]

Achievements of New Diplomacy: Phase of Democratic Reformism Versus Traditional Authoritarianism

A new Japan emerged after the World War I in the sense that democratic forces witnessed their growth as a counterblast to the established tradition of militarism in this nation-state. The rise and growth of democratic forces, though with intermittent ups and downs, looked like something fundamentally alien to Japanese experience. By the end of the War, the old oligarchs were out. Itagaki died in 1919; Yamagata and Okuma died in 1922; Mutusukata abandoned politics well before his death in 1925; and Saioniji, the only managing genro, expressed the appreciation of parliamentary democracy. The marks of the new wave had become evident even in the last few preceding years when many disingenuous intellectuals and men of letters had derided German militarism, advocated the cause of individual liberty, and strongly defended Wilsonian idealism. For instance, a noted editor like Yoshino Sakuzo defended his plan of a restructured polity under party

---

7. Schuman, op. cit., 616. Yoshida Shoin and a few of his disciples who became leaders of Meiji Japan espoused views which might be described as 'nationalistic' or even 'ultranationalistic' in the mid-nineteenth century but even in Japan it would be a mistake to suggest that nationalism in the modern sense had much of an impact before last third of the nineteenth century. It is said: "In spite of the island setting, the emperor system, the blatant preachings of Nichiren (1222-82) ... the ambitious schemes of Hideyoshi (1590s) ... and the anti-foreignism of Imperial party (1854-67), there was at most 'national consciousness' in Japan before 1868." But "there was little nationalism in the leadership of the Restoration." See Hilary Conroy: "Japanese Nationalism and Expansionism" in *The American Historical Review*, Vol. LX, July, 1955, pp. 820-21.

control; a jurist like Minobe Tatsukichi in very clear and powerful terms pleaded the case of constitutional monarchy in his country; and a novelist like Mushakogi Saneutsu reflected on the new spirit by commenting that only a country without absolute authority was 'liveable'. It all manifested that the victory of the Allies in the World War I "had infused Japanese democratic currents with new vitality."[8]

The new diplomacy of Japan yielded positive results satisfying both the Western powers and Japan for their own reasons. As a result of the agreements made at the Washington Conference (1922) Japan could restore as well as improve her relations with America, Britain, France and China, including Communist Russia. By the end of the year, Japanese forces left the mainland of Siberia that paved the way for its union with communist Russia. In June 1923 negotiations between Japan and Russia took place that culminated in the restoraion of relations between the two countries after the conclusion of a treaty on 20 January, 1925. Japan's relations with China also improved. In December 1925, when Kuo Sung-ling revolted against the ruler of Manchuria (Chang Tso-lin), Japan sent its troops to the area of Mukden to protect him. Again in April 1927, Japanese marines were used to resist Chinese mobs attacking the Japanese concession at Hankow. But Japanese naval forces did not join in the Anglo-American bombardment of Nanking in March 1927, despite the fact that the Japanese consulate had been wounded. "The crux of the Shidehara policy was a serious effort to reconcile China's aspirations with Japan's interests."[9]

But Japan's relations with Britain and the United States remained 'strained' in view of her obsession to increase her naval power. The consequences of the Washington Conference had left her in a disgruntled state and hence she wanted to develop her naval strength by hook or by crook. At the London naval conference Japan sought three fundamental claims—(a) a 70 per cent ratio relative to the US in 10,000 ton, 8-inch gun heavy cruiser; (b) a 70 per cent ratio in gross tonnage relative to the US in all auxiliary craft, and (c) a parity with Britain and the United States in submarine tonnage at the then high existing strength of some

---

8. Paul S. Clyde and Burton F. Beers: *The Far East: A History of Western Impacts and Eastern Responses, 1830-1975* (New Delhi: Prentice-Hall of India, 1977), p. 319.
9. Ibid., p. 327.

78,000 tons. And she could get much vide terms of the treaty of 1930 owing to an informal understanding of the United States. However, what irked Japan much was the anti-immigration law of the United States made in 1924 that excluded the aliens from acquiring American citizenship. The noticeable tension in growing US Japanese relations had its impact on sharpening Japan's hunger for armaments.

Obviously, Japanese diplomacy in the period following World War I rested on certain new foundations. The governments of Prime Minister Hara (1918-1921) and then of Kato (1924-26) followed the 'democratic line' of the 'Reformists' that saw a little tilt towards the line of the 'Militarists' when the government of Prime Minister Tanaka (1927-29) adopted a 'positive foreign policy' implying strengthening of Japanese position in Manchuria and adopting a tougher attitude towards Chinese nationalism.[10] During his two terms as Foreign Minister (1924-27) and (1929-31), Shidehara pursued a conciliatory policy tinctured with Japan's expansionist designs towards China by adhering to the following principles put by him before the Diet in January, 1927:

1. To respect the sovereignty and territorial integrity of China,
2. To promote solidarity and economic *rapprochement* between the two countries,
3. To entertain sympathetically and helpfully the just aspirations of the Chinese people, and
4. To maintain an attitude of patience and tolerance in the present situation in China, and to protect Japan's legitimate and essential rights and interests by all reasonable means at the disposal of the government.

---

10. Tanaka's purpose was to reassure his own people, but the hard line provoked anti-Japanese boycotts in China. Further touble appeared when officers of Japan's Kwantung army sought to deal on their own with the dangers of Chinese nationalism by assassinating the Manchurian warlord, Chang Tso-lin on the assumption that his successor would be more subservient to Japan. Premier Tanaka first told the young emperor that the army was not responsible. Later, with the support of his cabinet including the service ministers, he sought to punish the conspirators and re-establish discipline in the army, but he was blocked by the general staff and the powerful military affairs bureau. The conspirators were not punished and Tanaka's government resigned. It was a victory for irresponsible military officers and for the army's independent political power. Ibid., pp. 322-23.

By all means, the positive foreign policy of Japan inhered imperialistic designs. Prime Minister Tanaka made no bones when he declared that in the region of Manchuria and eastern Mongolia, Japan had 'special interests' and hence while Japan would have nothing to do with the on-going revolution and counter-revolution in China, it would at no cost shirk her duty to maintain peace and order in the eastern part of China.[11] The problem before the Japanese leaders was now to strike a beneficial compromise between Chinese nationalist aspirations and Japanese colonial interests. Since the Chinese government could not punish the assassins of Chang Tso-lin, the disgruntled elements in power sought to revive their military diplomacy. Hence, after the exit of Prime Minister Tanaka in July 1929, the course of Japanese foreign policy "was under the constant and increasing threat of extreme militarists and of a general staff that was unable or unwilling to restore discipline in its own service or to permit the civilian wing of the government to take steps to that end."[12]

Japan's Monroe Doctrine: Rise of New Japanism on the Warpath

The weak trend of democratism saw its eventual replacement by that of militarism in Japanese politics after the exit of Tanaka ministry in 1929. The army leaders with open and concealed support of the industrialists, the aristocrats and the peasants leaned towards the autocratic ideals and methods of the Fascists by repeatedly challenging the civilian authorities operating the vulnerable system of parliamentary democracy. The internal struggle for power between the liberal politicians and the ambitious army leaders went on uninterruptedly with the extremists attempting to intimidate the civilian authorities by means of propaganda and terrorism. The prime instrument of the militarists was war and they knew it well that to precipitate conflicts abroad

---

11. The manifesto of the Japanese cabinet adopted on 9 July, 1929 said: "Our government not only rejects a policy of aggression in any part of China but is prepared to render friendly aid to China for the attainment of the natural aspiration of China, but, it, of course, is the responsibility of the government to protect and preserve the legitimate rights and interests that are indispensable to Japan's existence and prosperity. The government believes that the Chinese people understand this fully." See H.B. Morse and H.F. MacNair: *Far Eastern International Relations* (New York: Houghton Mifflin Company, 1931), p. 772.
12. Clyde and Beers, op. cit., p. 327.

was always the best means of promoting temporary unity at home and increasing the influence of ultra-patriots and professional warriors. Thus, the resumption of Japanese aggression on the Asiatic mainland was engineered by the leaders of the army in search for land as well as glory and it was patently acquiesced in by the business groups interested in the spoils of the markets as well as by the zealous patriots devoted to the case of the glorification of their country. Hence, it is well pointed out that Japan's foreign wars since 1931 "have been less an instrument of national policy than weapons of domestic politics in the hands of the war lords."[13]

The invasion of Japan on Manchuria and then establishment of a puppet state with the name of Manchukuo there should be seen against this background.[14] Her withdrawal from the League of Nations in 1933 "created in the Far East a situation of growing tension."[15] After consolidating her conquest of Manchuria, she could well assert her position as a dominant power in the Far East. Now she could be capable of pursuing a forward policy based on the tenets of her 'special interests' and 'permanent interests' in the region sustained by her aspirations to be the sole guardian of peace and security in the Far East. Emboldened by the Manchurian adventure, a spokesman of the Japanese Foreign Office (Eji Amau) issued a policy statement towards China saying: "Japan would object as a matter of principle to any joint operations undertaken by foreign power even in the name of technical or financial assistance at this particular moment after Manchurian and Shanghai incidents are bound to acquire political significance. Undertaking of such nature, if carried through to the end, must give rise to complications.... Japan, therefore, must object to such undertakings as a matter of principle... Supplying China with war aeroplanes, building aerodromes in China, and detailing military instructors or military advisers to China or contracting a loan to provide funds for political uses would obviously tend to alienate friendly relations between Japan, China and other countries and to disturb peace and order in Eastern Asia. Japan will oppose such projects."

13. Schuman, op. cit., p. 618.
14. See Chapter 5.
15. Carr, op. cit., p. 242.

This important announcement, which came to be known as Japan's Monroe Doctrine, was forcefully repeated on subsequent occasions implying that in effect, henceforth, Japan alone would be the guardian of peace ad order in the Far East and also regard other countries of the region as her boroughs. Now the bellicose attitude of Japan, that had become one of the powerful factors in causing the failure of the World Disarmament Conference held at Geneva in 1932 and the breakdown of the International Economic Conference held at London in 1933, had its onward march in manifesting that this country had ridden roughshod over the reactions and assertions of the Western Powers. For instance, on 28 December, 1934, Japan exercised her privilege of giving two years' notice of her intent to denounce the Washington Naval Treaty of 1922 and also made it clear that at the new naval conference scheduled to be held at London in 1935 she would insist on naval parity with other powers. In the face of failure in making a new agreement, Japan withdrew from the London Conference and the treaty, which was signed on 25 March, 1936, by Britain, France and the United States, and became a set of death-grasp of naval limitations owing to the adherence of Japan and Italy. Consequently, the whole structure of international naval cooperation so assiduously constructed since the Washington Conference of 1922, collapsed. Instead, the naval race began which entailed ship construction and equipment, dock building, harbour dredging, and laying out of airfields from the Aleutians to the Mandated Islands.

Obviously, the political history of Japan after 1931 "is a history of extremist nationalism nurtured in a historically strong military tradition and directed by politically-minded, authoritarian military caste."[16] The success of the Manchurian expedition added to the weight of the demand for a stronger foreign policy and the activities of the ultra-nationalists became violent. They finished some leading political figures like former Finance Minister Inouye Junnosuke and Prime Minister Inukai in 1932 that entailed the resignation of the Seiyukai cabinet—the last vestige of party government. The new leaders stressed the point that Japan must establish her hegemony in Asia and follow a policy of 'Asia for the Asiatics' that alone could solve the problem of their search for

---

16. Clyde and Beers, op. cit., p. 366.

security. This policy implied that China be forced to recognise the puppet state of Manchukuo; her economic and military dependence on Western powers be terminated; and the country be brought into full cooperation with Japan for the good of both the countries.

From Glory to Grave : Militarism on the Path of War

It is true that Britain and the United States did not appreciate the Japanese Monroe Doctrine, yet they did nothing to thwart the ambitious claims of the Japanese rulers on account of their adherence to the course of appeasement of the aggressor with the long-range aim of effecting their collision eventually with the Red Empire of Stalin. Hence, nothing was done to prevent the further disintegration of China. With a resolve to finish China, Japan made an attempt to separate its northern provinces from the rest of the country. Although her efforts could not make headway on account of timely resistance of the Chinese, the local Japanese leaders were to set up a puppet government there under the name of East Hopei autonomous government. Attempts were also made by Japan to injure the Chinese finance by encouraging smuggling on a very large scale. On 25 November, 1936, Germany and Japan signed the Anti-Comintern Pact which Italy joined a year after followed by Hungary, Manchukuo and Franco's Spain.[17] "The war-lords of the

---

17. It consisted of a public declaration of three articles by the first of which the two Powers agreed to exchange information on the activities of the Comintern and to collaborate in preventive measures. They agreed in the second to jointly invite Third States 'where internal peace was threatened by the subversive activities of Communist International to adopt defensive measures in the spirit of this agreement, as to take part in the present agreement'. By the third article the Pact was to run for five years with provision for renewal. This public declaration was accompanied by a secret addendum also composed of three articles. The first of these provided that should either of the signatories become the object of an unprovoked attack or unprovoked threat of attack by the USSR, the other would do nothing which would have the effect of relieving the position of the USSR, while both would consult on the measures to be taken for the safeguard of their common interests. By the second article the two contracting Parties declared that except by mutual consent, they would not conclude any political treaties with the Soviet Union, which were not conformable to the spirit of the secret agreement, while this was in force. By the third article the secret agreement became operative at the same time as the public one and for the same period of five years.

Rising Sun thus befuddled the Western Powers and won political allies for despoiling them of their empires."[18]

In July, 1937 Japan made many advances into the Chinese territory that amounted to the prosecution of an undeclared war. A clash between Japanese and Chinese troops not far from Peking led to further incidents. Peking was evacuated and the Chinese, still resisting, were gradually driven back to the line of the Yellow River, while naval and air forces attacked Shanghai. By the end of the year Japan had captured Nanking. Aerial bombardment inflicted great slaughter on the defenceless multitudes. In the northwest of China they had controlled most of the Suiyuan. Alarming incidents occurred repeatedly. On 9 August, 1937, a Japanese naval officer and a seaman had been killed on ignoring, as the Chinese alleged, a warning not to approach the military aerodrome. A member of the Chinese Peace Preservation Corps was stated to have been shot by this officer. However, the immediate cause of hostilities was the arrival of large force of Japanese warships which had been ordered to Shanghai before this incident. In this adventure Japan succeeded and by the end of the year Nanking was under their occupation and the Yangtse under their control from Wuhu to the sea. Obviously, "though war was not then or indeed at any time officially declared, it may be considered for all practical purposes to have begun."[19]

The victim of the Japanese aggression (China) looked towards the League of Nations and, as had already happened in the case of the Manchurian crisis, nothing could be gained by her in this case as well. In September 1937, China appealed to the League invoking Articles 10, 11 and 17 of the Covenant. The matter was reported to the Far Eastern Advisory Committee which reported that the military operations carried on by Japan were out of all proportions to the incident that had occasioned the conflict; it was also in violation of the terms of the Nine-Power Treaty of 1922 and the Kellogg-Briand Pact of 1928. The League adopted this report on 6 October, 1937, with a resolution saying: "Members of the League should refrain from taking any action which might have the effect of weakening China's power of resistance, and should also consider how far they can individually extend aid to China." Under these

---

18. Schuman, op. cit., p. 622.
19. G.M. Gathorne-Hardy: *A Short History of International Affairs, 1920-39*, p. 333.

circumstances, it was hardly likely, however, that any utterance by the League "would be anything more than a *brutum fulmen*."[20]

Since the League failed to do the needful in this matter, the other workable option could be discovered in convening a meeting of the members of the Nine-Power Treaty that would also include the United States. In November 1937, the conference in the form of a promising expedient was held at Brussels without the attendance of Japan. Though the Soviet Union was no party to the Nine-Power Treaty, she accepted an invitation to take part in the deliberations. "But it was soon evident that the time had passed, if it had ever existed, when any of the nations concerned were prepared to go further than words in resistance to aggression, unless their own vital interests appeared to be directly involved. The Brussels Conference consequently produced nothing more useful than a reaffirmation of general principles, while its failure in this respect was one more notice to aggressors that they had nothing to fear from outside parties, whether alone or in combination, whose separate interests were not clearly endangered. It was perhaps significant that the adherence of Italy to the Anti-Comintern Pact between Germany and Japan, which converted the Berlin-Rome Axis into a Berlin-Rome-Tokyo triangle, took place on 6 November, while the Brussels Conference was in session."[21]

The military leaders had their full hand when the Emperor appointed Prince Konoe Fumimaro as the head of the new ministry

---

20. Ibid., p. 334.
21. Ibid. The Brussels Conference adopted a declaration on 15 November 1937. It rejected the Japanese view that the matter should be left to direct settlement between the combatants. It held that if Japan persisted in her refusal to cooperate, the States represented here should consider as to what would be their common attitude. But the net result went against the victim (China) by indirectly inciting the aggressor (Japan) to go ahead with her advances. It is well remarked: "It was rather worse than useless since it served only to irritate Japan without affording any concrete help to China. On 24 November the Conference adjourned *sine die* in order to allow time for the participating governments to exchange views and further explore all peaceful methods by which a just settlement of the dispute may be attained consistent with the principle of the Nine-Power Treaty and in conformity with the objectives of that Treaty. The Brussels Conference was more than a fiasco, it was a disaster. It contributed to the ruin of such chance as existed in 1937 of restoring peace between Japan and China." F.C. Jones : *Japan's New order in East Asia : Its Rise and Fall, 1937-1945*, (London: Oxford University Press, 1954), p. 55.

in 1937. On 3 November, 1938, he declared his plan of creating 'a new order in East Asia,' as the immutable policy and determination of Japan.' The actual terms that Japan intended to exact were released by Foreign Minister Arita in a report to the Privy Council on 29 November, 1938, laying down:
1. China would recognise the State of Manchukuo.
2. A Sino-Japanese military alliance would be concluded against the Comintern in furtherance of which Japanese troops would be stationed in Inner Mongolia and North China.
3. China would contribute to the upkeep of such forces.
4. Japan would exercise the right of supervision over Chinese land and water communications and would cooperate in the improvement and adjustment of the Chinese military and police forces.
5. Special zones of Sino-Japanese collaboration would be established in North China in the Yangtse basin and in certain islands along the South China coast.
6. Japan would control the exploitation of raw materials needed for national defence especially in Inner Mongolia and North China.
7. The Chinese currency, tariff and the maritime customer service would be reorganised to promote trade between Japan, Manchukuo and China.

The final paragraph of this important note said: "Japan at present is devoting her energy to the establishment of a new order based upon genuine international justice throughout East Asia.... It is the firm conviction of the Japanese government that in the face of the new situation fast developing in East Asia, any attempt to apply to the conditions of today and tomorrow inapplicable, ideas and principles of the past neither would contribute towards the establishment of a real peace in East Asia, nor solve the immediate issue."[22] It is clear that the whole purpose was to bring stability and coordination under Japanese leadership between Japan, Manchukuo and other occupied portions of China. In fact, it meant "Japanese hegemony in that region."[23]

The new policy had the long-range aim of bringing the whole of South-East Asia under the control of Japan's scheme of Greater

---

22. Ibid., pp. 78-79.
23. Ibid., p. 78.

East Asia Co-Prosperity Sphere. Its hardcore meaning grew soon evident as Japan started destroying all non-Japanese foreign business in China. In June 1939, Japan blockaded the British and French concessions at Tientsin, publicly stripping and searching foreigners as they entered or left the concessions. Even Germany, Japan's new partner, did not escape injury as the Japanese destroyed the West's economic interests in occupied parts of China. The aim of following such a policy was that Japan would be able to secure her political and economic interests. Hence, it is observed: "Japanese expansion into China and subsequently into South-East Asia was rooted in deep-seated feelings of insecurity. In a situation of great social and economic crisis, Tokyo's military leadership won popular support for the theory that Japan, despite a half-century of growth in her international status, was threatened by ever-growing crises."[24]

Since Japan "was haunted by its fears of population pressure, political discrimination and economic integrity, and determined to take whatever action seemed to be required for self-defence, she would strike out towards Siberia, deeper into China, or in the direction of the South Seas wherever the opposition seemed weakest."[25] China became the initial target. In 1938 and 1939 Japanese military victories in China continued with occasional ups and downs. Naturally, many attempts made by Japan aroused the protests of the Western Powers and did much danger to foreign property and trading interests. It became a patent reality that Japan

---

24. Clyde and Beers, op. cit., p. 372. As F.C. Jones comments : "Her assiduous copying of the West, especially in military and industrial techinque, had been stimulated in the main by fears of invasion and conquest by one or more of the Western Powers. In later years she had been at one with the rest of Asia in the demand for the recognition of racial equality and in her resentment at the barriers to Asiatic immigration imposed by the US and the British dominions. Since 1920 this sense of kinship with the rest of Asia had been strengthened by the abrogation of the Anglo-Japanese Alliance, by the American Immigration Act of 1924, and through the gradually deepening rift between Japan and her former allies and friends. In the early thirties this trend was greatly accentuated by the great depression and its aftermath of increasing trade barriers, by the Manchurian controversy, with subsequent Japanese withdrawal from the League of Nations, and by the breakdown of the Washington Conference agreements of 1921-22. All these events increased the Japanese sense of isolation and insecurity, conscious as they were of the great inferiority of their economic resources to those of the United States, the British Commonwealth and the USSR." op. cit., p.3.
25. C.A. Buss : *Asia in the Modern World* (New York : Macmillan, 1964), p. 401.

was bent upon converting China as a whole into her Manchukuo without bothering for the resentment of the Chinese people and the reactions of the Western Powers.[26] "As the Japanese stripped, insulted and slapped British subjects in the presence of Chinese (to impress the latter with the new importance of Japan), and advanced challengingly close to Hong-Kong, the British enlarged their credit advances to China and warned Tokyo of the future consequences of its acts. As the property of the United States was being destroyed through Japanese air attacks in various parts of China, Washington gave the required six months' notice of its intention to terminate the United States and Japanese Treaty of Amity and Commerce that had provided Japan with its much needed United States market and supplies. In Japan itself prices rose steadily, consumers' goods began to run short, and casualty lists mounted, nevertheless the military leaders ordered further tightening of the people's belts and persisted in their conviction that the new order in Asia was close at hand."[27]

In the later part of 1939 Japan played fast and loose with her foreign commitments in respect of honouring the territorial integrity of China and protecting the property and interests of the Western Powers like the United States and Britain. Though the Japanese warlords continued to make reassuring statements as to their intentions with regard to foreign interests, the military, who were obviously the controlling factor, used very different language, some of this speaking openly of a purpose 'to sweep from China the influence of Britain'. It was, therefore, deeply felt by Britain that the

---

26. Prince Konoe declared that 'Japan's one course is to beat China to her knees so that she may no longer have the spirit to fight'. In December 1937, he authorised the German ambassador to China (Dr. Trautmann) to present four points as the basic conditions for the solution of the affair:
    1. China to abandon her pro-Communist and anti-Japanese and anti-Manchukuo policies in their anti-Communist and anti-Comintern policy,
    2. Establishment of de-militarised zones in the necessary localities and of a special regime for said localities,
    3. Conclusion of an economic agreement between China, Japan and Manchukuo, and
    4. China to pay necessary indemnities.
    See C.A. Buss: *War and Diplomacy in Eastern Asia* (New York : Macmillan, 1941), p. 153.
27. Langsam, op. cit., p. 274.

forward policy of Japan "constituted such a menace to her vital interests as to render interference desirable, if only it were possible."[28] The ambitious warlords went on unrestricted in their advance marches and as a result of his forward policy Japan joined hands with Fascist Italy and Nazi Germany in causing the outbreak of the Second World War. In the appalling bloodshed which ensued, the invaders of Japan took city after city and province after province of China without caring for the fact that they had aroused the slumbering masses of this country to fierce patriotism. By the close of 1940, the Chinese war had become part of World War II and its outcome was clearly contingent upon the fortunes of battle in Africa, Europe and the Atlantic.[29]

Concluding Observations

A critical account of the Japanese foreign policy and diplomacy during the inter-war period, as contained in the preceding sections, leaves these strong impressions:

1. Japan is the first of the Asian countries to be influenced by the current of modern nationalism sustained and strongly flavoured by her traditional beliefs and practices. Beginning in the later part of the last century, the new leaders of Japan could build up a highly centralised political and economic order with all the trappings of nationalism and militarism that ascribed to their state the character of an autocratic system. They combined their policy of all loyalty to the Emperor with their policy of military adventurism so as to make their country a major power in the Far East that would eventually become a major power of the world. That is, by building up with all possible speed a strong central government based on industrial and military power, Japan could protect her sovereignty and gain recognition as a major power. "But in this process, the relatively mild type of state nationalism of the nineteenth century turned into virulent integral nationalism—once the safety-valve of expansionism had been opened."[30]

2. Though a victor like Britain, France and the United States, Japan became a disgruntled power like Italy as a result of the

---

28. Gathorne-Hardy, op. cit., p. 335.
29. Schuman, op. cit., p. 626.
30. Hilary Conroy, op. cit., p. 829, Also see Palmer and Perkins: *International Relations*, 1957 ed., p. 494.

agreements made at Paris and Washington Conferences. The Japanese were doomed to bitter disappointment by what they considered as the unfairness of the settlement at Versailles. The Washington Conference agreements frustrated Japan's dreams of controlling China and establishing itself as the dominant naval power in the Pacific. Japan's forward march was temporarily halted, and the world was relieved for a decade from the fear of general war which might result from recurrent conflicts in East Asia."[31]

3. Owing to this, shortly after the conclusion of the Washington agreements in 1922, the American-Japanese relations blew hot and cold. And though Japan signed the Kelogg-Briand Pact of 1928, her imperialistic designs became a patent reality after 1931 which had their first manifestation in the rape of Manchuria. In the face of an attitude of appeasement shown by the great Western Powers, the Japanese "considered their military venture as sound business, shrewd politics, sturdy patriotism and far-seeing statesmanship. Japanese military authorities took over the function of civil government in Manchuria and the operation of all radio stations, electric lights and power plants, coal mines, railways and the postal administration. Then the Japanese gave the world an unparalleled demonstration of the art of creating a puppet state."[32]

4. Unfortunately, the League of Nations failed in fulfilling its mission due to the wrong policy of the major Western Powers. The USSR could do nothing in the face of the appeasement policy being pursued by the great Western Powers that had its implicit aim of destroying the Communist State by the onslaught of the Fascist powers. The events of formation of the Rome-Berlin-Tokyo axis and the signing of the Anti-Comintern Pact were appreciated by the followers of the appeasement policy.[33] The authors of this

---

31. C.A. Buss, op. cit., p. 309.
32. Ibid., p. 382.
33. As H.M. Vinacke says: "An apparently fixed element in Japanese policy was that embodied in the Anti-Comintern Agreement with Germany and Italy of hostility to Communism and thus to Russia. The Agreement not only attached Japan to the Axis, thus giving her friends in Europe, but presented Russia with a two-front military dilemma and thus gave Japan what she needed, assurance against direct Russian action against her in the Far East." *A History of the Far East*, p. 611.

strategy could not take into account the fact that such a move could become counter-productive in the long run. The murderous assaults of Japan on China dragged on through dark and bloody years of the late 1930s and finally became a part of the Second World War.

Consequently the path of glory became the path of grave. Japanese nationalism was subverted by the force of militarism. The replacement of the shaky parliamentary democracy by traditional authoritarianism converted the 'positive' foreign policy of Hara and Shidehara into an aggressive adventurism. The imperialistic ambitions of Japan became a patent reality when her Foreign Minister (Arita) publicly declared in June 1940: "The countries of East Asia and the region of South Seas are geographically, historically, racially and ethnically very closely related to each other. They are destined to cooperate and minister to one another's needs for the common well-being and prosperity and to promote the peace and progress of their regions... Japan has responsibility as the stabilising force in East Asia."[34] When the United States suffered at the hands of Japanese aggression, President F.D. Roosevelt told the Congress on 15 Decemeber, 1941, that Japanese statesmen "talked of the 'new order in East Asia' and then the 'Co-Prosperity Sphere in Greater East Asia'. What they really intend is the enslavement of every nation within their power, and the encirclement, not of all Asia, not even of the common people of Japan, but of the warlords, who have seized control of the state."[35] Consequently, Japan herself invited the unfortunate situation entailing her downfall and destruction in a couple of following years.

---

34. See Alfred Crofts and Percy Buchanan: *A History of the Far East* (Bombay: Allied Pacific Private Ltd., 1958), p. 398.
35. Ibid.

13

CHINA

International cooperation has been a thorn in the Chinese flesh to the extent that it has usually meant cooperation of all the other nations as opposed to China in the conduct of diplomatic negotiations, in the actual carrying out of institutions, and in the imposing of Treaty settlements. The Powers would always support one another, knowing full well that a concession to anyone meant a concession to everyone through the operation of the most favoured clause. China had no opportunity to play both ends against the middle or to play one nation against another in the interest of selfish advantage.

—**Claude A. Buss**[1]

An account of the role of China in international politics during the inter-war period is both perplexing and interesting—perplexing because of rampant factionalism and strife in the ranks of the ruling warlords and politicians and interesting because of the role of some great leaders in converting this mighty land of the 'opium eaters' into a magnificent nation of the Far East. In the post-World-War I period China could not play a vigorous role on account of her domestic constraints and compulsions caused by a series of conflicts between the 'phantom warlord government' at Peking and the insurgent revolutionary government at Canton which under the leadership of Dr. Sun Yat-sen's Kuomintang (Chinese Nationalist Party) could formalise new nationalism of China at Peking after 1927. The prevailing conditions provided ample opportunities of her exploitation by the imperialists of Britain, United States and Japan. Though a socialist state, the Soviet Union sought to play a similar game in her own interest. It is, therefore, well commented:

---

1. C.A. Buss: *War and Diplomacy in Eastern Asia* (New York : Macmillan, 1941), p. 18.

"The China that emerged from the catastrophe of World War I was a paradox of indescribable chaos and of a magnificent rebirth.... Between the two political forces (one government at Peking and the other at Canton) and within each there were crusades of factionalism, duplicity, civil war and massacre. And between all of these and the foreign powers, there were intrigue and conspiracy in a battle for position, influence and control in the China that would emerge."[2]

Feudalism Versus Modernism: New Cultural Movement and the Leadership of Sun Yat-sen

For this reason, a background study of Chinese domestic politics becomes relevant in order to understand her foreign policy and diplomacy in the period following World War I. The revolution of 1911 had dealt a fatal blow to the principles upon which central authority had been based since long. Under the leadership of Yuan Shih-kai local armies had been permitted to swell on the theory that China's military power was thereby enhanced. Naturally, it bolstered local leadership often in opposition to the central government. The governor of the province of Shansi (Yen Hsi-shan) started a land reform movement by denouncing feudal gentry for their oppression of the peasantry and laying stress on imparting knowledge of science and technology. It smacked of the rise and growth of the trend of modernisation of China having its first manifestation in the New Cultural Movement that rested on the search for the intellectual underpinnings of a modern China.

One very important factor that played its part in the determination of China's role in international politics at this stage was the tussle going on between the forces of progressive right on the one extreme and the ultra-left on the other. While the former reflected the forces of modest reaction against the Confucian order, the latter represented the new forces of revolutionary reconstruction on the lines of Marxian socialism. While old-style scholars like Yen Fu and Hu Shih represented the former, Chen Tu-hsiu and Li Ta-chao represented the latter and subsequently got the credit of being the founders of the Marxist study groups. That is, while the former subscribed to the liberal line of John Dewey, the latter adhered to the radical line of Lenin and, hence, while the former preferred the

---

2. Paul H. Clyde and B.F. Beers: *The Far East : A History of Western Impacts and Eastern Responses* (New Delhi: Prentice-Hall of India, 1977), p. 330.

course of evolutionary change, the latter dismissed gradualism and instead the only radical solutions would serve the purpose of Chinese nationalists. The case of the latter became very strong when a Soviet representative (Adolph Joffe) arrived in Peking in August 1922. Curiously, both inspired by the trend of modernisation and the line of distinction between the two could be discerned in their preference for the pace of change with or without pursuing the line of Marxism. All pioneers of this movement held the view that Confucianism was dead and all its vestiges should be uprooted. "It was China, not her culture, that must be saved."[3]

Thus began the movement for the creation of a modern and nationalist China. The young students became the revolutionary agents of this movement. Despite some differences in their viewpoints, all sections of the young people asserted one point—"China was to be unified, to be relieved of the 'unequal treaties' which infringed her sovereignty, and to become the seat of new civilisation."[4] Under these conditions, the KMT (Kuomintang) whose members were bound by the ties of personal loyalty to Sun Yat-sen, got immense popularity and made its bid for power. Reference should, therefore, be made at this stage to the role of Sun who could successfully unite the tradition of Western liberalism with his philosophy of 'people's livelihood' that looked like a vague appreciation of Socialism sans Marxism. In 1922, a workable synthesis could be established between the thoughts of Sun and the Soviet representative Joffe who was engaged in establishing a rapport between the Peking regime and the Kuomintang as per instructions from Moscow. Clyde and Burr aptly comment: "Sun declared that neither communism nor the Soviet system was suitable for China, while Joffe, concurring in this view, assured Sun of Russian sympathy and support in the achievement of China's most pressing needs—national unifications and full independence. The Chinese Communist Party, which had been founded in Shanghai during the summer of 1921, pledged support to the Kuomintang, and Communists as individuals were permitted to join Sun's forces."[5]

3. Ibid., p. 332.
4. Ibid., p. 333.
5. Ibid., p. 334.

The Sun-Joffe alliance was like a marriage of convenience with selfish motives on both sides. While the Communists of Russia and China sought to create avenues for their entry into the KMT so as to eventually capture it, Sun adhered to his strategy of cashing capital out of any workable alliance in capturing power at home so as to repudiate all vestiges of imperial hold over his country. He knew it well that since he had a massive following of 150,000 members and the Communists were about 300 in number and 'youngsters' too, his hold over his party would remain unassailable. The arrival of another Soviet adviser (Michael Borodin) in 1923 in China also failed to deter him for such a reason.[6] The position of Sun was further strengthened when his trusted man Chiang Kai-shek took command of the army of the KMT. In 1924, Sun enunciated his basic manifesto setting the frame for future relationship between his party and government having three essential principles:

1. The first principle was *Min-tsu chu-i*, meaning people's nationhood or nationalism. In its original form it had held simply that the Manchus be ousted. But during the days of first Great War it also meant something more covering all points that would add to the solidarity of the Chinese people as a nation. Thus, in its revised form, it signified unity amongst all as Chinese, Manchus, Mongols, Tibetans and the minorities. And though Sun very carefully avoided the case of spelling out all implications of this

---

6. About the nature of partnership between Sun and Borodin, G.F. Hudson makes a fine observation: "A new element was introduced into the situation when Sun Yat-sen on his return to Canton in 1923 brought with him the Russian Communist Borodin to be political adviser to the Canton government. Thus began the four years' partnership of the Kuomintang and the Communist International, a marriage of convenience in which each side hoped, first to make use of and then to cheat, the other. The Kuomintang was primarily a party of the bourgeoisie; it was reformist and nationalist, but not Marxist. It aimed at reuniting China, at modernising the civil administration, and giving it a proper control over the army, at sweeping away the paraphernalia of an antiquated officialdom and liberating the productive forces of the country for the rapid development which was required for China's national resurgence but all on sound capitalist lines. The dictatorship of the proletariat was the last thing desired by the bankers, merchants, and contractors who gave financial banking to the party." *The Far East in World Politics: A Study in Recent History* (London: Oxford University Press, 1939), p. 214.

term, he laid stress on its sternly anti-imperialistic tone and character.

2. The second principle was *Min-chuan chu-i*, meaning people's power or democracy allowing no place for monarchy, even of a limited type. Its implications were manifold as they covered the tenets of Western republicanism, Swiss institutions of direct democracy as initiative, referendum and recall, democratic centralism of Russia as established by Lenin, and the Chinese maxims of examination and control. The last one was a typical feature of Chinese historical tradition implying tutelage of the leaders before being in power.

3. The third principle was *Min-sheng chu-i*, meaning people's livelihood or a crude form of socialism without any touch of Marxism. Sun openly and frankly reflected the Marxist tenets of economic determinism and class war and instead appreciated Mill's theory of economic rent implying taxation on unearned increments and socially- created values. He also appreciated the role of private capital in the reconstruction of economy and polity. In March 1925, Sun died, but his death "gave him a recognised status in China as the patron-saint of Chinese nationalism; and his name became a symbol of the national revolt against foreign control."[7]

Reactions to Peace Settlement : Emergence of Assertive Nationalism in China

While the Chinese people were engaged in bringing about their internal revolution after 1911, the foreign powers were engaged in expanding their political and economic hold over this country. The Treaty of Portsmouth (1905) had put Japan in a predominant position in the Far East. Moreover, while the Western powers were

---

7. Carr: *International Relations between the Two World Wars, 1919-1939* (London: Macmillan, 1952), p. 157. As a guide for his people, Sun "evolved his doctrine of the three stages of development: military rule, political tutelage, and constitutional government. The nationalism which Sun coveted was modern in pattern but devoid of imperialism and other excesses which marked Western nationalist movements; and it was based upon traditional Chinese virtues such as loyalty, filial piety, harmony and peace, and wholly compatible with internationalism." N.D. Palmer and H.C. Perkins: *International Relations: World Community in Transition* (Boston: Houghton Mifflin Company, 1957), p. 495.

seeking economic concessions in China and were investing their capital in railways and other undertakings, Japan was busy in effectuating territorial expansion. Already Japan had pushed China out of Korea. Apprehending a dangerous move from the side of Japan, China on 3 August, 1914, approached the United States to endeavour to obtain the consent of the belligerent European nations to an understanding not to engage in hostilities either in Chinese territory and marginal waters or in adjacent territories. However, considering that China's territorial integrity was vital to American interests, the Secretary of State (William J. Bryan) approached the European belligerents on an even more ambitious scheme "designed to neutralise the entire Pacific Ocean as well as China, and its adjacent water." Undeterred by any reaction of this kind, Japan presented a set of 21-Demands to China on 18 January, 1915, which, if accepted would have converted the latter into a vassal state of the former.[8]

At the Paris Peace Conference (1919) the Chinese delegates put forth their own claims. They sought to regain complete control over Shantung province made between Japan and China in 1915 and 1918 on the ground that their country had signed the agreement under conditions of threat. They also expressed the hope that in the spirit of Wilsonian idealism all limitations upon her sovereignty should be relinquished. But nothing could happen to their satisfaction. By the terms of peace embodied in Articles 156, 157 and 158 of the Treaty of Versailles, Japan acceded to the German position in Shantung, acquired under the agreements of 1858, and subsequent agreements including the lease-hold of Kiachow Bay and the economic rights enjoyed in the province. This succession was conditioned by a verbal promise given by the 'Council of the Three' that Japan would restore to China by direct negotiations all political rights in the province, retaining for herself only economic rights and privileges. China was relieved of all responsibility for the fulfilment of her obligations to Germany under the terms of the Boxer Protocol; she regained control of the German concession at Tientsin an Hankow; she was confirmed in her possession of the public properties of the German government in China, except those of diplomatic and consular character; and she secured the

---

8. See Chapter 12.

restitution of the astronomical instruments taken from Peking at the time of the Boxer rebellion.

Naturally, as the Chinese delegates tried to express their opposition to the award by signing the treaty with reservations as to the Shantung clauses, they were denied the right to sign the document with their dissenting notes. They left the Peace Conference empty-handed. An outwitted and betrayed China gave herself over in bitterness to a more violent and aggressive form of nationalism. As C.A. Buss comments: "The Chinese were so angry at their shabby treatment at the hands of the Allies that they refused to sign the Treaty of Versailles, although China became a member of the League of Nations by virtue of signing the Treaty of St. Germain with Austria."[9]

As a matter of fact, the claims of the Chinese leaders were not appreciated by any major power dominating the scene of deliberations at the Paris Peace Conference. The European allies as well as Japan looked upon the claims of the Chinese delegates with fear and suspicion as they felt that China was not really concerned with the problem of making peace with Germany and that she wanted to use this occasion to free China from her feudal and semi-colonial status. To the statesmen of the traditional and conservative school, this purpose was alarming inasmuch as it implied not only an attack upon Japan's 'special interests' but also upon the larger system of influence and the 'unequal treaties', in general, to which all the victorious Great Powers were parties.[10] Curiously, in addition to the mistrust of Japan, England and France "were further aroused because both before and during the peace Conference Wang and

---

9. Buss, op. cit., p. 27.
10. During the nineteenth century the Great Powers had imposed on China the so-called 'unequal treaties' by which China conceded a number of 'special privileges' to subjects of these Powers living and trading in the Chinese territory. Of these special privileges, two were of outstanding importance. Firstly, the Chinese customs tariff on imports and exports was limited by agreement to a maximum of five per cent. Secondly, the Great Powers enjoyed extra-territorial jurisdiction in China. Their nationals were not subject to Chinese law or to Chinese courts, and paid no Chinese taxes except such as were levied indirectly. Cases in which a foreigner was concerned either as accused or as defendant, were tried by judges of his own nationality under his own national law. Moreover, China had agreed to set aside in all the principal ports areas for foreign residence; and in several of the ports these areas had developed into 'concessions' and 'settlements' under foreign

Koo (leaders of the Chinese delegation) set out systematically to cultivate the sympathy and enlist the support of the American delegation which, in turn, was not loath to give the Chinese the encouragement they desired."[11]

While the Paris Peace Conference left China in a condition of utmost dissatisfaction, the consequences of the Washington Disarmament Conference (1922) were rather satisfying to her. Vide the terms of a treaty signed by 9 Powers (U.S., Britain, France, Japan, Italy, Belgium, the Netherlands, Portugal and China) the signatories pledged themselves to respect the sovereignty, independence and territorial and administrative integrity of China; to maintain and advance the principle of equality and commercial opportunity in China, and not to take or support any action designed to create spheres of interests or to provide for the enjoyment of mutually exclusive opportunities in the designated parts of Chinese territory. Besides, a treaty was signed by China and Japan on 4 February, 1922, whereby Shantung was returned to China and Japan was permitted to retain control of the Tsinan-Tsingtao railway for 15 years.[12]

It is rightly said that the results of the Washington Conference marked an event of great success in establishing peace in the Far East. The US and Britain could put an effective check on Japan's motives towards China. That is, Japan was forced to abandon her sole war gain on the mainland of China so that the framework of its republicanism could be saved from collapse and China could offer effective resistance to the new imperial power of Japan and also to the 'contagion' of the Soviet Union that lurked beyond the long Sino-Russian frontier. They agreed to the revision of the Chinese tariff, to relinquish the post offices they had maintained on the Chinese soil for many years; they withdrew their forces from Siberia and terminated their control of the Chinese Eastern Rail-

---

municipal administrations. At other places there were 'leased territories' of considerable extent, the leases amounting to a virtual cession of sovereignty for a period of 99 years to the foreign Power concerned. Before the First World War, these privileges had been keenly resented by the younger generation of educated Chinese; and when, at the end of the war, Germany and Russia were deprived of their special rights in China, the agitation for the cancellation of the other 'unequal treaties' grew apace." E.H. Carr, op. cit., pp. 155-56.

11. Paul. H. Cylde: *The Far East* (New York: Prentice-Hall, 1948), p. 406.
12. See Chapter 11.

way. The US displayed renewed interest in China's integrity and took steps to loosen the Japanese grip upon her. The policy of equality of economic opportunity was restated and, for the first time, legally defined. In this way, China could have a limited achievement of what her delegates had claimed as the powers united against these demands could agree to the extent of taking certain steps towards the ultimate relinquishment of their privileges. As a result, the actions taken at Washington "did lead to partial satisfaction of Peking's aims."[13]

Partial Success in Diplomacy: Termination of the Soviet Influence
The deliberations of the Washington Conference had their result in favour of China in the sense that the various treaties signed on this occasion liberalised the colonial hold of major powers over China and also paved the way for their eventual liquidation in the face of growing tide of assertive nationalism prevailing in the country. Henceforth, the pace of partial success and failure continued. For instance, on 19 October, 1925, China and Austria signed a treaty confirming the war-time ending of the latter's extra-territorial rights in the former; then on 26 October, 1926 China and Finland negotiated a treaty as equals. But in many other important directions the point of success remained overshadowed by the point of intermittent setbacks. It is evident from the fact that several assurances given to China at the Washington Conference by the major powers remained unfulfilled on account of their evasive attitude as well as due to the conditions of civil war prevailing in the country. For instance, at the Washington Conference Britain had agreed to surrender Wei-hai-wei as a means of facilitating a Sino-Japanese settlement on Shantung and though an Anglo-Chinese commission took up this matter, nothing fruitful could materialise until 1930.

Difficulties over repayment of the Boxer indemnity delayed until 1925 the implementation of agreements reached at Washington to raise China's tariff to an effective 5 per cent *ad valorem* level, to return to China the Kwangchow leasehold, and to set up a commission to reconsider abolition of extra-territoriality. Since the commission failed to set a deadline for the abolition of extra-

---

13. Clyde and Beers, op. cit., p. 338.

territoriality amounting to the termination of foreign jurisdiction in China, it became another potent factor of disappointment to the zealous nationalists of China. The commission could not go beyond recommending that the concerned powers should cooperate in the progressive modification of their extra-territorial rights. The mood of resentment of the Chinese nationalists could not be assuaged by the recommendation of the tariff commission, given in October 1925, that China should not be accorded tariff autonomy until the end of 1928. The reason was that the leaders of China had been demanding immediate abolition of the conventional tariff along with all other 'unequal treaties'. As a result, Peking "became increasingly aggressive in its efforts to revise China's treaty structure, but with only minor success."[14]

The noticeable point, however, is that the pace of intermittent success and setback in Chinese diplomacy at this stage played its own part in sharpening the trend of violent nationalism that had its synchronisation with the call for anti-foreignism propagated and fomented by the Soviet representatives staying in China. For instance, in early 1924 Borodin stated: "I believe that China is so backward, so different, that it is sorely in need of the civilising influence of the more forward countries. It serves as a justification for what the foreigner does here, for extra-territoriality, foreign courts, secessions, the customs being in foreign hands, and for the foreigners assuming the role of protectors of the integrity of China and of its sovereignty. It allows foreign publications in Chinese and maliciously to vilify and slander public men. It gives the innumerable servants of foreign interests here the opportunity of threatening the labour classes as if they belonged to an inferior race."[15] As C.A. Buss comments: "These words were music for the ears of the Kuomintang which caught the anti-foreign sentiments of the people and utilised every trick of slogans, symbols and propaganda in the pursuit of its objectives. The Party platform endorsed the Peking Professors 'Rights Recovery Movement' which advocated that all former treaties should be cancelled (not revised) and replaced with new ones giving equal treatment."[16]

---

14. Ibid., p. 338.
15. See C.A. Buss, op. cit., pp. 34-35.
16. Ibid., p. 35.

The interest of Communist Russia in the affairs of China had begun to unfold itself in 1918 with the Karakhan Declaration that appeared to concede China's political rights in the Chinese Eastern Railway zone while reserving Russia's financial and economic interests there. Later in 1920, the Russian government made a gesture of friendship by declaring that all treaties or agreements made by the Tsar government with China were null and void. Soon after his arrival in Peking in 1922, Joffe not only restored diplomatic relations but also sought Peking's approval of the new 'independent' People's Revolutionary Government which the Russians had set up in Outer Mongolia in 1920. He also tried to regain a position of influence in the Chinese Eastern Railway. With Japan's withdrawal from Siberia in 1922, the way had been cleared for the adherence to the Soviet Union of the eastern Siberian regime known as the Far Eastern Republic. Under such conditions, Peking was in no position to rebuff further Russian overtures presented by L.M. Karakhan in September, 1923 as a result of which a treaty was signed by Karakhan and Wellington Koo on 31 May, 1924.[17] A similar agreement was negotiated with the war-lord of Manchuria (Chang Tso-lin) on 20 September, 1924, since the Chinese Eastern Railway lay in that territory. "In effect, as a result of hard bargaining, Moscow had reclaimed much of the Tsarist position in North-east Asia."[18]

The Soviet representative with sworn anti-British motives waited for the opportunity and exploited it by fomenting anti-foreign activities. The firing of a Chinese mob on 30 May 1925 in the Shanghai International Settlement resulting in the death of a Chinese in a Japanese-owned cotton mill and shortly thereafter a

---

17. This treaty provided for the resumption of formal relations between the two countries. Its important features were : surrender by Russia of the extraterrirorial rights and of concessions at Hankow and Tientsin, restoration of Russian legations and consulates and property of the Orthodox Church, Russian recognition of China's suzerainty in Outer Mongolia, and withdrawal of Russian troops. In addition, Russia recognised Chinese sovereignty in the Chinese Eastern Railway zone and agreed that China might redeem the line 'with Chinese capital' in return for Chinese pledges that the futher disposition of the line would be determined by China and Russia to the exclusion of the third parties, and that management of the road would be a joint Russo-Chinese concern.

18. Clyde and Beers, op. cit., p. 339.

shooting incident on 23 June causing death of 52 Chinese in the island of Shamean, a portion of Canton, provided a pretext for the boycott of all British and Japanese goods. The repercussions of these events were felt throughout the country. A widespread boycott directed mainly against the British followed, and the demands of the Chinese for the abolition of foreign privileges were urged with increased impatience and vehemence. "The incident forms, in fact, a landmark in the history Chinese international relations."[19]

By this time the violent nationalism of China had assumed a patently anti-British form. A general strike of industrial labour in the city of Wuhan in November 1926, took such a serious turn that Britain proposed that the Washington Conference Treaty powers should: (i) do what Canton was already doing by agreeing to immediate dcollection of the 'sur-taxes' ; (ii) recognise and deal with regional governments; (iii) implement a grant of tariff autonomy immediately upon China's promulgation of a national tariff, and (iv) seek to develop better relations with China even while no national government existed there. But such gesture of concessions, far from satisfying the Nationalists, "spurred them to new outbursts of fury. The British policy was described as a design to weaken China by creating regional governments and by encouraging militarists to seize the ports and to profit by collection of the proposed sur-taxes."[20] It appears that the British government now had the wisdom to come to terms with the rising tide of nationalism that was the only real force in China. A British minister rushed to Hankow to meet the Foreign Minister of the Nationalist Government which signified the first move of Britain towards recognition of the Chinese government and then the British Legation at Peking issued a Memorandum emphasising the sympathy of the British government with the Chinese nationalist movement.

In pursuance of such a pragmatic policy, in January 1927, the British abandoned their concessions in Hankow and Kiukiang and they were immediately taken over for administrative purposes by the Chinese. It had its own repercussions on the diplomacy of other concerned powers. Soon US and Japan expressed their sympathy

---

19. G.M. Gathorne-Hardy: *A Short History of International Affairs, 1920-1939* (London: Oxford University Press, 1950), p. 244.
20. Clyde and Beers, op. cit., p. 340.

for the 'just aspirations' of China and indicated their willingness to help their attainment in an orderly manner. But what came to the satisfaction of Britain was the end of the Soviet influence over China when the Nationalists captured the Nanking government and turned out all Russian Communists, including Borodin from their country. Chiang Kai-shek became the supreme leader of the country in July 1927. The sudden and dramatic end of Borodin's influence showed that "the alliance between the revolutionary internationalism of Moscow and the patriotic nationalism of the Kuomintang had always been to some extent artificial."[21]

The establishment of a strong government at Nanking under the leadership of Chiang brought about a definite change in the conduct of China's foreign relations. Soon it issued a declaration calling for new treaties to be negotiated with full regard for the sovereignty and equality of States. It was not pleasing to other major powers like the United States, Britain and Japan, and yet it became so on account of their perception of the reality of the situation and, more than that, on account of the termination of the influence of the communists acting at the behest of their Russian comrades. In pursuance of a pragmatic policy, the US signed a treaty with China at Peking on 25 July, 1928, whereby it conceded tariff autonomy to China subject to most favoured nation treatment. Soon it was followed by similar agreements with other powers. Some such treaties signed with Belgium, Denmark, Italy, Portugal and Spain contained provisions for the abolition of extra-territoriality subject to a similar concession by all the powers. Accordingly, on 27 April, 1929, the Nanking government sent notes to the US, Britain, France, Brazil, the Netherlands and Norway requesting abolition of extra-territoriality at the earliest possible date. And since China could gain nothing in spite of her appeal to the League of Nations, she went to the length of declaring in a unilateral fashion that extra-territoriality would come to an end by 1 January, 1930.

One important point that should be taken note of at this stage is that while all major powers of the West could understand the reality of the situation and thereby sought to modify their diplomacy towards China, Japan remained adamant and looked for satisfying

---

21. Carr, op. cit., p. 159.

China

her colonial hunger that was suppressed at the Washington Conference. Already Japan had made much gain when the Chinese had staged the boycott of British goods. But the establishment of a strong government at Nanking and improvement in Sino-British relations had reversed the situation that brought about a fundamental difference between British and Japanese perceptions. As Carr notes: "Great Britain, whose interests in China were purely commercial, sincerely desired an orderly and united country where trade could prosper. Japan, whose concern in her neighbour's affairs was above all political, preferred to see China weak, divided and incapable of contesting. In particular, Japan regarded with distaste any prospect of North China coming under the effective control of a central government."[22]

The achievements of Chinese diplomacy by this time have been thus summed up: "By 1931, in addition to terminating the treaty tariff and opening negotiations looking to the end of extra-territoriality, the Kuomintang nationalist government could claim other successes in whittling away foreign privileges; the Shanghai Municipal Council and Mixed Court, long the exclusive preserve of the foreigners, had been given a Chinese voice; Nanking had issued new law codes and secured new treaties placing some foreign nationals under Chinese jurisdiction; Chinese control had been established over the Maritime Customer Administration, the Salt Revenue Administration, and the Post Office; and foreign concession areas had been reduced from thirty-three to thirteen. These achievements of the Nanking' government's early years, 1927-30, seemed to promise that China was finding a new, matured stability, that the day of the war-lord was gone; that the Russian bid for control had failed; that the unequal treaty system would be ended by force plus diplomacy, and, finally, that Sun Yat-sen's programme for a new China was assured."[23]

Manchurian Crisis and After : Formation of the United Front against Japan in a Grim Struggle for Survival
It is true that China improved her position after the establishment of the Kuomintang-Nationalist government at Nanking. Now Chiang Kai-shek could be in a position to thwart the hold of the

---

22. Ibid., p. 160.
23. Clyde and Beers, op. cit., p. 341.

Communists what they termed 'counter-revolution'. The Soviet Union struggled to retain its as little hold over China as possible, while Japan came out with its activity of territorial aggrandizement. Naturally, Russia and Japan posed serious problems for China and while the former retraced after a few years, the latter pushed matters to the point of war that became a part of World War II in a short course of time. The region of Manchuria became the theatre of conflict. Already in 1929, Russia had posed a threat to the position of Japan in its northern part where the Nanking government could do nothing more than to bow to the terms Russia had imposed on Manchurian authorities. But southern part of Manchuria created a very serious situation owing to the intervention of Japan since the assassination of Chang Tso-lin by the Japanese conspirators in June 1928. In 1931, the crisis of Manchuria broke out and in the following year Japan could establish a puppet state there with the name of Manchukuo.[24] No foreign power came to the help of China in the event of naked aggression of Japan and when during 1934-35 Japan's Kwantung army attempted to set up with the name of East Hopei Autonomous Government, an autonomous State around Peking, the Kuomintang-Nationalist government "played a delicate game of appeasement, neither obstructing the Japanese completely nor conceding all they asked. To this point the Kuomintang's policy was to placate Japan."[25]

In the middle of the 1930s the government of China was confronted with the difficult problem of first setting its own house in order by dealing with the Communists before facing the aggression of Japan that was out to finish the 'Middle Kingdom'. After establishing the East Hopei Autonomous Government in the summer of 1935, the Japanese started illicit trade in this region partly to pile up their pockets with enormous profits and partly to sap the resources and efficiency of the Chinese administration. Strengthened partly by the appeasement policy of the Western Powers like Britain, France and the United States and partly by being a party to the anti-Comintern Pact (signed with Italy and Germany), Japan made a series of invasions on China in 1937 that amounted to the prosecution of an undeclared war. On the night of 7-8 July, 1937, Japanese troops clashed with the Chinese troops

---

24. See Chapter 5.
25. Clyde and Beers, op. cit., p. 353.

at the Marco Polo bridge near Peking. Soon after, the Japanese government demanded from China that all Chinese troops be immediately withrawn from North China; that all anti-Japanese propaganda be stopped forthwith; and that cooperation against the Communists be extended. Within a short time hostilities spread over the whole of North China resulting in the death of thousands of innocent people. By the end of 1937, the Japanese captured the city of Nanking and established a provisional puppet government in the ravaged city. The Chinese rulers shifted their capital to Hankow and then to Changking.

The demand for having a united front against Japan became very strong at this stage, though it had been simmering since 1931 when anti-Japanese societies were formed in Shanghai, Hankow, Nanking and certain other places. The liberal elements of the Kuomintang desired a united front, including the Communists, while its conservative elements still adhered to the way of crushing them. The Communist government established in Kiangsi in November 1931, under the leadership of Mao Tse-tung and Chu Teh also desired a united front, but they offered no concessions to other groups to make such a front possible and did not do so until directed by the Comintern. In the face of growing bitterness with Japan, Moscow supported the idea of a united front and then negotiations started between the Kuomintang and the Chinese Communist Party, but no headway could be made as Japan renewed hostilities in July 1937.

Thus, on 29 July, 1937, Chiang Kai-shek gave a stirring call to his countrymen urging them 'to fight to the finish as one man'. The Soviet Union, whose interests were also threatened in the Far East by Japan, drew closer to China and concluded on 21 August, 1937, a non-aggression pact. Then on 22 September, the Kuomintang government and the Chinese Communist Party entered into an agreement pledging these points:
1. The Communist Party shall strive for the realisation of Sun Yat-sen's three principles which answer the present-day need of China;
2. It shall abandon the policy of armed insurrection against the Kuomintang regime, the policy of red propaganda, and the policy of land confiscation;
3. It shall abolish the Soviet government and institute a system of democracy that the nation may be politically united; and

4. It shall abolish the Red Army as such and allow it to be incorporated into the National Army and placed under the command of the National Military Council. The Red Army, thus recognised, shall await orders to proceed to fight on the front.

Thus came to an end the phase of fight between the Nationalists and the Communists and their troops fought jointly to save the country from Japanese invasions.

The fight of the united front could impart a setback to the ambitions of Japanese leaders. Although the Japanese troops could capture the city of Nanking on 15 December, 1937, they felt that a check had been put on their zeal. Hence, Tokyo sought the mediation of Berlin and offered terms of peace through German ambassador posted in China (Dr. Trautmann) which Chiang declined to accept.[26] Fighting was resumed in the spring of 1938. The Japanese army occupied the island of Hunan in February, 1939 and after a month seized the Spratly Island. Japan made another appeal to China to surrender and escape further bloodshed, but again she met with a rebuff. In March 1940, Japan established a new puppet regime at Nanking under the leadership of Wang-Chang Wei who had been expelled from the Kuomintang in July 1939, for his half-hearted loyalty to the country. In November, 1940 Japan recognised this government as the legitimate government of China and entered into a number of agreements with it. By this time the Chinese war had become a part of the Second World War.

Concluding Observations

A critical account of the foreign policy and diplomacy of China during the inter-war period, as contained in the preceding sections, leaves these strong impressions:

1. China became a modern nation-state in the early phase of the present century when her negative nationalism took a positive turn whereby the attitude of hostility towards the Manchus alone was replaced by the hostility towards all foreign elements engaged in the exploitation and subjugation of this vast country. Credit for

---

26. The terms of peace demanded that China should repudiate Communism, terminate the non-aggression pact with the USSR, recognise the State of Manchukuo, pay the costs of war, and appoint Japanese advisers to conduct her administration.

this goes to the personality and leadership of Sun Yat-sen, the celebrated Father of the Chinese Republic, who gave a new shape to his country after the Revolution of 1911. And though the leaders of the Kuomintang under Chiang Kai-shek and of the Communist party under Mao Tse-tung and Chu Teh had serious differences on many counts, all subscribed to the ideology of Sun who described China as 'a heap of loose sand' that needed the cement of nationalism to bind it together and give it the strength without which the Chinese people could not hope to escape foreign domination or divisive internal strife.[27]

2. China could not pursue a vigorous policy in the period following World War I on account of domestic constraints and compulsions. Things changed when Chiang Kai-shek could establish his hold after expelling the communists, including the Russian advisers, from the Kuomintang in 1927. From this time till the outbreak of Manchurian crisis in 1931, China could assert herself as a result of which her diplomacy witnessed a series of successess in the midst of setbacks. No major power came to the rescue of China and Japan could convert the province of Manchuria into a puppet state of Manchukuo. The League of Nations failed to deter the ambitions of Japan and the deliberations of the Brussels Conference "offered no inducement to make peace and there was no thought of collective force if she refused. The Brussels effort was still-born.[28]

3. Chinese diplomacy during the 1930s is so inextricably linked with the diplomacy of Japan that a description of one becomes automatically the description of another. Hence, what has been said here looks like a repetition of what has been said in the previous chapter. The militarism of Japan bent upon finishing China found its counter-force in the militarism of China urging all countrymen 'to fight to the finish as one man'. It appears that "the single dominating pupose of resisting Japan coloured every phase of China's national development."[29]

4. Japanese advances into China's territory after the rape of Manchuria brought about some shift in the foreign policy of Britain and the United States. Though both were following the course of

---

27. Palmer and Perkins : *International Relations*, p. 495.
28. Clyde and Beers, op. cit., p. 380.
29. Buss, op. cit., p. 51.

appeasement of the aggressors so as to encourage them to have their collision eventually with Communist Russia, both were also concerned with their political and economic stakes in China. Britain foresaw a time when Japanese militarism would menace her vast possessions and interests in South and South-East Asia and the Western Pacific. This assessment ushered in a new British policy of benevolent neutrality that favoured China by giving her moral support and limited material aid without causing a breakdown in her relations with Japan.[30] American President Roosevelt took the view that the events of China were symptomatic of worldwide tendency towards militarism. His well-known 'quarantine speech' (October, 1937) suggesting the isolation of the aggressors represented a possibly new direction in American foreign policy. But the US declined to go any further either in preventing Japan or helping China. That is, she neither conceded the American principle of opposition, nor encouraged his subordinates to seek a settlement with Japan. Preoccupied with efforts to end the great depression, the US leaned heavily towards a political philosophy of pacifism and isolation.[31]

5. The Soviet Union came to the rescue of China on many occasions with her own political and economic interests.[32] The Soviet leaders were not satisfied with the leadership of Chiang Kai-shek who had staged a 'counter-revolution' in 1927 and thereafter put a heavy hand on the activites of the Communists in his country. The terms of the Anti-Comintern Pact of 1936 had combined the fascist forces of Germany, Italy and Japan and this axis was a source of great anxiety to the Soviet leaders. Therefore, they looked towards China and could gain success when the Kuomintang-Nationalists and the Communists formed a united front in 1937 following the conclusion of a non-aggression pact with China.

---

30. See L.S. Friedman: *British Relations with China, 1931-1939*, pp. 18-42.
31. Clyde and Beers, *op. cit.*, p. 379. Also see Dorothy Borg: *The United States and the Far Eastern Crisis of 1933-1938 : From the Manchurian Incident through the Initial Stage of the Undeclared Sino-Japanese War.*
32. As H.M. Vinacke observes: "It was the Soviet Union which gave the most extensive material support to China during the first two years (1937-39) of the second Sino-Japanese war. Russia also gave China strong diplomatic support at the Brussels Conference called to seek a basis of accommodation between China and Japan." *Far Eastern Politics in the Post-War Period* (London: George Allen and Unwin, 1956), p. 78.

They did it at the cost of making peace with Chiang Kai-shek as a desperate measure of diplomacy. Thus the war against Japan "resulted not only in maintenance but also in an extension of the concentrated authority of Chiang Kai-shek modified by the need for balancing the claims of various factions in order to preserve the necessary national unity."[33]

After the fall of Hankow in October 1938, the war in the Far East "began to assume almost as much the character of a struggle between the Western Powers and Japan as between Japan and China."[34] China was faced with the problem of her survival as Japan had made it very clear that as she would not be involved in the European affair, she would bend all efforts to settle the China affair.[35]

---

33. H.M. Vinacke: *A History of the Far East in Modern Times*, p. 598.
34. Ibid., p. 604.
35. Clyde and Beers, op. cit., p. 381.

14

MIDDLE EAST

Aside from its location as the bridge of three continents, the Near East is strategically important because of the oil deposits of the Arabian peninsula. Control over them is an important factor in the distribution of power, in the sense that whoever is able to add them to his other resources of raw materials adds that much strength to his own resources and deprives his competitors proportionately.

—Hans J. Morgenthau[1]

The term 'Middle East' refers to the whole region of West Asia covering countries from Turkey and Egypt to Iran and Afghanistan. Sometimes, a geographical distinction was made between 'Near East' comprising Greece, Bulgaria, Turkey, the Leavant and Egypt, and the Middle East made up of the Arabian peninsula, Iran, Iraq and Afghanistan. But in the present century this distinction lost its significance and the entire world of Muslim countries from Afghanistan in the east to Egypt in the west formed the Middle East or South West Asia region.[2] Three great religions of the world—Judaism, Christianity and Islam—originated in this region and for hundreds of years it remained an arena of conflicting

---

1. Morgenthau: *Politics among Nations: The Struggle for Power and Peace* (New York: Alfred A. Knopf, Inc., 1954), pp. 115-16.
2. "The term 'South-West Asia' is probably, although less widely, used than either 'Near East', to which Americans are accustomed, or 'Middle East', the favourite British designation, which Americans are beginning to use. There is some doubt whether, for example, Iran belongs to the 'Near East' or whether Turkey can be placed in the 'Middle East', But there is no doubt at all that both are in Southwest Asia, Even this more comprehensive designation can include Egypt, as it must, only by certain amount of geographic license." N.D. Palmer and H.C. Perkins: *International Relations: The World Community in Transition* (Boston: Houghton Mifflin Co., 1957), p. 474. So say W.C. Langsam and O.C. Mitchell: "To define the Middle East is not easy. For more than a

interests of the imperial powers of Europe like Britain, France, Russia and Germany. The great importance of this region lies in the fact that under the arid soil of some of its sections are hidden the greatest single reserve of oil nicknamed as the 'black gold of nations'. Besides, it has its own strategic significance. It has remained the hub of three continents—Africa, Asia and Europe—and has provided trade routes for the peoples of different lands and, for this reason, become of special importance in the modern world of adventures and enterprise. A major portion of world trade passes through the Suez Canal constructed in 1869 that "very soon became the subject of endless controversies, negotiations, diplomatic incidents, and still unsolved problems. As a commercial artery, it has at all times been enmeshed in political considerations."[3] In this chapter an attempt has been made to discuss briefly the role of some of the important countries of this region in international politics during the inter-war period.

Turkey : Disintegration of the Ottoman Empire and the Establishment of a Secular Republic
When the First World War broke out, Turkey did not join it . But just a few days after the beginning of the conflict some young elements of the Tukish army entered into a secret agreement with Germany as they wanted the recovery of their country's lost territories (as Egypt, Cyprus, the Caucasus, Tunisia and Algeria) then under the control of Britain, France and Russia. When on 26 September, 1914, Turkey closed the straits and the next day Turkish destroyers under German command bombarded ports on the Russian Black Sea Coast, Russia declared war on Turkey and then Britain and France followed suit. Since Britain supported the Egyptians and the Arabs, they occupied the port of Aqaba on 6 July, 1916. The combined Arab and British forces occupied Palestine in September, 1916 and after a month also captured Damascus in Syria. The ruler of Nejd (Abdul Aziz Ibn-Saud) had already signed

---

century before World War I, it meant Persia, Afghanistan, India and Burma. After 1920, Middle East sometimes was applied to those lands where the Arab tongue was in common use. On other occasions, the term was used more broadly to refer to all those areas where populations followed the Muslim faith. The Middle East comprises the states of Saudi Arabia, Iraq, Iran, Syria, Lebanon, Jordan and Israel. *The World since 1919* (Delhi: Surjeet Pub., 1981) p. 677.
3. H.L. Holdins: *The Middle East* (New York: Macmillan, 1954), p. 40.

a treaty with Britain in December 1915 and had given them control over his foreign affairs. The real aim of Britain and France was to effect the disintegration of Turkish (Ottoman) Empire. For this reason, while Britain had promised independence to the Arab provinces of the Turkish empire, she had also made a pact with France (Sykes-Picot Agreement) that was approved by Russia as well. The main terms of this tripartite agreement were:

1. Russia would obtain the province of Erzerum, Trebizond, Van and Bitlis as well as territory in the southern part of Kurdistan, along the line Mush-Sairt-Ibn-Omar-Amadje Persian frontier. The limit of Russian acquisitions on the Black Sea coast would be fixed later at a point lying west of Trebizond.
2. France would obtain the coastal strip of Syria, the *vilayet* of Adana, and the territory bounded on the South by a line Aintab-Mardin to the future Russian frontier, and on the north by a line Ala Dagh, Kaisarya, Ak-Dagh, Jidiz-dagh, Zara, and Egin-Kharput.
3. Great Britain would obtain the southern part of Mesopotamia with Baghdad, and stipulate for herself in Syria the ports of Haifa and Akka (Acre).
4. By agreement between France and Britain, the zone between the French and the British territories would form a confederation of the Arab States, or one independent Arab State, in which the zones of influence were determined at the same time.
5. Alexanderatta would be proclaimed a free port.

In December 1918, Prime Minister Lloyd George of Britain and Clemenceau of France reached an agreement whereby Palestine and Mosul were to be considered as the British 'sphere of influence'.

Turkey emerged as a defeated power in the war. On 30 October, 1918, she signed the armistice with the Allies. In April 1920, the Allies offered to the Sultan of Turkey the terms of peace (that came be to be known as the Treaty of Sevres) with these main points:

1. Turkey was to surrender her sovereignty over practically all her non-Turkish population;
2. In Arabia, the kingdom of Hedjaz was to be recognised as independent;
3. Syria, Lebanon, Palestine and Iraq were to be administered as mandated territories;

4. Smyrna and South-Western Asia Minor were to be administered by Greece for five years, at the end of which a plebiscite was to decide their future status;
5. The Dodacanese and Rhode Islands were to be ceded to Italy which later on was to turn over the former to Greece;
6. Turkey was to recognise the independence of Armenian State to be constructed in the areas of Etzerum, Trebizond, Van and Bitlis, the frontiers of which were to be decided by the President of the United States;
7. Kurdistan was to receive autonomous government, or if a plebiscite so decided, independence; and
8. The Straits were to be internationalised and the adjoining territory demilitarised. Constantinople was to remain under Turkish sovereignty.

Though the Sultan of Turkey accepted these harsh terms, the Treaty of Sevres could not be implemented owing to the outbreak of civil war in the country that resulted in the assumption of power by a group of young military leaders. The fiery Turkish nationalists under the leadership of Mustafa Kemal Pasha staged a revolt and on 23 April, 1920, Kemal set up his own government at Ankara in opposition to the government of the Sultan at Constantinople. Soon the Communist government of Lenin supported the Kemalists and so they could push Greek forces out of Smyrna and take control of Thrace. The Kemalists also abolished the Caliphate and offered their new terms for peace which Britain and France accepted willy-nilly at the Lausanne Conference on 24 July, 1923. Its main terms were:

1. Turkey was to recover Eastern Thrace, including the city of Adrianople.
2. Constantinople was to be restored as an integral part of the Turkish State.
3. The zone of the Straits was to be demilitarised and opened to the ships of all nations in time of peace, and when Turkey was neutral in time of war. In the event of Turkey's belligerency, enemy vessels might be kept out of the Straits but not the neutral vessels.
4. The boundary of Syria, as agreed with France in 1921, was confirmed.
5. All Allied claims for reparations arising from the World War were to be renounced. All capitulations were to be abolished

on the promise that Turkey would soon introduce judicial reforms and adhere to the same provisions regarding minorities as they had been agreed to by other European countries.

6. The foreign control of customs was to be lifted. No restrictions were to be placed on Turkey's military, naval and air forces.
7. A small Anzac area on the Gallipoli peninsula was to be perpetually granted to Britain, France and Italy. Here the three countries might appoint custodians to watch over the graves of the soldiers who died in the campaign of 1915. The region, however, could never be fortified.
8. Turkey was to renounce all claims over Libya, Egypt, Sudan, Palestine, Iraq and Syria and she was to recognise British occupation of Cyprus. A supplementary Greco-Turkish convention provided for compulsory exchange of Turkish subjects in Greece and for Greek subjects in Turkey.

On 20 April, 1924, the government of Kemal adopted a new constitution whereby Turkey was made a secular republic and on 6 August the Treaty of Lausanne came into force. It is, therefore, rightly observed: "Had the Treaty of Sevres drawn up by the Allies and signed in 1920 by the representatives of Sultan Muhammed VI, gone into effect, the once resplendent Ottoman Empire would have been reduced to an insignificant region of desert and mountain in Asia Minor. But Fate, acting through the person of a young army officer named Mustapha, decreed otherwise."[4] The real importance of this treaty should be seen in this fact as well that it "is only one of the peace treaties which for thirteen years was accepted as valid and applicable by all its signatories and which even in 1936 was modified only by voluntary agreement and in one particular. Historically, it owed this advantage to several factors which distinguished it from other peace treaties. It came into being nearly five years after the end of hostilities when bitter passions had time to abate; it was not imposed but negotiated by a long process of bargaining between the parties; and it was signed, not in an Allied capital, but on neutral territory."[5]

---

4. W.C. Langsam: *The World since 1919*, p. 233.
5. Carr: *International Relations between the Two World Wars, 1919-1939* (London: Macmillan, 1952), p. 13.

Turkey's role in international politics during the inter-war period is hardly of any significance. Since the Communist Russia had rendered support to the regime of Kemal in the initial stages, Turkey had very good relations with the Soviet Union. But when the Communists carried on their subversive activities, the government of Kemal suppressed them with force in 1929. It paved the way for Turkey's better relations with Western countries. Already in 1927 when the Permanent Court of International Justice had rendered a favourable award to Turkey in a dispute with France over responsibility for the collision of a French steamer with a Turkish ship, there developed a gradual amelioration in Turco-Western relations that caused the Turkish republic in 1932 to accept an invitation to join the League of Nations. In 1923 Turkey and United States discussed a Treaty of Amity and Commerce that could not be approved by the Senate. But a *modus vivendi* providing for the restoration of diplomatic and consular relations was concluded in 1927. Soon thereafter the High Commissioner, who had represented the United States interests in Turkey since 1919, was replaced by an ambassador. Commercial treaties followed in due course.

During the early 1930s, Turkey sought to refortify the region of her Straits demilitarised under the terms of the Treaty of Lausanne. In 1936, she did lay before the signatories of this treaty and the League a request for revision of the appropriate treaty terms. Partly because of the general feeling against Italy's Ethiopian venture and her apparent aims in the eastern Mediterranean, and partly out of gratification over the legal rather than unilateral method employed by Turkey to gain her ends, the Allied Powers promptly agreed to consider her wishes. The result was the Montreux Straits Convention that permitted the refortification of the zone in question.[6] Turkey now lost no time in refortifying the strategic area connecting and separating the Black Sea and the

---

6. As a matter of fact, the remilitarisation of the Rhineland by Nazi Germany had changed the entire scene and for this reason the Powers at the Montreux Conference took a conciliatory view. As Gathorne-Hardy observes: "In place of a fresh initiative of unilateral repudiation, the Montreux Conference provided a welcome precedent for treaty revision by the general and deliberate consent of the parties. For this reason, the request which Turkey put forward, not for the first time, in April 1936, for the modification of the Straits Convention embodied in the Treaty of Lausanne won the approval of revisionist and *status*

Mediterranean. Turkey continued her policy of cementing friendship with all other powers and of non-aggression and mutual cooperation with her near and eastern neighbours. Remembering the lessons of the First World War, Turkey signed treaties with Britain and France in 1939 providing for mutual assistance in the event of an attack. A few weeks after began the Second World War.

Egypt: From a British Protectorate to a Sovereign State

Egypt was a part of the Ottoman Empire. But it became partly an independent state under Mohammed Ali (a governor of this Turkish province) who broke away from the Turkish Emperor. Though occupied by the British since 1882, Egypt continued to remain under the nominal control of the Sultan of Turkey. The British suppressed the nationalist movement started by Arabi Pasha demanding 'Egypt for the Egyptians'. Thereafter, Britain and France came to an agreement that while the former would not interfere in the matters of Morocco, the latter would allow unrestricted control to the former over Egypt. In 1914, Britain converted Egypt into her protectorate, because Khedive Abbas Hilmi showed his fealty to the Sultan of Turkey who at that time was the lawful suzerain of Egypt. As a result, this country "was flooded with inexperienced British army officers and civil officials who treated Egypt almost as an occupied territory in which the rights and wishes of the inhabitants counted for little."[7]

During the war period, Egypt remained under the control of Britain. The Treaty of Versailles (1919) recognised Britain as 'ultimately responsible for ensuring the execution of the Suez Canal Convention.'[8] Immediately after the end of hostilities the Egyptians started an agitation for independence under the leadership of Saad Zaghlul Pasha. The British administration suppressed the agitation by force and deported Zaghlul to Malta. The Egyp-

---

quo Powers alike; of the former because of the end , and the latter because of the means. The principle of the sanctity of the treaties was upheld, while at the same time the provisions of this particular instrument were subjected to peaceful change." *A Short History of International Affairs,* p. 426.
7. G.E. Kirk: *A Short History of the Middle East,* p. 132.
8. It was signed on 29 October, 1888, by Britain, France, Germany, Austria, Russia, Turkey, Spain, Italy and the Netherlands so as to ensure that the Canal should always be free and open to every vessel without distinction of flag in peace as well as in war times.

tians resented this action and so, in order to give a dose of satisfaction to them, the British Government appointed a commission under Milner. In the light of the report of this Commission, the British Government released on 28 February, 1922, a Declaration of Policy for Egypt with these important provisions:
1. The British protectorate over Egypt would be terminated and Egypt be declared an independent sovereign state.
2. But some matters would be absolutely reserved to the discretion of His Majesty's Government until such time as could be possible by free discussion and friendly accommodation on both sides to conclude agreement between His Majesty's Government and the Government of Egypt.[9]

It was followed by a pronouncement that 'any interference in the matters of Egypt by any foreign power would be regarded by Britain as a menace to her own security.'

The Egyptians received this declaration without gratitude as 'merely an instalment of independence'. It was nothing more than half-independence and Prof. Arnold Toynbee commented that it 'amounted to less than Dominion Status'. And yet the Egyptians could feel a little satisfied when on 15 March, 1922, Sultan Faud was declared their monarch and on 23 April, 1923, a new constitution was promulgated. In January 1924, first parliamentary polls were held in which the Wafd party got majority and so its leader Zaghlul Pasha became the Prime Minister of this country. Soon he demanded repeal of the 'reserved subjects'. Since Turkey under Kemal could gain much by the terms of the Treaty of Lausanne, the Egyptians felt encouraged and on 19 November, 1924, the extremist elements killed Sir Lee Stack (Governor-General of Sudan and the commander-in-Chief of the Egyptian army) in Cairo.[10]

In 1927, the British government offered two more concessions, namely, to convert the British personnel in the Egyptian army into a military mission, and to maintain British officials in the Departments of Police and Public Security pending the reform of

---
9. These subjects were—security of the communications of the British Empire, defence of Egypt against all foreign aggressions and direct or indirect interference of any other power, protection of foreign interests and immunities in Egypt, and control of Sudan.
10. In retaliation the British Government sent an ultimatum to the Egyptian government and a fine of £ 500,000 was exacted. Then Zaghlul resigned and Ahmed Ziwar Pasha formed a new cabinet.

the Capitulations. But Mustapha an-Nahas Pasha, who succeeded Zaghlul, rejected these offers. Thereupon in May 1929, the British Government issued another policy statement saying: "Because the interests at stake are of supreme importance to the safety and well-being of the Empire, His Majesty's Government reserved, by the Declaration of 1922, certain matters for its own determination, but even in these cases it is the desire of His Majesty's Government, respecting in the largest possible measure, the liberties and independence which by the same Declaration they conceded to Egypt." It was not appreciated by the Wafdists. The people became restive again and then, at the resignation of Nahas Pasha, came Ismail Sidki Pasha who behaved dictatorially. He dissolved the Parliament and promulgated a new constitution in 1930.

Sidki resigned in September 1933, and was succeeded by Muhammed Tewfik Nessim Pasha. The situation became tense in 1935 owing to anti-Christian outbursts in the country and Italy's invasion on Ethiopia. With a view to create political unity in the country King Faud restored the original constitution of 1923, reconciled terms with Wafdists, and formed a 'united front' of all parties. In March 1936, negotiations started with Britain as a result of which Anglo-Egyptian Alliance was made on 26 August, 1936. By the terms of this treaty, British military occupation of Egypt was terminated. Britain was allowed to fly RAF planes over the country for training purposes and to maintain their air bases. The ground troops of Britain were also allowed to be sanctioned in a special zone along the Suez Canal for 20 years and at the naval base at Alexandria for 8 years; they were to be withdrawn from the interior of the country. Mutual assistance on a very large scale was also provided in it. Britain promised to support Egypt's candidacy for admission to the League of Nations, agreed to an exchange of ambassadors, and undertook to confine the troops in Egypt to a zone of northern end of the Suez Canal. Joint rule over Sudan was to be re-established with the right of unrestricted immigration for the Egyptians. In return, Egypt agreed to accord to Britain all facilities and assistance in the event of a threat or outbreak of war. She also undertook not to enter into any treaty with a foreign power which might be opposed to this alliance. The treaty could be discussed for revision after 10 years provided both parties agreed, and after 20 years on the demand of any party.

In accordance with another treaty Britain helped arrange for a meeting of those powers with extra-territorial rights in Egypt at Montreux in May 1937. There a convention was signed providing for complete abolition of extra-territoriality in Egypt by 1949 with certain steps to be taken at once. Shortly thereafter on 26 May, Egypt became a member of the League of Nations and Farouk was installed as the first king of independent country. In 1938 an agreement with Britain was signed concerning the accommodation of British troops which under previous agreements were stationed to protect the Suez Canal; and Egypt, while upholding her independent position, remained fully loyal to her obligations to Great Britain. The moderate elements of the Wafdists won majority in the election of 1938 and so Mahmud headed a cabinet until his death in August 1939. Then a military government with wide powers was instituted. The increasing gravity of the Palestinian situation also interested the Egyptians who now joined Iraq and Saudi Arabia in an expression of sympathy for the cause of the Arabs.

The story of Egypt's role in international affairs during the inter-war period is, therefore, by and large an account of British diplomacy in this part of the Middle East. The British sought to maintain their hold over this country in the light of their interest in having access to the countries of Asia through the Suez Canal and also to make terms with the growing tide of Arab nationalism. Once a protectorate under British control, then a semi-independent country, Egypt gained full freedom after the alliance of 1936 and since the British acted judiciously in dealing with the challenge of Arab nationalism, they managed to retain their hold over this country even after independence that yielded positive results during the Second World War. It is, therefore, well commented: 'The history of Anglo-Egyptian relations during this period is that of a series of unsuccessful attempts to employ the expedient which had achieved at least moderately successful results in Iraq. When British diplomacy, with its native love of compromise, wishes to retain the substance of control while conceding the shadow of independence, it is apt to resort to the method of a treaty."[11]

---

11. Cathorne-Hardy, op. cit., p. 235.

Iraq: From a British Mandated Territory to an Independent State

Iraq, once known as Mesopotamia, became a part of the Ottoman Empire in 1639 and remained like that until it became a mandated territory under British control after the First World War.[12] When in November 1914, the Sultan of Turkey joined the war on the side of Germany, an Indian army brigade under British Command landed. On the one hand, Britain promised independence to the Arab provinces of the Ottoman Empire through Hussain-Macmahon correspondence she also agreed under Sykes-Picot agreement to partition Iraq between two powers in a way that Britain would get Southern Mesopotamia with Baghdad and France having the rest of the country. Another secret agreement was arrived at whereby Lloyd George of Britain and Clemenceau of France agreed that the province of Mosul (under the Sykes-Picot agreement going to France) would be included in the British sphere of influence and that France would be allowed share in the oil deposits of this country. On 8 November, 1918, Britain and France declared that Iraq would be granted independence after the end of hostilities. It was in clear opposition to the above agreements. As a result, Iraq was placed under the Mandate System of the League of Nations and its control was entrusted to Britain. The British government invited Faisal (the son of Sherif Hussain who had been expelled from Syria by the French in 1920) to accept the throne and he was formally inducted into it on 23 August, 1921.

The Iraqi people, influenced by the wave of Arab nationalism, did not appreciate the arrangement and so they agitated against the system of mandate imposed on their heads. The British High Commissioner (Sir Percy Cox) thus dealt with the grave situation. On 10 October, 1922, Britain imposed a treaty on Iraq that incorporated the provision of a 'mandate' and guaranteed Britain's special interests in this country. In order to make up for the abolition of Capitulations, special judicial guarantees were given to the British

---

12. The status of the first British mandated territory (Iraq) "was from the outset anomalous." No formal mandate was ever granted, its place being taken up by a treaty between Great Britain and Iraq, which was approved by the League, and under which Great Britain promised to afford Iraq "such advice and assistance as may be required... without prejudice to her national sovereignty." Carr, op. cit., pp. 234-35.

nationals living in Iraq. Britain undertook to use her good offices to secure the admission of Iraq to the League of Nations, but the nationalist elements rejected this offer. Yet the British went ahead with their move and created a constituent assembly. It framed the new constitution that came into effect on 21 March, 1925. On 30 June, 1930, Britain forced Iraq to sign another treaty that provided for cooperation in foreign affairs and mutual assistance in the event of war, including Iraq's provision of communications and other facilities, assistance and passage to British troops. Under this treaty Britain was authorised to construct aerodromes near Basra and west of the Euphrates and she was permitted to station her troops at Habbaniyah and Sahibah.[13]

In 1932 Britain sponsored the case of Iraq for the membership of the League of Nations. The Council of the League appreciated this move provided Iraq make a declaration guaranteeing minority rights, administration of justice, international law and other safeguards. Iraq signed the declaration and became a member of the League on 3 October, 1932, and then came the end of the British mandate over this country. But the harsh treatment of the Iraqi government meted out to the Kurds and the Assyrians and, more than that, the growing influence of Nazi Germany over this country became the source of anxiety for Britain as well as the League of Nations. The Iraqi people also resented British policy towards Palestine and heavy influx of the Jews into the Arab territory. When their king (Ghazi) was killed in a motor accident in April 1939, they suspected the role of British authorities. But Iraq acted wisely in breaking off her relations with Germany when the Second World War broke out, though the political opinion in the country remained divided on the point of rendering help and cooperation to Britain as pledged in the Anglo-Iraqi treaty of 1930.

---

13. The original treaty of 1926 had contemplated admission of Iraq to the League of Nations in 1928, but this date was postponed to 1932 and made conditional upon continuous progress in the political development of the country. A new treaty, signed in 1927, remained unratified, and a new term translated as 'the perplexing predicaments' was coined to cover the numerous and striking anomalies qualifying ostensible independence by practical control. In June 1930, a new treaty of alliance was concluded (that was ratified on 26 January, 1931) to take effect on the termination of the mandate by the election of Iraq to League's membership. See G.M. Gathorne-Hardy, op. cit., p. 233.

Palestine : Jewish Zionism Versus Arab Nationalism
Palestine is the only country of the Middle East where the rival claims of the Jews and the Arabs (Muslims) have created a dilemma of immense complexity and, for this reason, has been a centre of international rivalry intermittently since the beginning of human history. Though numerically smaller than the Arabs in the wake of the present century, the Jews managed to swell their strength by immigration under the protective umbrella of British 'mandate' over this territory that saw its end in 1948. Inspired by the ideal of Western nationalism, the Jews also began to think in similar terms and an Austrian journalist (Theodor Herzl) gave to it a definite shape that came to be known as Zionism.[14] Thousands of Jews living in European countries migrated into Palestine as a result of which their population reached the figure of 80,000 in a total population of 700,000 in 1914.[15]

The sympathy of the British for the cause of the Jews became quite clear when the Foreign Secretary (Lord Balfour) gave an important statement on 2 November, 1917, stating : "His Majesty's government view with favour the establishment in Palestine of a National Home for the Jewish People, and will use their best endeavours to facilitate the achievement of this object, it being

---

14. As the legend says, Mount Zion is the place where Yehweh, the God of Israel, dwells. Zionism signifies Jewish homeland, symbolic of Judaism or Jewish national aspirations. As a Jewish nationalist movement, it has had its goal the creation of and support for a Jewish national state in Palestine, the ancient homeland of the Jews. Though Zionism originated in Eastern and Central Europe in the later part of the nineteenth century, it is in many ways a continuation of the ancient and deep-felt nationalist attachment of the Jews and of the Jewish religion to Palestine, the promised land where one of the hills of ancient Jerusalem was called Zion. The Haskala ('Enlightenment') Movement of the late eighteenth century urged the Jews to assimilate into Western secular culture. But Herzl regarded assimilation as most undesirable and, in view of anti-semitism, impossible to realise. Thus he argued that if the Jews were forced by external pressure to form a nation, they could lead a normal existence only through concentration in one country. In 1897 he convened the first Zionist Congress at Basel in Switzerland which drew up a programme stating that Zionism 'strives to create for the Jewish people a home in Palestine secured by public law'. *Encylopaedia Britannica*, Vol X, 15th ed., 1974 Ptg., p. 886.
15. In March, 1925 the Jewish population in Palestine was officially estimated at 108,000 and had risen to about 238,000 by 1933.

clearly understood that nothing shall be done which may prejudice the civil and religious rights of the existing non-Jewish communities in Palestine or the rights and political status enjoyed by the Jews in any other country." It was implicit in this declaration that the Jews would be given their 'homeland' in course of time.[16] Surprisingly, it occurred before the British forces captured Palestine on 9 December, 1917, and then permitted systematic immigration of the Jews into this country.[17] Arthur Koestler, therefore, hailed it a document in which one nation solemnly favoured to a second national the country of a third people. As a matter of fact, the Jews got this bonanza in return for financial support to Britain during war times from the Jews of the world. Lord Balfour assured the Jewish leader (Rothschild) that the British government was in favour of creating a Jewish 'homeland' in Palestine. Obviously, such a declaration was made to please only 8 per cent of the total population of this country in total disregard to the feelings and sentiments of 92 per cent of the Arab (Muslim) population there.

The problem of Palestine engaged the attention of the peacemakers at the Paris Conference in 1919. In accordance with a proposal advanced by President Wilson of the United States to the Supreme Council of the Allied Powers at the Paris Conference, a commission was sent to Palestine to ascertain the public opinion there. Fearing the results of such an exercise, both Britain and France abstained. But the two American members of this Commission (Henry C. King and Charles R. Crane) reached Palestine on 10 June, 1919, and they submitted a report stating that "a national home for the Jewish people is not equivalent to making Palestine into a Jewish state, nor could the execution of such a Jewish state be accomplished without the gravest trespass upon the civil and religious rights of the existing non-Jewish communtites." And yet a Zionist organisation was allowed to put its case before the Supreme Council of the Allied Powers.

---

16. Two important figures of the Jewish community (Chaim Weizmann and Nahum Sokolow) were instrumental in getting the Balfour Declaration.
17. The sympathy of the British government for the Jews is evident from the fact that in 1903 it had offered 6,000 sq. miles of land in Uganda for the Jews to settle down there, but the Zionists rejected this gesture and instead held out for Palestine.

In 1920 Palestine was placed under Class A 'mandate' of Britain which was endorsed by the League of Nations two years after. By the terms the Mandatory Power was put under an obligation to place this country under such political, administrative and economic conditions as will secure the establishment of the Jewish national home, while at the same time safe guarding the civil and religious rights of all the inhabitants of Palestine. Naturally, it annoyed the Arab Muslims who resented the promise of awarding a 'homeland' to the Jews and they found little consolation in the phrase that "nothing shall be done which may prejudice the civil and religious rights of the existing non-Jewish communities." Thereafter, the British High Commissioner (Sir Herbert Samuel) promulgated a constitution. It provided an appointive executive council and a legislative body in which Muslims, Christians and Jews would be represented. The Arabs denounced the whole arrangement and since they boycotted all elections for the composition of such a body, the British High Commissioner continued to administer with the help of an appointed advisory body.

The British government looked at these developments with alarm and in 1922 it issued a Statement of Policy with regard to Palestine. Since it was drafted by the new Foreign Secretary (Churchill), it came to be known as the Churchill White Paper on Palestine. It repudiated Weizman's interpretation of the Jewish home that 'Palestine should become as Jewish as England is English' and declared that His Majesty's government had no such aim in view, nor did it contemplate the disappearance or subordination of the Arab population, language or culture in Palestine. But it further stated that the establishment of the Jewish national home "required that the Jewish community in Palestine should be able to increase its numbers by immigration which, however, should not be so great in volume as to exceed whatever may be the economic capacity of the country at the time to absorb new arrivals."

It could afford some satisfaction to the Muslims. However, increasing Jewish immigration into Palestine tested their patience. The resentment of the Arabs took the shape of violent disturbances in August 1929, in which about 116 Arabs and 133 Jews were killed and 6 Jewish agricultural settlements were totally destroyed. The government appointed a commission of inquiry under the chairmanship of Shaw that condemned the policy of 'too much of Jewish immigration', but it laid all blame on 'the Arab feeling of animosity and hostility towards the Jews.' The League Mandates Commission, however, claimed that outburst was directed as much against Great Britain as against the Jews and blamed the British for failure to provide adequate military and police protection.

The Arabs enumerated their specific grievances against both the authorities and the Jews. Their main grouse was that the legislation enabled the Jews to buy up large portions of the limited arable soil and threatened the existence of thousands of Arabs. They objected to the favourable attitude of their government towards Jewish immigration and also claimed that most of the immigrants were poor and radical. Another point of dispute was related to the Wailing Wall in Jerusalem.[18] Meanwhile, the British government had some conflict with the World Zionist Organisation and the Jewish Agency for Palestine. Thus, in order to balance and counter-balance the claims of the Jews and the Muslims, the British Government issued another Statement of Policy in 1930 which stressed rather the obligations of the Mandatory Power towards the non-Jewish inhabitants of Palestine. Dr. Weizman protested that the White Paper was inconsistent with the terms of the Mandate, whose main purpose was the Mandatory's obligations towards the Jews. He resigned from the presidentship of the

---

18. At this wall, supposedly a relic of Solomon's temple, the Jews had been accustomed to worship and to mourn. Since the sacred Al Aqsa mosque of caliph Omar adjoined the wall, it often became the centre of dispute between the two communities when they offered prayer at one and the same time. In 1930, British government appointed a neutral commission to find out a solution to this problem. It reported that the wall and its adjoining pavement were Muslim property, but that with certain restrictions, the Jews should be granted free access to it. It was promptly implemented. That which was the 'Wailing Wall' to the Jews on the ground that it was the last surviving vestige of their Temple was to the Muslims the stable of the Buraq the beast which had carried the Prophet Mohammed to heaven on the 'Night of Power'. The scene of the Jewish devotions is part of the retaining wall of the Haram-esh Sherif, an enclosure of special sanctity in Muslim eyes, as the starting point of the Prophet's celestial journey and as containing the Dome of the Rock and the Mosque of Aqsa. The inflammatory possibilities of the situation were increased by the fact that the Jewish fast in commemoration of the destruction of the Temple coincided with the date of the Muslim celebration of the birthday of Mohammed." Gathorne-Hardy, op. city., p. 231.

Zionist organisation. In order to assuage the feelings of the Jews, Prime Minister Ramsay MacDonald felt obliged in February 1931, to write a letter to Weizman stating that His Majesty's Government did not intend to prohibit the acquisition of additional land by the Jews and that it had no intention of going back on the promises made to the Jews. The result was that while the Arab Muslims had felt a little satisfied with the new Statement of Policy issued in 1930, they resented the move of the Prime Minister and denounced his note as 'black letter'.

What, however, came as a sop to the Arabs was the move of the British authorities to put a kind of check on the immigration of the Jews into Palestine. The authorities suspended for an indefinite period immigration permits already issued to more than 2,000 prospective Jewish immigrants. The ban was imposed pending a study of the economic conditions of Palestine by a commission under Sir John Hope Simpson. It gave its report in October 1930, and on its basis a fresh White Paper on statement of policy was issued. It maintained that too much haste had been shown in the upbuilding of the Jewish homelad and that, as a result, the future welfare of the Arabs had been put in jeopardy. It was also said that rapid immigration of the Jews had caused shortage of land for further colonisation. It was also given in this report that the Jewish Foundation Fund, which leased land to Jewish colonies, had forbidden Arabian labour on its soil and the Central Federation of the Jewish Labour had adopted the policy of importing Jewish workmen rather than employing landless Arabs.

The implementation of a check on the immigration of the Jews into Palestine became slow after the persecution of the Jews in Nazi Germany in 1933-34 as a result of which the Jews rushed to Palestine in greater numbers. It is evident from the fact that while in 1932 the number of average immigrants was about 9,000 a year, it rose to 62,000 in 1935. In such a situation of extreme resentment, the Arabs came forward with three demands—establishment of democratic government in Palestine, prohibition of land transfer from the Arabs to the Jews, and an immediate stop at the spate of immigrations. Since the British High Commissioner failed to give any satisfactory reply, disturbances broke out in April 1936. The Arabs declared a National Political Strike and an Arab Higher Committee was set up to direct the campaign. The strike went on for 6 months and resulted in the death of about 400 Jews. Thereupon, the British government appointed a commission under Earl Peel to ascertain the underlying causes of the disturbances.

The Peel Commission wrote a report on the basis of 'a small mountain of evidence' plus the knowledge that Palestine was strategically important to Great Britain. The British also had to consider the effect of any decision upon the attitude of the Jews throughout the world and of the Muslims scattered throughout the British Empire. The report was approved by the British cabinet and released in 1937. It declared that "the obligations Britain undertook towards the Arabs and the Jews some twenty years ago... have proved irreconcilable and as far ahead as we can see, they must continue to conflict.... We cannot—in Palestine as it now is—both concede the Arab claims to self-government and secure the establishment of the Jewish National Home." The most important point of the Peel Report was its proposal for the partition of the country. As it said : "Inasmuch as neither race can fairly rule part of it, Partition offers a chance of ultimate peace. No other Plan does .... A radical solution of the surgical operation, dividing the country into a Jewish and an Arab State, with a small residuary enclave from Jaffa to Jerusalem left in charge of the Mandatory."

The Peel Report proposed termination of the mandate over Palestine and its division into three parts—a new Jewish state occupying about one-fourth area of this country, an Arabian section including most of the remainder of Palestine in union with Trans-Jordan, and an area under British administration including Jerusalem, Bethlehem and other holy places. It angered the Jews and the Arabs alike. While the Jews called it an act of betrayal the Arabs cried out that 'the richest zone was to be given to the Jews, the holiest to the British, and the most barren to the Arabs.' Now the militant Arabs got the support of the Italian fascists and so violent disturbances broke out in many parts of the country resulting in the casualty of moderate elements who appreciated the Peel proposals.

The matter was seriously debated in the British Parliament and it was resolved to refer it to the League of Nations. As a result, the League took up the matter and set up a commission under Sir John Woodhead so as to draw up a more precise and detailed scheme for solving the problem. It opposed the partition plan because it appeared impossible to recommend the boundaries for the suggested areas that would afford a reasonable prospect of the eventual establishment of the self-supporting Arab and the Jewish states. It found that the plan was unworkable as it was impossible to give the Jews a workable area without leaving unfairly large Arab minority and the bulk of the Arab-owned citrus areas in the Jewish State, while the residual Arab state would not be economically self-supporting. Instead, it proposed a scheme of 'economic federalism' under which the Mandatory Power would determine the fiscal policy for the Arab and Jewish areas which otherwise would be autonomous. Thereupon, the British government decided that the surest foundation for peace and progress in Palestine would be an understanding between the Arabs and the Jews.

Early in 1939 the British government invited the Jews and the Arabs to take part in a Round Table Conference at London, but both parties declined the offer. Thus, in May, 1939 the British Government issued another white paper unequivocally declaring that "it was no part of Government's policy that Palestine should become a Jewish state, regarding it as contrary to their obligations to the Arabs under the Mandate." The paper, however, proposed the creation of an independent Palestinian state in treaty relations with Britain at the end of 10 years, 75,000 Jewish immigrants to be admitted in the first five years after which further immigration was to depend upon Arabs' consent. The Jews condemned it as an 'outrageous breach of faith' and it asserted that it denied them the right to reconstitute their 'national home' in Palestine. The Arabs had their own grouse. But as the British were faced with the conditions of the Second World War, they sought to evade the whole proposal of partition of Palestine so as to win the support of the Arabs, while the support of the Nazis was taken for granted in the context of stern condemnation by the British people of the persecution of the Jews at the hands of the Nazis in Germany. In the midst of violent disturbances in Palestine came the news of the start of another great war.

Transjordan : From a British Mandated Territory to an Independent State
Transjordan was also a part of the Ottoman Empire that was placed under British mandate after the disintegration of the Turkish Empire as per the decision of the San Remo Conference held in April, 1920. Curiously, it was done according to the wishes of the

Jews, though the mandatory power was permitted to exclude it from the area of Jewish settlement. It was, of course, a kind of compromise between the Zionist ambitions which always covered Transjordan and an arrangement made vide the Sykes-Picot Agreement that explicitly excluded any part of Transjordan from Palestine. The territory mandated to Britain was divided geographically by the river Jordan—Transjordan on the east and Palestine on the west. In 1922 Britain constituted a semi-independent Arab kingdom of Transjordan subject to the control of British High Commissioner posted at Jerusalem. Now the second son of Sharif Hussain (Abdullah) was installed as the ruler. On 25 May, 1923, the creation of the new state was proclaimed.

The relations between Britain and Transjordan were settled by a treaty (signed on 20 February, 1928) whereby His Majesty's Government recognised the government of Transjordan as 'independent' and its ruler (Amir) was obligated to be guided by the advice of Britain in foreign relations and to follow an administrative, financial and fiscal policy so as to ensure the stability and good organisation of the government and its finances. It was supplemented by another agreement on 2 June, 1934, whereby the ruler of this country was permitted to appoint consular representatives in other Arab States. In May 1939, the British Government came out with a new and more important Policy Statement on Palestine which provided for the establishment of a Council of Ministers. Each member of this body was put in charge of one department of government and owed accountability to the Amir. This body came into being on 6 August, 1939, as a solid mark of an independent government of Transjordan. Thus, by all means Jordan, as now called, became an independent state and the British mandate came to an end.

Syria : From a French Mandated Territory to an Independent State

"The experiences of France in her Syrian mandate, an important silk-producing area, were almost as troublous as those of Great Britain in Palestine."[19] In 1516 Syria became a part of the Ottoman Empire. But after the defeat of Turkey in World War I, it was placed

---

19. Langsam, op. cit., p. 250.

under the mandate of France as per the decision of the San Remo Conference held in April 1920. A little earlier in 1919, British General (Allenby) had installed Amir Faizal as the ruler of Syria, but when the French established their mandate, he was driven out of the country. Right from the very beginning, the French sought to suppress national movement by adopting the policy of divide and rule. The country was divided into five (later four) demonstrative areas each with a different name and law system, but all subordinate to one High Commissioner.[20] Martial law and censorship were imposed and French was made the language of the law courts.

The policy of exploitation and dismemberment of Syria at the hands of a mandatory power like France was keenly resented by the Syrian Arabs and so violent agitations broke out from time to time. All protests lodged with the French High Commissioner were treated with a discourteous rebuff and many Syrian leaders were put behind the bars on the charge of being 'conspirators'. Matters reached a point that French troops bombarded Damascus in October 1925; martial law was imposed over all disturbed centres of the country and the 'rebels' were suppressed by force. The Mandates Commission of the League of Nations reacted by criticising French activities there. Taking note of such a development, the French High Commissioner convened a constituent assembly in 1928 to draw up an instrument of government. But the effort was given up when the nationalists demanded establishment of an independent republic. In 1930 the French High Commissioner (Henri Ponsot) at his own instance promulgated a constitution setting up a republic restricted only by the mandatory powers of France and by French control of its foreign affairs.

In 1933 the French made an unsuccessful attempt to get the Syrian Parliament to accept a treaty that would have assured that for the next 25 years France would continue to supervise foreign, military and financial affairs of Syria. In 1936 France and Syria

---

20. The whole mandate was first sub-divided into five separate States—Greater Lebanon, the territory of the Alouites, Aleppo, Damascus, and the Jebel de Druse. "This step was itself open to criticism, as being based rather on the maxim *divide et impera* than on an intention to facilitate that cooperation upon which progress towards complete autonomy depended." Gathorne-Hardy, op. cit., p. 130.

signed another treaty providing for Syrian independence after three years.[21] Thereupon, Turkey requested that an autonomous regime be set up in new Syria for the district of Alexandretta, including the city of Antioch, that was inhabited by a large portion of the Turks. This matter was referred to the Council of the League of Nations which proposed that Alexandretta should remain under the control of Syria with the latter controlling its foreign relations and customs. However, the district was to have its own legislature with Turkish as official language. All these principles were incorporated into a statute and a Commission of League was sent to this place to prepare for elections in 1938. But the Turks objected to the methods of this Commission on the ground that it would give them the status of a minority in the assembly. Disturbances broke out and the Commission had to leave the place. France and Turkey signed an agreement at Ankara stipulating that Alexandetta should become an 'autonomous state' under Franco-Turkish control and then it became the Republic of Hatay which the French preferred to cede in favour of Turkey in 1939 so as to pay a price for the support of Turkey during the time of war.

Such an action angered the Syrians who raised the point that France had no right to cede a part of the mandated territory to another state. The rulers of Fascist Italy and Nazi Germany criticised it on the ground of being against the provisions of the Covenant of the League of Nations. The Mandates Commission of the League also censured France. But France did not bother for such criticism. The French High Commissioner suspended the constitution and assumed full control in his hands in July 1939. He appointed a council of five Directors to run the administration of Syria. Military defence was controlled from Paris. In June 1940, metropolitan France fell to Germany and the Vichy regime was inaugurated. Under such conditions, on 8 June, 1941, General Catroux, on behalf of the Free French, proclaimed the termination of the mandate. Thus, Syria became an independent state.

---

21. As a matter of fact, the grant of independent sovereignty to Iraq and its admission to the League of Nations in October, 1932 "made it very difficult to defend the continuance of the mandates in Syria and the Lebanon, where the inhabitants were, to say the least, as fitted for autonomy as were the Iraqis." Ibid., p. 296.

Concluding Observations

A study of the role of some of the important countries of the Middle East in international politics during the inter-war period, as contained in the preceding sections, leaves these strong impressions:

1. The importance of this region lies in its strategic location and its richness in terms of oil resources. The case of these countries can be cited to prove how important a place natural resources occupy in the context of power. The Arab nations, which may not be of much consequence otherwise, are very carefully treated by great powers only because of the oil which they possess. It is aptly commented: "The relatively important part the States of the Arabian peninsula are able to play in international affairs rests not on anything resembling military strength. Aside from a precarious solidarity with the Moslems of Africa and the rest of Asia, and the strategic location of the Arabian peninsula, the importance of the Arab States derives exclusively from their control of, and access to, regions rich in oil."[22]

2. The countries of this region could not play a part of any significance in the sphere of international politics owing to their weak political position. Turkey became very weak as a result of the disintegration of her Empire and the areas liberated from the Ottoman Empire could not assert their voice owing to the tutelage, protection and supervisory control of the European powers. Thanks to the growing power of Arab nationalism, these States secured complete independence in course of time and thereby managed to take a stand of their own in the period following World War II.

3. Palestine's case has its uniqueness in the sense that here continued a struggle for 'homeland' as demanded by the Zionists and its fierce opposition by the Arab nationalists. Though a mandatory power, Britain exercised her administrative control with ostensile sympathy for the cause of the Jews. The proposal of partition, as mooted in 1936, satisfied the Jews, it was stoutly opposed by the Arabs. And though the matter remained in abeyance during the war time, it prepared the ground on which further developments took place and the Jews eventually managed to have their own State with the name of Israel in 1948.

---

22. Morgenthau, op. cit., p. 116.

Obviously, the politics of the Middle Eastern countries during the inter-war period is contained in the role of the major Western Powers engaged in the practice of oil diplomacy.

15

LEAGUE OF NATIONS

So I say of this document (Covenant of the League of Nations) that it is at one and the same time a practical document. There is a pulse of sympathy in it. There is a compulsion of conscience through it. It is practical and yet it is intended to purify, to rectify, to elevate... Many terrible things have come out of this war, gentlemen, but some very beautiful things have come out of it.

—Woodrow Wilson[1]

The end of the First World War led to the birth of the first international organisation called the League of Nations; the end of the League led to the birth of the Second World War. Obviously, a study of the League in a study of international relations and politics during the period of two World Wars has a relevance of its own. Such a study becomes more thought-provoking when we take note of the fact that while President Wilson played the most instrumental part in the creation of the League, the United States withdrew itself from the liability of the international organisation in the name of its traditional adherence to the policy of 'isolationism'. And yet the US statesmen played their part in a negative way to offset the menace of Bolshevism. While they supported the restoration of Germany so much so that she became a member of the League in 1926 with a semi-permanent seat in the Council, they kept the Soviet Russia at bay until 1933. The then major powers of the world, like Britain and France, failed to subject their national interests to the dictates of international peace and security, while the dictators of Italy, Germany and Japan frankly and most unabashedly took to the path of aggression. The result of all these

---

1. Cited in Temperley (ed.): *A History of the Peace Conference of Paris* (London: Oxford Univ. Press, 1952), Vol. I, p. 65.

developments was the end of the first international organisation as a bold proof of the fact that the founders of the League did not claim to have abolished war from the sphere of international relations completely; they only gave mankind at least the right to hope that war would not occur so frequently.[2]

Birth of 'A Living Thing': Triumph of the Wilsonian Idealism

The adoption of the Covenant of the League of Nations at the Paris Peace Conference was not at all a sudden development. Behind this we may trace a long history of the rise and growth of the ideas of international unity, harmony and cooperation. We may refer to the times of ancient Greeks when they had evolved some agencies of arbitration for the settlement of their disputes like the Delphic Oracle, the Amphicytonic League, the Athenian League, the Peloponnesian League and the Achaean League. Numerous thinkers like Dante of Italy, Pierre Dubois of France, Grotius of Holland, Kant of Germany and Bentham of England offered their designs of an international system for the maintenance of peace or avoidance of war. However, an institutional form of this idea came for the first time in 1815 when the powers of Britain, Russia, Austria and Prussia formed the Quadruple Alliance that became the Concert of Europe. The parties decided to meet from time to time in diplomatic congresses to discuss their problems and seek their settlement without going to war. Thus, the first congress met at Troppau in 1820, the second at Laibach in 1821, the third at Verona in 1822, and the fourth at St. Petersberg in 1823. But then it had its end on account of the involvement of other partners in the politics of Latin-American countries that was opposed by Britain.

Apart from this, some other bodies of international cooperation (like Danube Commission of 1856, International Telegraphic Union of 1865, Pan-American Union of 1890, International Institute of Agriculture of 1905, and International Health Office of 1907) came into being. More important are the Hague Conferences of 1899 and 1907. The latter established the Permanent Court of Arbitration. Movement in this regard gathered momentum in England. In 1905, Sir Henry Campbell proposed the creation of a League of Peace. In 1911 Foreign Secretary Sir Edward

---

2. C.K. Webster: *The League in Theory and Practice* (London: George Allen & Unwin, 1933), p. 121.

Grey emphasised the need for the formation of a concert of nations. Prime minister Asquith spoke in similar terms. The Fabian Committee headed by L.S. Woolf produced a comprehensive plan for this purpose. In 1916, Lord Cecil forcefully suggested this idea to the War Cabinet. On 5 January, 1918, Prime Minister Lloyd George emphasised the need for the creation of some international organisation to limit the burden of armaments and diminish the danger of war.

This movement had its remarkable development in the United States. On December 2, 1913, in his first annual message to the Congress, President Wilson hailed "many happy manifestations of the growing cordiality and sense of a community of interests among the nations." In June 1915, the American League to Enforce Peace was founded in Philadelphia under ex-President Taft. On 22 January, 1917, Wilson addressed the Senate on the 'World League for Peace' when he proposed four points: (i) peace negotiations after the war to include some concert of powers that might avoid similar catastrophies again, (ii) extension of the Monroe doctrine so as to embrace the whole world, so that no nation should seek to extend its policy over any other nation, and that all people be left to determine their own way of development unhindered, unafraid and unthreatened, (iii) all nations to avoid entangling alliances which dragged them into competition for power and a net of intrigues and selfish rivalry, and (iv) a government with consent of the governed, freedom on the seas and armaments to be limited to the needs of international peace and security. Its best example was contained in the last item of his 14-Point Programme given on 8 January, 1918. It said: "A general Association of Nations must be formed under specific covenants for the purpose of affording mutual guarantees of political independence and territorial integrity to great and small states alike."

The peace movement took a more positive turn towards the end of the first great war. In March 1918, the Lord Phillimore Committee produced the Draft Convention of a League of Nations that was appreciated by President Wilson and his confidential adviser (Colonel House). At the same time, Gen. Smuts of South Africa brought out his monograph *The League of Nations—A Practical Suggestion*. On the basis of these two papers, Wilson prepared his own design. On 25 January, 1919, the Preliminary Peace Conference, as it was then called, favourably considered the proposal

moved by Lloyd George for the creation of the League of Nations. It resolved that:[3]
1. "It is essential for the maintenance of the world settlement which the Associated Nations are now to meet to establish that a League of Nations be created to promote international cooperation, to ensure the fulfilment of expected international obligations and to provide safeguards against war.
2. "This League should be created as an integral part of the General Treaty of Peace and should be open to every civilised nation which can be relied upon to promote its objects.
3. "The members of the League should periodically meet in international conferences and should have a permanent organisation and secretariat to carry on the business of the League in intervals between the conferences."

After this, the Conference appointed a committee of Associated Governments to work out the details of the constitution of the proposed international organisation.[4] This body accepted the design prepared by Sir Cecil Hurst and David Hunter Miller that eventually became the Covenant of the League of Nations. It was incorporated into the Treaty of Versailles as it first chapter on 28 April, 1919. (It was also appended with other peace treaties.) In this way, the Covenant of the League of Nations "emerged as the distilled essence of this vast cloud of discussion, debates, drafts, and counter-drafts, based on such a mass of political, economic and social antecedents, going far back into history, the resultant of so many hopes, endeavours, achievements, failures, efforts and conflicts."[5]

As a matter of fact, the adoption of the Covenant at the Paris Peace Conference boldly demonstrated the triumph of the Wilsonian idealism. He not only struggled hard for the adoption of the constitution of an international organisation, he also saw to it that it should become an integral part of the peace settlement. In the prevailing circumstances, "It might well have been expected that

---

3. See F.P. Walters: *A History of the League of Nations* (London: Oxford University Press, 1952), Vol, p. 32.
4. This committee consisted of 15 members, namely, USA, Britain, France, Italy, Japan, Belgium, Brazil, China, Portugal and Serbia. Greece, Poland, Rumania and Czechoslovakia were added to it later.
5. C. Howard-Ellis: *The Origin, Structure, and Working of the League of Nations* (London: George Allen and Unwin, 1928), p. 99.

the work of drafting the Covenant and setting the League in motion would be left on one side at least until the territorial questions had been decided. Without doubt, it would have been so left but for the influence of Wilson and House. But even before the President left for Europe, he made it plain that he was prepared to insist not only on making the League a constituent part of the peace settlements, but also on giving this task priority over all other business of the conference."[6]

That it was backed by certain pertinent reasons is not difficult to take note of. As Walters says: "Wilson had strong reasons for this attitude. In the first place, he believed that if the Covenant were not adopted in the early stages of the conference, but were left to the end, it might never be adopted at all. He foresaw that American influence, overwhelmingly powerful at the moment of the Armistice, would gradually diminish as the hope of the various delegations were fulfilled or disappointed; and he suspected that none of the European powers cared much about starting the League, so that it could only be brought into existence by strong American pressures.... In the second place, Wilson counted on the League to correct the inevitable imperfections of Peace Treaties and to facilitate the solution of questions on which agreed decisions proved impossible. In this he was so abundantly justified: as the work of peace-making continued, one deadlock after another was resolved by reference to the League. Wilson's third reason arose from the political situation in the United States. He knew that there would be opposition to the Covenant, but he did not expect that the Senate would refuse to ratify the terms of peace with Germany; he determined therefore so to interwine the Covenant with the rest of the Treaty that it would be impossible to reject the first without destroying the second."[7]

One important reason that had its impact on the minds of major Allied Powers at this stage was the fear of Bolshevism. They very cautiously took note of the fact of growing revolutionary tendencies among the workers in different leading countries of the world and, in particular, their demand that the new world order must be based upon social justice. Thus, Wilson said: "The poison

---

6. Walters, op. cit., p. 31.
7. Ibid.

of Bolshevism is being absorbed as a protest against the way the world has worked. It will be our business at the Peace Conference to fight for a new world order. That order must be based upon and guaranteed by League of Nations." In his Confidential Memorandum', Lloyd George noted: "The whole of Europe is filled with the spirit of revolution. There is a deep sense not only of discontent but of anger and revolt amongst the workmen against pre-War conditions." While speaking at the Paris Peace Conference, Wilson frankly uttered: "It is, however, not enough to draw up a just and farsighted peace with Germany. If we are to offer Europe an alternative to Bolshevism, we must make the League of Nations into something which will be both a safeguard to those nations who are prepared for fair dealings with their neighbours and a menace to those who would trespass on the rights of their neighbours whether they are Imperialist Empires or Imperial Bolsheviks."

The anxiety to make the world safe for democracy and to perpetuate the era of peace strengthened with a resolve to improve the conditions of the international working class created a situation in which the reason of Wilson prevailed. All sharp differences were removed[8] and, as Wilson proudly declared, 'a living thing' was born. Webster well observes: "Nevertheless, the authors of the Covenant, even though they sometimes, as was only natural, were not aware of all they were doing, had made a wonderful structure. They had interwoven the various ideas of world organisation into one strand and each could strengthen the others. Above all, they had avoided too much definition and left for future the development of their institutions.... But, above all, the great thing was that the League was made, and made in such a way that it must be given a chance to function. This was the greatest of all President Wilson's decisions in 1919, for without his determination it is clear that the League could not have come at once into existence."[9]

---

8. On this point J.R.M. Butler makes an observation: "The real divergence lay between the adherents of the rigid, the definite, the logical, in other words, the judicial point of view and those who preferred the flexible, the indefinite, the experimental, the diplomatic: between those who feared human nature and were content to trust the future, between those who desired written guarantees and those who desired moral obligations only to be cynical; between those who expected to give, in a word, between the Continental point of view and the Anglo-Saxon." Cited in Temperley, op. cit., Vol. 6, p. 441.
9. Webster, op, cit., pp. 54-55.

Structure: Principal and Allied Organs of the League

In 1920 the League of Nations came into being with three principal organs—the Assembly, the Council and a permanent Secretariat. It was given in the Covenant that the League would perform its functions through the instrumentality of these three important organs. Let us discuss the organisation and functions of each briefly in the following manner:

Assembly

It consisted of the representatives of all the members of the League. Each member had a right to send three representatives who would cast their vote collectively. It elected its own president and made its rules of procedure in consonance with the provisions of the Covenant. Though its agenda was prepared by the Secretary-General, it could make necessary modifications in it. It was to meet at stated intervals from time to time as occasion arose to transact its business. Its seat was at Geneva. It was a sort of world parliament. Thus, it usually followed the principles of parliamentary procedure and operated through the committees, six in number, on constitutional and legal questions, technical organisations, reduction of armaments, budgetary matters, social and humanitarian questions, and political matters.

Its functions were of three kinds. In the first place, it had some functions relating to elections. It could admit new members by a two-thirds majority of its members. It elected annually three of the nine permanent members of the Council. While the Council appointed the Secretary-General, the Assembly approved it. For 9 years it in conjunction with the Council elected 15 judges of the Permanent Court of International Justice. The cooperation of the Assembly and of the Council was required for the nomination of additional permanent members of the Council, or for increasing the strength of the Council. Second, it had constituent powers. It could adopt amendments to the Covenant by a majority of its members. The amendments were also to be ratified by the Council. Last, its deliberative powers were important. It had to make deliberations on international political and economic matters likely to endanger world peace. From time to time, it had to advise reconsideration by the members of treaties that had become inapplicable. It had the power to supervise the working of the Council and technical commissions and revise the budget of the

League prepared by the Secretariat. It made an apportionment of the expenses of the budget among the members. It is obvious that all these functions and powers made the Assembly the dominant organ of the League of Nations.

Council

It was like a cabinet or an executive committee of the League. Its seats were to be divided among the Principal Allied and Associated Powers (U.S., U.K., France, Italy and Japan) and the four members of the League, the former having them permanently and the latter by the formula of rotation. In 1920, it was decided that four non-permanent seats should be assigned to Belgium, Brazil, Greece and Spain, but their successors were to be chosen periodically by the Assembly. Since the US did not join the League, one permanent seat remained vacant that became the bone of contention. When it was given to Germany in 1926 in the 'semi-permanent' capacity, it was resented by Brazil and that eventually led to her withdrawal from the international organisation. In 1922, two more non-permanent seats were created that were given to Poland and Yugoslavia. In 1933, Japan withdrew herself from the League as a result of which one more seat became vacant that, after some time, was given to the USSR. In 1933, Germany left the League and Italy followed suit after three years. The USSR was 'expelled' from the League in 1939. Thus, at the time of its demise in 1940, the Council had only two permanent members—Britain and France.

Each member of the Council had one vote. The presidency of the Council changed at each session, one country succeeding another in an alphabetical order. It had its meetings in public, though meetings in *camera* could also be held. The minutes of the meeting were published. It appointed one of its members to act as the rapporteur. It met whenever the occasion demanded. Any member of the League, not being represented in the Council, was requested to send a representative to sit as a member in any meeting of the Council during the consideration of a matter, especially affecting its interest. Most important of all was the voting system. It was given in Art. 5 of the Covenant that decisions in any meeting of the Assembly and the Council would require agreement of all the members represented in the meeting. But this unanimity rule did not cover matters of procedure in the meetings of the Assembly and the Council including the appointment of committees to investigate particular matters.

The Council had the power to deal with any matter affecting the peace of the world. The scope of its functions could be settlement of international disputes and maintenance of international peace and security. We may refer to its other functions also. It had the power to:

1. formulate plans for the reduction of armaments for the consideration and action of the States after taking account of the geographical situation and circumstances of each State;
2. advise how the evil effects of the manufacture of munitions and implements of war by private enterprise could be prevented;
3. advise on the ways and means by which the obligations of the members to respect and preserve as against external aggression the territorial integrity and existing political independence of all the members could be performed;
4. make report after inquiry on any dispute arising between the members likely to lead to rupture within 6 months of the summation of the dispute to it;
5. recommend to the several concerned governments what effective naval, military or air force of the members of the League should severally contribute to the armed forces to be used to protect the Covenant of the League in case any member resorted to the course of aggression;
6. institute an inquiry into the disputes and recommend such action as may seem best and most effectual in case any dispute between a member of the League and a non-member or between the non-members existed; and
7. define the scope of authority, control or administration to be exercised by the mandatory power over the Mandated areas.

Secretariat

The League had a permanent secretariat under the charge of a Secretary-General and such secretaries and staff as may be required. The Secretary-General was appointed by the Council with the approval of the League Assembly. The members of the Secretariat enjoyed diplomatic privileges and immunities, but they retained their own nationality in spite of being the members of the international civil service. All appointments of the Secretariat were made by the Secretary-General with the approval of the Council. The Secretary-General with two Under-Secretaries-General and two Deputy Secretaries-General was charged with the duty of compilation and publication of all international problems coming for consideration before the League. It had divided its work into 11 sections dealing with the matters of law, economics, politics, transit, administrative commissions, minority questions, mandates, disarmament, health, social problems, and international associations. It registered every treaty and international agreement entered into by any member of the League so as to give it a binding force. Its seat was at Geneva. Its expenses were borne by the League members in proportion as decided by the Assembly.

In addition to these important organs of the League of Nations, mention should be made of two important allied organs—the Permanent Court of International Justice and the International Labour Organisation.

Permanent Court of International Justice

Conscious of the limitations of the Permanent Court of Arbitration as set up by the Second Hague Convention of 1907, some statesmen at the Paris Peace Conference strongly desired a more effective machinery for the judicial settlement of international disputes. For this purpose, Art. 14 of the Covenant said that the Council "shall formulate and submit to the Members of the League for adoption plans for the establishment of a Permanent Court of International Justice." Thus, the Council appointed a Committee of Jurists in February 1920 to frame the Statute of the Court. This committee met at the Hague. It prepared a report and a draft that was submitted to the Council. It adopted the recommendations of the committee and then transmitted the same to the Assembly with its own proposals of modification. Thereupon, the Assembly set up its own committee that submitted its recommendations. As a result of this, all formalities were completed on December 13, 1921, and then the PCIJ came into being on 15 February, 1922.

The Statute of the Court had 64 articles. It was composed of 11 judges and 4 deputy judges elected by the Assembly, in conjunction with the Council, for a term of 9 years. On the recommendation of the Council, the Assembly could increase the number of judges to 15 with 6 deputies. In order to ensure impartiality and independence of the judges, they were elected concurrently by the Assembly and the Council from the lists of candidates nominated by the national groups of members of the Permanent Court of Arbitration. It was also laid down that the 'whole body should represent the main forms of civilisation and principal legal systems of the world.' A judge of the Court could be removed by a unanimous vote of all fellow judges. All judges were given diplomatic privileges and immunities. They were eligible for re-election. Its venue was the Hague where it met every year from June 15 onwards, though its special session could be convened at any time by the President. It worked with the help of three special chambers—Summary Procedure, Labour, and Transit and Communications.

As laid down in the Statute, only States could be a party to the case before the Court. It was also given that the Court was open to the members of the League and any other State whose name was included in the Annexe.[10] That is, to such States the Court was open as a matter of right. In May, 1922, the Council decided that any other State could also appear before the Court, provided it deposited with the Registrar of the Court in advance a declaration by which it accepted jurisdiction of the Court and also undertook 'to carry out in goodwill its decisions and not to resort to war against any State complying therewith.' Then, the States could bring a case before the Court either by 'unilateral application' or by 'special arrangement'. The former meant by request from a party, and the latter by agreement between various parties to submit a particular case to the Court.

A pertinent question arises at this stage as to which law was administered by the Court. The framers of the Statute well thought over this question and they defined it as follows in Art. 38 whereby the Court should apply:
1. International Conventions, whether general or particular, establishing rules expressly recognised by the contesting States;
2. International Customs as evidence of a general practice accepted as law; and

---

10. The Statute of the Court was signed by 52 States or all members of the League at that time (including two ex-members namely Brazil and Costa Rica) except by Argentina, Honduras, Nicaragua and Peru. Moreover, of all the States signing the Statute it was not ratified by Bolivia, Colombia, Costa Rica, Dominican Republic, Guatemala, Liberia, Panama, Paraguay, El Salvador, Luxembourg, and Persia (Iran).

3. General principles of law recognised by civilised nations subject to the provisions of Art. 59, judicial decisions and teachings of the most highly qualified publicists of the various nations, as subsidiary means for the determination of the rules of law.

Apart from this enumeration, the Court had the power to decide a case as per its esteemed judgement in case the parties agreed thereto.

The jurisdiction of the Court was of three kinds. Vide 'voluntary' jurisdiction, it could settle all cases which the parties referred to it and all matters especially provided for in the Treaties and Conventions in force. So wide was the jurisdiction of the Court under this clause that it could hear and settle any dispute of an international character which the parties submitted to it. Vide 'compulsory' jurisdiction of the Court, the signatories to the Covenant or to the Annexe of the Court could declare that they recogised as compulsory *ipso facto* and without special agreement in relation to any other Member or State accepting the same obligation, the jurisdiction of the Court in all or any of the cases concerning interpretation of a treaty, international law, existence of any fact which, if established, could constitute a breach of an international obligation, and the nature and extent of the reparation to be made for the breach of an international obligation. It was also stipulated in Art. 36 of the Statute that the Court alone could settle the controversy whether a particular matter fell within its jurisdiction or not. Then, Art. 37 said that when a treaty or a convention in force provided for the reference of a matter to a tribunal to be set up by the League, the Court would act in that behalf. Finally, the Court had 'advisory' jurisdication. Art. 14 of the Covenant enjoined the Court to give an advisory opinion upon any dispute or question referred to it by the Assembly or the Council. The opinion of the Court was not binding, though it had a great persuasive value of its own.

Finally, one may ask about the nature of the relationship between the League and the Court. The Court was the result of a decision taken by the Council and the League. But its composition and working were determined by its own Statute. While the Council and the League could elect its judges, or they could increase their number, they could not remove them. The Statute of the Court was brought into operation by the direct act of the individual signatories. The independent position of the Court was evident from the fact that it could exist and function even if the League went out of existence. Any State of the world could join the Court without being the member of the League of Nations. The judges of the Court were under no obligation to enforce decisions of the League. Their salaries were, of course, fixed by the League, but these were subject to the condition that they might not be decreased during the period of service of a judge. And yet the relationship of the Court to the League was somehow intimate. "The budget of the Court was a part of the budget of the League and subject to control by Assembly of the League. The Court was open as of right only to members of the League and to States mentioned in the Annexe of the Covenant of the League. Moreover, the Court might give advisory opinions on disputes or questions referred to it by the Council or the Assembly of the League."[11]

A critical examination of the working of the Court shows that it could not perform remarkable services as was expected by the people of the world. The reason was that, being a child of the League of Nations, it remained subject to same tugs and pulls that vitiated the working of its creator. As the League of Nations saw its doom in the Second World War, so happened with the fate of this Court. But as the League witnessed its rebirth in the United Nations in a refined form, so happened with the case of this Court in the form of International Court of Justice. However, we may not ignore some positive achievements of the Court. During the short term of its existence, it tried 65 cases, handed down 32 judgements on diputes, gave 27 advisory opinions and several hundred orders as endorsed by one of its judges.[12] It may, however, be true that none of the cases was of any great significance if it were taken to refer to the 'bright hopes of the better world'. "They were the undramatic, unspectacular run-of the-mill cases which any court, international or national, is primarily equipped to handle. They were, since the Court's jurisdiction was limited to cases which the disputant States

---

11. C.G. Fenwick: *International Law* (New York: Appleton-Century-Crofts, 1948), III Ed., p. 523.
12. M.O. Hudson: "The World Court" in H.E. Davis (ed.): *Pioneers in World Order* (Columbia Univ. Press, 1944), p. 67.

were willing to have adjudicated, cases on which the States concerned were willing to take the chance of losing."[13]

International Labour Organisation

Apart from maintaining peace and security in the world, the idea of improving conditions of the working class also gathered weight ever since some socialist intellectuals like Robert Owen in England, Colonel Frey in Switzerland and Blanqui in Farnce engaged the attention of the people in this important direction. But what immediately attracted the attention of the statesmen was the triumph of Marxism in Russia in 1917. Lenin's programme of establishing the Third International had its electrical effect. The British leader at the Versailles Conference told his fellow-delegates about the urgency of amelioration of the conditions of labour, because new thoughts "are surging all around". Such a realisation laid stress on the fact that international peace was integrally bound with social peace. Class war within the States was in itself a great source of danger to the peace and security of the world. The delegates of the Allied and Associated Powers realised that the solution of purely political problems "would be sterile, unless some solution could also be found to the social problem which the war had brought into sharp relief in every country, belligerent or neutral, and upon which the fires of the Russian Revolution had thrown a lurid light."[14]

For this reason, in the Preamble to Part XIII of the Treaty of Versailles, it was said that 'universal and lasting peace can be established only if it is based upon social justice.' In order to give effect to this sole realisation, Art. 23 (a) of the League Covenant said that its members "will endeavour to secure and maintain fair and humane conditions of labour for men, women and children, both in their own countries and in all countries to which their commercial and industrial relations extend, and for that purpose will establish and maintain the necessary international organisations." On January 5, 1919, the Paris Peace Conferece took an important decision to set up an international commission for labour legislation and to draft its constitution. This commission submitted its

---

13. Grant Gilmore: "The International Court of Justice" in *Yale Law Review*, Vol. 55, No. 5 (August, 1946), pp. 1053-54.
14. Temperley, op, cit., Vol. 6, p. 462.

report after about two months that was accepted by the Peace Conference on 29 April. Thus, the constitution of a new international body, called International labour Organisation (ILO), was adopted as Part XIII of the Treaty of Versailles covering articles from 387 to 427 and thereby showing the ILO as an integral part of the League of Nations.

The constitution of the ILO highlighted its objective as "to gain recognition for workers as human social beings rather than as mere commodities to be bought cheaply and to be exploited in the process of industrial and agricultual production. "It could be achieved through several measures like improvement in the working conditions, assurance of economic security through adequate terms of labour as an active participant in the policies of production, and provision of welfare services for the workers and their families. The agreement among the member-states, that created the ILO, stated that "the central aim of national and international policy should be the implementation of the principle that all human beings, irrespective of race, creed or sex, have the right to pursue both their material well-being and their spiritual development in conditions of freedom, of economic security and equal opportunity."

Art. 427 of the Treaty of Versailles contained certain general principles that the signatories accepted to ameliorate the conditions of labour in their respective countries. Popularly known as the 'Labour Charter', it included these important points:

1. Labour should not be regarded merely as a commodity or an article of commerce.
2. The right of association for all lawful purposes by the employed as well as the employers should be recognised.
3. The payment to the employed of the wage adequate to maintain the reasonable standard of life, as this, as understood in their time and country, should be guaranteed.
4. An 8-hour day or a 48-hour week should be the standard to be aimed at where it had not already been allowed.
5. A weekly rest of at least 24 hours, which was to include Sunday, wherever practicable, should be provided.
6. Child labour should be abolished.
7. The principle that men and women should receive equal remuneration for work of equal value should be enforced.

8. Each State should make provision for a system of inspection in order to ensure the enforcement of the law and regulations for the protection of the employed.
9. Workers should be protected against disease and injury arising out of employment.

The ILO functioned through an International Labour Conference, a Governing Body, and an International Labour Office. The meetings of the Conference were held at least once in a year, though its meetings could be called at any time as the occasion arose. It was composed of the national delegations of four, of whom two were government delegates and the two represented the employers and the workers each. Every delegate had the right to cast his vote individually on all matters that were taken into consideration by the Conference. Though its venue was Geneva, the meeting could be held at some other place too as per its decision by two-thirds majority of votes at the previous meeting. Its main function was to establish international social standards in the form of international labour conventions and international labour recommendations. It designated the members of the Governing Body, adopted the annual budget and examined the application of conventions. As a matter of fact, it was the principal policy-making body of the ILO.

The International Labour Office with its seat at Geneva was under the charge of a Director appointed by the Governing Body. He appointed his own staff from different nationalities of the world. Its functions were:

1. To collect and distribute information on all subjects relating to the international adjustment of conditions of industrial life and labour, and particularly the examination of subjects which it was proposed to bring before the Conference with a view to the conclusion of international conventions, and the conduct of such special investigations as were ordered by the Conference,
2. To prepare the agenda for the meetings of the Conference, and
3. To edit and publish a periodical paper dealing with problems of industry and employment of international interest.

The staff of this body rendered assistance to the Secretary-General of the League of Nations.

The Governing body of the ILO consisted of 32 persons—16 representing governments, 8 representing employers, and 8 representing the workers. Its term was 3 years. It was like an executive committee. Its meeting could be requisitioned at the request of at least 12 representatives. It had its own committees to deal with particular problems. Its functions were : to determine policy and work programmes, making of agenda for the Conference in so far as it was not prepared by the Conference itself, to prepare the annual budget of the ILO, to supervise the work of the International Labour Office and its various committees and commissions.

The ILO performed significant services during the inter-war period. By 1939 its ILC adopted about 73 recommendations and 67 conventions to be submitted for consideration and implementation to the member-States. These covered different problems of labour policy like employment, general conditions of labour, working of women and children, industrial health, safety and welfare, social insurance, industrial relations, and administration of social legislation. In 1919, it adopted four important conventions in its meeting at Washington relating to working hours (8 in a day and 48 in a week), minimum age of children for industrial employment, employment of women before and after child birth, and employment of females during night. In 1925 in its meeting at Geneva it adopted a convention of workmen's compensation for occupational diseases and in 1934 it adopted another convention ensuring benefits or allowances in case of involuntary employment.[15]

In the end, the question arises about the nature of relationship between the ILO and the League. Since the ILO had its own constitution and that it was free from the control of the Council, it enjoyed a sort of autonomy. Despite this, it was an integral part of the League for several reasons. Its membership was bound with the membership of the League in the sense that only a member of the latter could become the member of the former. Its expenses were met out of the budget of the League. In theory the office of the ILC was separated from the Secretariat of the League, in practice the two worked in close collaboration. Some noticeable change took place in due course. For instance, Japan and Brazil continued to remain the members of the ILO even after quitting the League, and the United States joined the ILO in 1935 without getting the membership of the League. Though the League had its demise in

---

15. Fenwick, op. cit., pp. 491-92.

1940, the ILO survived and became an important allied organ of the United Nations in 1945.

The Mandate System: Inauguration of the Decolonisation Process under the Auspices of the International Organisation

One of the complex problems before the peace-makers at Paris was as to what should be done to the territories detached from the defeated powers of Germany, Austria-Hungary and Turkey. The paradox of the situation lay in the fact that while the major Allied Powers like Britain and France had often declared during the war period that they had no ambition to annex the territory belonging to the Central and Axis Powers inasmuch as their objective was to liberate the people from the 'tyranny of the autocrats', at the same time, they were concerned with the weight of public opinion that desired utmost possible suppression of the defeated powers for the sake of compensating war losses. More important than this was the problem of fulfilling the terms of secret treaties whereby Italy and Japan had now come forward with their powerful claims. Such an affirmation naturally clashed with their pretended declarations in favour of their solemn resolve for granting self-determination to the people of the areas detached from the enemy powers. However, the most gigantic problem before them was the idealism of President Wilson contained in his 14-Points that insisted on 'a free, open-minded, and absolutely impartial adjustment of all colonial claims.'

A way out to this dilemma was discovered in the plan of Gen. Smuts of South Africa. It was embodied in Art. 22 of the Covenant whose Para (1) said: "To those colonies and territories which as a consequence of the late war have ceased to be under the sovereignty of the States which formerly governed them and which are inhabited by peoples not yet able to stand by themselves under the strenuous conditions of the modern world, there should be applied the principle that the well-being and development of such peoples form a sacred trust to civilisation, and that securities for the performance of this trust should be embodied in this Covenant." However, as different territories were in different stages of development, they were placed in three categories as follows:

1. In category 'A' were placed those parts of the Turkish empire that had reached a stage of development where their existence as independent nations could be provisionally recognised

subject to the rendering of administrative advice and assistance by a Mandatory until such time as they were able to stand alone. It was also stated that the wishes of these communities must be the principal consideration in the selection of the Mandatory.

2. In category 'B' were placed other areas, particularly those of South Africa that were in such a stage that a Mandatory must be responsible for the administration of the territory under the conditions which would guarantee freedom of conscience and religion, subject only to the maintenance of the public order and morals, the prohibition of abuses such as slave trade, the arms traffic and the liquor traffic and the prevention of the establishment of fortifications, or military and naval bases and of military training of the natives for other than police purposes and the defence of the country, and would also secure opportunities for the trade and commerce of other Members of the League.

3. In category 'C' were placed territories that owing to the sparseness of their population or their small size or their remoteness from the centres of civilisation, or their geographical contiguity to the territory of the Mandatory, and other circumstances could be best administered under the laws of the Mandatory as integral portions of its territory subject to the safeguards above mentioned in the interests of the indigenous population.

While the complex question could be solved, the fate of the ex-Turkish possessions still remained undecided. The Supreme Council (comprising the United States, United Kingdom, France, Italy and Japan) could take a decision in regard to the placement of territories in 'B' and 'C' categories on 7 May, 1919, at Paris, but the fate of the former Turkish possessions could be decided by the Supreme Council on 25 April, 1920, at San Remo. The delay in this matter occurred owing to differences among the Allied Powers and, more important than that, owing to the revolutionary conditions in Turkey. Thus, by the summer of 1920 the whole picture became clear and different territories were placed in different categories under the charge of different powers of the world.

In order to keep the Mandatory powers under the supervision of the League of Nations, it was provided that each Mandatory power would submit its annual report to the Council about the management and welfare services rendered by it in that area. The Council was also empowered to set up a permanent commission to receive and examine the annual report of the mediators and to advise the Council on all matters relating to the observance of the mandate. For this purpose, the Council passed the constitution of the Permanent Mandates Commission (PMC) on 1 December, 1920. It consisted of 9 members the majority of them being nationals of non-Mandatory powers. In no respect these Members were the representatives of their governments, or they could be called upon to act as such. Moreover, the PMC had the power to summon technical experts to act in advisory capacity for all questions relating to the application of this system.

Mandated Areas	Categories	Mandatory Powers
1. Syria	A	France
2. Lebanon	"	"
3. Palestine	"	Great Britain
4. Transjordania	"	"
5. Iraq	"	"
6. Cameroon (one-sixth)	B	"
7. East Africa (Tanganyika)	"	"
8. Togoland (one-third)	"	"
9. Cameroon (five-sixths)	"	France
10. Togoland (two-thirds)	"	"
11. Ruanda-Urundi	"	Belgium
12. South-West Africa	C	Union of South Africa
13. Western Samoa	"	New Zealand
14. Nauru	"	British Empire (Britain, Australia and New Zealand)
15. Former German Pacific Islands (South of the Equator)	"	Australia
16. Former German Pacific Islands (North of the Equator as Marshal, Carolines and Marianas)	"	Japan

The PMC had its seat at Geneva. It received annual reports of the Mandatories through duly authorised representatives who would be prepared to offer supplementary explanations or information that it might request. It examined each individual report in the presence of the duly authorised representatives of the Mandatory Power from which it came and then forwarded it to the Council along with its own observations as well as the reactions of the duly authorised representative. These reports were considered each year by the Assembly as well as by the Council and necessary instructions were issued to the Mandatory Powers. In 1926, the PMC suggested that the reports should be on the basis of a more extended questionnaire so that more accurate and specific information concerning conditions in the mandated territories might be collected. In the same year it admonished France for her action in Syria as a result of which she liberalised her administration for the betterment of the Syrians. In 1932, Britain relinquished her mandate over Iraq. She got independence and then became a member of the League.

In defence of the Mandate System, it may be said that it certainly marked a definite step in the way of the decolonisation process adopted under the auspices of the League of Nations. "Viewed in the context of complex problem after the termination of war, it could satisfy all parties to some extent."[16] It was taken as "compromise between anti-colonial feeling and annexationism in the Allied countries."[17] It was also looked at as an approach

---

16. E.B. Haas: "The Reconciliation of Conficting Colonial Policy Aims: Acceptance of the League of Nations Mandate System" in *International Organisation*, Vol. VI, 1952, pp. 521-36. While speaking at the Paris Peace Conference, President Wilson said: "We undo with annexations of helpess people, meant in some instance by some Powers to be used merely for exploitation. We recognised in the most solemn manner that the helpless and undeveloped peoples of the world, being in that condition, put an obligation upon us to look after their interests primarily before we use them for our interests; and that in all cases of this sort hereafter it shall be the duty of the League to see that the nations who are assigned as the tutors and advisers and directors of these peoples shall look to their interests and their development before they look to the interests and desires of the mandatory nation itself." Cited in Temperley, op. cit., Vol. I, p. 64.
17. P.E. Jacob and A.L. Atherton: *The Dynamics of International Organisation* (Homewood, Illinois: The Dorsey Press, 1965), p. 626. As a matter of fact, this system was "a half-way house between outright Allied annexation of the former colonies, which the more idealistic climate of the times seemed to rule out, and their internationalisation which was considered too novel and impractical." See F.S. Nothedge and M.J. Grieve: *A Hundred Years of International Relations* (London: Duckworth, 1971), p. 39.
18. Jacob and Atherton, op. cit., p. 627.

towards international peace. The optimists considered that it would stop any further international tension over colonies. In other words, it represented an admission of the fact that the colonies were "a responsibility to be administered in accord with the international standards and under the supervision of an international organisation."[18] In this way, it "represented a distinct improvement in colonial policy and administration."[19]

Despite this all, the Madate System was inherent with certain grave shortcomings. The existence of the discredited system of imperialism could not be ruled out altogether. Some of the Mandatory powers gave a proof of the fact that their mentality could not be affected by this system of superficial international supervision. For instance, in 1923, Lord Curzon openly said in the House of Lords: "It is a mistake to suppose that under the Covenant of the League or any other instrument, the gift of a Mandate rests with the League of Nations. It rests with the powers who have conquered the territories which it then falls to them to distribute." Likewise, when the PMC circulated a questionnaire in 1926, British Prime Minister (Austen Chamberlain) opposed it on the plea that it "was definitely more detailed, infinitely more inquisitorial than that which was being used." He went to the length of asserting that the PMC was threatening to extend its authority to a point where the government would no longer be vested in the Mandatory Power but in the Mandates Commission. Thus, Britain frankly pursued the policy of 'divide and rule' in Palestine and thereby allowed this land to be the scene of frequent massacres. The Union of South Africa treated South-West Africa as her colony. For all practical purposes, the 'C' mandates were taken as outright annexations. For these reasons, the critics dubbed it as like 'a hollow mockery' and 'a hypocritical shame' designed to disguise old imperialistic wolves in new sheep's clothing.

As a matter of fact, the Mandate System could not place effective restraints of the League over the Mandatories. The people of the mandated territories had no right to send their petitions of grievances direct to the League Secretariat. There was the prohibi-

---

19. See Quincy Wright: *Mandates under the League of Nations* (Chicago: Chicago University Press, 1932). H.W. Harris observes that the Mandate System "marks a new departure in colonial administration and creates a new status in international law." *What the League of Nations Is* (London: George Allen and Unwin, 1925), p. 104.

tion of any kind of inspection tour by the PMC. The whole system was dominated by the wishes of the Mandatories themselves. The PMC felt powerless to exert an effective influence. It acted like purely an advisory body to an overcautious and ever-weaker Council. It had no power of coercion. Its weak position becomes evident from the fact that despite the ban that the principles of demilitarisation and no recruitment of the natives for military service in the territories of 'B' and 'C' categories were established, Japan fortified the Pacific Islands under her mandate and used them effectively during the Second World War. As Carr says: "But its function was limited to friendly criticism. Since it did not grant the mandates, it clearly could not revoke them. Where the sovereignty over the mandated territories resided was an insoluble legal conundrum."[20]

Achievements of the League: Maintenance of International Peace, Security and Cooperation

As universally acclaimed, the League of Nations came into being for the purpose of maintaining international peace and co-operation. The Preamble to the Covenant affirmed the resolve of the High Contracting Parties to accept it for the 'prescription of open, just and honourable relations between nations,' and 'for the maintenance of justice and a scrupulous respect for all treaty obligations in the dealings of organised peoples with one another.' Bringing out the implications of these glorious words, Prof. F. P. Walters says: "The three essential principles of the system established by the Covenant for the maintenance of peace are:

1. To provide that in time of crises open consultation and discussion must take place not only between the States immediately concerned, but with the participation of States whose only interest is peace and justice;
2. To provide impartial tribunal to settle disputes by law or by statesmanship, and
3. To resist by common action and attempts to settle disputes by the use of force."[21]

---

20. E.H. Carr: *International Relations between the Two World Wars* (London: Macmillan, 1952), p. 16.
21. Walters: "Introduction" to H.S. Morrison: *The League and the Future of the Collective Security System* (London: George Allen and Unwin, 1937), pp. 1-2.

Thus, soon after its creation, the League started doing work for the great cause. Some of the achievement of the League in this connection may be enumerated as under:

1. In 1920, Germany submitted to the Council a series of protests against the cession of her territories of Eupen and Melmedy to Belgium. The Council discussed the matter and then instructed Germany on 2 February, 1921, to accept the dictate of the Versailles Treaty.
2. The States of Sweden and Finland developed differences over the Aaland islands. The cause of dispute was that while the islands, located at the mouth of the Gulf of Bothnia, belonged to Finland, the majority of the people were Swedish. The government of Finland claimed sovereignty over these islands, for these were ceded to her vide Peace Settlement. It also invoked the plea of theirs being under her 'domestic jurisdiction'. The Council appointed a Commission of Jurists to investigate into the matter that refuted the plea of 'domestic jurisdiction' as raised by Finland. Then, a commission was sent for an on-the-spot study. Upon receipt of its report, the Council on June 24, 1931, ruled that the Swedish charter of the people must be recognised along with the fact of sovereignty of Finland over it.
3. Poland and Lithuania had a dispute over Vilna. The Council got success in referring this matter to arbitration whereby it was given to Lithuania. But the Polish forces occupied it on October 1, 1920. Poland did not accept the Council's advice for holding a referendum there on this question. The matter was, finally, decided by the Conference of Ambassadors on 15 February, 1923, whereby it was awarded to Poland.
4. Britain and France had a dispute over the question of nationality of persons born in Morocco and Tunis. France made a rule that a person born in a territory under her colonial rule would become a French citizen, while the English rule was that a child born of the English parents would be a British citizen. When Britain desired a matter to be taken to arbitration, it was rejected by France on the plea of her 'domestic jurisdiction'. It was taken to the Permanent Court of International Justice that rejected the plea of 'domestic jurisdiction'. However, the matter could be settled by negotiations.

5. When the Delimitation Commission was engaged in the task of demarcating boundary line between Greece and Italy, one Italian was killed on the Greek soil on 23 August, 1923. The Italian government under Mussolini demanded huge indemnities, while Greece agreed to meet them to some extent. At this Italian naval authorities bombarded and then occupied the island of Corfu at the mouth of the Adriatic sea as a guarantee of reparations. The matter was seized by the Council. But by the time it could take any decision, it was settled by conference of the ambassadors. Greece was ordered to pay to Italy 500 million lire as compensation. Then, Corfu was evacuated by the Italian forces.
6. When on October 19, 1925, a commander of the Greek frontier post and one of his men were murdered by the people of Bulgaria, Greek army marched into Bulgaria. She at once appealed to the Council. The Council instructed the Greek government to withdraw its troops from the soil of Bulgaria. It also requested Britain, France and Italy to depute their military officers for an on-the-spot study. Then, the Greek forces left the place and Greece was made to pay compensation for this wrong.
7. Britain and Turkey developed a dispute over the petroleum, rich district of Mosul in Iraq. Vide the Treaty of Lausanne of 1923, it was stipulated that Britain and France would demacate the boundary line between Iraq (that was then under British mandate) and Turkey and if it could not be done, then the matter would be decided by the Council. Since Turkey demanded her full control over this area, the matter was referred to the Council. The Council sought advisory opinion of the Permanent Court of International Justice that upheld the right of the Council to settle the dispute. Thus, the Council appointed an investigation commission on the report of which the boundary line was drawn. It was not acceptable to Turkey. However, the Mosul dispute came to an end when the Treaty of Angora was signed on June 5, 1926, between Turkey and Britain whereby Turkey got a small portion of this area and some share of royalty on oil.
8. The basin of Saar was a very big industrial area known for coal mines. Its three-fourths population was German and it was a part of Germany, but it was placed temporarily under French

ownership as a partial compensation for the 'deliberate destruction wreaked by the German army upon the coal mines in northern France.' Its charge was given to a Commission of the League that would work for 15 years and then a plebiscite would be held. In 1935, the plebiscite took place under the charge of this Commission and then it was given to Germany.

Significant was the work of the League in the economic sphere too. One of the important points of Wilsonian idealism was 'the removal of all economic barriers and the establishment of an equality of trade conditions.' Thus, the Council on 13 February, 1920, decided that soon an international conference of the powers interested 'in the financial and exchange crisis should be held to consider and ease the situation.' Thus, a conference of 39 States took place at Brussels in September, 1920. (It was also attended by an American observer.) It made some important recommendations like balanced budget, stopping inflation, returning to gold standard, removing barriers to international trade, improving transport facilities and making good economic relations among nations. Its key recommendation was the establishment of an Economic and Financial Committee that was soon implemented by the League.

Another world economic conference was held in the city of Geneva in May 1927, that made important recommendations like free movement of labour and capital in all countries of the world, cooperation as aim of the industry, abandonment of useless customs duties, industrial agreements among the States for the regularisation of production, and rationalisation of industry. Its deliberations gave birth to the International Relief Union. It helped India during the earthquakes in 1934 and China during the floods in 1938. However, the World Economic Conference of June 1933 held at London is the last event in this regard, for it met under the shadow of worldwide economic depression. But so sharp were the differences that it failed to achieve its purpose. It dragged on till the end of July, concluding subsidiary agreements about the marketing of wheat and the price of silver. It adjourned *sine die* after performing the important function of demonstrating beyond any manner of doubt that the world economic crisis could not be cured by any universal formula."[22]

---

22. Carr, op. cit., p. 150.

Apart from all this, the League also rendered useful services in economic and financial restoration of Austria and Hungary. Commenting upon the successful activities of the League, a learned commentator observes: "Within the period of only a couple of decades, governments moved from comparative isolation to intensive collaboraion through international organisation or their common economic and financial problems. For the first time in history, the agenda of international meetings was crowded with economic questions, tariffs, depressions, access to raw materials, cutoms formalities, and financial reconstruction. This did not mean that the programmes were undertaken in all these spheres or that concrete policies resulted. Nevertheless, it was of great significance that these subjects were being discussed and discussed jointly by organs established by them. This was a far-reaching step in the direction of greater international economic collaboration."[23]

The achievement of the League in social and cultural spheres may also be referred to at this stage. Its Health Committee made many important researches in serious diseases like tuberculosis, prevented the spread of typhoid syphilis, cancer and malaria. An Epidemic Commission prevented the spread of typhus through Poland to Europe and smallpox among the Greek refugees immigrating from Turkey. For this purpose, it set up Epidemiological Intelligence Service at Singapore. In 1925, the Assembly requested the Committee on Intellectual Co-operation to consider and coordinate the means for making arrangements for a scientific study of international relations. It set up a committee under Dr. Nansen for restoring half a million war prisoners to their homeland. Similar services were rendered to the refugees of Greece and Bulgaria.

In 1926, the Assembly adopted a convention for the abolition of slavery. It also adopted a convention on the prohibition of traffic in opium and other dangerous drugs. At the Barcelona Conference in 1921 it adopted a convention which laid down that transport, originating in one State and crossing a second into a third should enjoy complete liberty of transit with equal treatment for all flags and freedom from customs duties and vexatious dues. Another

---

23. L.L. Leonard: *International Organisation* (New York: McGraw Hill, 1951), pp. 335-36.

conference held at Geneva in 1923 dealt with international railway traffic, equality of shipping in maritime ports and the transmission of electric power. The Maritime Ports Convention contemplated for equal treatment of all States in port dues and regulations, while the Railways Convention simplified frontier formalities for passengers and goods traffic.

As a matter of fact, the phase of 1920-30 looks, what Walters calls, like the 'halcyon days' of the League. It is rightly said: "The years 1924 to 1930 were the period of the League's greatest prestige and authority."[24] While delivering an address at the University of Oxford on 9 October, 1929, Gen. Smuts expressed his impression in these words: "Looked at in its true light, in the light of the age and of the time-honoured ideas and practice of mankind, we are beholding an amazing thing, we are witnessing one of the great miracles of history.... The League may be a difficult scheme to work, but the significant thing is that the Great Powers have pledged themselves to work it, that they have agreed to renounce their free choice of action and bound themselves to what amounts in effect to a consultative parliament of the world. By the side of that great decision and the enormous step in advance which it means, any small failures to live up to the great decision, any small lapses on the part of the League, are trifling indeed. The great choice is made, the great renunciation is over, and mankind has, as it were one, bound and in the short space of ten years, jumped from the old order to the new."[25]

Failure of the League: Breakdown of the System of Collective Security

The most significant measure of preventing another great war was contained in Articles 10 to 16 of the Covenant that sought to materialise the idea of collective security. The word 'security' indicating the goal and the prefixed word 'collective' suggesting

---

24. Carr, op. cit., p. 98.
25. Cited in Walters, op. cit., p. 413. In a statement on 10 September 1927 British Prime Minister Sir Austen Chamberlain said: "The League is the judgement of the highest tribunal to which here on earth any nation can appeal to justify its action, and on whose approval any nation will have infinite need in the moment of trial and trouble." Cited in Webster, op. cit., p. 119.

the nature of the means to be employed for its achievement constitute an important concept of international politics that may be defined as "a machinery for joint action in order to prevent or counter any attack against an established order."[26] The whole concept is based on the maxim that an attack on any one state is an attack on all. It is an international translation of the principle 'one for all and all for one'. It implies, in simple terms, that a war anywhere, against anyone and by anyone is a war against everyone and everywhere. Its underlying assumptions are: (i) war is likely to occur, and (ii) it can be prevented only by an overwhelming power. "It is, for this reason, not the elimination of power but the management of power."[27]

The Covenant had some very meaningful provisions for the maintenance of collective security system. For instance, Art. 10 said that all members of the League would respect and preserve, as against an aggression territorial integrity and existing political independence of all and, in the event of any menace, the Council would suggest measures for this purpose. Art. 11 said that any war or threat of war was a matter of concern to all members and it could be brought to the notice of the Assembly, or of the Council, by the Secretary-General or by any member. Art. 12 desired that all disputes should be settled by judicial methods; in no case a State should resort to war until three months had lapsed after the non-compliance of award given by the arbitrators or adjudicators. By virtue of Art. 13, the members agreed to carry out in good faith such award and the Council was asked to take suitable action in case a State flouted the view of the Permanent Court of International Justice or the Court of Arbitration. Finally, Art. 16 laid down that the Council would recommend to several concerned governments what effective military, naval and air force was to be contributed by different States to protect the Covenant in the event of an aggression. It empowered the Council to impose financial and economic sanctions against the aggressor. It could expel a Covenant-breaking State by a majority vote concurred in by the Representatives of all other members of the League represented thereon.

---

26. George Schwarzenberger: *Power Politics* (New York: Praeger, 1951), p. 494.
27. Inis Claude: *Power and International Relations* (New York, 1963), pp. 6-7.

One may form an impression that the Covenant had made several arrangements for the maintenance of international peace and security. Particularly in Art. 11, "indeed, lay the heart of the League idea, the revolutionary notion that in the twentieth century peace is indivisible; that war anywhere could spread anywhere. And that all States were involved in the defence of peace and could no longer detach themselves from the struggle to maintain the peace by rational discussion or by force, through policies of neutrality or isolation."[28] Unfortunately, it all went in vain when the League was, as Walters says, 'caught in difficulties' after 1930. The Manchurian crisis of 1931 laid the foundation of the League's demise. "Thus, at the moment when its first great conflict was approaching, the League was trebly weakened—first by the economic crisis which forced each country to devote its chief energies to its own internal problems; secondly, by the bitter ill-feeling between Germany and her neighbours; thirdly, by the fact that it had become a highly unpopular institution in wide sections of public opinion. There were many who openly or secretly rejoiced in its reverses and hoped for its failure, without any clear idea of their own and their countries' fate might thereby be affected."[29]

We have already discussed the crises of Manchuria, Ethiopia, Austria, Czechoslovakia and Spain in preceding chapters that eventually entailed the doom of the League. We may, therefore, now make a passing reference to these great tragic events as a result of which the whole system of collectively security broke down. The first such instance occurred in 1931 when Japan raped Manchuria and there established a puppet state of Manchukuo. When the Council asked the disputants to withdraw their troops, it was ignored by Tokyo. When the Lytton Commission held Japan guilty of the act of aggression, her government rejected its findings and then left the League in March 1933. It had a very bad effect. "The small powers, in particular, had learnt to doubt, not so much the efficacy of the League system, as the will of the great powers to apply it.... The whole structure of the League, never fully recovered the respect and authority which it had lost through its weakness and uncertainty in the early days of the conflicts.

---

28. Northedge and Grieve, op, cit., p. 155.
29. Walters. op, cit., pp. 459-60.

The second powerful jolt to the collective security system was given by Italy when she invaded Ethiopia in 1935 and captured it in the following year.[30] Surprisingly, sanctions were imposed for the first time against a Covenant-breaking State, but they could not be effective as the then major powers (Britain and France) were determined to appease the dictator of Rome. Thus, the Italian invasions of Ethiopia "sealed the fate of the League as an agency for the preservation of peace. So far from sanctions being forcefully applied under leadership of the great powers, the French assisted by the British, made clear to the Italian government that they would be willing to compensate Italy in the time-honoured manners, by portions of Ethiopian territory if the Fascist authorities called off the war."[31]

Finally, the actions of Hitler played their own part in the destruction of the collective security system. Neither Britain nor France could check the dangerous moves of the dictator of Berlin when he left the League in October 1933, introduced conscription and remilitarised the Rhineland in 1935, abrogated Locarno agreements in 1936, occupied Austria and then devoured Czechoslovakia in 1938, and, finally invaded Poland in 1939 that signalled the commencement of the Second World War. Likewise, when Hitler and Mussolini openly supported the revolt of Gen. Franco in Spain, Britain and France incapacitated the League by sticking to the course of 'non-intervention.' All these tragic developments demonstrated that now the idea of collective security "seemed to have been but a dream from which men now awakened to the old world of bilateral diplomacy and power politics."[32]

Thus, the League failed. Now let us enumerate the main causes that led to this end. These are:

1. *Withdrawal of the United States*
The greatest cause of the downfall of the League of Nations lay in the defection of the United States in spite of the fact that President

---

30. *Ibid.*, Vol. II, p. 499.
31. Northedge and Grieve, op. cit., pp. 159-60. It is rightly remarked that sanctions were not applied automatically, simultaneously and comprehensively; they were applied only haltingly, gradually and piece-meal." Schwarzenberger, op. cit., p. 498.
32. Northedge and Grieve, op. cit., p. 160.

Wilson was its principal architect. On November 19, 1919, the Senate rejected the Treaty of Versailles. It automatically entailed American non-participation in the first international organisation in view of the fact that the Covenant was an integral part of the Treaty signed by the Allied and Associated Powers on the one hand and Germany on the other. The 'isolationists' led by Henry Cabot Lodge had their triumph.[33] "The racial sentiments of Irish-Americans and German-Americans, fear of Japan and indignations over the treaty provisions concerning Shantung, Italo-American sympathy with the frustrated hopes of the Indian delegation in Paris—these and other influences began to bring formidable reinforcement to the limited group of pure isolationists or of irreconcilable partymen. Every word of the Covenant was submitted to a microscopic examination. Some concluded that the League would be an impotent debating society; some that if the United States were a member, her soldiers would be ordered off to fight in Ireland or Arabia in defence of the British Empire, her immigration laws would be dictated by Japan, and her tariffs controlled by her competitors."[34]

2. Aggressive Nationalism

Great injustice was done to Germany under the Peace Settlement and the Covenant of the League was conjoined with it. Naturally,

---

33. The isolationists were drawing inspiration from the classical affirmation of President Washington who in his farewell address (1896) had said: "The great rule of conduct for us in regard to foreign nations is, in extending our commercial relations, to have with them as little political connection as possible. So far as we have already formed engagements but they be fulfilled with perfect good faith. Here let us stop. Europe has a set of primary interests which to us have none or a very remote relation. Hence, she must be engaged in frequent controversies, the causes of which are essentially foreign to our concern. Hence, therefore, it must be unwise for us to implicate ourselves by artificial ties in the ordinary combinations and collisions of her friendship or enmities." Cited in J.H. Latane and D.W. Wainhouse: *A History of American Foreign Policy* (New York: Odyssey Press, 1940), p. 99.
34. Walters, Vol. I. op, cit., p. 69. He futher opines that the United States "seemed to be marked by circumstance and by character, for moral and political leadership. First in power, she was also unique in her freedom from ancient feuds, from present embarrassments, and from fears of the future. She had no desire for military glory or for territorial expansion. There, with the support of the British Commonwealth, she would have pointed the way to reconciliation." Ibid., p. 72.

it was an eyesore to the people of Germany. But the victors of Italy and Japan had their own grievances. While Germany complained of excessive suppression, Italy and Japan took vigorously to the path of revision of the peace settlements, for their hopes had been frustrated by the obduracy of Wilson. The secret treaties made during the war by Italy and Japan with Britain and France remained unrecognised. Naturally, it left them like highly unsatiated powers. It was for this reason that though these countries could digest their resentment in 1920, they anxiously and eagerly looked forward for the opportune time to realise their irredentism. Thus, when Japan took the first chance, the second was taken by Italy, and the last by Germany. The 'period of crisis' (1931-1939) showed that the aggressive nationalism of these three Fascist powers was the sole motivating force behind their claim for the revision of peace settlements. They "were bitterly dissatisfied with the *status quo* and were swept along by a fever of romantic, swashbuckling nationalism into attempts to change it by force which at first, at least, were successful."[35]

3. *Appeasement Policy*

The aggressive nationalism of Japan, Italy and Germany could make success on account of the policy of 'impotence' pursued by Britain and France directly and by the United States in an indirect manner. The ultimate motive to see the destruction of Communist power in Russia at the hands of the Fascist dictators of Tokyo, Rome and Berlin informed the statesmen of London, Paris and Washington to invoke the plea of 'purchasing peace at any price.' The dishonest British statesmen like Viscount Cecil, Gilbert Murray, Stanley Baldwin, Samuel Hoare, Neville Chamberlain and Winston Churchill and French leaders like Bonnett, Laval and Daladier ever "regarded the League as much more than claptrap of the hustings to which public defence had to be paid while traditional diplomatic processes still went on in private. The British Conservative leader, L.S. Amery, true to his style of thinking, once likened the League to the legend of the Emperor's New Clothes; everyone had to pretend to see something in it, no one was honest enough to say that it was an optical illusion."[36] In other words, the 'guiltymen

---

35. Northedge and Grieve, op. cit., p. 162.
36. Ibid.

idea' was very much at the base of this notorious policy of appeasement. The spectre of Communism had so much haunted their minds that they desired its destruction at any cost. Thus, the aggressors marked that collective security system could and in this famous occasion did turn out to be a potential friend against the more dangerous aggressor which threatened the peace by methods the League system was not designed to prevent."[37]

4. *Power Politics*
Another factor was that the major powers of the world could not subordinate their national interests to the great cause for which the first world organisation was established. While Britain and France suppressed Germany under the Treaty of Versailles, the former sought to restore the position of Germany in the comity of nations so much so that Germany was not only included in the League, she was given a seat in the Council (lying vacant owing to American withdrawal). With this development Brazil had to quit the League in protest in 1926. Even the United States supported the case of Germany in a different way.[38] What happened at Geneva in 1926 had its rehearsal at Locarno a year before.[39] The Soviet Union denounced the League of Nations as a 'band of robber nations', but her attitude in this regard changed after the remilitarisation of Germany under Hitler. Suffering from the pangs of worldwide economic depression, the United States cared more for her economic interests and thus recognised the USSR in 1933. Then in 1934 the USSR joined the League "only to be expelled, the only member-State to suffer this experience, when her forces invaded Finland in 1939."[40] Whenever occasion arose, the great powers of that time demonstrated their unwillingness to subordinate their own inter-

---

37. Ibid., p. 163.
38. It is well commented: "But the road did not, as Count Bernstoff had envisaged, lead via the League of Nations to a *rapprochement* with the West, but on the contrary the *rapprochement* with the Western powers led German into the League of Nations." Gerhard Schultz: *Revolution and Peace Treaties, 1917-20* (London: Methuen, 1972), Translated from German into English by Marvan, Jackson, p. 227.
39. It is aptly commented: "Locarno was an admirable achievement, but Locarno must be brought into the framework of the League, not the League into the framework of the Locarno." Walters, op. cit., p. 138.
40. Northedge and Grieve, op. cit., p. 138.

ests to the peace of the world."[41] Later, Gen. Smuts thus recalled: "What was everybody's business in the end proved to be nobody's business. Each one looked to the other to take the lead and the aggressors got away with it."[42]

5. Gaps in the Covenant

Finally, we come to the theoretical part of this study. There were serious shortcomings in the text of the Covenant. While the important provisions desired Members to have a pacific settlement of international disputes, they did not make the Council powerful enough to check an aggressor effectively. Surprisingly, war remained legal if it was waged after the prescribed period of three months, or it was waged against a State not complying with the resolution of the Council or with the award of the Permanent Court of International Justice, or it was waged in the circumstances in which the arbitral or judicial body had been unable to give its award, or in which the Council had failed to give its unanimous report. Unsuccessful attempts were made to fill up these gaps as by the Draft Treaty of Mutual Assistance of 1923 and the Geneva Protocol of 1924. Only Kellogg-Briand Pact could be a successful effort, but even this did not prohibit war in the case of self-defence. Moreover, it failed to set up a machinery for the prevention of war. At the most, it lived like a moral precept. The association of the United States with the pact for the outlawry of war was certainly widely hailed. Quitting the world body became the most non-serious affair and "the rate of withdrawal of States from the membership reflected the progress of a fatal disease."[43]

---

41. Grant and Temperley: *Europe in the Nineteenth and Twentieth Centuries* (London: Longmans, 1952), p. 583.
42. Gen. Smuts: "Thoughts on the New World", being a speech to the members of the Empire Parliamentary Association on November 25, 1947, ibid.
43. F.L. Schuman: *International Politics* (New York: McGraw Hill, 1948), IV. Ed., p. 313. As Jean Reay puts it: "We are convinced that this timidity of the authors of the Covenant has serious consequences and puts in jeopardy the new system which they tried to erect. As a matter of fact, since the contrary opinion was not clearly expressed, it remained tacitly admitted that war is a solution, the normal solution, of international conflicts. The obligations, as a matter of law, are presented only as exceptions; the implicit rule is the recourse to war." Cited in H.J. Morgenthau: *Politics among Nations* (Calcutta: Scientific Book Agency, 1966), p. 472.

Membership of the League of Nations

Original Members (1920)	Subsequent Members		Withdrawal of Membership (effective after two years' notice)	
1. Argentina	1. Afghanistan	Sept., 1934	1. Brazil	June, 1926
2. Australia	2. Albania	Dec., 1920	2. Chile	June, 1938
3. Belgium	3. Austria	Dec., 1920	3. Costa Rica	Jan., 1925
4. Bolivia	4. Dominican Republic	Sept., 1924	4. El Salvador	Aug., 1937
5. Brazil	5. Ecuador	Sept., 1934	5. Germany	Oct., 1933
6. Bulgaria	6. Egypt	May, 1937	6. Guatemala	May., 1936
7. Canada	7. Estonia	Sept., 1921	7. Haiti	April, 1942
8. Chile	8. Ethiopia	Sept., 1923	8. Honduras	July, 1936
9. China	9. Finland	Dec., 1920	9. Hungary	April, 1939
10. Colombia	10. Germany	Sept., 1926	10. Italy	Dec., 1937
11. Costa Rica	11. Hungary	Sept., 1922	11. Japan	March., 1933
12. Cuba	12. Iraq	Oct., 1932	12. New Zealand	June., 1936
13. Czechoslovakia	13. Ireland	Sept., 1923	13. Paraguay	Feb., 1935
14. Denmark	14. Latvia	Sep., 1921	14. Peru	April, 1939
15. El Salvador	15. Luxembourg	Dec., 1920	15. Portugal	July, 1940
16. France	16. Mexico	Sept., 1931	16. Spain	May, 1939
24. Liberia				
25. Lithuania				
26. Netherlands				
27. New Zealand				
28. Nicaragua				
29. Norway				
30. Panama				
31. Paraguay				
32. Persia (Iran)				
33. Peru				
34. Poland				
35. Portugal				
36. Romania				
37. Siam (Thailand)				
38. Spain				
39. Sweden				

17.	Greece	40.	Switzerland	17.	Turkey	July, 1932
18.	Guatemala	41.	South Africa	18.	USSR	Sept., 1934
19.	Haiti	42.	United Kingdom			
20.	Honduras	43.	Uruguay			
21.	India	44.	Venezuela			
22.	Italy	45.	Yugoslavia			
23.	Japan					

17.	Venezuela	July., 1938

---

1. Austria was annexed in March 1938 by Germany.
2. Albania was annexed in April 1939 by Italy.
3. USSR was expelled by the League Council in December 1939.

Source : *Encyclopaedia Britannica*, Vol. 13, 1963 Ed., p. 833.

6. Race for Armament

The mere existence of an international organisation is not enough for the maintenance of international peace and security; it is equally necessary that major States of the world sincerely observe the call for disarmament. Taking it into consideration, President Wilson in one of his 14-Points called for national armament to be reduced to the lowest point consistent with domestic safety. It got its way into Art.8 of the Covenant that desired reduction of armament to the lowest point consistent with national safety and the enforcement by common action of international obligations. The League made some effort in this important direction. In 1925, the conclusion of the Locarno treaties, one of the purposes of which was to hasten effecting disarmament, paved the way for the establishment of the Preparatory Commission. As a result of this, the World Conference on Disarmament started at Geneva on February 2, 1934, in which 61 States took part.

But the whole purpose was frustrated when the major powers got themselves involved into complex issues like distinction between offensive and defensive weapons, alignment of the disarmament goal with the system of collective security, treatment of land, air and naval forces as separately or jointly, reduction of arms in a direct way or in an indirect way by drastic cuts in the budget, inspection of armaments by some international agency or not, and the like. France insisted that any movement for disarmament must be accompanied by a system of more effective guarantee for security, while Britain and America insisted that any progress in the direction of disarmament would automatically bring security. Opposed to both, the Italians and the Germans demanded equality in respect of national armaments, while the Russians proposed complete disarmament and an inspection system. The deadlock occurred that could not be broken even by the proposal of President Hoover that certain highly destructive weapons should be abolished and all others be reduced by one-third. The whole effort came to an end when in October 1933, Germany withdrew from the League and its Disarmament Conference and frankly took to the path of remilitarisation.[44] In 1934 it became evident that the League

---

44. Reduction of national armaments and maintenance of collective security were 'incompatible principles' like an attempt 'to square the circle'. Lord Davies: *The*

was proving impotent to insure peace and the States were falling back on their own right arms to protect themselves against the growing threat from Germany, Italy and Japan. "The letters of FAILURE written large over the portals of successive disarmament conferences during the two decades after Versailles, became letters of impending catastrophe for the Western World."[45]

In short, the negative role of the three major powers (Britain, France and USA) coupled with the destructive role of three other powers (Japan, Italy and Germany) entailed the end of the first international organisation. It could never recover from the blow of the Ethiopian war, for instead of checking a third-rate power like Italy, the great appeasers of London and Paris showed an anxiety to avoid war with a Fascist country at almost any cost that proved to be 'the decisive factor'.[46] The situation deteriorated more after the surrender at Munich in 1938 that forced the League to 'maintain a shadowy existence' until 1946 when it was formally dissolved.[47]

Concluding Observations

It is true that the League failed after giving a proof of being like 'a dishonourable daughter of a disreputed mother' (Norman Bentwich). The Treaty of Versailles, with which the Covenant was appended, was an ill-fated document combining with it contempt, spite, vengeance, idealism of Wilson, imperialism of Lloyd George, and materialism of Clemenceau. Its burden was hypocrisy. Moreover, since the Covenant was made an integral part of other treaties as well, it proved to be a matter of serious disadvantage. All defeated countries "became prejudiced against the League simply because it was so closely tied to the Paris peace settlement."[48]

Nevertheless, it cannot be lost sight of that even during this small span of some 20 years, the League could make some noticeable success. While writing in 1939, the American Secretary of State (Hull) said that the League "had been responsible for more hu-

---

    Problem of the Twentieth Century: A Study in International Relationships (London: Ernest Benn, 1934), p. 227.
45. See Schuman: *International Politics*, V.Ed., 1953, p. 233.
46. C.G. Haines and J.S. Hoffman: *The Origins and Background of the Second World War* (London: Oxford University Press, 1943), p. 385.
47. N.D. Palmer and H.C. Perkins: *International Relations* (Calcutta: Scientific Book Agency, 1965), p. 347.
48. W.C. Langsam: *The World Since 1919* (Delhi: Surjeet Publications, 1981), p. 25.

manitarian and scientific endeavour than any other organisation in history."[49] And Arthur Sweetser declared in 1940 that "the experience has been deeply valuable, for it marked a phase in the slow transition of mankind from international anarchy to the world community."[50] Potter's observation runs: "If measured by what other international organisations had accomplished in the past, the League's performance even in the security field, rates very high, indeed higher than that of any other international institution, with the exception of a very few highly special and limited agencies."[51]

The League "did not prevent the outbreak of a Second World War in 1939; indeed, after the fiasco of economic sanctions against Mussolini's attempt to conquer Ethiopia in 1935-36, the League was for all practical purposes dead. Nevertheless, by 1939 the League idea, if not the League itself, had become a permanent feature of the international landscape and there was no question among the victorious Allies in the Second World War than that a future attempt should be made to preserve peace through a general international organisation. This second attempt, the United Nations Organisation, is certainly better endowed with resources and legal authority than the Old League, but it is founded upon much the same general lines and had borrowed many features and principles from its predecessors, despite the protests of many statesmen present at San Francisco Conference to draw up the UN Charter in May-June, 1945 that they were beginning on an essentially clean sheet."[52] Again: "...if a woman hopes to marry a multi-millionaire and only succeeds in winning a millionaire, she can hardly be described as a failure.... The League was a tender plant; it had to survive in an Arctic blizzard and with very many of those who actually worked in it, as politicians or diplomats, sceptical as to whether it would survive, even in the most clement of times."[53]

It is indisputable that "the greatest general contribution of the League was its influence in spreading the idea of international co-

---

49. See Warren O. Ault: *Europe in Modern Times*, p. 643.
50. Sweetser: "The Non-Political Achievements of the League" in *Foreign Affairs* (October, 1940), p. 192.
51. P.B. Potter: *An Introduction to the Study of International Organisation* (New York: Appleton-Century-Crofts, 1951), p. 252.
52. Northedge and Grieve, op. cit., p. 140.
53. Ibid., p. 160.

operation."[54] A great authority on this subject endorses his esteemed judgement in these words: "As a living thing, it was born; it experienced growth, success and power; it inspired love and hatred; it met with failure and defeat.... Although the League's span was short and troubled, its success transitory, and its end inglorious, it must always hold a place of supreme importance in history. It was the first effective move towards the organisation of a world-wide political and social order, in which the common interests of humanity could be seen and served across the barriers of national tradition, racial differences, or geographical separation."[55] In fine, that the failure of the League "did not doom the whole process of international organisation is, as has been remarked, at first not surprising .... It was possible to see the League not an especially a promising one. This was cheerily the case in such areas as the development of international law and the range of issue arising out of economic independence, but even in relation to international security matters, the League had developed a variety of peace-keeping mechanisms which could perhaps be built upon."[56]

We may conclude our study with these words of a learned writer : 'The League of Nations represented both a radical and a conservative trend in the development of international relations. It was radical because, for the first time, the ideas and ideals of several philosophers who had advocated a universal organisation for promoting peace and cooperation among nations were incorporated into state policy. It was radical because it dared to encompass within a single organisation, the means for dealing with

---

54. Langsam, op. cit., p. 33. H.A.L. Fisher says that the League could give "the maximum of international cooperation which its Member-States desired at any time." Cited in Northedge and Grieve, op. cit., p. 144.
55. Walters, op. cit., p. 1. Elsewhere this writer says that "in its purposes and principles, its institutions and its methods, the United Nations bears at every point the mark of the experience of the League. Its judgments upon the records of the League and all that it did, this truth must always be borne in mind. Whatever the fortunes of the United Nations may be, the fact that, at the close of the Second World War its establishment was desired and approved by the whole community of civilised peoples, must stand to future generations as a vindication of the men who planned the League, of the thousands who worked for it, of the many millions who placed in it their hopes of a peaceful and prospeous world." ibid., Vol. II, p. 812.
56. David Armstrong: *The Rise of the International Organisation: A Short History* (London: Macmillan, 1982), p. 48.

League of Nations

a wide range of problems on which international action was desirable if not imperative. It was radical because it was innovative in creating the political, judicial, economic, social and administrative agencies that would serve basically as a model for the United Nations. The lessons of the League's twenty years of experience also served well to modify and strengthen the pattern of the United Nations. The trend in establishing the League was conservative because it was based on an existing international order and no attempt was made to redirect the sources of authority and power. The sovereignty of national states remained undisturbed in an organisation based primarily on the principle of voluntary co-operation among those states. The innovations of the League did not include any radically new practices. The methods for settling disputes, the use of conferences, the techniques of international administration, and the principles of equality of states and of the right of a state to be bound only by its own consent were long established features of the international scene. The new element was the superimposition upon the existing order of a comprehensive and permanent system of periodic conferences and continuous administration.... If the League of Nations is measured against a yardstick of hopes and possibilities for achieving world peace and cooperation, it fell short of its goal. If, on the other hand, it is measured by the standard of previous advances towards world order, it represented a breakthrough in the development of international organisation. If the process of development does not reverse itself, the League will continue to stand as a landmark in the evolutionary process of achieving a more orderly world."[57]

---

57. A. LeRoy Bennett: *International Organisations: Principles and Issues* (New Jersey: Prentice-Hall Inc., 1988), IV ed., pp. 36-38.

APPENDIX A

The Covenant of the League of Nations
The High Contracting Parties,
    In order to promote international cooperation and to achieve international peace and security,
    By the acceptance of obligations not to resort to war,
    By the prescription of open, just and honourable relations between nations,
    By the firm establishment of the understanding of international law as the actual rule of conduct among Governments,
    And by the maintenance of justice and the scrupulous respect for all treaty obligations in the dealings of organised peoples with one another,
    Agree to this Covenant of the League of Nations.

ARTICLE 1

    1. The original Members of the League of Nations shall be those of the Signatories which are named in the Annexe to this Covenant and also such of those other States named in the Annexe as shall accede without reservation to this Covenant. Such accesssion shall be affected by a Declaration deposited with the Secretariat within two months of the coming into force of the Covenant. Notice thereof shall be sent to all other Members of the League.
    2. Any fully self-governing State, Dominion or Colony not named in the Annexe may become a Member of the League if its admission is agreed to by two-thirds of the Assembly, provided that it shall give effective guarantees of its sincere intention to observe its international obligations and shall accept such regulations as may be prescribed by the League in regard to its military, naval and air forces and armaments.
    3. Any Member of the League may, after two years' notice of its intention to do so, withdraw from the League provided that all

its international obligations and all its obligations under this Covenant shall have been fulfilled at the time of its withdrawal.

Article 2

The action of the League under this Covenant shall be effected through the instrumentality of an Assembly and of a Council, with a permanent Secretariat.

Article 3

1. The Assembly shall consist of the Representatives of the Members of the League.
2. The Assembly shall meet at stated intervals and from time to time as occasion may require at the seat of the League or at such other place as may be decided upon.
3. The Assembly may deal at its meetings with any matter within the sphere of action of the League or affecting the peace of the world.
4. At meetings of the Assembly, each Member of the League shall have one vote, and may have not more that three Representatives.

Article 4

1. The Council shall consist of Representatives of the Principal Allied and Associated Powers,[1] together with Representaives of four other Members of the League. These four Members of the League shall be selected by the Assembly from time to time in its discretion. Until the appointment of the Representatives of the four Members of the League first selected by the Assembly, Representatives of Belgium, Brazil, Spain and Greece shall be members of the Council.
2. With the approval of the majority of the Assembly, the Council may name additional Members of the League whose Representatives shall always be Members of the Council; the

---

1. The Principal Allied and Associated Powers were—the US British Empire, France, Italy and Japan.

Council with like approval may increase the number of Members of the League to be selected by the Assembly for representation on the Council.

2A. *The Assembly shall fix by a two-thirds majority the rules dealing with the election of the non-permanent Members of the Council, and particularly such regulations as relate to their term of office and the conditions of eligibility.*[2]

3. The Council shall meet from time to time as occasion may require, and at least once a year, at the seat of the League, or at such other place as may be decided upon.

4. The Council may deal at its meetings with any matter within the sphere of action of the League or affecting the peace of the world.

5. Any Member of the League not represented on the Council shall be invited to send a Representative to sit as a member at any meetings of the Council during the consideration of matters specially affecting the interests of that Member of the League.

6. At meetings of the Council, each Member of the League represented on the Council shall have one vote, and may have not more that one Representative.

Article 5

1. Except where otherwise expressly provided in this Covenant or by the terms of the present Treaty, decisions at any meeting of the Assembly or of the Council shall require the agreements of all the Members of the League represented at the meeting.

2. All matters of procedure at the meetings of Assembly or of the Council, including the appointment of Committees to investigate particular matters, shall be regulated by the Assembly or by the Council and may be decided by a majority of the Members of the League represented at the meeting.

3. The first meeting of the Assembly and the first meeting of the Council shall be summoned by the President of the United States of America.

---

2. This Amendment came into force on 29 July, 1926, in accordance with Art. 26 of the Covenant.

Article 6

1. The permanent Secretariat shall be established at the seat of the League. The Secretariat shall comprise a Secretary-General and such secretaries and staff as may be required.
2. The first Secretary-General shall be the person named in the Annexe; thereafter the Secretary-General shall be appointed by the Council with the approval of the majority of the Assembly.
3. The Secretaries and staff of the Secretariat shall be appointed by the Secretary-General with the approval of the Council.
4. The expenses of the Secretariat shall be borne by the Members of the League in proportion decided by the Assembly.[3]

Article 7

1. The Seat of the League is established at Geneva.
2. The Council at any time may decide that the seat of the League shall be established elsewhere.
3. All positions under or in connection with the League, including the Secretariat, shall be open equally to men and women.
4. Representatives of the Members of the League and officials of the League when engaged in the business of the League shall enjoy diplomatic privileges and immunities.
5. The buildings and other property occupied by the League or its officials or by Representatives attending its meetings shall be inviolable.

Article 8

1. The Members of the League recognise that the maintenance of peace requires the reduction of national armaments to the lowest point consistent with national safety and the enforcement of common action of international obligations.
2. The Council, taking into account the geographical situation and circumstances of each State, shall formulate plans for such

---

3. This amendment came into force on 13 August, 1924, in accordance with Art. 26 of the Covenant and replaced the following paragraph:
"The expenses of the Secretariat shall be borne by the Members of the League in accordance with the apportionment of the expenses of the International Bureau of the Universal Postal Union."

reduction for the consideration and action of several Governments.

3. Such plans shall be subject to reconsideration and revision at least every ten years.

4. After these plans shall have been adopted by the several Governments, the limits of the armaments therein fixed shall not exceed without the concurrence of the Council.

5. The Members of the League agree that the manufacture by private enterprise of munitions and implements of war is open to grave objections. The Council shall advise how the evil effects attendent upon such manufacture can be prevented, due regard being had to the necessities of those Members of the League which are not able to manufacture the munitions and implements of war necessary for their safety.

The Members of the League undertake to interchange full and frank information as to the scale of their armaments, their military, naval and air programmes and the condition of such of their industries as are adaptable to warlike purposes.

Article 9

A permanent commission shall be constituted to advise the Council on the execution of the provisions of Articles 1 and 8 and on military, naval and air questions generally.

Article 10

The Members of the League undertake to respect and preserve as against external aggression, the territorial integrity and existing political independence of all Members of the League. In case of any such aggression or in case of any threat or danger of such aggression, the Council shall advise upon the means by which this obligation shall be fulfilled.

Article 11

1. Any war or threat of war, whether immediately affecting any of the Members of the League or not, is hereby declared a matter of concern of the whole League, and the League shall take any action that may be deemed wise and effective to safeguard the

peace of nations. In case any such emergency should arise, the Secretary-General shall on the request of any Member of the League forthwith summon a meeting of the Council.

2. It is also declared to be the friendly right of each Member of the League to bring to the attention of the Assembly or of the Council any circumstance whatever affecting international relations which threatens to disturb international peace or the good understanding between nations upon which peace depends.

Article 12

1. The Members of the League agree that if there should arise between them any dispute likely to lead to a rupture, they will submit the matter either to arbitration or judicial settlement or to inquiry by the Council, and they agree in no case to resort to war until three months after the award by the arbitrators or the judicial decision or the report by the Council.

2. In any case under this Article the award of arbitrators or the judicial decision shall be made within a reasonable time, and the report of the Council shall be made within six months after the submission of the dispute.

Article 13

1. The Members of the League agree that whenever any dispute shall arise between them which they recognise to be suitable for submission to arbitration or judicial settlement, and which cannot be satisfactorily settled by diplomacy, they will submit the whole subject matter to arbitration or judicial settlement.

2. Disputes as to the interpretation of a treaty, as to any question of international law, as to the existence of any fact which when established would constitute a breach of international obligation, or as to the extent and nature of the reparation to be made for any such breach, are declared to be among those which are generally suitable for submission to arbitration or judicial settlement.

3. For the consideration of any such dispute, the Court to which the case is referred shall be the Permanent Court of International Justice, established in accordance with Article 14, or any

tribunal agreed on by the parties to the dispute or stipulated in any convention existing between them.

4. The Members of the League agree that they will carry out in full good faith any award or *decision* that may be rendered, and that they will not resort to war against a Member of the League which complies therewith. In the event of any failure to carry out such an award or decision, the Council shall propose what steps should be taken to give effect thereto.

Article 14

The Council shall formulate and submit to the Members of the League for adoption plans for the establishment of a Permanent Court of International Justice. The Court shall be competent to hear and determine any dispute of an international character which the parties thereto submit to it. The Court may also give an advisory opinion upon any dispute or question referred to it by the Council or by the Assembly.

Article 15

1. If there should arise between Members of the League any dispute likely to lead to a rupture, which is not submitted to arbitration or judicial settlement in accordance with Article 13, the Members of the League agree that they will submit the matter to the Council. Any party to the dispute may effect such submission by giving notice of the existence of the dispute to the Secretary-General, who will make all necessary arrangements for a full investigation and consideration thereof.

2. For this purpose the parties to the dispute will communicate to the Secretary-General, as promptly as possible, statements of their case with all the relevant facts and papers, and the Council may forthwith direct the publication thereof.

3. The Council shall endeavour to effect a settlement of the dispute, and if such efforts are successful, a statement shall be made public giving such facts and explanations regarding the dispute and the terms of settlement thereof as the Council may deem appropriate.

4. If the dispute is not thus settled, the Council, either unanimously or by a majority vote, shall make and publish a report

containing a statement of the facts of the dispute and the recommendations which are deemed just and proper in regard thereto.

5. Any Member of the League represented on the Council may make public a statement of the facts of the dispute and of its conclusions regarding the same.

6. If a report by the Council is unanimously agreed to by the members thereof other than the Representative of one or more of the parties to the dispute, the Members of the League agree that they will not go to war with any party to the dispute which complies with the recommendations of the report.

7. If the Council fails to reach a report which is unanimously agreed to by the members thereof, other than the Representatives of one or more parties to the dispute, the Members of the League reserve to themselves the right to take such action as they shall consider necessary for the maintenance of right and justice.

8. If the dispute between the parties is claimed by one of them, and is found by the Council, to arise out of a matter which by international law is solely within the domestic jurisdiction of that party, the Council shall so report, and shall make no recommendation as to its settlement.

9. The Council may, in any case under this Article, refer the dispute to the Assembly. The dispute shall be so referred at the request of either party to the dispute, provided that such request be made within fourteen days after the submission of the dispute to the Council.

10. In any case referred to the Assembly, all the provisions of this Article and of Article 12 relating to the action and powers of the Council shall apply to the action and powers of the Assembly, provided that a report made by the Assembly, if concurred in by the Representatives of those Members of the League represented on the Council and of a majority of the other Members of the League exclusive in each case of the Representatives of the parties to the dispute, shall have the same force as a report by the Council concurred in by all the members thereof other than the Representatives of one or more of the parties to the dispute.

Article 16

1. Should any Member of the League resort to war in disregard

of its Covenants under Articles 12, 13 and 15, it shall *ipso facto* be deemed to have committed an act of war against all other Members of the League, which hereby undertake immediately to subject it to the severance of all trade or financial relations, the prohibition of all intercourse between their nationals and nationals of the Covenant-breaking State, and the prevention of all financial, commercial and personal intercourse between the nationals of the Covenant-breaking State and the nationals of any other State, whether a Member of the League or not.

2. It shall be the duty of the Council in such case to recommend to the several Governments concerned what effective military, naval or air force the Members of the League shall severally contribute to the armed forces to be used to protect the Covenant of the League.

3. The Members of the League agree, further, that they will mutually support one another in the financial and economic measures which are taken under this Article in order to minimise the loss or inconvenience resulting from the above measures, and they will mutually support one another in resisting any special measures aimed at one of their members by Covenant-breaking State, and that they will take the necessary steps to afford passage through their territory to the forces of any of the Members of the League which are cooperating to protect the Covenant of the League.

4. Any Member of the League which has violated the Covenant of the League may be declared to be no longer a Member of the League by a vote of the Council concurred in by the Representatives of all the other Members of the League represented thereon.

Article 17

1. In the event of a dispute between a Member of the League and a State which is not a Member of the League, or between the States not Members of the League, the State or States not Members of the League shall be invited to accept the obligation of membership in the League for the purposes of such dispute, upon such conditions as the Council my deem just. If such invitation is accepted, the provisions of Articles 12 to 16 inclusive shall be applied with such modifications as may be deemed necessary by the Council.

2. Upon such invitation being given, the Council shall immediately institute an inquiry into the circumstances of the dispute and recommend such action as may seem best and most effectual in the circumstances.

3. If a State so invited shall refuse to accept the obligation of membership in the League for the purposes of such dispute, and shall resort to war against a Member of the League, the provisions of Article 16 shall be applicable as against the State taking such action.

4. If both parties to the dispute when so invited refuse to accept the obligations of membership in the League for the purposes of such dispute, the Council may take such measures and make such recommendations as will prevent hostilities and will result in the settlement of the dispute.

ARTICLE 18

Every treaty or international engagement entered into hereafter by any Member of the League shall be forthwith registered with the Secretariat and shall, as soon as possible, be published by it. No such treaty or international engagement shall be binding until so registered.

ARTICLE 19

The Assembly may from time to time advise the reconsideration by the Members of the League of treaties which have become inapplicable and the consideration of international conditions whose continuance might endanger the continuance of world peace.

ARTICLE 20

1. The members of the League severally agree that this Covenant is accepted as abrogating all obligations or understandings *inter se* which are inconsistent with the terms thereof, and solemnly undertake that they will not hereafter enter into engagements inconsistent with the terms thereof.

2. In case any Member of the League shall, before becoming a Member of the League, have undertaken any obligations

inconsistent with the terms of this Covenant, it shall be the duty of such Member to take immediate steps to procure its release from such obligations.

ARTICLE 21

Nothing in this Covenant shall be deemed to affect the validity of international engagements, such as treaties of arbitration or regional understandings like the Monroe Doctrine, for securing the maintenance of peace.

ARTICLE 22

1. To those colonies and territories which as a consequence of the late war have ceased to be under the sovereignty of the States which formerly governed them and which are inhabited by the people not yet able to stand by themselves under the strenuous conditions of the modern world, there should be applied the principle that the well-being and development of such peoples form a sacred trust of civilisation and that securities for the performance of this trust should be embodied in this Covenant.

2. The best method of giving practical effect to this principle is that the tutelage of such peoples should be entrusted to advanced nations who by reason of their resources, their experience, or their geographical position can best undertake this responsibility, and who are willing to accept it, and that this tutelage should be exercised by them as Mandatories on behalf of the League.

3. The character of the mandate must differ according to the stage of development of the people, the geographical situation of the territory, its economic conditions and other similar circumstances.

4. Certain communities formerly belonging to Turkish Empire have reached a stage of development where their existence as independent nations can be provisionally recognised subject to the rendering of adminstrative advice and assistance by a Mandatory until such time as they are able to stand alone. The wishes of these communities must be a principal consideration in the selection of the Mandatory.

5. Other peoples, especially those of Central Africa, are at such a stage that the Mandatory must be responsible for the

administration of the territory under conditions which will guarantee freedom of conscience and religion, subject only to the maintenance of public order and morals, the prohibition of abuses such as the slave trade, the arms traffic and the liquor traffic, and the prevention of the establishment of fortifications or military and naval bases and of military training of the natives for more than police purpose and the defence of territory, and will also secure equal opportunities for the trade and commerce of other Members of the League.

6. There are territories, such as South-West Africa and certain South Pacific Islands, which, owing to the sparseness of their population, or their small size, or their remoteness from the centres of civilization, or their geographical countiguity to the territory of the Mandatory, and other circumstances, can be best administered under subject to the safeguards above mentioned in the interests of the indigenous population.

7. In every case of mandate, the Mandatory shall render to the Council an annual report in reference to the territory committed to its charge.

8. The degree of authority, control,or administration to be exercised by the Mandatory shall, if not previously agreed upon by the Members of the League, be explicitly defined in each case by the Council.

9. A permanent Commission shall be constituted to receive and examine the annual reports of the Mandatories and to advise the Council on all matters relating to the observance of the Mandates.

Article 23

Subject to and in accordance with the provisions of international conventions existing or hereafter to be agreed upon, the Members of the League:
a) will endeavour to secure and maintain fair and humane conditions for men, women, and children, both in their own countries to which their commercial and industrial relations extend, and for that purpose will establish and maintain the necessary international organisations.
b) undertake to secure just treatment of the native inhabitants of territories under their control;

c) will entrust the League with the general supervision over the execution of agreements with regard to the traffic in women and children, and the traffic in opium and other dangerous drugs;
d) will entrust the League with the general supervision of the trade in arms and ammunition with the countries in which the control of this traffic is necessary in the common interest.
e) will make provision to secure and maintain freedom of communications and of transit and equitable treatment for the commerce of all Members of the League. In this connection, the special necessities of the region devastated during the war of 1914-18 shall be borne in mind; and
f) will endeavour to take steps in matters of international concern for the prevention and control of disease.

ARTICLE 24

1. There shall be placed under the direction of the League all international bureaus already established by general treaties if the parties to such treaties consent. All such international bureaus and all commissions for the regulation of matters of international interest hereafter constituted shall be placed under the direction of the League.

2. In all matters of international interest which are regulated by general conventions but which are not placed under the control of international bureaus or commissions, the Secretariat of the League shall, subject to the consent of the Council and, if desired by the parties, collect and distribute all the relevant information and shall render any other assistance which may be necessary or desirable.

ARTICLE 25

The Members of the League agree to encourage and promote the establishment and cooperation of duly authorised voluntary national Red Cross organisations having as purposes the improvement of health, the prevention of disease and the mitigation of suffering throughout the world.

Article 26

1. Amendments to this Covenant will take effect when ratified by the Members of the League whose Representatives compose the Council and by a majority of the members of the League whose Representatives compose the Assembly.

2. No such amendments shall bind any Member of the League which signifies its dissent therefrom, but in that case it shall cease to be a Member of the League.

APPENDIX B

Treaty for the Renunciation of War (Kellogg-Briand Pact or Pact of Paris, 1928)

The President of the German Reich, the President of the United States of America, His Majesty the King of the Belgians, the President of the French Republic, His Majesty the King of Great Britain, Ireland and the British Dominions beyond the Seas, Emperor of India, His Majesty the King of Italy, His Majesty the Emperor of Japan, the President of the Republic of Poland, the President of the Czechoslovak Republic

Deeply sensible of their solemn duty to promote the welfare of mankind;

Persuaded that the time has come when a frank renunciation of war as an instrument of national policy should be made to the end that the peaceful and friendly relations now existing between their peoples may be perpetuated;

Convinced that all changes in their relations with one another should be sought only by pacific means and be the result of a peaceful and orderly process and that any signatory Power which shall hereafter seek to promote its national interests by resort to war should be denied the benefits furnished by this Treaty;

Hopeful that, encouraged by their example, all the other nations of the world will join in this humane endeavour and by adhering to the present Treaty, as soon as it comes into force bring their peoples within the scope of its beneficent provisions, thus uniting the civilised nations of the world in a common renunciation of war as an instrument of their national policy;

Have decided to conclude a Treaty and for that purpose have appointed as their respective plenipotentiaries who having communicated to one another their full powers found in good and due form have agreed upon the following articles:

Article 1

The High Contracting Parties solemnly declare in the name of their respective peoples that they condemn recourse to war for the solution of international controversies, and renounce it as an instrument of national policy in their relations with one another.

Article 2

The High Contracting Parties agree that the settlement or solution of all disputes or conflicts of whatever nature or of whatever origin, they may be, which may arise among them, shall never be sought except by pacific means.

Article 3

The present Treaty shall be ratified by the High Contracting Parties named in the Preamble in accordance with the respective constitutional requirements, and shall take effect as between them as soon as all their several instruments of ratification shall have been deposited at Washington.

The Treaty, when it has come into effect as prescribed in the preceding paragraph, shall remain open as long as may be necessary for adherence by all the other Powers shall be deposited at Washington and the Treaty shall immediately upon such deposit become effective as between the Power thus adhering and the other Powers parties hereto.

It shall be the duty of the Government of the United States to furnish each Government named in the Preamble and every Government subsequently adhering to this Treaty with a certified copy of the Treaty and of every instrument of ratification or adherence. It shall also be the duty of the Government of the United States telegraphically to notify to such Governments immediately upon the deposit with it of such instrument of ratification or adherence.

In faith whereof the respective Plenipotentiaries have signed this Treaty in the French and English languages both texts have equal force, and hereunto affix their seals.

Done at Paris the Twenty-seventh day of August in the year one thousand nine hundred and twenty-eight.

Index

Albania, 227, 234, 247-51, 268
Anglo-Japanese Treaty of 1902, 366
Anglo-Russian Convention of 1907, 3
Anti-Comintern Pact, 241-42, 375
Austria, 6, 52-53, 131-36, 165, 213-15, 221, 224, 243-4, 319, 321, 360
Austro-Hungarian Empire, 4, 5, 6, 7, 8, 11, 15, 17, 18, 20, 35, 51, 52, 223

Balance of power, 2, 15; in British foreign policy, 256-59
Balkan wars, 14, 17, 54
Berlin Treaty of 1878, 7,
Bismarck, 4, 5, 6, 136, 251
Bolshevism, 1, 2, 15, 217

Chamberlain, Austen, 109, 113, 202
Chamberlain, Neville, 139-42, 147, 149, 151, 206, 215, 216, 221, 255, 256
China, 8, 119-25, 156, 384-403; resurgence under Sun Yat-sen, 385-88; rise of assertive nationalism after First World War, 388-92; termination of communist influence, 392-97; Manchurian crisis, 397-400; critical estimate, 400-03
Churchill, Sir W., 11, 92, 219, 255, 259, 298
Clemenceau, 30, 32, 33, 34, 35, 48, 49, 61, 63, 68, 191, 219, 222, 302
Czechoslovakia, 28, 136-44, 150, 152, 175, 183, 184, 187, 189, 202, 215-17, 221, 234, 245, 286, 321, 360

Dawes Plan, 78, 82, 93, 101, 162
Draft Treaty of Mutual Assistance, 98-101

Egypt, 410-13
Entente Cordiale (Triple Entente), 3, 4, 5, 6, 7, 9, 17, 18
Ethiopia (Abyssinia), 125-31, 237-40, 275, 319-20

Fascism, 207, 212, 213, 232-35, 274, 317
Four Power Pact, 238, 247
France, 2, 4, 9, 10, 176, 191, 222; search for security, 192-96; policy of coercion, 196-99; accord with Germany, 199-201; policy of appeasement, 201-07; Abyssinian crisis, 207-210; civil war in Spain, 210-13; Austria and Czechoslovakia, 213-17; invasion on Poland, 217-19; critical estimate, 219-22
Franco, Gen. of Spain, 207, 212, 144-49 (see Spanish Civil War)

Geneva Protocol, 101-06, 108, 200, 221
George, Lloyd, 30, 32, 33, 35, 49, 60, 61, 63
Germany, 3, 4, 5, 8, 12, 15, 17, 18, 20, 26, 27, 31, 111-36, 136-42, 156-90; rise of Nazism, 156-60;

Index

policy of fulfilment, 160-65; great economic depression, 165-68; Nazi ideology, 168-74; main propositions of Hitler's foreign policy, 176-80; phase of resurgence, 179-82; phase of aggression, 184-88; Rome-Berlin axis, 241-47, 247-51, 282-85

Hitler, Adolph, 49, 92, 96, 110, 118, 131, 136-44, 150, 152, 156, 157, 167, 169, 175, 176, 200, 204, 205, 208, 209, 211, 212, 213, 215, 217, 218, 245, 246, 247, 249, 252, 256

Hoover Moratorium, 86-88

Imperialism, 9-10
International Labour Organisation, 441-45
Iraq, 414-15
Italy, 5, 6, 11, 125, 131, 221-54; irredentism, 227-31; fascist ideology, 232-35; Mussolini's policy, 235-37; conquest of Abyssinia, 237-40; Rome-Berlin axis, 241-47; pact of Steel, 251-52, 279-82

Japan, 3, 8, 20, 119-25, 156, 277-79, 366-83; policy in the period after First World War, 367-69; phase of democratic reformism, 369-72; Japan's Monroe Doctrine and Rape of Manchuria, 372-75; aggression on China, 375-81; critical appreciation, 381-83.

Kellogg-Briand Pact (Pact of Paris), 111-117, 362

League of Nations, 33, 37, 38, 97-105, 110-17, 122, 126, 128-31, 149, 162-65, 175, 178, 180, 181, 195-96, 201, 208, 211, 214, 220, 228, 237, 265, 269-71, 311, 317, 346, 356, 377, 428-69; genesis and birth, 429-33; Assembly, 434-35; Council, 435-36; Secretariat, 436-37; Permanent Court of International Justice, 437-41; International Labour Organisation, 441-45; Mandate System, 445-50; Achievements, 450-55; Failure, 455-66; critical estimate, 466-69

Little Entente, 28, 196, 234, 237, 247

Locarno Pacts, 106-11, 162, 163, 181, 199, 200, 214, 221, 235, 267, 268

Lytton Commission, 121-22

Manchurian crisis, 8, 114, 119-25, 244, 268, 290, 318, 319, 372-75, 400-03

Mandate System, 29, 445-50
Mazzini, 6, 226
Middle East, 404-27
Militarism, 11-14, 381
Monroe Doctrine, 332-39
Morocco, 4, 35
Munich Pact, 140-42, 216-17
Mussolini, Benito, 118, 125, 127, 146, 180, 184, 208, 212, 214; (also see Italy)

Napoleon Bonaparte, 4, 198, 256
Nationalism, 10, 11, 381, 388-89
Nehru, Jawaharlal, 2, 15, 29, 62

Orlando, 32-34, 61, 63, 225

Pact of Steel, 247-51
Paris Peace Settlements, 33-64; organisation of the Conference, 34-38; Treaty of Versailles, 38-51; Treaty of St. Germain, 52-54; Treaty of Trianon, 54, Treaty of Neuilly, 54-55; Treaty of Sevres and Lausanne, 54-57; and the question on minorities, 57-59; critical appreciation, 59-64, 98,
Permanent Court of International Justice (World Court), 104, 166, 437-41
Poland, 28, 149-50, 175, 182-83, 186-87, 217, 218, 286

Reparations and inter-allied war debts, 65-96; meaning and divergent motives, 66-71; German liability, 71-75; determination and realisation, 75-77; Dawes Plan, 78-82; Young Plan, 82-85; Hoover's moratorium, 86-88; inter-allied debts, 89-94; critical estimate, 93-96, 101, 159, 160, 197, 289
Russia (USSR), 4, 5, 7, 8, 21, 22, 27, 100, 137, 144, 151, 153, 156, 163, 167, 183-88, 189, 217, 222, 252, 253, 292-327; ideology and national interest, 293-96; phase of war communism, 296-304; Lenin's peace proposals, 299-301; policy of peaceful co-existence, 301-10; Stalin's policy, 310-16; United Front Strategy, 316-22; policy of neutrality and defence, 322-25; critical estimate, 325-27, 394-96

Secret Treaty of London of 1915, 36
Spanish Civil War, 144-49, 183, 210-15, 246, 320, 321
Shimsonian doctrine, 123
Syria, 423-25

Transjordan (Jordan), 422-23
Turkey 5, 8, 15, 55-57, 202, 224, 405-10
United Kingdom (Britain and England), 3, 4, 6, 12, 17, 49, 86-88, 219, 220, 224, 255-91; policy of balance of power, 256-59; search for peace and security, 259-63; Chamberlain's policy, 267-69; pre-appeasement phase, 267-71; ramifications of appeasement policy, 271-76; appeasement policy in practice, 276-85; end of appeasement policy, 285-89; critical estimate, 289-91
United States of America (USA), 20, 26, 27, 49, 86-88, 89-90, 92-93, 100, 111-14, 196, 218, 328-65; broad aims of foreign policy, 329-32; Monroe doctrine and policy towards Latin America, 332-39; policy towards Far East and Washington treaties, 339-48; economic foreign policy, 348-52; policy towards Europe, 352-57; on path of appeasement 357-61; critical estimate, 361-65

Versailles Treaty, 37-51, 92, 149, 156, 166, 188, 190, 194, 198, 200, 205, 228, 272, 353, 354, 389, 410, 451

Index

Vienna Congress, 4

Washington Conference and treaties, 339-48, 368

Wilson, Woodrow, 2, 20, 22-25, 26, 31, 32, 34, 36, 49, 59, 60, 62, 67, 112, 188, 223, 224, 227, 228, 303

World Disarmament Conference, 180

World War I, 1-32; background or prelude, 2-9; specific causes, 9-14; Balkan wars, 14-17; course of war, 17-28; consequences, 28-32, 34, 64, 85, 87, 191, 200, 224, 225, 229, 335, 348, 353, 367

World War II, 152, 155, 182, 183, 329, 338, 467

Young Plan, 82-85

Zinoviev (and his letters), 61, 104, 264, 309, 315